TETHERED SOULS

THE INFINITE CITY #6

TIFFANY ROBERTS

TETHERED SOULS

Kier and Kayl only foresee one fate for themselves.

For Kier is wrath.

And Kayl is vengeance.

They have but one purpose—slay the pirate Vrykhan at any cost. They expect to give their own lives in pursuit of their revenge...

But they never expected her. Aileen.

Their *na'diya*. Their mate.

Their missing piece.

They never imagined a different fate. Is it too late to claim the future they never dared hope for?

KIER + KAYL
TETHERED SOULS

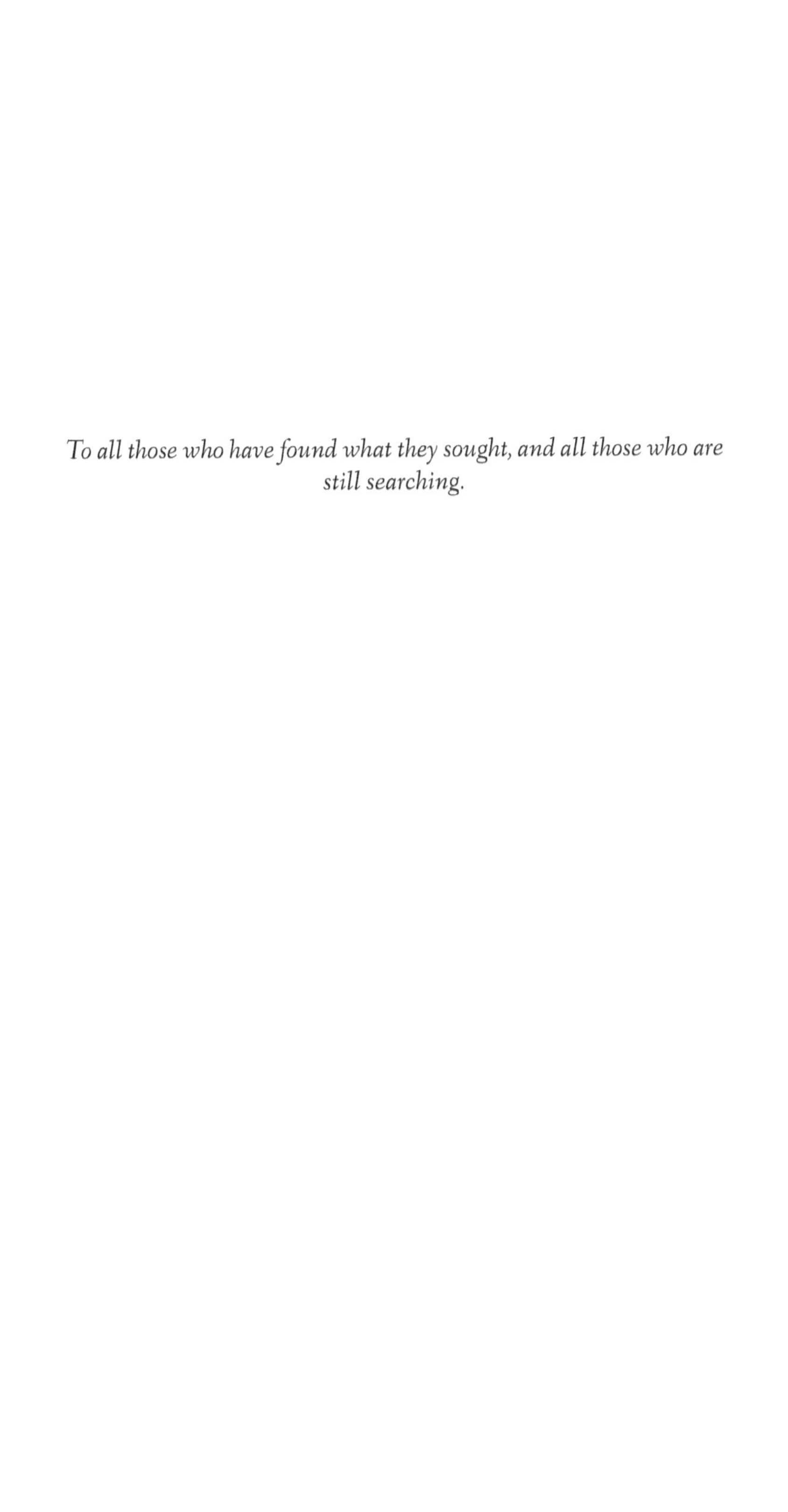

To all those who have found what they sought, and all those who are still searching.

ONE

Aboard the starship Fang
   Somewhere on the fringes of Consortium-ruled space
   Terran Year 2108

Kayl swept his hands through the holographic star map, adjusting the angle. Vrykhan's last attack had been launched from the center of the Ultris III star system. Had the pirates lain in wait, or had they attacked fresh from a jump?

He shifted the map again and tilted his head, following the potential trajectories with his gaze. Perhaps the pirates had cut close to the star? That would've made their ship more difficult to detect, and they could've taken advantage of the star's gravitational field to grant themselves a burst of speed.

The cockpit floor vibrated under Kayl's feet, keeping time with a heavy drumbeat. Dissonant, punishing instruments accompanied the beat—sonic claws raking the air with no regard for the damage they might cause.

Tail flicking from side to side, Kayl forced his focus back to the map. With more hand movements, he marked the pirates' potential routes and sought places in the star system where they could have hidden the huge battle cruiser that served as their command ship.

Kayl and his twin had been hunting Vrykhan for years. They'd traced his movements, tracked down his contacts, and documented every reported encounter. But in all that time, they'd never caught up to the pirate.

There had to be a pattern in Vrykhan's activities. There had to be something Kayl had missed, a key that would unlock the secrets, had to be—

The music rose to a blistering crescendo, so loud and fast that it rattled Kayl's bones. Guttural voices roared and growled amidst the instruments.

In response, Kayl's heart beat faster, heavier—he could just feel it through the vibrations. He dropped his hands to the console beneath the projected map. As the music continued its relentless assault, Kayl's fingers curled, and his claws scraped the console.

"Kier," he said.

The music devoured his voice.

"Kier!" Kayl turned his head to look at his brother.

Kier sat in the gunner's seat at the front of the cockpit with his booted feet propped on the control console, bobbing his head to the music. The holo screens arranged before him, which monitored the *Fang's* various sensors and systems, commanded none of his attention.

Kayl clenched his fists, slammed them down, and blasted out a single word with his mind.

Kier!

Kier sat up with a jolt, dropping his feet to the floor. His loose hair flopped into his face; he swept it back as he spun the seat to face Kayl. His mouth opened, his lips forming a question Kayl understood perfectly even if he could not hear it—"What?"

Kayl stilled his restless tail and held his brother's gaze. *Turn. It. Off.*

Scowling, Kier folded his arms across his chest. His *aerys*—the voice of his soul, projected psychically through their bond—sounded clearly in Kayl's mind. *This music is a reflection of my current mood.*

With teeth clenched—which only intensified the way the music rattled them—Kayl pulsed, *Deafness is not a mood, Kier. I cannot hear my own thoughts amidst this noise.*

Kier smirked. *Would that I could not hear your thoughts amidst this noise.*

Releasing a huff, Kayl shoved away from the projector console and strode to his brother's chair. He braced a hand atop it, leaned over Kier, and tapped the stop icon on the music player's holo screen.

The abrupt silence was a salve upon Kayl's irritated soul. "Would that Thargen had not introduced you to such auditory abominations."

"Would that you had developed an appreciation for art," Kier replied as Kayl straightened.

Resisting the reflexive itch threating to set his tail into restless motion again, Kayl stalked back to the star map. *Vorgals screaming and banging is not art.*

"You are hardly qualified to make such a determination, Kayl."

"And you are?" Kayl turned to look at his brother.

Kier rose smoothly from the chair, lifted his arms over his head, and arched his back in a languid stretch. Graceful as his movements were, they bore a subtle stiffness, a barely masked frustration. "More so than you. Your idea of music is only good for inducing unconsciousness."

A shame it does not work on you, Kayl pulsed. *And my preferred music has no bearing on my ability to recognize what is or is not art.*

Dropping his arms, Kier turned a palm toward the ceiling and strolled closer to Kayl. "I will cede you that point. It is your inability to experience emotion that renders you unable to recognize art."

Kayl's tail stiffened, but he stopped himself from clenching his fists. He refused to grant Kier the satisfaction of seeing how the comment had irked him. "So, we are now resorting to juvenile insults?"

"No. It is simply mature, uninhibited honesty."

"I would laugh if—"

"If you possessed a sense of humor?"

Kayl pointed at the holographic star map. "What time have we for humor while Vrykhan still roams the stars sowing terror?"

Time enough for you to absorb some culture, Kier pulsed, his smirk reflected in his mind-voice.

Drinking with Thargen and the others is not absorbing culture, Kier. Through his teeth, Kayl added, "There is much to be done."

"And we can do so with music on."

Kayl shook his head and folded his arms across his chest. "Not with that cacophony."

I am wrath, Kier pulsed with unexpected solemnity—solemnity that crumbled when he walked back to his seat and reached for the music controls. *And so are these vorgal battle ballads.*

Battle ballads? Was that really what such music was called? Who had chosen to violate the meaning of the word *ballad* by making such a classification?

With another shake of his head, Kayl dislodged those pointless wonderings. Such questions were unimportant. *Do not, Kier.*

Locking his gaze with Kayl's, Kier extended a finger and slowly moved it toward the holo screen.

"We need to focus on finding a new lead," Kayl said.

"No, we do not." Kier's finger eased closer to the play icon.

Kier...

"Something will arise. Until then..." The tip of Kier's claw drew another centimeter closer to filling the cockpit with sounds that would do naught but make Kayl eagerly look forward to his inevitable demise.

That is not how it works, Kier. Jaw clenched, Kayl watched that finger with all the intensity and anxiousness he would've afforded it had it been creeping toward a trigger.

"This? Of course it is. I simply press the icon and—"

"The hunt," Kayl growled. "Leads do not simply materialize. We must work for them. Opportunity will not seek us!"

The control console chimed. The twins snapped their gazes to the holo screen in front of Kier as the music player was replaced by the animated icon for an incoming commlink call. The lack of identifying information on the call could only mean one thing.

"Can we not go even two full days without him calling?" Kier asked.

Kayl strode across the cockpit to join his twin. "It is difficult enough to focus with you around all the time. He makes it nearly impossible."

Kier's extended finger still hovered near the screen—now directed at the *DENY CALL* button. He glanced at his brother; no words, whether spoken or thought, needed to be exchanged for Kayl to understand the unasked question.

And it was tempting. As grateful as Kayl was for the assistance Arcanthus and the others had provided over the last six months, he was in no mood for one of the sedhi's laidback, rambling, pointless conversations right now.

It had always been Kier and Kayl. Though they'd learned to trust Arcanthus, Thargen, and the rest of their crew, the twins could only truly rely upon each other.

For I am vengeance.

And I am wrath, Kier's *aerys* intoned.

"But he has provided useful information many times," Kier continued out loud.

Yet here we are, adrift, with nothing to show for all that information. Kayl clenched his jaw, staring at Kier's finger and the icon beyond it.

"We can tell him we have little time," Kier said. "Tell him to be brief."

As though that would ever work with him.

Kier smirked. He shifted his hand aside and touched the accept icon.

"Had to think about it, did you?" Arcanthus asked before his holographic image had even appeared.

The sedhi was leaned back in a chair, clad in a satiny robe that revealed most of his chest and his upper abdominal muscles. His long black hair was swept aside to hang over one shoulder. The intricate marks on his gray skin—called *qal*—glowed golden.

His terran mate, Samantha, sat on his lap, one arm cradling her rounded belly. Her cheeks were pink, usually a sign of embarrassment in her kind, but her gentle smile suggested only contentment, especially when she glanced at Arcanthus.

Something deep and hungry stirred inside Kayl, accentuated by a sour pang in his chest. Bitterness. Jealousy. Longing.

Distance.

Much of it had come from Kier...but not all of it.

"We were occupied," Kayl said.

Arcanthus grinned and chuckled. "You were bickering again, weren't you?"

Kayl only just prevented himself from exchanging a glance with his brother.

Are we truly so predictable? Kier pulsed.

Kayl had no satisfactory answer. All he could do was try to mask the discomfort lurking at his core. He and his twin knew each other, heart, mind, and soul. They'd been linked even before they'd been born. But to have someone else be so familiar with them...

"Hey Kier," Samantha said cheerfully with a wave. "Hey Kayl."

Kayl nodded in greeting.

"Hello, Samantha," Kier said with a smile that fell as he turned his attention to the sedhi. His tail bumped Kayl's leg before swinging away. "Do you need something from us, Arcanthus?"

"No. The opposite, in fact."

Kayl's chest constricted, and his heart quickened. "What have you found?"

Leads do not simply materialize, hmm? Kier pulsed.

Shut up.

Arcanthus lifted a cybernetic hand and delicately brushed some of Samantha's loose hair behind her rounded ear. "How are you two doing? You've been out there a long time."

Now Kayl's tail flicked; just once, but the lapse in control only heightened his irritation.

Be easy, brother, Kier's *aerys* warned.

Is the information he has provided worth wasting all this time? Kayl replied. *Every moment Arcanthus spends blathering, Vrykhan's trail fades further.*

"You asked us that the last time we spoke, Arcanthus." Kier leaned forward, placing his hands atop the console. "We are fine."

Arcanthus's grin took on a lopsided tilt. "A lot can change in a couple days."

"Little has changed."

Shifting his arm so his hand was on Samantha's belly, Arcanthus drew her more snugly against him. "What little?"

Kayl's attention dipped to Arcanthus's hand. How could the sedhi's hold on the terran seem so relaxed and loving and yet so protective and possessive? Kayl's awareness of his missing piece intensified in that moment; the *daevalis* he shared with his brother would forever be unbalanced and incomplete. There would forever be a void in their souls. They would never have their *na'diya* to complete their triad.

They would never hold their mate like that, would never see her belly grow with a youngling. They would never know peace and comfort like Samantha and Arcanthus provided one another.

They would never be whole.

Is that why we stay away?

Kier's voice, with a hint of smugness layered over that old, persistent pain and longing, slipped into Kayl's mind. *Shall I gloat over the fact that I must be the one to tell you to focus, brother?*

Kayl bit back his thoughts and lifted his gaze to the sedhi's face. "Are you asking for a definition of the word little?"

Arcanthus laughed. "Kier said little had changed. I'm only asking what is different."

Why can he not simply be direct? Kayl pulsed.

He is, Kier replied. *You are just frustrated and distracted.*

Oh? Kayl frowned.

Fine. We are frustrated. After a brief silence, Kier begrudgingly added, *And distracted. We are both frustrated and distracted.*

He is staring at us with that knowing grin, Kier. Say something to him.

Ba'shanaal, Kayl, you have a mouth of your own.

"Nothing of note," Kier said.

Arcanthus scoffed. "There must be more. You're out there hunting notorious space pirates and liberating slaves, and don't have a single story to share?" He stroked Samantha's belly with undisguised reverence.

"We missed you both at the Conquerors table last night," Samantha said.

"Razi is still convinced you two were cheating telepathically. He might push to ban you from being able to play separate factions when you return. I say he's just being grumpy."

Kier tilted his head. "Why is he grumpy?"

"Someone must have died on that volturian show," Kayl said.

With a laugh, Arcanthus asked, "When doesn't someone die on that damned show?"

Samantha's smile widened. "It's because you two almost beat me last time, but Razi hasn't come close in months."

"We were not cheating," Kier said with a smirk, "and *Kayl* almost beat you."

"So Kayl almost beat me, then. But almost doesn't count, does it?"

Kier chuckled. "Is that a challenge?"

She gave Arcanthus a sidelong glance. "I haven't had one of those in a while."

Dipping his head, Arcanthus nibbled at Samantha's neck, making her giggle. He growled, "You ignite a fire in me when you talk like that, terran."

Again, Kayl felt that bitterness, that jealousy, that...emptiness. But it was almost all his own this time.

Kier had mingled with Arcanthus's crew with relative ease. He'd watched shows, played games, shared meals, and even trained with them. Kayl had tried to follow his brother's example. He had made the effort, but he'd always felt that distance. He'd always felt anxious, restless, out of place.

Because that leisure time had delayed the hunt. It had allowed Vrykhan to get farther away, for the trail to fade, for the opportunities to dwindled and die. The twins had one purpose.

Playing Conquerors and drinking did not fulfill that purpose.

Arcanthus's expression shed its mirth—and most of its hunger. "Your hunt has faltered again."

"What would you know of it?" Kier's voice held a hard edge.

"My work benefits from knowing many things," Arcanthus said with a casual flick of his wrist. "But more importantly, it is much easier to protect the people I care about when I remain suitably informed."

Vague as always, Kayl pulsed.

Kier glanced at Kayl from the corner of his eye. *He learned to speak thusly to survive the criminal underworld, brother. Would it not benefit us to do the same?*

"What, then?" Kayl demanded. "Spying upon us?"

Tact, Kayl, came Kier's *aerys,* thin with impatience. *Perhaps you should research the term when you have a moment to spare.*

Arcanthus's jaw fell open in mock shock, but the gleam in his eyes was decidedly mischievous. "Spying is such a loaded word, Sol'Kayl. Bristling with negative connotations. After Drakkal, Shay, and Leah were kidnapped and Thargen disappeared without a trace, I simply prefer to keep in contact with my friends. To know where they are. Why do you think I call so often?"

"Because you enjoy the sound of your own voice."

Kier grimaced outwardly, but he laughed in his mind.

Samantha made no such effort to hide her amusement. She laughed aloud, and her laughter only strengthened when Arcanthus regarded her with an arched brow. "What? It's true. You do. You can't deny it."

"Truly, Arcanthus, we are busy," Kier said when his mental laughter had finally subsided. "What have you found?"

Arcanthus returned his attention to the twins. "Why does everyone seem to think they can insult me and then ask me to do something for them?"

"Goodbye, Arcanthus." Kayl leaned forward and reached for the holo screen.

"You'll regret it." Arcanthus's smirk reclaimed its rakish slant.

No, I will not.

Kier caught Kayl's hand, stilling it, and sent an image through their psychic link—the star map that loomed only meters away. The star map dotted with incidents the twins had tracked over the years, the map comprised overwhelmingly of the dark, empty, impossibly vast space between those marks.

When Kier released his hold, Kayl lowered his hand.

"There is a place called Eternal Paradise," Arcanthus said, "located in neutral space along one of the many routes to the Entris Dominion. Originally established as a refueling station, but the current owner has made it into something...more."

"We are aware of it," said Kayl.

"Entertainment. Attractions. Intergalactic cuisine," said Kier. "Parties, music, and gambling."

"A very popular place." Arcanthus glanced at his terran mate, gaze softening. "Appears legitimate on the surface. Nice enough for travelers to stop and stay, even with children. But underneath..."

"Drugs and prostitution. A loosely kept secret." Kier waved a hand. "But we have found no connection to our quarry."

"Ah, but not all connections are so readily apparent."

"The owner does not keep slaves."

The sedhi's eyes darkened. "Not all slavery is readily apparent either."

"What does Eternal Paradise have to do with our hunt?" Kayl asked, tail twitching.

Arcanthus frowned, and his nostrils flared with a heavy exhalation. "Could you at least allow me the satisfaction of building up to that?"

"No."

Samantha chuckled and lifted a lock of Arcanthus's hair, tucking it behind his pierced, pointed ear before resting her head on his shoulder. Her eyelids drooped, and her lips parted with a yawn that she stifled with the back of her hand.

"Your tretin deals in much more than slaves," Arcanthus said flatly.

Kier's tail swished with burgeoning excitement, hitting Kayl's leg each time it came near. "Vrykhan offloads other illicit cargo at Eternal Paradise?"

"Yes. Drugs, primarily. And I believe in return he's given information on ships, cargos, and passengers that pass through. Eternal Paradise is far enough from any claimed territories that he can act with little fear of retaliation from governmental entities."

"We've never found a place where he obtains intelligence *and* moves goods," said Kier. His excitement intensified, but Kayl sensed him holding back, restraining his blossoming hope.

"It would seem you have been searching for the wrong goods."

"How do you know all this?" asked Kayl, fighting back his own hope.

Arcanthus grinned. "I have my methods."

Kayl frowned.

So what if he is vague? Kier pulsed. *All the information he has provided before has proven correct. However he does it, he is better at this than we are.*

You are correct, Kier.

Now Kier frowned. *Why do you never say things like that out loud, Kayl?*

"We will chart a course presently." Kayl moved his hand toward the commlink's *END* icon.

"There's more," Arcanthus said hurriedly. He adjusted his hold on Samantha, gently shifting her aside so he could sit forward. "The owner of Eternal Paradise, a vroca named Saduuk, has almost doubled his security in the last week."

"Good to know. Goodb—"

"There is word that Vrykhan is going to Eternal Paradise, Sol'Kayl. In the flesh."

Everything within Kayl stilled, everything fell silent. For the first time in his life, no thoughts passed through his psychic bond with his twin—because Kier was in the same stunned state.

The information couldn't be real. After all these years, all this searching, it couldn't be so easy.

One of the twins uttered a single word. "When?"

Kayl didn't know whether he or his brother had spoken, and he didn't care. Only the answer mattered.

"Six days," Arcanthus said. "But I need you two to listen to me, because—"

Kayl terminated the call. He leapt into the pilot's seat and grasped the controls; Kier was already in the gunner's seat, setting a course for Eternal Paradise.

The incoming commlink alert appeared on one of the console's holo screens.

Kier dismissed it without looking away from his work. He pulsed, *For I am wrath.*

And I am vengeance, Kayl answered.

Their minds completed the mantra in perfect unison as Kayl turned the *Fang* toward its new destination.

And our only fate is to slay the tretin called Vrykhan.

TWO

Aileen forced herself to sit perfectly still, keeping her heels to the floor, her hands in her lap, and her eyes closed. She visualized herself as a picture of utter serenity, an unmoving statue.

Think of the ocean waves you once played in, of the wind blowing through your hair and the kiss of the cool, salty spray upon your face. Think of the lush fields of heather, of that fresh, earthy fragrance filling your senses.

She had to think of anything but the upcoming show. Of anything but what would come after the music stopped.

It was never like this. I was never like this.

No, she hadn't been. She'd loved to perform; it was in her blood. Her parents had been performers, and they'd passed that talent, that passion, on to Aileen. She'd reveled in the thrill of the show, the energy in the air, the delight upon the audience's faces. She'd cherished the bliss and freedom of losing oneself in song.

But she didn't have that here, in this prison. The joy she'd once felt in singing had been stolen from her.

Everything had been stolen from her.

She curled her fingers and dug her nails into her bare thighs. The pain didn't help. Her stomach twisted, and it took everything within Aileen to swallow the bile down.

Think of the ocean. Think of the sweet fields of lavender. Think of—

A soft-bristled brush swept over her eyelids. Aileen flinched.

Tulaya huffed, and the brush dropped away. "Aileen, you must hold still!"

Aileen snapped her attention up to the volturian woman, who glared down at her. Even with her eerie, opalescent eyes narrowed in frustration, Tulaya was gorgeous. Her pale purple skin, long white hair, and intricate white *qal* marks on her body and face leant her an effortless, otherworldly beauty.

"Sorry." Cringing, Aileen sat back in her seat. "I'm trying."

Tulaya's expression softened. "I know. I know." She sighed and lifted the brush once more, applying the finishing touches to Aileen's eye makeup. "But Saduuk will be here soon, and he expects you ready. If you're not..."

"Then we'll both be punished for it."

Tulaya pressed her dark purple lips together and nodded.

They both knew Saduuk's preferred method of punishment.

Aileen touched her fingertips to the dark choker around her throat. Anyone looking at it would see a beautiful, intricate piece of jewelry, a symbol of elegance and riches. And it did symbolize wealth —Saduuk's wealth. It was a sign of his power, his ownership. His cruelty.

All Aileen saw in it was an expensive collar...and the promise of pain.

Once Tulaya finished applying the eyeshadow, she leaned away to survey her work. She nodded with approval. Setting the brush and color palette on the vanity, she picked up a comb and stepped behind the chair, running her fingers through Aileen's hair. "He is anxious today."

"Did he...come to you?" Aileen asked.

Tulaya's fingers stilled. Aileen could only imagine what was going through the volturian's head, could only imagine what the woman had suffered since coming here. Being selected by Saduuk meant an elevation in status on Eternal Paradise, but that supposed prestige was superficial, and it came at a heavy price.

Dropping her gaze, Tulaya shook her head.

Aileen released a relieved breath. She should've been grateful for her position. At least, that was what Saduuk had told her. She was doing what she loved. What more could she have asked for? As long as she kept Saduuk happy, she got to sing on stage in front of an audience every night, she had her own room, and she was never hungry.

Of course, keeping him happy usually meant performing private...*encores* for his favored guests.

Don't think.

Closing her eyes, she focused on the memory of running through the heather with her mother, on the feeling of flowers brushing over her legs. On the sweet, mossy fragrance that had filled the air, the warm sunshine that had caressed her skin.

Tulaya resumed her work, her fingers deftly weaving thin, bead-adorned braids into Aileen's hair. Her voice wavered with a mixture of pity and relief when she said, "Saduuk currently favors Almun. It was he who confided in me."

The volturian's touch, though gentle, and her words, though softly spoken, forced Aileen back to the present. Despite the decadence and revelry of Eternal Paradise, Aileen couldn't forget. The friendships she'd made, the rush of performing for an eager crowd, the drugs Saduuk sometimes forced on her...none of it was enough to make her forget. There was a void inside her, a massive black hole that had expanded every day since she'd lost her parents, and it would not be ignored.

They'd be horrified to know where you ended up, Aileen.

This isn't what I sought. This isn't what I wanted. Not at all.

She'd left Earth to escape the pain, to find herself, to seek the source of the siren song luring her out into the stars. To fill the void. At first, she'd thought she had found her place here. Everyone had been so kind. Especially Saduuk. And for a short while, this place had helped her forget that pain. She'd thrown herself into performing, into the shallow wonderment and spectacle, into the cheers and applause.

And she'd mistaken those distractions for healing. She'd been naïve enough to think that not looking her pain in the face would make it go away.

It had been too late by the time she realized her pain was only intensifying, that its roots were sinking deep into her soul. It had been too late by the time she realized she didn't belong here.

It had been too late by the time she realized the choker Saduuk had given her, marking her as part of the staff, didn't come off.

"What did Almun say?" Aileen asked.

Almun was a young dacrethian with golden hair and skin, both of which shimmered like the precious metal they resembled. He was often requested by patrons not only for his beauty, but because of his four arms. At least while he had Saduuk's favor, he'd be off limits to others.

"Not much," Tulaya said. "Only that Saduuk was rougher than normal today. That he almost seemed...scared."

"Scared?" Not once in all the years Aileen had been trapped here had Saduuk shown even a hint of fear.

"He made a mess of his room and demanded even more security for tonight. That is all Almun could say."

Aileen tilted her head at Tulaya's guidance and studied her reflection in the mirror in front of her. The pale, ghostly blue of her eyes was made ethereal by her makeup—black eyeliner with outward swept wings; glittery, vibrant shades of blue, green, and violet on her eyelids; intense blue lipstick. Those colors were contrasted by the dusting of pink blush across her cheeks. But none of that could hide the shadows lurking in her eyes.

"Is Saduuk expecting trouble?" she asked.

Tulaya stilled again. "I...I think someone is coming tonight. Someone...important."

Aileen met Tulaya's gaze in the mirror.

The volturian's delicate brow was creased, and her lips had fallen into a deep frown.

Someone important.

Aileen's skin prickled like something was crawling over it, and the fine hairs on her arms rose. Dread pooled in her belly. Someone important visiting Saduuk always meant one of those private encores after the show. It always meant...

She shivered.

How could she keep going on like this? How much more could she take? How much more could she allow *them* to take?

Tulaya firmly grasped Aileen's head on both sides and stroked a thumb across Aileen's brow. "You need to stay strong, Aileen. Do not lose yourself."

I'm already lost.

"Do not let him break you...not like he broke me." Tulaya continued, her voice dropping to a ragged whisper.

Tears burned behind Aileen's eyes. "Tulaya, I—"

The door behind them slid open. Thumping music blasted into the room, rattling the cosmetics on the vanity, its beat in time with Aileen's pounding heart.

A towering figure stepped inside, spreading his arms wide. "Ah, my beautiful songbird. Are you ready for tonight's performance?"

The door slid shut behind him, plunging the room into silence.

Aileen clenched her jaw and dug her nails deeper into her thighs.

Tulaya turned Aileen's chair toward Saduuk, dropped her arms, and stepped back, eyes on the floor. "She is ready."

Saduuk's craggily face split into a wide grin as he approached, revealing his sharp teeth. Numerous short spikes protruded from the sides of his bald head, forming a crown of pointed bone that he'd adorned with gold paint in contrast to his dusk-gray skin. He wore his loose, flowing shirt open at the collar, its hem tucked into pants that hugged this thick, muscular legs. The look was capped off with a pair of tall, polished black boots.

He'd reminded Aileen of a pirate when she'd first seen him.

If only she'd taken that as a warning before he'd used that suave tongue to entice her into *working* for him.

Stupid, naïve, lonely Aileen.

She rose to her feet, smoothing her hands down her short, glittery blue skirt to hide their trembling. The thin strands along the bottom of the skirt tickled her skin.

"Let me see." Saduuk caught her chin with his fingers and tilted her face up, turning it from left to right. His callused grasp was rough as he ran his scrutinous yellow eyes over her face. "You did well, Tulaya. She'll shine bright tonight."

"Thank you, Saduuk," Tulaya murmured.

He shifted his thumb to press a claw against Aileen's bottom lip. "I need you to be perfect tonight, my songbird."

Aileen glared up at him. "Aren't I always?"

You fucking bawbag.

His smile twisted into a scowl, and his grip on her chin strengthened. "I would prefer not to have these conversations with you, terran."

"And I'd prefer not to have any conversations with you at all."

Baring his sharp teeth with a growl, he bent down and drew her closer until their noses nearly touched. "Do not test me. I have no patience for your defiance tonight. You will perform, and you will do so perfectly. And when I summon you for an encore, you will perform again with a fucking smile on your face."

Aileen grasped his wrist with both hands. "Fuck you."

"Aileen..." Tulaya beseeched.

Saduuk snarled, swung Aileen around, and slammed her back against the wall. The breath fled her lungs as icy, slithering fear crept into her heart. Saduuk thrust his free hand into his pocket, withdrew a small vial, and held it up to Aileen's face. The contents glowed a soft red.

Rhapsody.

Battling back the threatening tears and panic, she clawed at his arm and shook her head—at least as much as his iron grip allowed. "Please, Saduuk, no. Please, stop. I don't want this."

"My guest tonight is a tretin," he said, popping the stopper off the vial with his thumb. "You know what that is, little songbird?"

Aileen's eyes widened, and her breath hitched. She'd heard horror stories about the tretin. Brutal conquerors who only took and took and took, who killed and raped without remorse. They were huge, horned beings—demons sprung right out of old Earth stories.

"You do. I see it in your eyes." Saduuk squeezed her cheeks, forcing her mouth open, and poured the rhapsody in.

The cold liquid spread across her tongue. Saduuk forced her mouth shut, pinched her nose closed, and tilted her chin up to make her swallow. The chill slid down her throat. Only then did he ease his hold enough for her to suck in a frantic breath.

Saduuk leaned his face close to hers. "You're going to get on that stage and give the performance of a lifetime, Aileen." He stroked his thumb over her bottom lip. "And then you're going to meet with my guest and give a performance that may save your life. You're going to provide him with everything this soft little body of yours can give."

The drug pooled in her belly, where the coldness gave way to growing warmth that spread through her limbs. But it was nothing like what was to come.

Holding his gaze, she rasped, "I hate you."

Saduuk's grin returned, but it was strained, teetering on the edge of becoming a grimace. He tilted his head and wrapped his fingers around her collar. "And I own you, songbird. You will do everything I command." His grip on her was harsh enough to leave a bruise. Through his teeth, he asked, "Do you understand?"

She nodded, unable to stop her trembling. "I understand."

Saduuk released her so abruptly she fell to the floor, catching herself on hands and knees. "Thirty minutes, songbird. Find whatever control you need to find. You know what you'll be doing if you fuck this up."

The door opened. That powerful music assaulted Aileen again, thumping down into her bones, making her heart seize. Then Saduuk was gone, and the door slid shut.

Aileen brought a hand to her jaw, where she still felt the phantom grip of his cruel fingers. Inside, the rhapsody-induced heat spread, but it didn't take away the growing, sickening dread of her upcoming performance...and what would come after. She curled her fingers into a fist and press them against the floor.

The first stage of a rhapsody high was a wave of joy and elation, a shedding of worries and cares, but even that wouldn't be enough to kill her fear. Even that wouldn't be enough to let her lose herself in song the way she used to, the way she so desperately wanted to. But once the heat kicked in fully, it would consume her—there'd be no happiness, no fear, nothing but uncontrollable desire and fiery oblivion.

There'd be no Aileen.

She'd come to Eternal Paradise with almost nothing...and Saduuk had taken what little had remained.

A gentle, steadying hand settled on her back. Tulaya said, "It will be okay."

Aileen shook her head, tears burning her eyes. "How? How will it be okay? Look at me! Look at what I've become, Tulaya. What *we've* become." A sob escaped her. "It'll never be okay."

THREE

Any operation the twins undertook in a place like Eternal Paradise would normally have seen days, if not weeks, of preparation. The space station was in neutral territory, meaning its private security force was beholden to no laws or regulations, and the place could serve as a haven for illicit activity. There would be hundreds of staff and thousands of civilians aboard at any time. It was impossible for the twins to ignore the enormity of the task before them as the *Fang* approached Eternal Paradise.

There were surveillance and security systems to hack, floor layouts and staff schedules to study, and a constant stream of spacecraft arriving and departing to monitor. All that before any considerations were made to minimize the danger to bystanders. With a notorious pirate and an unknown number of his crew added into the equation, only one outcome was likely—disaster.

And the twins had already endured more than their share of disaster as of late. The incident on Sotera half a year ago had been a failure. Most of the slaves they'd sought to liberate had died, the smugglers they'd intended to interrogate about Vrykhan had been slain before revealing anything, and the twins and their newfound companions had barely escaped the planet with their lives after an attack by hundreds of battle-frenzied skeks.

Yet when Kier suggested he and Kayl simply walk into Eternal Paradise and seek Vrykhan, Kayl agreed without hesitation.

Because there hadn't been time to prepare. This was their first chance at killing Vrykhan after fifteen years of hunting, and they refused to miss it.

The *Fang* scanned the many ships docked at the space station, searching records from the Consortium and hundreds of other intergalactic governments and organizations to trace ownership records, passenger and cargo manifests, and incident reports. Information flitted across the holo screens faster than Kier could read.

His chest tightened with anticipation. He knew it wouldn't be as simple as Vrykhan having docked an identifiable ship here—it couldn't be. But he could not stop that glimmer of hope, a tiny flame that nonetheless burned blindingly bright.

Everyone made mistakes sometimes. Even merciless pirates with decades-long terror sprees left in their wake.

"Nothing," Kayl said, releasing the controls to flick through the information on screen.

The *Fang* continued its approach on autopilot, angling toward the dock assigned by Eternal Paradise's traffic control.

"There must be something," Kier replied as that tightness intensified. "This is the day."

Voice strained, Kayl said, "It is. We may be late."

"Or early."

Kayl's only response was the faintest downtick of one corner of his mouth as he set new parameters for the *Fang's* search, attempting to trace any of the present ships back to any one of the many parts of Vrykhan's expansive network that the twins had uncovered over the years.

The *Fang* slowed and turned around, removing Eternal Paradise from the cockpit's forward view. The space station appeared on a central holo screen, relayed by the rear holo recorders as the ship backed toward it.

Though neither twin allowed the thought to fully form, it lingered in the backs of their minds, slinking along their psychic bond unbidden—this was likely another dead end. Another lead that would result in nothing.

How many more such failures could they endure before their will finally faltered and they accepted that they were not equal to the task of killing Vrykhan?

The mantra Kier and his brother had repeated countless times nearly formed in his mind, but he silenced it. All his anticipation, fear, fury, and anxiety, all his sorrow and pain, swirled along the edges of his thoughts, and somehow, he knew that mantra would empower rather than suppress them now.

"Still nothing," Kayl said. "I will expand the—"

Something stirred inside Kier, a sensation unlike any he'd ever felt. His brow furrowed, and his tail—which had been in ceaseless motion since Arcanthus had tipped them off about Vrykhan coming to this place six days ago—stilled.

It felt like...like a thread had been pulled taut inside him. One that wound through every bit of his being, anchored in an unbreakable coil around his heart. Though the sensation was faint, it was warm, and the tug on that thread was undeniable. It was leading him into the space station.

This is where we are meant to be.

Kier turned his head to find Kayl already looking at him.

This is the place, Kier pulsed.

Kayl nodded. Cold fire flooded his eyes, and his expression hardened. *This is fate.*

With a faint rumbling, the *Fang* halted. Kier could just make out the muted whisper of machinery in motion. A notification appeared on the central screen, announcing that the docking sequence was complete. It was replaced by another notification almost immediately.

Accept incoming message from Eternal Paradise?

Kayl touched the accept icon.

A vroca with gray skin and short bone spikes on the sides of his head appeared before them, his holographic image backed by a pair of polished stone columns and a balcony overlooking a lower level cluttered with gaming tables and crowds of gamblers.

Kayl's *aerys* said, *Saduuk. The owner.*

"As the proprietor of Eternal Paradise," Saduuk said with a sharp-toothed grin, "I'd like to welcome you to my little piece of paradise out here in the stars. Whatever your pleasure, Eternal Paradise has something to satisfy your appetites. Whether you're here for the live shows, the award-winning intergalactic cuisine, the games"—he threw his arms wide, indicating the gambling floor below —"or enjoyment that runs a little...deeper, we're here to ensure your experience is the best possible."

The background behind the vroca changed, becoming a long, carpeted corridor with many doors, all of which were numbered in universal speech. Saduuk strolled along the hallway, passing more columns and alcoves in the walls containing exotic plants and shimmering fountains. "If you need anything during your stay here, whether in our expansive dining hall or one of our luxurious rooms, all you need to do is call upon one of our attentive staff members"—a pair of scantily clad volturians, one male, one female, wearing matching chokers appeared to Saduuk's sides—"and we'll meet your every desire."

Kier extended an arm, brushing his fingers through the projection. The controls that normally appeared in response to such gestures failed to materialize. "How do we skip this?"

Kayl sat forward with a frown. "You simply touched a spot the projector did not recognize." He reached toward the holo.

"All exits are marked," Saduuk continued, now standing before a door that read *exit* in Universal and several other languages. "In case of emergency, we ask that you follow the instructions of staff members so we can get you safely back to your ships."

Nothing happened when Kayl's hand touched the projection.

"Yes, because the problem was that I did not touch it correctly, Kayl," Kier said. His heart pounded, its thumping permeating his body, and heat gathered just beneath his skin. His tail snapped from side to side.

Worse, that odd sensation became more insistent—the pull had grown stronger.

Saduuk's location had changed again; he now stood on a stage, bathed in bright spotlights. "Now hey, I know nobody likes to be told what to do, but I have a few rules here at Eternal Paradise that are for your safety. All business matters must be arranged through one of our liaisons, who you can contact by—"

"If we were not late already, we certainly will be after this," Kier growled. "Power down the ship."

"You want me to shut the *Fang* down so you do not have to watch this?" Kayl asked.

"Yes! *Zor atkoshai*, we do not have time for this, brother." Kier jabbed a finger toward the rear of the ship. "If he is not in there already, he will be soon. Will we miss our opportunity for *this*?"

He looked at the holo again. A pair of tall, burly onigox, one with bright blue skin and the other with deep red skin, flanked Saduuk. Both were dressed in tailored, volturian style suits that looked ridiculous on their burly, four-armed frames, mostly because there'd been no attempt made to disguise the combat armor beneath their clothing.

"—will be confiscated by security," Saduuk said. "So keep your weapons on your ship. We don't tolerate violence here at Eternal Paradise. At least...not for free." The vroca's lips split in a wide grin again.

After lingering on Saduuk for much too long, the holo ended, and the central screen reverted to normal.

"No violence on his Eternal Paradise, but he knowingly deals with Vrykhan?" Kier demanded.

"We have encountered many of his sort, brother," Kayl replied. "They are driven purely by greed."

Kier stood, claws scraping the arms of his seat. "Perhaps he should be taught the true price of his crimes." He turned toward the rear of the ship.

Kayl caught Kier's upper arm, halting him. "He is not our target, Kier."

Fury roiled in Kier's chest, rising above the other tangled, roaring emotions. And still there was that strange pull, its gentle coaxing slowly building, building; how long before it was a compulsion, a command?

Our destiny is here.

Kayl's eyes narrowed. *Our destiny is to kill Vrykhan.*

Kier's lips peeled back, baring his teeth. "And I will not miss the chance to bring down those who have enabled Vrykhan for all these years along the way."

"Focus." Kayl guided Kier to turn toward him. "Vrykhan first. Then the rest."

If we outlive our revenge, both twins thought in unison.

Kier stared into his brother's eyes—one blue, one magenta, mirrors of his own. The torrent of emotion that swirled at Kier's core was echoed in Kayl, he knew it, but he could barely feel it, and he saw only the slightest hint of it in Kayl's gaze. Kier's nostrils flared, and his throat tensed with the sudden urge to yell at his twin. To ask why Kayl couldn't just...*feel.* Why he couldn't give himself over to those emotions, if only for a few minutes, so Kier could truly know that he was not alone in his feelings.

To ask why he insisted on shielding part of himself from his twin.

After releasing a heavy breath through his nose, Kier said, "They will have scanners at the entry checkpoints."

"Armor in stealth mode."

"And weapons? We have blaster pistols we can shield from the scanners, but you will be without your rail gun."

Kayl's lips twitched into the ghost of a frown. "Why voice questions to which you already know the answer?"

Because Kier was angry. Anxious.

Impatient.

The twins knew what had to happen; their *aerysi* spoke the words as one.

Even if we are unarmed, he will not escape our vengeance.

They hurried to their quarters and prepared, donning the form-fitting black suits that housed their retractable combat armor and stashing compact blasters in the suits' cloaked storage compartments. They put on the loose, flowing clothing their people preferred over the suits—silky tunics with low hems, baggy pants tucked into tall boots, and long, colorful wraps around their necks and shoulders.

Such attire was part of their heritage, their culture, and yet Kier always felt like an impostor when wearing it. They'd lived among other daevahs for such a brief time as children, and when they'd finally returned to daevah society as adults who'd fought their way out of slavery, they'd never felt at home. Their second stay with their kind had been far shorter than the first. What ties did they truly have to their people?

Shed your doubts, said Kayl's *aerys. Focus.*

Kier adjusted the wrap's position around his neck. *It would not kill you to lose focus every now and again.*

Kayl's reply was quick and cold. *It would kill us both.*

"I am ever so grateful that ego plays no part in our relationship," Kier said as he and his brother strode to the *Fang's* aft.

"Your sarcasm is hollow." Kayl used the holocom on his wrist to open the rear ramp while he and his brother descended into the cargo hold. "Ego does not play a part in our relationship."

"Perhaps it should. Changing things up a little might do us some good."

"We are meant to work as a team, Sol'Kier."

Hurrying ahead of his brother, Kier looked over his shoulder and snapped, "We are, but that does not mean we have to be happy with one another."

Kayl did not respond, following Kier down the ramp and toward the space station's entry door. Kier's annoyance sputtered and faded even as that unknown pull strengthened. He slowed his pace, allowing his brother to again fall into step at his side.

It is almost done, Kayl pulsed.

I know, Kayl. I can feel it. We are nearing the end.

If only they knew what end that would be.

Old memories stirred in the back of Kier's mind, but he shut them out. There could only be now—there could only be this place, this moment, this convergence of destiny's unfathomable paths.

The large airlock door slid open at their approach. The twins crossed the threshold, entering Eternal Paradise.

The wide reception area was lit with vibrant neon lights. Shimmering décor mingled with clusters of exotic plants, many of which glowed beneath the neon. More airlock entries stood along the wall to either side of the twins, each leading to a docking gate. Travelers entered and exited those gates all around.

It is busy, Kier pulsed. *That will not make this easy.*

We never expected easy, replied Kayl.

A large eatery stood on the other side of the chamber, its seats largely occupied by patrons with weary airs—likely travelers just passing through, stopping to refuel and have a meal before plunging back into the vast, empty stretches of space. Not far from the eatery was a service counter, and beside that, the security checkpoint leading deeper into the space station.

The twins followed the flow of people, entering the queue for the service counter. Kier watched to one side, Kayl to the other, their psychic link opened wide to share their sight with one another. Kier studied the faces within that expanded field of view, seeking anyone familiar, anyone suspicious—anyone with four jagged horns, four blazing eyes, and a mouthful of pointed teeth.

Each beat of his heart sharpened his focus, deepened his impatience, and heightened his anxiety, marking another lost moment. Fate called ever louder, luring him onward.

Half of them may well be criminals, but none wear it outright.

Kayl's tail brushed against Kier's. *Remain vigilant.*

You can see through my eyes, Kayl. You know I am being vigilant.

Yes. I only ask you to remain so, Kier.

Kier clenched his jaw. *Shall we twine our tails and hold hands, or will you trust me to do the bare minimum required of me?*

Before Kayl could respond, they reached the counter, where they were greeted by a cheerful female volturian dressed in a white uniform tailored to accentuate the body beneath without revealing much of it. The other two employees nearby, both males, were similarly attired.

Kier summoned a smile from the depths of his soul and perused the list of services the female provided, several of which were purposefully vague—especially considering *Entertainment* and *Pleasure* were separate.

It would seem revenge is not on the list.

No more jokes, Kier, Kayl replied, his psychic voice as flat as his spoken voice usually was.

It took a startling amount of willpower for Kier to hold back a retort. Somehow, he kept his smile in place, hoping it looked as warm, nonchalant, and natural as he needed it to, and selected refueling and entertainment from the services list.

He paid the balance up front, and he and Kayl were directed to the security checkpoint. The guards eyed the approaching twins with detached scrutiny. Kier clamped down on his emotions, managing to ease the stiff, restless movements of his tail. Both he and Kayl passed through the body scanner, neither allowing his thoughts to tumble down the slope of what-ifs over which they were perched.

They would not get caught here. They would not have to fight their way inside. And if they did...they would not be stopped before their purpose had been fulfilled.

The guards waved the twins through. Kier and Kayl walked along a hallway in which the walls and ceiling were deepest black, run through by streaking blue and purple lights reminiscent of stars speeding past a spacecraft.

Darkness loomed ahead. The formerly open space now felt too small, too tight, and unease coiled in Kier's gut. That odd sensation in his chest urged him onward, mixing his unease with burgeoning desperation...and still, only darkness awaited.

But Kier and Kayl had known that all along. They'd long since accepted it. They'd vowed long ago to throw themselves into the abyss if that was what it took to find and kill Vrykhan.

Fate. Purpose. Finally, we are where we were meant to be.

Kayl's *aerys* held a hint of unsteadiness, of barely restrained emotion. *The darkness holds no terror for us. Let this be done. For I am vengeance.*

And I am—

"Welcome," said a soothing, feminine voice from all around, "to paradise."

The darkness ahead split open, and light so bright that the twins had to shield their eyes spilled through. But their strides did not falter, remaining in perfect unison, carrying them to meet their fate.

The strange thread in Kier's chest tingled and warmed as he and his brother exited the dark corridor. Their eyes quickly adjusted, and they lowered their hands to take in their new surroundings.

Straight ahead stood the stone columns that had backed Saduuk at the beginning of the holo. Beyond them was a sleek, dark railing, seeming to hang in the air, overlooking an immense room filled with gaming tables and island bars. But the other details were clear now—vibrant plants, neon lights, and water fountains, some of which were garish and colorful, while others looked like waterfalls tumbling down rock formations. The ceiling overhead was shrouded by an immense hologram depicting a partly cloudy sky bearing the violets, reds, and oranges that heralded sunset on so many planets.

All the walls and walkways were reminiscent of building exteriors, many with eateries, clubs, and more gambling machines visible through wide display windows and arched entryways. Hundreds of people milled about gambling, talking, and drinking, creating a din of conversation that even the sound dampeners couldn't fully contain. The staff working the tables wore black uniforms tailored just like those of the service desk workers, but the servers carrying drinks and food around the floor were in the revealing outfits that had been in Saduuk's holo, with matching chokers around their necks.

The place was a strange blend of coastal vacation village and Undercity nightclub, and it left Kier oddly disoriented.

Together, the twins stepped forward and braced their hands on the railing to scan the concourse. Finding their target in that mass of bodies would've been difficult were Vrykhan not a tretin. Standing at nearly two and a half meters tall with a powerful build and those characteristic horns, the pirate would be easy to spot even in a crowd as diverse as this.

But he is presumably here for business, Kayl pulsed. *It is unlikely he will conduct said business in the open.*

Kier raked his gaze over the aliens below; they quickly blurred together despite hailing from countless different species. He curled his fingers around the railing, digging his claws into its underside.

So we find the owner. Saduuk.

The staff is not likely to share his location, Kier.

But they may provide unwitting answers all the same.

Kayl turned his head to look at Kier.

Once more, Kier felt a hint of his brother's emotions, all of which were tightly held down—whispers of desperation, anger, yearning. There was no telling whether they'd find Vrykhan, but this was the closest they'd ever been. They both felt it.

As one, the twins lifted their gazes to look across the space. The level upon which they stood formed a ring around the gaming floor below, complete with its own décor, shops, restaurants, bars, gambling, and private rooms. Numerous staircases and elevators bridged it to the lower level. But one spot on the opposite side of the concourse commanded their attention, where a massive staircase led up to a wide, tall entryway bordered with sleek columns, colorful plants, and alluring lights.

The glowing sign overhead read *Saduuk's Theater – Shows and Fine Cuisine.*

There, Kayl pulsed.

Kier drew in a deep breath. That internal pull intensified, squeezing his heart, seizing his lungs. That was the place. Logic said he couldn't possibly know that, and reason insisted he ask around to gather intelligence, but logic and reason had never been Kier's guiding forces—and it seemed even Kayl had abandoned them for now.

"We did pay for entertainment," Kier muttered.

Pushing away from the railing, he and Kayl strode toward the theater, dodging guests, ignoring the staff seeking to fill their tables, and declining the servers' offers to fetch refreshments.

Kier kept his eyes fixed on the theater's entrance. That was their destination, their destiny. Each step closer was heavier, yet somehow easier, than the last. That invisible tether led the twins along faster and faster.

Muted music struck them as they reached the theater's entrance.

Kier's heart sped to match its beat. The entrance was closed by a thick, lavish curtain with a satiny sheen and faintly glowing embroidery.

For what must've been the millionth time, Kier considered what he would say to Vrykhan when he was finally standing face to face with the tretin. So many years of struggle and sacrifice had led to this, and so many people had suffered and died because of Vrykhan in that time. What were the perfect words with which to deliver justice?

Kayl extended an arm to part the cloth, but his hand passed straight through—the curtain was just another hologram.

The twins exchanged an unamused glance and stepped forward to meet their long-awaited fate.

The music struck them full force the instant they crossed the threshold. Kier's brows fell, and he clamped his jaw against bass that vibrated down into his bones. He felt Kayl stiffen beside him; Kier couldn't help but smirk at that.

The theater was a large, tiered space with a high, domed ceiling beneath which dozens of free-floating holo lights swirled in ever-changing formations. The stage lay directly ahead, its sleek, black floor backed by flashing lights and abstract holos that all kept time with the music. A troupe of dancers of various species also moved to the music atop the stage. That their costumes were mere threads away from nudity certainly didn't detract from the sexual suggestiveness of their choreography.

The twins moved deeper inside, Kier scanning the right half of the theater, Kayl the left, again combining their vision psychically.

The floor in front of the stage was clear of furnishings, and it pulsed with synchronized patterns and lights beneath the feet of a writhing crowd of dancing patrons. Farther back were rows of seats, which extended up to the next level.

Dining tables dominated the remaining two tiers, the uppermost of which held several private booths that were elevated from the rest. Servers hurried between the tables, delivering food and drink, collecting dirty tableware, and taking orders.

With staff included, there were several hundred people present—a far from ideal situation considering what was likely to happen.

If opportunity arises, Kayl pulsed, *we must not ignore it for any reason.*

You have certainly developed a talent for stating the obvious, Kayl.

Kier's roving gaze halted on one of the booths—the only one that had Eternal Paradise security guards posted around it. Several individuals reclined on the plush seating within, including a bare-chested, four-armed dacrethian with golden skin. Beside him was a gray-skinned vroca with gold painted head spikes.

Saduuk, the twins thought in unison.

Saduuk lifted a glass from the table, tipped his head back, and drained the glowing drink in a long draft. His eyes darted around the room as he set the glass down.

Kayl's *aerys* pierced the surrounding noise. *We are early.*

The course was clear now—observe Saduuk, follow him if necessary.

The twins continued forward, looking around the theater as though for a place to sit.

Guards at every doorway, Kayl pulsed. *Understandable on the game floor, perhaps, but in a theater?*

Kier nodded, tail swaying. His muscles thrummed with anticipatory heat, assuming a looseness that occurred only in the face of a coming battle. It was contrasted by a deep, unsettling tension in his gut, a looming guilt as inevitable as the violence that would erupt when Vrykhan showed himself.

There would be casualties beyond the tretin and his pirates. Innocents would come to harm.

Kayl led Kier to an empty table on the uppermost level, one with an unhindered view of Saduuk's booth. Kier ordered drinks from the server who approached them, asking for the first that came to mind—void venom, a particularly potent beverage that Arcanthus's crew was fond of when they really wanted to do what Thargen described as *cut loose.*

Both daevahs turned their eyes toward the stage, though neither truly looked at it; Kayl watched the entrances within his view while Kier kept Saduuk in sight at the edge of his vision.

Restlessness coursed through Kier from top to bottom, making his skin itch beneath the surface. Bodies moved on stage, lights flashed, and music thumped, though the latter had faded now that the twins were at a table.

Saduuk grinned; the expression did not reach his troubled eyes. Dragging the dacrethian closer, he grasped the golden-skinned alien's chin in one hand while the other tugged the dacrethian's leg over his lap. Saduuk ravaged the dacrethian's mouth with his own and slid his hand to palm the dacrethian's ass.

Kier again surveyed the room, scrutinizing every audience member within his altered field of view. His leg threatened to bounce, so he held it down with a firm hand. When his tail lashed the seat cushion beside him, he curled it beneath his thigh, pinning it in place.

Focus. It is not yet the time to unleash my wrath.

In response, that unknown force pulled hard on his heart. For an instant, he was hollow, alone, incomplete, and was certain those feelings would tear him apart.

Something deep within—deeper than his mind, something buried in his soul—whispered.

This is where you behold your fate.

This is where you are made whole.

His eyes suddenly shifted to the stage of their own accord, settling not upon the panting performers but the unseen space beyond. Something awaited the twins backstage, something profound, and it beckoned them.

All Kier could hear was the pounding of his own heart. Heat skittered through him, crackling out from his center to flood his limbs, flowing to the tips of his fingers, toes, and tail.

Focus, Kayl pulsed, his psychic voice uncharacteristically strained.

Kier clenched his teeth and curled his fingers, pressing his claws into his thigh. Before he could question what was happening or what he felt, a flurry of movement at Saduuk's booth drew his attention in that direction. Several more security guards clustered around the booth, and Saduuk barked orders that were swallowed by sound dampeners long before they reached the twins.

The twins watched as Saduuk, eyes repeatedly shifting toward the main entrance, continued speaking. The vroca shoved the golden dacrethian aside to emphasize his words with harsh gestures—mostly aggravated pointing. Yet more security staff entered the theater from the side doors.

Never easy, Kier pulsed.

The universe does not understand easy, Kayl replied.

Battling the pull to look back at the stage, Kier turned his head just enough to bring the main entryway into view, where the guards appeared to be talking over commlinks.

Had there been time, the twins would've hacked into the security comm system.

Kier's fingers twitched, moving toward the hidden blaster on his thigh. But his eyes strained toward the stage again—toward that mysterious psychic magnet. None of the signs indicated Vrykhan would approach from that direction. Why did Kier want to keep looking that way? What was he missing?

He was only vaguely aware that the music had stopped, the flashing lights had given way to soft, unwavering blues and purples, and the dancers had retreated backstage to scattered cheers. He was only vaguely aware of the hush that fell over the room.

But he did notice the thickness of the air and the electric current with which it was charged. He noticed the jumbled emotions inside him, making him feel on the verge of explosion. And he could not ignore that unrelenting pull toward the stage.

This is our destiny...

Kier turned his head directly toward the entrance; Kayl did the same. The tips of their tails thumped the floor, their breath grew ragged, their hearts beat faster, harder, and their eyes narrowed.

After all these years, they would finally end their hunt. They would finally be done.

The holographic curtain at the entrance shimmered, and the nearby guards turned toward it.

Placing his hand over the hidden blaster, Kier drew in a deep breath.

The lights in the theater went out, plunging the place into utter darkness.

Alarm flared in Kier—both his own and Kayl's. He slid his hand through the slit on the side of his pants, reaching for the blaster as a curse clawed out of his throat.

A voice cut through the dark, but it wasn't the voice the twins had expected—it wasn't the rough, malicious voice of a tretin pirate. Kier's hand stilled. This voice was high, clear, lyrical, producing a wordless sound that came from everywhere at once. As it wove a soft melody, it slid gently higher and louder, gaining energy.

Kier's ears twitched, his eyes widened, and his tail curled. That voice reached inside him and wrapped around his heart, caressing it even as it sparked electricity along his every nerve and drove him mad. It was the most beautiful sound he'd ever heard.

The twins' heads snapped back toward the stage. Something was there—*someone*. In that pitch black, Kier could just make out a shape, a figure, a female...

Her voice rose to a high, powerful peak, and the stage lit up with brilliant teal, purple, and blue accents. A raised platform, itself ringed by vibrant lights, was positioned at the center of the stage with a female standing atop it.

Her short, blue skirt and revealing top, which was shaped like colorful wings cradling her breasts, shimmered in the light. It was complimented by the intricate metalwork of the choker around her neck, similar to the others the twins had seen but somehow *more*. She held her arms high as she prolonged that note, her eyes closed to display her multihued eyelids. Vibrant red hair hung in spiraling tresses and beaded braids around her shoulders, standing out fiercely amidst all the blue, purple, and black.

Something stirred in Kier, that deep, primal thing he must have always known was there but had never acknowledged, and his pulse permeated his body.

The female on stage ended the note. Her blue-painted lips stretched into a dazzling, blissful smile, and she opened her eyes. They were the purest, palest blue Kier had ever seen—and they stared right at him.

The audience cheered enthusiastically.

Kier's groin ached, and that pull demanded he rush onto the stage and carry her away; this female was not for the crowd to gawk at. She was for him. For Kayl. For *them*.

Without meaning to, he shifted his hand from his blaster to his groin. His fingers closed around his hard, throbbing cock, which was currently battling the restrictive bodysuit. It was so erect it hurt.

He hissed through his teeth as he squeezed his shaft. Kayl's *aerys* joined Kier's, ragged with shock, disbelief, and longing, sharing words that should never have been theirs to use.

The missing heart of our daevalis.

Our na'diya.

The twins met each other's gazes, fire and ice swirling through them in an uncontrollable torrent.

Our mate.

FOUR

Kayl couldn't move, couldn't breathe, couldn't think. He'd always maintained tight control of his emotions, but this... This went so far beyond emotion that he didn't know what to call it.

Fate. It is our fate.

She *is our fate.*

Upbeat music blared over the sound system, the theater lights pulsed and flashed in synchronization, and the audience cheered louder, but nothing could distract him from her.

The female on stage was radiant, a brilliant star in an expanse of empty black. For Kayl, there was nothing but her in that moment. He doubted there'd ever be anything but her after this.

Kayl's heart stuttered, and the feeling that had led him here—that had led *them* here—coiled in his chest. Heat thrummed inside him, racing along his limbs in electric jolts, and his cock ached. He clenched his jaw to stifle a groan and pressed down on his groin to alleviate the pressure. His touch only made it worse.

He'd not experienced an erection in years. Not since...not since he and Kier had been slaves, since they'd been drugged to force arousal. Male daevahs could become aroused naturally by only one thing—their mate.

The female strutted forward, moving her hips with the beat. Kayl's muscles tensed. His body was eager to rush to her, to embrace her, to bring her into the *daevalis.*

But she was a terran. Was it even possible for daevahs and terrans to form such a bond, to complete a *daevalis?*

Why was he wasting time on such thoughts? He and Kier were not meant to complete their *daevalis.* Their destiny was to slay Vrykhan, to deliver justice, to exact vengeance.

They weren't supposed to find a mate. Weren't supposed to have a *na'diya.*

Yet now all he could think about was taking this terran far away from this place so she could become their heart, their soul.

The terran resumed singing. Her voice rose above the music, shoving everything else into the background, and enveloped Kayl in warmth, in beauty, in joy. His translator implant conveyed the meaning of her words, but he recognized their sound even without it —it was the same language used by the other terrans he'd met.

She lifted her foot. A thin, glowing platform appeared in the air beneath it, and she stepped up. Once she stood at the center of the small platform, it rose into the air, lifting her high above the crowd that had gathered around the stage. As she raised her voice into something powerful and uplifting, the platform carried her forward.

The crowd roared in response.

A growl rumbled in Kayl's chest. He only stopped himself from charging toward the terran by bracing his free hand on the table.

She was his, she was Kier's. She was not for these people.

That flare of jealousy, of possessiveness, was reflected in his brother, but Kayl could not fool himself this time. His own reaction had been just as strong as Kier's.

Each time the terran shifted her weight, a small, faint aura of light appeared beneath her foot— cloudy luminescence reminiscent of distant galaxies in blues, violets, and teals. With every passing second, the platform brought her a little closer to the twins, a little closer to the *daevalis* she was meant to complete.

Focus.

But that word had lost its meaning. All words had lost their meanings.

The platform halted only ten meters away from the twins' table, placing the female on the same level as them. Her eyelids fell shut, and her voice soared again.

"Welcome to paradise!" She drew that last word out into some-

thing triumphant, majestic, and moving, all through the power of her entrancing voice.

Tingles spread across Kayl's skin. Only when the terran's eyes opened again did he realize he and Kier had stood up. That unseen force stretched tight between the twins and the terran, making the space separating them seem impossibly vast.

Her gaze fell upon them. Those eyes, so stunning a blue, bore an odd glossiness, a lack of focus, a...distance, but all that faded when they rounded and her smile fell, lips parting slightly. Her delicate eyebrows drew closer together, forming a tiny crease between them.

Time halted as Kayl stared into her eyes. The space station could have crumbled around him, the whole universe could have collapsed, and he wouldn't have looked away.

Something clawed at the back of his mind, urgent and desperate.

Our only destiny is to...is... Our destiny is...

Her, Kier pulsed.

The terran blinked and started, the movement making her red tresses sweep across her cheeks and shoulders and the glittering strands of her skirt brush across her pale thighs. Then she spun away, launching into the next verse of her song.

Kayl's gaze dipped, fixing upon a marking on her right ankle—a sprig of some flower with small violet petals and tiny green leaves. His fingers twitched, palms thrumming with the desire to touch her skin, to feel its warmth, its smoothness, its softness.

But the platform was carrying her away. Kayl stepped forward to give chase, bumping the table and rattling the utensils and drinks.

It was enough to snap Kayl back to reality. Though the terran and her voice remained brightest and clearest of all, his awareness expanded to all the other sights and sounds, to the sharp, stinging scent of the void venom that had spilled on the table.

He looked at his brother. Kier wore Kayl's feelings in his expression—lingering shock, arousal, and an uncertain blend of hope and disbelief. Neither of them spoke, not out loud or in their minds.

Of all the things they could have expected to find here, of all the things they might've hoped to find, neither would ever have imagined meeting their mate in this place. And though Kayl had long relied upon his keen senses, they must have been deceived.

None of this could've been real.

She could not have been real.

And yet there she was, singing above the crowded dance floor, her body swaying to the music. Kayl's heart was still pounding, his limbs were still tingling, his hard cock was still throbbing.

Kier's gaze shifted to look past Kayl, and he bared his teeth. Rage swelled in him, a firestorm barely contained by something cold and heavy—dread.

Kayl's fury rose in response. It was more concentrated than Kier's, a sharpened shard of ice rather than an inferno, but it too was encased in dread. He knew what he'd see when he turned. He'd spent most of his life anticipating this moment, imagining what he would do, how it would feel. He'd dreamed about the satisfaction it would bring, had yearned for the closure. Now that it was here, he wasn't sure if he wanted it.

Because when he turned and beheld it with his own eyes, it would mean all this was undoubtedly real. It would mean the twins' *na'diya* was in the same room as *him*.

Kayl clenched his jaw and spun around. For the second time, everything halted, and his focus narrowed on a single person, blocking out the rest of existence.

A two-and-a-half-meter-tall tretin walked toward Saduuk's booth, his stride unhurried, his thick, powerful tail swaying behind him. The tretin seemed unconcerned with the half-dozen security guards surrounding him with hands on their holstered blasters. Kayl recognized that nonchalance for what it was—the confidence of a predator that had broken into the cage of its helpless prey.

Two curving horns jutted from the tretin's forehead, with another pair sweeping outward from the sides of his head. His four eyes gleamed, crimson irises contrasted by black sclera. The tretin's body was broad and powerful, but he wasn't overly bulky —his kind were amongst the most feared warriors in the universe, and they were built for agility as much as they were for strength.

Vrykhan.

None of the few holos and still images of the infamous pirate had prepared the twins for seeing him in person again. During their first and only direct encounter, Kayl and Kier had been children, and Vrykhan had been a gigantic, nightmarish figure, too terrible to be overcome by mere mortals.

The tretin was still nightmarish and terrible, but he wasn't quite so big as Kayl recalled...and he'd never been anything more than flesh and blood.

Kayl's hand shifted to his thigh, sweeping aside the fabric of his tunic and parting the slit on his pants to reach for the hidden blaster. Vrykhan strode past the twins' table, coming closer to them than the terran had.

A hand clamped around Kayl's wrist, halting his arm before he could open the weapon compartment. Kayl glared at his brother, whose fiery gaze remained on the tretin.

Not yet, Kier pulsed; his *aerys* was a ragged, bristling growl.

This is our chance, Kier. Here. Now.

The muscles of Kier's jaw ticked. His eyes shifted toward the floating platform—toward the terran performing upon it.

"Not for any reason, Kier," Kayl said. "We agreed. Not for *any* reason."

Kier met his brother's gaze and bared his teeth, tail flicking erratically. "I never knew she could be a reason, Kayl. We were not supposed to find her. She was not supposed to exist."

With a huff, Kayl tore his arm free from his brother's grasp, leaning aside to seek Vrykhan. The tretin was walking straight for Saduuk's booth.

We cannot ignore what we have found here, Kier pulsed.

I am not. We found exactly what we came for, and I am going to kill him.

Kier shifted his body to match Kayl's stance. Jumbled, raw emotions radiated from him in waves, battering what little control Kayl had reclaimed.

They could not let the tretin slip through their fingers. They could not let Vrykhan escape. Not after all this time, not after what Vrykhan had done, after what the twins had been forced to do.

Not after everything they and so many others had lost.

It will spark chaos, Kier said through the psychic link. *She is only one of many who may come to harm.*

Kayl stared at the tretin. In his memory, he relived that night—he heard the screams, smelled the blood and scorched flesh, tasted his tears. He saw his parents, his mother and fathers, die. But those memories couldn't help him ignore the pang of guilt in his heart brought on by the thought of the terran being hurt.

Many more will suffer if we fail. It ends here, Kier. It ends now. And she...she is not for us.

Kier's tail bumped Kayl's calves in its restless swinging. Kayl sensed the stiffness in his brother's posture, the tension gripping his brother's body, the roiling frustration and indecision in his brother's heart.

She cannot be a distraction from our purpose, Kayl pulsed.

Kier snorted. *She is meant to be our purpose.*

A cold, slithering thing wrapped around Kayl's heart and squeezed it. *Our* na'diya *deserves more than a broken pair. Deserves better than us.*

The deep wounds on Kayl's soul, that old, inescapable pain, was mirrored in Kier. Different as they were, they shared those invisible scars. They carried that crushing weight. Alone, neither would have been able to do so.

With a huff, Kier dropped a hand to his thigh. "Fine. Let us end this."

Kayl swallowed the hot, bitter lump in his throat and returned to his seat.

Kier narrowed his eyes, lips peeling back to reveal his fangs. "What the fuck, Kayl?"

Keeping his arms below the tabletop, Kayl touched a control on his holocom. A tiny, spherical drone detached from its docking station on the holocom and floated into the air, vanishing as its cloaking function activated. Kayl directed the drone toward Saduuk's booth.

Kier dropped into his chair, arms slamming on the table to jar everything atop it. "After all your arguing, we are going to sit here and watch?"

Watch and listen, Kayl corrected.

Kier's *aerys* echoed Kayl's earlier words, laced with venom. *It ends here. It ends now.*

As you have pointed out, Kier, she is but one of many bystanders present, and Vrykhan is surrounded by guards. We will kill him, but we will act only when we can be sure the plasma bolts meant for him are not intercepted by his escort...or an innocent bystander.

The drone's audio feed came on in Kayl's ear commlink just as Vrykhan halted a few meters away from Saduuk's booth.

Saduuk flicked a control, likely manipulating the sound dampeners that normally restricted conversations to the confines of his private booth.

Vrykhan spread his arms, palms turned toward the ceiling. When he spoke, his voice was relayed to the twins through the drone. "This is how you welcome me, Saduuk?"

A chill crept down Kayl's spine. He clenched his fists, digging his claws into his palms, and gritted his teeth as that chill merged with his rage. After all these years, he still recognized Vrykhan's deep, gravelly voice. Even if he lived forever, he'd never forget it.

Kier growled and squeezed the tablecloth in one hand.

Saduuk stood up and lifted his hands to match Vrykhan's gesture. He stepped out of the booth; despite there being six guards around the tretin, two more fell into place on Saduuk's flanks as he advanced.

"Dangerous times, my friend, dangerous times." Saduuk wore a smile, but his eyes gleamed with unease. He gestured toward the booth. "Come and sit. Have a few drinks, and we can address whatever business you've come to conduct."

The guards are focused on the tretin, Kier pulsed. *We can strike before they realize what is happening.*

Kayl's hand again drifted to his blaster, this time slipping through the slit on his pants and opening the compartment. *We will have our moment.*

All Kayl needed was an instant, a clear shot, and it would be done. A single plasma bolt in response to decades of terror, death, and suffering.

Hardly adequate.

But the armored security staff were still packed around the tretin, and a few of them were nearly as large as him.

"Always quick to jest, aren't you?" Vrykhan lowered his arms, his tone somehow warm despite the threat with which it was laced.

Saduuk tilted his head and narrowed his eyes, smile wavering. "Not sure what you mean."

Vrykhan took a single step toward the vroca. The security guards shifted with him, making no apparent attempt to impede his advance.

"And the jokes keep coming," Vrykhan rumbled.

Saduuk's arms fell, and the remnants of his smile fell with them.

The music shifted into a new song, and the terran's voice

changed with it, producing low, sultry notes that spread tingles along Kayl's flesh. He gritted his teeth, neck tensing as he fought the urge to fix his gaze upon her and never look away.

Vrykhan turned his head toward the stage, granting a glimpse of his predatory grin to Kayl. The tretin's four blazing eyes followed the female's movements.

Rage erupted inside Kayl, doubled by his brother's fury to become a supernova that seized his every muscle with searing heat and halted his heart. Before he'd realized he'd moved his hand again, his fingers were wrapped around the grip of his blaster, loosening it in its hidden holster.

Vrykhan was not allowed to look upon their female that way. He was not allowed to threaten her.

Kayl's eyes flicked to his brother. Kier was pushing himself up from his seat, pulling his weapon free, a firestorm alight in his mismatched eyes.

Kier!

Kier faltered, angling his face down.

Not yet, Kayl pulsed. *We must be patient.*

If ever there was a time to act, Kayl, it is now!

"Do you like what you see?" asked Saduuk. "You can have her for tonight. A sign of our friendship."

"Your little distractions aren't going to get you out of this," Vrykhan replied.

"What are you getting at, Vrykhan?" Saduuk's stance had grown rigid, and he'd twisted slightly away from the tretin; he was an animal confronted by a predator, poised to flee.

"You know exactly why I'm here, Saduuk." Vrykhan returned his attention to the vroca. "You're stupid, but not that stupid."

Saduuk scowled. "You come to my place and insult me, and—"

"We're far beyond insults, old friend."

A short, bitter laugh escaped Saduuk. "Look around. You want to call someone stupid? You're the one threatening me while you're alone and unarmed in a room with thirty of my guards. Out there, you might be the boss, but this is *my* place. I'm on top here."

Vrykhan took another step toward Saduuk, again unhindered by the guards, who simply moved with him. "We're beyond threats, too."

Saduuk backpedaled, eyes wide. "What the fuck was I supposed to do? What the fuck did you expect?"

Kier lifted his gaze, meeting Kayl's. *We are missing our chance.*

Patience, Kayl replied.

Anger creased Kier's brow. He flattened his empty hand atop the table and leaned toward his twin. *It is always patience until you are focused on something, Kayl. We have not gone through all this, we have not hunted for all these years, just to watch someone else gun him down!*

The terran female's voice became a breathy moan, backed by primal, pulsing drums in a sensuous beat. Each note reached straight into Kayl, coiling arousal low in his belly. His blood heated, and his breaths grew shallow. He needed to claim her, needed to—

Needed to focus. Needed to fulfill his purpose.

His finger crept behind the trigger guard of his blaster, settling over the trigger. One plasma bolt...

"Tell me when that fucking volturian showed up," Vrykhan growled. "You've been getting breaks on merchandise for years, and the one thing I asked—"

"Ship manifests, passenger lists, and routes." Saduuk jabbed a finger at Vrykhan. "That's what you asked for, and I've always delivered."

"I told you what to do if that volturian came here. I told you to hold him and contact me." Vrykhan's shoulders rose with a deep, harsh breath. "I was very clear in my instructions. And then I hear that he did come through. That he was here, and you knew about it." The tretin leaned forward bared his fangs. "You didn't hold him. Didn't contact me."

Those guards need to stand aside. Kier's psychic voice was strained; he was barely holding himself back.

Anger flashed across Saduuk's features, though it didn't overpower the glimmer of fear in his eyes. "And you didn't tell me that Syntrell Volcair Vantricar was a former commander in the Dominion military or that his father is the fucking Dominion ambassador to Arthos!"

"We're not in Arthos, Saduuk."

"You think the Dominion couldn't hit me out here if they wanted to? I don't cause them trouble. That's why I'm still in business!"

"But you caused me trouble. That's why you're no longer in business."

Saduuk shook his head, releasing a disbelieving laugh. "Not great with numbers, are you?"

In that moment, Kayl understood the truth of the situation, which he should have realized the moment Vrykhan walked into the theater.

Vrykhan had evaded pursuers for decades—not just the twins, but countless bounty hunters, mercenary forces, and elite teams of soldiers dispatched by various intergalactic governments. In person, the tretin was huge, powerful, dominant without exerting effort. He was a warrior capable of overpowering almost any foe who challenged him. But it was not strength that had made him so elusive, it was cunning.

Kayl's insides knotted and sank, and his tail stiffened. He tugged his blaster free. *This is about to get much, much worse.*

He felt eyes upon him, sparking heat along his spine and rekindling his arousal. He could not stop himself from glancing over his shoulder.

The female terran was still on the transparent platform, which had again stopped close to the twins' table, and she was looking right at Kier and Kayl as she sang. There was a light flush to her cheeks, and something gleamed in her eyes—a hint of uncertainty, a spark of curiosity.

Kayl's every cell thrummed, drawn toward her by a force greater than the gravitational pull of a black hole. His legs tensed; he refused to give in to that urge. He was here to deal with Vrykhan, not mate with this terran. He was here to end a fifteen-year-long hunt.

"Oh, I'm fine with numbers, old friend. But unlike you, I understand that numbers aren't everything," Vrykhan said.

Kayl wrenched his attention away from the terran only by using of every shred of his willpower.

The security guards in front of Vrykhan raised their blasters, directing them toward Saduuk.

Vrykhan chuckled. "It takes more than credits to earn loyalty."

Saduuk's eyes nearly popped out of their sockets. The guards fired. The vroca recoiled, ducking his head and throwing his arms over it as blue-white plasma bolts zipped through the air around him. Those bolts struck the booth, hitting the dacrethian who'd been with Saduuk; they hit the guards to either side of him; they hit the other guards who'd been stationed around the booth.

The high whine of the blaster fire mingled with the music, accompanied by screams from nearby patrons.

And the terran continued singing, already bathed in the flashing lights that went with her show.

At least a dozen curses in nearly as many languages raced through the twins' psychic link simultaneously, but they could all be summed up by one word.

Fuck.

Kayl swung his left hand to his right wrist, tapping the controls for his armor without releasing his blaster. Kier did the same. The twins stood up simultaneously, their chairs falling away as their segmented combat armor expanded and shifted into place, fitting itself snugly around their bodies and tails.

Saduuk, untouched by the onslaught of plasma, shouted a command to his security.

The music continued playing, though the panicked cries of the audience was now competing with its volume, and fresh blaster fire sparked around the room. Kayl saw enough of the chaos in his peripheral vision to understand what was happening—security guards battled one another along with armed members of the audience near every door, half a dozen small firefights occurring at once. Panicked bystanders rushed for the exits, but there seemed to be nowhere safe to flee.

Vrykhan's pirates had infiltrated Eternal Paradise in every sense.

The tretin strode forward. The guards around him kept close, covering his advance—an armed and armored barrier standing between the tretin and the twins' revenge.

"Pass on the word," Vrykhan said as the guards in front of him stepped aside. "Take everything, everyone. As much as we can. We burn the rest."

Two of the guards nodded and broke away from the group.

Saduuk retreated from the tretin. His heel struck the step leading up into his booth, and he fell, landing hard on his backside. Before he could recover, Vrykhan was over him.

The tretin clamped a huge hand around the Saduuk's neck and lifted him. "You can't buy loyalty, old friend. You earn it by taking care of your own. I will avenge any wrong done to my crew, and Syntrell Volcair Vantricar killed nine of them. It's been too long on that score. He needs to die. But you wouldn't understand that, would you?"

Vrykhan raised Saduuk higher. The vroca clawed at the tretin's thick forearm, legs flailing with feet nearly half a meter over the floor. His face rapidly darkened.

The terran's singing halted abruptly, allowing the continued blaster fire to become the dominant sound. Those shrill, piercing notes were a poor replacement for the terran's voice.

A blast of confusion and panic slammed into Kayl, strong and sudden enough to nearly throw him off balance. It wove through all his other emotions and settled in as though it had belonged there all along. But that confusion and panic weren't his—and they didn't feel like Kier's either.

Could they have come from the terran?

No, that wasn't possible. They'd not completed their triad, hadn't mated with her. How could she already be so firmly lodged in their *daevalis?*

"Oh shite," she said.

Those words, so brief, sounded different—a different lilt to them, a different accent. Kayl yearned to hear more of it, to compare it to her singing voice, but...

But this is not the time, damn it! What is wrong with me?

FIVE

W*HAT IS WRONG WITH* us, Kier pulsed, raising his blaster. *It is now or never, Kayl.*

Kayl released a growl and clamped his free hand on the edge of the table; Kier grasped the opposite side. They opened fire on Vrykhan's guards as they tipped the table over.

Plasma bolts struck armor, leaving bright, orange glows, and scorched through flesh. As the guards turned to face the twins, two of them fell with smoke curling from their smoldering wounds.

Vrykhan's head snapped aside, and two of his eyes locked on the twins. His lips twisted into a fanged scowl as he squeezed Saduuk's neck. His claws sank into the vroca's throat.

Saduuk twitched, his struggles taking on a new urgency. Dark, frothy blood bubbled from his mouth, and he made a choked grunt. The tretin tightened his grip; Saduuk's throat crunched, and his struggles halted.

Vrykhan flung Saduuk's body over the railing. Seemingly unconcerned with the plasma bolts flying only meters away, he bent down to wrench an auto-blaster from the hands of a dead guard.

Kayl's throat constricted with a swell of rage. He focused it down to a fine point, and felt Kier's rage consolidate around it, creating a deadly weapon.

The guard's return fire punched through the table to either side of Kayl, leaving sizzling, melted plastic dripping down its surface. Kayl fired two shots faster than thought; Kier fired simultaneously.

The two remaining guards were each hit by a pair of plasma bolts through the eyes. One continued firing his auto-blaster into the floor as he fell.

The barrier was down. The way was clear. Finally, there would be justice. There would be vengeance.

Kayl swung his blaster toward Vrykhan.

The tretin fired his auto-blaster from the hip as he spun toward the twins, spraying a torrent of plasma bolts at them. The projectiles blasted through the table, leaving misshapen holes and melting plastic. They hit the floor, charring the carpeting and creating orange-ringed grooves in the metal beneath, and struck the twins' armor, creating dull impacts on Kayl's torso, legs, and right arm.

The thump of an explosion sounded from the other side of the theater, and the music cut out.

Smoke stung Kayl's nose; his tunic had been ignited by the plasma breaking on his armor.

Ducking behind the table, he activated his helmet and grasped the loose fabric of his tunic and wrap as the faceplate slid into place. The helmet's display immediately populated a heat gauge—a small icon in the shape of the armor showing the points of impact and the heat building up on the segments.

Even advanced armor had limits to the punishment it could withstand. But it would hold. It *had* to hold until this was done.

Kayl tore off the burning clothing and threw it on the floor, wadding the fabric and stomping on it to snuff out the flames. Beside him, Kier struggled to remove his smoldering tunic, which had caught between two of the armor segments on his back.

Grasping his brother's garment, Kayl ripped it free, leaving behind only a scrap of dangling cloth.

Kier slapped his holocom. His helmet extended from his neck armor in pieces, enclosing his head fully within a fraction of a second.

"So what are you?" Vrykhan asked. Another burst of plasma struck the table, and more bolts broke upon the twin's armor. "Bounty hunters? Special forces? Stupid kids with something to prove?"

"We are wrath," Kier spat.

Kayl shifted his head to peer through one of the many holes in the table. The glimpse of the tretin's gray flesh was all he needed; he angled his blaster toward it. "We are vengeance."

He squeezed the trigger, firing through the table. Vrykhan unleashed a furious roar and returned fire. The scattered shots struck all around the twins, hissing and sparking.

We need to be quick, Kayl, Kier pulsed. *His crew will be converging on us soon.*

Now who is pointing out the obvious, Kier? Kayl activated the drone's holo feed. A window appeared in his helmet display, sharing the drone's viewpoint from near Saduuk's booth.

It showed Vrykhan's back as the tretin charged toward the twins.

"*Zor atkoshai,*" Kier snapped.

He leapt to the right, Kayl to the left, just as Vrykhan smashed the table into pieces with a heavy kick.

"Not something to prove," Vrykhan growled, storming through the wrecked table to place himself between the twins. "Someone to avenge."

Kayl landed on one knee, tail straight out to solidify his balance, and swung his blaster up. The tretin used his auto-blaster like a club, slamming it into Kayl's extended arm. The blow blasted him with bone-deep pain and knocked the weapon from his hand.

Kier found his footing quickly and bent his legs to leap. Vrykhan's tail lashed out, hammering into the side of Kier's head to send him reeling.

Vrykhan stared down at Kayl. Only charred, smoking flesh remained where two of his crimson eyes had been. He bared his sharp teeth. "The worst kind. Always making things personal."

"You murdered our parents," Kier snarled, firing his blaster as he angled it toward Vrykhan. A bolt struck the tretin's tail.

Vrykhan snarled and spun with startling speed, releasing the foregrip of his auto-blaster to catch Kier's wrist. Kier grunted as the tretin wrenched on his arm, angling the blaster away. Kayl's heart stuttered. He lunged at Vrykhan, who kicked him hard in the chest, forcing all the air out of his lungs and sending him to the floor.

"I've murdered many parents," Vrykhan said, his deep, harsh voice raking across Kayl's very soul. "Brothers and sisters, cousins, friends. And all the people who came to avenge them."

Helplessness gathered in Kayl's core, curling into a dense,

impossibly heavy ball laced with that near-immobilizing panic that could only have come from the terran. This was how he'd felt the day Vrykhan had attacked his home. This was how he'd felt as a child.

Had nothing changed?

At the edge of the drone's visuals, something moved—the terran. She was on her hands and knees, trapped atop the floating platform high over the dance floor.

Kayl's chest constricted, and his inhalation burned his throat and lungs.

We are not helpless.

"We have hunted you, tretin," Kier said, his rage flowing stronger, brighter.

"For fifteen years," Kayl continued, rolling onto his belly and pushing himself up.

Vrykhan maintained his hold on Kier's arm and kept the auto-blaster aimed at Kayl. His expression twisted into a scowl. "You're the ghosts. The ones who've been fucking with all my contacts."

"We are your death," the twins said in unison.

"You might've lived a little longer if you hadn't fucked with my crew," Vrykhan said. "Might've earned slavery instead. But I'm just going to kill you. Which one wants to be first?"

The twins were moving before Vrykhan had finished his question. Kayl got his feet beneath him and whipped his tail forward, wrapping it around the tretin's ankle; Kier twisted to hook his free arm around Vrykhan's. The tretin snarled. His auto-blaster fired, hitting Kayl's helmet and shoulders.

Kier rolled away from Vrykhan, using all his weight to pull the tretin's arm. It might not have been enough to have an effect had Kayl not rolled in the opposite direction that same instant, yanking on the tretin's leg.

Vrykhan's foot slipped off the floor, and the hulking tretin flipped. His leg escaped Kayl's hold as Vrykhan fell on his back with a great crash, crushing pieces of the table beneath him.

Kier rode his momentum to get atop the tretin. Growling like a beast, he rained lightning-fast blows upon Vrykhan, striking with claws and the grip of his blaster.

Kayl snatched his fallen weapon off the floor and stood up. His arm darted out, and he squeezed the trigger. Kier leaned aside, clearing a path for Kayl's shot. But Vrykhan shifted with him. The bolt hit the floor centimeters to the side of the tretin's head.

Kier fired a shot of his own, missing by the same distance to the other side of Vrykhan's head.

Vrykhan's huge fist connected with the side of Kier's helmet. The *thunk* of the impact was so strong that it resonated in Kayl's skull, making his head ache, but somehow, Kier did not fall. When the tretin attempted to raise his auto-blaster, Kier caught it with his free hand, halting it. His muscles trembled as he leaned forward, using all his strength and weight to counter the tretin's might.

Vrykhan's empty hand swung back, elbow bent to block Kier from aiming his weapon. Those thick, claw-tipped fingers wrapped around Kier's throat.

"There are conquerors," Vrykhan said through bloodied teeth. "And the conquered. You should've remembered your fucking place."

Paralyzing emotion welled within Kayl. He and his brother had risked death countless times, but this was different. This was the end. The twins had always known their deaths were likely, perhaps even necessary, to achieve their goal. As long as Vrykhan died...

But seeing his brother at the mercy of their nemesis triggered something in Kayl he'd not anticipated. He didn't want to die. More than that, he didn't want his brother to die. Willingness to give their lives for their cause did not mean they had to yearn for their deaths. It did not mean they should stop fighting to live. It did not mean they should throw their lives away.

We are not done, Kier pulsed. *Assistance would be appreciated.*

Despite everything, Kayl's lips twitched into a smirk. He closed the distance to Vrykhan in two steps and fired three shots into one of the few parts of the tretin not shielded by Kier's body—his leg.

Vrykhan roared in pain. His leg stiffened, and bits of ashen fibers crumbled around the charred edges of the plasma holes in his right thigh. Kier's blaster went off again; the tretin whipped his head aside. The plasma bolt sheared off the top few centimeters of one of his horns.

Before Kayl could fire again, Vrykhan's tail swept across the floor, directed at the daevah's feet. Kayl leapt backward, avoiding the limb. But he could not dodge the next attack.

Muscles bulging, Vrykhan threw Kier off. Kier's limbs flailed as he flew backward. His heels came down on the floor, and he stumbled back, nearly catching his balance, but he collided with Kayl before he could stop.

The twins tumbled, Kier atop Kayl, halting only when Kayl's back struck the railing at the edge of the tier. They scrambled to right themselves.

Vrykhan grabbed a chunk of the ruined table and flung it at the twins. Kier and Kayl raised their arms. Even with their armor, the impact was immense, slamming Kier into Kayl and Kayl into the barrier, jolting bones and punishing joints.

People shouted nearby, their voices drawing closer. Figures appeared in the drone's feed, navigating overturned tables and chairs on their way toward the twins. Kayl doubted they were guards coming to apprehend the tretin.

We cannot fail, Kier.

Not for her, Kier replied.

Her could only be one person—the terrified terran trapped several meters in the air behind them. A terran who had clearly never been exposed to the world in which the twins had been immersed for nearly half their lives.

Because if Vrykhan was victorious, she would not leave this place a free being. She would see suffering even greater than anything the twins had endured.

Together, Kayl and his brother shoved the heavy piece of table aside.

Vrykhan was on one knee, bloody teeth bared. He lifted his autoblaster, depressing the trigger before the barrel was even directed at the twins. A spray of plasma bolts swept across the floor as he adjusted his aim.

The twins raised their weapons and fired. Vrykhan's bolts struck their armor and everything around them, making Kayl's heat gauge flare. Kier's shot hit Vrykhan's shoulder, Kayl's his arm. The tretin growled, jerking back, and the stream of plasma swung up and aside.

Kayl hissed at a sudden flare of pain in his gut, a flash of searing heat that stole his breath. Kier made the same sound, body tensing.

Kayl's helmet display highlighted several incoming threats—the armed individuals who'd been advancing. Gritting his teeth, he looked down. Several spots on his armor glowed with cooling plasma impacts, but the armor itself was unbroken.

Kier.

It was not me, Kier pulsed.

Vrykhan's auto-blaster ceased firing as the tretin attempted to right himself. His features contorted in pain and rage as his wounded leg buckled and he fell aside, catching himself by dropping his hand —which still clutched his weapon—to the floor. He growled and glared at the twins.

This was the moment. The monster Kayl and his brother had spent so long hunting was before them, vulnerable, wounded. All they had to do was finish him.

But Kayl could not focus upon Vrykhan. Nor could he focus upon the plasma bolts being fired at him by the approaching pirates. All that hardship, all that searching, all the fighting and suffering...it meant nothing, because he knew just then where the pain in his gut had come from.

The twins grasped the railing and stood up. Though all his deeply rooted rage protested, Kayl glanced over his shoulder. Kier did the same.

The terran female lay atop her transparent platform, curled on her side with her arms around her belly and her back toward the twins. Those shimmering red locks were in disarray, and her chest and shoulders rose and fell with rapid, shallow breaths.

A plasma bolt had hit just above her hip, burning away a large chunk of flesh and leaving everything around it a raw, blackened mess.

What passed between the twins in response to that sight was beyond Kayl's ability to describe. It transcended words and thoughts, and though a torrent of emotions came with it—fear, fury, guilt, and a driving desperation—it was so much more than emotion.

Something had awakened in their cores, and it seized control.

The twins had only one purpose. A new purpose.

They acted without conscious thought. Kayl passed Kier his blaster and grasped the railing. With a blaster in each hand, Kier fired a barrage of plasma at the approaching foes, many of whom ducked behind cover—Vrykhan included.

Kayl hopped up, planting his feet atop the railing. His tail moved behind him to preserve his balance as he sank into a crouch, muscles coiling. He leapt off the rail with every bit of strength he could muster. Blue-white plasma bolts darted through the air around him, punctuated by the whines of firing blasters and the pained, terrified cries of people elsewhere in the theater.

But all his attention was on the female. On their terran.

His feet hit the platform with a heavy *thunk*, and it dipped and bobbed under his weight, causing him to slide. Reflexively, he activated his armor's climbing pads and slapped a hand down.

His legs swung off the far edge of the platform, but the climbing pad caught and halted his momentum before he could fall off. He fixed his eyes on the terran and pulled himself to the center of the platform.

Kier roared and kept shooting, his hands in constant motion to send white-hot plasma in the direction of every target before him. He moved with preternatural speed, producing a rate of fire to match any auto-blaster.

Kayl hurriedly placed himself between the terran and the pirates, knelt, and scooped her trembling body into his arms. She started, eyes flaring; her pupils were so large that they swallowed almost all the pale blue of her irises.

He could not help but notice her features, could not help but admire the lines of her nose and jaw, so delicate and yet so strong, and the fullness of her lips. He could not help but lose himself, if only in small part, in her eyes.

She stared up at him, her terror peaking for a heart-crushing instant, but something shifted in her gaze.

"Finally," the terran rasped. She whimpered and curled against his chest with her arms clamped around her midsection, body shivering.

Some piece of Kayl recognized what he was doing, and it fought him, but it could not overcome the thoughts repeating in his mind on an endless loop.

You will be all right, terran.

Please be all right.

You must be all right.

Clutching the wounded female securely against him, Kayl jumped off the platform. His knees bent as he landed on the next tier down, legs absorbing the impact of the three-meter drop. The terran released a strained, pained breath, tensing in his hold.

Kayl stood upright as Kier landed beside him. Shouts sounded from the upper level, answered by more from around and below the twins.

They did not need to speak their new purpose. They understood what had to be done, understood what was driving them now—instinct. Instinct that Kayl was powerless to deny. That he did not want to deny.

They needed to get their female, their *na'diya*, to safety.

Kier ran, and Kayl followed half a step behind.

Be all right.

SIX

Kɪᴇʀ's ʜᴇᴀʀᴛ thundered in his ears, setting a frantic rhythm that urged him onward ever faster. Countless thoughts tumbled in his mind, colliding and careening, forming impenetrable chaos amidst his anger and desperation, but the twins' purpose remained clear above the jumble—save the terran.

Save their *na'diya*.

His helmet display marked hostile targets all around. Plasma bolts darted past, fired from above, from below, from all sides. Kayl remained close behind, his steps in perfect synch with Kier's. Their bodies were her shield.

Hold on, female.

He envisioned his goal—the large entryway through which they'd entered the theater—as he fired both blasters, answering every enemy shot with several of his own. The overturned furniture and unmoving bodies scattered across the floor sped by; he gave them his attention only when they obstructed his path.

The emotions roiling under the surface of his mind swelled. Immense pressure spread through him, more than enough to make him burst, but his stride did not falter.

A male dressed like one of Saduuk's security guards emerged from behind a low divider wall ahead, placing himself in front of Kier.

Kier's hands snapped forward. Before the guard had fully raised his weapon, Kier fired half a dozen plasma bolts into his head. The guard, now lacking anything resembling a face, remained on his feet until Kier knocked him aside with his shoulder.

She is losing consciousness, Kayl pulsed.

Kier's heart stalled. He clamped his jaw shut and kept his feet moving, leading Kayl up a carpeted ramp to the highest level of the theater. Eight more hostiles appeared at various places in his display, four of them at the entryway.

She will be fine, Kayl.

She will, Kayl replied.

Kier didn't find Kayl—or himself—very convincing. He shot at every target presented to him, unable to hold back the bitter taste from his mouth, unable to stop his stomach from churning.

Vrykhan's booming voice filled the theater. "Kill them!"

The hostiles at the door turned toward the twins. Two wore security suits and armor, the other two simple civilian clothing, but all carried auto-blasters. Kier didn't need to absorb any details beyond that. He charged forward, letting out a wordless, raging battle cry.

Kier's tail brushed the terran's back as he fired. Plasma bolts struck his armor, and he made himself as large a target as possible to intercept them all.

Vrykhan was still shouting. That the tretin was alive and well enough to produce such noise gnawed at Kier's tumultuous mind, but that fact was overshadowed by the memory of searing pain in his gut—by the knowledge that the terran was also alive. That her time was limited.

Throbbing aches permeated his hands, but he kept shooting. All he could do was shoot.

One of the unarmored enemies at the entryway fell, chest smoldering with fresh blaster holes. A fake security guard staggered back as he was hit, his auto-blaster firing in a wild arc that struck the other plainly clothed pirate in the leg. Then Kier was upon them.

He shot the leg-wounded pirate in his uninjured leg, driving the bastard to his knees. The only uninjured foe lunged at Kier. Kier ducked aside.

Kayl reacted instantly, kicking the lunging foe in the chin.

The holographic curtain rippled as plasma bolts fired from deeper in the theater went through it. Kayl turned his back to the shots, shielding the female. Kier's arms swung to the sides, and he squeezed the triggers of his blasters, shooting the two pirates in their heads.

The armored pirate who'd shot his companion recovered just in time for Kier to jab both blasters under his chin and fire.

Vrykhan's roar was bestial, a sound of fury and bloodlust that seemed to shake the entire space station.

Again, something within Kier tried to speak, tried to tell him to turn around and finish what the tretin had begun all those years ago. Vrykhan and his pirates were here now, and there would not be another opportunity.

But the terran was hurt. The terran was...dying.

No! Not dying.

His thought was one with Kayl's, a desperate exercise of willpower and hope. A chance at Vrykhan was not what would be lost here—it was the chance of saving their mate that they needed to seize, because if she was lost before they'd even forged their *daevalis*...

Kier turned toward the entryway. He saw the innocent people huddled against the wall nearby with their terrified, pleading eyes directed at him and their arms restrained behind their backs. Guilt lodged in his throat, jagged, cold, and bitter. He knew the sorts of lives they would have when the pirates dragged them out of here.

But he and Kayl could not battle Vrykhan's entire crew. Especially not with their mate critically wounded.

He swallowed his guilt and darted through the entryway with Kayl immediately behind him.

The concourse was chaotic. Firefights occurred in pockets where station security and pirates battled from the cover of the shops and restaurants, innocents ran for the docking gates or cowered behind whatever cover they could find, and more pirates roamed with shock staffs and tranquilizer guns, incapacitating their victims. Some of the guests had taken it upon themselves to fight back, but they were largely unarmed and outmatched.

Alarms blared overhead, cutting through the screams, shouts, and blaster fire. Debris was scattered across the concourse floor, interspersed with unmoving bodies—some unconscious, others undoubtedly dead.

Kier and Kayl sprinted along the upper level, not allowing their eyes to linger on the scene below. If they stopped to help, they would die. *She* would die.

"That's them!" someone shouted ahead, drawing Kier's attention to small group of armed individuals standing in front of a shop with shattered windows. Kier fired his blasters, sending a volley of bolts at the pirates that gave them time to do nothing but widen their eyes in shock before they were hit.

Even through his armor, Kier felt the heat radiating from his weapons. He flicked the heatsink switches with his thumbs. The small vents along the tops of the blasters slid open, and small clouds of steam hissed out as the blasters cooled themselves.

The female groaned. The pain in that sound pierced Kier's chest, striking him harder and deeper than any physical wound he'd ever suffered.

We must hurry.

Kayl's response was not without sarcasm. *Have we not been doing so?*

Kier released a humorless laugh. *This is the moment you finally choose to develop a sense of humor?*

We may discuss inappropriate timing at length, Kier, after she is safe.

The twins quickened their pace, as did Kier's heart. Alerts and targets flitted through his helmet display. That Eternal Paradise's concourse had been designed to resemble a village only made it harder for him to hold off the memories of the day his birthplace had been destroyed by Vrykhan's pirates, when he'd seen those once quiet streets littered with rubble, blood, and corpses.

The blasters' heat vents snapped closed. Kier gritted his teeth and squeezed the weapons' grips; their heat had flowed into him, feeding his blazing fury.

He was not carrying the female, wasn't tending her, and that was maddening. There was only one way to vent his heat.

Kier fired at every enemy in his path, letting his body function as a weapon. No thought, no hesitance; only action. He compensated for inaccuracy with volume.

There was no way but forward, and the path had to be clear.

Blue-white bolts darted past the twins from behind. Despite the cacophony, Kier heard Vrykhan's voice coming from near the theater.

No way but forward.

No way without her.

More shouts sounded from all around, and more bolts sped toward the twins. Kayl moved closer to Kier to better shield the terran between their armored bodies. His racing pulse sounded in time with Kier's, two hearts pumping for one soul.

Three hearts, Kier corrected. *We must ensure it becomes three.*

The entrance to their section of the docking gates stood unguarded just ahead—proof that fortune could sometimes bend in the twins' favor. But a group of pirates was charging up the stairs close to that exit, one of them barking orders to the rest. These were armored not in the fashion of Saduuk's security, but in rough, pieced together combat armor, the sort common for warriors stuck on long, grueling campaigns that forced them to scavenge parts and improvise repairs.

Too many, Kayl pulsed, *and they will be on our heels as we exit the concourse.*

Growling, Kier aimed his pistols at one of the thick stone pillars standing at the top of the steps. The blasters were unlikely to hold out much longer; the continuous fire had undoubtedly drained the power cells significantly. There was only one chance. He fired at the column about a meter from its base, pouring bolt after bolt into it.

The stone smoked and melted. At the top of the pillar, the ceiling cracked, bits of it falling to the floor. The pillar began to tip, its top tearing free.

Kier rushed to the pillar and slammed a foot into it. The pirates on the stairs yelled and fired up as the stone scraped and cracked. Kayl fell into place beside Kier, and they kicked in unison.

The pillar toppled off its severed base. It hit the floor at the top of the stairs with a quaking thud and fell down and to the side, one end striking the handrail. The pirates' aggressive shouts gave way to curses and startled exclamations as the pillar rolled down the steps.

The twins did not linger to witness the results. They ran for the docking gates, and the cacophony faded, leaving Kier to hear only the blistering beating of his heart and the ragged breaths fighting their way into and out of his lungs.

Each step forward was one closer to getting the female to safety. Each second passed was one closer to her death.

That thought reignited Kier's fury, and he used it to fuel a fresh burst of speed. They would outrun death. They had to.

He darted through the entryway. The dark corridor that had led the twins into *paradise* was no longer streaked with purple and blue stars; they had been replaced by an ominous, unwavering crimson glow that somehow made the space feel even more cramped than before.

Almost there. A little farther...

A new sound cut through Kier's focus—a startled grunt from his brother.

Kier's heart ceased beating, and the air caught in his lungs, making his chest burn. A thousand horrible thoughts battled to enter his conscious mind as he skidded to a halt. Foolish as it was, only one of those thoughts was able to break through.

The sound Kayl had made was exactly like those uttered by characters in Razi's volturian melodramas when they'd been literally stabbed in the back.

Kier twisted to look back at his brother; the burning sensation rose into his throat.

Kayl stood in profile, two thirds of his body having passed through the entryway. The concourse was not visible through the opening. There was only that white light, meant to dazzle newly arrived guests. That white light...and the terran.

From the shoulders up, she remained on the far side of the entryway.

With a low growl, Kayl planted his lead foot and leaned farther through the opening. The terran moved with him, but the instant her choker reached the threshold, it locked in place. Kier's eyes widened as the choker slid up her neck and pressed into the delicate flesh on the underside of her jaw.

Her eyelids fluttered open, and her eyes rolled in their sockets. She let out a choked cry.

Kayl froze, head snapping toward her. He rasped, "Fuck."

He retreated through the opening, vanishing in the blinding light. Kier raced after him.

The noise and chaos of the concourse assaulted Kier immediately upon his reentry. He held his blasters up, raking them across his surroundings as he scanned for threats. Then his attention fell to his brother and the female. Their mate.

Their *na'diya*.

Kayl was on one knee with the terran's backside resting on his thigh, holding her torso upright as she gulped down wheezing breaths. The choker had fallen back into place, but the skin under her jaw was red and irritated. Her lashes were still fluttering, and her pupils were wildly dilating and contracting. She clawed weakly at her neck with one hand; the other hand was on Kayl's shoulder, clutching at his armor.

The twins had investigated Eternal Paradise in the past, but they'd been unable to find any evidence of Saduuk purchasing slaves, whether from Vrykhan or other sources. He'd clearly been involved in several unsavory business practices and dealt in illegal goods, but none of that had been the twins' focus.

Not all slavery is readily apparent. That was what Arcanthus had said.

But Kier and Kayl had noticed the chokers on the workers here—on the entertainers, on the scantily clad servers. They'd noticed them and not given them a second thought, even after seeing countless people restrained by slave collars over the years. Even knowing that such collars came in many styles.

How could we have missed it? How could we have been so blind? Kier pulsed.

Just get it off her, Kier, Kayl replied.

Kier stowed a blaster on the magnetic holster at his hip, freeing his right hand, and accessed his holocom. He sank into a crouch as he brought up the collar-breaker program.

The female's gaze shifted to Kier. She blinked, and her eyes drifted away, only to snap back to him again when she sucked in a sudden breath. "I...I'm..."

"Easy," Kier whispered. His fingers moved quickly to select her collar as the target and initiate the hack. "You will be all right, terran. We have you."

A series of shouts sounded from the lower level, followed by volleys of blaster fire and the *whump* of an explosion.

Kayl turned his head toward the sounds. *We have little time, Kier.*

But the real meaning of those words was apparent. *She* had little time.

"Who..." The female's brow creased, and her eyes fell shut again. "I'm ready. Ready...ready to go..."

"*No,*" the twins growled in unison.

Tiny lines of code streamed across Kier's holocom screen as the program attempted to decrypt the collar's security. Kier willed it to go faster, urgency and anger crackling through his body and sizzling along every nerve.

"Stay with us, *na'diya*," Kier said, touching his fingertips to her cheek. Her face looked ashen and clammy. He wished he could touch her without the armor on, wished he could feel her skin, wished he could comfort her as she needed.

"Home," she muttered. "Ready to...go home. Please."

The constriction in Kier's chest strengthened tenfold, locking everything up. He could not breathe, could not think, could not do anything but stare at her, at the female destiny had deigned to give the twins today of all days—at this wounded, dying, broken person.

The cracks that had formed in his heart all those years ago deepened and spread.

"Hurry," Kayl growled.

Kier gritted his teeth and withdrew his hand from the terran, flicking through the program's commands. "*Zor atkoshai.*"

What is it? Kayl pulsed.

The encryption on this collar is more advanced than any I have seen, Kier replied.

So it will not work?

It will. But it may take hours.

"We do not have hours, Kier," Kayl snarled.

"I am well aware, Kayl. What would you have me to do?"

"Call Arcanthus."

Releasing a huff through his nostrils, Kier pulled up his holocom contacts and selected Arcanthus's code. The screen flashed and displayed a message in large, clear characters.

NO SIGNAL. CALL ABORTED.

Kier tried again, and again, and each time received the same message. He curled his right hand into a fist, barely stopping himself from slamming it into the holocom. "Of course they're jamming communications."

"Hold her upright," Kayl said.

Pressing his lips into a tight line, Kier shifted closer to his brother and slipped his arms behind the female's back. Kayl freed his hands and moved them to either side of her neck, hooking his fingers under the collar. His knuckles pressed into her flesh; the collar allowed little room.

Kayl growled and pulled outward.

A small light flashed on the front of the collar, preceding a crackling electric current. The female let out a strained grunt as her back arched, her head fell backward, and her limbs writhed stiffly.

Stinging pain echoed through Kier's limbs, contracting his muscles. It radiated from his core—from his delicate connection to this terran.

It was only a fraction of the pain she was suffering.

"Stop!" Kier snapped.

Kayl abruptly withdrew his hands, and the electricity ceased. The female's body sagged, slumping on Kayl's leg and Kier's arms. She let out an agonized whimper. Kayl's hands remained in the air, fingers curled, as he stared down at her.

Emotions roiled on Kayl's end of the psychic link; Kier sensed their power, their depth, their darkness, but Kayl did not allow them through.

"Find them!" Vrykhan bellowed. His voice echoed across the concourse, seemingly unhindered by the numerous sound dampeners.

Kier looked at his brother. With Kayl holding back his emotions, it was difficult to determine his state of mind, especially since even the subtlest clues that might've crept into his expression were now hidden behind his helmet.

We need to move, Kayl.

A tremor ran through Kayl's fingers. He stilled them by clenching his fists. *We do. Can you access the* Fang?

Kayl slipped one arm under the terran's legs and the other behind her back, allowing Kier to withdraw his arms from beneath her and operate his holocom.

"Yes," Kier said.

"Engage full cloaking." Kayl stood, clutching the female against his chest.

Her head lolled, and her limbs hung limp. She made no indication that she felt Kayl moving, didn't so much as attempt to open her eyes or say a word. Kier swallowed his dread; she was still breathing. She still had some time.

"They have undoubtedly seen the ship already, Kayl."

They must not see it again, Kayl pulsed. *They will ransack every craft that is docked here. Without the* Fang...

They both looked at the terran. There was no need to complete the thought.

Kier engaged the *Fang's* cloaking field on full power, switched the collar-breaker program's readout to his helmet display, and drew the blaster from his hip.

The twins ran. They did not know where they were going, did not know what they would find, but their purpose remained unchanged.

They would save their *na'diya.*

SEVEN

Beyond the central concourse, Eternal Paradise was a labyrinthine jumble of corridors and rooms where everything was masked in a veneer of luxury and exoticism. But the cracks were showing now—the hallways were littered with fallen items and debris. Potted plants had been tipped over, spilling dirt across the floors, and plasma burns marred every surface. Occasionally, the overhead lights flickered, often preceded by the distant thump of an explosion.

But most noticeable to Kayl, even more so than the scattered bodies, were the faltering sound dampeners. Without those dampeners active, these corridors became catacombs haunted by the ghostly, echoing screams of innocent people who'd been left to the mercy of Vrykhan's pirates.

Those screams were far too reminiscent of what the twins had heard in the streets when Vrykhan attacked their village.

All those sounds seemed to come from distant reaches of the space station, but it was difficult to determine their true distances and directions. Vrykhan must have had his entire crew involved for them to be seizing so large a place, for them to be capturing and killing so many people.

Kayl held the female terran a little tighter. In the minutes since the twins' failed attempts to remove her collar, she'd regained consciousness twice, and had remained awake for mere seconds each time. He could only hope he was not causing more damage to her wound—for all his agility and athleticism, he could not prevent her limbs from flopping with his hurried gait.

The harsh realities of the situation battered Kayl's awareness from all sides.

Eternal Paradise was being overrun by Vrykhan's forces. What resistance remained would soon crumble as the pirates focused their efforts on clearing the place.

Communications were down, and the space station was in neutral territory. There was no help coming.

Vrykhan was alive, injured but reinforced by his crew.

The twins could not reach their ship while the terran was collared. And the terran...

One matter at a time.

Kier, who'd taken the lead as they'd traveled these corridors, slowed his pace. Kayl's heart quickened, and anxiety soured his gut. They'd been fortunate enough to avoid their enemies since leaving the concourse, but they were still too exposed, too vulnerable.

An open door, Kier pulsed, gesturing ahead with a blaster.

Kayl silenced his misgivings and matched his brother's speed, following as Kier stalked along the wall.

More screams echoed through the hallway, culminating in a blood-curdling cry of anguish and grief. Kayl clamped his jaw shut. He would not allow himself to relive those memories again, would not acknowledge how similar that wail had been to the ones his fathers had made when his mother was killed.

Kier reached the doorway. Blackened impact marks from dozens of plasma bolts were scattered across the doorframe and the surrounding wall, more concentrated and in greater number than elsewhere the twins had seen.

Kier flattened himself against the wall, blasters at the ready, and checked the corner of the room adjacent to him. Then he swept the weapons around, scanning the rest of the room to the opposite corner with his gaze.

It took him no longer than a second; that seemed like a second more than could be spared.

Kayl drew in a steadying breath.

Vrykhan lives.

His jaw tensed.

But our mate is dying.

Those thoughts warred within Kayl, making him more aware of the unconscious female in his arms. Though he could not feel her skin directly, he had the unshakable sense that it was cold. That she was cold.

Clear. Looks like a security station, Kier pulsed. He turned his head, angling his face toward the terran. His brow furrowed. *There may be first aid inside.*

Kayl's heart stuttered. He checked along the corridor behind them. In its ruined state, it served only as a jarring testament to what had undoubtedly been the most terrifying moments of many people's lives...and in some cases, the final moments.

Kier stood aside, covering the hall as Kayl entered the room.

A console stretched along one wall, its controls flashing and flickering. Several of the projectors atop it emitted unstable holograms in the air—feeds from surveillance recorders. Many more were dark. Erratic sparks sprayed from sections of the console that were blackened, melted, and smashed.

Kier entered immediately behind Kayl. The door closed with a grinding rumble that Kayl felt through his feet.

There is another door, Kayl pulsed, nodding toward the closed door in the rear corner of the room.

I know, Kier replied.

So you have checked it?

Obviously not, Kayl. You came in here before me.

Kayl released a huff and spun toward his brother, fingers curling to again strengthen his hold on the terran. *Then why did you say it was clear?*

Kier put his arms out to either side, turning his palms toward the ceiling. The gesture lost some of its meaning considering that he was still holding his blasters. He strode forward, sinking easily into a combat stance, and stopped at the interior door. He didn't press the button until Kayl had shifted aside to get out of sight of the doorway.

The door opened on a small, dark room. With weapons raised, Kier stepped inside, lifting his feet high to clear something on the floor. When Kier's shadow cleared the doorway, Kayl was able to identify the object. A booted foot.

Kier's armored tail, the only part of him Kayl could see, rippled. Then Kier emerged from the room with his blasters fastened at his hips and a plastic case in one hand. He closed the door behind him without looking back.

Well? Kayl pulsed.

Kier retracted his helmet, revealing his face. His hair was slicked back and sweat dampened, and his eyes brimmed with more emotion than seemed possible. *Storage room. Currently stocked with the guards who were posted here.*

He strode to a table tucked in the corner of the room and swept away the holoprojector discs and drinking glasses that had been atop it. The items clattered onto the floor, the glasses clinking but not breaking. "Place her here."

Kayl moved to his brother. He looked down and hesitated; a filthy table in a security room on an illicit space station was no place for her. She deserved so much better.

"Now, Kayl," Kier said.

Growling, Kayl laid the terran atop the table as gently as he could. Those vibrant red tresses, all tousled now, settled around her, starkly contrasting her too-pale skin. Her ragged breaths were shallow, barely strong enough to move her chest.

He retracted his helmet and inhaled. Though the air filtration system had likely cleared the worst of it, the tang of burned electronics lingered in the air. But the terran's scent was stronger. Exotic, sweet, and feminine, it made Kayl long to lean over her and draw that fragrance in directly from her skin, made him want to—

The table rattled as Kier slammed the plastic box atop it, jolting Kayl from his consuming longings.

Kier opened the case, revealing an array of first aid supplies. Both twins quickly assessed the case's contents before looking at the female's wound.

The damage was more apparent beneath this clear, cold light. Nothing in the first aid case would be enough to save her. The only thing that had allowed her this much time was that the plasma bolt had cauterized the wound.

"It does not matter," Kier said, shaking his head. "We do what we can. Everything and anything."

Heat skittered across Kayl's skin, making his bodysuit and armor feel like it was squeezing him, suffocating him, crushing him. The only response he could offer was a nod as strained and shallow as the terran's breathing.

He and Kier removed a wound-sealant dispenser and a disinfectant spray from the case.

With as much speed and care as possible, they rolled the female so her wounded side was facing the ceiling. She moaned weakly and pulled her arms in over her chest as shudders wracked her body. Her shaky breaths quickened.

Kier readied the spray. His finger twitched on the button, but he did not press it.

"Everything and anything," Kayl said.

Kier huffed and pushed the button. The clear spray struck the terran's burned flesh.

She screamed and arched her back, face contorting in pain. Kayl leaned over the table, bracing one hand on her hip and the other on her shoulder to pin her down.

Her pained cries escalated as Kier continued spraying, covering the wound as thoroughly as her writhing allowed. Agony radiated along Kayl's side, a searing sting that penetrated to his core. His every muscle went taut—just like hers. Kier fared little better; his teeth were clenched so tightly that Kayl swore he heard them grinding even over the female's sounds.

Cracks formed around Kayl's heart. Knowing she was in pain, sensing it, was worse than anything he'd experienced in his life.

I do not even know her.

And she is the reason Vrykhan lives.

She is why we abandoned our hunt when we were perched on the edge of victory.

Tossing the spray into the case, Kier hurriedly picked up the wound-sealant dispenser. He managed to keep his hands steady enough to power on the cylindrical device.

The terran whimpered. She'd grasped her own shoulders with such desperation that her fingers had left deep indentations on her skin, each with a fresh red scratch from the bite of her nails.

Kier held the dispenser over her wound and activated it. The bluish scanner light swept across her flesh, preceding the pale, translucent substance the dispenser laid over the ruined tissue.

She hissed and twisted away, but Kayl's hold was firm, and she had little strength remaining. The twins seamlessly alternated between operating the device and keeping the terran still, stopping only when the entirety of her raw, burned flesh was covered.

The female sagged atop the table. The twins eased her onto her back. Sweat glistened on her pale skin, droplets of it following the path her tears had traced across her cheek.

Our mate. Our na'diya.

Why had Vrykhan been able to continue the fight while she had been reduced to this? Why did she have to suffer, why was her life hanging by a thread? No one made it through life without committing some wrongdoing, but there was no way hers came anywhere close to Vrykhan's. She was not the one who deserved this.

She should not have been here. Not tonight.

"Not ever," Kier rumbled. With a touch of his holocom, he retracted his suit's armored gloves, baring his hands. He placed his fingertips on her cheek, and his already dire frown deepened before he shifted his hand to the side of her neck. "Her skin is cool, and her pulse is racing, but it is weaker with each moment."

He pressed his lips into a tight line and leaned his hands on the table. *She is slipping away.*

Kayl's dread stirred in the pit of his stomach.

They were going to lose their mate right after they'd found her, without ever learning her name, having a conversation with her, hearing her laugh or seeing her truly smile. All they would have would be memories of her beautiful voice...and of her final, agonized moments.

And Vrykhan was alive. All this would be for naught. No mate, no vengeance, no justice.

Growling, Kayl grabbed the first aid case and dragged it closer. He tore through its contents, throwing the items aside. He barely heard them clattering on the table and floor. Something in the case had to be of use, something would help her, something would make a difference so the twins could leave this place having saved at least one of the innocent people who'd been caught up in this, so they could—

He grasped a tool on the bottom of the case and pulled it out just as one of Kier's hands darted in to retrieve something else. They held up their finds side-by-side—an auto-injector and a cartridge marked ulturine, commonly referred to as liquid rage.

A thousand unspoken words raced along the twins' psychic link, thrumming with anger, with fear, with trepidation and desperation.

There were undoubtedly risks in injecting the terran with ulturine, but what was the alternative?

Doing nothing would guarantee her death. Doing this would grant her a chance at life.

Kayl flicked the control on the side of the injector, opening the breech. Kier slid the cartridge into the opening and pressed it firmly in place. When Kayl hit the control again, the breech snapped closed, and a small holo screen projected from atop the injector, noting the currently loaded substance and indicating the device was ready.

The twins met one another's gazes. Everything that had happened before now fell away; their reason for being in Eternal Paradise to begin with ceased to matter. The goal, the obsession that had driven Kayl forward for most of his life had been replaced.

Only the female on the table was important. Only her life. And no one could ensure she'd survive but Kier and Kayl. There was no time to reflect upon why it had come to this, or to consider what had been risked today, or to count all that had been lost.

They had this one chance to stop anything else from being lost. To stop *her* from being lost.

"Everything," Kier growled.

"And anything," Kayl responded. He swung his attention to the female, pressed the auto-injector to her neck, and pulled the trigger.

The injector clicked as its needle pierced her skin, and with a brief hiss, it emptied the ulturine into the terran. Those small sounds were amplified in the otherwise quiet room, carrying a weight and power that should not have been possible.

A blue light flashed around the tip of the injector, and Kayl lifted it away.

The twins stared at the female, their breaths caught in their throats as hers struggled on. Kayl's lungs burned, and everything in his chest was taut, about to collapse around his heart.

Seconds passed, marked only by her weak, rapid breaths. Apart from the shallow rise and fall of her chest, she lay unmoving.

The cracks in Kayl's heart deepened and spread further.

None of this should have happened.

Her eyes snapped open.

· · ·

Aileen gasped, back arching as her lungs filled with a great rush of air. All she could see was pure, blinding white, but she couldn't look away, didn't want to look away. Her memory of darkness was too fresh. She refused to go back to that. *Couldn't* go back to it.

The air left her in a *whoosh* as her body fell back onto the hard surface beneath her. She panted, drawing in one desperate breath after another, and still, she did not pry her gaze from that light.

"Easy, terran," someone said in a deep, gentle voice. The words were followed by a light touch on her shoulder that sent tingles across her skin.

Aileen jerked away, and her eyes rounded as they settled upon the two males clad in black, segmented armor standing beside her. Her already pounding heart quickened. There was a strange fluttering in her belly, and it spread heat through her, making her core clench.

It's them.

The daevahs from the theater. She'd never seen them before tonight, and yet, there was something so, so familiar about them. Aileen had felt a strange pull the instant she'd locked eyes with them.

She'd seen other daevahs at Eternal Paradise. The males were always in pairs—twins.

This pairs' faces were identical. They had the same short eyebrows resting over the same eyes, the same defined cheeks and jawbones, the same noses, flatter than a human's, with two pairs of thin slits above their nostrils, and the same teal skin. Both had facial markings—one set of lines running from the corners of their mouths up to their pointed ears, another leading over their lips and down through the centers of their chins, one coming down from their hairlines to cut across the centers of their eyes and continue to their cheeks.

Each daevah had one magenta eye and one blue eye, the colors mirrored between them, and their pupils were narrow slits focused on Aileen. Both had purple hair with teal streaks running through it, but that hair was where they differed; one had the sides of his head shaved and his hair pulled back in a ponytail, while the other's hair was loose and tousled, with some longer strands woven into a braid that dangled beside his face.

"W-Who are you?" she breathed.

"I am Sol'Kier Sevris," said the one with the wild hair, tapping his chest. He gestured to his companion. "And this is my brother, Sol'Kayl Kortanis."

"Kier and Kayl will suffice," said the second daevah. His voice was flatter than Kier's, harder. Colder.

"What is your name?" asked Kier.

She pushed herself up to sit, slowly swinging her legs over the edge of the table. "Aileen. Aileen...McConnell."

"Aileen," he purred as his lips curled up into a smile, granting her a glimpse of his fangs. But that smile quickly faltered, succumbing to a grave light in his eyes. "Everything is going to be all right, Aileen. You have my word. But we need you to trust us through what is to come."

What was to come?

Frowning, she dragged her gaze away from them to look around the room—the very damaged room. This was one of the security stations scattered around Eternal Paradise, where Saduuk's guards monitored surveillance feeds and communications. Why was she here? Why wasn't she on stage?

"What's going on?" she asked. "I'm... I'm not supposed to be in here. I'm supposed to be performing."

The daevahs exchanged a glance. Kier frowned; Kayl betrayed no emotion at all, save for in the erratic twitching of his long tail.

"Do you not recall what happened, Aileen?" Kier asked gently.

"I was on stage singing. And I..."

I saw you, both of you. And I...I wanted to stop that song right then so I could go to you.

You sound crazy, Aileen. You don't know who these two are. And you're...you're high on rhapsody.

"You were injured," said Kier.

"You *are* injured," said Kayl.

Aileen's brow furrowed. "What?"

All at once, the memories flooded her mind—Saduuk, the plasma shots, the screams, the fear, the *pain.*

Don't look. Do not look, Aileen.

I have to look.

No... Don't look. None of this is real if you don't look.

She grasped her thighs, twisted, and looked down at her right side. Her pale skin was covered by a large patch of white reminiscent of the synthetic skin she'd seen on robots back on earth. It was flexible; it bent, stretched, and wrinkled, but it didn't do any of those things quite like real skin should have.

With a whimper, she brought a trembling hand to it and, after a moment's hesitation, pressed her palm over the synthetic skin. She felt...*nothing* beneath.

Why is there no pain?

Releasing a shaky breath, she closed her eyes. In her mind's eye, she saw what lurked beneath that artificial white covering—charred, ruined flesh. A literal piece of her body had been burned away by plasma, destroyed, taken from her. And that searing pain echoed through her soul, stealing her breath and making her heart stutter just as it had when she'd been hit.

"I was shot. I was shot," Aileen said, opening her eyes, voice growing more frantic with each word. "Oh my god, there's a *hole* in me."

A hand settled on her shoulder, rough and strong but reassuring. Heat spread across her skin beneath that touch.

"You will be all right, Aileen," Kier said, his voice edged with a growl.

She looked at him, eyes wide with panic, body shaking. "Why can't I feel it? Why can't I feel the pain?"

He shifted his hand, sliding it to the side of her neck as he crouched to get closer to her eye level. The pad of his thumb brushed across her cheekbone, and the tip of his claw grazed her flesh. "We did what was necessary to keep you going."

"Am I going to die?"

"We injected you with ulturine," Kier said.

Take it, songbird. Make it easy on yourself. Because you're doing this either way.

Aileen's heart quickened. That was Saduuk's voice in her memory, those were the words he'd said the first time he'd made her take rhapsody. The first time he'd forced her to...

"What is that?" she demanded, catching Kier's wrist and drawing his hand away from her. "What did you put in me?"

He held up both hands without breaking her hold on his wrist, displaying his palms. "It is simply to keep you moving for a little longer. It is like...adrenaline, only much stronger."

"So it's not...it's not a drug? It's not going to mess with my head?"

With one long finger, he pointed to something beside her on the table. "It is from the first aid kit."

She looked down at the kit. It had been ransacked, with its supplies strewn haphazardly on the table and the floor. "Okay." Aileen released her hold on Kier, tension easing. Her trembling, however, did not subside. "Okay. I just... This is a lot, isn't it? I need a minute to"—her fingers flexed on the synthetic skin covering her wound—"absorb all of this."

Kayl huffed, shaking his head. "We do not have time. *You* do not have time, Aileen." He stepped closer, looking down at her with that unreadable expression. "If we do not get you into a medpod very soon, you will die."

Kier glared at his brother and bared his fangs. "You will not die, Aileen. We will not allow it."

But Kayl didn't look at him; he held Aileen's gaze firmly. "You are frightened. Confused. There is no time for that either. You must do as we say if you want to survive this."

"Kayl, what are you trying to accomplish?" Kier demanded, standing up to turn toward his twin. "What is wrong with you? *Ba'shanaal!*"

Kayl faced his brother, jaw muscles ticking. They stared at each other in silence, but Aileen had a strange sense that there was a great deal being communicated between the two—and not merely in their eyes and body language. She was almost certain they were...talking.

Really, Aileen? This isn't the time to lose your grip on reality. No matter how horrifying reality might be...

"The goal has changed," Kier growled suddenly, making Aileen start.

"It never should have," Kayl replied with a hint of venom in his voice—but that hint seemed so out of character for him that it was even more unsettling than Kier's growl.

She looked from one twin to the other and back again. She didn't know them, had no reason to trust them, and should've been launched into fight or flight mode by their strange behavior, but something in her hated seeing them like this. Hated seeing them out of harmony.

Aileen opened her mouth to ask what they were arguing about, but something across the room caught her attention—one of the flickering holo screens on the damaged console.

The feed pulsed with noise and distortion, but she could make out the hallway and the group of people walking along it. She could make out the figure at the center of that group.

Her mouth went suddenly dry, and the remembered pain again flared on her side, followed by an odd numbness that permeated her body. She slid off the table and walked between the twins, barely registering their confused expressions as she continued to the console.

The group in the surveillance feed drew closer. They were clad in armor, holding weapons, all clearly dangerous, but the male at the group's center was the one who made ice form in her heart, who made her knees feel weak.

The tretin. The tretin who had killed Saduuk. The tretin who had shot her. He was being helped along by his companions, limping, but that did not rob him of his ferocity and menace. That didn't make him seem weak or less threatening.

Somehow it was worse.

She sensed Kier and Kayl to either side of her before they stepped into her peripheral view. Their armored tails swung restlessly, lightly bumping the backs of her calves before moving away again.

"We're safe here, right?" she asked, barely managing a whisper.

"That is the corridor outside," Kayl said.

Kier touched the controls, but the image only flickered more intensely, and the damaged electronics spat fresh sparks. He pressed the buttons faster, harder. "It will not switch the feed."

"Slamming on it will not fix it, Kier," Kayl snapped.

"It works sometimes!"

"If you focus for more than two seconds, we—"

The holo screen buzzed, the image breaking into digitized fragments, and flickered to a new angle. This one showed a door in the hallway, its face and the wall around it blackened with the impacts of many plasma bolts. The tretin and his companions were moving toward that door.

Kier and Kayl snapped their mouths shut, teeth clacking.

Brow creasing, Aileen swung her gaze from one twin to the other. "Is that—"

Before she could finish the sentence, Kier's palm covered her mouth, silencing her, and his other arm snaked around her waist. He lifted Aileen off the floor, hitching her body close to his. She felt that heat again where his skin touched hers, but the unexpected pleasure of the sensation was offset by the chill of his hard armor and the strange, numb pressure in her side.

Kayl raced to the back of the room, where he opened a door leading into a dark room. Kier hurried after, carrying Aileen with him, and preceded his brother through the doorway. He stepped aside and flattened himself against the wall. Aileen glimpsed a storage locker standing on the opposite wall, partly shrouded in shadow. Kayl placed himself next to Kier, and the door closed with a soft *whoosh*, plunging the room into total darkness.

No. No, no.

She'd only just risen from the darkness. She didn't want to be back in it, didn't want to lose herself, didn't want to...didn't want to die.

Aileen reached up to grab Kier's hand and dropped her other hand to the arm around her waist. Her heart was pounding, her breaths were coming short, fast, and shaky, and there was a thrumming beneath her skin, an anxiousness to move, to flee.

To *live.*

Kier's hold eased infinitesimally. He gently lowered her so her feet were on the floor again, but he did not withdraw his hands; instead, he coiled his tail around her calf. It left an odd thrill in its wake despite being covered in armor.

Nostrils flaring, she took a deep breath.

The primary scent filling her lungs was *him*—fresh earth and ocean mist. There was something heady and soothing about it, and it would have calmed her nerves were it not for the taint of a foul, underlying smell—the stench of scorched flesh.

She slid a foot forward. The toe of her shoe bumped into something heavy and yielding.

Oh God, is that... Is that a body?

With a squeak, she yanked her foot back, kicking her heel against Kier's armored shin.

He drew her against him more securely and leaned his head down so his mouth was beside her ear. His breath was warm against her skin as he whispered, "Easy, Aileen. I have you."

"Not a sound," Kayl rasped.

Aileen closed her eyes and nodded. Despite the adrenaline and fear pumping through her, the gentle stroke of Kier's thumb over her cheek eased some of her panic. She didn't understand the pull she felt toward these daevahs. They were total strangers, and based on their armor and the way they moved, they were *dangerous* strangers.

But she felt safe with them. Perhaps it was just a matter of being out of Saduuk's clutches for the first time in three years, but it seemed like more than that. It seemed deeper than that. And there was a voice within her, a soft, warm, quiet voice, that somehow cut through all her confusion and fear to deliver a message...a message that just felt *right*.

Trust them.

EIGHT

Our mate is *in my arms.*

A bitter smile twisted Kier's lips. The one thing he and Kayl had always missed, the one thing they'd never dared hope for, was with them now—was here in Kier's arms—and *everything* was wrong.

They'd found their *na'diya,* and they couldn't take even a modicum of joy in it. Their relief upon her regaining consciousness was the closest they'd come to happiness, and it had been swiftly crushed by their knowledge of her dire condition.

Their mate was not meant to be hurt. She was not meant to be dying. She was not meant to be trapped in a place like this, where she had undoubtedly been abused and forced to serve against her will. A place now brimming with pirates who would appreciate another terran to sell.

Terrans were relatively new in the intergalactic community. That exoticism, paired with their impressive adaptability, ensured they fetched high prices at slave markets. The twins would not allow that to happen to Aileen.

Our mate is in my arms, dying, while we hide in a supply closet full of corpses to evade the monster who killed our family and enslaved us, the monster we have hunted for so long. The monster we have failed to slay.

Still your mind, Kayl pulsed.

Kier gritted his teeth and looked in his brother's direction. He couldn't see Kayl, but he could sense him; their shoulders were within centimeters of touching.

The terran trembled against Kier's body, and her warm breath fanned across his palm. This was his first feel of her breath on his skin, the first time he had her body pressed against his, and all of it was wrong. All of it was—

A metallic grinding sound came from the other room, barely audible through the closed door. The pirates had entered the security room. Heavy footfalls and muffled voices followed that first sound, the latter of which was too muted for Kier to pick out even a single word.

Aileen tensed further, leaning back against Kier as though she could disappear into him. He stroked his thumb over her cheek again and curled his tail around her leg more snugly. He wished he could vanquish her fear. He wished he could make everything better *now*.

But his heart was pounding, and it was a struggle to keep his breathing silent and even. Though Kier did not fear death, he did not want to die, and the mere thought of Kayl or Aileen dying instilled him with near-paralyzing dread.

The voices in the next room grew louder, and the footsteps approached the supply closet.

Fire rippled through Kier's muscles, flooding them with fresh strength. If Vrykhan was approaching the room...

Not Vrykhan, Kayl pulsed, his mind voice rough and raspy. *The gait is too even.*

Kayl dropped his left hand to Kier's waist, tugged the blaster free of the magnetic holster, and held the weapon at the ready.

The door opened, and light spilled in, bright enough compared to the darkness that had enveloped Kier that he had to slit his eyes against it. Aileen's breath hitched, and her body went impossibly still. The twins looked toward the open doorway to their right.

A long shadow fell across the patch of light.

The barrel of an auto-blaster crossed the threshold, followed by a large, scarred hand on the foregrip. A flashlight clicked on, emitting a beam of light from just beneath the weapon's barrel. The light swung downward.

Aileen's head shifted, following the flashlight's beam. Her hold on Kier's arms tightened, and she trembled anew. The dead security guards—five in total—lay just as they had when Kier opened the door only minutes before, with their flesh melted and blackened around plasma wounds and their limbs tangled and bent to unnatural angles. They'd been thrown in this room without any respect.

Not that they'd deserved any.

Saduuk had kept slaves—likely hundreds of them. And Kier did not doubt that the security staff had been employed as much to keep those slaves in line as to maintain the peace.

The auto-blaster shifted, its barrel angling toward the twins and their mate. The flashlight beam stopped on the corpses in front of the trio. Aileen turned her face away. Kier didn't restrict her movement, but neither did he remove his hand from her mouth.

Kayl clutched his pistol against his chest, aiming it in the direction of the doorway with his finger on the trigger.

"It's clear," said the being holding the auto-blaster.

"Anything good in there?" asked another pirate.

The blaster-bearer chuckled. "Some of ours must've cleared this room already. Tossed the waste in here." The weapon withdrew from the entryway, and the shadow receded, allowing the light from the next room to fall unbroken upon the bodies near the entryway.

"Well, were any of ours hurt?" asked a third. "Someone's made a mess of this first aid kit."

"Won't know until we regroup," the second pirate said. "Comms are a mess right now."

"There wasn't supposed to be this much resistance," a fourth pirate grumbled.

"Doesn't matter," Vrykhan said, voice deeper and rougher than those of his companions. For the second time tonight, something deeply buried and terrible roused within Kier, instilling him with equal measures of fear and fury.

A single word pulsed from Kayl's mind, unguarded—*kill.*

The dread in Kier's gut grew larger and heavier. His eyes rounded, and he released Aileen's waist, hand snapping out to close over Kayl's blaster and halt its movement.

Release me, Kayl pulsed.

No, Kier replied.

"Saduuk tried to fuck me over. He hemorrhaged credits to improve security, and it doesn't matter." Vrykhan grunted, and metal groaned across the floor, as though the table were being shifted. "He's dead. And two of his mercenaries will be dead for every wound our crew takes tonight."

The other pirates growled their approval.

Kayl exerted some force on the blaster, fighting Kier's hold. *Release me, Kier.*

Rage rumbled along their psychic link—the cold, hard rage that had dwelt in Kayl's core for so many years, that had fueled him, that had preserved his focus through the worst the universe had thrown at the twins. And it spoke directly to Kier's anger, even though the two were such different expressions of the same emotion.

He is right there, Kier. Release me and I will end this.

Movement sounded from within the other room; people walking, items being shifted, picked up, and dropped, the click of the auto-injector's breech opening.

"RAGE," said one of the pirates. "Someone must've gotten really fucked up."

"Or really wanted to fuck something up," suggested another.

That triggered a chorus of harsh laughter that only encouraged Kayl to increase the strength of his resistance.

"Don't worry about the fucking spray," Vrykhan spat. "Patch me up and get another shot of ulturine loaded. We're not leaving until I have my hands around those daevahs' scrawny necks."

Release me, Kier.

Zor atkoshai, Kayl, what do you think you'll accomplish?

Kayl snapped his face toward Kier, scowling. *Our mission!*

Aileen's shaky exhalation tickled Kier's skin. He clenched his jaw.

His mind was ablaze. Vrykhan was right there, not ten meters away, already wounded. If not for Aileen, he would have been dead already. If not for Aileen...

The pirate who'd checked the supply closet let out a long, low growl. "They took the terran, too. She'd bring in a lot of credits."

If not for Kier and Kayl, Aileen wouldn't be cowering in this room waiting to die. If not for the twins, she would not have been harmed like this. But she would have experienced far worse.

And the twins would never have known.

Aileen turned toward Kier. He didn't stop her, dropping his palm from her mouth and settling it on the back of her neck as she tucked herself against his chest and clutched him. The side of his hand touched the collar; the memory of its electric jolt only intensified his determination.

She is our mission now, Kayl.

We have only one fate, Kayl pulsed. *To kill the pirate Vrykhan and avenge those he has wronged. If we must die to accomplish that—*

Enough! Kier's grip on his brother's weapon tightened, muscles trembling.

He is right there, Kier. Two chances in one night after fifteen years of nothing, and you expect me to give this up? I cannot let him walk away. Not again. I refuse.

"It's all right. Once we take down the slave collar system, we'll get all Saduuk's slaves loaded up with our haul," a third pirate said. "One terran is nothing compared to what the rest will earn."

"Not about the credits anymore," Vrykhan said. "Though they'll wish it was before I'm through with them."

Kayl strained toward the door, his thoughts ceding to that icy rage.

Kier wanted to give in. Wanted to finish this. Wanted to make Vrykhan finally face the consequences of his countless crimes.

Kier released Kayl's arm, lifted his hand to cup the back of his brother's head, and forced Kayl closer. Kayl didn't struggle as much as he could have; even now, neither was willing to move so suddenly or strongly that they'd create unwanted noise.

Kayl's *aerys* was ragged. *We were always willing to die for this.*

But we never needed *to, Kayl. And that...that was before.*

We cannot lose sight of our purpose. We must not.

Perhaps we never truly had sight of it. Kier held his brother's gaze. *If you do this, she will die too.* His gut churned, roiling with sourness, with bitterness, and his muscles smoldered with unreleased energy. *If we allow Vrykhan to leave, there can always be another chance at him. The hunt will continue. If we let Aileen die, there is never another chance with her.*

Kayl's hard-set expression endured for a few more heartbeats before wavering. First was a slight twitch of his brows, then a brief flare of his nostrils and nose slits, and then the corners of his mouth dipped. His eyes shifted, pupils dilating further as they fell upon Aileen.

She lifted her chin to look up at Kayl. Her breathing was still heavy, but it had slowed considerably.

In the other room, the injector made a click-hiss.

Vrykhan let out a long, low, rumbling growl. "Another."

The pirates responded with a chorus of laughs and cheers that rolled into boisterous conversation and bragging, largely about the quality of the *merchandise* they'd obtained here—and what they'd like to do with said merchandise.

Kayl pressed his lips into a tight line, blaster trembling in his hand.

Aileen shook her head. The gesture was so subtle that it was barely perceptible, but it made Kayl freeze. Hesitantly, she placed a hand on Kayl's forearm.

"Stay," she whispered. "Please." Her voice was so soft, so quiet, especially compared to the pirates', that Kier couldn't be sure if he'd actually heard her speak or had somehow felt the words.

She and Kayl stared at one another until finally, with her gentle guidance, he lowered his weapon.

Impossibly, Kier's heart quickened further—and it had nothing to do with fear now. There was something so warm and comforting about what had just occurred, something so right. It was a small taste of the connection the three of them were meant to have in their *daevalis*. A glimpse of a life they'd never known was possible.

But Kier wasn't allowed time to dwell upon those feelings. Another click-hiss from the injector yanked him back to the present situation, where their enemies were just on the other side of the wall at the twins' backs, where every second gone by meant one less to get her to the *Fang*.

Where the life they'd never dreamed possible, which they'd discovered not an hour ago, was already under immediate threat.

Vrykhan roared. There was an immense bang, and objects clattered across the floor. Aileen started, pressing her forehead against Kier's chest armor.

"We've got ghosts to hunt," Vrykhan growled. "Get moving!"

The pirates produced noise enough to drown out a herd of stampeding beasts as they exited the room, but Vrykhan's voice still carried over the cacophony as he called, "And if you find the terran *ji'tas*, bring her to me. I've decided to take Saduuk up on his offer."

Never her! She is ours!

Fueled by a maelstrom of emotion that had erupted in the twins' cores, that thought blasted through their psychic link in a ferocious roar. Just the notion of Vrykhan touching Aileen, of even looking upon her, was more than Kier and his brother could tolerate.

Kier bared his fangs and strengthened his hold on Aileen. Vrykhan had already taken everything else from them. He wouldn't get Aileen.

The twins met each other's gazes. Though their link was ablaze, they slowly focused their emotions, molding them into what was required—the drive to achieve their sole objective.

Save Aileen.

They nodded to one another and waited, still and silent, until they could no longer hear the pirates.

Kayl used his free hand to gently break Aileen's grip, sank low, and crept out of the supply room. When she reached for him, Kier held her in place.

"He is scouting," Kier whispered.

Aileen stared at the doorway, brows drawn. "What if the tretin is still in there?"

The room is clear, Kayl pulsed. *They are moving away along the corridor.*

"They are gone," Kier said.

She frowned at him. "How do you know?"

He offered her a half smile, wishing he could give her more. Wishing there was a reason for joy. "Because Kayl is scouting."

The confusion in her expression deepened.

Kier brushed the back of a finger across her soft cheek. "We will have much to talk about, Aileen, when there is time." Easing his hold on her, he stepped away from the wall. "Come."

Despite her obvious reluctance, she followed his lead, keeping her chin up as they stepped over the bodies and exited the supply closet. Kayl was standing near the security room door, which was still open, blaster raised.

"Wow," Aileen breathed.

Kier followed her stunned gaze to the table they'd laid her upon minutes before. It was now a mangled wreck; its thick metal surface had been bent severely inward at the middle, nearly folding it in half, and its legs jutted out to the sides. Shallow gouges on the floor marked where those legs had scraped when the table had buckled under the immense force of Vrykhan's blow.

The first aid case was overturned nearby, its contents scattered around it on the floor. Withdrawing from Aileen, Kier strode over to it, crouched, and checked through the items, inspecting the remaining injector cartridges. He picked up the final cartridge, checked the name, and let it roll off his fingers; it clinked on the floor.

No more ulturine, he pulsed, clenching his fists.

And soon there will be no time, Kayl replied.

Aileen folded her arms across her chest, looking from Kier to Kayl and back again. "Um, so...what's the plan?"

Kier drew in a steadying breath and stood up. "We need to get you to our ship."

"Your ship?"

"We have a medpod on board that will heal you."

Kayl's tail whipped aside hard. "We cannot waste time discussing this. If we fail, you will—"

"Die." She released a shaky breath. "I'm on borrowed time. Got it."

Do not be an asshole, Kayl.

Kayl glared at Kier. *Are you really insulting me now?*

I am not insulting you. I am telling you to not be an asshole.

"And there *is* discussion to be had," Kier said, "as we cannot enter the docking gates while your collar is on."

Aileen caught her bottom lip between her teeth and carefully brushed her fingertips along the metal slave collar. A pained light sparked in her eyes.

"But we have no means of removing the collar. Standing here will not solve that," Kayl added before leaning forward to peer into the hallway.

Kier stepped closer to Aileen again, tail swinging restlessly. "Perhaps one of these guard stations has a control, or there is a chamber where the collars are attached and removed?"

Aileen closed her eyes, shoulders rising with a deep breath. "Saduuk."

"What about Saduuk?" Kier asked.

"He gave all his security guards control enough to shock us or restrict our movements with the collars, but he is...*was* the only one with the key to remove them. That bastard always kept it with him."

"You know of no other way?" Kayl asked.

She shook her head. "He liked to be in control."

Kayl sighed and lifted his free hand to rub his temples. "To be clear, our plan is to navigate a space station swarming with pirates to return to the theater we barely escaped with our lives, *hoping* that Saduuk's corpse is still there with the key."

"Yes," Kier said.

"I know a way to possibly avoid the pirates," Aileen said.

Kier and Kayl looked at her, asking in unison, "How?"

NINE

Aileen had walked Eternal Paradise's staff corridors many, many times over her years here. There'd always been activity within them—security guards hurrying to respond to an incident, servers bringing food to a room, performers moving to take their places, whether on stage or in the private room of whatever guest had paid for them that night.

She'd never seen them so empty. So quiet. So...eerie.

There were many signs that people had been through the corridors recently. Pieces of costuming, food carts, serving trays, and other items lay scattered all over, abandoned, forgotten. Somehow, it was worse to see that here in these unadorned, gray passages than it had been up in the plush, luxurious resort.

As Aileen and the twins passed sealed doors that led into maintenance and storage rooms, she couldn't help but wonder if anyone was behind them, huddled in the dark, praying that this would all be over soon, that they would get out of it alive. Her heart ached at the thought.

Not everyone who worked here was a slave, but almost all of them had been victims in some way. Saduuk had had methods of keeping people around without slipping collars around their necks. How many of the dealers, bartenders, and courtesy staff had been caught in crushing debt earned at Saduuk's gaming tables or had developed addictions to drugs that Saduuk himself supplied?

I might die here. I might be trapped here forever.

Aileen touched her palm to her bandaged side. She remembered the pain from the plasma that had burned away her flesh and torn up her insides, she could still *smell* it, but she could barely feel it. A wound like the one she'd received should've left her in shock...or dead. Yet that she was on her feet, that she was conscious at all, seemed impossible. Whatever that ulturine stuff was, it was powerful.

But it wouldn't save her. She knew that in her heart, and her certainty had to do more with what she sensed within herself than what she'd been told.

Aileen glanced at the twins—at Kayl, who stalked the corridor in front of her, and Kier, who followed closely behind her. When he met her gaze, Aileen quickly faced forward again.

Why are they helping me?

Why not Tulaya, or Almun, or any of the other people who'd been trapped here against their will? Why Aileen when so many others deserved freedom too?

And why did they look at her and touch her with such familiarity? Why did she find comfort in their presence when she was literally dying and the place that had been her prison was plunged into chaos and horror?

You can figure that out later.

If you survive this.

Kier's words, laced with passion, fury, and determination, rose from her memory. *You will not die, Aileen. We will not allow it.*

"Take a right," Aileen said when they reached an intersecting corridor. "We're almost there."

She couldn't tell for sure, but she swore the twins shifted just a little closer to her. That suspicion was confirmed when she felt the brush of Kayl's tail against her shin. With all she'd experienced in this place, that should've made her uncomfortable, should've triggered her mental alarms.

Yet somehow, it only made her feel safer.

When they reached the door at the end of the hall, memories assailed Aileen from all sides. How many times had she stood here and stared at that doorway as she struggled to catch her breath before going on stage? How many times had she stood here with rhapsody buzzing in her mind, wondering why she couldn't feel her fear for what would come after the show?

Was that why she was so calm now? Was the rhapsody still at work?

"This leads into the trap room," she said.

The twins exchanged a glance over her head.

"Trap room?" Kayl's brows fell low. His finger slipped behind the trigger guard of his blaster.

Aileen arched a brow. "Not a literal trap. It's what they call the area under the stage."

"Why call it a trap room?"

"Because the trap doors on the stage lead down to it. It's where I get on the platform that lifts me up onto stage."

"Please, Kayl, stop looking so confused and check the room," Kier said.

Kayl turned back to the door—after glowering at his brother—and readied his weapon again. Kier stepped in front of Aileen as Kayl opened the door. She could only glimpse darkness beyond the two daevahs.

Kayl stalked into that darkness with measured, deliberate movements. He wasn't afraid; he was methodical. Disciplined.

Deadly.

The corridor was silent, so silent that Aileen barely allowed herself to breathe. She sensed the danger all around her, thickening the air, but her mind couldn't quite wrap around its enormity. She was a singer. A performer. She was not supposed to be sneaking around a captured space station with twin commandos. She was supposed to be on stage, making people happy, connecting with them through song.

But it hasn't been like that for a long time, has it Aileen?

For the last three years, she'd only gone on that stage because she'd been forced to. Whatever joy she should've experienced by performing had been stolen from her.

"Stay close, Aileen," Kier said, his gentle words shattering the silence and startling her.

"Okay," she replied.

He glanced down the corridor in the direction from which they'd come and then stepped into the trap room. Aileen followed immediately behind him.

Usually, the room was lit by the glow of all the electronics used to control the stage lights and effects. Usually, there were people down here—performers waiting for their cues to head up, technicians ensuring everything operated smoothly, security guards keeping everyone in line.

But it was dark and still now, far too much like some long-forgotten tomb for Aileen's comfort.

Kier led her toward the stairs that went up to the backstage area, where Kayl awaited them with his tail continuing its stiff, erratic motions. Kayl met Aileen's gaze briefly before looking at his brother. He nodded and crept up the steps, pausing as soon as his head was high enough to see the next level. Kier followed him up, waving Aileen along.

Backstage was deserted and even messier than elsewhere, clearly having been evacuated in a panicked rush. Kier fell into place behind Aileen again as she followed Kayl toward the stage, which was blocked off by the thick backing curtain that had been lowered during her performance. She tried not to look at the objects scattered on the floor; she couldn't bear the sorrow of thinking about the people who'd dropped the items in their desperation to escape.

At the edge of the curtain, Kayl halted. He remained there for a long while, head turning slowly as he peered out, scanning the theater. The silence was overwhelming. No part of Eternal Paradise had been so quiet in all Aileen's time here, especially not this theater. Saduuk had insisted on there being a performance going almost every minute of the day, allowing the audience only brief windows to, as he'd put it, *refill their drinks and drain their cocks.*

Kayl glanced at Aileen over his shoulder. "Quickly and quietly, terran."

She nodded and drew in a steadying breath. Her stomach was in knots, her throat was tight, and her heart was racing. She'd stepped on this stage countless times. Why should it be any different now?

You know why it's different, Aileen.

And now there were no pulsing lights or thumping music to distract her from the truth of the situation.

Kier's tail brushed the back of her calf before he softly touched his fingers to the side of her neck. He leaned close and whispered, "Focus on Kayl. You need not let your eyes stray."

Unbidden warmth spread through her at his every point of

contact with her skin. His scent, that blend of earth and ocean, of sunshine on sand and crisp sea wind, enveloped her. Something urged her to move closer, to touch him in turn, but she kept firmly in place, allowing herself only a nod in response.

That wasn't the heat. It couldn't be, not so soon. She knew she'd been in and out of consciousness, but Saduuk had only given her the rhapsody a couple hours ago at most.

Kayl drew the curtain aside and slipped through. Aileen forced her feet into motion to follow him. Stepping out onto that stage after all that had happened, with all that was happening, was surreal. In her mind's eye, she saw dancing lights, and her body thrummed with the memory of pounding bass...but too quickly came the screams of terror, and flashes all around that had been caused by blaster fire instead of stage lighting.

She did as Kier had said and pinned her gaze on Kayl's back, not allowing her eyes to wander. But in her peripheral vision, she saw the unmoving forms on the dance floor, slumped in and over the chairs, and sprawled at the tables. The stench of smoke and burnt flesh filled her nose.

Swallowing thickly, she forced herself onward as Kayl neared the edge of the stage. Her knees wobbled, and a deep, aching throb coursed through her wounded side.

Kayl hopped down smoothly, landing on the dance floor without making a sound. He moved as though to continue walking but faltered mid-stride. Righting himself, he turned toward Aileen, met her gaze, and raised a hand to her.

Aileen glanced toward the main entrance, expecting someone to step through it at any moment. Taking a deep breath, she returned her attention to Kayl, sat on the edge of the stage with legs dangling, and placed her hand in his. Tingles crackled through her palm and along her arm.

Using Kayl for balance, she slid off the stage. Though he supported most of her weight on the way down, the impact of her landing still jarred her. She hissed, pressing her hand to the bandage on her side as the pain flared, blurring her vision and making her knees nearly give out.

A burning sensation, dull but impossible to ignore, radiated between her hip and her ribs.

She didn't hear Kier drop down beside her, but he was suddenly there, slipping an arm around her back in support.

Kayl's grip on her hand tightened. "Aileen?"

"I'm okay," she said, taking in a long breath and releasing it in a steady exhalation. "Let's...let's find Saduuk."

But she wasn't okay, and she knew it. The pain was getting harder and harder to ignore. It was a constant hum, amplifying a little with each thump of her heart.

The ulturine was wearing off.

Aileen lifted her head. Kier and Kayl were looking at each other, their features tense. Once again, she had the odd sense that the twins were speaking with each other, that a whole conversation was occurring between them, though neither spoke a word.

Kayl's fingers flexed around Aileen's hand, squeezing gently, before he released his hold and turned away. He continued onward without a backward glance.

Kier kept his arm around her as he followed his brother. "I have you, Aileen. We're almost through this."

She leaned into the shelter of his body a little more than she'd intended. "Thank you."

They crossed the dance floor with cautious swiftness. Aileen fixed her gaze upon Kayl's back again, refusing to look at the bodies on the floor as Kier guided her over and around them. But she couldn't hide from the smell. It was the same stench as in the supply closet, the same stench she'd smelled from herself after being shot.

Some part of her brain acknowledged that the nearby corpses were the people who'd been jumping, cheering, and dancing during her performance. A pang of sorrow pierced her chest; all that life, all that energy and enthusiasm, had so quickly and cruelly been ended. But another part of her—thankfully the stronger one—couldn't believe any of this had happened, couldn't believe everyone had been captured or killed.

Couldn't believe that she was all but dead, even though she felt it.

With each step, her legs became a little less stable. Nausea gripped her stomach, and bile threatened to rise in her throat, but she kept walking. As she climbed the ramp to the next level, a chill raced up her spine and skittered outward across her skin. What began as a faint tremor soon escalated into bone-deep shivering.

Aileen leaned on Kier more and more. He remained at her side, steady and solid, accepting her weight without complaint.

Why couldn't I have met him a few years ago? Before...all this?

They ascended to the second highest level, where they turned left, working their way around the ring.

She let out a shaky breath, and her eyes flicked up, focusing on a section of the uppermost level's railing. Numerous holes had been shot through the railing, most of which had trails of melted material beneath them reminiscent of candle wax that had trickled down before cooling. Only a few meters away from that spot, the free-floating platform still hovered in the air, its edges visible only due to the light reflecting on them.

That was where she—

Aileen groaned, knees buckling as the pain on her side sharpened. Kier tightened his hold on her; he was the only thing keeping her upright as she breathed through the pain with teeth clenched.

Cold sweat beaded on Aileen's back, and tremors wracked her in gradually intensifying waves.

It wasn't just the pain. Her right side felt overly taut, like too little skin had been stretched across too large an area, and a maddening itch coursed just under the surface.

"A little farther," Kier said, helping her stand up straight.

"Sorry," she whispered, shaking her head. Despite the fire pulsing from her wound, she was cold. She clutched at Kier and continued walking, wishing his armor wasn't between them, that it was just his skin against hers, sharing his warmth.

Ahead of them, Kayl halted, his gaze settled on the face-down body at his feet. Aileen recognized that gray skin and those gold-painted head spikes. A new sort of heat sparked in her belly.

Kayl wedged a foot under Saduuk's body and quite unceremoniously flipped him onto his back.

The vroca's swollen tongue was jutting out from between his lips, his eyes were bulging from their sockets, and dark, congealing blood was smeared across his face and his discolored, misshapen neck.

She straightened her back, dropped her arm from Kier, and clenched her fists at her sides. The pain and discomfort faded, driven back by surging anger. Shrugging off Kier's arm, she stepped forward. After all Saduuk had done to her, after all he'd forced her to do, she had no sympathy for him.

She'd never hated anyone until him. That had been Saduuk's gift to Aileen—hatred. Suffering and trauma, too. Oh, he'd wrapped them up in compassion and kindness, had pretended that he was just helping her, giving her a break, but she'd only realized that wrapping had always been paper-thin.

She kicked Saduuk's ribs hard, making his body sway. The impact caused a dull ache in her foot and triggered a pang of agony in her side, but she kicked him again, and again, wanting to make him hurt, *needing* to make him hurt. When her knees buckled again, she didn't fight for balance; she dropped onto them and embraced the fresh swell of anger.

Her body was failing because of him. She was *dying* because of him.

Teeth clenched, she battered Saduuk's torso with her fists, barely noticing the pain she caused herself.

Her breath was ragged, her wounded side ablaze, and her vision blurred with gathering tears, yet she kept hitting him, unable to forget the last three years, unwilling to forgive. Everything she'd kept inside for so long came out—and it was only more infuriating that Saduuk took it all without a sound, without feeling even a shred of the agony he deserved. A sob escaped her.

Strong hands grasped her arms, halting her blows. Her nostrils flared with a heavy exhalation as she pitched herself forward. There was still so much anger, so much hatred, so much pain—and she was just one of many people Saduuk had harmed. Just one of many people he'd tricked, enslaved, and abused.

"Easy Aileen," Kier said as he pulled her back. His hold was firm —she couldn't have broken it if she wanted to—but it was so, so gentle. "He can do you no further harm, but you will hurt yourself more if you continue."

Those tears, which had somehow remained in her eyes despite her movements, finally spilled. She squeezed her eyes shut, forcing more moisture from them. Spots danced in the darkness behind her eyelids, and the room tilted beneath her.

Cloth rustled in front of her. She opened her eyes to see Kayl crouched on the other side of Saduuk, checking the vroca's pockets with his free hand.

"I'm...I'm done," she rasped, tugging on her arms.

She felt Kier's gaze upon her, felt his concern, his reluctance, but he released her. Aileen didn't allow herself to focus on the body before her; she couldn't let herself see Saduuk anymore. It was just a corpse.

Her hands trembled as she reached forward, grasped the collar of Saduuk's shirt, and pulled it down, revealing the polished platinum necklace that had been hidden beneath. The object attached to the necklace was small, oval-shaped, and unassuming. And that little thing was the key to her freedom—to her survival.

She tore the controller off the necklace. For a moment, she held it on the palm of her hand, staring down at it. Blackness encroached on the edges of her vision, which blurred for a moment as the room again tilted. She blinked away her dizziness.

How could something so small and so light be so important?

"Do it, Aileen," Kier said.

Kayl cupped her hand with his, guiding it higher. "Claim your freedom."

Aileen met his gaze. He'd been curt, blunt, and grave throughout the short time she'd known him, but there was something in his eyes now that spoke of such impossible depth—that spoke of fire in his soul.

She curled her fingers around the key, lifted it to the choker on her neck, and pressed the release button.

With a dull, unassuming click, the collar opened. More tremors coursed through her hand as she tentatively touched her fingertips to the metal; the collars produced electric shocks any time they were tampered with.

But there was no shock now. She grasped the thin, intricate choker and pulled it away from her neck, letting it fall from her hand. It struck the floor with a dull thump that resonated in her heart.

Whatever happens...I am free.

"Now we must go." Kayl rose and strode back in the direction from which they'd come without a backward glance.

Kier placed his hands beneath Aileen's elbows and helped her stand. The burning in her side intensified. Her legs were weak and shaky, and her head spun, eyelids fluttering. She turned toward him, bracing a hand against his chest to steady herself.

"Are you all right?" he asked, carefully sweeping rogue strands of hair from her face.

She shivered. She wished it had been a reaction to his touch.

"We can go," she said, blinking repeatedly in a vain attempt to clear the black spots from her vision. Growing impossibly colder, she stepped away from him—or thought she did, at least. Everything was suddenly fuzzy, and she felt herself tipping, falling, spinning out of control.

But she didn't hit the floor, even though she swore it was rushing to meet her. For an instant, she was weightless. When her vision cleared, she found herself looking up into Kier's face from her place in his arms, held securely against his chest.

"Hold on, Aileen." His deep, smooth voice possessed a hard edge, making it impossible to ignore.

She somehow lifted her arms, hooking them around his neck, and leaned her face against his shoulder. The theater bounced and jostled around her, the objects within flitting by.

He's running. Is he in a hurry?

Is someone...hurt?

In response, her side roared with agony and fire, stealing her breath, making her queasy, and tensing her every muscle. Darkness pressed in on her from everywhere, even thicker than before. She willed it away; there was little else she could do.

"Stay with me, Aileen," Kier said raggedly.

All she wanted in that moment was to say she would. Yes, she would stay with him, stay with him forever. Stay with him anywhere, so long as it wasn't this place.

Nothing came out when she opened her mouth but a pained whimper.

Aileen curled against him, clutching his armor as fresh tears ran down her cheeks. That thought from earlier echoed through her clouded mind.

Whatever happens, I am free.

If only that could've been enough.

TEN

Aileen.

Kier's mind-voice broke Kayl's stride, making his boots skid on the floor. Heart racing, Kayl slapped his free hand on a table, halting his momentum, and twisted to look back.

Kier held Aileen in his arms. Her skin had again gone ashen, and it glistened with a sheen of sweat. Despite Kier's firm hold on her, she was shivering, making those now chaotic tresses bounce and sway.

Only meters away was the spot where the twins had failed to kill Vrykhan. This place should have been the site of their greatest triumph, of the fulfillment of their destiny. It should have been the site of a victory that was the culmination of years of hunting, investigating, and fighting.

Only meters away is the spot where a plasma bolt intended for us struck Aileen.

Kier's tail swung up. It coiled around the blaster on his hip, tugged the weapon free, and tossed it to Kayl.

Shoving away from the table, Kayl caught the blaster by its grip.

His gaze met Kier's, and their minds interfaced, establishing a connection that was beyond words, beyond thoughts. It was true unity—another taste what it would be like to complete their *daevalis*.

The blasters' power cells were nearly depleted, Kier's arms were full, and Eternal Paradise was bristling with pirates, but the twins would not be deterred.

They would get Aileen to the *Fang*.

They would heal her.

Kayl and his brother ran side-by-side to the railing. They leapt simultaneously, their leading feet coming down atop the railing, and launched themselves over it. Kayl landed on the floor of the next tier, and he did not allow his pace to falter. Forward. Only forward.

Kier landed atop a table, rattling tableware that had somehow not been knocked off in the battle, and used a nearby chair as a step to get down to the floor. They jumped the next railing as well and raced across the silent, still dance floor without slowing.

They mounted the stage, pushed through the curtain, and descended into the trap room, where Kayl took the lead. The empty, drab corridors seemed impossibly longer, as though he had to take ten steps now for every one he'd taken on their journey to the theater, and it all looked so similar. How could anyone tell which corridor was which, how could anyone navigate this place?

Focus.

"Aileen," Kier said, a guttural undertone breaking through his otherwise gentle voice, "we need you to stay awake. You need to show us the way to the docking gates."

The sounds of the twins' ragged breathing and frantic footfalls faded from Kayl's awareness, leaving only the thumping of his heart. Countless thoughts circled his consciousness like predators sizing up their surrounded prey. None of them would help. Nor would the roiling emotions at his core, which threatened to blaze to the surface in an inferno at any moment.

Aileen...

"Right," she murmured.

Kayl turned the next corner, his speed carrying him into the wall. He pushed away from it with his elbow before the impact could break his stride and continued onward even faster, drawing from reserves of strength he hadn't known he possessed.

That torrent of thoughts kept swirling, those volatile emotions kept churning, and the pressure inside him built with his every step. Though he sensed Kier close behind, Kayl had to fight the urge to look back.

He needed to see Aileen, to know she was still with them. But part of him didn't want to see her like this.

Kier's worry flowed into Kayl—not that *worry* was adequate to describe the emotion anymore. This was panic, this was alarm, this bordered on terror. It didn't have to come with coherent thoughts for that to be clear.

Their footfalls echoed along the empty corridors. The naked ducts and conduits overhead only made the hallway seem longer, a sense that wasn't helped by the uniform doors that varied only in the tiny signs denoting what lay behind them. The gray walls and floor gave little indication of distance crossed.

And that pressure kept building.

Aileen guided them through a few more turns; each time Kier asked her the way, her answer came slower than the last. Kayl could *feel* her fading.

Kayl had been acquainted with death since childhood. He'd seen it more times than he could count, had held innocent people as they'd taken their last breaths, had delivered death to slavers, smugglers, and pirates. But Aileen dying was worse than all that. His chest felt like it had been caught in a trash compactor, and the only thing keeping it from being crushed was the shallow breaths with which he filled his lungs.

Finally, they reached a staircase leading up.

Aileen's head lolled. Her eyelids fluttered, and beneath them, her eyes were glossy and unfocused, pupils dilated. She looked worse than she had before the ulturine injection. Whatever life the shot had instilled in her was gone; whatever extra time it had afforded her was spent.

She rasped, eyes closing, "To the...concourse."

The concourse. They had to go through it to reach the gates, and it was there they'd be most exposed—it was there that the pirates had been herding most of their prisoners. The twins had barely reached the entrance to the gates the first time.

Plan? Kier pulsed.

Go fast, Kayl replied.

The corner of Kier's mouth hitched up in a joyless smirk that was hidden an instant later when both twins activated their helmets, enclosing their heads in armor.

Kayl adjusted his hold on the blasters and bounded up the steps. He didn't hesitate to open the door at the top of the stairs. He checked to either side of the doorway, weapons at the ready.

He recognized the railing ahead, the pillars, the lush greenery and faux village sprawled out below—though it was now populated by overturned gaming tables, scattered chairs, trash, and motionless corpses instead of an enthusiastic crowd enjoying the vices Saduuk had on offer.

Voices rose in shouts from below and to the sides, and Kayl could make out faint sobbing and cries from somewhere, but there were no pirates in view.

He stepped through the doorway and turned left, running for the docking gates. To the right, he spied the melted base of the pillar Kier had kicked down the stairs; it felt as though that had occurred a lifetime before.

Somewhere on the lower level, someone shouted in a guttural voice. A chorus of panicked cries responded, escalating into screams after the high whine of a blaster firing cut through the noise.

There were dozens, if not hundreds, of people being held down there. Being threatened. Being killed.

Kayl fixed his gaze on the entrance to the docking gates and did not look away.

No way but forward.

No way without her.

Whether those words had come from his mind or from Kier's did not matter. They were true.

Kayl passed through the entryway without a backward glance. The ominous crimson glow in the corridor beyond did not faze him; he would not allow the morbid thoughts it might otherwise have triggered to rise to the surface of his mind.

Kier followed Kayl even more closely than before. Their bodies were Aileen's only shield, her only protection.

A voice on the overhead sound system calmly told all guests to return their ships in an orderly fashion and stand by for clearance to depart.

Based on the series of screams and urgent voices ahead, those instructions were not being followed.

"Shut up and get down on the floor!" someone yelled. The command was followed by blaster fire and more screams. The sounds echoed faintly in the relative quiet between the announcement system's nonchalant directions.

Kayl kept his weapons raised as he and Kier passed the security checkpoint, where the guards who'd allowed the twins entry lay dead and the scanner system stood smoking, riddled with holes.

The wide space beyond the checkpoint had been packed with travelers when the twins first arrived. Now it was strewn with debris and bodies. To the sides, pirates stood with weapons trained on huddled groups of survivors—people who'd come so close to escape only to have their hopes dashed at the last instant.

That will not be us.

Never, Kier's *aerys* replied.

Despite the resistance they'd faced and the destruction and death they'd wrought, the pirates would leave Eternal Paradise with hundreds, if not thousands, of captives to sell on the slave markets and an untold amount of material wealth.

And Vrykhan was still alive to oversee it all.

Biting back a surge of rage and the bitter, bilious taste of failure, Kayl charged toward their docking gate.

Vrykhan was alive, but so was Aileen. Keeping her that way was the only success they could hope for in this situation. Nothing else matter beyond that.

"Fuck, that's them!" one of the pirates yelled.

On either side, pirates turned toward the twins, bringing their weapons to bear. Kayl extended his arms and fired a torrent of bolts. The bolts hit their targets, and pirates fell, but his right blaster only managed four shots before its power cell failed. The left held out for seven.

The pirates' retort to Kayl's fire came in a spray of plasma bolts. Kayl felt them hit his shoulders, legs, and head, and the heat gauge in his helmet display lit up as it registered the impacts. None of the bolts broke through, but his chest constricted in fear regardless—he was armored, but Aileen was not.

We are almost there, Kier pulsed. *She will be fine once we get there.*

She has to be, Kayl thought. *She has to be.*

Only twenty meters to the door that led into the *Fang's* docking corridor. Twenty meters was nothing after journeying countless light years, after traversing the universe galaxy by galaxy in pursuit of Vrykhan for fifteen years.

Kayl lowered his arms, dropping the depleted blasters to the magnetic holsters on his hips, and pinned his focus on the airlock door. His helmet display flashed with indicators marking hostiles to the left and right. The pirates were advancing, firing their weapons without concern for where the stray bolts struck.

They will not have her. He will not have her.

Kayl felt every millimeter of distance. Each thunderous beat of his heart produced a twinge in his gut, an echo of the terran's pain, and the pressure at his core had far surpassed the bursting point.

Those twenty meters felt longer than the lifetime that had led the twins to this moment.

His feet slid as he reached the door; he stopped himself by slamming his palms on the doorframe and tensing his muscles. A plasma bolt struck the upper frame. It was halted by shielded tristeel, pooling in a glowing orange hole no more than a centimeter deep.

Kayl slapped the door control. Before the door had even fully opened, he pushed his brother through, following immediately behind. Several more bolts struck the door and the wall around it, spraying flecks of hissing plasma and molten metal onto the floor.

He paused only long enough to hit the control panel inside the corridor. The airlock door reversed its motion, sliding shut. Kayl yanked his tail in close. The closing door brushed its tip, nearly catching it.

The relative silence was jarring—no screams or blaster shots, no shouting pirates or computer-generated announcements. Here there was only the twins' ragged breaths, their thumping heartbeats, and the thudding of their boots as they sprinted to their ship.

Aileen didn't make a sound.

Using his holocom, Kayl opened the *Fang's* rear ramp. Familiar cool white light spilled from the cargo hold. He found little comfort in it.

Kier carried Aileen onto the ship. She'd been curled up tight against him for most their journey from the theater, but now she was limp, with arms and legs dangling. Though it may have been because of the light, Kayl swore she looked even paler than she had only minutes before.

Far behind Kayl, the airlock door opened. A pirate fired his autoblaster toward the twins. Plasma bolts cut molten paths along the corridor's walls, ceiling, and floor.

Kayl bounded up the ramp, sending the command to close it

through his holocom. The corridor pulsed with flashes from the pirate's continued fire until the moment the ramp was sealed.

Vrykhan was still aboard Eternal Paradise. He'd escaped retribution, had escaped justice. And even knowing that, even knowing Kayl's lifelong enemy, the target of all his ire and hatred, was right out there somewhere...

We need to get the ship away from here, Kayl pulsed.

We need to get her to the infirmary, Kier pulsed simultaneously.

The twins retracted their helmets at the same time and looked at one another. Kayl saw his own urgency and desperation in his twin's eyes. Their shoulders rose and fell with their strained breaths, their tails lashed from side to side, and their jaw muscles ticked as they clenched their teeth.

And Aileen remained unmoving, unresponsive.

She must survive.

Their *aerysi* had spoken as one, echoing their hope, their yearning, their will. Their need.

Without a word, the twins ran up the steps into the ship's upper level. Kier split off at the infirmary while Kayl continued to the cockpit.

Kayl's holocom thrummed with a silent alarm, likely the *Fang* detecting hostiles attacking its aft. But those auto-blasters wouldn't penetrate the ship's defenses. The pirates didn't matter. The tretin didn't matter.

Only the terran was important.

The infirmary's cold, clinical lights came on as Kier entered the room. It was the opposite of Eternal Paradise in so many ways—function over form, designed to be clean and efficient. He brought Aileen to the medpod and activated it with a touch of his tail. The glass cover receded silently to expose the pod's interior, a concave bed with a white, padded surface. A wide holo screen appeared beside the pod, displaying the controls and settings.

He laid Aileen on the bed. Though he longed to study her face, to comb his fingers through her hair and gently work out the tangles and braids, his eyes moved immediately to the bandage on her side. When he and Kayl had applied the wound sealant, the material had been paler than her skin. Now it was an almost perfect match.

His throat constricted, and his side throbbed with remembered pain.

Underfoot, he felt the faint hum of the *Fang's* engines powering up.

Kier retracted his armor and moved a hand to her cheek.

The female's skin was damp and cool, especially compared to Kier's, and her breathing was shallow and irregular. He pressed a fingertip to her neck, locating her pulse. Faint but rapid. Kier's heart sped to match that rhythm.

The ship rumbled, making Kier sway and the terran's head loll. Alerts buzzed on his holocom.

What was that, Kayl?

Kayl's psychic voice held undeniable strain beneath its usual calm. *Eternal Paradise's automated traffic control expected us to wait for clearance to depart.*

So what did you do?

I...told it to fuck itself.

Shaking his head, Kier turned to the controls and hurriedly searched the presets for terrans. The species had only been accepted into Arthos, and thus the wider universe, for a few years, and many devices and databases had not been updated to accommodate them.

His eyes flicked to Aileen. Her vibrant makeup, though smudged and fading, contrasted her ashen flesh more with each passing moment. Faint blue veins were visible beneath her skin. That could not have been normal.

You will be all right, terran.

Please be all right.

You must be all right.

"We are not going to lose you, Aileen," he growled.

He finally found a relevant entry on the list—*TERRANS, FROM URGAND'S RECORDS.*

Why would the preset on this medpod mention the vorgal medic from Arcanthus's crew? This had been state-of-the-art military technology developed by a private organization, and according to Thargen, Urgand had simply been one of many medics in the vorgals' Vanguard.

Kier released a huff through his nostrils. *Arcanthus.* Arcanthus had accessed their ship's systems and added the information into the database without telling them.

Thank you, Arcanthus.

Kier tapped the selection and turned back to Aileen. Her color-ful, glittery top hugged her body like a second skin, and the shimmery strips of fabric that comprised her skirt were tangled and folded over her thighs. Both garments bore scorch marks; the trajectory of the bolt that struck her had left damage from hip to ribs. Her clothing would only get in the medpod's way.

The backs of his fingers brushed the cold flesh between her breasts as he grasped the upper edge of her top. Before he could remove the garment, the ship shook violently, rattled by a deafening explosion.

Kier's eyes rounded. He threw himself over her, grasped the opposite side of the medpod with both hands, and pressed his legs against it, pinning her in place.

The lights flickered out, plunging the room into darkness that was broken by random, blinding flashes. Everything around him quaked, and gravity tugged him in every direction, threatening to break his grip. He used every muscle in his body to hold on and keep Aileen in place.

All the while, his holocom vibrated with alerts, a tiny mockery of the greater chaos.

What is happening, Kayl? What did you do?

The cloaking field failed when we broke away. They fired on us before I could reengage it, Kayl replied. Only a shred of control remained in his *aerys*; this was the closest thing to outright panic Kier had ever sensed from his brother.

Finally, after a rumbling that Kier felt down to his marrow, everything stilled.

I will take the gunner's seat, Kier pulsed as he lifted his head and eased his hold on the medpod. His limbs were stiff from the exertion, and faint tremors ran through them—aftershocks of the quaking.

We cannot outgun them, Kier. The fire came from the Azkazor.

Kier did not know an oath in any language adequate to utter in that moment. As difficult as it was to find information regarding Vrykhan, the *Azkazor*—a century-old tretin war cruiser the pirates had heavily modified—was infamous. Rumors alleged it had destroyed several modern battle cruisers dispatched by various intergalactic governments over the years.

The *Fang* was a highly advanced, extremely capable military spacecraft, but it could not stand against anything like the *Azkazor*.

Kier stood upright, keeping his hands on the edge of the medpod, and glanced at Aileen. She remained unconscious; unaware of her surroundings, unaware of the danger, unaware of the dire price she had already paid for being in the wrong place at the wrong time. Kier could not help but curse fate for putting her in their path today of all days.

You need to initiate a jump, Kier pulsed.

I know, Kayl replied.

So why have you not done so?

Kayl's mind-voice was harsh as he replied, *Because it is exactly what you would do, meaning it is quite likely to kill us!*

Kier clenched his jaw, fingers tightening on the edge of the medpod. He did not remove his eyes from Aileen. *You feel exactly what I do, Kayl. If we stay here, it is guaranteed death. If we jump, at least there is—*

A chance, Kayl pulsed.

Kayl's mind-voice resonated within Kier as the lights flickered and went dark again. The ship rumbled and rattled, metal groaned, and the engines roared distantly, impotently. Kier again threw himself over the terran and shut his eyes.

The *Fang* would hold together.

Aileen would be all right.

The noise around him built. Violent vibrations ran through his muscles, coursed through his bones, buzzed along his every nerve. A high sound, like the whine of a giant blaster, underscored it all, soon growing so powerful that it was unbearable. Kier was certain his eardrums would explode, was certain Kayl had been right—this jump was the end.

Just as the pain and pressure would surely have undone him, everything went utterly silent and still.

For Kier, there was only darkness. His stiff limbs refused to move immediately, and his eyelids were too heavy to open, but he felt his chest heaving with his hoarse breaths, felt the blood pumping through his veins.

He forced his eyes open.

Aileen lay beneath him, the braids and ringlets of her red hair gathered around her head in a chaotic cloud. Only the faintest of breaths passed between her parted blue lips.

Tearing his hands off the medpod, Kier hurriedly sliced her garments with his claws and tore them off. One of her shoes had fallen off during the jump. He tugged the other off and tossed it aside.

Part of him knew this was wrong; this was not how he was meant to see his *na'diya's* naked form for the first time. She was the embodiment of beauty, meant to be admired and worshipped, but he could take no pleasure in the sight of her now. All he could see was the bandage—and, in his mind's eye, the blackened and mangled flesh beneath.

He stepped back and engaged the automatic care sequence.

ELEVEN

The glass lid slid back into place, sealing Aileen inside the pod. The bed lit up in soft white as its antigrav field engaged. Her body rose, hovering a few centimeters above the bed. Her long, red tresses floated around her head, curls and braids rippling as though on the surface of a peaceful pool.

Kayl entered the room and strode over to Kier. Silently, they watched the scanner lights sweep across her body from head to toe and back again, their pale bluish glow painfully reminiscent of the plasma bolt that had done this to her.

A second light came on, focusing into a thin line on the edge of her bandage. As the light moved along the bandage's length, the pale material burned away, revealing the horrific wound beneath.

Data streamed across the holo screen at the corner of Kier's vision, but he didn't look away from Aileen. The tightness in his throat spread up into his face; his lips pressed together, his brow furrowed, and his nose slits flared. He balled his fists and squeezed as hard as he could, making his arms tremble.

Why now? After all this time, why find their mate *now*?

A display appeared on screen detailing the processes the medpod would undertake to tend to its patient. Kier kept his attention on Aileen's face as robotic tendrils emerged from the bed to inject her with medications and begin the procedure.

Kayl turned his head and to look at the screen. He didn't speak, didn't allow even a single conscious thought through the psychic bond, but Kier felt his brother's acknowledgement of the truth—Aileen would have died had it taken any longer to get her here. She would have died without the ulturine injection.

Though Kier had known that truth all along, it slammed down on him now with crushing weight.

Kier settled a hand on the medpod's smooth lid. It was cool to the touch, just like Aileen's skin. He swallowed thickly, forcing down his dread and pain to rejoin the maelstrom of emotions raging at his core.

She needed to be well. Then everything else could be addressed.

Kayl's eyes returned to the terran, and he folded his arms across his chest. One of his fingers tapped the armor on his bicep.

The medpod worked with speed and precision no flesh and bone hands could match, rebuilding and repairing damaged organs and tissues from the inside out. Time and again, Kier's emotions swelled, threatening to break out of the cage in which he'd locked them. Somehow, he kept them contained. Perhaps it was for her; perhaps it was because of her.

But he knew his self-control was only temporary. The air thickened with each passing second, crackling with unsettling energy. His tail swung erratically, gradually gaining speed.

The robotic tendrils reconstructed her skin in a series of sweeping, crisscrossing motions, almost like they were weaving threads into fabric. The result was a large patch of fresh, pinkened flesh on her side, healthy and smooth but distinguishable from the surrounding skin. The tendrils made a final injection at the center of the wound and retracted into the bed.

The scanner lights came on again, sweeping over her body from all sides. Once they switched off, Aileen slowly descended onto the bed, where she lay like a rare object on display behind glass.

The twins turned toward the holo screen. According to the scans, the procedure had been successful, and Aileen's vital signs were nearing acceptable levels for her species.

But none of the pressure inside Kier had eased, none of the tension in the air had dissipated.

Kayl drew in a deep breath and held it.

Everything erupted at once—years' worth of emotions Kayl had never shared, all his compounded doubts and frustrations, all the pain, sorrow, and hatred he and Kier had carried in their hearts.

A harsh growl tore out of Kayl's throat, and he spun away from the medpod and slammed a fist into the wall. The sound of the impact was insignificant compared to all the feeling behind it.

"*Ja'skaal*," Kayl snarled. He hit the wall again and again, each blow sending jolts up his arms and working his hair loose of its tie.

Wary, Kier turned toward his twin. He'd long dealt with his own intense emotions, and didn't always succeed in mastering them, but this was new. And it was jarring.

Kayl's psychic voice repeated the same word over and over, its volume increasing with each punch.

Fuck!

"Kayl."

Another blow, and now a lock of hair hung in front of Kayl's blue eye.

Kier gritted his teeth. Tension rippled through him, suffusing him with heat, and bile rose in his throat. "Kayl!"

Kayl spun toward Kier, more hair falling into his face. His eyes were ablaze, but they were somehow...dark. He raised his hands and bent his fingers like talons. "He was right in front of us! Right in front of us, and we failed."

"We did what we—"

"We *failed*, Kier." Kayl moved closer, nose slits flaring. "The one thing we were meant to do, the one purpose we were meant to fulfill, the one task we have spent our lives preparing to complete, and he is still out there! How many scores of foes have we slain upon this path, but the one"—he straightened a finger—"we *needed* to kill has escaped justice."

Kayl's furious gaze dipped to Aileen, and the gleam within it intensified. Through bared teeth, he said, "If not for her, Vrykhan would be dead."

"And so would we," Kier said, clenching his fists at his sides.

"A sacrifice we were always willing to make, brother. Now we have forsaken our purpose for her. For *nothing*."

Kier's heart stopped. With limbs trembling, chest constricted, and fire roiling in his lungs, his gut, his veins, he stared at his twin. For all their arguing and disagreements over the years, he'd never once wished harm upon Kayl. But now it took every sliver of willpower in Kier's possession to prevent himself from hammering a fist into his brother's jaw.

Kayl's brows rose slightly, and his mouth fell open. He inhaled; his breath hitched, and his tail fell limp. *Kier, I—*

"Go," Kier snapped, thrusting a finger toward the door. "Tend to the *Fang*. I will see to this...*nothing*."

The word was bitter on his tongue. Kayl flinched, swaying back. Kier did not let himself feel remorse. *Nothing* had been Kayl's word, and so Kayl could be the one to suffer its weight.

But Kayl's expression quickly hardened. He clamped his mouth shut, turned on his heel, and stalked out of the room.

Kier sensed the wall going up. He felt it as though it were a physical thing—an imposing barrier of jagged ice blocking off the psychic bridge that connected him to his brother. Nothing would breach that wall, nothing short of the threat of death...and that hurt. Despite everything, Kier did not care for this silence.

He forced his eyes away from the empty doorway and looked down at Aileen, who remained motionless in the medpod.

"I understand," he said, voice strained. "We have been on this hunt for so long, and to draw so close only to fail..." With a sigh, Kier placed his hands on the medpod's lid, closed his eyes, and bowed his head. "We were never supposed to find you. Never supposed to have you."

Kier brushed a thumb across the smooth surface. "I know so little about you, Aileen, but you are not *nothing*. You will never be that. He knows it too. He just...needs time."

When he opened his eyes again, the terran was exactly as she'd been a few moments ago—in silent repose, her red hair wild around her head.

So unused to silence that I am speaking to an unconscious stranger...

Was she truly a stranger though? Part of him recognized her as strongly as it recognized his twin; she was their *na'diya*. He'd seen it in her eyes when she'd looked upon him and Kayl during her performance, and he had seen it again and again during the brief time she'd been conscious afterward. She'd felt a connection too. But what difference could that make if none of them really knew what it meant?

Kier still sensed nothing from his brother, but he ignored the feeling of rejection and tamped his anger down. He would confront all that later. Success, failure, purpose, fate... What did Kier understand of such things? It was much too late to do anything differently, and there was far too much to be done to waste time being devoured by regret.

Pushing away from the medpod, he strode to the cargo hold. The sound of the ship's engines, usually a barely perceptible hum, was more pronounced than ever, accompanied by a deep, irregular whirring.

If the Fang *is damaged enough, none of this will matter...*

Kier grunted and opened the storage locker, searching the clothing within for something suitable for a terran. He settled on pants and a top that had been tailored in traditional daevah style. Aileen was shorter and somewhat curvier than the average female daevah, but the clothing would do.

She could always choose other garments once she was awake and moving about.

He laid the clothing out in the spare crew quarters, gathered an extra blanket, and returned to the infirmary. According to the medical readout, she had stabilized and was clear to exit the pod. Kier wished he could be relieved by that. He wished that things had gone differently, wished that he and Kayl had met Aileen anywhere but Eternal Paradise. He wished that one of his earliest memories of his mate would not forever be of her curled up on that platform with a smoking blaster wound through her abdomen.

He opened the medpod. Aileen's skin was still quite pale, but a hint of pink had crept back in some places.

Fire stirred in him again, this time low in his belly. His cock throbbed, hardening with each beat of his heart, and resonated with a deep ache. He longed to touch her, to explore her body. To feel every bit of her skin beneath his fingertips.

To know that she was real.

Kier halted his hand mere centimeters from her face. A tremor ran through his arm, and his tail curled. His fingers stretched, reaching for her of their own accord.

Not this way. Not now.

He snatched his arm back, grasped the blanket in both hands, and draped it over her, covering her naked body. Before his resolve could crumble, he slipped his arms beneath Aileen and lifted her off the medpod. Her weight settled easily within his arms—like she belonged there.

But she was still limp and unresponsive, still too cool for his liking, and the medication in her system would keep her unconscious for a while longer.

Cradling her against his chest, Kier carried her to the spare quarters. He laid her on the bed, propping her head upon the pillow, and withdrew his arms from beneath her.

Aileen's head fell to the side as Kier straightened the blanket. He didn't let his eyes linger when patches of her flesh were exposed by his adjustments, didn't sate his curiosity. He just tucked the blanket around her, ensuring she was covered from her neck to her toes.

He glanced up at her face to find spiraling strands of sweat-dampened hair lying across it.

Bracing a hand on the bed, Kier leaned over her. He held his breath as he hooked a finger beneath those wild locks and swept them behind her rounded ear.

Her features were relaxed; no more terror or pain. Only her smudged, sweat-streaked makeup remained as evidence of the trials she'd undergone.

Plucking a sanicloth from the nightstand, he gently wiped away the makeup. She looked so different with those bright colors gone. Just as beautiful, but...softer. Realer. This was his mate's true face; the makeup had been a mask, a version of herself she wore on stage. She did not need it to be vibrant in his eyes.

Kier cupped the side of her face with his palm. He stroked her cheek with his thumb, marveling at the smoothness of her skin, and took in a deep breath that was laced with her alluring scent. Her fragrance—her real fragrance—was soft and lush, reminding Kier of the blue aza flowers that grew along the coast near his childhood home.

Warmth blossomed beneath his hand and spread, tingling, up his arm. It flowed straight to his core and expanded outward in waves. For a few blissful moments before he severed that contact, Kier was untroubled by the universe.

"Never nothing," he whispered.

Maybe...everything.

Kayl leaned on his arms and curled his fingers, scraping their armored tips across the top of the control console. He bowed his head, squeezed his eyes shut, and took in a breath that was meant to steady him, but it burned going down.

He'd raked his gaze over the readout in front of him half a dozen times already, hoping that he'd misread it, that the situation couldn't possibly be so bad. But those hopes had proven as foolish as the twins' decision to assassinate Vrykhan in a crowded public space without even a modicum of planning or preparation.

The information on the display hadn't changed, and Vrykhan was alive.

The pirate who'd murdered their parents, who'd sold the twins into slavery, who'd destroyed and ended so many lives, had escaped death. And everyone who'd survived the assault on Eternal Paradise would pay for that. Everyone the tretin encountered afterward would pay for it.

Kayl and Kier should have done what they'd always intended to do—they should have fought to the end. They should have given *everything* to ensure Vrykhan was killed.

Now we have forsaken our purpose for her. For nothing.

Kayl's words echoed in his head, slicing his soul like a flurry of blades.

Aileen was the reason they'd failed. She was the reason they were stuck here, exposed, with a furious tretin warlord undoubtedly out for their blood. She was the reason everything was crashing down.

He opened his eyes and looked at the readout again. The *Fang's* status was the same as it had been the last six times he'd looked—completely fucked.

One plasma bolt. A single bolt through the tretin's head, and it would have been over.

Kayl had taken countless shots on countless targets, and he'd hit nearly all of them. Why had he failed to do so when it mattered most? Why had his concentration faltered in the hour of his greatest need, why had the focus he'd held for fifteen years crumbled?

Because of one plasma bolt. The bolt that hit her.

The soft clank of footsteps behind Kayl wrenched him from his thoughts. His tail stilled, and his fingers flexed. He'd forgotten how jarring it was to have himself closed off. How strange it was for Kier to be able to sneak up on him.

"I will figure this out," Kayl said without looking back. "Apply yourself elsewhere."

Kier's footsteps drew nearer, stopping just behind Kayl.

Their psychic link flickered, and a burst of emotion flooded from Kier into Kayl. Kayl's barrier wavered. No matter how hard he concentrated, he could never hold it for long. He released it like he would have let out a breath held too long—with a little discomfort and a lot of relief.

He was not surprised by what he felt from his brother.

Sighing, Kayl said, "I have no desire to—"

"We do not deserve her. That is the truth of it, Kayl. But she is here regardless."

Kayl's jaw muscles ticked. "Correct. We do not deserve her. And we have already paid far too high a price for her."

"Look at me."

Standing straight, Kayl clenched his fists at his sides and turned to face his brother.

"Do not speak of Aileen that way," Kier said through bared fangs.

"You know what I mean, Kier."

"And I expect you of all people to be precise in your language, Kayl. She is not a thing to be bought and sold. After what we have experienced, after all we have seen, you know better than to speak in such a manner."

"Because precise wording is important right now?" Kayl gestured toward the aft of the ship—vaguely in the direction of Eternal Paradise. "Fifteen years of hunting, and that was our first chance to kill him. *Fifteen years.* All gone in a few minutes. We let him get away because—"

One of Kier's hands darted up, finger raised, and his lips peeled farther back. "Do not say it. She is our *na'diya.*"

"We are not meant to have a *na'diya.* Our *daevalis* was never meant to be completed."

"Yet she is here"—now Kier gestured toward the ship's rear—"and she is ours."

...for nothing.

Fury hardened Kier's expression. "Do not even think those words again."

Kayl's anger was an expanding star at his core, taking up far too much space, putting out far too much heat. And it was directed... everywhere. At himself most of all. Because his mind kept flashing back to those desperate moments when it had seemed like Aileen would die. Those moments when he'd realized that his willpower couldn't alter reality—that wanting something with all his being made no difference in whether he could have it.

And because he didn't know what he wanted anymore.

He let out a long, heavy breath. "We have far more pressing matters with which to concern ourselves at present, brother." Stepping aside, he waved toward the diagnostics readout.

Kier scowled, but the expression softened to a frown as he looked over the screen.

Life support leaking oxygen.
Communications array destroyed.
Engines at forty-three-percent functionality.
Fuel reserves leaking.

The solemnity on Kier's face was further proof that the information was indeed real. "All this from one hit?"

"Any other ship this size would have been destroyed. The damage is not immediately dangerous"—Kayl turned to face his brother from the side—"but all of it together, compounding over days..."

"Death." Kier shook his head. "We have time. We can have the ship repaired. There must be somewhere close."

"There is. I think."

Kier looked at Kayl, brows falling low. "You *think?*"

Kayl reached out and indicated one of the lines on the diagnostic report. "With communications down, we have lost our long-range scanners, and the ship's navigation has defaulted to the star maps preloaded in the computer system. Such maps are not often updated for areas like this."

"Like this? Where did that jump take us, Kayl?"

"The Faladore Omega system, on one of the outer reaches. Frontier space."

"So, we can jump again. Move closer to a population center."

Kayl folded his arms across his chest. "We survived one jump by sheer luck. Are you willing to risk a second?"

Kier's frown deepened. The memories that flashed through their psychic link came from both twins—the smuggler ship they'd followed from Arthos, the smugglers jumping despite their ship being damaged, the terrible crash on a hostile planet caused by that jump.

Innocent lives had been lost. People who'd been just like Kier, Kayl, and Aileen, kidnapped and enslaved...

"And where is this possible settlement?" Kier asked.

"A planet called Omega IV. According to the map, it is the base of an old corporate colony called Navaire."

"How old?"

"I do not know."

Kier's nostrils and nose slits flared with a sigh. "You have us enroute, then?"

"Yes. We can only hope the colony still exists, as it is the only one in this star system. And that the parts and skill necessary to repair the *Fang* are available there."

"How long?"

"Approximately five days."

Kier leaned toward the holo screen, settling his gaze on a particular section—the life support. He made a troubled grunt and pushed away from the console. "And until then?"

Kayl swept his eyes around the cockpit. This ship had become home to them, and it was unsettling to have their home in such a state. "See to whatever repairs we can make from inside the ship."

"Fine." Kier strode toward the exit without a backward glance, pausing before he crossed the threshold. His *aerys* was firm. *I will check on the female. You are better suited to other matters.*

Very well, Kier.

Kier continued forward, leaving Kayl's sight, and a hard, cold blade pierced Kayl's chest, penetrating to his core.

Despite knowing he could not hold it for long, Kayl forced his mental barrier up again.

We have forsaken our purpose for her. For nothing.

He gritted his teeth, braced his hands atop the console, and let out a strained breath. How did Kier function while allowing himself to feel so much?

She is not nothing. *Not at all.*

But...I may be nothing without this hunt.

TWELVE

AILEEN'S LASHES FLUTTERED. Her eyelids were heavy, and the deep, dreamless sleep from which she'd just emerged threatened to drag her back under, but she forced her eyes to remain open. As soon as her vision cleared, her brow furrowed. The ceiling didn't have the intricate carved patterns and luxurious flourishes she usually awoke to; it was smooth, unadorned gray with plain white lighting squares.

I'm not in my room.

She sat up with a gasp, and the blanket that had been covering her fell around her hips. Cool air caressed her bare chest.

Bare?

Heart thumping, she swept the blanket off her lap. She was completely naked beneath.

Alarms blared in her head, and a wave of panic crashed over her. White noise filled her ears, and her chest constricted, making every breath a struggle. She thrust a hand between her thighs.

How many times had she awoken naked in a strange room after a performance? How many times had she found herself bruised and covered in crusted seed with no memory of what had happened? How many times had she been violated, abused, *raped*, while she'd been completely unaware?

But her careful probing of her sex brought no pain, no tenderness.

Removing her hand and closing her eyes, Aileen clutched the

bedding in her fists and drew in several big, calming breaths, willing herself to relax.

Stay with me, Aileen.

That deep, soothing voice rose from her memory, and a pair of kind but fiery eyes flashed in the darkness behind her eyelids. Blue and magenta—the most beautiful eyes she'd ever seen. There'd been strong arms around her, cradling her to a solid chest.

Kier.

She'd been with Kier and his brother Kayl, hadn't she? And they hadn't hurt her. They'd...

Aileen opened her eyes and dropped her gaze to her side, where a patch of pink flesh stretched from her hip to her ribs. It was bordered by a thin white line, and almost looked like birthmark. When she raised her arm, that new skin pulled taut, and a dull itch ran under its surface.

They'd *saved* her.

She touched her hand to her side. The pink skin was warm and smooth, but it only felt her touch distantly, like it was mostly numb. If not for her memories of what had happened during her perfor-mance—terror and confusion, a demonic tretin with crimson eyes, blue-white flashes of plasma, and searing, consuming pain—she might've thought it all a nightmare.

She trailed her fingers over the slightly raised outline of the healed wound. The twins had told her they needed to get her aboard their ship so they could get her into a medpod. Thankfully, it seemed they'd succeeded. If only the medpod had been able to erase those horrible memories too.

Those horrible memories go back a lot further than what happened tonight, Aileen.

Rubbing a hand over her face and combing back her tangled hair, she looked around the small room.

The bed she was sitting upon was tucked in a corner. On the other side of the room stood a little table, atop which rested a pile of folded clothing, and two chairs. A shower stall occupied the left corner. There was a cabinet built into the wall just past the foot of the bed, and the wall straight ahead had a closed door at its center. There was no décor, no colors but black, white and gray. This was nothing like her extravagant room on Eternal Paradise, and yet it was infinitely more welcoming.

Aileen shifted her legs over the side of the bed and settled her feet on the floor. There was a slight ache in her side, but it was nothing she couldn't deal with. Bracing a hand on the bedframe, she stood. Her limbs were weak and wobbly. The heaviness she'd felt in her eyelids upon waking permeated her whole body, trying to drag her down. She moved her hand to the wall to steady herself as she stepped away from the bed.

Though the air in the room wasn't particularly cold, her sleep-warmed skin prickled with goosebumps, and a shiver trailed down her spine.

When she reached the table, she picked up the top article of clothing from the pile; it was a simple dark green halter top. The other garment was a pair of harem style pants with gold embroidery around the waist and loose, billowing legs that were cuffed at the ankles.

Once she'd dressed, she adjusted the waistband of the pants to sit below the wound on her side; even the slightest brush of the soft fabric felt like a scratch to that hypersensitive skin. The top was a little snug, especially around her breasts, but the leggings were comfortable.

Aileen moved to the mirror beside the shower. Her vibrant makeup was gone, her skin was far, far too pale, and her hair was a mess. Using her fingers, she unraveled some of the looser braids, worked out a few tangles, and tamed some of her curls. The result was far from perfect, but it would have to do.

It was time to find her twin rescuers.

She retrieved the blanket and drew it over her shoulders, wrapping herself in it before padding to the door. When she pressed her hand to the touchpad, the door slid open silently, vanishing into the wall. She poked her head out.

A large metal door stood only a few steps to the right, blocking off the corridor. To the left, the corridor continued past several doors just like the one to this room before reaching an open entryway at the far end, through which came a bluish glow that didn't match the white overhead lights everywhere else. Though the corridor was deserted, voices drifted to her from beyond that entryway, too low for her to make out any words.

Something unfurled in her chest, triggering a spark of warmth at her core. Even if she couldn't understand what they were saying, those voices were familiar, and their low hum comforted her. She had a strange longing to get closer, to listen to them for hours and hours...

Clutching the blanket, Aileen stepped into the corridor and walked toward those voices. Her bare feet whispered across the cold, hard floor; an insistent, invisible tether pulled her onward, filling her with the sense that she belonged with the people who were speaking.

"...all I can," one of the voices said.

Aileen's heart skipped a beat. That was Sol'Kier.

"It will be close," replied the other—Sol'Kayl. "Too close."

"We do not have the parts, Kayl, and I am not a mechanic."

"That is obvious enough that I should have been the one to say it, at least by your logic."

Aileen forced herself to stop just before the entryway, hiding her body behind the wall as she looked through. The blue glow came from the many holo screens and control panels all around the room. She couldn't begin to guess what all the readings and gauges were for. A long window—no, not a window, another hologram—wrapped around the three walls she could see, displaying the inky black expanse of space dotted with tiny, twinkling stars.

This was the control room of their ship.

"Of all the words we have exchanged, Kayl, those are the ones you refuse to let go?" asked Kier.

"You said I had developed a talent for pointing out the obvious, yet it would seem yours is unrivaled," Kayl replied.

Aileen shifted her gaze to the daevahs. They were at the front of the control room—Kayl standing before a holo screen with his back to Aileen but his head turned toward his brother, who sat in a chair nearby, leaned back with his arms folded across his chest and his long tail lazily swinging behind him.

That spark of warmth at her center expanded.

She settled a hand upon her chest as though it could stop the sudden quickening of her heart. Aileen had felt this same sensation then when she'd first locked eyes with the twins during her performance. She hadn't understood it then, and she still didn't understand it now, but she couldn't tear her eyes away from them.

"Lashing out at me will not change our situation," said Kier. He wore snug navy-blue pants tucked into black boots. His sleeveless white shirt had a low-cut collar, its fabric loose and billowing. The outfit—light on top and dark on bottom—was tied together by a wide violet sash around his waist, the ends of which lay across his thigh.

Like most daevah she'd seen, his limbs were long and lean, but his arm muscles were well defined. She couldn't help but admire how the purple stripes on his teal skin seemed to complement his musculature.

"Advice you might have offered yourself a thousand times before this," Kayl replied. His tail was also in motion, but it was more erratic, more restless. He wore dark pants and boots that matched his brother's, but his attire wasn't nearly as casual. The navy-blue fabric of his tunic was run through with subtle patterns that gave hints of purple. The garment's hem hung to his knees, its high collar stopped just under his jaw, and its long sleeves ended in bracer-like pieces of leather that enclosed his forearms.

The daevahs were mesmerizing, and with every second Aileen gazed upon them, her urge to move closer to them strengthened. That desire had caught her off guard while she was performing, but from the moment she'd seen the twins, she had wanted to get near them. She'd longed to meet them, to learn about them, to touch them.

And here, now, without the pulsing lights, the music, the audience, the chaos, what reason did she have to stay away? What reason did she have for the nervousness tangled in her gut, for her hesitance?

Something about this, about them, *feels too big. Too deep. Too...right.*

Kier's tail flicked faster, and his jaw muscles bulged. "What would you like me to say? We both know that we are fucked—"

"You did not speak that way before we met Thargen," Kayl said.

"I apologize, Kayl, for offending you." Kier spread his arms, turning his palms up. "Can you offer a more apt term? Because it seems like *fucked* is the perfect word for this situation. And yet we are here because—"

"Because of the terran," Kayl snapped, baring his fangs and turning his body toward his brother.

Aileen started, eyes widening at the venom in his words.

Kier bolted to his feet, stalking across the distance that separated him from Kayl. He bared his own fangs. "Aileen is not at fault. This is because of the choices *we* made, Kayl. Because of what we did."

Kayl's stance was stiff with restrained aggression. "And did we make those choices with clear minds? Did we really choose at all?"

"Yes! And the sooner you accept that, the sooner we may move on to address everything at hand."

"That is all I have been doing, Kier."

Kier shook his head. "You have been brooding. *Bitching*, as Shay would say."

"I do not need to hear what everyone else would say," Kayl growled, leaning toward his brother. "Vrykhan escaped. We failed. Yes, we are fucked. And it is because of the terran. If not for her, we would have accomplished what we set out to do."

Kier released a huff through his nostrils. "If not for her, we would be dead. Have you not considered that she may be a blessing, Kayl? That we may have a second chance?"

"The only second chance I need is another shot at Vrykhan. Have you forgotten what this is all about? What he did? Have you forgotten our purpose?"

Kier growled. "Of course I have not forgotten!" Lifting a hand, he raked his fingers through his hair, sweeping it back but leaving it no less messy. "What if we were wrong about our purpose?"

Kayl's brows fell, and something entered his eyes that chilled Aileen—shards of ice so, so cold and hard that they couldn't possibly be real. "You would forsake our family? You would shun all those who deserve justice for what they have suffered?"

"I would spit in the face of those who made us suffer by daring to claim happiness." Kier's voice was low, run through with barely contained emotion. "I would find the courage to live, Kayl. We did not die when Vrykhan attacked our home...but we have not lived in all the time since. He does not need to be our end. He is not worth our lives."

"And she is not worth forsaking justice."

"Do not pretend it is about anything but revenge."

Kayl's nostrils flared. "Then she is not worth forsaking our revenge."

Those cold, cold words obliterated the strange, comforting warmth Aileen had felt upon hearing their voices. A sense of rejection flooded her, squeezing her heart and stealing her breath. She didn't understand why Kayl's words hurt so much. She *couldn't* understand. Aileen didn't know these daevahs. She'd never seen them before her last performance—and if her life as a traveling performer had taught her anything, it was to shake off the opinions of strangers, to quickly shed such hurt and move on.

But these twins had saved her. They'd taken her from a situation she had been desperate to escape, tended her wounds, and kept her alive through their willpower and tenacity. All that was far more than enough to make their opinions matter to her, and yet something about this was so much deeper. Kayl's words had burrowed into Aileen and lodged themselves in her heart.

Saduuk's voice rose from her memory.

You're lucky I have a soft spot for you, terran, or you'd be putting on that performance every night.

He'd said that the morning after he'd first drugged her with rhapsody. After she'd succumbed to the heat for the first time and woken, confused and sore, in a random room. After he'd first...*rented* her to the highest bidder.

She was nothing. Just a lost, broken performer, a shade of who she'd once been, a mockery of what she could've become. A toy for people like Saduuk to play with as they saw fit.

The daevahs stiffened, tails stilling, and turned their heads in perfect unison to look at her. Their eyes rounded, their short eyebrows rose, and Kayl's lips parted in shock.

Aileen's heart beat faster still. Looking into their eyes made her want to run to these daevahs, to shelter herself against their bodies, but...but no. She couldn't ignore the hurt.

Saduuk had walked all over her, but he was dead, and Aileen was still here.

Despite everything, she was still here.

She was still *here*.

Alive.

And she didn't deserve Kayl's scorn.

Tears of pain and anger stung her eyes as she stepped out from behind the wall. "I didn't ask you to save me." She met Kayl's gaze. "I didn't ask you for anything."

Kayl pressed his lips together, expression hardening—but vulnerability gleamed in his eyes. "Yet we saved you all the same."

"And I'm grateful for that. But however worthless my life might be to you, I don't deserve the blame for what *you* chose."

He strode toward her, angling his chin down. "Hundreds may be dead, a great many more enslaved, because—"

Kier clamped a hand on Kayl's shoulder, halting his brother. "Because Vrykhan is evil, Kayl."

Kayl turned his head slightly toward his twin, but his eyes remained locked with Aileen's. "He would be dead had we continued fighting."

"*Ba'shanaal!* For someone who rarely talks, you seem not to know when to shut up," Kier growled. "She would be dead too if we had continued. But we did not. And given the chance to go back and relive those moments, I would make the same decision without hesitation."

Aileen tightened her grip on the blanket. "I'm sorry. I don't really understand what happened back there, and I don't know what I messed up for you, but I'm sorry." Looking away, she curled her lips in and bit them, battling back fresh tears. "Thank you for what you did. For...patching me up. You can just drop me off at the nearest spaceport, and I won't be a bother to you anymore."

The daevahs' tails fell, and they both took a step closer to her. They spoke a single word, their voices layering with one another perfectly, instilling it with such strength and passion that it made Aileen rock on her heels. "No."

She looked up at them, brows drawn. "What do you mean *no?*"

Kayl opened his mouth, but snapped it shut immediately when Kier glared at him. Kier's expression softened as he returned his attention to Aileen and moved toward her. "We cannot take you to a spaceport."

"What? Why?"

"There are none within range."

"Can't you just...make a jump?"

Kier halted, leaving several meters of distance between himself and Aileen. That tail of his was swaying again, slowly, fluidly, almost hypnotically. "This ship is damaged. It would not be able to make a jump."

"We would not survive a jump," Kayl said.

"Oh." Aileen pulled the blanket a little more securely around her shoulders and met Kier's mismatched gaze; his eyes had no sclera, only dark pupils amidst vibrant color. "What's going to happen then?"

Kier tangled a finger in the braid hanging beside his cheek and tugged on it. "We are traveling to a nearby settlement. Hopefully, they will have the means to repair our ship. For now, that is our only plan." Kier looked over his shoulder at his brother. "If you have opinions, share them aloud."

He and Kayl stared at each other for a time before Kier said, "Because it is considered rude, Kayl. It does not help build trust."

Aileen glanced between the two of them. "I...don't understand."

Kier walked directly up to Aileen. Her eye level was at his collarbone; his low-cut collar granted her view of his sculpted chest muscles. This close, she could smell his earth-and-ocean scent, which settled her nerves.

"Twin daevahs share a psychic bond." He swept the loose strands of her hair back from Aileen's face, tucking them behind her ear, then brushed the backs of his fingers over her cheek, leaving tingles in their wake. It was such an affectionate gesture, and wholly unexpected. Warmth flared in her core. Kier had acted without hesitation, as though him doing this were the most natural thing in the world.

"It is part of what we call our *daevalis*." He inhaled; his pupils became slits that divided his eyes in half. "It means—"

"That we have no respite from one another's thoughts," said Kayl, striding over to them.

Kier closed his eyes briefly and pressed his lips together. "You will find that my brother excels at identifying the negatives of any situation."

Aileen again looked from one twin to the other. "So you can... speak to each other? In your minds?"

"Yes. It is...deeper than that, but that is the easiest way to describe it." Kier withdrew his hand from her, curled it into a loose fist, and lowered his arm.

Oddly enough, the knowledge that Kier and Kayl shared a telepathic connection was by far the easiest part of this who situation to accept. The other questions tumbling through her head were far more dire. Where in the universe were they right now? Where were they going? What had happened to everyone else on Eternal Paradise, what had happened to the few people who'd been genuinely kind to her? What had happened to Tulaya?

What was going to happen to Aileen now that she was no longer in Saduuk's possession?

I need to stop thinking like that. Not what will happen to me, but...

What will I do?

And somehow that question was even more worrisome than the rest, because she had nothing, no one.

"I have been...overly harsh," Kayl said, drawing Aileen out of her thoughts. He was standing beside Kier now, his eyes upon her, unwavering, his expression betraying nothing. "I..."

"Am sorry?" Kier suggested. "Apologize? Regret my words? Any of those would do."

Kayl glared at his brother, lips peeling back to bare his fangs. "All of them." That display of aggression was already over when he looked at Aileen again. "This situation is far from ideal, but we will keep you safe, Aileen."

Aileen shifted on her feet, turning her toes in and curling them against the hard floor. The twins were so close, their gazes so intent, and despite Kayl's hurtful words from earlier, the heat within her core was intensifying. They just... God, they smelled *so* good.

"Why me?" she asked.

They tilted their heads—Kier to the right, Kayl to the left.

Kier asked, "What do you mean?"

"Why did you save me and no one else? Why did you bring me here?"

The movement of their tails slowed. She had the sense, not for the first time, that thoughts were passing between them, that they were having a conversation to which she was not privy.

"The shot that struck you was meant for us," Kier finally said, dipping his chin toward her.

Aileen gently pressed her hand over the taut, pink flesh on her side. The recollection of that pain remained strong, almost enough so to make her wince, almost enough so to bring tears to her eyes, but all she really felt now was the slight discomfort of a freshly healed wound. "There were other people hurt, other people in danger."

"There were." Kier's voice was strained, raw. "Many others."

"More than we could help," Kayl added. His voice was flat, devoid of emotion.

"That doesn't answer my question. Why me and not one of the others?" Somehow, Aileen kept her words steady. "Why did I deserve to survive, to be healed, instead of them?"

"It is not a matter of who deserved to live," Kayl replied, a hint of something hard creeping into his tone, "or the one who did all this would have been dead long ago."

"We had to...to choose"—Kier's eyes flicked toward his brother—"and there was no time to waste in doing so. You were hurt. Dying. And you were right there."

Aileen nodded, lowering her gaze to the floor. Her voice was soft when she said, "Thank you."

Please let Tulaya be all right.

Aileen's chest constricted. If Tulaya had survived, she was likely going through far worse than what they'd endured under Saduuk.

Kier settled his hand on the side of her neck. Though its strength was apparent, his touch was gentle and warm, and it sent a thrill through her. "We wish things had gone differently, Aileen, but we must make the best of what has happened. You may consider this ship your home. There is food, spare clothing, and you likely saw the shower stall in your room."

The longer Kier's hand remained upon her, the stronger that sensation—that heat—at her core became. The closest comparison she could make was to the heat brought on by rhapsody, which triggered irresistible sexual urges in users in its later stages.

Saduuk had given her rhapsody before her performance. But how long ago had that been? And could the fear and stress she'd endured, the ulturine injection, and the surgery she'd undergone in the time since have had any effect on it? Maybe all that had combined to delay or diminish her response to the rhapsody, or even nullified the drug completely?

Because this felt different. This felt *real.* It felt like something that had been inside her all along, something that had been waiting for the right person to awaken it.

And its power unnerved her.

Aileen took a step back, forcing Kier's hand to fall away. "For what? What do you want in return?"

Kier's hand lingered in the air, fingers curved as though cupping her neck. His short eyebrows drew closer together as he lowered his arm. "I do not understand."

"Are you asking if we want payment?" Kayl asked, his expression still betraying nothing.

"Why wouldn't you? Nothing is free," Aileen said. "Saduuk

always found a way to make us pay for what little *kindnesses* he gave us."

The twins exchanged a glance. Aileen once more sensed a whole conversation occurring during their brief eye contact, but she couldn't glean any of it.

"We ask for nothing," Kier said when he met Aileen's gaze again. "Our only concerns are your safety and comfort. And for now, you require rest."

"Your wound has been healed, but it is a taxing process," Kayl added.

"And we have a long journey ahead."

It all seemed too good to be true. Kayl had acted like she was a nuisance, and he'd made it clear that he and his brother had risked their lives—and failed their mission—to save her. How could they not want *anything* in return?

And yet some part of her believed them.

Can't really trust your own judgement though, can you Aileen? Didn't go so well last time.

But one thing was undeniable—she did need rest. In every bit of her body, she felt the sort of pervasive weariness she hadn't experienced since she and her parents had decided it would be fun to perform at six different state fairs in a week.

Aileen frowned. "You said we were traveling to a nearby settlement. How long until we get there?"

Kayl's tail swung to the side and whipped back to a neutral position. "Five days."

She nodded. That would give her time to figure out what she was going to do when they got there. That would give her time to...to sort herself out.

Guess they'll have to put up with me just a little longer.

"Okay. I'll just"—she took another step back and pointed over her shoulder—"head back to my room and leave you both to, well..." She waved toward the control room. "I'll let you get back to doing what you were doing. I'll try to stay out of way until we get to wherever we're going."

The twins stared at her with their heads still slightly tilted.

"You do not need to go," Kier said.

"You were right. I just... I need to get more rest."

Kier flicked a scathing glance at his brother. "If we have made you feel unwelcome, Aileen—"

"No. No, I'm fine. Everything is fine. I really am tired after all...*that*."

The twins' bodies were tense, their tails agitated, and concern poured from them, somehow radiating into her. By the set of their brows and their frowns, they were entirely unconvinced by her words.

"So...I'll see you two later." She took another backward step and then turned, hurrying down the corridor to her room.

Silence followed her until she'd arrived at the door and was reaching for the button to open it.

"The, uh...the lavatory is the first door to your right," Kier said. "Feel free to use it. If you need to. I mean—"

"Time to stop speaking, Kier," Kayl muttered.

Cheeks ablaze, Aileen slapped the control and rushed through the opening door.

THIRTEEN

Kayl watched as Aileen entered her quarters. He squeezed his fists to fight the itch racing across his palms and into his fingertips—it was the urge to reach for her, to touch her, to offer her simple physical comfort, like Kier had...and to take a little of it himself.

But that was a fantasy. There was only one sort of comfort Kayl could provide, only one sort he could receive, and it lay solely in killing Vrykhan. The tretin's death would be a relief for the entire universe and an end to Kayl's worries. And for a long time, he would've been content for it to also be the end of himself.

Who would protect her if we were gone?

Something coiled through his chest and constricted. Aileen had seemed all right on the surface—as all right as anyone could be after suffering a traumatic event, anyway—but there was much more going on inside her. He'd felt her emotions, albeit in brief flashes. He'd sensed deep pain and sorrow, had sensed desperation and fear, had sensed defiance.

And he'd also sensed a spark of...arousal.

Her image appeared behind his eyelids when he closed them. That tousled shock of red hair contrasting the drab gray blanket over her shoulders, the healthy, alluring pink of her cheeks, those full lips and pale, entrancing blue eyes. Despite her obvious weariness, she'd moved with poise and grace.

And he'd been unable to stop himself from imagining the body beneath those coverings. Even now, those imaginings made his groin ache.

Aileen.

She was beautiful, and now that she'd left his sight, Kayl realized just how strange that was for him to have noticed. He'd understood beauty as something other people saw in one another and the universe around them, but he could not recall having ever considered anyone or anything beautiful himself.

Not before her.

It had never mattered before, and it shouldn't have mattered now. Beauty could not aid his hunt, could not assist in the kill.

And yet he wanted to see her again *now*. He wanted to drink in her form with his gaze, to memorize the exact shapes of those delicate eyebrows and enticing lips. He wanted her soulful eyes to meet his so he could peer into the even deeper beauty shining within them. He wanted to explore all of her—body, mind, and soul—to learn of the wonders she held within.

His cock throbbed. He took in a shaky breath, clenching his fists tighter still to stop himself from reaching for the source of that ache.

Losing control, Kayl? Kier pulsed.

Kayl glanced at his brother to find him smirking. *You started these feelings, Kier.*

You would have felt this regardless had you stepped close enough to smell her.

Kayl's tail whipped from side to side. *I did smell her.*

So, you are not as indifferent as you pretend to be, Kier replied.

Kayl turned to face his twin, gritting his teeth. *Were you not so insistent upon speaking aloud, we might have avoided that situation.*

Kier laughed and shook his head. *The problem is not that she overheard us, Kayl.*

You are correct. It is that she is here in the first place.

Kier shifted closer, his face coming within centimeters of Kayl's. "You do not believe that."

With nostrils flaring, Kayl held his brother's gaze. "You presume much about what I believe, Kier."

"I know what you believe, Kayl. As much as you try to hide it, I know. And *you* know quite well that the real problem is you being an insufferable asshole to her."

Those words struck Kayl hard, but they did not make him reel; they were the truth.

I apologized to her, he pulsed, trying—and failing—to still his restless tail. *What more can be expected of me?*

"To make amends," Kier said. "But first you need to admit it to yourself."

Kayl sighed and ran his tongue over his teeth. All of this was a distraction from the twins' purpose, an unnecessary, unwarranted delay. They should have been spending this time repairing the ship or making plans. Flatly, he said, "I am an asshole."

"Delighted as it makes me to hear you finally say so, that's not what I meant."

Everything inside Kayl grew tighter, hotter, and an immense pressure built at his core. When he spoke again, it was through his teeth. "What, then, would you have me say?"

One corner of Kier's mouth shifted aside, and his brows fell over narrowed eyes.

The pressure inside Kayl expanded.

"You are doing yourself harm," said Kier, voice low. "That must be even more unpleasant for you than it is for me."

We have much to do. We are wasting precious time.

Kier folded his arms across his chest. "We have done all we can. This must be addressed now, Kayl, or else we will be unable to move forward."

"We are quite literally moving forward, Kier."

Kier tapped his foot on the floor in a rhythm that was slow, steady, and wholly impatient.

Growling, Kayl lifted a hand, burying his fingers in his hair, and raked his claws across his scalp as he paced away from his brother. The inner pressure, the heat, was too much now, and the sliver of self-induced pain did nothing to distract him from it. Stepping back toward Kier, he threw his arms to the sides and hissed. "She is our mate."

"And?"

"And saving her was the right thing to do. Is that what you were waiting to hear?"

Placing a hand on the side of Kayl's neck, Kier drew him closer. "No. It is what I was waiting for you to say. *You* needed to hear it, Kayl."

Kayl's heart pounded. He stared into his brother's eyes, which were so like his own and yet so different, and the warmth within him grew and spread, wrapping around his core.

This feeling is new for me, too, Kier pulsed. *It is big, and powerful, but it does not need to be crushing. It does not need to be constrictive.*

Kayl cupped the side of his brother's neck, creating a tiny circle; the circle they'd always shared, the circle that had included them and only them for their entire lives.

The circle that had always been meant to become a triangle...a completed *daevalis.*

Closing his eyes, Kayl tipped his forehead against his brother's. *She is not daevah, Kier. She is a terran. We do not know if she can truly complete our* daevalis, *do not know if she will even accept us as we are. We know nothing about her.*

"Come, brother." Kier pulled away and walked along the corridor.

Kayl followed, hesitating only as he neared Aileen's room. He could feel her in there. It was in that growing sense of warmth within him, it was in that tug in his chest, in the rhythm of his heart.

He drew in a breath and continued after his brother, who opened the large door at the end of the corridor and descended into the cargo hold.

Kier gestured to the items inside—cots and bunks neatly folded and stowed along the walls, storage chests with bedding and pillows, lockers filled with spare clothing, a small ration pantry. "This ship was built for war, but what have we done with it?"

"We have waged a war of our own," Kayl replied.

"I am astounded at how immensely you have missed the point. Please, Sol'Kayl. What have we done with the *Fang?*"

Kayl frowned. "I do not appreciate being spoken to as though I am a child, Sol'Kier." But he studied the items all the same, taking in all the details. And in his mind's eye, he saw people here. Hundreds of people, dozens of species, many of them bewildered, broken, battered, but all possessing the same light in their eyes—a spark of hope.

"We have liberated slaves," Kayl said.

"Yes. We have helped people, Kayl." Kier settled his hands on his hips and looked around space. "People who were at their lowest point. People who thought their lives would never be their own again."

"Because you pushed for it, Kier. Because you insisted upon doing so."

Kier's laugh lacked its usual humor as he turned to face Kayl. "But still, you are the stubborn one. We have ever worked toward the same goal, Kayl, and the aid we have provided would never have happened had you not known at heart that it was the right thing to do. Because every time we have raided a slaver ship or discovered slaves in smuggler cargo..."

Kayl ground his teeth together, fighting back the images that threatened to burst from his memory. Kier's words might have summoned them, but they belonged to Kayl. They had shared those traumas without any need for their psychic link.

We see ourselves, Kayl pulsed. *And we wonder how things might have been had someone rescued us. Had someone spared us the horrors we faced.*

Kier nodded. Pain and sorrow were etched upon his features as he looked down. "And the truth of it, Kayl, is I cannot say I would choose to have been saved. Even after all we have been through, I cannot say it."

A pang of guilt arced across the twins' psychic link, lodging itself deep in Kayl's chest.

"If given the chance to do so," Kier continued, "I cannot say I would change what happened. What does it say about me that I would consider allowing the deaths of our parents, our family, our friends, that I would choose for us to suffer for all those years, to be..." Kier's voice grew thick, cutting off his words. He did not continue until he'd drawn in a heavy breath, let it out slowly, and lifted his gaze to Kayl's. "I would not change our past."

Kayl squeezed his fists and forced his tail to still. That guilt was still there; it had come from Kier, but it did not belong to Kier alone. Kayl embraced it.

"Because we have helped so many as the result of our suffering," Kayl said.

Kier nodded and stepped closer, taking the sides of Kayl's face between his hands. "We felt Aileen before we had even docked at Eternal Paradise. We were drawn to her before we ever knew she existed. And when we saw her for the first time..."

He chuckled, smiling softly, though his expression quickly sobered. "We felt her fear and panic. Felt her pain when she was wounded. And just now, we felt so much more from her."

"We do not know her," Kayl said, "and we do not know how any of this works. *If* it works."

"But we know she is troubled, even if we do not know why. We know we have a connection to her."

Kayl lifted his hands, grasping his brother's wrists and tugging them down. "We should focus on important matters, Kier. The ship. The hunt. Vrykhan is still out there, and he will seek revenge for what we have done. Aileen is...a complication." He hurriedly added, "Through no fault of her own."

"She is our mate," Kier replied gently. He shifted his arms to clasp Kayl's wrists, keeping them connected. "We escaped slavery fifteen years ago, Kayl. For all the lives we have saved, we have never reclaimed our own."

"We are broken. Used. She..." Kayl clenched his teeth. "She deserves better."

"She deserves a choice. And we deserve a chance, do we not? A chance to live. To be fulfilled, to find happiness, to claim a new life, as have so many of the people we saved."

Kayl shook his head, again battling the pressure, the warmth, the sensations that were so familiar to him and yet so terrifyingly foreign. "What if we cannot have any of that? What if..."

What if I am nothing without the hunt?

"What if we never try?" Kier's question was spoken softly, but those words held impossible weight. "That seems worst of all to me."

"Our purpose is to end Vrykhan."

"It was for many years. But what if we can change our purpose? Redefine it?"

Kayl searched his brother's eyes, though he did not know what he was looking for. Perhaps for a hint of Kier's madness, or perhaps for a reflection of his own. Perhaps he sought an argument to make, a weakness to exploit, a hint of doubt upon which to pounce.

But all he could see was that spark of hope—the same spark he'd seen in the eyes of so many of the people they'd saved.

When the twins were young, their lives had been the same as those of most daevah children—carefree and innocent. They'd spent their days studying, playing, and exploring the countryside around their quiet village. As they'd neared adolescence, they'd assumed they would have grown into their natural roles as part of a *daevalis*. They'd not known enough to truly hope for it, but it had seemed destined.

They'd assumed they would find their *na'diya*, make their bond with her, and do whatever it was that adults did while enjoying the happiness and serenity of a completed *daevalis*, just like their mother and fathers had.

A simple life. A content life. That was all they'd wanted, all they'd imagined. The twins had never dreamed of riches or glory, had never craved adventure and danger. They'd never pictured themselves fighting. In their youth, they'd have been perfectly happy to have never left their village.

"We have known nothing but the hunt, Kier," Kayl said, his voice ragged.

"The terrans have a saying. *It is never too late.*"

"That is easily proven untrue."

The ghost of a smile curled Kier's lips. "It is a figure of speech, Kayl. It is not meant to be taken as an immutable, scientific fact of the universe. Samantha, Shay, and Yuri said it means that so long as one is alive, it is not too late to learn. To grow, to change."

How had Kayl been so blind to what was right in front of him? How had he missed the desires Kier had made no attempt to hide?

The signs had been there for so long; Kier wanted to *live*. He wanted friends and family, wanted joy and happiness, and he'd wanted those things for a long while. Kayl had seen him with Arcanthus's crew, socializing and joking, building new relationships, slowly filling in the holes that had been torn in their lives so many years ago.

Kayl had felt like an outsider in Arcanthus's compound. His focus had always been on vengeance, on the fury and hatred he'd carried in his heart for most of his life. Every interaction he'd had with other people for as long as he could remember had been for the purpose of furthering his goal. He'd seen anything else as a waste of time.

But that hope in Kier's eyes, that longing... That wasn't foolish. That wasn't a waste. It real, and pure, and *good*.

If Kayl had been an outsider, it was because he'd made himself one. But had he ever really wanted that? Had he ever asked for such loneliness? Deep, deep in his soul lay the truth—Kayl yearned for the same thing as his brother. Perhaps it wasn't too late to learn. To...change.

To live.

The twins released their hold on one another, and Kayl sighed. "Where would we even begin?"

Kier shrugged, turning his palms up.

But Kayl knew the answer; perhaps he'd known before he'd even posed the question. Fresh guilt solidified in his heart. "The truth. We begin with the truth."

"We do not know how she will react."

"But nothing lasting can be built upon a broken foundation."

Tail swinging behind him, Kier nodded. "I agree. And perhaps it will make her more willing to be open with us."

A shared memory flashed along their psychic link—the conversation they'd just had with Aileen, the emotions they'd sensed from her, the pain and trauma beneath those emotions. The twins could guess at what had happened to her as Saduuk's slave.

Fury and protectiveness roared inside Kayl, rising from his core. Kier's lips peeled back, baring his fangs; the rage was mutual. But Saduuk was dead, Eternal Paradise was behind her, and only those emotional scars remained.

They understood as well as anyone the scars left behind by being enslaved. They understood the degradations, the despair, the nauseating sense of having been violated in every way imaginable. And to overcome all that, she'd have to revisit those traumas. She'd have to tear open the old wounds. She'd have to look at them directly and choose to move on...and even then, it would be hard. So, so hard.

Fifteen years later, Kayl and his brother were still working through their own pain.

They both frowned. The force that had drawn the twins to Aileen wrapped around Kayl's heart and squeezed.

"Of course," Kier said, "that does not address the matter of how we should present the truth."

"What is the issue, Kier?" Kayl pointed toward the steps leading back to the upper deck. "We go to her room and speak with her. Simple."

Kier scoffed. "She is our mate, Kayl. She deserves more thoughtfulness from us than that."

"Openness and honesty are not thoughtful?"

"Ah, my brother"—Kier slapped Kayl on the shoulder, making him sway—"you have much to learn about wooing a mate."

Kayl stared at his twin, eyes narrowing. "I know as much about it as you, Kier."

Kier's brows fell. "Don't you dare say—"

"Which means I know absolutely nothing."

"I would have you know I spent our recent time on Arthos quite productively." Kier flipped his messy hair back; most of the strands fell into their prior positions immediately. "Compared to you, I am an expert in romancing a mate. I have studied it extensively."

Kayl dragged his hands down his face. "Must I really point out that watching volturian melodramas with Razi while drinking that vile *gurosh* does not count as study?"

Kier smirked, cocking his head. "You need not feel threatened by my expertise, brother. We are not in competition. My skills will be of benefit to us both."

Kayl scoffed, turned away from Kier, and walked toward the stairs. "We must at least allow Aileen time to rest before you ply her with your romantical wiles."

Kier's footsteps sounded over the floor, soft and quick, behind Kayl. "I would not dream of disturbing her prematurely. And it will allow us time to prepare."

"We went after a notorious space pirate who has killed thousands without a plan, but we need to strategize before attempting to woo our would-be mate?"

"Thoughtfulness, Kayl." Kier slapped Kayl on the back as he fell into step beside him. "Before we do anything else, you should check the computer for a definition of the word."

Zor atkoshai, what have I just agreed to?

I heard that, Kier pulsed.

Kayl glared at his twin. "I know."

FOURTEEN

Large, callused hands glided over Aileen's belly, their claws grazing her skin and leaving delightful, torturous tingles in their wake. Liquid fire coursed through her veins. Opening her eyes, she gazed up at the tall, lean figure above her, her attention drawn by disheveled hair and intense, mismatched eyes.

Kier.

"Please," she whispered.

His palms cupped her breasts, kneading the soft flesh, and he teased her hardened nipples with his thumbs. Aileen gasped, arching into his touch. Lowering his head, he brushed his lips across her temple, her cheek, and her jaw until his hot, wet tongue teased beneath her ear. She whimpered and tipped her head back, lashes fluttering as she relinquished herself to the sensations, to the blazing heat inside her.

Every stroke of his fingers, every prick of his claws, every lap of his tongue sent an electric current straight to her core.

Her fingers delved into his wild hair, clutching him to her.

Another pair of hands settled upon her knees. Their touch was just as fiery as Kier's, leaving their searing mark upon her soul like a branding iron.

She looked down her body. Kayl pushed her knees up and to the sides, spreading her wide as he crawled between her legs. His eyes locked with hers; they gleamed with passion as he trailed his palms *toward her cunt. Something long wound around her ankle, holding it to the bed—his tail.*

Curling a finger, he ran the back of his knuckle over her sex, gathering her slick. Aileen moaned, pressing her breasts into Kier's palms as she undulated her hips to grind against Kayl's finger, craving more.

But Kayl did not touch her clit. He did not grant her relief.

"More," she rasped.

Kayl's gaze dipped, tracing a heated path down her body. She reached for him, but Kier caught her arm with his tail and drew it back to kiss her palm.

"Please," Aileen begged over the roar of her inner flames. "I'm burning."

Kayl's claws dug into her thighs as he opened her wider still. Baring his teeth, he dropped his head, pressed his mouth to cunt, and sucked her clit between his lips.

Aileen jolted awake with a gasp, clenching the blanket in her fists. Her sex pulsed as tremors wracked her body. Even the brush of the sheets against her skin elicited pleasure.

When her orgasm ebbed, she lay panting, and stared up at the dull gray ceiling. Sweat coated her body and dampened her hair, making her bedclothes and the sheets cling to her, and her inner thighs were coated with her slick. The insistent throb of her sex did not relent; the fire within her did not fade.

It's happening.

No.

Her rapid breaths broke the silence in the dim room. She sat up and hissed. Her nipples were tight, achy points, so responsive that the merest movement of her shirt over them induced sparks of pleasure-pain, and the light press of her thighs against one another was enough to heighten the throbbing in her core. Aileen should have known this moment would come. There was no escaping the heat. Whatever reprieve she'd been granted was over. The delay had only been temporary.

She should have anticipated this, and now that it was here...

She *hated* it. She hated Saduuk, hated herself, hated what was to come. At least this time she would suffer the heat alone.

"You've made it through this many times before. You can do it again. You're safe here. This time...should be easy."

She just had to endure.

Kicking off the blanket, Aileen climbed out of bed, pausing to release a soft moan as her clothes rasped over her skin and swollen breasts.

She gritted her teeth and tore the halter top off over her head and shoved her pants down her legs. The air, though no cooler than it had been before she'd gone to bed, was freezing against her burning skin.

Moving to the door, she engaged the lock, pressed her forehead against the cold metal, and closed her eyes. "I can do this."

She just needed to stay inside this room and let the rhapsody run its course.

"I'm safe here," she whispered. "Safe."

Pushing away from the door, she padded to the shower, opened the stall, and turned it on to the coldest setting. Droplets from the spray splashed upon her. She shivered and groaned when her nipples tightened further. Taking a deep breath, she stepped inside.

Aileen slapped a hand over her mouth to muffle her pained cry. The water felt like jagged shards of ice battering her heated flesh, stinging, stabbing, freezing. Her body trembled uncontrollably, and she struggled to breathe. But as the heat inside her intensified, that water became a balm.

She drew her arms in close to her body as she eased down onto the floor. Tipping her head back, she closed her eyes and let the water fall upon her, let it cool her, let it calm her.

Perhaps it wouldn't be so bad this time. She'd allow it to take control, allow it to consume her, and be done with it. What good would it do to resist? This was nothing like the other times Saduuk had forced rhapsody upon her. It was nothing like the times when he'd used it to demonstrate how much power he'd held over her, when he'd brought her into Eternal Paradise's underbelly and allowed his clients to—

No. Don't think about it. Just...just forget.

"I can do this," she whispered again.

But the heat kept rising, and the sensation of water falling upon her became stimulating instead of soothing. She felt her mind slipping. Thoughts tumbled through her brain—thoughts of hands stroking her body, of slick skin against skin, of tongues, of sex.

Thoughts of Kier and Kayl.

She recalled her dream. It'd been both of them with her, touching her—Kier fondling her breasts, Kayl hands on her thighs while his mouth...

Aileen moaned as her fingers dipped into her cunt. She was hot and soaking wet. She imagined Kayl's lips closing around her clit, imagined him sucking and licking as she stroked herself. Her other hand squeezed her breast, and though it felt nothing like Kier's touch in her dream, it heightened her pleasure all the same.

Her breaths came in harsh pants as her belly tightened. Within moments, she cried out with her orgasm. Squeezing her knees together, she willed her fingers to continue their assault upon her clit, pushing over one peak and on to another. She envisioned only them —Kier and Kayl.

But it wasn't enough. She needed more.

Aileen cupped her mound and opened her eyes. Her vision swam, blurring on the edges, merging with the images running through her mind—and those images warped. She shook her head as Kier and Kayl grew more indistinct, as her pair of imagined lovers became a trio; then four, five, a whole crowd of shadowy, leering faces surrounded her with the twins no longer in sight.

These weren't imaginings anymore. They were *memories*.

"No. Please. Please just...just forget. Forget!"

But the heat at her core only grew.

She stroked herself again, speeding her fingers. Her heart raced fast enough to match the blistering tempo of the water droplets falling upon her. Something dark twisted and sank in her gut, and her breaths became ever more desperate.

The shadowy figures from her memory stood over her, laughed at her, and pawed at her skin with rough hands, using her body just as they had when they'd paid Saduuk for a private encore.

And she hadn't told them to stop.

Even though the pain had outweighed the pleasure, she'd begged for more. Her body had not been hers to control. Some small part of her, lucid despite the building heat, had watched helplessly, too weak and quiet to intervene. And it hadn't been long before that part of Aileen had been swallowed in the fiery haze of her rhapsodic heat too.

A sob shook Aileen as she yanked her hand out from between her thighs. She pounded her fists against the shower floor, splashing frigid water. "No! No, no, no! Stop... Please stop."

She dropped her forehead onto her hands, grasping her wet hair as she struggled to ignore her insistent need, the wretched cramping of her core, the quivering of her thighs, and the ache in her breasts.

"I can't do this."

She could feel herself slipping, slipping, and all the pain she'd somehow ignored for the last three years was closing in on all sides, sinking its claws into her soul, tearing her apart from within, all while her body demanded more, more, more...

Aileen screamed.

FIFTEEN

Kier was leaping out of bed before his eyes had fully opened and his conscious mind had realized what was happening. His bare feet slapped down on the floor; the stark contrast between that unyielding cold and the inferno raging at his core blasted him to awareness.

A scream. Aileen's scream.

He could not know if he'd heard it with his ears or sensed it through her burgeoning link to their *daevalis*, but it had been real. And it had been chilling.

His heart was pounding, his breath was ragged, and his groin throbbed with a dull, insistent ache. His cock strained against the confines of his undershorts.

Ba'shanaal, why was he aroused? That anguished scream had pierced his very soul and triggered upon his deepest instincts, which demanded he act, demanded he help her.

On the other side of the room, Kayl stood beside his bed with his chest heaving, one fist braced against the wall, and his hair partly dangling in his face. Like Kier, he was clad only in a pair of black undershorts.

Flashes of their dream crackled through Kier's mind—he and his brother with Aileen, pleasuring her. Preparing her to seal their *daevalis*. He could almost feel her hands on his skin, could almost taste her tender flesh on his tongue, could almost—

Kier, Kayl pulsed.

The twins met one another's gazes and rushed out of the room. Side by side, they darted across the corridor to her quarters, where Kier slapped the door control.

The panel flashed red.

The door did not open.

Intense emotions radiated from the other side of that door. Consuming lust assailed Kier mercilessly, impossible to ignore despite the pain, fear, and desperation swirling around it. He hit the control again, harder this time, and still nothing happened.

Kier moved his face close to the door. "Aileen!"

There was no response.

He hammered a fist against the door. The dulled pain that pulsed up his arm was lost in the torrent of emotions flowing from her.

Kayl shoved Kier aside and brought up an override menu on the door control. Kier's tail swung erratically behind him, and he bounced on his heels, clenching his fists at his sides to keep himself from attacking the door again. "What is happening?"

"I do not know, Kier," Kayl replied without looking away from the controls.

Kier's dread intensified with each thunderous beat of his heart—as did his arousal. How could the two exist simultaneously? How could they both be strengthening? "Get it open!"

"I am!"

The control panel flashed blue, and the door slid open with a muted *swoosh*. Kier rushed into the room, eyes darting to the bed—atop which lay only rumpled bedding. A familiar sound tugged at his attention, but he was distracted by his first inhalation inside the room.

Kier's cock stiffened with an ache so intense that his knees nearly buckled; the air was redolent of arousal, of sex. Of Aileen.

Kayl groaned behind him.

Clenching his jaw, Kier clamped a hand over his shaft. For the first time in over fifteen years, he was on the verge of spilling his seed, and that internal pressure was far too much to bear. He closed his eyes.

Images of the dream he'd shared with his brother flitted behind his eyelids—Aileen's pale skin; her full breasts; her pink lips parted in pleasure; her blue eyes half-lidded and gleaming; her cheeks flushed with desire.

He needed to mate with her. *They* needed to mate with her. They needed to complete their *daevalis*, to make her theirs, to make three into one.

The shower. That sound is the shower.

Whether the thought had come from Kier or Kayl did not matter —it broke through that lust haze, letting Aileen's anguish flood back in and restoring a modicum of Kier's lucidity.

Not just the shower, Kayl pulsed.

Moaning. Aileen was moaning, her voice raw, passionate, and tortured. Fire roiled through Kier's veins.

He forced his eyes open and turned to the shower. The glass door was spattered with droplets of water, but they did not hide the figure sitting in the corner with her back against the wall, her knees drawn up, and her hand between her thighs.

Electric tingles raced just beneath Kier's skin. Aileen's wet hair hung about her shoulders, brushing her bare breasts as she rocked her hips and twisted her torso. Her body moved with an unsettling blend of sensuality and desperation.

This...this is a private moment. We should not be here.

But something is wrong.

Something is very wrong.

Despite their own overwhelming arousal and flaring instincts, the twins could not pretend the other emotions flowing from Aileen were gone. Kier could not pretend that the dread in his belly had faded.

They had to think past that maddening, lustful scent, past the sight of their mate pleasuring herself. They had to act. Because even if the twins had no idea what was wrong with Aileen, she unquestionably needed help.

The twins raced to the shower stall. Every step closer heightened the pain they felt from Aileen, the fear, the *desire*.

Kayl tore the stall door open. Icy water sprayed out, spattering Kier's skin and sending a shiver along his spine.

Aileen had her eyes squeezed shut and her head tipped back. Her right hand continued stroking her sex, its pace quick enough to match Kier's thumping heart, while her left kneaded and clawed the flesh of her thigh, which was marred by angry scratches—several of them seeping blood that was diluted by the falling water.

Kier's dread reached up from the depths of his soul, wrapped a cold hand around his heart, and crushed it.

"Aileen," he rasped.

She did not respond.

Kier stepped into the stall and hissed through his teeth. The frigid water pooled on the floor made him shiver again as he crouched directly before Aileen. Despite the water washing everything away, her scent struck him anew. That instinctual hunger, that primal yearning, growled at his core.

He repeated her name louder, this time with Kayl saying it simultaneously.

Aileen snapped her head up, eyes opening, and stilled her hands. Her gaze met his, but it was glossy. Vacant. She was looking at him, but she wasn't *seeing* him.

Worse, he didn't see *her* in those eyes. Her pupils had dilated, shrinking the soft blue of her irises into hair-thin rings and forming dark pits in which no trace of the female they'd spoken to earlier could be found.

She lunged at Kier. His eyes flared, and his breath hitched as she slammed into him, sending him tumbling backward. He wrapped his arms around her instinctively, ensuring he took the brunt of the fall. He landed on the floor half outside the stall. Aileen came down atop him, thighs straddling his hips, breasts pressed to his chest.

Her skin was feverishly hot despite her having been sitting under freezing water. She smoothed her hands up from his shoulders, delving her fingers into his hair as she buried her face against his neck. She took in a deep breath.

Smelling me. My mate is smelling me.

Purring, Aileen clenched Kier's hair and ground her sex along his hardened cock. Her tongue trailed a wicked line up his throat.

Pleasure spiraled outward from his groin. He shuddered again, dropped his hands to her hips, and squeezed, pricking the soft flesh of her ass with his claws. The heat of her slit wrapped around him. Aileen moaned and undulated her pelvis, gliding her sex up and down along his shaft. Her hot slick soaked through his undershorts.

An amorous haze enveloped Kier's mind. The sensations and raw emotions were overpowering his rationality, were sweeping him away on a rising tide, and all he could see was her, all he could feel was her —fire, pleasure, pain. Lust so powerful it hurt. *Need.*

Her mouth came down over his, and she sucked and nipped at

his lips between her desperate breaths. She slid a hand down Kier's body and hooked her fingers under the waistband of his shorts.

Need her. Need her now.

He tightened his hold on her hips and lifted his head to seize control of the kiss.

Wrong, a voice rasped in the back of his mind. Though low and soft, it pierced that haze, reawakening Kier's awareness of his lingering dread.

What was wrong? Everything he needed was here; all he needed was her. With a spray of icy water, his tail swung up off the shower floor to caress the outside of Aileen's thigh.

Wrong, the voice repeated louder, sharper.

Something moved over Kier, beyond Aileen—a teal figure made indistinct by his desire.

The figure took Aileen by her upper arms and lifted her torso away from Kier.

Kayl.

Shocking cold swept over Kier's skin in the absence of that contact, but the chill couldn't deter him, not with such heat bearing down on his shaft.

Aileen continued grinding against Kier even as her hands darted to Kayl's crotch and clawed at his shorts. Grunting, Kayl seized her wrists, forcing her hands away.

Beneath all the pleasure and desire, Kier sensed something was wrong, something was off, something was...missing. But Aileen was here, and her breasts, so lush and round with their pink tips, were right above his face, begging his attention.

"Aileen," Kayl said.

Grasping her wrists in one hand, Kayl caught Aileen's jaw with the other, angled her face toward his, and leaned close, staring into her eyes. She strained toward him without slowing her pelvis, her breath growing more ragged.

Her continued gyrations built the pressure in Kier to an unbearable level. His fingers flexed on her hips, and his tail curled around her leg. It was too much. He was going to burst, was going to break apart into a million pieces, was going to—

"Fuck," Kayl snarled. He wrapped his arms around Aileen's midsection and tore her away from Kier.

Gasping, Kier slapped his palms on the floor and raked his claws across it, thrumming on the edge of climax, but now there was only frigid water touching his skin. His groin pulsed with an ache that stole his breath and tensed his every muscle. Arching his back, he angled his head to find his mate.

Kayl was striding to the bed, carrying Aileen, who had wrapped herself around him. Her breaths came in shallow, rapid pants as she undulated against Kayl's abdomen. Her features were set in pleasure —eyes closed, brow creased, full lips parted.

Need her. Need more.

Kier rolled over, braced his hands on the floor, and pushed himself up, getting his feet beneath him, gaze fixed on his brother and their mate.

Just before Kayl reached the bed, Aileen cried out. Her nails dug into his back, and she dropped her head, clamping her teeth down on his shoulder. He staggered; she shuddered, the movements of her hips becoming erratic and more frantic. Kayl clamped a hand on the back of her head, holding her mouth there as he bared his teeth in a snarl.

The scent of her arousal intensified. Kier rushed toward her, his cock throbbing all the harder.

With another curse, Kayl tossed Aileen onto the bed. She bounced into the air and was already reaching for him before she landed again, but Kayl pressed a hand on her chest, pinning her down. She caught hold of his head just long enough to pull his mouth toward her breast before he escaped her grip and turned his face toward Kier.

Aileen's hands caressed every part of Kayl within their reach before one dipped to her sex again. She moaned.

Wrong. Wrong. Something wrong.

When Kier drew close, Kayl stopped him by extending his arm and flattening his palm against Kier's chest. Kayl's breathing was heavy, his tail lashed furiously, and his expression was strained. The tendons in his neck stood out clearly.

"Stop," Kayl rasped.

The distressed, pleading note in Kayl's voice blasted a hole in Kier's lust; it was only then that he realized he could not sense his brother's thoughts, that the link between them was closed.

That wasn't right. He and Kayl needed to be open to one

another, needed to function as one to complete their *daevalis*. That's what it meant—three hearts, three minds, three souls as one.

Kier's gaze swung to Aileen.

"No," Kayl spat. His body shook as he leaned toward Kier while still somehow keeping Aileen in place. "Listen to me, Kier. You need to close the link."

Need. Need her. I need...we need...

"Look at me, Kier! Close it off. Now."

Kier stared into his brother's eyes. He saw arousal in their gleam, saw pain, saw...fear.

Wrong. This is wrong. Something is wrong.

Drawing in an unsteady breath, Kier squeezed his eyes shut and focused on the psychic link—on blocking it. His instincts rebelled. This wouldn't merely be closing himself off to his twin, but to their *na'diya*, who they'd only just found. This would be closing himself off to all these sensations and emotions, to—

"Trust me," Kayl whispered. "It is for her."

Kier clenched his jaw and severed the link. The fierce emotions that had been radiating from Aileen since the twins had awoken ceased, but their echoes lingered, and his arousal did not fade. How could it, when her scent dominated the air?

He opened his eyes, blinked away the remnants of that haze, and looked past his brother to the female writhing atop the bed. He saw the still-bleeding scratches on her thighs, saw the glistening essence coating her sex, where her fingers continued stroking her reddened, swollen flesh, saw the wet hair spread on the rumpled bedding and clinging to her flushed skin.

He saw the empty but desperate light in her hooded eyes.

The horror that descended upon him then was all his own. Aileen's behavior, his reactions, this whole situation...

"Focus, Kier," Kayl said firmly but not ungently, drawing Kier's attention back to him. His abdominal muscles also glistened with Aileen's essence. She'd worked herself to climax rubbing against him.

Kier stomped down the rising memories this situation had summoned; he could not help her if he allowed the past to swallow him. He looked at Aileen again. "She is harming herself."

Kayl offered a shallow nod. "Help me restrain her."

Kier climbed onto the bed and positioned himself on his knees beside their *na'diya*. He took hold of her right arm and leg, pinning the former at her side; Kayl did the same for her left limbs.

She resisted with surprising strength, and her struggles brought out hints of the lean muscles beneath her otherwise delicate skin, but the twins were stronger. She lifted her head to strain toward Kayl, then Kier, and back again repeatedly.

"Aileen," Kier said.

Her face snapped toward him. She pumped her hips in his direction and ran her tongue across her pink lips.

"We need you to talk to us, Aileen," Kier continued.

"We want to help you," Kayl added.

Again, she strained toward each of them, but when she could reach neither, she growled and fought harder. The twins grunted and leaned more of their weight upon her limbs.

Kier's nostrils flared. "Aileen, please. Speak to us."

She only continued struggling, her growls interspersed with desperate, breathy cries. More of her hair swept into her face as she swung her head from side to side; she seemed not to care. The bed shook beneath her.

"We must face the truth, Kier." Kayl looked at his brother, loose strands of hair falling to obscure one of his eyes.

"No. Not her, Kayl." Kier met his brother's gaze. "Not her, too."

Kayl's jaw muscles ticked. "She has been drugged."

"We do not know that!"

"We do not know what with, but it is clear, Kier."

Aileen's cries escalated into screams, each of which pierced Kier's chest and made his heart stutter. He and Kayl held on as she thrashed. Her chest heaved faster and faster, and the color on her cheeks darkened. Again, Kier looked at the bloody scratches on her thighs, at the abused flesh of her sex; again, dark memories threatened to well up.

"We have seen similar reactions," Kayl rasped. Even with their psychic link silenced, Kayl's unspoken words were apparent—*we have experienced similar ourselves.*

Kier gritted his teeth and bowed his head. He shut his eyes again, but no matter how tightly he did so, it could not change anything. The twins' mate was still writhing in their hold, her skin pouring out heat while her yearning, tortured cries battered their hearts and souls.

"What do we do, Kayl?"

"We need to determine what is in her system."

Kier opened his eyes and met his brother's gaze. "The medpod will have her scans on record. It would have noted any traces of foreign substances."

Kayl's nostrils flared with a huff. "I should have examined the reports more closely. We could have anticipated this."

"The blaster wound through her midsection was our priority, and rightly so. We were not looking for anything else."

Kayl turned his head away, brows falling low and jaw bulging. "Her wounds were *your* priority. I cannot pretend mine were so noble."

"It is in the past, Kayl," Kier said gently. "We cannot waste time lamenting choices made during a crisis while a new crisis is occurring. You are here with her. She is your priority now. That has to be enough."

Aileen arched her back and screamed, tugging on her arms. The twins again found themselves struggling against her unexpected strength.

"We need to fasten her down," Kayl said.

Kier swung his gaze from Aileen to his brother, tail thumping on the bed. After everything they'd seen and experienced in their lives, the thought of securing this innocent female—their *mate*—to the bed against her will was nauseating. It was the sort of thing slavers and pirates did, not something the twins did.

"We are not doing her any good like this," Kayl said, apparently guessing Kier's thoughts even without having access to them. His eyes were fixed upon Aileen, and his lips were downturned in a tight frown.

"*Ja'skaal,*" Kier growled. "Go. I will hold her until you return."

Kayl nodded, his expression becoming even more strained. The tension in his muscles undoubtedly stemmed from much more than the exertion of keeping Aileen restrained. Kier had never seen such uncertainty in his brother's eyes—not since they were children.

Kier released Aileen's leg and threw himself over her body, laying his side atop her pelvis and grasping her left arm just above his twin's hand. Intense, desirous heat flowed from her, saturating Kier, and stirred instincts in him to which he could not succumb, to which he *would* not succumb.

With her leg free, her resistance strengthened, and she bucked her hips against Kier's weight. He kept himself firmly in place.

So intense were her struggles that Kier did not immediately notice someone else had also remained in place—his brother. Kayl was staring down at Aileen with that troubled look on his face, unmoving but for the subtle flexing and relaxing of his jaw.

"Kayl!" Kier snapped.

Kayl started, inhaling sharply through his nose. A crease formed at the center of his brow, small but unignorable; that tiny change made his expression tenfold grimmer and more tortured.

"I will not be able to hold her for long," Kier said. "Go now."

With a final uneasy flick of his tail, Kayl released Aileen. His hands paused in the air just above her skin, trembling faintly. Kier's pounding heart marked the seconds of his brother's inaction. Kayl snatched his hands back abruptly, released a shuddering breath, and raced out of the room without a backward glance.

Aileen moaned, panted, gasped, and thrashed. Her hardened nipples brushed Kier's chest, sending tingles across his skin that produced a sourness in his gut. She kicked her legs several times in an effort to angle her hips so she could rub against him again, but he held himself in place with teeth gritted.

Her thighs and knees struck his back several times, hard enough to make him grunt and send dull pain along his spine.

She is like a wild beast.

He hated himself for that thought, but he could not dispute it.

"I am sorry," he rasped as he wrapped his tail around her legs at her knees and drew them together. It was not strong enough to still her, but it restricted her motions just enough to stop her from striking him.

We did not bring her here to be our prisoner...

Kier shoved that thought aside. This was different. They were not imprisoning her, they were helping her, they were protecting her, both from herself and the instincts she'd awakened in them.

He drew in a steadying breath. The air was laden with her sweet, heady scent, eliciting a growl of hunger from him. And her skin was so hot—especially her sex, which radiated the heat of a blazing sun, beckoning him closer.

His mental walls trembled. Aileen's emotions continued their assault on his defenses, and though they'd not yet broken through, they needed only the smallest chink through which to flood.

Hurry, Kayl. Ba'shanaal, *hurry.*

Aileen released a pained cry. Kier closed his eyes so he didn't have to see the tortured pleasure upon her features, so he didn't have to see the void in her gaze. So he didn't have to see his mate like this.

An eternity passed, and each of the infinite moments comprising it tormented him with temptation, pain, and helplessness, dismantling his resolve bit by bit. He knew that only seconds had gone by, but to his heart, his soul, and his raging instincts, each of those seconds spanned unfathomable years.

Finally, Kier heard his brother's bare feet padding across the floor. He opened his eyes to find Aileen staring at Kayl, again straining toward him. In her current state, her reasoning must have been simple—Kier was currently denying her needs, but Kayl was not.

Kier glanced over his shoulder.

Kayl held a pair of cuffs in each hand, and now wore his holocom on his right forearm. He did not meet Kier's gaze as he reached the foot of the bed, leaned over it, and wrestled Aileen's legs—which were still bound by Kier's tail—into stillness to clamp a cuff around each ankle.

The sounds of those cuffs closing should have been insignificant, especially given the noises Aileen was making, but they were as loud and jarring as metal blast doors slamming shut to Kier.

Moving toward the headboard, Kayl grasped Aileen's left hand and slipped one of the remaining cuffs around her wrist. He passed the other cuff to Kier, who released her left arm and shifted his weight, fastening the binding around her right wrist.

Kayl lifted his hands away from her, reaching to access the controls on his holocom. That instant of freedom was all Aileen needed. Her hand darted out and clasped Kayl's wrist, and she yanked him closer. He grunted and stumbled. His leg caught on the edge of the bed, and his upper body pitched forward. His shoulder struck Kier's, knocking him aside, which allowed Aileen to raise her hips.

She thrust Kayl's hand between her thighs.

Kayl's breath stuttered. The muscles of Aileen's forearm stood out in strong definition as she pressed his fingers between her slit, clamped her thighs around his hand, and bucked, using the bounce of the mattress to add force to her motions.

The cries that emerged from her were a heart-wrenching blend of pleasure and insatiable need.

Kayl's lips peeled back, baring his fangs, and fire sparked in his eyes. He threw himself forward, seeking Aileen's mouth with his own.

Kier spat a curse and dove at his twin. He caught Kayl's loose hair in one hand and hooked the other around Kayl's arm, dragging him back. The twins tumbled off the bed; Aileen followed.

The three of them fell in a tangle of limbs. All three were panting; Kier could not tell his own breaths from those of Aileen and his brother. Their hearts raced, and their thumping pulses blended into one frantic, punishing beat. And the heat...it baked into Kier from every direction, heightened by the feel of Aileen's skin against his, of her groping hands and raking nails, of her teasing tongue and nipping teeth.

He could not understand how she seemed only stronger after her prolonged struggles, could not understand how his cock was still throbbing, how his yearning ache had deepening further.

He could not understand why part of him wondered if this jumble of bodies was what it would be like to seal their *daevalis*.

Still wrong. This is not her, not our na'diya. *This is but her shell.*

Growling, Kier finally found what he sought in the chaos—his brother's arm. He pulled on it hard, wrenching Kayl's hand away from Aileen's sex. She gasped in pain, in panic, but Kier did not allow himself to hesitate.

He braced a foot on the side of the bed and shoved off, forcing Kayl onto his back. Kayl snarled and bucked beneath his twin, straining to reach Aileen, his muscles taut. Aileen grasped Kier's legs and backside as he pinned his brother's arm to the floor and activated the holocom. His fingers flew through the commands on screen.

Aileen gasped as the cuffs activated and pulled her body away from Kier. He heard her hit the bed; the sound might as well have been that of a plasma bolt piercing him.

I am sorry, na'diya. *Sorrier than I can ever say.*

Kayl's struggles halted. Kier stared down at him, and Kayl stared back, their chests heaving, their lungs burning, their hair utterly disheveled. Clarity gradually returned to Kayl's eyes as his pupils expanded from the tiny slits they'd become.

Kier pushed himself onto his feet and helped Kayl up. They turned to face Aileen simultaneously, each with the same brief hesitation, each with the same stiffness.

She sat with her back against the bed, her arms pinned to it on either side of her, and her legs pressed together. Each cuff displayed a small green light; the invisible energy tethers had been formed.

With her gaze locked on the twins, Aileen fought the restraints, hair falling over her shoulders and chest to cover her breasts. When her efforts amounted to nothing, she keened. The voice that had so moved Kier when he'd first heard it, that had stunned him with its beauty and expression, now twisted around his heart like a thorny vine.

Kayl swept his hair back and dragged his palm down his face. He stiffened, hand freezing as his fingers reached his nose; their tips glistened with Aileen's essence. Kayl's pupils shrank into slits again. He dipped his hand farther, parted his lips, and extended his tongue.

Kier caught his brother's wrist and tugged that hand away from Kayl's mouth. "*No. Not like this.*"

Rocking on his heels, Kayl blinked, eyes again clearing. His nostrils and nose slits flared. "I..."

The words Kier needed to speak did not come easily, but he forced them out. "We need to leave."

Because eventually we will falter at the same time, and then we will be undone.

They glanced at Aileen again. Her anguished cries continued as she scraped her heels on the floor, twisting her waist and rubbing her thighs together. Her features were strained and pleading, though her eyes were still empty—empty save for the tears welling in them.

Keeping hold of Kayl's arm, Kier turned away and hurried for the door. His brother stumbled along for a few meters before falling into step. When they reached the threshold, Aileen's cries grew louder and more desperate.

Kayl tensed, resisting Kier's lead. Kier felt that same reluctance in himself, felt that same pull toward Aileen, the same drive to soothe her and fulfill her every need.

To relieve her suffering.

But that would have been *wrong*. She wasn't aware. She wasn't...*there*.

Kier didn't allow himself to look back. He didn't allow himself to take another glance in her direction, as he knew what it would cause.

The twins drew in simultaneous breaths and stepped into the corridor. They closed the door behind them, muffling her cries, but Kier still felt her emotions slamming into his mental shield. He only released his hold on Kayl after they'd entered the infirmary and were standing in front of the medpod.

Kayl braced his hands on the medpod's lid, closed his eyes, and took several deep breaths, shoulders heaving and nostrils flaring. "I can still smell her. Still *feel* her. I almost—"

"But you did not." Kier raked his fingers through his hair, tugging it back and holding it in place.

"I am the one who maintains control, Kier. I am the one who maintains distance. When we were slaves..."

"You kept us sane. You kept us grounded. I know, Kayl." Dropping his hands, Kier shook his head. His body was abuzz, his psychic shields were crumbling, and his own emotions were already so chaotic, so conflicted.

"And yet," Kayl said, bowing his head, "I have faltered. I cannot control myself with Aileen."

"Because this is the not the same. She is our mate. We are not meant to hold back with her. Bodies, minds, souls, we are meant to share it all with our *na'diya*. Everything we are, everything inside us, demands we complete our *daevalis* with her. When it comes to Aileen...our resistance is destined to fail."

The image of Aileen bound against the bed flashed in Kier's mind's eye, chilling his core. He and Kayl had used those restraints to hold slavers, smugglers, and pirates. They had used them during interrogations which had marked them with blood. And such bindings were often used on slaves.

Now the twins had used them on their mate. Kier knew why they'd done so, knew why it was necessary, but his heart could not reconcile that necessity with the fact that those cuffs were only used on villains or slaves.

Aileen was not a villain, and the thought of her being a slave constricted Kier's heart.

Aileen didn't deserve this.

She deserved so much better than Kier and Kayl could give.

Ba'shanaal, *no! This is not helping.*

Kier pushed those thoughts away and settled his hand upon his twin's shoulder. "Right now, she needs our help."

Kayl's jaw muscles ticked a final time before he nodded, stood up straight, and removed his hands from the machine. Kier activated the medpod, and the twins stepped to the holographic control screen that appeared beside it.

Folding his arms across his chest, Kier willed his tail to still and his body to relax as he watched his brother navigate the on-screen menus. It felt like hours passed in the few seconds it took Kayl to access Aileen's medical scans.

The list of chemicals and compounds meant little to Kier, and it couldn't have meant much more to his twin, but when it was filtered to display only foreign substances, the brothers' eyes snapped to the same item immediately.

Rhapsody.

Everything within Kier went utterly still and deathly silent.

The silence was overcome by a ringing in his ears as molten fury pooled in his gut. Kier's tail coiled around his leg and squeezed, but the pain didn't change the words on the holo screen.

The scan is wrong. It has to be wrong.

"No. There must have been...an error." Kayl shook his head, hurriedly exiting the report to pull up another scan that had been taken just before Kier removed Aileen from the medpod. And that word was there again. *Rhapsody.* "It does not make sense."

The twins had been aware of the drug for years. It was popular throughout the universe, considered a party drug, something people used to have a good time. It induced a euphoric state that left users completely carefree, unburdened by worries, by sadness, by grief or fear. There was only joy.

But it was even more popular amongst the sorts of people Kier and Kayl had dedicated their lives to hunting—slavers. In that euphoric state, individuals were far more open to suggestion, far easier to control. Far more compliant, friendly, and forgiving. Yet it was the second stage of rhapsody's high that made it so appealing to slavers and slave masters.

"If she was using rhapsody, she would have taken it sometime before her performance," Kier said, voice tight. "The heat should have hit her hours ago."

"It does not make sense," Kayl repeated. His voice was low, strained, furious.

"The timeline does not match the drug's effects." Before he'd even finished speaking those words, Kier knew they were a waste of breath. They could not change the truth. His anger, frustration, and stubbornness could not alter reality, could not make it so this had all been a terrible dream.

"We know such things are not universal," Kayl said, dragging his fingers through his still-loose hair. "Terrans may experience delayed effects, or...or her body simply held it off longer."

Kier stared at the mepod. In his mind's eye, he saw Aileen inside, her skin blackened by the plasma bolt that had nearly killed her. "The anesthetics and painkillers. They may have temporarily blocked the rhapsody's effects."

Kayl's lip curled, baring his fangs, and a deep line formed between his eyebrows. A harsh growl tore out of his throat, and he stalked away from Kier with fists balled. He paced along the wall, his movements uncharacteristically restless, erratic, and stiff.

As Kier watched his twin, the cracks in his psychic shield widened. Whispers of emotion crept through—lust, despair, desperation, confusion, pain. Each bore the particular note that marked them as Aileen's; her feelings were distinct from Kier's and Kayl's in the same way her voice was distinct from theirs.

And Kier hated that her current emotions had become so familiar to him in so short a time.

He forced his attention to the holo screen and stared at that word —rhapsody.

Do you like what you see? You can have her for tonight.

Those had been Saduuk's words while Vrykhan stared at Aileen. She'd been drugged not so she would be a compliant performer, but in anticipation of Vrykhan's arrival—she'd been meant as a gift of appeasement for the pirate. Saduuk had wanted her to succumb to the heat. He'd wanted her willing and eager to please the tretin.

Fury rumbled from the depths of Kier's soul, sending tremors along his limbs. Tears of rage, guilt, and sorrow stung his eyes. "She was a slave in Eternal Paradise, and even now, she is not yet free."

Kayl shook his head, loose hair falling into his face. "If we had... If *I* had..."

Kier's emotions were briefly amplified by an echo from his brother. Their psychic link closed again almost immediately, but that brief lapse in control from Kayl was jarring—jarring enough to provide Kier with sudden clarity.

The twins swung their gazes toward each other simultaneously, locking eyes. Their mental bond opened wide. A torrent of thoughts and emotions roared through, but now Kier and Kayl's were stronger, clearer, and more dominant than Aileen's.

Those emotions were no more pleasant than they'd been a moment before, but they were far more bearable, far less overwhelming.

Because the burden was again being shared.

It was necessary to close ourselves off in that situation, Kayl pulsed.

But it is foolish to believe we can continue functioning that way, Kier replied. He turned fully toward the medpod. It had healed Aileen's body when she'd been on the brink of death, but physical wounds weren't the only sort she'd suffered. The other wounds required something more.

"We are meant to be a *daevalis*," Kier said.

"Three parts made one." Kayl's tail thumped the side of the medpod.

"Your burdens are mine, Kayl, and mine are yours."

"And so too must Aileen's burdens become ours."

Kier smiled, embracing the flutter of hope in his chest. If all three of them were broken, incomplete, wounded, they could only find wholeness together. They could only find fulfillment as a *daevalis*. "Because she is ours."

Kayl's voice was uncharacteristically uncertain when he replied, "And we...are hers."

Smile widening, Kier slapped his brother on the shoulder. "Someone I know once told me the universe does not understand easy. This will be difficult, Kayl, but it *will* be worth it."

Kayl exhaled slowly. "I will try, brother. I will try as best I can... for her."

SIXTEEN

A THICK FOG of sleep blanketed Aileen, threatening to press her deeper and deeper until she was enveloped in impenetrable, inescapable darkness. She could only perceive two things through that fog—a spark at her core, emitting flickering heat, and a desperate need to wake up, to escape this void.

With every ounce of resolve she could summon, she dragged herself up.

She opened her eyes. Her eyelids fought to close again, each weighing a thousand kilos, and whispering tendrils of that thick fog beckoned her back into the abyss, but she willed herself to hold on. To remain awake.

Aileen stared up at a familiar gray ceiling.

She'd done this before. She'd awoken in this bed, looking up at that plain ceiling, disoriented and with no memory of how she'd wound up here. Except this time, there was no part of her body that didn't hurt. Her throat and mouth were dry, her stomach was hollow, and her limbs ached. Worse still was the raw, stinging sensation of her sex.

What had happened? What—

The heat.

No. Oh no, no, no.

Her pulse quickened, and her breathing became ragged.

But I was in the shower. I wasn't in bed. I...I...

I don't remember. Oh God, I don't remember.

And that was familiar too, wasn't it? Every time Saduuk had sold her body to a client, he would drug her with rhapsody. Aileen would be forced go through that initial euphoria, usually while performing on stage, unable to acknowledge the voice from the furthest reaches of her mind screaming that this was wrong, that she should have been terrified.

Occasionally, she'd been given to her owner for the evening before the heat had fully taken control. She would remember going to opulent rooms, escorted by Saduuk and his burly security guards. Would remember leering, alien faces, hungry stares, probing hands, revolting touches. But once the heat consumed her...

There'd be nothing until she woke up, naked, in an unfamiliar place, her body sore and stiff, typically marked with bruises, scratches, and bite marks...and the dried fluids left behind by her temporary owner.

Tulaya had often said not remembering was the one good thing about the heat, but she'd always spoken those words with a haunted look in her eyes—a look that resonated right down to Aileen's very soul.

She'd been spared the experience of being a spectator in her own body as it actively participated in her own rape. But waking up with all that evidence there, all the lingering sensation, and no memory of how she'd been used, abused, and violated... That was its own sort of torture. It was a nightmare that could not be overcome, because the human mind didn't let the unknown rest—it only offered possibilities that were worse and worse, darker and darker.

And in the moments of her greatest horror and self-loathing, Saduuk would always come to remind Aileen who she was, what she was.

You are mine, little songbird.

A sob caught in her throat, and tears spilled from the corners of her eyes.

Something brushed over her cheek. "Aileen?"

Aileen started, flinching away from that touch, but she didn't get far. Her wrists and ankles caught, holding her in place and producing flares of pain. Heart racing, she looked first to Kier, who sat on the edge of the bed at her hip, and then to the metal cuffs binding her wrists and ankles.

"W-What did you do to me?" she asked, trembling. Her movements had caused the blanket covering her to slip, revealing her naked body, but she couldn't lift her arms and legs even a millimeter off the bed to cover herself. "What did you do?"

"We restrained you," said Kayl, drawing her attention to him. He stood with his back against the wall and arms folded across his chest, but as their eyes met, he straightened and walked toward the bed.

"You were harming yourself, Aileen." Kier raised his left arm and activated the holocom around his wrist, flicking his fingers through the controls. "We did not know what state you would be in when you woke, so we did not think it wise to free you."

There was a series of soft, rapid clicks, and the cuffs on her limbs opened and fell away. She hurriedly sat up and lifted her arms only to pause when she saw the angry red skin ringing her wrists. That was when she felt the sting; the cuffs had rubbed her flesh raw. Hands trembling, she pulled the blanket up to cover her chest, squeezed her thighs together, and drew her knees to her chest. That simple movement brought a whisper of pleasure—and a wave of soreness—to her sex. "Did...did you..."

"*No*," rasped the twins said unison.

"You tried to..." Kier's cheeks darkened, and he looked down at the ground.

"You were..." Kayl's cheeks also darkened; he looked toward the ceiling. "You were a bit...forward."

A cry burst from her. She wrapped her arms around her legs and buried her face against her knees. Shame, disgust, and self-loathing flooded her, overshadowing her relief at knowing the twins hadn't taken advantage.

Aileen had thought herself safe while locked in this room, but she should've known she couldn't control the heat. There was no avoiding it, no escaping what Saduuk had forced upon her. "Why did y-you have to come in here? I l-locked the door. I tried...I tried..."

"We thought you were hurt," said Kier.

His response only made her cry harder.

Kier settled his hand on her upper back. Though it was rough with calluses and brimming with strength, his touch was nothing but gentle, warm, and soothing. "It was not you, Aileen," he said softly. "It was not your fault. You have done nothing wrong."

"We are sorry you had to wake up like this," Kayl said.

"We are sorry you have gone through any of this at all."

The bed shifted slightly beneath her as Kayl knelt on the foot of the mattress. "You have no reason to be ashamed."

"I'm sorry," Aileen rasped. "Whatever I did to you, I'm sorry."

"Aileen." Kier's hand shifted up, fingers sliding into her hair, and cupped the back of her head. With continued gentleness, he guided her head up and turned her face toward his.

She blinked and wiped the moisture from her eyes.

"You did nothing wrong. Do not apologize," he said in that deep, smooth voice. He brushed a tear off her cheek. "Nothing happened."

Aileen didn't know how or why, but she trusted those words—she trusted the twins. She barely knew them, but somehow, she knew in her soul they were not lying.

Kayl leaned closer, lightly settling a hand on her foot over the blanket. "You are the victim in this."

"What was done to you, what was forced upon you, was not right," Kier said, lowering his hand to her shoulder, "and it was not your fault."

"And we understand. More than you know, we understand."

Bottom lip trembling, Aileen sniffled and nodded. "I was alone, lost, and hurting when I arrived at Eternal Paradise, and Saduuk... I was singing by the docking gates, playing my da's guitar. Just trying to earn enough credits to keep moving on. I don't know if he was told about the crowd that had gathered or what, but Saduuk showed up.

"He offered me a job with full room and board, and said I'd perform on his main stage. I mean, *how* could I say no to that?" Aileen wiped more tears from her cheeks. "I didn't know the trap had been set, and I walked right into it. I was such an eejit. He collared me before my first performance. I thought the choker was just part of the costume. I didn't know that...that it'd make me his slave."

The twins' hands flexed, their hold on Aileen briefly tightening. Kier's eyes flicked toward Kayl. Aileen felt unspoken words passing between them.

"But he was not content with you merely performing on stage," Kier said, a hard edge in his voice.

She clenched her fingers, digging her nails into her legs through the blanket, and looked away as fresh tears blurred her vision. Shame skittered over her skin and made her stomach churn.

"Easy, Aileen," Kayl rumbled.

Aileen had become all too familiar with shame during her time in Eternal Paradise. It always found some place to linger—in the pit of her stomach, in the back of her mind, deep in her chest. Sometimes it lurked in the lyrics of a song, waiting for her to sing the words before springing out on her.

"He got greedy." She laughed bitterly. "No, he was always greedy. But for a little while, I made him enough money singing that he turned down the offers he was getting. Some of the other...slaves, they would overhear sometimes and tell me.

"I knew what was going on down in the underbelly. The sex and drugs and all that. But I was the star of his show, and he needed me singing on that stage every night because everyone wants to see a terran. I thought I was safe from that...that part of his business. I think even after I understood what the collar was for, I didn't understand what it meant. Because as soon as someone offered him the right price, he looked at me differently." She touched her fingers to her throat; she could almost feel the phantom weight of the collar there. "Any defiance on my part earned harsh punishment from then on."

Though the sound was barely audible, she swore she heard a growl from one of the twins—perhaps both. Their postures were rigid, their tails curled stiff, their jaw muscles bulging.

Aileen shouldn't have felt a rush of arousal from those growls, not after what she'd just gone through, not with the story she was sharing, but the sounds coaxed a response from her body nonetheless. She rubbed her thighs together, triggering a tiny, tantalizing thrill in her sex.

What is *wrong* with me?

It's...it's the remnants rhapsody. It has to be.

"Saduuk realized I could bring in an audience for my shows *and* earn top credits for my... For people to..." She pressed her lips together and drew in a slow, deep breath. Something roused inside her—something at once blazing hot and biting cold, something primal, restless, dangerous. Something...violent.

Anger. The anger she wished she could've expressed while she was on Eternal Paradise. The anger she wished could have made a difference.

"For people to fuck me," she continued. "And it didn't matter that I refused. He'd just have me restrained, pour rhapsody down my throat, and let it run its course. And I... God, I didn't want to do it. I never wanted *any* of it."

Kier's fingers flexed infinitesimally. The prick of his claws created a wicked, intriguing sting that sent a shiver down her spine. A guttural growl rumbled in his chest.

Kayl's hand stiffened around her foot, and she felt it trembling as though with immense exertion. He also growled, but the sound was different from Kier's—lower, subtler, more felt than heard.

Aileen looked from on twin to the other. Their lips were peeled back to bare their fangs, and their eyes burned with predatory light. Their pupils had narrowed to slits that were nearly swallowed by the surrounding blue and magenta. The cords of their necks stood out beneath their teal skin, and their short eyebrows were angled sharply downward.

Kayl's claws raked Aileen's skin through the blanket as he abruptly pulled away. He was off the bed and on his feet almost faster than she could perceive, and he set immediately to pacing along the far wall with his tail lashing. The grace with which he and his brother usually moved was absent. Kayl's entire posture was stiff and bristling with fury—head bowed, shoulders hunched, his fingers curled and tense with claws at the ready.

Kier slowly withdrew his hand from Aileen, settled it on his lap in a fist, and released a heavy breath through his nose. "Were he alive, I would go back and kill him myself."

"Death was not punishment enough for him," Kayl snarled.

Though he was still sitting on the bed, Kier's posture matched his brother's. His voice was thick with more than anger when he spoke. "This should not have happened. It should never have happened. Not to her. Not to our *mate.*"

Aileen whipped her face toward Kier.

Hold up a minute. Their what?

"And what could we have done, Kier?" Kayl paced faster. The tip of his tail thumped the wall as it swung, creating an erratic, unsettling rhythm.

"Search for her," Kier growled, shoving himself off the bed. "We should have searched for our *na'diya.*"

"We should have forsaken everything to search for someone we did not believe existed?"

"Anything to protect her!"

"But we were not there!" Kayl turned toward his twin and threw his arms to his sides. "We did not protect her. Shall we add it to the list of our failures?"

What is this? What are they talking about?

They...they can't mean me... Can they?

Kier advanced on Kayl. Something dark trickled from his clenched fist—a tiny trail of blood. "It is at the top of that list, and forever will be. She"—his voice faltered, becoming raw and rough—"is ours. Our fate. She is all that should have mattered."

Kayl drew directly up to Kier; they stood nose to nose now, both bristling with rage, and the air around them crackled with aggression. Aileen's heart raced. She didn't like them fighting, especially when their whole argument seemed to be about her.

Especially when she had no clue *why* they were arguing about her.

"Fate?" Kayl demanded. "You want to speak of fate, brother? Fuck fate!"

With a snarl, Kier lunged at his twin, grasping the front of Kayl's tunic and pulling on it hard. "I told you not to speak of her that way!"

Aileen's eyes widened. "Stop."

"I speak only of fate!" Kayl roared. He thrust a finger toward Aileen. "She is our fate. And what has the universe done to make that so? What suffering have the three of us endured to get here? Fate, Kier, dictated that she suffer. Fate demanded it. Because everything that has happened to us and to her was necessary to bring us together. Fate led her to that place, and it kept her there, where she was manipulated, used, broken!"

Used.

Broken.

"Please stop," Aileen whispered a little louder, gathering the blanket in her fist. All this discord, fury, and guilt made her stomach roil.

"I accept everything that happened to us," Kayl continued, his voice now barely more than a rasp, "but everything that happened to her? I am through with fate, Kier. She is ours, and *I* will ensure she does not suffer again."

Kier bared his teeth, and his grip on Kayl's tunic relaxed infinitesimally. "All the more reason we should have *looked*. Should have tried to stop all this from happening to her. We should have... Should have…" He shook his head and hung it, shoulders heaving with a shuddering breath.

Aileen threw her legs over the side of the bed and stood up on shaky legs, clutching the blanket to her chest. "That's enough!"

The twins snapped their heads toward her, eyes rounded.

"Just stop it," she said, extending a hand to brace against the wall for support. Weakness threatened to drag her back down. "Stop fighting. Please. You have no reason to feel guilty for…for what happened to me. Neither of you owes me anything."

Kier released Kayl's tunic. His hand lingered in the air for a moment before he lowered it, stretching his fingers and then curling them loosely. Aileen glimpsed tiny spots of blood on the heel of his palm—the results of his claws puncturing his flesh.

With jaw muscles ticking, Kayl straightened his tunic. There was a small blood stain on the fabric where Kier had grabbed it.

The twins turned to face Aileen fully and approached her.

"It is not about owing you," Kier said in a gentle tone.

"When our home was attacked, we could not protect our friends, our family. We could not protect ourselves," Kayl said. "Now we have strength. We have skill. We have the capability."

"But we could not use it to spare you from your suffering," Kier continued. "The one person we are meant to protect above all others."

Our mate.

They were fighting because they believed Aileen was their mate? *Their* mate, as in…shared?

Aileen's brow creased. "What are you talking about?"

The twins looked at each other again, mouths falling into identical frowns, cheeks darkening. They nodded to one another in unison.

"We have much to discuss with you, Aileen," Kier said as he and his brother returned their gazes to her.

"But this is neither the time nor the place," said Kayl.

She again looked from one twin to the other. They were conversing telepathically, hiding something from her.

"Please don't keep me in the dark," she said. "You referred to me as your…your mate. That's not something you can just say and then brush off until later."

"You are correct." Kier drew closer and settled his hand on the side of her neck, stroking her jaw with the pad of his thumb. "We want nothing more than to be open and honest with you."

"We simply wished to allow you a chance to recover from your ordeal first," Kayl added.

"The last twenty-four hours have been harrowing," Kier continued. "You have been through so much, Aileen, and we did not wish to burden you with anything more until you had time to process what has happened."

Aileen looked up at Kier. His eyes were soft, his expression tender and understanding. Warmth radiated from his touch, spreading whispers of pleasure through her, but also offering a comfort that made her chest ache.

When was the last time she'd been touched like this? When was the last time she'd been treated like she really mattered? Like her feelings mattered, or were even valid?

Tulaya had done what she could, but she and Aileen had been prisoners restricted by circumstance—and Saduuk never liked it when his *employees* got too close to one another.

Unable to help herself, Aileen closed her eyes, covered Kier's hand with her own, and guided it up, nuzzling cheek against his palm. She didn't know what compelled her to do so, but it just felt right.

Was she that starved for affection?

"Please tell me," she said.

Something soft trailed delicately across her wrist, just beneath the raw skin.

Kier's next breath came out heavier than the last. "Allow me to tend your wounds, and we will explain as I do so."

Wounds?

Aileen opened her eyes and lowered her hand to look at her wrist. Her skin was red and irritated, with abrasions and deep grooves where the cuff had dug into it. "How long was I..."

"You struggled for hours." Kayl had straightened, shedding the anger that had dominated his posture, though his tail continued its erratic motions behind him. "The cuffs kept you from...fulfilling your needs to the point of self-harm."

He crossed an arm over his chest and curled his fingers over his shoulder. When his eyes met hers, they glinted with fire, but that heat was immediately replaced by his typical cool indifference.

What had she done?

Kier gently withdrew his hand, the faint scrape of his claws as he did so made Aileen shiver. He gestured to the bed. "Sit, Aileen."

Catching her bottom lip between her teeth, Aileen sat down on the bed.

Kayl stepped over to the table, opened a small case atop it, and took out a medtool—a cylindrical device that curved on one end, leading to a little disc. Kier knelt before Aileen and took her hand as Kayl brought the device to him.

Kier activated the medtool. The disc on its end lit up with blue lights, and tiny beams swept over her raw skin, producing a faint warm tingling sensation.

"How did you know something was wrong?" Aileen asked.

At the edge of her vision, she saw Kayl look away.

Kier kept working, guiding the little lasers over her wound. "We were dreaming of you. Of pleasuring you. Then you screamed...but there was no pleasure in the sound."

Heat suffused her cheeks, and her clit pulsed with the memory of that dream. She squeezed her thighs together. What pleasure might have come with the remembrance was dulled by the lingering soreness of her abused sex. "I was dreaming the same. How...how is that possible?"

The twins glanced at one another, and their expressions spoke volumes—there was no brotherly bickering now, no sniping at one another, just two people absolutely in sync with each other and united in purpose. Their eyes settled upon her, magenta and blue thrumming with energy, with determination, with...desire.

"When you asked us why we saved you earlier, our answer was not a lie," Kier said.

"But it was not the full truth," Kayl continued.

Voices intertwining, they said, "You are our mate, Aileen."

Aileen blinked. There was that word again. *Mate.* It was so small, so inconsequential. She'd heard that word often in her youth traveling around Scotland, England, and Wales. It was a friendly term, that was all.

But the way the twins said it implied so, so much more.

No. They must've misspoken. Maybe...maybe it's one of those lost in translation things, and they're just misusing the term.

If that's the case, why are they looking at you that way?

They're...intense, that's all. Just two intense males, with intense muscles and intense stares. The hunger in their eyes...

It didn't mean anything. Couldn't.

They're aliens, Aileen. You've heard about aliens and their mates plenty over the years to know what it means. Don't be dense.

But that couldn't be right... She was a human!

A light, nervous laugh escaped her. "Now you're pulling my leg."

Kayl's short eyebrows drew closer together as he glanced down at her legs, which were covered by the blanket. "I am not pulling your leg. Nor is my brother."

"I don't mean literally. It's a saying. It means you're joking with me. Because that's what you're both doing. Joking, pulling one over on me. Ha ha?"

They stared at her, expressions unchanging.

Aileen's brow furrowed as she shifted her gaze from twin to twin. "Right?"

"We are not, Aileen," Kier said gently. "Kayl is not even capable of joking."

"And how does that help the situation, Kier?" Kayl let out a huff. "You are our mate, Aileen. Our *na'diya*."

Wait, wait, wait.

Our mate. Not my mate or his mate. Our mate.

So she hadn't misheard that first time.

Aileen curled her toes against the floor. "S-So when you say *our*, you mean *both* of you?"

"Yes," the twins replied.

"A *daevalis* is three parts made one." Kier paused his work with the medtool. Pink, healed flesh had been left in the wake of its tiny lasers, a stark contrast to the remaining damaged skin. Tucking the tool against his palm with his two smallest fingers, he used the fore-fingers and thumbs of both hands to form a triangle. "Two *na'divali* balanced by their *na'diya*."

Aileen opened her mouth to speak, but the words didn't come immediately as she tried to process what they'd told her. "How...how is this possible? How can I be your mate? I'm not a daevah."

"We do not know," Kier replied.

"But you are," Kayl added.

"We feel it." Kier tapped his chest. "And I think you feel it also, Aileen."

She did feel it. That magnetic pull had been there since just before she'd gone onstage for her last performance at Eternal Paradise, and it hadn't let up in all the time since. It had drawn her directly to the twins. "I... I don't... How does that explain the dream?"

The corner of Kier's mouth curled up, making her belly flutter. He resumed his work on her wrist. "Though you are not yet bonded to us, Aileen, there is already a connection. We have felt your emotions when they are strong."

Aileen focused on the laser. "Are there others who could have been a match to be your...mate?"

The medtool reached the end of the wound. Kier released his hold on her arm and switched to her other wrist. "No. I do not believe that is how it works...not that I can claim to understand much of it at all." His eyes flicked up, meeting hers briefly. "You are ours, Aileen. We felt it before we knew what it was and recognized you the moment we saw you."

"I don't understand either. Humans don't get that certainty, but we do get choice. We don't just...*feel* it when we meet someone. So many of us don't even believe fated mates exist."

"Do you?"

Didn't she believe? Hadn't she spent most of her life longing to find the sort of love her parents had shared, longing for that moment when she would see her soulmate and just *know* they were meant to be together?

Of course she'd believed—before she'd fallen prey to Saduuk. In the time since, those dreams had faded; each day in Eternal Paradise had poisoned her hope a little more. If she still believed in fate, her opinion on it was much closer to Kayl's.

Fate was cruel.

Yet here she was with not one but two males who claimed she was their fated mate.

You felt it when you saw them, Aileen. You feel it right now with Kier kneeling before you, like something is drawing you closer to him. You feel it in Kayl's distance, in your quiet but insistent longing for him to close that gap.

"I would like to believe," Aileen said. "It's just..."

"Some wounds cannot be healed by technology," Kayl said, his tone surprisingly soft and warm.

Kier lifted his gaze, again meeting hers. "Openness and honesty, Aileen. That is what we promise you. We are not telling you all this to force you into a decision."

Kayl crouched, putting his face closer to Aileen's eye level. "We know what it is like to have our choices taken from us. We will never take yours."

"Never," Kier echoed with a hint of a growl.

Tears pricked her eyes, and her bottom lip trembled. "Thank you."

Kier finished with her wound, switched the medtool off, and placed it on the bed beside Aileen. His hands, with those long, claw-tipped fingers, rose to cup the sides of her face, and his thumbs swept across her cheeks to catch the first tears that escaped her eyes.

"We cannot blame ourselves for what is beyond our control," he said, his voice falling low. He smiled again; the expression was just as alluring as before, but it held a hint of sorrow now. "I think all three of us know that at heart, but it is never so easy, is it? Perhaps we may help each other accept those words. To live them."

The tenderness in his touch and his voice made her chest constrict. She wanted what they were offering, she just didn't know how to reach for it. How to accept it.

You're complete strangers, Aileen. You know nothing about them. Haven't you learned anything?

But they're...they're not Saduuk.

Kayl placed a hand on her knee, grasping it gently through the blanket and drawing her attention to him. "You need not trouble yourself with all this now, Aileen."

Kier withdrew his hands and tipped his head toward the night-stand beside the bed, where a tall black canister with a dull metallic gleam stood "There is water if you are thirsty. We gave you some periodically while you were unconscious, as you were sweating for most of that time."

"Shower. Get dressed. Relax if you are able." Kayl pulled his hand back and stood up.

Kier rose alongside his brother. "We will return to you soon. Perhaps to share an evening meal?"

Keeping the blanket tucked beneath her arms, Aileen inspected her wrist, moving her hand around to test it. There was no pain. She offered them a smile. "I would like that."

Kier grinned. His eyes flicked toward his twin, and that grin only grew. "We will go prepare, then."

Kayl's brow creased, and he narrowed his eyes at his brother.

Bracing a hand on Kayl's shoulder, Kier shoved him in the direction of the door. Kayl scoffed and shook his head, but walked along all the same. Their tails swung behind them in perfect sync. Kayl opened the door and stepped into the corridor.

Kier paused before following him through and looked at Aileen over his shoulder. "If you require anything, come find us."

Then he was gone. The door slid shut, and the room seemed suddenly so much larger, so much colder.

And yet Aileen smiled. For the first time in so long, she had something to look forward to.

SEVENTEEN

AILEEN STOOD with her head bowed, her eyes closed, and her hands flat upon the wall as hot water cascaded over her back and shoulders. It had been a couple hours since the twins had left her, but whispers of her rhapsody high lingered. She felt it in the ripples of sensation the falling water sent across her skin, which roused echoes of her desire, felt it in the tenderness of her sex, where the slightest friction sparked phantom thrills.

But she was not compelled to chase those sensations. She was in control again, and she'd never have to take even a single drop of rhapsody for the rest of her life.

I'm free.

A sob escaped her, and her body shook with it.

If only she could turn back the clock to three years ago, to the time before she'd ever set foot in Eternal Paradise, before she'd ever met Saduuk and fallen prey to him.

If only she could go back years more to when her parents had been alive. If only she could listen to her father's jokes in his thick Scottish brogue, hear her mother's light, tinkling laughter, and see them look at one another with that undying, everlasting love. If only she could feel their arms around her as they sang together, just like they'd done since she was a child.

It's all my fault.

"I'm so sorry," she rasped. "I miss you both so much. I need you."

But there were no soft words of comfort from her mother, no words of encouragement from her father. They were gone. They'd been dead for years.

Aileen opened her eyes and stared at the water swirling down the drain at her feet. She'd been alone for all that time. Even on Eternal Paradise, where she'd had a couple people she cared about, she'd been alone—because they'd all been trapped, all been enslaved. They'd all been held there against their will.

What had become of them? What had become of Tulaya? Had she and the others been taken from one shitty situation straight into another? Had they even survived?

Aileen dropped a hand to the scar on her side.

If not for Kier and Kayl, she would have died on that platform.

You are our mate, Aileen.

She was still reeling from that revelation.

Being Saduuk's slave had killed all hope of ever living a normal life again. Just the notion of living *her own* life had become unrealistic and unattainable, and thinking about it had only caused her more anguish. She'd stopped dreaming of finding that perfect someone.

She'd stopped dreaming entirely.

But then, on what had been perhaps the worst—and very nearly the last—night of her life, two males had materialized from the ether to whisk her away and say she was theirs?

How could that have been real?

Aileen drew in a shuddering breath and held it in as she tilted her face up, letting the shower wash away her tears.

That wasn't how life was supposed to work, was it? How could she reconcile the horror and pain of that night with the twins' warmth and caring?

Her father's voice did come to her then, risen from the depths of her memory.

Life gives us good and bad, Aileen. You take the good and tell the rest, 'Awa' an bile yer heid!'

Away and boil your head—her father's way of saying fuck off.

Aileen grinned.

After she'd finished washing herself and brushing her teeth, she turned off the shower. A few moments later, the automated dryer came on, its warm light evaporating the moisture from her skin. She closed her eyes, taking pleasure in the warmth, pretending it was the sun shining down upon her while ignoring the hunger pangs cramping her belly.

Once her hair was dry, Aileen stepped out of the stall and put on the clothes Kier had left out for her. Despite the heaviness of her thoughts, she felt a little better, a little more human, after a nap and shower.

Standing before the mirror, she frowned at her reflection. She was still a bit too pale, and her eyes were faintly red from her tears. There was nothing to cover it up, no mask to hide behind, no music and lights in which to lose herself. She wasn't an exotic terran performer here. She was just...Aileen.

Do I even know what that means anymore?

With a sigh, she ran her fingers through her hair, combing out as many of the tangles as she could.

A knock on the door startled her. Her fingers snagged in her hair, tugging at her scalp and making her hiss. Nose wrinkling, she rubbed away the sting. The pain was a good thing—because it didn't come with a flare of arousal.

Carefully, she freed her hands from her hair, dropped her arms to her sides, and turned toward the door. Her stomach fluttered, and Aileen caught her bottom lip between her teeth. She knew who was on the other side.

How am I supposed to act?

What do you mean how are you supposed to act? Just be yourself!

But I...I don't know how to do that anymore. Who am I?

Aileen crossed her arms over her chest, hugging herself.

"Why are you being like this?" she whispered. "You're a stage performer. You've been in front of thousands of people since you were born."

But this was different. It *felt* different. This wasn't a performance; it was her life... And the daevahs on the other side of that door were the ones who had saved her. The ones who had cared for her.

The ones who said she was their mate.

"Oh God," she groaned, squeezing her eyes shut and tipping her head back. "What am I going to do?"

The knock came again, followed by Kier's muffled voice. "Aileen?"

Shite, shite, shite. Get it together, Aileen.

She took in a deep breath and exhaled it slowly.

You got this. Go get them, lass.

Aileen opened her eyes, and her feet were moving before she even realized it; they carried her across the room, and she tapped the control button on the wall.

The door slid open to reveal the twins standing, shoulder-to-shoulder, in the corridor, both dressed in the semi-formal attire Kayl seemed to favor. Their mismatched eyes met hers.

That fluttering in her belly intensified. They were so...*striking*.

Aileen grinned and awkwardly leaned against the doorframe, sliding her hand up along it. "Oh, um, hi!" Not sure where to put her hand, she floundered for a moment before resting it behind her head.

You call that flirting? What the hell was that?

I'm out of practice!

Kier tilted his head, lips curling in a roguish smile. His hair was neater than before—the wild strands were swept back in more or less the same direction. "Well, it looks like you are feeling better."

Kayl arched a brow, flicking a glance toward his brother and then looking at Aileen again. "Is everything all right?"

Aileen self-consciously jerked her arm down and straightened, clasping her hands in front of her. "Yeah. I'm great. Well, as good as I can be after all...that. You know?" She curled her toes and twisted her foot back and forth. "You mentioned something about food earlier?"

The corner of Kayl's mouth ticked down, but the change was tiny and fleeting. "Yes. Come eat."

Kier nudged his twin with his elbow. "What Kayl means to say is that we would be delighted if you were to join us for a meal."

"I said as much in fewer words," Kayl muttered.

Shoulders sagging, Kier rolled his eyes. "There is a difference between offering an invitation and issuing a command, Kayl."

Aileen looked at Kayl. "I could just...grab something and bring it back here. I don't want to bother you."

"Out loud, Kayl," Kier whispered over his shoulder.

Kayl huffed in frustration, but his expression softened, if only slightly. "We would not have asked if we found your company bothersome, Aileen."

"Oh. Well, in that case"—she smiled and stepped in between the twins, offering them her arms—"kindly escort me to dinner, gentle-men. I'm *starving*."

The twins turned to face her. Kayl looked down at her arm, brow creasing. "What does *gentlemen* mean?"

Warmth flooded Aileen's cheeks. "A gentleman is a male who takes the arm of his lady—his female—to lead her to dinner. Because she is very, very hungry." She wiggled her arms. "That means you two."

Kayl hesitantly lifted a hand. He'd been so blunt and decisive on Eternal Paradise. It was almost endearing to see him uncertain and a little self-conscious, and it went a long way toward easing her own nervousness.

Kier showed no such hesitancy. He touched his fingertips to the side of Aileen's elbow and slid them down her forearm, eliciting a thrill along her skin. She managed only a quick glance at his face—his expression was serious, his eyes heated—before her gaze became transfixed by the slow, deliberate movement of his hand.

He said, "Our *na'diya* has spoken, and I am more than happy to oblige."

She'd heard that word from them before, and though she didn't know what *na'diya* meant, the way Kier said it in that deep, husky voice made her core clench.

His hand touched hers, fingers sliding along and then between her own. Aileen's cheeks heated, her heart quickened, and her skin prickled in awareness.

Clearing her throat, she smiled up at Kayl. "Still starving. Better hurry before I decide to take a bite out of you."

Aileen inwardly cringed.

Why did I just say that?

Kayl's eyes widened, his cheeks darkened, and he looked away quickly, drawing in a sharp breath. He took her hand with none of Kier's deliberate smoothness. His tail swung restlessly, brushing the backs of her legs.

Kier laughed as he laced his fingers with Aileen's. Kayl glared at him and squeezed her hand a little tighter.

"This way." Kier gestured down the corridor with his free hand and began walking. Despite the bit of friction between the twins, Kayl fell into perfect step with his brother.

Aileen followed their lead.

During her time in Eternal Paradise, Saduuk's guards had often escorted her from place to place. The huge, hulking aliens would position themselves to either side of her as they walked, always setting a brisk pace. Were she to fall even a step behind—which was all but guaranteed given her shorter stature, impractical costumes, and uncomfortable footwear—they would take her arms in viselike grips and half drag, half carry her to their destination. They'd been more like mobile cages than escorts, frequent reminders that she couldn't go anywhere Saduuk didn't want her to go.

The twins caged her in from both sides, but she didn't feel trapped, and she couldn't help but notice that they seemed to be staggering their strides to accommodate her shorter legs. Their closeness was protective, their hold on her hands was comforting, and nothing about their lead was demanding or dominant. She had the sense that they'd cut down anyone or anything that dared threaten her.

Short as their journey was, she felt safe throughout.

Just before they would've reached the control room, they stopped, and the twins released Aileen's hands. Kier moved to the entryway on the right and, with a wave equally graceful and exaggerated, guided her into the room.

She stopped short when she stepped inside.

The dining space matched the other parts of the ship she'd seen—sleek, sparse design, all blacks and grays. A long table took up the center of the room with eight swivel chairs bolted onto the floor around it. A counter ran along the far wall, with cabinets arranged above and below. Several trays lay upon the table, each of them covered by another tray flipped upside down, with three table settings arranged nearby complete with metal bottles.

Aileen's brows rose. "Ehm..."

The lights dimmed, but the gloom was swiftly broken by holo projectors switching on atop the table. Aileen's eyes rounded as holographic images took shape there—three stout candles in glass jars, spaced evenly on the surface. Each had two wicks lit with small flames that gave off a warm orange glow.

It was almost like this set-up was an attempt at being...romantic.

She looked back to see Kayl standing in the doorway and Kier in front of a control screen on the wall. He was looking at her, his lips tilted in a decidedly seductive smile, as he touched another icon on the screen.

Thunderous music blared from unseen speakers, attacking Aileen with growls, bone-rattling drums, clanging cymbals, and guitar-like instruments so dissonant and down-tuned that they made her teeth ache.

Kier frantically tapped options on the screen, mouth moving as though he were speaking—not that Aileen could hear his voice. Kayl raised a hand to his forehead, squeezing his temples between forefinger and thumb.

The music stopped abruptly. The muffled silence that followed was pierced by an uncomfortable ringing in her ears.

"—know that was on there," Kier was saying, his voice slowly growing clearer to Aileen as he fiddled with the controls, sliding something down that must've been the volume. "I am very sorry for that. I meant to play *this*."

A new song came on. Soft and soothing, it was an unobtrusive melody, played on wind and string instruments that almost sounded familiar to Aileen.

"That's lovely," she said.

Kayl stepped into the room, offering Kier an unmasked glare as he passed. He gestured to the table. "Please sit, Aileen."

Aileen padded across the room and took a seat on the far side of the table. She ran her gaze over the table settings, amazed at how those little tweaks to the décor and lighting completely altered the mood of the room. It was sweet.

It'd been years since she'd seen a candle from Earth, and though these weren't real, they still gave her a sense of nostalgia. Her mother adored candles and would light them every night as they sat outside beneath the stars. Her father would play his guitar, the three of them would sing together. Though they'd earned their living as traveling singers and had performed on a stage of some sort almost every day as far back as Aileen could remember, the times when it was just her and her parents had always been her favorites...because those songs had been just for them.

A pang of grief filled her chest, and she had to blink back the tears misting her eyes.

The twins moved quickly and silently—so much so that she didn't realize what they were doing until they were seated to either side of her, close enough that she was enveloped by their intoxicating scents—earth and ocean from Kier, sandalwood and spice from Kayl.

Their eyes were fixed on her, and their mouths were set in identical frowns.

"What is wrong, Aileen?" Kier asked gently.

Embarrassed, she leaned back and brushed the moisture out of her eyes. "Nothing. Just...a memory." She waved toward the table. "This is really nice."

At the corners of her vision, she saw Kier and Kayl look at one another, saw their frowns tick down a hair further. Again, she sensed them communicating—but it was beyond a sense now. It almost seemed like she could reach out and touch the thoughts that were passing between them, like if she tuned her mind just right, she'd hear them too.

Wanting to lighten the mood, Aileen smiled big. "Och, don't you know it's rude to talk past someone like they're not even there?"

Kayl tilted his head, the tiniest crease forming between his eyebrows. "We did not say anything."

She tapped her temple.

The crease smoothed as his brows lifted, and a hint of purple stained his cheeks. It was really quite adorable. It made him appear less...somber. "We do not intend to be rude."

"Communicating telepathically is natural for us," Kier said, drawing her attention back to him. Though his cheeks displayed that same faint blush, he grinned. "And rudeness is natural for Kayl."

"She implied both of us," Kayl grumbled.

Kier only shrugged.

Aileen chuckled. "I was only poking fun. I don't mean for you to...to change your ways for me."

"We have been trying to change the habit for a long while," Kayl said.

"And despite Kayl's resistance, we have made great progress." Kier leaned closer to Aileen, and she felt his warm breath on her neck when he whispered, "Though I do not believe his abrasiveness will ever change."

Kayl shifted closer as well. "And he claims it is I who is rude?"

Aileen's breath hitched as Kayl's thigh came in contact with hers. His heat radiated into her through the material of their clothing, and that warmth made her skin tingle with awareness and her core ache. Kier turned his seat slightly just after, his thigh touching her other leg.

Rhapsody is definitely not to blame now.

"Our journey will offer more than enough time for Aileen to decide that for herself," Kier said.

"It will," Kayl replied.

Aileen looked down. Kayl's tunic had parted, allowing her a glimpse of his muscular thigh, over which his pants were drawn taut. His hand rested upon the same leg, and she couldn't help but admire his long, claw-tipped fingers, his defined knuckles, and the play of tendons under his teal skin.

She flicked her gaze to the right; Kier's hand was resting upon his own thigh, so, so close to touching hers as well.

They really do have sexy hands…

Her fingers twitched with the urge to reach out and touch them while her mind played with images of their hands upon her. She longed to feel them sliding sensuously over her body, to feel them cupping her breasts and stroking her nipples, to feel them between her thighs, dipping into her cunt and—

Aileen clenched her fists as desire stirred deep in her belly.

The twins' fingers flexed, making those tendons stand out even more. A low, rumbling sound, barely audible over the soft music, emanated from Kayl's chest—and from Kier's at the same time.

She slowly dragged her gaze up to meet Kayl's. His lips were slightly parted, and his half-lidded eyes gleamed with hunger. She swung her attention to Kier to find an equally intense light in his eyes. He'd caught his lower lip with a fang.

Her nipples hardened as that desire unfurled in her core. Her body thrilled in every little touch—the brush of the twins' clothing against her arms, the press of Kayl's leg along hers, the whisper of their breath over her skin. She was hyperaware of *them*.

She swallowed and placed her hands on the tabletop. "Okay! I'm hungry. Are you hungry? I mean for food. Of course, I mean food. What else could I possibly be hungry for?" Her cheeks warmed with her every word, leaving Aileen certain that she was about to burst into flames. Hadn't she already threatened to bite Kayl? She laughed nervously. "Let's eat."

"Are you all right?" Kier asked. Had his voice grown a little huskier, or was it Aileen's imagination?

She flashed him a smile. "Fine. Just starved."

In more ways than one.

Shut up!

Kier's eyes dropped to her mouth. "Ah."

How had he made that small, insignificant sound so sexy?

Because it's the sort of sound he might make during sex.

Oh, God, why did I even think the word sex?

Aileen squeezed her thighs together and pressed her hands firmly on the table, refusing to let them roam anywhere else. Thankfully, the twins didn't notice anything else amiss—or at least didn't question her on it.

"Allow us to present your meal." Kier leaned forward, grasping the makeshift lids on two of the four trays, but he did not lift them away immediately. After a few moments in that position, he cleared his throat and shot a glare at his brother.

Kayl grunted, lips dropping into that slight frown that seemed to be his default expression, and took hold of the other two makeshift lids.

"We took the liberty of preparing the finest foods in our stores," Kier said.

"By *preparing*, he means rehydrating," Kayl muttered.

Kier hissed at his brother, brows low and eyes narrowed, and then looked at Aileen again, his expression instantly brightening. "If he wants to be technical, *I* rehydrated them while he watched. So *I* have prepared this meal for you, Aileen."

He lifted the lids away; Kayl did the same for the pair he held, though he was a fraction of a second behind his brother. They moved those lids aside, Kier with a little flourish, revealing...food for which she had no name.

There were brown and white slabs of meat sitting in a glistening pool of dark sauce, long, flat violet strips that reminded her of bamboo shoots, orange beans flaked with green herbs, and a blue, pudding-like substance filled with little pink orbs reminiscent of tapioca.

"It's certainly colorful," Aileen said. She picked up the fork that had been set on her left and moved it toward the tray with the purple strips.

Kayl closed his hand around hers, halting it before the fork reached the food. Aileen's heart fluttered; Kayl's hand engulfed her own, and though his grip was not ungentle, his warm skin was rough and callused.

"Allow us," Kier said.

Guiding Aileen's hand back to the tabletop, Kayl released his hold—though his palm lingered there briefly before he lifted it away. He and Kier set about filling her plate with almost eerie grace and odd delicacy, piling the various foods as though they were chefs crafting their signature dishes.

"The quiya is truly delicious," Kier said as he carefully spooned more of the blue pudding onto Aileen's plate. "It is quite sweet. I have been told terrans enjoy sweetness, do you not?"

"But the evodu has a more balanced flavor," Kayl said as he tilted his spoon, dropping a few more beans into the pile he'd already made on her plate. "Excessive sweetness can become overwhelming."

"And what would you know of excessive sweetness, Kayl?"

"Only what I just said, Kier."

"I cannot help but sense an underlying meaning to your words, dear brother." Kier jabbed a fork into one of the chunks of meat a little harder than seemed necessary and cut it into several bite-size pieces.

Kayl scooped violet strips off their tray. "We can hear one another's thoughts, Kier. You know exactly what I meant."

"I, uh, like both savory and sweet," Aileen chimed in, trying hard to hide her grin.

Kier huffed and shook his head. "No, Kayl, I would not consider you savory anymore than you would consider me sweet."

"What?" Eyes rounding, Aileen gestured to her plate. "I...I meant the food!"

"Yes. The food." Kier added more meat to Aileen's plate, which was fast running out of space—especially as Kayl was still adding violet shoots onto it.

Without looking at his twin, Kayl said, "I am sure we can allow Aileen to enjoy her meal without being subjected to our bickering, can we not?"

"We can, so long as you refrain from starting arguments with me."

Kayl released a long, slow breath through his nostrils.

Suddenly, the twins stopped filling Aileen's plate. They set down the serving utensils, and each touched his fingers to one side of the plate, sliding it closer to her.

She blinked down at it. There was more food heaped in front of her than she'd be able to eat.

Well, I told them I was hungry.

"Thank you," she said.

Despite the questionable appearance of the meat, the smell wafting from the steaming food was appetizing. She poked a piece of purple bamboo and raised it to her mouth. She stopped the fork short when she looked up to find the twins intently watching her with their hands clamped on the edge of the table and their plates empty.

Why had they not served themselves? Why were they just sitting there watching her?

"Are...you two going to eat?" Aileen's eyes widened as a thought occurred to her. How could she be so stupid? Was she destined to repeat her mistakes? She leaned back and dropped the fork as though it burned her. It clanged atop the table, the purple shoots flying off to land next to Kier's hand. "Is it drugged?"

Kier blinked down at the violet strips on the table, a small crease appearing at the center of his brow. But there was something in his eyes beyond that confusion—a flicker of hurt? Kayl, on the other hand, betrayed nothing in his expression.

Lifting his hand, Kier plucked up the purple shoots between the claws of forefinger and thumb. He met Aileen's gaze and held it as he raised the food, opened his mouth, and tossed it in. He chewed slowly. After he swallowed, his pointed tongue slipped out to run across his lips. "We understand your lack of trust, Aileen."

"But we truly mean you no harm," Kayl added.

Aileen lowered her eyes, shame heating her face as she picked her fork up. "I'm sorry. And I'm grateful for all you've done, grateful for all this. I just... Seeing you sitting there, not eating, all I could do was think the worst, especially after Saduuk... When he'd..."

How often had Saduuk slipped drugs into her food and drink to make her more...manageable? She was certain it had been far more often that she'd realized—it wasn't exactly easy to keep track of such things when one's mind was so clouded.

Tension radiated from the twins. She felt it where their thighs touched hers, saw it from the corners of her eyes in the way their tails flicked behind their chairs.

"We truly do understand," Kier said. "That is all behind you now. No tricks."

Kayl's fingers twitched toward her leg. "You are safe with us, Aileen."

She didn't know why, but their reassurances calmed her, their voices and presence wrapping around her like a cocoon.

Aileen stabbed a piece of meat, slipped it past her lips, and bit down on it as she withdrew the utensil. The meat was warm and savory, and it tasted far better than Aileen had expected. She looked up at the twins and smiled. "It's actually really good."

Kier's mouth curled in that easy grin of his, and even Kayl's lips crept upward. They continued staring at her as she took her next bite, coaxing an awkward chuckle from her.

"Please eat," she said, waving to their empty plates. "It's not really sharing a meal if you don't have anything yourselves."

Kier's grin widened. "We simply want to ensure you are satisfied before we partake."

"Just take some food, Kier," Kayl said as he helped himself to the selections laid out before him.

Kier huffed even as he transferred a piece of meat onto his plate. "I would say that is another point in favor of you being the rude one, brother."

Aileen laughed, and a real smile spread across her lips. "Are you two always at odds with each other like this?"

"Yes," Kayl replied.

"No," Kier said simultaneously.

The twins glanced at one another.

"No," Kayl corrected.

"Yes," Kier said over him. He sighed and shook his head. "Ours is a complicated relationship."

"But we are in sync when it matters."

"We complement each other nearly as much as we infuriate each other."

Aileen tilted her head. "I imagine it can get frustrating always having someone in your head and never getting a moment's privacy."

It's crowded enough as it is in my head. I'd go crazy if I had to hear someone else's thoughts too.

She pushed the food around on her plate. "Though it must be nice to know that someone is always there for you. To not feel so...alone."

Having scooped some of the blue quiya onto his plate, Kayl set the serving spoon down and placed his hand on the table, sliding it closer to Aileen's left hand. Tentatively, he touched his pinky to hers. It was such a tiny gesture, such a gentle, comforting one, but it sent a thrilling tingle along her arm.

"There is still loneliness," Kier said. "We are two parts of a greater whole. We are incomplete. As close as we are to one another..."

"There is always a missing piece," Kayl concluded.

"You're talking about your *daevalis*, right?" Aileen asked. "You said it's two *na'divali* and one"—her eyes widened as the terms lined up in her mind—"*na'diya*. That's why you've called me that. Because you think I'm your...mate."

Kier brushed his tail along the back of her arm, making her breath hitch. "We do not think it. We know."

Aileen's chest constricted with emotion; she couldn't identify it, couldn't tell if it was happiness or sorrow, if it was doubt or certainty, excitement or fear. For Kier to say something like that without wavering, without hesitating... "How? How can you possibly know that?"

"As I said earlier, Aileen, we feel it. It is a...a sense, like sight, smell, or hearing," Kier replied.

Kayl pressed his hand a little more firmly against hers. "It is a pull. We are drawn to you every moment."

"Even when we are already close to you," Kier continued, "that extra sense drives us to get closer still."

"So, it's a compulsion?" She released her fork. "Like some kind of animal instinct? A forced attraction?"

Kayl said, "It is a complex biochemical process that—"

"It is fate," Kier said firmly, silencing his brother—though he did not take his eyes off Aileen. "Whatever hormones or reactions might be behind it, it comes down to fate. In the history of our people, we have never been able to explain why, Aileen. But...what difference would *why* make? It is deeper than such questions."

"So you think it's fate... Meaning that everything that happened" —a torrent of memories struck her; the loss of her parents, her arrival on Eternal Paradise, everything she had endured under Saduuk, the attack that had left so many dead—"was just so...so we could meet?"

Kayl's muscles tensed. He covered her hand with his, curling his fingers around it. "Whatever you have been through, and all that we have been through... It was not because we needed to meet.

We would have met regardless. Our paths crossed *now* because of all we have suffered, but they would always have crossed eventually."

Kier covered her other hand with one of his. "And that crossing of paths is a bright point in the darkness. A blazing star in the void of space."

Aileen stared down at their hands, so starkly different from her own and yet so perfect. Why did their touch feel so right, so comforting, so grounding?

"This is a lot to take in," she said quietly.

Kayl's fingers flexed. "Humans...take only one mate, do they not?"

"Most do. Many humans prefer monogamous relationships."

Since she was young, Aileen had pictured herself having a relationship just like her parents', full of respect, laughter, love, and adoration. As she'd grown into a teenager, she'd longed to meet someone who would look at her the same way her father looked at her mother—as though she was the very heart of his existence. Ethan and Lila McConnell had lived for one another.

But in those imaginings, she'd never actually envisioned her significant other, had never been able to. That role had been filled by...by a *sense*, an idea. A vague notion that one day, when the time was right, fate would fill in the blank.

Or *blanks*, perhaps.

What would it be like to have *two* men love her with equal fervor? What would it be like to have them both?

What would it feel like to make love with them both at the same time?

Four hands, two mouths, two bodies moving over hers, two voices growling her name...

Blood rushed to the surface of her skin as a restless energy filled her.

She squeezed her thighs tighter together and curled her fingers to stem the sudden, wicked stirring in her core. Yet how could she combat her desires when the twins sat so close to her, touching her? When their strong, long-fingered hands lay over hers so solidly, so possessively?

How could she resist when her every breath was laced with their essences? When something buried deep, deep inside her cried out for them and strained toward them every moment, just as Kayl had described?

"But some people," she continued, her voice a little breathy, "are open to taking more than one partner."

Something brushed her left calf, sending a thrill across her skin that nearly made her jump.

Kayl's tail. That was Kayl's tail.

Four hands, two mouths, two bodies...and two *tails*. For all the alien beings she'd seen at Eternal Paradise, how had she never considered what sinful delights could be wrought with tails?

"And what about you, Aileen?" Kier purred.

Her heart quickened, and her rapid pulse thrummed in her veins, heating Aileen further and sending a tremor through her. The twins' warmth radiated into her, and their scents enveloped her, flooding her senses; the twins' mere presence stoked the flames of her desire to greater heights than ever before.

How should she have answered his question? What was she supposed to have said? She wouldn't lie to herself—the idea of being with them aroused her. But Aileen didn't know anything about these men.

What if she said no? What if she denied being their...their mate? Would they force her anyway, would they keep her prisoner?

No. Stop it. Stop comparing them to Saduuk. Don't let him continue to hold you prisoner.

But I can't just jump into this.

"I don't know." She withdrew her hands from beneath theirs, ran her fingers through her hair, and settled her hands safely on her lap. "I just... This is too much. We're strangers. To go from that to...to mates overnight is just a lot."

Their hands lingered in the air, still curled as though resting atop hers, and frowns tugged down their lips, Kier's a little deeper than Kayl's.

"Before we saw you, we thought we would never find our *na'diya*," Kier said, "that we would never complete our *daevalis*. This is a lot for us also, Aileen."

"We do not know how to navigate this." Kayl dropped his hand to his own lap. "But we want to try."

Kier dragged his fingers through his chaotic hair. "Everyone begins as strangers, do they not? Allow us the duration of this journey to come to know each other better, to show you that we would be good mates. To woo you."

"Woo me?" she asked. "Do people still use that word?"

"Of course they do."

Kayl scoffed. "We are hardly experts on modern slang, Kier."

"Well *you* certainly are not, Kayl."

Aileen smiled. Even if the pull they felt toward her was merely biological or instinctual, perhaps, in time, something more would grow between them. Something real. And she found that she wanted that—she wanted to try. Because whatever it was they felt, she felt it too.

"So you'll give me time?" she asked. "To get to know you both? To...get used to the idea?"

"However much time you need," Kier said.

Aileen nodded, flicking her eyes between them. "Okay. I can do that. Though humans usually call it dating, not wooing."

Kier's lips split in a grin. Kayl smiled, the expression much more muted and yet just as powerful as his brother's.

Though Aileen knew these two daevahs were hardened, dangerous males—that they'd been in Eternal Paradise to kill a pirate and had managed to escape that chaos unscathed was proof of it—there was a decidedly childlike glimmer in their eyes. She could almost feel hope pulsing from them.

Kier placed his fingertips on the edge of Aileen's plate and slid it a little closer to her, his grin unwavering. "We would be poor daters were we not to ensure you have enough to eat."

Kayl leaned forward, bracing an elbow on the table. "Is *daters* the correct term?"

"I do not know, Kayl. I have never tried dating."

"So why would you assume the terminology?" Kayl took another scoop of the violet strips and deposited it on Aileen's plate without looking away from his brother.

Aileen blinked at the pile. How much food did they expect her to eat?

"I am simply trying to be more accommodating of Aileen's culture." Kier picked up a metal bottle and unscrewed the lid, setting it before Aileen. "Her comfort is my primary concern."

"Then should we not ask her the proper terminology so we may learn her culture?"

They turned their intent, expectant gazes toward her.

She reached out, grabbed the bottle, and lifted it to her lips. "Um, boyfriends. You'd be my...boyfriends." Why did that word sound so *wrong?*

Mates *really does have a nice ring to it...*

Almost as nice as na'divali.

Shut up, Aileen! No one asked you.

Well, technically I did...

Shush!

Kayl's eyebrows sank. "We are not boys."

"No, you're definitely not," she muttered, skimming her eyes over his broad shouldered but lean frame. The tunic accentuated his body perfectly. She forced her eyes away and took a hasty drink as the heat in her core intensified. The cold, fruity liquid did nothing to quench her sudden thirst.

I am in so much trouble.

Double trouble.

EIGHTEEN

"Thank you for the meal. I really enjoyed it. And I enjoyed my time with you too," Aileen said as she walked toward the doorway with the twins behind her. It'd been so long since she'd shared a meal and real conversation with anyone—since she'd truly bonded with anyone

Dinner had been fun, and the twins, with their often-conflicting personalities, had put her at ease and made her laugh more than she had in years.

But they'd long since finished eating and cleaned up the dishes, and now it was time. Wasn't it? That was how these things worked. Didn't want to overstay your welcome. Especially when all three of them were still feeling out this new relationship and what it meant, what it could mean...

She didn't want to go. She didn't want to retreat to the room they were letting her use, where she'd have nothing to do but think— nothing to do but stare at the walls and remember everything that had happened over the past few years.

Her life had once been filled with music and laughter. She couldn't bear going back to silence again.

And she wanted to learn more about Kier and Kayl, wanted to explore this...this *daevalis*.

All I have to do is say something. All I have to do is ask if they'd

like to spend more time together. All I have to do is tell them I don't want to be alone.

At the door, she hesitated, dropping her gaze to the floor. The things she should've said danced at the forefront of her mind.

Just be casual, Aileen. Be...smooth. Lay on some of the ole Glaswegian charm.

"I...guess I'll return to my room?"

Really? That's what just came out of my mouth?

"No," Kayl said brusquely.

There was a dull *thwap* behind her, like someone had been hit. Brow furrowing, she turned to face the twins only to find them much closer to her than she'd anticipated—barely half a meter separated her from them.

Kayl rubbed his arm, glaring at his brother. Kier returned that glare for an instant before looking at Aileen and offering her a smile. "This ship is your home for now, Aileen. We would like you to treat it as such. You need not confine yourself to your quarters."

Aileen clasped a hand around her elbow. "I'm not even sure where else I'd go, and I really don't want to get in your way or touch anything I shouldn't."

"You will not be in the way," said Kayl.

Kier chuckled. "And where is the fun in not touching anything?"

Kayl folded his arms across his chest. "Kier, we are aboard a damaged spacecraft hurtling through space at immense speeds. This is exactly the time to *not* go around touching things."

"But that is exactly what I am about to do." Kier shifted closer to Aileen, locking his gaze with hers as he took her hand. His thumb brushed across her knuckles. "I must check on the emergency repairs and ensure everything is functioning, but my brother will gladly give you a tour of the *Fang* so you can familiarize yourself with your new home."

"We agreed to do that together."

Kier's smile tilted into a smirk. "I am sure your natural charisma will see you through this, brother. And my absence will allow you the chance to be very thorough on what Aileen should and should not touch."

Aileen arched a brow in Kayl's direction, unable to contain her own sly smirk.

I wouldn't mind touching them...

Shhh! Stop it. Too soon.

Spoilsport.

Kayl's cheeks colored slightly. The change was more muted on Kier's face, but it was still there.

Kier glanced back at his brother before leaning close to Aileen and whispering, "Be easy on him. He has no idea what he is doing."

Kayl scowled. "I can hear you, Kier."

Aileen chuckled, easing closer to Kier, and loudly whispered, "I think he's doing just fine."

Laughter danced in Kier's eyes. "I will be sure to let him know."

"I can still—" Kayl cut off his words with a frustrated growl and shook his head. "If you have something to do, Kier, begone."

Snickering to himself, Kier shifted as though to move away only to pause, gaze lingering on Aileen. "I...will see you soon."

She nodded, her smile softening. She reached up and gave Kier's braid a gentle tug. "Okay."

Heat smoldered in his eyes, which dipped briefly to her mouth. His lips parted. He caught the lower one with a fang, tipping his head infinitesimally closer.

Aileen's breath hitched, and she stared at his mouth, at that wicked fang. What would it feel like for his fangs to graze her skin? For his lips and tongue to follow? A sudden ache permeated her core.

There was another heavy *thwap*. Kier grunted and released Aileen's hand, staggering aside as he clutched his shoulder, where his twin had punched him. "That was rude, Kayl."

Kayl lowered his fist, one corner of his mouth ticking upward. "I am vengeance, Kier."

Kier laughed, but his laughter faded all too soon, and somberness crept into his expression. "But you do not need to be."

There was deeper meaning behind their words, much deeper, just as there was behind the change in Kier's expression, but Aileen couldn't guess at what it was.

Kayl frowned. He was silent for a time, looking just as solemn as his brother, and then said, "You did deserve that, though."

Kier scoffed. "I did not."

"You kind of did though," Aileen said.

"What? How?"

Aileen chuckled. "Because you punched him first."

"But *he* did deserve it."

Kayl lifted a hand to his face and massaged his temples. "Please, Kier. If you are going, just go."

"Fine, fine." Kier waved a hand dismissively. "I understand, Kayl. You want our *na'diya* to yourself. Behave, brother." Without a backward glance, he stepped around Aileen and strode into the corridor, brushing his tail across her belly and hips as he passed.

Once Kier was gone, Aileen turned her face toward Kayl and smiled wide. "Looks like it's just you and me."

Releasing a heavy breath, Kayl brushed his hands down the front of his tunic, smoothing the wrinkles. "Yes."

Aileen closed the distance between them, looped her arms through one of his, and tilted her head back to peer up at him. "It's okay, Kayl. I won't bite."

His cheeks darkened, and his features tightened.

He'd had a similar reaction when she'd jokingly threatened to take a bite out of him earlier. What was going on here? Did he...want her to bite him?

She cleared her throat. "I mean, unless you...want me to? If you're into that?" Her eyes rounded and her face burned. "I mean, not *now*! But, I mean..."

Oh, God. Did you really just go there, Aileen?

Yep, I went there.

What the hell?

Kayl's tail flicked wildly from side to side. His nostrils—and the smaller slits above them—flared with a sharp inhalation. "You did bite me, Aileen."

Her brow furrowed. "What? When did I—" Her heart stilled. "Oh. *Oh*. Oh God." She snatched her arms back and retreated. She hadn't known, couldn't remember any of it. What else had she done to them while consumed by the heat? "I'm so sorry."

But Kayl turned toward Aileen fully and followed her, shaking his head. "Do not apologize." He extended his hand and cupped her cheek in his rough, warm palm. The tip of his pinky claw grazed her neck as he tipped her face up. "It was not you. And it"—his tongue slipped out to wet his lips—"was not unpleasant."

Kayl's tail hooked around her leg and trailed along her calf. "If you choose to bite me again, I would welcome it."

"Oh," Aileen breathed. She stared at him, heart racing. He stared back, his pupils shrinking to slits, his gaze roiling with hungry fire. A rogue strand of hair fell before his magenta eye. She reached up and brushed it aside, tucking it behind his pointed ear, upon which her fingertips lingered as she traced its tip. "Maybe next time...you could bite me."

His fingers twitched, pricking her skin with their claws. His ravenous eyes searched hers, peering into her heart, into her soul, and she wanted nothing more in that instant than to bare herself to him in every possible way.

He bent down and drew in another deep breath. She knew he was breathing her in, drinking in her scent, knew that the low rumble from his chest was in response to it.

Aileen turned her face toward him and inhaled. Sandalwood and spice filled her nose, underlaid by an exotic, wholly masculine scent. Her nipples tightened and her sex pulsed; between that sound and his smell, she couldn't stop her body's reaction.

His thumb brushed across her bottom lip slowly, reverently, and the hunger in his eyes intensified. His tail pulled her closer.

"Aileen..." His voice had become a purr, deep and gravelly, thick with desire.

Was he going to kiss her?

There were likely many reasons for Aileen to put a stop to this, but despite her efforts, she couldn't think of a single one. That invisible tether compelled her even nearer to him. She found herself tipping her lips up, flattening her palms against his chest, and closing her eyes.

Kayl's body pressed against Aileen's, solid and warm. She felt his face above hers, felt his breath on her lips, felt the fires at his core blazing just as intensely as her own. And her soul shivered with want.

But something dark and heavy was closing in on her. Her skin prickled with an ominous sensation. It dampened the heat Kayl had ignited within her, chilling her from the inside out, constricted her lungs and stole her breath.

With a gasp, Aileen's eyes snapped open, and she shoved away from Kayl, turning to steady herself against the wall. Staring at the floor, she drew in ragged breaths.

No, no, no!

I will not let Saduuk continue controlling me like this. I will not let them.

The shadows receded, but their claws had sunk deep, and they did not retreat without a fight. Dark memories and cold fear crept along the edges of her consciousness, seeking a way in.

Aileen clutched a hand to her chest and whispered, "Don't think of them. Don't think of them. He's not *them*."

Gradually, her awareness returned; she was *here*, not *there*. She was with Kayl, not Saduuk.

Kayl's tail fell away, severing that last bit of physical contact between them. She sensed his hand reaching out to her, sensed it hesitate and it fall away without touching her.

Kayl rasped, "Aileen, I... I am sorry. I did not mean to..."

No, something within her cried.

This is my *choice. I want this.*

I need this.

I want this.

I want him. I want them.

Aileen spun toward Kayl and without another thought cupped his jaw between her hands, pulled his face down, and pressed her mouth to his. His lips were hot and firm, sparking tingles that raced through her body in a thrilling current. All that sensation channeled straight to her clit.

With a gasp, Aileen drew back, breaking the kiss. She looked up at Kayl.

He stared down at her, slitted pupils bisecting each of his mismatched eyes. His lips were parted, his shoulders heaved with ragged breaths, and that violet tinge remained upon his cheeks. In the moments of silence that spanned between him and Aileen, she swore she could *feel* the rapid beating of his heart layered over her own.

Kayl's upper lip twitched, granting a glimpse of his fangs.

Her inner heat flared.

The small distance she'd opened between them vanished as he shifted forward. Her heart fluttered, but she didn't back away again—she leaned toward him, driven by some deep, undeniable instinct.

He dropped one hand to her hip and cupped the back of her head with the other, burying his long, claw-tipped fingers in her hair. His tail coiled around her leg possessively as he moved her backward.

She felt like she was floating, even when her back met the hard wall. Kayl's body pressed against hers just before his lips crashed down upon her mouth.

The kiss was hard and demanding, bruising and hungry. Aileen closed her eyes and opened to Kayl. She thrust her hands into his hair as she returned the kiss with equal fervor, loosening the tie that bound the strands, and clutched him closer. She needed more. Her tongue traced the markings upon his lips before flicking inside his mouth.

Kayl growled and tightened his hold on her hair, grazing her scalp with his claws. He angled her head back to allow himself deeper access, leaned against her, and took the lead with his tongue, coaxing hers into an intimate dance. He explored Aileen's mouth, tasted her lips, devoured her, and his hot, wet kiss filled her with searing heat.

Her tongue traced the point of his fang, sending a rush of excitement through Aileen. She yearned to feel those teeth on her skin, brushing, scraping...*biting*.

He dug his fingers into her hip. The prick of his claws produced another small but overwhelming sensation, eliciting a moan from Aileen. His tail slid higher, brushing along her ass before hooking around her inner thigh, and he shifted one of his legs between hers. His thigh pressed firmly against her throbbing clit.

She mewed. The sound would've embarrassed her to death at any other time, but she didn't care now. All she wanted to do was chase these feelings, this pleasure. All she wanted to do was lose herself in Kayl.

Aileen had never experienced anything like this. She'd never been so consumed by need—the need to feel his skin on hers, to imprint his scent and taste upon her senses, to have him *inside* her.

But hadn't she? Hadn't rhapsody turned her into a mindless, sex-crazed beast, desperate for any physical contact she could get? Hadn't the heat instilled her with a need so immense that it had swallowed her consciousness and forced her to do things she even now refused to imagine?

She stiffened, her fingers tightening in Kayl's hair as she broke the kiss and leaned her forehead against his. Those shadows, those dark thoughts and darker memories, licked at the edges of her consciousness, threatening to pull her under again.

I didn't want that. I didn't want any of that.

Another growl rumbled from Kayl. His fingers eased their grip, and he removed his hand from her hair to grasp her chin. He rasped against her lips, "Stay with me, Aileen."

The darkness retreated from his voice, and Aileen opened her eyes, meeting his vibrant magenta and blue gaze.

Her body was molded to his, soft against hard, and there was no mistaking the thick bulge pressing into her belly through his clothing.

What did we just do?

Aileen's eyes flared, and she drew her head back. "I kissed you. We...we kissed."

So much for taking things slow, huh Aileen?

Oh my God, I'm almost dry humping a stranger!

But he's supposed to be one of your mates.

So? What does that even mean? It's...it's just some biological instinct for them!

And what about you? How do you explain what you're feeling, Aileen?

Heat burned her cheeks. "We *kissed*."

Kayl's eyes, alight with hunger, were locked on her. A corner of his mouth quirked in a crooked smile that, paired with his tousled hair, reminded her of Kier—Kayl's walls were down completely in that moment, allowing Aileen a glimpse of the person he hid deep inside.

"We did," he said.

And based on the way he was looking at Aileen and holding her, he was about to do it again.

Too fast. We're going too fast.

But damn if she didn't want to feel his mouth on hers again.

Aileen licked her lips. All that did was grant her another taste of him.

Kayl's gaze dropped to her mouth.

I'm so fucked.

Oh, you will be, Aileen.

Stop it!

She reluctantly released his hair and settled her palms upon his shoulders—his strong, broad shoulders—trying to ignore the teasing stroke of his tail on her inner thigh. "H-How about that tour?"

"Tour?" He blinked a few times, and his pupils expanded slightly. When his tongue slipped out to trail over his upper lip, it was nearly Aileen's undoing, but somehow, she held herself still until he finally withdrew from her.

Her fingers itched to grab hold and drag him back.

"Yes, the tour." Kayl straightened and smoothed the front of his tunic. He lifted his hands, removing his loosened hair tie before gathering up those purple and teal locks, sweeping them back, and resecuring them in a neat top knot. He cast Aileen another glance; the glint in his eyes suggested his inner fires still burned as hot as Aileen's.

He clenched his jaw and turned away, gesturing vaguely toward the rest of the room. His voice was flat when he said, "This is the mess..."

NINETEEN

WE KISSED.

Aileen watched Kayl walk along the corridor just ahead of her. He kept a slow, easy pace, but it didn't hide his natural grace and prowess. She knew those long, lean limbs were capable of impressive bursts of strength and speed, and she couldn't deny that she felt a little thrill at the thought.

Only his tail contradicted the deliberate rhythm of his stride. It swept from side to side faster than his pace justified, curling up at the apex of each swing.

After the awkward silence following the start of his tour, he'd led her from the mess into the control room, which he'd referred to as the cockpit. He hadn't lingered there long, muttering that she'd already seen it before moving on to the galley, which was directly across the corridor from the mess. Those three rooms had doors, but they were left open, making the front of the ship feel a little bigger and more welcoming.

He'd led her to the next set of doors down the corridor. The first, which was beside the mess, was the exercise room, which he'd said had been converted from a spare crew bedroom.

With her skin still heated from their kisses, Aileen hadn't allowed herself any time to think about the twins in that room exercising, bare chested, with sweat dripping down their muscled bodies...

Too fast. This is all too fast.

That had become her mantra during the tour, but repeating it hadn't helped.

Kayl's distant demeanor had faltered again after they stepped into the infirmary. There, his expression had softened, a shadow had darkened his eyes, and a raw edge had entered his voice as he told her that she'd been very near death when Kier placed her in the medpod.

The cracks in his shield were small, but through them she sensed his sorrow, his pain, his guilt.

He'd continued along, indicating the lavatories, one on each side of the corridor, and another bedroom across from hers—the room he shared with Kier.

Again, she'd made a point of not allowing herself to think—this time about their room, about their beds, about the things she might've wanted to do in there.

Slow down, Aileen.

Kayl stopped in front of the big door at the end of the corridor. Aileen stepped up beside him, studying him from the corner of her eye as he reached for the control panel.

He was reserved, sometimes even cold, especially compared to his brother. But throughout their time together, Kayl had given her glimpses of the male within that hard shell.

A male who was thoughtful, focused, attentive, and even a little... vulnerable. A male who had been hurt. He was also a male who harbored intense passion at his core—and she knew it would be an unstoppable force once he unleashed it.

The thought of that stoked the flames inside Aileen.

You're supposed to be getting your mind off that kiss, Aileen, not getting all hot and bothered again.

She moved her gaze over his profile, appreciating the glinting silver earring dangling from his ear, the sharpness of his jaw, the downward curl of his mouth, and his teal-streaked, purple hair. Though alien, he was attractive. Exceedingly so.

And he could be mine.

They *could be mine.*

His blue eye slid toward her.

Aileen started as their eyes met and looked forward again just as the big metal door split, its halves sliding into the wall on either side. Warmth filled her cheeks.

Slow, Aileen. Take it slooooow.

Had it been possible, she would've given her inner voice the side-eye. She was allowed to look. Where was the harm in admiring an attractive male, especially when he was supposedly her mate? Well...*one* of her mates.

The corridor continued for a couple meters, reaching a set of stairs that led down into a larger, more open space.

Kayl strode forward, tail swinging faster than before, and cleared his throat as he reached the top of the stairs. "Watch your step," he said before descending.

Aileen followed him, and despite his warning, kept her eyes fixed on him. She smiled. She'd seen Kayl and Kier fighting in the theater, if only briefly, had glimpsed their speed and skill. They were dangerous. They'd been horribly outnumbered in Eternal Paradise, and they'd been carrying her on top of it, but their tenacity and bravery had still seen them through and saved her life.

That Kayl, a veteran warrior, blushed under Aileen's gaze was endearing, and only made it harder for Aileen to resist her yearnings.

But as they reached the bottom of the steps, Aileen couldn't stop her gaze from wandering. There was a large bay door straight ahead, the sort that dropped down to make a ramp when it opened. The layout and flooring in the large room were indicative of a cargo room, but there was no cargo within—just several storage lockers and chests and at least a dozen cots folded up and against the walls. It was like this room had held soldiers instead of goods and supplies.

"What is all this for?" Aileen asked, running her fingers over the frame of a cot.

Kayl stood in the center of the room and swept his gaze around. His tail slowed as he did so, and his posture stiffened slightly. "It is for liberated slaves."

Her eyes widened. "You free slaves?"

"We hunt slavers," he replied. "Sometimes, that results in freeing slaves."

"And Vrykhan, that pirate you're after..."

His nostrils flared as he released a long, slow breath. "He has murdered and enslaved thousands. We have vowed to slay him."

Then she is not worth forsaking our revenge.

The words she'd overheard Kayl speak still stung, but she understood the anger behind them, and this information added another piece to the puzzle. For Kayl, this was about more than all those lives that had been—and would be—taken. It was personal.

She couldn't imagine what suffering the twins had endured to make them seek vengeance so fervently.

Aileen crossed one arm over her chest, grasping her other elbow, and bowed her head. "And you failed because of me."

On the edge of her vision, she saw his tail still.

"Aileen." His voice called her attention up to him. He dragged a hand down his face, fingers rasping over his cheek. "I did not mean what I said."

She turned to face him fully, lips curling into a small smile. "You did. I don't know you, Kayl, but you really don't seem like the type to say anything but exactly what you mean. And it's okay. I understand."

He tilted his head and studied her with fresh intensity. "Open and honest. That is what we told you, and I have already failed." Kayl took a step closer, tipping his chin down as he neared to hold her gaze. "You are correct. I meant those words when I spoke them... but I did so in anger. Anger that should never have been directed at you."

Aileen clutched her arm. As much as she wanted to look away from his intense, mismatched eyes, she didn't. "What did Vrykhan do to you?"

Kᴀʏʟ's ᴄʜᴇsᴛ ᴄᴏɴsᴛʀɪᴄᴛᴇᴅ. He clenched his fists at his sides and looked away from Aileen, but he was blind to the cargo hold around him.

He saw flames beneath a smoke-blackened sky. He saw blood running over paving stones and pooling in the dirt. He saw the lifeless forms of friends and neighbors, plasma wounds still smoldering, saw shattered windows and battered doors. He saw nightmarish monsters prowling through the destruction, snatching survivors off the ground and dragging them away.

His lungs refused to fill with air as he saw his parents, his fathers and mother, forced onto their knees in front of their ruined home. He glimpsed Kier's face, and he recognized his own heart-crushing terror in it.

He saw a towering beast approach through the smoke, saw its

jagged horns and a predatory grin, and watched again—as he had every single day of all the years since—as Vrykhan grasped the twins' mother by her hair, drew her head back, and stared down at her with blazing eyes.

And Kayl heard that voice, powerful and terrible.

They're worthless if they're mated, but the whelplings will more than make up for it.

Another voice cut through the memories, piercing straight to Kayl's core.

We are not there, Kayl. Kier's *aerys* was strained, but its strength was grounding. *That pain has long since passed.*

It has never passed, Kayl pulsed. *It will never pass.*

But it need not be our master, Kayl. It cannot be allowed to consume us. Why now, of all times?

Aileen asked what happened. Asked what Vrykhan did.

Kier was silent; it must only have been for a few moments, but it seemed an eternity to Kayl. Finally, Kier pulsed, *So tell her. If sharing the pain with me is not enough...perhaps it will be enough to share it with her too.*

Something touched Kayl's chest, light but firm. "Kayl?"

That suddenly, Kayl was back in the cargo hold—back in the present. Aileen stood before him with her hand, so warm and delicate, on his chest. Her features were drawn; brows pinched, mouth downturned in concern, eyes intent upon him.

He released the breath that had been trapped in his lungs and sucked in another, blinking away the lingering visions. His next inhalation carried the sweet fragrance of aza flowers. It was soothing, alluring, the scent of home.

Aileen's scent.

He'd not smelled aza flowers since...since Vrykhan attacked their village.

Neither twin had ever shared the details of that day with anyone, not even Kier, who'd always had an easier time connecting to others. But the thought of telling Aileen, of telling...

Our na'diya...

Who else could they share their greatest pains with? Who else could they share their sorrow, their doubts and fears, their hopes and joy with? They needed to trust her with everything, for without trust, there could be no bond. There could be no *daevalis*. There could be no peace.

Kayl covered her hand with his, squeezing gently. His tail swept forward to brush her ankle. "Vrykhan attacked our home when we were children. Our people usually eschew violence. Daevahs are scientists, philosophers, artists, scholars. Our planet was not fortified, protected by only a token defense force. Yet we thought ourselves safe.

"He proved that wrong. His crew raided the settlement, killing, pillaging, abducting. Our family was dragged outside"—he fought the growing tightness in his throat, struggled to keep his tail from coiling around Aileen's leg—"and shoved onto our knees. Vrykhan himself grasped my mother's hair, declared mated daevahs worthless, and cut her throat with our fathers, myself, and my brother watching."

Kayl gritted his teeth. "The wails of pain our fathers released were the most haunting sounds I have ever heard."

"Oh, my God," Aileen rasped. She turned her hand and curled her fingers, lacing them with his.

"I still feel them here." He placed his free hand on his abdomen. "A sinking feeling. A...hopelessness. Our fathers fought, but they were not warriors. I cannot recall them once raising their hands in violence before that day. And Vrykhan killed them as though they were no more than insects. Vermin to be crushed under his heel. Kier and I were taken away and sold as slaves."

"I'm so, so sorry. I..." Aileen shook her head and looked down, but not before Kayl glimpsed the tears glistening in her eyes. "You came to Eternal Paradise to make him pay for what he did, and because of me—"

He caught her chin and tilted her face up again. Seeing those tears in her eyes, feeling the emotion radiating from her...somehow, it hurt more than anything else; somehow, it was worse than his fathers' agonized cries. It was only further proof how deep a bond he and Kier would form with their *na'diya*. "We made our choice, Aileen, but you were never given one. Know that I mean exactly what I say now—I was wrong. You are not to blame."

Her lower lip trembled. She nodded, curled her fingers around his hand, and closed her eyes. "This is why you liberate slaves." Her lashes lifted, and her pale blue eyes searched his face. "Because of what you and your brother suffered."

His chest rumbled. "Everything we have done has been to find Vrykhan. I cannot pretend to be a hero, Aileen. I am driven by vengeance. Freeing slaves was never my goal. It merely comes as a result of our hunt."

"But you're still doing good." She swept an arm to the side. "All this...this is you and Kier. This is you giving hope to those who had none. Despite what you think you've done, or your intentions, you've saved people, Kayl." She dropped her gaze to their intertwined hands. "You saved me."

Kayl lowered his eyes as well. All those lives saved, including hers, had been because of Kier. For Kayl, there'd only ever been the end goal—the death of Vrykhan. Nothing they could have done would ever be more important or impactful than killing the tretin.

At least that was what he'd thought. Kier's pushback on that notion had been what saved those innocent lives over the years, and Kayl had always opposed his brother.

But my opposition never lasted. I always helped regardless. Does that not mean anything?

Of course it does, Kier pulsed. *You are not heartless, Kayl.*

Aileen gently squeezed Kayl's hand, bringing his attention back up to her. She was smiling at him, her pale blue eyes alight, and Kayl's chest constricted.

"Thank you," she said. "For everything you and Kier have done for me."

He could only bring himself to nod; any words he might have spoken, any words he *wanted* to speak, lodged in his throat and refused to emerge.

She withdrew from him, releasing his hand, turned, and stepped away to explore the hold.

Heartless.

That had been Kayl's aim, hadn't it? Emotions could only get in the way of the twins' purpose. Relationships, attachments to others, were a weakness, a vulnerability. Everything within Kayl had been turned toward revenge. Toward justice.

But Kier was right; Kayl was not heartless. Kayl carried those emotions deep inside him—pain, sorrow, anger, loneliness. Even if he'd managed to hold them in the cage he'd constructed at his core, he'd never eliminated them. All he'd managed to do was keep himself disconnected. Isolated. Alone.

He'd kept himself alone even in the company of the one person he trusted in all the universe, the one person with whom he should have been open. The one person who'd understood exactly what he'd experienced because those experiences had been shared.

And now he was here with the one who could complete their *daevalis*, with their mate, and he had no idea what to do.

How was he supposed to proceed? How was he supposed to read her, this female who was almost instinctively familiar and yet entirely unknown to him? He couldn't provide the emotional support she needed, wasn't equipped to form a relationship, wasn't sure how to connect with her or if he even could.

He wasn't sure if he could connect with *anyone*.

You did not seem to have a problem connecting your lips to hers, Kier pulsed.

Kayl clenched his teeth. His face warmed and his lips tingled with the memory of the kiss. *That...that is not the issue, Kier.*

Is it not? Kier replied.

Aileen approached one of the storage lockers, head turning from side to side as she studied her surroundings. The *Fang* was plain and unadorned, but perhaps that held its own sort of wonder for her considering the gaudy place she'd been trapped in for so long?

I do not know what to do, Kier. Do not know how to decipher her, how to form a bond with her, how to give her what she needs.

Kier's mind-voice came edged with concern. *Should I come, Kayl?*

Kayl curled his hands into fists, glancing at the doors to either side of the stairs that lead into the ship's underbelly, where Kier was checking the repairs. *I...do not know. I think...*

That is the issue, Kayl. Thinking.

Kayl's brow furrowed. *How is thinking my problem? If anything, it is your problem.*

Kier chuckled through their psychic link. *You had no problem with the kiss, remember?*

Again, that is a separate matter.

But it is not, Kayl. When you kissed her, you were not thinking. You were acting upon instinct.

Aileen opened the locker in front of her. She made a soft, thoughtful sound—a hum that reminded Kayl of just how lyrical her voice was—as she studied the clothing hanging inside.

She was beautiful. More beautiful than Kayl could describe, more than any words could do justice. And his heart recognized her. His soul called out to her.

So I am to give over to instinct? he pulsed. *Surrender to it completely?*

No, Kier replied, *but you should learn to trust it more when it comes to her. You do not need to plot every step, every conversation, every interaction, Kayl.*

Kayl's heart quickened. Heat crackled beneath his skin, and his insides felt twisted and heavy. He clenched his fists; his claws bit into his palms. *I do not even know what she needs! She deserves better than I can give.*

What is all this, Kayl? Ba'shanaal! I am coming. I will be—

No! Kayl drew in a breath, willing his heart to slow. The heat under his skin receded, albeit slowly. Overthinking. He was overthinking because he was dealing with a situation he'd never encountered, a situation he'd never imagined. *No. I...must learn to overcome this. I must learn...her.*

And you will, Kier replied. *You are. You just need to* be. *She is our* na'diya. *However hard it is to accept, we are meant to be enough.*

A different sort of warmth flowed through Kayl as he watched Aileen spread the clothing in the locker and lift the sleeve of a tunic to study its fabric.

Can we be enough? We are broken.

We have to be. Whatever it takes, Kayl, we have to be. We will come to know her in time, and she us.

It seems we scarce know ourselves, Kier.

We will find our true selves as well. However difficult that process may prove, know that you are not alone, brother.

Kayl forced his hands to relax and released a long, slow exhalation. All he needed to do was speak with her. That was how relationships were built, wasn't it? Conversation. How difficult could that be?

Kier's laughter echoed through their link. *It is not difficult for most people. But you are not most people, Kayl.*

Kayl frowned. *Thank you for expressing your confidence in me.*

I am confident you will succeed, brother. Some day. Do not allow yourself to be discouraged by the many missteps you will undoubtedly make along the way.

Fingers twitching, Kayl fought both the reflexive urge to massage his temples and the petty desire to raise his mental walls and block Kier out again. Because, despite his sarcasm, Kier was correct. Kayl could admit that much to himself.

Aileen glanced at Kayl over her shoulder. "Are these for the people you save?"

Ignoring the dryness in his throat, Kayl replied, "Yes."

She faced the locker again and resumed her perusal of the clothing. "And you said liberating them was only a result of the hunt." She let out a quiet huff. "These are all new."

Aileen has nothing, Kayl, Kier pulsed. *She likely does not even count the clothing she is wearing as her own.*

Kayl's memory flashed back to their first attempt to escape Eternal Paradise—when the collar around Aileen's neck had prevented her from entering the docking area. When Kayl had realized with no small amount of panic and rage that she had been a slave there.

Her experiences were like those of so many of the people Kier and Kayl had rescued, were like what the twins themselves had endured. She carried deep scars on her heart.

But their *na'diya* wasn't alone now, and neither were the twins.

Kayl stepped closer to Aileen, clasping his hands behind his back to keep his fingers still. "Also at my brother's insistence, though I cannot argue against his reasoning. It is a simple thing to allow a freed slave to choose their own clothing from these lockers, but it is a profound moment for many of them. A small but powerful assurance that they are free. That they have a choice."

Aileen paused and clenched the fabric in her hand. She bowed her head.

"Select anything you would like," Kayl said gently, stopping a meter behind her. "It is for you to choose, Aileen."

And as soon as we are able, we will provide for your every want and need. We will open the entire universe to you, na'diya.

She raised her head and looked at the clothing again. "It's been three years since I last picked my own clothes—since I had anything to call my own. Saduuk was particular about what costumes I wore for every show...and what I wore in between."

Rage rumbled in Kayl's core, echoed by Kier through their

psychic link. Kayl gritted his teeth, but didn't allow his body to tense, didn't allow himself to clench his fists or lash his tail.

No matter the strength of Kayl's fury, no matter the power of his longing to make Saduuk pay, there was nothing to be done. The vroca had wronged Aileen in unforgiveable ways, but Saduuk was dead.

"Your choice will never be taken from you again," he vowed.

Eyes misty with tears, Aileen looked at him. Even without any real bond formed, Kayl felt Aileen's gratitude and relief, flowing straight form her heart.

Aileen released an unsteady breath and faced the locker again. Lifting her arms, she gathered her long, thick hair, swept it over one shoulder, and combed her fingers through it. "I have no idea what to pick."

But Kayl didn't look at the clothing—his gaze had caught on the tattoo on her back, positioned between her shoulders. All his doubts fell silent; all his anger and pain burned away. That tight, heavy feeling spread into his chest, even more overwhelming now because it was brimming with hope. With a sense of...destiny.

The tattoo was simple—a single thick cord twisted into knots to form a three-pointed design, wrapped in a shape he recognized as the terran symbol for heart. Interwoven, unbroken. Complete.

Kayl closed the little distance remaining between himself and Aileen and lifted a hand. A faint tremor ran through his fingers as he lightly touched their tips to her skin, tracing one of the curves on her tattoo.

Aileen gasped and went still.

"What is this marking?" he asked.

She shivered but didn't withdraw from him. "My tattoo? I got it when I turned eighteen. It, uh... It's a Celtic symbol that represents love."

"Love?" He clenched his jaw, holding back a burst of assumptions—and a torrent of alarmed questions from Kier's *aerys*. "You... had a mate?"

"What?" Aileen regarded him briefly, brow furrowed, before her eyes rounded with realization. "Oh! No, I didn't have anyone. I've actually never been in a romantic relationship. Nothing ever felt right, you know?"

Kayl told himself that his relief wasn't so extreme as it felt; that sentiment was belied by the shakiness of his next exhalation. Though he meant to lower his hand, he could not bring himself to do so, and instead traced the next loop of the design. "What meaning does it have for you then?"

Pink tinged her cheeks, her lips parted, and her pupils dilated. She quickly looked away. Still, she did not withdraw from him. If Kayl hadn't known any better, he might have thought she'd even leaned back into his touch infinitesimally.

"It meant hope," she said softly. "Hope that I might one day find the same kind of love that my parents shared."

"Shared. They are gone."

"Yes."

Fresh pain and sorrow struck Kayl, strong enough to make his throat constrict and his chest ache. He knew the emotions were from Aileen even though they were so powerful, even though they were so terribly familiar. As desperately as he'd clung to his cold, focused rage, grief, emptiness, and hopelessness had dwelled in his heart for many years.

I am coming, Kier pulsed.

No, Kayl replied.

How can you expect me to stay away when I am being bombarded by these intense emotions, Kayl? Even if some were not from her, feeling it from you is concerning enough.

She is opening to me, Kier. I will not have it disrupted.

Then open to me. She is our na'diya, *and these moments should be ours to share.*

Surely the universe had turned upside down on Kayl sometime over the last week—there could be no other explanation for Kier being correct so often lately.

Kayl took in a deep breath and relaxed his control on their psychic link. He felt it expand, felt the flow increase as every thought, every sensation, every sensory input became shared. Usually, they only opened to each other this way when they were in combat.

And though he'd never admitted it openly, Kayl had always found it to be a comfort.

Releasing that breath, Kayl shifted his concentration briefly to suppressing the senses coming from Kier's end; he did not need to see, feel, hear, and smell what his brother was experiencing now. He needed to focus on what stood before him. On Aileen.

And still he could not bring himself to withdraw his hand, though he resisted the urge to press it more boldly against her back. "Tell me about them."

Aileen pulled away from him, breaking that physical contact. Kayl curled his fingers and lowered his hand, clenching it at his side. Every instinct inside him and his brother roared for him to touch her again, to draw her against him, to forge their *daevalis*.

Crossing her arms over her chest, Aileen sat down upon one of the storage chests, eyes downcast. She appeared so small, so fragile. "My maw told me she'd always dreamed of seeing the world since she was a wee girl. She was only five years old when aliens made first contact with Earth, and she grew up during a time when humans were seeing their universe explode outward. All the other kids around her would talk about going into space, exploring distant galaxies, but she just looked at the planet she was on and knew there was more beauty there than any single person could see in a lifetime. But she was keen to try anyway.

"She always told me that if I wanted to make my dreams come true, I'd have to take a leap of faith. That I should never, ever just wait for the right moment because it might never come. That it would never be the right time unless I made it the right time. And that's what she did. When she was eighteen, she scraped together all the money she'd made working as a barista in the States and took her leap.

"She went to Scotland with nothing but a backpack and barely enough money to eat, and she never regretted it. Not for a single moment. Of all the places she'd wanted to see, that was top on her list. She used to joke that just being there was sustenance enough for her in those first few weeks."

Aileen smiled as she lowered her hands to her lap. "My mother was sightseeing in Glasgow when she heard someone singing and playing a guitar. She said she'd never heard such a deep, beautiful voice in her life, so she followed it around a corner, and when she saw the singer... She said it felt like fate. Like that was exactly where she was meant to be in that moment.

"That man made eye contact with her, and he stumbled over his words like he'd forgotten the lyrics. When he recovered, she started singing along with him, and he gave her the biggest, most dazzling smile. And that was it. It was like they were two halves of the same soul, and they both knew in that instant that they were meant for one another."

Kayl's heart skipped a beat; his brother's did the same. Perhaps it was a case of cultural differences—of terrans and daevahs using similar terms to describe things that weren't really the same—but what she'd described resonated with the twins.

A new batch of questions blazed along the twins' psychic link, fueled by a surge of hope. If terrans could recognize their mates down in their souls, if Aileen could feel what the twins felt...maybe that meant she really could complete their *daevalis*.

"My da told me," she continued, "that from that day onward, she was his world—and he hers. They got married a few months later, and not too long afterward I was born. My parents traveled all around Scotland, England, Wales, and Ireland, performing at small shows and festivals, and I was there for all of it."

She looked off to the side, her eyes unfocused, and chuckled. "I remember one time there was a May Pole set up where we were performing. That's a tall post with ribbons attached to the top. Me and my mother grabbed onto those ribbons and started spinning around the pole while my father was playing a pan flute, and he kept speeding up his rhythm so we'd go faster and faster until we finally fell down on top of each other, grinning and laughing like fools.

"When I was ten, we moved to the United States, where my maw was from. My parents bought a big van that they fixed up, and that was our home as we traveled all over, performing all across the States and Canada.

"It wasn't much, and I don't think we ever made a lot of money, but we were happy. We had everything we needed. We had each other, we had love, we had music. I played instruments and sang with them on stage, and then most nights we'd sit together and sing just for ourselves. And every time my parents looked at each other, I saw that light in their eyes. Saw their love. And it grew brighter and brighter with every passing year.

"So when their twentieth wedding anniversary was coming up, I wanted to do something special to celebrate. Something just for them. We'd been away from Scotland for ten years by then, so I followed my mother's example and scraped together all the money I could. I worked odd jobs at festivals, helping set up and take down equipment, covered shifts at concession stands here and there, anything I could do to earn a little extra on my free time. When I finally had enough, I booked a trip for them—airfare and a stay at a bed and breakfast in Glasgow, Scotland for two weeks. They were so, so happy."

That sharp, stabbing pain returned, tightening Kayl and Kier's hearts. Aileen gripped her thighs as she curled her lips in and bit them, the hurt intensifying. Kayl pressed a palm to his chest, but it did nothing to soothe the ache.

Because the pain is coming from her, Kier pulsed.

"I drove them to the airport, gave them big hugs, and said goodbye," Aileen said, her voice thick. She looked up at Kayl. Her eyes, so full of anguish, glistened with tears. "It was the last time I saw them."

She looked down as a sob tore from her throat. Her shoulders shook, and she used the back of her hand to wipe away her tears. "I didn't find out until f-four days later that they were gone. Struck by a drunk driver at a crosswalk. They were just...gone, and I... God, I didn't know what to do. I felt like I was in a dream, a nightmare, one that I still haven't woken up from. And the only people who could have made me feel better are dead...because of me."

Everything within Kayl was twisted, knotted, tangled, run through with emotions too powerful to overcome. He'd felt this way only once before—when his own parents were killed. Even now, as an adult, it was too much. Even now he could not break free of it.

Instinct demanded he go to her, demanded he comfort her. That was his purpose. *She* was his purpose. But his legs would not move, and he did not know how to give her what she needed. Something within him, something so deep a primal that there was no real name for it, insisted that he existed for her, but he didn't know how to do that. He didn't know if he could.

All he'd known for so long was his pursuit of vengeance. All he'd known was conflict and battle...all he'd known was the hunt.

Go to her, Kier's psychic voice growled. Everything Kayl felt was mirrored in his brother, amplified and redirected back to him, making it only more unbearable.

Kayl's muscles tensed; for a moment, they continued their stubborn refusal. Then he forced himself to look at Aileen—her posture, her expression, her beauty and the way it was colored by her sorrow. She was their mate. Their *na'diya*.

And she was in pain.

How could he stand here and do nothing? How could he not try, whether or not he knew what he was doing? The twins' parents were gone; her parents were gone. But Kier, Kayl, and Aileen were not. They were here.

Kayl strode to his mate, stopping in front of her. His hands remained curled into fists at his sides, his tail moved stiffly, and his heart thumped unreasonably fast and loud, but his voice was steady when he said, "It was not your fault, Aileen."

She sniffled and looked up at him. Her pale blue eyes stood out amidst the red, and her cheeks were flushed and wet with tears. "How isn't it? If I hadn't bought those tickets, if they hadn't left…"

"It was not your fault," he repeated more firmly. "You gave a gift from your heart. That is more than many people could ever hope to receive, Aileen."

You call that comfort? Kier asked.

Shut up, Kier.

Gritting his teeth, Kayl knelt so he was at eye-level with her. The hurt, lost expression on her face only strengthened the ache in his chest. He wiped the tears from her cheeks with the backs of his fingers. "I will not lie and tell you the pain will go away. Ours has not, and it has been many years. But…we are here for you now, Aileen. You need not carry it alone."

Aileen searched his eyes. "Thank you." She drew in a deep, shuddering breath, looked away, and sniffled again. "I'm sorry. I didn't mean to dump all that on you."

That is what we are here for, Kier pulsed.

"You may dump on us all you wish," Kayl said.

Kier telepathically sighed. *I wish you had not worded your response that way.*

Aileen laughed. She pressed her lips together quickly to silence it, but the sound burst from her again. It was a delightful sound, coming from low in her belly but still bearing the innate musicality of her voice.

It seems to have worked, Kayl pulsed.

Not in the way you intended, Kier replied.

"Sorry. I know what you mean, but it just sounded..." She shook her head.

I require an explanation, Kier.

Kier's laughter rolled along the open link. *Ah, brother, you do not need my help. I am sure you will figure it out on your own eventually.*

Aileen's laughter faded, but her smile—along with the light it had sparked in her eyes—remained as she held her hand out to Kayl.

Tilting his head, Kayl regarded her hand. He did not doubt he could lose himself in studying it—he could lose himself in studying any part of her, and even now he longed to do so. Her fingers were long and slender, and the blunt nails at their tips were painted the same blue her lips had been during her performance.

But it was unlikely that she'd offered her hand just so he could memorize its every line and contour.

He lifted his gaze to hers.

"We're supposed to be dating, right?" she asked. "You know, the wooing?"

Kayl nodded.

The corners of her mouth rose just a little more. "Well, couples on Earth like to hold hands, and I'd...I'd like to hold yours."

I fail to see why your ineptitude should be rewarded, Kier pulsed.

You volunteered me to give her a tour, Kier. You have only yourself to blame.

And yet a moment's hesitance kept Kayl's hand still; all those doubts clawed up from his subconscious again, all those questions of what she deserved, of what he could give her.

Aileen's brow creased, and her smile fell as she withdrew her hand. "Sorry, you don't have—"

His hand darted forward, catching hers before it was out of reach. Aileen's hand was warm, and her skin was so soft, but he sensed the strength and confidence in her fingers. His heart pounded faster, louder.

What would it be like to have her hand touch him elsewhere? What would it be like to touch her elsewhere...to touch her *everywhere?* His mind leapt back to their kiss—her body pinned between him and the wall, her lips molded to his, their breaths mingling, heat pulsing between her thighs.

His cock stirred, forcing him to fight back another wave of tension threatening to seize his muscles.

Control, Kayl, said Kier's *aerys.*

Hearing that from Kier was jarring enough to restore some of Kayl's discipline.

"All this is new to me—to us," Kayl said. "Not just terran customs, but the way we feel. I cannot navigate it as well as my brother can, but I want to try."

"It's okay. This is new to me too." She laced her fingers with his. "Shall we continue with the tour?"

He held her hand a little tighter, his worries crumbling in the face of the rightness of this—of the way her hand fit so perfectly in his, of the flutter her smile produced low in his belly, of her presence. "We shall."

She's ours, Kier pulsed.

Ours.

TWENTY

AILEEN WOKE LATE the next morning. She hadn't meant to sleep in, but she was grateful for the rest regardless. When was the last time she'd been allowed to lounge in bed? The last time she hadn't had to worry about punishments for being late?

With a smile, she stretched, and the newly healed skin on her right side pulled taut. She released a sigh as she settled back onto the bedding. Slipping a hand beneath the oversized tunic she'd slept in, she touched her side. Though it'd only been a few days since the twins had healed her, the scarring along the edges of the wound had diminished greatly.

I almost died.

It was horrifying to think about how close she'd come to death. It was just more proof that life could be so fleeting, that it could be snuffed out in that short, delicate space between heartbeats.

Wasn't that more than enough reason to embrace whatever time she had left? To *live*, to place herself firmly in every moment, to appreciate every bit of joy, sorrow, pain, pleasure, and beauty the universe offered? To seize the opportunities presented to her and create those that weren't?

Wasn't that more than enough reason to take that leap her mother had talked about years ago?

Eagerness had Aileen springing out of bed—eagerness to see Kier and Kayl, to spend time with them, to get to know them. After eating a ration bar to tide her over, she brushed her teeth, combed her hair with the brush Kayl had given her yesterday, and dressed in a pair of leggings and a light, airy tunic. She paused at the mirror, studying her reflection.

Without all the glitz Saduuk had forced upon her, without the makeup and flashy costumes, and after a lot of rest, she looked...like herself. It had been a long, long time since she'd looked in the mirror and seen Aileen McConnell staring back at her.

It had been a long time since she was able to recognize anything of herself in her own reflection. Even if it was still just a glimmer, it was there, and it was real.

Aileen's lips curled in a small smile as she left the room to search for the twins.

They weren't in the mess, cockpit, or the galley.

Maybe they're making repairs on the ship?

She walked back toward the cargo hold, meaning to check the lower decks, but hadn't made it far when something brought her to a halt.

Vibrations. A faint thrumming in the walls, in the floor, and almost perceptibly in the air itself. Thrumming...with a rhythm. She took a step backward, placing herself at the closed training room door. The vibrations seemed just a tiny bit stronger. Aileen tapped the entry button on the wall.

Music blasted her as the door slid open, making her jump. It flowed into her body, quickening her heart, rattling her bones, devouring her with sheer, forceful sound. It was savage, raw, rousing.

Aileen stepped into the room, but her stride faltered the instant her eyes fell upon Kier.

He was hanging from a pull-up bar attached to the ceiling, his feet nearly half a meter off the floor. His back was partially turned toward her; even seeing his face in limited profile, she couldn't miss the concentration in his expression, the intensity. Except for a pair of form-fitting black shorts and odd, bulky cuffs around his ankles and wrists, he was unclothed.

She stared at Kier as he drew his chest to the bar; his long tail curled beneath him, and the muscles on his back, arms, and shoulders bulged. Once he was there, he lifted his legs, bending them to bring his knees in, nearly touching the bar with them as well. Then he extended his legs and lowered himself with deliberate slowness.

He repeated those motions, and Aileen watched—she watched the way his body moved, the way his muscles flexed, the way sweat glistened on his purple-striped, teal skin. It was a mesmerizing display of the strength and control in his lean body. Each time he pulled himself up, his lips peeled back to reveal his fangs.

She caught her bottom lip between her teeth as her eyes dipped. The material of his shorts clung to his ass like a second skin, leaving little to the imagination.

It's like he's wearing nothing at all...

Desire stirred within her belly, and heat pooled between her thighs. She curled her fingers, clenching her fists as she battled the urge to reach for him—or to touch herself.

Kier's momentum faltered in the middle of another pullup, and he shuddered as though releasing a heavy breath. Without lowering himself—ensuring those muscles remained deliciously taut—he turned his head toward Aileen. His eyes rounded as they locked with hers, pupils narrowing.

Something Kier had told Aileen rose from her memory. *We have felt your emotions when they are strong.*

Oh...

A different sort of heat suffused her cheeks. She wasn't sure if she'd ever get used to her feelings flowing freely through this bond, wasn't sure if she'd ever understand how it all worked. It was disconcerting that she couldn't hide things from the twins. It should've been downright mortifying, especially while she was standing here ogling Kier.

But what was there to be embarrassed about? What was there to hide? Kier was a tantalizing male, a strong, virile male, and he...he was hers.

My mate.

Rather than shy away or make a hasty retreat, Aileen took another step forward, smiled, and waved.

Kier released the bar, dropping onto the balls of his feet. He turned toward her fully, and Aileen's mouth went dry. There was no missing the defined bulge in his shorts. Apparently, there was no looking away from it either, as her eyes remained fixed on it as he raised his arm and activated the holocom clamped on his wrist beside one of those cuffs.

The tiny digital numbers displayed on the cuffs went dark. After a few more flicks of Kier's finger, the cacophonous music fell silent, leaving Aileen's skin thrumming with the memory of the punishing percussion.

He lowered his arms and walked over to her; she still could not look away from that bulge. The material of his shorts was thicker there, tantalizing her with that outline but offering no real details, and her imagination was on the verge of running wild.

Get hold of yourself, Aileen. You're acting like you've never seen a naked man before.

None of those men were Kier.

But he's not even actually naked!

So?

She exhaled shakily before taking in another deep breath. This situation was different. The twins were different. She couldn't explain it, but everything felt more potent with them, more profound.

Kier touched the pad of a finger to Aileen's chin and tilted her head up. As her gaze rose, it raked over ridges of muscles glistening with perspiration—his chiseled abdomen, his broad chest, his powerful shoulders—until final meeting his eyes. He searched her face; Aileen's flesh tingled beneath the heat of his stare.

His scent, made even more intoxicating by his sweat, enveloped her. She breathed him in greedily. Her eyes yearned to roam, to drink in his form, and her fingers itched to touch him, to feel him, to explore him.

He leaned closer, close enough for Aileen to feel his breath on her skin, and purred, "Hello."

"Hi," Aileen breathed.

Kier's finger curled, grazing the underside of her jaw with its claw. His mouth tilted in a roguish smirk. "Did you come to watch?"

The heat under her skin intensified. "No. I...I haven't been here long. I didn't mean to interrupt you."

He touched his fingers to the side of her neck and trailed them down as his tail brushed the outside of her calf. A shiver coursed through Aileen.

"Ah, my *na'diya*, you have not interrupted." He grinned, flashing those wicked fangs. "You may stare at me any time you wish."

Aileen didn't know how she was going to survive the attention of not one, but *two* of these incredibly sexy daevahs.

Her gaze dipped down his body and slowly rose, taking in every muscle, every scar, every purple stripe. "It's been a long time since I had a hobby. Just figured I'd try a new one."

Kier chuckled, and his cheeks—already tinged violet from his workout—darkened. His hand came to rest between her shoulder and neck, and his thumb stroked the hollow of her throat, making her pulse race. Now his eyes dipped. "I am sure we can find other ways to entertain you."

Aileen leaned into his touch. Her nipples hardened, turning into achy little points that begged for his hands. She knew they were visible through the flimsy material of her tunic by the way his pupils shrank when his gaze reached her breasts. The playfulness of his expression gave way to something far hungrier and more intense.

What happened to the whole taking it slow thing, Aileen?

I don't know, guess I lost it somewhere between their lickable bodies and fuck-me eyes?

She wanted the twins, wanted a relationship with them, more with each beat of her heart—and it was beating pretty fast right now. She wanted to take the leap. She wanted to be their mate. But sex... that was too much, too soon. Aileen wanted—*needed*—an emotional connection first. She needed it all to mean more than just mutual attraction and lust.

A low growl came from Kier's chest. "I feel your desire, Aileen. But I feel your struggle also." He curled his tail around her leg. "What are you thinking?"

Aileen reached up and lifted his hand off her shoulder, lacing her fingers with his. His hands, tipped with those deadly-sharp black claws, were large compared to hers, but she knew they would be nothing but gentle with her. She knew deep in her soul that neither Kier nor Kayl would ever raise their hands to her, would ever hit her or punish her.

"I'm just overwhelmed. I'm...adjusting," she replied.

Kier raised his free hand, hooked several loose strands of her hair, and tucked them behind her ear. He smiled that easy, warm smile. "I understand. It is the same for us. As natural as it feels to have you here, as right as it feels, we are still learning. Any discomfort or trepidation you may experience, Aileen, you may speak to us." He caressed the rounded shell of her ear. "We can adjust together."

She barely suppressed the delightful shiver roused by his words and touch. Biting her bottom lip, she brought their intertwined hands up, holding them over her heart. "Thank you."

Aileen released his hand and retreated, causing Kier's tail to fall away. She tore her eyes from him to look around the room. Along with the bar attached to the ceiling, there were several other pieces of exercise equipment, most of which were reminiscent of equipment she'd seen on Earth. And unlike the rest of the ship, the floor was warm and padded—a change welcomed by her bare feet.

"So is this what you and Kayl do to keep yourselves busy?" she asked. "I mean, you guys spend most of your time on this ship, right?"

Kier followed her gaze with his own. "We do spend most of our time aboard the *Fang*, yes. There is little with which to occupy ourselves here, and our focus has always been on hunting Vrykhan, so we often pass the hours by exercising and sparring."

"Sparring?" She looked at Kier and chuckled. "Must be hard when your opponent knows every move you're going to make."

His grin took on a mischievous tilt. "It is not quite that simple. We can close ourselves off to one another when necessary, though Kayl is admittedly much better at doing so. Yet in combat...it is more about instinct and muscle memory than thought. It is difficult to read one another's intent in battle without willingly opening our connection."

"What's it like? Opening yourself to someone so completely?"

He caught the braid dangling beside his cheek and tugged on it as his eyes lost their focus. "It is...natural, as we have said. It can be comforting. I suppose it is the opposite of loneliness, is it not?" He chuckled, but there was little humor in the sound. "We flow together as one, but we do not lose ourselves. It is...liberating. And it also makes the times we are closed off to one another much harder. The silence can be unbearable."

Aileen frowned at the sadness in his Kier's voice. More than anything, she wanted to take away that hurt, to comfort him. "Does Kayl close himself off to you often?"

Kier met her gaze again, a wistful smile settling on his lips. "Far more often than I care for. But I cannot blame him for it. He does not do so out of spite, at least not usually. I think..." He sighed and shook his head. "I think he is afraid to share what he truly feels at times. He has always been the steady one, and some part of him cannot bear to reveal that he is not always grounded. That he is not always in control."

She couldn't help but think of her parents. They'd made every day a joy, but as she'd grown up, Aileen had learned how difficult that had sometimes been. It was hard to not overhear quiet conversations about finances or impossible schedules when they were living out of a van—hard not to hear the times, usually late, late at night, when her father would voice his concerns that they wouldn't be able to stretch their money far enough to eat before their next show.

But they'd always sheltered Aileen from such worries, even when she'd asked about them directly. They'd always made sure she had what she needed no matter how difficult things were. And even when she'd tried to make little sacrifices to help them, they'd smiled, hugged her, and told her it was okay.

"We try to shield the ones we love most," Aileen said softly. "But we don't always realize when that sometimes hurts the people we're trying to protect."

Kier tilted his head, regarding her with a thoughtfulness she'd not experienced in a long, long time. After her years on Eternal Paradise, it was strange, almost unsettling, to be seen—not as a performer, not as an exotic piece of flesh, but just as herself. For someone to look at her as she was and think she was enough.

"It would be a lie to say it does not hurt," Kier said, "but it is not my pain that most concerns me. I worry for what he does to himself. For what he holds inside. That weight is too much for one person to carry alone. I would gladly help shoulder any of Kayl's burdens. And I do. All our experiences are shared, so I do not understand why he so stubbornly tries to hold all of it inside."

"Have you talked to him?" Aileen asked.

"The subject has come up. We are moving forward. Slowly but undeniably forward."

Aileen smiled and flattened her hand upon Kier's chest, feeling the steady thumping of his heart beneath her palm. "Change takes time, and it isn't easy. But Kayl knows you're there for him and always will be. That's what's important."

He returned that smile, flashing his fangs. "You are correct,

Aileen." He cupped her jaw, stroking her cheek with his thumb. "And now we have you too."

Something fluttered in her belly. It wasn't unlike the anxiety she'd sometimes felt before a show, but at the same time it was entirely different. This was so much larger, so much deeper, so much more hopeful.

She felt like she had so much more to lose.

Aileen pressed her cheek more firmly against his palm. "You do."

TWENTY-ONE

Kɪᴇʀ's sᴍɪʟᴇ widened into a grin.

You do.

Those two words carried so much more meaning and weight than should have been possible. He knew they didn't mean everything, knew there remained a long way to walk on the path toward completing their *daevalis*, knew she wasn't yet ready to become one—and that he and his brother weren't truly ready for that either.

Kier, Kayl, and Aileen all bore deep scars. The act of physically joining with their mate...

No. He wouldn't let the past taint this moment. He wouldn't let those dark memories prevent his heart from soaring.

Aileen was accepting them. Aileen wanted them. That...that gave Kier more hope than he'd had in a long, long while.

What happened? Kayl pulsed. Their psychic link had been open, but it had been quiet as each twin attended his own tasks. The only surprise was that Kayl had not responded directly to Kier's near overwhelming desire a few minutes before.

Kier relayed the memory to his brother; it was one that would remain clear in his mind for the rest of his life.

And now we have you too.

You do.

Kier's elation was amplified and reflected at him through his bond with Kayl; it now belonged to his brother as well.

We must not overreact, Kayl pulsed, his *aerys* brimming with excitement despite his clear attempt at a neutral tone. *But this is a step forward.*

A great step forward, Kier replied.

It seems my efforts to be open with her are paying off.

Kier nearly laughed aloud at that, maintaining his composure only due to Aileen's proximity. *I know the real reason, and so does she.*

He leaned closer to her and said, "I knew you could not resist my charms, Aileen."

She laughed. "You are very persuasive." Her eyes flicked between his. "You're talking to Kayl now, aren't you?"

It is not a matter of your charms, Kier, Kayl pulsed.

Do you not have work to do, Kayl?

It is difficult to focus when I am being assailed by a constant barrage of emotions, whether good or ill.

Shall I bring up what occurred between you and Aileen after dinner yesterday while I was working?

Kayl's memory flashed along the link, undoubtedly without him intending to share it—Aileen's body tucked against his, Aileen's lips pressed against his, all that heat, all that desire. The secondhand taste of *her* rekindled Kier's longing. He'd not yet enjoyed such intimacy with Aileen. But he could be patient. This was not a competition; he and his brother were working together toward the same goal.

"I am," Kier said. "Is there enough of a delay in my replies for you to tell?"

"There is a little." Aileen brushed her fingers across his brow, sweeping aside damp locks of hair. "But I can tell by the look in your eyes."

"Oh?" He smirked. "Does it look as though I am being bored to death whenever I telepathically converse with him?"

Aileen laughed again. It was melodic and sweet, and Kier vowed to himself that he would do everything his power to hear more of that sound.

"He's not boring," she said.

"I have to disagree with you on that. Perhaps you will change your opinion after a few more days with him."

Kayl sent a weary sigh through the psychic link.

She grinned. "We'll have to wait and see. Where is he now?"

"He is on the lower deck, reinforcing some of the repairs."

"Tell him I said hello and that I'm sorry I slept past breakfast."

A wave of warmth flowed from Kayl, a feeling more serene and wholesome than anything he'd ever shared with Kier. Was it truly possible for Kayl to show signs of change after only a couple days?

"He says hello, and he does not want you to worry about breakfast," Kier said. "You needed rest, and neither of us wanted to disturb you."

Her smile softened. "Thank you. So"—she glanced toward the pull-up bar—"since I interrupted your work out, why don't you spar with me?"

His eyes rounded, and his tail whipped the air. "What?"

What? Kayl demanded simultaneously.

Aileen chuckled. "Don't look so horrified."

"We would *never* strike you, Aileen," Kier said hoarsely. "Never."

"I don't mean for you to fight me, but..." She withdrew from him and shrugged, brow creasing as she rubbed her forearm. The light in her eyes dimmed. "Could you show me how to defend myself?"

Kier knew that her thoughts had turned dark; he felt it. How could he not relate to that sense of helplessness? How could he not relate to feeling powerless and vulnerable? In many ways, those feelings had driven him and his brother to seek revenge just as much as their anguish and grief had.

Looking into her eyes now granted Kier a glimpse at something buried deep inside him. If he'd been able to look at his younger self, after his parents had been killed, he would've seen something similar in his expression.

He placed a hand over hers, halting its motion. "Though we will do all we can to ensure you never have to employ such skills, I can teach you. But they can only be developed over time."

The corners of Aileen's mouth curved upward. "I'm willing to learn. And we have plenty of time, right?"

Kier ran his gaze over her again and grinned. "We do." He held his hand out to her, palm up. "Shall we begin?"

She placed her hand in his, yelping in surprise when he yanked her toward him. She bumped into him, breasts against his upper abdomen, pelvis against his thigh. He looped his arm around her back without releasing her hand.

Their eyes met. Kier could not look away—not that he wanted to—and Aileen seemed just as incapable of breaking that eye contact.

Her long tunic created scant separation between their skin, allowing her delicious heat to flow into him. That heat sparked fire in his core, which swiftly spread outward. Kier's nostrils flared as he breathed her in.

His cock pulsed against her belly, hardening with a deep, maddening ache. He curled his fingers, claws lightly pricking her skin through her tunic.

Lips parting, Aileen released a soft breath.

She and Kayl fit together so perfectly. *This* was their natural state—bodies flush, warmth shared, hearts pounding. Each moment they spent apart was unnatural. Each moment when their skin was not in contact, when he could not feel her softness—those were wrong, all wrong, and always had been. He simply hadn't known it until now.

Kier, Kayl's psychic voice growled, *focus.*

Focus.

Kier had a task to attend. Though on the surface it ran counter to his instincts, at heart it was fulfilling them. Teaching Aileen to defend herself was a means of protecting her. He didn't want to imagine a scenario in which he and Kayl failed to safeguard their little mate, but if anything were to happen, if she were ever put in another dangerous situation like she had been on Eternal Paradise, she needed some means of defending herself.

He exhaled through his nostrils and let out a low, rumbling sound. "Failed your first test."

"Failed?" she rasped, her wide eyes searching his.

"Yes. I caught you."

She smirked and braced her free hand against his chest. "Not fair." Though she shoved, she did not break his hold.

"There is no such thing as a fair fight." Kier drew her hand, still in his grasp, upward to rub against his cheek. "Especially not with the enemies we have made. Now escape."

Aileen pushed harder against his chest, at the same time tugging on her trapped hand. "I understand. My da told me a few stories about his wild days rollicking around the pubs in Glasgow, even though Maw didn't approve. He bloodied his fists a few times back then."

Kier grinned. "I see. Did he impart any wisdom to his daughter?"

"Just a bit."

She moved quick, quicker than Kier had expected, thrusting her knee up toward his crotch. But he was faster still. He squeezed his thighs together, catching her leg before that knee could strike the more sensitive bits of his anatomy.

He laughed, tail swinging with burgeoning excitement. "Not bad, Aileen. But even if you connect, it will not work on everyone. Now what?"

Grunting, she pulled on her arm and leg while pushing with her braced hand. Kier swayed, but shifted his weight slightly away from her, keeping his stance remained firm.

Zor atkoshai, *to have a part of her that close to my cock ...*

She tried to knee you in the testicles, Kier, Kayl pulsed. *I fail to understand the excitement in that.*

Were you in my place, Kayl, you might understand.

"What do you feel as you try to pull away?" Kier asked.

She bared her teeth and gave another mighty tug. Kier simply leaned back farther to counter her force, allowing her to gain nothing.

"You're just using more of your strength. Tightening your hold," she replied.

"Pay attention to my body, Aileen. Not just my strength."

She eased her struggles, though she did not cease her resistance, and tore her gaze away from his. Her eyes dropped to his chest, shifting back and forth.

"I am using my weight far more than my strength," he said.

Aileen's brow creased. Her fingers bent, digging those blunt nails into his chest briefly before her eyes rounded. At the bottom edge of his vision, he saw her reposition her foot on the padded floor, and he sensed her altering the tension in her muscles, preparing herself. His grin did not fade. All the signs suggested that she'd never fought before, but she had good instincts regardless.

Aileen abruptly reversed her momentum, throwing her weight toward Kier. As he'd already been leaning back, her body, however slight, was enough to disrupt his balance.

Her leg fell free first, and she slammed her foot down firmly before ducking low, escaping the arm he'd held around her back. Her hair fell into her face as she pushed hard against his belly. He staggered backward a couple steps before catching his balance and halting.

Their eyes met. Aileen was panting lightly, her arm extended—her hand still caught in Kier's.

"Using your weight is just as important as using strength or speed," he said. "But the larger your opponent, the less difference it will make."

"So what, then? I'm just out of luck?" she asked.

"Not out of luck. Just at a great disadvantage. You will prevail only by remaining calm and relying upon technique to seize whatever opportunities you may."

"That and fighting dirty, right?"

"Yes. And fighting dirty." With a smirk, he released her hand and lowered his arm. He immediately missed the warmth of her palm, missed the reassurance of her grip, missed that closeness, even though she stood not two meters away.

There will be many chances to have my hands upon her over the coming minutes.

Thrilling as that knowledge was, it could not silence his body's instinctual protest of her being just out of his reach.

He stood up straight and forced that smirk into a smile. *Adjusting.* They were all still adjusting, and that was all right. Learning to cope with these powerful new instincts, to prevent them from taking control, was part of that process.

"Let us begin in earnest, Aileen," he said.

She scoffed, lifting her palms in exaggerated exasperation. "Are you saying none of that counted?"

"Consider it a skill assessment, *na'diya*." Kier shifted his stance, turning his body perpendicular to hers. "Now we will build those skills."

Aileen raked her eyes over his body and changed her position, mimicking his stance with just a touch of uncertainty. But there was no uncertainty in her voice when she said, "Which implies I have some skills."

"I did not say—"

"Oof." Aileen winced and straightened, turning toward him again. She braced her hands on her hips and shook her head. "You were about to say you never claimed I have any skills, weren't you?"

Kier's brow furrowed, and he tilted his head. "I—"

"Because if you were, I mean, that would have been bad for the whole wooing thing you're going for, you know?"

Cheeks heating, Kier dropped his fighting stance and lifted a hand, raking his fingers through his hair as he frowned. "It is not my intention to—"

Aileen's mouth stretched into a grin that displayed her straight, white teeth an instant before she lunged at him. She aimed low; her shoulder struck his abdomen, and she threw her arms around his middle, driving with her legs to push him back.

Kier caught hold of her arm and spun to the side, breaking her hold and using her momentum to drive her forward and to the floor. She let out a yelp just before she hit the mat face down, and Kier immediately straddled her back, pinning her hips and legs with his body.

She wiggled beneath him and let out a huff that blew wild locks of her red hair toward Kier's face.

"What was that?" he asked.

Aileen turned her head, resting a cheek on the floor to look up at him with one eye. She was pouting. "Fighting dirty."

Kier laughed; even in his humor, it was impossible to ignore their current position. It was impossible to ignore the thin fabric separating their bodies, or that his still-throbbing cock was tucked against the generous curve of her ass. He was thankful his shorts were reinforced in the front to keep everything...restrained.

Perhaps she is not at quite as much of a disadvantage as I assumed...

He smoothed a hand up her back. When his fingers reached her hair, he took it in a gentle but firm grasp and lifted her head. Kier leaned forward to place his lips close to her ear. "What will you do now, Aileen? I have you where I want you."

He didn't miss the shudder than ran through her.

Flattening her palms on the floor, she pushed and twisted, grunting as she tried to dislodge him, but Kier just pressed his other hand on her back and forced her onto the floor again.

She growled; he very nearly groaned. He couldn't ignore the sensations caused by her struggles—couldn't ignore the sweet friction.

Kier, Kayl's *aerys* intoned.

Shut up, Kier replied. *I am fine.*

Kier moved his hand to her face, grazing her cheek with his

claws. "For most beings, the head and neck are vulnerable points. Protect them as best you can."

Her pale blue eye still stared up at him, bright with a glint of frustration, a spark of excitement, and a flare of determination. He did not grant her any leeway as she tried to move her arms up to shield herself. She bared her teeth, letting out another frustrated growl, but managed to cage her head between her bent arms.

"Good," he said.

She attempted to buck her hips, prompting Kier to lean more of his weight upon her.

"You need to get onto your knees," he said. "That is your next goal. Do not focus on forcing me off, just on getting your knees beneath you."

"How do I do that?" she asked, a touch breathlessly.

"Any way you can," he replied.

Aileen dipped her chin in a shallow nod, drew in a deep breath, and renewed her struggles with surprising vigor. Rather than trying to buck him off, she moved her legs and twisted her hips. Kier clamped his thighs around hers, but the hold was not firm enough to last long. She quickly raised her backside and slipped her legs out from beneath him, bracing her knees on the floor.

"Excellent, *na'diya*," Kier rasped as he altered his hold, wrapping his arms around her torso and leaning over her.

"I'm still trapped," she said.

"Weight and momentum," Kier replied. "Heed my movements, my balance. Use it against me."

Against me. Perhaps I should consider the way I word my instructions...

With a grunt, Aileen shoved herself toward Kier and swung her legs in front of her, forcing herself into a sitting position that knocked him backward. She rolled to the side before he could solidify his stance again. Kier tumbled with her, maintaining his hold around her midsection until her hands and knees came down again.

She wrenched hard, throwing all her body weight and force against the weak point of his grip—his interlocked hands. They broke apart, and she scrambled away.

Strands of her tousled hair fluttered with her panting breaths as Aileen stood on her knees, grinned, and pumped her fists in the air. "I did it!"

Kier's chest swelled, brimming with pride, tingling with excitement and arousal. "You did, Aileen." He crawled toward her, brushing her hair out of her face. "Shall I use more strength on the next one?"

"Jerk," she said with a laugh, knocking his hand aside. "Show me some more."

You are conflicted, Kayl pulsed.

Of course I am, Kier replied, careful not to betray his inner thoughts in his expression as he got onto his feet. *My every instinct is to protect her. This feels too close to trying to harm her.*

It feels too close to something else also, based on what I have sensed from you, Kier. Take care to control yourself.

Kier spread his arms and rolled his shoulders, stretching his tail out behind him. His exercise had left a satisfying ache in his muscles, which thrummed with heat—though the heat he felt now was only partially due to exertion.

I am sorry you are not present to enjoy this, brother, but treating me like a child will not change that, Kier pulsed. He turned to face Aileen, who'd also pushed herself onto her feet. She swept back her hair and tucked it behind her ears.

My absence is not the issue, Kayl replied.

Nor is my self-control, Kayl.

Something cracked in Kayl's often stoic telepathic voice, letting unmasked concern seep through. *She is not ready.*

I know. Kier offered Aileen a smile, which she returned so brilliantly that his heart skipped a beat. *Neither are we.*

But all three of them would be ready before long. Whether they realized it, whether they understood it, they would soon be ready to forge their eternal bond. Kier knew it as a fact much the same way he knew his heart was always beating, or that stars were constantly burning through their fuel. The same way he knew Aileen was their mate.

Kayl sighed through their psychic link. *I meant no insult, Kier.*

I know, Kayl. I have taken none. But you can trust me.

I do trust you. See to your training, brother. I will offer no further distraction.

The link did not close, but it fell quiet again. Not silent—Kier still felt the usual unobtrusive thoughts trickling through, felt the tiny flutters of emotion, felt his brother's physical presence elsewhere on the ship. He turned all his attention back to Aileen.

"Tell Kayl we're busy," she said with a smug yet alluring smirk. "If he wants to talk, he can march up here and do it in person."

Kier laughed and shook his head, marveling at the female before him. He still knew so little about her, but each new thing he discovered made him yearn for her even more. With each new layer of herself she revealed, she exceeded Kier's wildest imaginings, making him question how this could possibly be real. How *she* could possibly be real.

"He has left us to our work, little terran." Kier put on his own smirk, reassuming a fighting stance. "There is no one else to save you. You are all mine."

Those words felt so right coming from his mouth. Fire sparked in Aileen's eyes as she again copied his stance, making their otherwise soothing blue into something ravenous and seductive.

Ba'shanaal. *She is a challenge I could never have anticipated.*

He allowed himself no further hesitation; he rapidly closed the distance between them and caught Aileen—who was far more alert and evasive now than at the onset of their impromptu training session —in another hold.

Kier felt her pulse quicken when he drew her body against his. Ignoring her racing heartbeat and ragged breaths required all his willpower.

He coached her through escaping the hold, answered her questions, and led her through more exercises. A few times, he initiated attacks without warning, testing her reflexes and composure. Other times, he guided her into positions likely to occur if she were accosted. In all cases, his speed, strength, and experience left him largely in control.

Though instinct insisted he hold everything back to shield her from harm, he refused to fully restrain himself. Partly because it would have required far too much concentration, which he'd already had to apply to prevent his body's natural reactions to her touch, her warmth, her scent, her closeness.

But it was also because she would not benefit from being handed victory. Daevahs were known for their agility, but they were far from the biggest, strongest beings in the universe. Even exerting every shred of strength in his body, he could not have hoped to match someone like Vrykhan. The disparity would be even greater for Aileen.

Regardless, something shuddered in Kier's core each time he took Aileen to the floor. When she struggled against him, it was like a blade twisting in his gut, its point sinking deeper and deeper. Her every grunt, groan, and hiss of pain made his heart skip a beat.

But his discomfort was assuaged by Aileen's determination. For every hold Kier applied on her, every situation he simulated, every sparring match he conducted, she fought to the end. Whenever she went down, she found the strength within herself to get back up. Even when her muscles trembled with weariness, even when she was panting and her skin glistened with sweat, she kept going.

And just in that short time, she showed improvement. She did not have the conditioning of a fighter, did not possess the size, strength, and speed natural to so many other races, but she learned swiftly. Kier found himself utilizing more and more of his own speed and skill to ensure she remained consistently challenged.

Of course, to his disappointment—but not his surprise—his arousal scarcely diminished throughout. While he could suppress his reactions to her, he could not eliminate them. Fortunately, she was still too inexperienced to recognize the mistakes he made because of his lingering desire...or at least he'd thought so.

As he was taking hold of her from the side to demonstrate a different angle of attack, she turned slightly; it was just enough to press her breast against his side. The hardened bud of her nipple teased at his skin through her tunic, speeding his already racing heart.

Their tumbling and wrestling had confirmed that she wasn't wearing anything beneath that tunic, and with his hand on her hip, all he would have to do was lift the hem...

That moment of distraction was enough. Aileen hooked his arm, pivoted her feet, snaring one of Kier's legs with her own, and cocked her hips. The leverage allowed her to throw him with relative ease. He came down on his back, stunned by her sudden counter—but he did not release her.

Aileen rolled with Kier, coming down atop him before he used his weight to continue the roll. Their positions flipped, with Aileen beneath him, but her control of the situation was superior; she clamped her thighs around his waist, ankles crossed at his back, and used her lower body to swing him into a final tumble.

Kier's back again hit the mat. Aileen straddled him, bracing a forearm across his chest. Her hair fell around them, blocking out the rest of the universe. She stared down at him. Kier stared up at her. Their chests heaved with their ragged breaths and sweat tricked over their heated skin. Her weight was centered on his pelvis, her sex bearing down on his erection, which refused to ease.

Aileen's cheeks were flushed, her eyes half-lidded, and her lips parted. He'd seen that light in her eyes before. Something within him stirred at the sight, something hot and primal.

He should have said something, should have complimented her. Yet all he could do was gaze into those pale blue eyes. They were deep and mesmerizing, threatening to swallow him, and his soul welcomed it. He wanted to lose himself there. Wanted to lose himself in her.

Would her eyes change when they forged their *daevalis?* Female daevahs were born with colorless eyes, taking on the eye colors of their mates after bonding. The twins' mother had had a swirl of their fathers' magenta and blue that blended to a rich violet around her pupils.

It would be a mark upon Aileen. A sign for all the universe that she was theirs. Kier wanted that, craved the sight of it, but the blue of her eyes was so striking. Could he bear for it to vanish?

Kier's hands flexed upon her hips. "Aileen..."

Her eyes dipped. He felt a flicker of need from her an instant before her mouth was on his.

Electricity crackled outward from that point of contact, sizzling beneath his skin, and stilled everything within him. His breath caught in his lungs, his heart ceased beating, and his mind stalled, unable to comprehend what was happening.

Our na'diya *is kissing me.*

She is kissing me.

Heat blazed in the wake of those electric arcs, suffusing Kier to his core. Her lips were soft, her breath sweet, and he tasted a hint of salt from her sweat. Her enticing floral scent enveloped him in a lustful cloud. Every inhalation filled him with her essence.

Aileen's hands delved into his hair, and she raked her nails across his scalp as she leaned further into the kiss. Her mouth caressed and nipped, soothed and teased, and he reciprocated eagerly. His tail brushed along her leg before coiling around it, securing her to him.

Their breaths mingled. The desire simmering at Kier's center intensified, consuming him from within. There were no words to describe what he felt—his elation was too immense.

Right. Everything about this kiss, this moment, was right.

Our na'diya...

Her lips parted. At the first flick of her tongue over his fang, Kier's tenuous grip on his restraint snapped, and instinct took over.

He cupped the back of her head, holding her firmly in place as he slanted his mouth and took a deeper taste. His tongue swept past Aileen's lips to dance with hers. A low, rumbling growl built in his chest. She was more delicious than he could ever have dreamed. She was divine.

And he wanted more.

His cock pulsed. It was trapped, aching, taunted by the heat radiating from her, tormented by the pressure of her sex nestled atop it.

He *needed* more.

Placing his other hand on the small of her back, Kier pressed her body down, and ground himself against her sex. Pleasure flared outward from his shaft, chased by echoes of Aileen's. He shuddered.

Aileen gasped, body tensing and fingers squeezing his hair. She raised her head, abruptly breaking the kiss, and looked down at him. Her cheeks were red, her lips kiss swollen and glistening, but her eyes...

They were flooded with guilt.

"I kissed Kayl," she blurted.

Kier's brow furrowed, and he blinked at her.

"Y-yesterday, before he showed me around. I kissed him."

A smirk tilted Kier's mouth. "I know, Aileen."

Now, her brow creased. "He told you?"

Kier tapped his temple, smirk widening.

Her gaze skittered away, but not quickly enough to hide her uncertainty. "Of course. But...you're not mad that I...that I kissed him first?"

Kier frowned. Her uncertainty was endearing, but it was also saddening. That she already felt so strongly about the twins only fed his joy, but he never wanted her to feel so conflicted, to feel so guilty. To feel so torn.

With as little conscious thought as it took to breathe or blink, Kier opened himself fully to Kayl. He sensed that this conversation was important for all three of them. Kayl also needed to know their mate's feelings so they could ensure, together, that she'd never have to face such again.

Kayl accepted the widening of their link without comment, immediately picking up on the weight of the situation and refusing to interrupt. In this, he and Kier were one. United and in harmony.

Kier smoothed his hand over Aileen's hair. "Why would I be mad? It always would have been one or the other first. Kissing us at the same time would be something of a challenge, wouldn't it?"

She laughed softly, looking back at him. "It would be." Her humor faded. "So you're not jealous? And you don't...think poorly of me?"

He uncoiled his tail from her leg, trailing it slowly up and down her outer thigh as he shifted his hand to her cheek. "I could never think poorly of you, Aileen. And there is no jealousy between me and my brother. We are your mates. Every moment spent with you belongs to all three of us. Every touch, every glance, every word, every kiss, is *ours*. You are ours. To resent you or Kayl for that kiss would be as foolish as resenting you for breathing the same air or looking upon the same sky."

Kier brushed his thumb over her cheek and smiled. "Once we are bonded, you will feel it too. You will feel us."

Aileen closed her eyes and turned her face into his palm, pressing her lips against it in a soft kiss. "I'm sorry. This is new to me. I know I said there were relationships similar to this where I came from, but growing up, all I saw was my mother and father. I...I couldn't imagine another coming between them."

"Ah, *na'diya*." He guided her head down until their foreheads were touching and closed his eyes also. "In a *daevalis*, no one is between the others. It is not two males vying for a female's attention. It is two males finding balance in their female. It is two males loving their female more than any one person ever could."

Kier's chest constricted, but he forced the next words out regardless. "That is what we hope for with you. If you allow us."

"I want it too," Aileen whispered. A soft laugh followed, and she lifted her head, prompting him to open his eyes. She met his gaze.

"It's crazy. We're strangers, and yet we're already talking about binding our lives together after a few days."

Kier pressed his palm to her chest, over her heart. "Strangers in body. In mind. But not in heart. Our souls recognize yours, Aileen, as though we were always meant be together."

She covered his hand with hers. "I feel it too. All my life, I've always felt like something was missing, some part of me. But when I saw you and Kayl, it was like that something clicked into place. My mind says this can't be real, that we're moving too fast, but...my heart says it's the two of you."

In answer to her words, Kier and Kayl's hearts sang in unison—because it was her, it had always been her, it would always be her.

Their *na'diya*.

TWENTY-TWO

Are you nearly done? We are going to shower, Kier pulsed as Kayl approached the last stop on his maintenance tour of the *Fang's* lower deck.

Kayl clenched his jaw at the memory that forced its way to the surface—Aileen, her bare skin blazing despite the icy shower she'd been pulled from, clinging to Kayl, grinding against him, wild with abandon as she marked him with her essence. Her arousal perfuming the air, her cries filling the room when she climaxed.

The feel of her body against his, fitting so perfectly even in their struggles, had been overwhelming. And that heat, the slickness of her essence, the tickle of her ragged breath on his flesh, and her little teeth clamping on his shoulder...

He'd been so close to tasting her, to joining her, but he hadn't. Thankfully, he hadn't. Because that hadn't been *her*. Her eyes had been devoid of all but unthinking desire, fueled by a drug.

Knowing that she hadn't been in control of herself, that she'd been lost to the rhapsody, Kayl had still been tempted. And in that temptation, he'd allowed his defenses to crumble. His instant of weakness had been more than enough—Aileen's lust had invaded him, the rhapsodic heat had flooded him, both compounding with his already powerful desire for her.

He'd lost himself utterly.

Since that night, his desire, shame, and arousal had not faded, all made worse by the truth of his soul—if not for Kier's intervention, Kayl would have succumbed to those overwhelming desires, no small part of which had been his own, and committed an unforgivable act.

He gritted his teeth and tamped the memory down. He wouldn't let it diminish his joy and wonderment at the words Kier and Aileen had exchanged only minutes ago.

My heart says it's the two of you.

The twins were the missing pieces of her soul. They were what she'd sought all her life without knowing, and she was the same for them. Even if Kayl couldn't fully let go of his frustration over their recent encounter with Vrykhan, even if he couldn't shed the anguish, sorrow, and fury he'd carried for so long, there was no denying that Aileen was meant for him and his brother.

I have but one more issue to check. But was it not decided that we are taking this slowly, Kier? Kayl asked, keeping his *aerys* stern—which proved surprisingly difficult considering their shared elation.

Yes, it was, Kier replied. *What is the issue?*

Kayl stopped in front of the maintenance compartment, disengaged the lock, and grasped the door handle.

His imagination presented a new image—Aileen standing in the shower with hot water cascading over her naked body, eyes hooded and dark with arousal as hands, the twins' hands, caressed her soft skin, washing away her sweat and teasing her thighs, her breasts, her belly, her sex.

His blood heated, rushing to his groin to make his cock ache. His hand would've trembled were it not clamped on the handle.

Kayl pulsed, *Neither of us could resist the temptation were we to—*

Kier's laughter echoed along their psychic link. His underlying arousal, hardly faded from only seconds ago, added a strained edge to the sound. *She is showering in her quarters, and myself in ours.*

Zor atkoshai, Kier, why did you not specify that sooner?

Kier laughed harder still. *Because I take petty satisfaction in your discomfort. But in all seriousness, Kayl, we are going to share a meal after we have cleaned up. You should join us in the mess when you are done.*

Kayl released a huff through his nostrils. *I will.*

The connection between the twins fell quiet, leaving Kayl to himself. Leaving him at the mercy of his feelings.

Now more than ever, he was glad to have Kier for his brother. Navigating his own emotions was hard enough for Kayl; navigating this burgeoning relationship with Aileen would've been impossible without Kier.

Kayl turned the handle, unfastening the airlocked latch, and tugged the door open. It revealed one of several compartments containing core components of the ship's various systems and machinery.

He secured the door in its fully open position, braced a hand on the doorframe, and leaned his head into the compartment, turning to look at the pipes and conduits overhead. His helmet display overlaid translucent blueprints in his vision, distinguishing the various parts and their purposes.

So much of what should've been there was damaged or destroyed. Frayed wires and broken pieces of metal and plastic dangled everywhere, and many of the neat, intricate lines in the blueprints were disrupted or outright severed.

He and Kier had both come down here many times since their escape from Eternal Paradise. The damage the *Fang* had sustained had seemed almost fitting to Kayl—a physical representation of everything having gone wrong. A metaphor for the hunt. For his life.

My heart says it's the two of you.

How wrong he'd been to think his life had been damaged, that everything had been ruined. Nothing had been destroyed; they were simply thrown off-course, forced onto a different path. A path which, perhaps, they should've been following all along.

But can I walk it? Do I deserve to?

Even after all that had happened, Kayl was still uncertain. But he wanted to try. He wanted to be worthy of Aileen.

Finally, he located the line that the latest diagnostic check had identified as ruptured. He switched on the helmet's holo scanner and slowly raked his gaze along the conduit, allowing the scanner to search for damage his naked eye could not detect. The line appeared surprisingly intact—likely the only reason the leak hadn't been detected by the computer sooner.

The scanner didn't pick up anything until it reached the spot where the conduit connected to the life support filtration system. A hair-width breach in the coupling was leaking infinitesimal amounts of oxygen.

Over hours, days, or weeks, even so tiny a leak would add up to something significant. That was a problem when the ship's computer had calculated that there'd be enough breathable oxygen to sustain its passengers through the journey to Omega IV and little farther. They'd have mere hours of air left by the time they reached their destination.

Left unattended, this leak would only shrink the room they had for error. It would only heighten the risk that they'd suffocate before reaching Omega IV.

He shifted his position, anchoring his legs and tail on the edges of the opening so he could pluck the fusion tool off his belt with his left hand and raise it to the coupling. He tightened his abdominal muscles to steady himself and activated the tool. Brilliant blue sparks illuminated the cramped space as the tool bonded the damaged metal on a molecular level, sealing the leak.

Bonding.

Strange how that word struck him differently now, when he would never have given it a second thought a few days ago.

A maelstrom of doubts swirled just beneath the surface of his mind, each fighting to claim his attention. What was he without the hunt? What could he and his brother truly offer a mate after they'd been...sullied, used, tainted? Would Aileen—

He cut off those thoughts and stuffed them into a tristeel vault which he sank deep in the recesses of his mind. When it had come to his goals, Kayl had never doubted himself—he'd always operated under the certainty that he and his twin would succeed. Failure was not acceptable.

It could be no different when it came to their mate. Torment and struggle lay ahead, but they would see the journey through, and the end result would be their completed *daevalis.*

But we did fail. We had Vrykhan right there, and we failed.

Failed to kill him...but succeeded in saving her. We made a choice. The right choice.

Now we just need to keep her alive.

As dependable as the *Fang* had been, the damage it had suffered was immense. There was no guarantee that the ship would reach its destination. So many of the variables were outside Kayl's control now. There was so much he could not change, so little he could do.

Frowning, he flicked off the fusion tool and reactivated the helmet scanner, checking for any traces of the leak. When the scanner detected nothing, he ran it again, just to be certain.

This ship will hold together. It will see us to where we must go.

We will land together, alive and well, and then we will decide how to continue forward. How to make our bond.

He would do everything he could to see Aileen and Kier through this. He would do the *best* he could. And as far as the *Fang* was currently concerned, he'd done everything possible.

Kayl slipped the fusion tool into its holder and shifted again, meaning to slide out of the compartment. But he halted when his gaze dropped.

The compartment floor was gone. He'd seen it during his prior inspections, but something about the sight now was particularly gripping. There was jagged, scorched metal all around the hole, some more dangling wires and bits of broken machinery, and then...the universe.

Countless stars twinkled amidst cloudy nebulas of varying colors and vibrancy, each an impossible distance away, each representing a vastness his eyes should never have been able to perceive, and between all that was impenetrable, endless darkness.

Only the *Fang's* invisible energy shields stood between Kayl and the unfathomable reaches of space, acting as a surrogate hull to contain the ship's atmosphere and maintain pressurization. He knew that, knew he was in no danger, and yet he could not help but look through that breach with something akin to dread gathering in his belly.

The twins had been traversing that void for years, tiny and alone. They were specks of dust in an infinite universe.

But now we have her.

And everything was different. The universe didn't seem quite so vast, didn't seem quite so cold, didn't seem quite so unforgiving.

"That will only be true so long as we keep her safe," he rasped. The closed helmet amplified his voice, making it sound harsher and less steady.

The twins would do everything in their power to protect Aileen, but would that be enough? Because somewhere out there, Kayl and Kier's oldest, truest enemy lurked amidst the darkness. Vrykhan had survived, and he would not forgive what had happened on Eternal Paradise.

The hunters had become the prey. How long did they have? Where could they go that would be safe? What could the twins do if Vrykhan turned the full strength of his pirate force toward destroying them and their *na'diya*?

There is no point in concerning yourself with such matters now, Kier pulsed.

Sighing, Kayl swung his gaze back up, reengaging the helmet scanner to check the other lines for unreported damage. *Ignoring the problems standing before us will not make them vanish, Kier.*

I am not so naïve as to believe they would, Kayl.

No, you are not. I am sorry to imply such, brother.

Do not apologize. Kier's *aerys* was soothing, gentle, empathetic. *My point is that we cannot currently change those things. For the time being, it is best to focus on the present. To focus on what we have here, now.*

Kayl frowned. He'd always been their stone, their shield, their unwavering foundation. He'd been the one to keep them in control, to keep them sane. But in all that, he'd lost sight of Kier's contributions to their survival.

If Kayl was their shelter, protecting them from the outside world, Kier was their fire, their food; he was the one who'd sustained them. Kier had tended the emotions Kayl walled off at his core, Kier had kept the twins from becoming just as terrible and merciless as the slavers they'd hunted.

Kier was the one who'd kept enough hope and compassion in their hearts for them to accept the mate they'd found against all odds.

I...will consider your words, Kayl pulsed.

Do not delay too long, Kier replied.

Kayl continued his inspection, slowly moving his head to allow the scanner access to different portions of the compartment. He willed his heart to slow, his mind to steady, and his soul to still, and he was not surprised to find that his willpower alone was not strong enough to achieve those aims.

There was a terran saying Kier had picked up, which the twins had debated about during one of their many long, quiet journeys through space—*live for the moment.*

For Kier, it was a relatively carefree philosophy. Exist in the present, and find joy, excitement, and thrills in it. But it had meant something very different to Kayl.

For Kayl, the moment—the *only* moment—had always been Vrykhan's death. That was the moment for which he'd yearned and raged, for which he'd fought and bled, for which he'd lived. Every second leading up to Vrykhan's death could only have been in service to that ultimate, defining moment.

Switching off the scanner, Kayl let out a long, slow breath that warmed his lips and nose as his mask reflected it.

During their argument over that simple terran saying, both twins had refused to budge. But even then, Kayl had known in his heart that his interpretation wasn't true to the intention of the phrase. That he had...twisted it to suit his own mindset rather than acknowledging that there were other ways to view the universe.

Kayl grasped the upper edge of the compartment opening in both hands and slipped back into the walkway, drawing in a shaky inhalation as his feet touched the floor. He closed the door and secured the latch. The flip of a switch engaged the mag lock, sealing the compartment fully.

Removing the fusion tool from its holder, he crouched and returned it to the toolbox. After he closed the lid, he picked the toolbox up, turned, and surveyed the corridor.

This part of the lower deck had always been tight, dark, and oddly lonely, and the damage wrought by the *Azkazor* had only enhanced that atmosphere. Several of the walkway lights were no longer functional, whole sections of the floor were uneven or warped, and half the mechanical compartments had red warning lights over their doors to indicate system errors.

Focus on what we have here, now.

And here, now, we have Aileen.

He strode forward, navigating the altered walkway with care where the damage was most evident. At the end of the walkway, he pressed the door control; there was a brief delay before the door opened as the ship ensured the pressurization and atmosphere were equalized between the lower deck and the rest of the ship.

Kayl stepped into the hold, placed the toolbox in its locker, and deactivated his armor. The segmented pieces retracted swiftly, exposing his face to the cool caress of the air. His mind responded with a ghostly sensation—tingling warmth across his lips. The distant echo of the kisses he'd shared with Aileen.

Heat blossomed at his core. Despite all his worries and guilt, his happiness endured. Aileen was theirs.

Theirs.

Perhaps he didn't truly know what that meant. Perhaps he didn't truly know what to do about it, or where to go with it. But it was real, it was right, and he would find a way forward. He would find a way to live for the moment.

He walked up the stairs and into the main corridor. Faint music echoed from one of the chambers at the far end of the hall. Kayl strode to the quarters he shared with Kier, where he paused, tilting his head to listen. Whether it was too low or Kier had actually activated a sound dampener in a rare display of courtesy, Kayl couldn't make out much more than the muted strumming of some sort of string instrument with a higher, reedier sound accompanying it.

Entering their shared quarters, Kayl changed out of his bodysuit, donning loose pants, a sleeveless undershirt, and a long, form-fitting tunic. Once dressed, he studied himself over in the mirror. He fixed a few rogue strands of his hair, straightened his clothing, and glanced down to adjust his belt; when he looked up again, he caught a smile on his own lips.

There was a heated, fluttering energy in his chest, threatening to spread through his limbs and make them shake. But it wasn't a surge of adrenaline, wasn't a growing sense of panic. It was eagerness.

He was about to spend more time with his brother and their mate. Was about to spend more time as a soon-to-be *daevalis*.

When was the last time he'd been eager to share anyone's company? When was the last time he'd had something positive to look forward to?

When was the last time he'd been happy?

The smile on his lips changed; it widened, but there was a glimmer of sorrow in his eyes. All those years hunting... Had they been wrong? Had they been wasted?

Could the twins have found Aileen sooner?

Letting out a huff, Kayl thrust those questions aside and exited the room, hurrying down the corridor toward the source of the music. Though Kier had told him to meet them in the mess, the sound was coming from the galley across the hall.

He stopped just before the galley's threshold to take in the sight in front of him.

Kier stood at the center of the room, grinning and holding one of Aileen's hands high as he twirled her about. Her long white skirt and loose red hair flared around her, and her delighted laughter rose over the music.

As Aileen spun, her gaze flicked toward Kayl. Her features brightened. She stumbled to a stop and turned toward him, smile widening, eyes sparkling. Kier's smile also widened as he looked at Kayl.

Something shifted in Kayl's chest. Those cold, hard walls he'd built around his heart fractured and crumbled. Warmth pervaded him—warmth generated by the caring, excited gazes of the two most important people in his life, warmth flowing from the center of his soul.

Their mate was waiting for him.

Are you coming in, brother, or do you plan to remain in the corridor? Kier pulsed.

Unable to keep his mouth from curling upward, Kayl crossed the threshold. The music enveloped him; it was simple, upbeat, and lively, harkening back to an era that certainly predated him and his companions. But that simplicity was oddly appealing, and the beat was just quick enough to urge his body to move. It seemed to have little in common with the songs the twins had heard Aileen perform in Eternal Paradise, and it suited her so much better.

"How is the *Fang*?" Aileen asked, cheeks flushed. "Will we survive another day?"

Kayl allowed his smile to form fully. "So long as Kier refrains from playing any more of his *music*, I believe the ship will hold."

Kier's eyebrows rose, and his eyes rounded. "I do not know if I have ever seen you smile like that, Kayl."

"As evidenced by your lack of a retort," Kayl said, expression softening. "I suppose I have not had reason to. Not for a long while."

"And you do now?" Aileen asked.

He met her gaze; within it, he saw all the things he felt but could not express, all the things for which he yearned but had not yet claimed, he saw everything he would ever want or need. "I do."

She grinned and reached out, brushing her fingertips over his chest. "Let's see if we can make you laugh next." Aileen grasped his hands and drew him closer. "Dance with us."

Though he did not resist her pull, he shook his head. "I am no dancer, Aileen."

"Everyone can dance, Sol'Kayl." She stepped in close to him, pressing her breasts to his chest, and spread their arms outward. Her fingers laced with his. "You just need to move your body."

She swayed her hips, brushing against him in time with the music. The friction between their bodies speared him with pleasure. Her response to his stifled growl was a knowing, mischievous grin before she pulled away, releasing one of his hands. She twirled and moved behind him. Kayl went after her, unwilling to let her out of his sight, unwilling to relinquish her.

She offered a hand to Kier.

With a laugh, Kier took her hand. Aileen tugged the two of them along. Kayl scarcely knew what his feet were doing; he followed her lead almost instinctually as the room spun around them and her lyrical laughter filled the air. Time again, she spun or twisted away, but her eyes always returned to the twins, shining brighter with each passing second.

The music quickened, tempo becoming a delightful frenzy. Before Kayl understood what was happening, Kier had grabbed his free hand, and the three of them were facing each other in a ring. Without need for a word, they danced in a circle, speeding to match the pace of the song.

Kayl's eyes flicked toward his brother. For an instant, a memory emerged from the depths of his mind—he and Kier as children, holding hands much like this as they spun each other in circles. He recalled the wind on his cheeks, ruffling his hair, recalled the long grass swishing around them, recalled the clouds spiraling overhead. And he recalled the fluttery feeling in his gut that was even now returning.

He, Kier, and Aileen moved faster still, so fast that everything else was a blur. All that remained were those bright eyes, those broad smiles, those warm hands.

The universe pulled on them from every direction, but they spun in defiance of it. What need had they for the universe? They were a *daevalis*; they were one another's universe.

All at once they fell, tumbling to the floor atop one another in a jumble of limbs. Aileen's shriek turned into giggles as she fell across the twins, her wild hair in Kayl's face. His cheeks ached from the smile he'd worn the whole time, and his heart outpaced the song's rhythm.

He laughed. The sound came straight from his belly, straight from his soul.

It is good to hear you laugh, brother, Kier pulsed.

It...is good to laugh, Kayl replied.

He felt light, free, content. Revenge had never been the thing that would complete Kayl and his brother. It was Aileen. Only Aileen.

Forever with Aileen.

Kayl brushed Aileen's hair from his face. Breath ragged, she smiled at him, and his heart stuttered.

For the first time since Vrykhan had come into his life, Kayl had happiness within his grasp. All he had to do was reach out and take it. All he had to do was allow himself to have it.

TWENTY-THREE

"No!" Aileen cried, struggling against the crushing grips of the guards who held her down. "I don't want this!"

Saduuk caught her chin, forced her to look at him, and leaned close. "You are mine, songbird. Caged with your little wings clipped."

Tears streamed down her cheeks and nausea curdled her belly. No matter how much she begged, no matter how much she pleaded, she couldn't stop the inevitable. Couldn't stop him. "Please, Saduuk. Please don't. I'm begging you. I can't...I can't go through that again. I can't."

Saduuk squeezed, claws biting into her cheeks as he pried her jaw open. His grin displayed a mouthful of sharp teeth as he raised the glowing vial of rhapsody. "This will make it all better. And you will sing, luring clients into my den of carnal delights."

He tipped her head back and emptied the vial into her mouth.

Cold liquid slid down her throat. She shivered, and choked, but she couldn't stop it. The instant that cold hit her stomach, it erupted in searing heat that spiraled through her body. The world blurred around her in a fiery haze. She lusted, she craved, she burned. Shadowy figures surrounded her. Leering and laughing, they reached for her with rough, demanding hands, they groped her flesh, they invaded her body.

Aileen screamed. All her terror, desperation, and shame went into it, and it tore apart her chest and throat, making her burn hotter still. But no sound came out. There was only pain, only pressure.

She was trapped, trapped inside her mind, where it didn't matter how much she screamed and cried, didn't matter how much she struggled and thrashed. She was trapped in a cage stronger than any metal.

Aileen's eyes snapped open as she was awoken by a sound—her own soft cry. Another quiet sob escaped her, and she turned, curling atop the bed and clenching the blanket to herself. Tears spilled from her eyes, running down her already wet cheeks.

They're gone. It's over. It's all over. They'll never hurt me again.

But she could not forget the unwanted touches she'd so often suffered in the maddening minutes before the heat would consume her. Nor could she stomach the horrifying oblivion that had followed each of those memories, those periods of utter nothingness that her imagination sought to fill with all the terrible things that might've happened to her while she'd been consumed by rhapsodic heat.

Sometimes, she'd wished the heat would take her faster, so she wouldn't have to experience *any* of it. But the evidence of what had occurred had always been there, waiting for her when she woke.

She sniffled and looked around the darkened room. It was quiet save for the low, ambient hum of the ship. She'd never felt so alone as she did in that moment. Aileen squeezed her eyes shut and tucked her chin down.

Go to them, Aileen.

Her breath hitched.

Kier and Kayl were asleep in their room just across the hall. The invisible tether that had snared her heart tugged insistently, coaxing her to follow it. To go to them.

What would it be like to wake up in their arms? Would their presence, their soft touches, and their reassuring words chase away her nightmares?

Her mother's voice spoke across all the years that separated them. *If you want something badly enough, Aileen, you have to reach out and grab it. Take a leap of faith. Because if you wait for the right moment, you'll just spend your entire life waiting.*

Aileen looked at the door. Kier and Kayl were so close, and yet, that distance seemed vast. But she'd decided. She wanted what they'd offered, wanted to be their mate.

She wanted them.

Wiping the moisture from her cheeks, Aileen sat up, threw off the covers, and slipped out of bed. The hem of her sleeveless nightshirt fell to brush her thighs. Cool air teased her bare legs as she padded to the door and pressed the control button. The light from the corridor spilled through, and she narrowed her eyes against the brightness as she stepped out. She didn't stop until she reached the twins' room.

Lifting a hand, she curled it into a loose fist.

The door slid open before her knuckles could make contact. Aileen started, her gaze darting up to meet that of the male on the other side of the doorway—Kier. His hair was even messier than usual, and he wore only a pair of those tight black shorts, but his eyes were alert, and his features were strained. The room beyond was dimly lit.

"Aileen," he breathed.

"I don't want to be—"

He stepped forward and wrapped his arms around her, drawing Aileen against his chest in an embrace that was at once crushing and soothing. "You are not alone, *na'diya*. Never alone."

Her tumultuous emotions swelled, making her chest burn and her throat constrict. She clutched at Kier, pressed her face to his velvety skin, and cried.

She was only distantly aware of Kier shifting his hold on her and lifting her off the floor. Her natural response was to hook her legs around his waist and cling to him even tighter, seeking solace in his warmth, his solidness, his presence. He and Kayl possessed all the strength necessary to behave just like the lewd, callous figures from her memories, but they did not.

They were as far from those terrifying shades as anyone could have been.

Kier sat down, settling her weight on his lap. One of his arms remained securely around her while he smoothed a hand over her hair and down her back in gentle, comforting strokes. His tail did the same to one of her legs.

She didn't think about how her nightshirt had ridden up and bunched around her hips, or how her sex was bearing down on Kier's pelvis with nothing but the thin materials of their undergarments as a barrier, or how her skin pebbled at the brush of his tail. Her attention was absorbed by his nearness, his embrace, by the way his touch assured her that she was not alone.

Once the storm inside her calmed, Aileen drew in a deep, shuddering breath. That sea and earth scent filled her senses. She raised her head and met Kier's gaze.

His short eyebrows were low over his mismatched eyes, which gleamed with both concern and fiery anger. Aileen turned her head and sought Kayl; he was pacing not far from the bed Kier had sat upon, his movements stiff and tail swinging erratically. His lips were drawn back to bare his fangs, and his fingers were bent like he was about to shred something with his claws.

As though sensing Aileen's gaze, he stopped and looked at her. His eyes, normally so shielded, blazed just as brightly as his brother's, brimming with fury, worry, and helplessness.

But as he stared at her, Kayl's expression softened. He stepped to Aileen and dropped onto his knees, lifting both hands to wipe the tears from her cheeks. "Do not cry, *na'diya*."

Kier continued the soothing motions of his hand and tail. "The dream has passed."

"We have you."

Aileen stilled, eyes wide as they flicked back and forth between the twins. "Y-you... What?"

"Whether dream or memory, it has passed," Kier replied. "You are with us. You are safe."

Kayl frowned. "We shared your dream again."

"That is why we were already awake."

All the heat drained from Aileen. How could she have forgotten that they'd shared her dream the other night? How could she have forgotten the blossoming strength of their connection? And for them to have shared *this* dream, to have witnessed that memory, to have experienced it...

Kayl swept his thumbs over her cheeks, catching the freshly falling tears. His features tightened. "We feel your distress, Aileen. And we..." He glanced at his brother, and his frown deepened. "We understand. We understand what you have suffered. We...have suffered the same."

"We are meant to share your burdens. You are not meant to hurt alone," Kier said as he combed his claws through her hair.

Aileen's lower lip trembled, but she forced it to still. Reaching out, she cupped Kayl's cheek with one hand, and Kier's with the other. Neither of them looked away from her, and she could not look away from them. There were so many emotions swirling in the depths of their eyes that she could not even begin to name them all, but it was their compassion, their loneliness, and their hopeful longing that shone brightest.

She saw herself reflected in their eyes, saw her desires. She saw her need for a true connection.

"Can I stay with you tonight?" Aileen asked softly.

That quickly, shock superseded the other emotions on their faces. Their short eyebrows shot up, their mismatched eyes rounded, and their lips parted.

"Yes," they said in unison.

Kier smiled. "This night—"

"And any other." Kayl tucked Aileen's hair behind her ear.

Eyes misting anew, she smiled. "Every night."

The twins closed their eyes, faces easing with relief. They leaned close to Aileen, tipping their foreheads against hers, and said together, "As it was meant to be."

Aileen had been happy as a child. Happy and *loved*. But there had always been something missing, there'd always been a hollow in her chest, in her soul...

What she felt right now wasn't that empty space being filled, but the pieces were aligning, and she knew they would fit. This was the closest she'd ever been to putting them in place.

Kayl withdrew his hands, rose, and walked across the room to the other bed. Kier also stood up, keeping hold of Aileen until he was fully upright. With great gentleness, he guided her legs down from his waist and settled her on her feet.

He ran his palms down her arms. "Give us a moment."

Aileen nodded and watched as the twins dragged their mattresses off their beds, laid them on the floor at the center of the room, and pushed them together. Kayl then opened a compartment built into the wall and pulled out an extra blanket and two more pillows, the former of which he draped over the mattresses to cover the seam between them.

The makeshift bed took up most of the floor, creating a much larger sleeping space—a space for all three of them.

Kayl knelt upon the bed and held a hand to her. "Come, *na'diya*."

Aileen placed her hand in his, and he curled his fingers around it, helping her step across the mattresses and settle down in the center of them. Releasing his hand, she grasped a blanket, slipped her legs beneath it, and drew it up her body as she lay down.

Kier dimmed the lights further and strode over.

He lowered himself on Aileen's right while Kayl settled on her left, each lifting her blanket to slide their bodies beneath. They lay on their sides, facing her, and scooted close, cradling their heads on the crooks of their elbows as each draped an arm over her midsection. Kier's tail coiled around one of her legs, Kayl's the other.

Aileen settled her hands on their arms. Their mingled scents and delectable body heat enveloped her. She sank into the mattress, and she would've been content to melt right there, for her last sensation to be that of Kier and Kayl holding her in the dark.

For a dreadful instant, she feared her nightmare would return, that it would plunge her into terror and warp the twins in her mind's eye, turning them into shadowy, faceless figures with cruel hands and leering grins. She feared she'd be dragged down by those horrid shades, suffocated by them.

But all she felt was...peacefulness.

"You are safe, Aileen." Kier's voice was low and deep as he stroked her belly with his thumb.

"We have you," Kayl rumbled, brushing the sensitive flesh on the inside of her knee with the end of his tail.

In all her life, she'd never felt so protected. So...wanted. After her parents died, she'd traveled to so many places, had crossed the universe in search of whatever she was missing, in search of the place where she belonged.

She'd finally found it. Right here, nestled between Kier and Kayl, this was her spot. This was where she belonged. This was where she *fit*.

Aileen closed her eyes and let herself feel the twins, smell them, hear them—their soft breaths, the rasp of their skin moving against her clothing, of their fingers and tails caressing her. Though she longed to drift to sleep, to let different, more...pleasurable dreams fill her head, something kept her mind in motion, holding her weariness at bay.

We understand. We understand what you have suffered. We...have suffered the same.

Aileen's heart clenched. Surely they hadn't...

She opened her eyes and stared up into the darkness. "You said you were meant to share my burdens."

"We are," Kier replied.

"Then I'm meant to share yours too." She curled her fingers around their forearms, squeezed gently, and asked a question that filled her with dread. "What did you mean when you said the two of you had suffered the same as me, Kayl?"

Their soothing ministrations faltered, and each twin let out a long, slow breath.

Aileen frowned, fingers twitching, throat tight. "If you don't want to talk about it, I understand. I don't mean to dredge up painful memories. I should know more than anyone what that feels like. I just... I want you to know that I'm here for both of you too, just like you've been here for me. And I want to know you. The good and bad, the pleasant and unpleasant... Everything."

The twins were silent and still but for their racing pulses, which Aileen felt through every place where their bodies touched hers.

Oh God, why had she asked? Of all the ways to spoil the moment, she'd picked the most insensitive. Instead of just lying here with them in peace and quiet, instead of enjoying the contentment they'd found, she'd decided to ask *that*.

Tears stung her eyes. "I'm sorry. Forget I asked. You don't owe me anything, especially something so—"

Kier lifted his arm from her and pressed a finger to her lips. "We have told only one person what happened to us, Aileen, in all our lives."

"And even he did not receive the full story," Kayl said, voice uncharacteristically strained.

"Not nearly. But you, Aileen..." Kier sighed and stroked her lips before brushing his knuckles along her cheek. "You are our *na'diya*. We do not wish to lay our sorrow and pain upon you."

Kayl moved his hand up, cupped her opposite cheek with his warm, callused palm, and turned her face toward him. His eyes— mere suggestions of magenta and blue in the gloom—met hers. "Yet neither do we wish to keep anything from you."

She covered their hands with her own, holding them more firmly to her face. "The way you explained a *daevalis*... Isn't all your sorrow and pain mine too? And all your joy, and all your hopes? Your everything?"

Though she could not see either of the twins well enough to know for certain, she swore she felt them smile—she felt it through a blooming warmth in her chest.

"Ah, *na'diya*. Would that we had found you sooner," Kier said. "All three of us might have been spared some suffering."

"My maw always used to say that those long, dark nights always made the sun seem so much brighter in comparison," Aileen said, fighting back fresh tears. "That the hardships and struggles make all the good times that much sweeter."

"And we three are no strangers to hardship," said Kayl.

The twins shifted closer to her, returning their arms to her middle and resuming their leisurely stroking. Aileen folded her hands over their arms again and closed her eyes.

"Our village was called Itheria," Kier began. "It was beautiful. Peaceful. So far removed from the rest of the universe, and yet... It felt like an entire universe unto itself. It was..."

"Full of wonder," Kayl said.

"Yes. Full of wonder. My brother told you of Vrykhan's attack." Kier's fingers curled slightly, his claws pricking Aileen's belly through her nightshirt.

"He did," she replied softly. "He told me about your parents, and that you were taken."

"We were dragged to the pirates' dropships, along with many of the youths from our village. Children with whom we had played, learned, and grown. With whom we had laughed. Those ships brought us to the *Azkazor*, Vrykhan's flagship, which had been in orbit over Tilara.

"With the blood of our parents still wet on their hands, the pirates put collars on our necks and prodded us into pens in the cargo hold."

The twins' tails tightened around her legs, and Aileen felt a strange sensation around her neck—a phantom chill, a ghostly weight —that made her skin break into goose bumps. She knew what it was like to be forced to wear one of those collars. She'd felt its metal against her flesh every second of every day, had suffered its terrible, electric jolts. It didn't matter how pretty the thing had looked when its only purpose was enslavement.

Kayl resumed where his brother had left off. "We were given buckets in which to relieve ourselves and were forced to share scraps of food and brackish water between hundreds of us. Our struggles and eventual conflicts provided our captors great amusement."

Kier caught the fabric of Aileen's shirt between finger and thumb and plucked at it absently. "Despite their cruelty, they did not let any of us die. That made them only crueler in my eyes. To willfully inflict such suffering on anyone, especially children..."

"They brought us to a place called Caldorius," Kayl said. "A planet where all manner of illicit goods are bought and sold under the watch of the universe's most powerful crime syndicates. The males were kept in pairs as we were brought to the auction blocks."

"That we were not separated is the only blessing in all of this." Kier's voice was raw. "The females from our village...they were torn away from their siblings. They were torn away from all they had left. They were made more alone than Kayl or I can ever imagine, and then they were sold."

"We were lined up and brought forward to be displayed for sale one pair at a time," Kayl continued. He let out a quiet, heavy breath that warmed Aileen's ear. "We saw Vrykhan out there, watching with a grin on his face as his *merchandise* was sold to the highest bidders. Unmated daevahs...a valuable commodity on Caldorius."

"We understood little of what was happening at the time," said Kier. "We knew only fear, grief. Pain. We were purchased and ushered away, bewildered. They cleaned us, clothed us, fed us. And fools that we were, we thought it meant our ordeal was over. That we had been saved."

Aileen's eyes stung, and her aching heart pulsed with sorrow. "You weren't fools. You were *children*. Children who didn't deserve to go through any of that."

"No one deserves to go through that," Kayl replied, "and yet so many do. So, so many."

Kier curled his hand around Aileen's hip. Though it still thrummed with tension, his claws did not press into her flesh again. "They brought us to another ship, this one full of well-dressed and well-spoken staff instead of leering pirates. They told us nothing of where we were going or who they were, but they began instructing us immediately after takeoff."

Kayl shifted a leg up, his knee pressing against Aileen's lower thigh. "They taught us to serve. We complied."

"What else could we have done?" Kier asked. "We were glad to be clean, to be warm, to have our bellies filled. And it provided a distraction. It gave us something to focus on apart from the chasm that had been torn in our lives.

"Our journey ended on a planet called Helviorus. We disembarked the ship on a private landing pad and were led into an opulent mansion, larger than any home we could ever have imagined in every way."

A low growl sounded in Kayl's chest. "Everything there was pristine. Perfect. Polished and gleaming, not a speck of dust out of place. Everything was…"

"Cold," Kier said. "Everything was cold. And…oddly large. To us, Vrykhan had been a giant. A terrible creature of nightmare."

"And our owner would have towered over Vrykhan. She was a raishen named Lystai."

Aileen had seen members of larger species from time to time on Eternal Paradise. But nothing that would have *towered* over Vrykhan. She couldn't imagine how that must've felt to two children who had lost everything they'd known, who'd already felt so small.

"A raishen? I…I don't think I've heard of them," she said.

"They tend toward isolationism," Kayl explained. "They believe themselves superior, and therefore above most other species. They often conduct affairs across the universe through non-raishen agents."

"They are shaped more or less like you or I," Kier said. "Two arms, two legs, a head. Hands and feet. But they are somewhat larger."

"Lystai stood four meters tall."

Aileen's eyes shot open—*wide* open. Her mouth was suddenly dry, her heart beating faster. "Four meters?"

"Yes," Kier replied. "When we were first brought to her manor as children, we scarcely stood taller than her knees. And she looked upon us as lesser lifeforms. As pitiful creatures scuttling at her feet."

"She was not kind," said Kayl, "though she often proselytized her kindness.

"She was not. The closest she came was in the rare relaxation of her cruelty, which is not the same as kindness." Kier's next exhalation came out in a growl. "We acted as her personal servants. As her exotic pets. As her…*toys*. She kept us near when she had guests, showing how handsome and well-trained we were. Any mistakes we made, however slight, were harshly punished. Especially if she believed our error could affect her social status in any way."

Tension radiated from both twins, but Kayl seemed particularly stiff. "As we grew, her interest in us shifted."

"No, Kayl. Her interest did not shift. We merely matured into it."

Aileen's stomach churned, and bile threatened to rise in her throat. The sorrow that already had her heart caught in a viselike grip squeezed impossibly tighter.

No, please. Don't let that have happened to them...

The twins were silent, but anguish radiated from them like a song heard from a great distance; sad, heart-wrenching, haunting. Aileen felt its notes in her soul.

Kayl broke the silence. "We were instructed in different matters. Taught to please her in different ways. Physical ways." His next words sounded as though they were spoken through clenched teeth. "But she was displeased because we were not capable of reacting to her satisfaction."

"We daevahs do not experience arousal with anyone other than our mates," Kier said softly. "Whether a biological matter or a spiritual one, it is simply how we work. We may recognize beauty and appeal elsewhere, but sex and attraction function only within a *daevalis*."

Though her mouth was dry, and the words were difficult to get out, Aileen asked, "Is that why they said your parents were of no value to them?"

"In part. But it has more to do with the workings of a *daevalis*. Together, mated daevahs cannot be broken. They are strong, they flourish, they endure. But remove any piece of the *daevalis*, sever any thread..."

Kayl tipped his face closer to Aileen. His nose brushed her cheek, and his breath was warm on her neck. "They wither away."

Pressure gathered behind her eyes, and she closed them, turning her head toward Kayl. She knew the twins were thinking of their parents. Of their mother being killed right in front of her mates, her children, of the agony their fathers had felt when she'd been taken from them. Aileen felt the echoes of their pain in her heart.

"I'm so sorry," she whispered.

Kier pressed his face to Aileen's hair and breathed deep. "Our parents are many years gone. But were they here... There is such joy in your heart, Aileen. Even if it has been battered by tragedy and suffering, it is there, shining like a beacon. Whenever you shed your troubles and let that joy out, when you laugh, when you dance, there is nothing more beautiful in this universe."

"Our parents would have adored you," Kayl said.

Aileen smiled, letting out a short laugh. "Even though I am human?"

"Why would that ever make a difference?" Kier's arm slipped around her more firmly. "You are ours."

Warmth flooded her chest, and she stroked their arms. "You don't have to tell me more if you don't want to."

"Ah, *na'diya*. We want to share everything with you, just as you said."

Aileen pressed her lips together and nodded.

"We were drugged," Kayl said. "Drugged to induce arousal, so she could use our bodies fully. So she could...*reward* us as she saw fit."

Aileen squeezed her eyes shut and tightened her hold on the twins.

Kier released a ragged breath. "And no matter how we railed against what was happening, no matter how wrong it felt, we complied. We had no choice. If one of us resisted, she would punish the other. If we both resisted... It mattered little. She always got what she wanted in the end, whether we fought or not.

"Every waking moment, we felt as though we were betraying our mate, as though we were wronging a female we had not yet met. We felt like we were violating something sacred."

"I felt the same," Aileen whispered. "Every time they touched me, every time they... It was wrong. So, so wrong. It was always meant to be you. I was always meant to be yours."

The twins moved closer still; Kier pressed his lips to the back of her head, Kayl pressed his to her shoulder, and the heat around and within Aileen intensified for the brief time their mouths were on her. When they withdrew, they said, "You are ours, *na'diya*."

"And we are yours," Kier rasped.

Aileen and the twins had known each other for mere days, but in her heart, it felt as though she had known them forever. Her soul had known them since before the dawn of the universe.

She turned her face toward the ceiling again; the twins' breaths tickled her ears and flowed teasingly along the sides of her neck. She didn't want to ruin this moment, didn't want to drag their minds back into darkness. But where else could they discuss such things if not here, tucked under a blanket together, sharing this warmth, this closeness, this security? This was the best place. The safest place.

"How did you escape?" she asked.

"The raishens ruled Helviorus," replied Kayl. "Their size, wealth, and technology afforded them all the advantages, but they were greatly outnumbered by their slaves. And despite what they believed, they were not invulnerable."

Kier angled his head down, brushing his cheek against Aileen's shoulder as he combed his fingers through her hair. "We were with Lystai for many years. Toward the end of that time, we began hearing rumors. Whispers of slaves turning on their masters. Of revolt. We knew better than to hope, but we could not help doing so. We were not warriors. We had resisted her, but we had never been violent. And yet we had the memory, forever emblazoned in our souls, of our fathers making their desperate attempt to avenge our mother...and we had rage."

"It had been planted deep within us," Kayl said, "taking root over the years. Long overshadowed by grief and fear."

"But it had grown strong. So, so strong." Kier's tail tensed around Aileen's leg. "We knew that we needed to use it. That it was our only chance."

Kayl moved his hand, splaying his long fingers across Aileen's stomach. The faintest of tremors ran through them, and Aileen could deny neither the fluttering in her belly nor the spark of heat his touch ignited. His voice was devoid of emotion as he said, "Death was all but certain."

"Yet what point was there to life if all we had was suffering and subservience? We were but two of many slaves in her household, but two of many who had been forced to satisfy her appetites. As long as she lived, none of us would know peace, none of us would know joy."

"Fortunately," Kayl said, "we were not the only ones to have heard the whispers. We were not the only ones to find hope in the stories, or the only ones to yearn for freedom. Soon, the liberated slave armies had pushed into the surrounding city. The fight for freedom was happening all around us, and the raishen were scared."

"So, we staged a revolt of our own," Kier continued. "Lystai had paid staff and security, and some slaves remained loyal to her despite what she had done to all of us. But we...we silenced those who would have given our cause away and confronted our master. It took a score of us to wrestle her to the floor. Kayl and I stood at her head. We saw the fury in her eyes, the fear. She directed it all at us."

"We did not hesitate." Now there was something more in Kayl's tone, something primal, creating a rough, raw edge.

Kier's voice was low, strained. "We do not regret what we did. We do not feel remorse for her, do not feel pity. We felt..."

"Satisfaction," they both said.

Aileen's chest constricted with the torrent of emotion emanating from the daevahs—emotion only enhanced by her empathy.

"Lystai's blood was still warm when the liberated armies breached the manor," said Kayl. "They congratulated us, welcomed us into their fold, and ushered us out into the chaos on the streets."

Kier's tail crept a little higher on her leg, but its hold relaxed. "We recall little of the few days that followed. We were...numb. It was not until the liberated armies withdrew from the city that we understood what was happening, what we were involved in."

"We had become part of the revolt. We had become soldiers," Kayl continued. "There was little time for training. We were forced to learn in the field, and we employed every means available to overcome our stronger, better equipped foes. To kill them."

Kier shook his head. "The details do not matter. It was war, though to many of the raishen, we must have amounted to little more than an infestation of vermin to be exterminated. Many people died, most of them on our side. We held for months, and every day saw suffering, but it was a different sort of suffering. We were exhausted, near starving, often sheltering in filth and ruins, but we were *free*.

"And all the rage we carried... How else was it to get out? What else was it good for? We were using it to fight for something worthwhile. To give hope to others. And we took well to combat. To... killing. Within a short while, we were counted amongst the best warriors the liberated armies had at their disposal."

A low, sorrowful sound rumbled from Kayl. "But the revolt was doomed from the start. It had spread so quickly at first, catching the raishen off guard, but once they organized, our cause was doomed. So, some of our leaders changed their goal. We were not to overthrow the raishen, but to evacuate as many freed slaves as we could from Helviorus."

"It was no simple undertaking," Kier said. "The skies were controlled by our enemies, as was the surrounding star system. We turned to smugglers, most of whom were raishen themselves, to help. There was no other way. Many of them kept their word and transported our comrades off the planet."

Kayl sighed and curled a finger, trailing a claw down her belly. "Many more did not. They turned in their would-be passengers for bounties, or immediately betrayed their contacts in the liberated armies the instant they faced any sort of scrutiny from their rulers."

"Thousands of lives were saved by those smugglers. Thousands more were lost, as our dealings with them revealed the location of our final stronghold on Helviorus. Kayl and I were aboard the last ship to depart. We watched through the holo screens as the raishen military obliterated that stronghold with orbital strikes. They destroyed hundreds of square kilometers of their own planet just to ensure the revolt was annihilated."

Their story—their lingering pain, trauma, and anger—made perfect sense to Aileen. The twins had left that planet long ago, but it remained with them inside, in their hearts and minds. It was one of many burdens they'd silently carried. And though their fight in that slave revolt had ended, their fight against slavery had never stopped.

Aileen mourned for the loss of the gentle souls her mates had once been, mourned for the peaceful, contented lives they should have led, but at the same time she was fiercely proud of them. They'd had the courage to fight, even in the face of terror and hardship, and had continued fighting for all this time.

"We eventually found our way back to a daevah planet," Kier said. "It was not our homeworld, but it was our people. Yet it did not feel that way. They welcomed us, treated us with compassion and caring, but we did not feel as though we belonged. Our own culture seemed strange to us. They told us to rest, to recover..."

Kayl let out a harsh, heavy breath. "But we could not. We could not bear to remain idle knowing what was happening in the universe. Knowing that we had the skills to make some difference, however small. We could not rest knowing Vrykhan could still be out there. But we did not know what to do, or how to do it."

"And the more time we spent idle, the more we thought about

Vrykhan. That led us to check what records were available to us, where we found reports of him conducting raids as recently as a few months before." Kier grunted, and his teeth clicked together in a decidedly agitated sound. "That anger we'd held rekindled. He was alive, and he was still doing harm."

"We could not accept that," Kayl growled.

Aileen frowned, the ache in her chest only deepening. "So it became your mission to kill him. Your purpose."

"Yes. We told ourselves it was to enact justice, to protect others. And it was. But more than that, it was revenge."

"To answer blood with blood," intoned Kier. "Lystai and the raishen were vile, but it all began with Vrykhan. It would end with him also. That was our vow to ourselves. We did what we could to gather resources, but it was difficult."

"Our people had provided for us," Kayl said. "Food, shelter, clothing, comfort. But we needed guns. We needed a ship. And we needed information."

Kier continued, "So, we did what had been done on Helviorus. We went to the unsavory groups, the smugglers, the criminals, to find what we needed." Kier laughed, the sound a mixture of sorrow and amusement. "What fools we were. We knew little of such matters. Our attempts were easily discovered, and we were apprehended by law enforcement.

"While we were being held, we received visitors. They introduced themselves as part of a military organization they refused to name, and said they were familiar with our story...and our skills. They lamented the inability of intergalactic governments to truly combat piracy and slavers due to territorial disputes, conflicting jurisdictions, and the vast amount of space to be covered."

"I told them to make their point or leave," Kayl said.

Aileen chuckled, lips curling into a smile despite everything.

Of course he did.

"And they did make their point," Kier continued. "Our people could not reliably dispatch forces against the likes of Vrykhan because the instant they chased him out of our own territory, our military was in violation of intergalactic treaties. But many governments had placed bounties upon slavers and pirates, enabling independent actors to hunt such criminals almost anywhere to deliver justice."

Kayl's palm came to rest on her pelvis, the pads of his fingers a breath away from the top of Aileen's sex; her breath hitched. He said, "They offered to supply us with the best military equipment available, including weapons and a ship, and ensured we had no want for credits in exchange for hunting slavers."

"Of course, they made certain that we understood we were not working for them in any way," added Kier. "In the case of any issues with law enforcement or outside governments, the daevah military would deny any ties to us. We were free to go where we needed because we would not be acting in any official capacity on behalf of our people."

"And we did not care about any of that," Kayl said. "Our purpose was clear, and they provided the equipment to act upon it."

"We were sullied." Kier smoothed his hand up Aileen's chest, guiding it between her breasts, and settled his palm over her heart. "We had been forced to betray our mate before ever meeting her. While we had imagined having quiet lives in a *daevalis* as children, we were no longer worthy of such an existence. It was no longer within our reach."

"We forsook our fate to chase another," Kayl rasped. His fingers flexed and pricked her with his claws, making her shiver. "We forsook you."

"Yet every day we felt the void that you were meant to fill. Every day, without ever realizing it"—Kier moved his mouth close to her ear, voice becoming low, husky—"we yearned for you, Aileen."

Her heart sped, beating as swift as a hummingbird's wings, and heat pooled between her thighs. Was it wrong to feel this way after what they'd told her? For her body to grow excited by their touch, their words?

She caught hold of their chins and turned their faces toward hers. "What happened to you wasn't your fault any more than what happened to me was mine. We had no control. It was taken from us." She stroked their jaws with her thumbs and gazed into their eyes. Even in the dark, she could see some of that color, that depth, that vulnerability. That gleam of yearning. "We are not sullied, or tainted, or unworthy. Each of us is exactly what the others need."

"Aileen," Kier rasped, shifting as though to prop himself up. His hand moved down from her heart to the swell of her breast, palm rasping over her nipple. A jolt of pleasure coursed through her, racing straight to her core.

Aileen gasped. Kier stilled, lips parting. His fingers curled to cup her breast, and his breath caught, eyes wide. Kayl's expression was exactly the same.

Kier's lips twitched like he was about to speak, but no sound emerged. Clamping his mouth shut with jaw muscles bulging, he began to pull his hand away, and Kayl did the same, claws grazing her pelvis.

Her body cried out—it could not bear the absence of their touch, could not bear to have that contact severed, that pleasure ended. She could not stand distance between them, no matter how small.

Stomach fluttering, Aileen released their chins and swiftly covered their hands with her own, pinning them in place. "No."

Their brows fell, and their bodies tensed.

"No," she repeated, softer than before. She ran her tongue over her lips and exhaled. Fire roared inside her, hungry, lustful, consuming. "I... Our choices were taken from us in the past, and we all suffered for it. But we can make our own choices now. And I want this. This moment with you. I want you to touch me, I want you to learn me. I want *you*."

Aileen looked Kier in the eyes and held his gaze pointedly before doing the same with Kayl. "I want both of you. That's my choice. What do you want?"

TWENTY-FOUR

THE TWINS' chests swelled with simultaneous inhalations as they stared at her, eyes ablaze. They tipped their heads close, nuzzling her hair and cheeks, their breath was hot against her skin as they rasped, "You, *na'diya*."

Kier squeezed her breast, pressing his palm firmly down on her nipple. "We want you."

Kayl teased the flesh just above Aileen's sex with his claws. "Only you."

Their voices were raw and husky, thick with desire, heat, and yearning, but there was more beneath all that. So much more—a hint of pain, yes, but also hope and promise. She knew they didn't just mean here and now.

When the twins said they wanted her, they meant it in *all* possible ways, in this moment and every other.

A heavy ache permeated her core, and her skin warmed, tingling in the places it touched the twins. Restless energy buzzed within her. All she had to do was arch her back, and her nipple would rub against Kier's rough palm; all she had to do was tilt her hips, and Kayl's fingers would glide over her cunt.

But she wouldn't. Not after everything they'd just told her. She would leave this up to the twins, would allow them control.

And it was her choice to do so. It was control not taken, but freely given. Though she'd known Kier and Kayl for only a few days, she trusted them with every bit of her being—heart, body, and soul.

Aileen turned her head, skimming her lips across Kier's brow. "Then you can have me. In any way you desire."

Kayl lowered his face to her neck, brushing his mouth over her flesh, and breathed deep. He growled; Aileen felt his chest vibrate against her arm, and the sensation only heightened her need. She lifted her chin, allowing him more access as her eyelids fluttered shut.

But as soon as her eyes were closed, those imposing, malicious shadows pressed in all around the edges of her consciousness. Aileen tensed, breaths quickening, pulse raising.

No. No, not now. Not with them.

Warm lips pressed to her temple before Kier's voice beckoned her, chasing away those shadows. "Stay with us, Aileen. There is no light or darkness, no future or past. Only this moment."

"Only you and us," Kayl rumbled. One of his fangs grazed her neck, and Aileen's lips parted with a shaky exhalation as her core clenched.

Kier pushed himself up. His free hand slid beneath Aileen's head, cradling it, while his other hand lifted from her chest to sweep the hair out of her face. "Open your eyes."

She obeyed, and found herself looking up at his face, which was mere centimeters from her own. His eyes, half-lidded and gleaming, were focused on her—solely on her. And as she held his gaze, the shadows retreated. Her heart did not slow, but its rapid pace was no longer due to fear.

"All that we have shared," he purred, "and all that we will share is beautiful, *na'diya*. Nothing will taint our time with you. Never." He lowered his head and settled his mouth over hers. Though he hadn't moved with speed or aggression, the press of his lips was as confident, firm, and demanding as it was soothing.

Aileen opened to him, releasing a sigh that he breathed in and returned to her. Her eyelids fell shut again, but the darkness behind them was no longer filled with shadows—it was tinged blue and magenta. She curled her arm around Kier, fingers delving into his hair. There was a hunger buried in his kiss that belied his outward calm.

While Kier kissed Aileen, Kayl traced a burning path down her neck to her shoulder, his lips and fangs teasing her, taunting her, thrilling her.

The blanket draped over Aileen was suddenly whipped away, baring her to the cool air and making her even more sensitive to every little touch from the twins. Kayl shifted lower, extending that erotic trail along her arm as he curled a hand around her hip.

Kier grazed the tips of his claws down her throat. Shivers of delight coursed through her. Her nipples hardened further, and the hollow ache in her core intensified. When his fingers reached the collar of her nightshirt, they brushed back and forth along the fabric's edge, each pass building her excitement higher.

Kayl took hold of her leg and guided it up. He slid beneath it smoothly, positioning himself between Aileen's thighs. Hands spanning her hips, he hooked his fingers around her panties, lifted her backside off the mattress, and drew the garment down.

The first whisper of air against her naked sex was like a kiss itself. Aileen broke away from Kier's mouth to look at Kayl. He was kneeling before her, his body silhouetted by the dim baseboard lights, with hints of color gleaming in his eyes. His gaze did not leave hers for even an instant as he dragged her panties along her legs.

Kier's mouth fell to her neck, and his hand slid lower, gliding over her breast and her budded nipple. She shuddered again, releasing a soft moan as her pleasure and anticipation leapt. But his hand did not pause there; it continued down her belly, stopping only to grasp the fabric of her nightshirt.

His knuckles brushed over her abdomen as he pulled the nightshirt up, hand moving with the same deliberate, tantalizing slowness as Kayl's. The twins' touches sparked tingles across her skin.

Aileen raised her arms, assisting Kier while he propped himself up and removed her shirt. Her hair fell around her head and shoulders just as Kayl slipped her panties off her feet and tossed them away. She lowered her arms on either side of her head.

Curling his fingers around her inner thighs, Kayl pressed Aileen's knees to the mattress, spreading her wide open.

Everything fell still and silent. Aileen lay there, naked and vulnerable. As much as she wanted this, wanted the twins, as much as she craved more of their touch, she could not quiet the whispers in the back of her mind.

Did they like what they saw? Did they find her human body strange, or unappealing?

Did they find her...wrong?

Aileen had never much cared what others thought of her, but when it came to Kier and Kayl, it mattered. It mattered *so* much. She curled her fingers, digging her nails into her palms, and caught her bottom lip between her teeth. Her thighs trembled; they attempted to close of their own accord, but Kayl held them firmly in place.

"No," he said with the same vehemence Aileen had used when she'd told them not to pull away earlier. His expression was fierce, primal, that of a predator staring at prey. "Let us look upon our mate."

Kier settled his hand upon her belly, splaying his fingers. "Let us look upon what we have been gifted."

The air seemed electrified as the twins' fiery gazes raked over her. As surely as she felt their physical touches, she felt their eyes on her, heating her skin bit by bit, awakening her to subtle new sensations, to new pleasures. Warmth coursed through Aileen, suffusing her body, pooling in her core.

The way they looked upon her during those breathless moments was more intimate than any touch she'd ever received, than any words that could ever have been spoken. Kier and Kayl were looking at her as though she were everything, and her doubts and insecurities withered beneath their intense stares.

"Never have I gazed upon such beauty," Kayl said, voice low, thick, as his claws pressed on the flesh of her thighs.

"I never imagined it possible," Kier said in the same tone, hand gliding toward her hip.

Together, they snarled, "And she is *ours*."

Aileen's reaction to their rough declaration was swift and powerful; her pulse skittered, her skin thrummed, and her belly clenched as arousal swallowed her.

"All ours." Kier gently smoothed his hand over the scar on Aileen's side.

Kayl slid his hands along her inner thighs. "Every part."

. Kier cradled her breast in his palm. He caressed the giving flesh teasingly at first, but his touch grew steadily firmer. "Our *na'diya* is so soft."

Aileen turned her face toward him, but his eyes, dark with

possessiveness, were fixed on her body. He captured her nipple between his thumb and forefinger and pinched. She started with a gasp as a rush of excitement swept through her.

Kayl leaned closer, nostrils and nose slits flaring with a deep, ragged inhalation. "And she smells so sweet."

Aileen blushed, fixing her attention upon Kayl even as Kier's continued ministrations built her desire higher and higher.

Hunger glinted within Kayl's eyes as he dipped his head farther. He trailed the back of a finger up along her wet folds. When his knuckle brushed her clit, pleasure sizzled through Aileen, making her breath hitch and flooding her with more liquid heat.

Kayl paused. His brow arched, and his eyes flicked down.

"What was that?" Kier asked, his hand slowing briefly.

A rumbling sound, at once thoughtful and ravenous, came from Kayl's chest as he placed his finger and thumb to either side of her sex and spread her wide. Using his other hand, he stroked her clit with the pad of a finger.

Aileen released a throaty moan, lashes fluttering, and she tipped her head back. Kayl continued his exploration, circling that little bud slowly, leisurely, building those whispers of pleasure into something far more potent. All the while, Kier continued teasing her breast.

Aileen clutched the bedding in her fists. The twins watched her raptly; soon, she was panting and undulating her pelvis, seeking ever more as pleasure coiled in her core.

The twins released shaky breaths and ceased the small, maddening motions of their fingers.

"Pleasure," Kayl said, the merest quiver in his voice. "It is pure pleasure."

Squeezing the blanket harder, Aileen struggled to keep her hips still, to prevent herself from bucking against Kayl's hand in desperation for more of that delicious friction. She was trembling, awash in sensation and burning with heat. Kayl's touch had been far too fleeting.

Kier's lips stretched into a grin, but his eyes remained half-lidded and smoldering. His fingers tightened infinitesimally on her nipple, nearly making her cry out in yearning. He purred, "Nothing has ever felt so good."

"You...felt it?" Aileen asked breathlessly.

"Echoes." Kayl spread her cunt wider, heightening the contrast between the cool air and his fiery touch. He dipped a finger to her entrance, gently gathering her essence. Having part of him poised there, even just his finger, only made her more aware of the aching emptiness at her core that needed to be filled, that *he* needed to fill.

He withdrew his finger. Everything within Aileen screamed for her to give chase, but she could only watch as Kayl brought his finger to his mouth, extended his pointed tongue, and slowly licked her glistening essence from his skin.

Kier growled, baring his fangs and tightening his hold on her breast as his eyes fell shut. "She is delicious."

Kayl's claws bit into Aileen's thigh. Keeping his gaze on her cunt, he parted his lips and slipped his finger into his mouth. When he drew it out again, he rasped, "Delectable."

The look of utter bliss on the twins' otherworldly faces was breathtaking.

A puff of air escaped Aileen as her sex clenched and her body trembled. She was left on the edge, so, so close to tipping and falling into a sea of pleasure vaster than she could ever have imagined, but she couldn't get there alone.

She'd felt such torment before. She'd felt such desire, such consuming need, but it had never been ignited by anyone's touch—she'd only experienced it during that unwelcome rhapsodic heat.

But this...this was *real*. This desire was hers. It was her body reacting to Kier and Kayl because she wanted them, not because some drug had seized her mind.

Aileen slid a hand into Kier's hair, needing something more to hold onto. "Please," she begged. "Don't leave me like this."

"Never, *na'diya*." Kier reverently brushed his fingers across her cheek. He leaned over her, caught Aileen's gaze with his own, and lowered his mouth onto hers.

She opened to his kiss without hesitation, welcoming the press of his lips, welcoming his warm, spicy breath, and pulled him closer as she closed her eyes. She felt Kayl moving between her legs, but Kier's kiss distracted her from what was happening until she felt the heat of Kayl's breath against her sex.

Kier lifted his head, breaking the kiss. Aileen kept hold of his hair while he trailed kisses along her jaw to her chin, then down her neck and across her collarbone, all while Kayl's breath teased her most sensitive flesh. Anticipation had her heart racing; everything she felt was already too much. Anything more would shatter her mind...

And she wanted it. She wanted it so, so much.

Kayl's fingers curled around her inner thighs, the tips of his claws again pricking her skin. She shivered as tingles spread outward from those points.

Somehow, she found the willpower to open her eyes and look down at Kayl.

He lay between her thighs, eyes aglow with hunger and lust. Strands of his normally neat hair dangled in his face.

"We will never leave you wanting again," he said, squeezing her thighs.

Kier's kisses finally reached Aileen's breast. Just as he closed his lips around her nipple, Kayl's mouth came down upon her sex.

Speared by searing pleasure, Aileen gasped and arched into their touches. Her thoughts scattered, leaving nothing behind but ecstasy —and the twins. She clutched Kier's hair as he sucked her nipple, his every hard draw sending a bolt of pure pleasure straight to her core, where Kayl eagerly licked.

Though the sensations made her eyelids flutter, she refused to let them shut. She would not look away from Kayl. She watched, trans-fixed, as he dragged his hot, delectable tongue along her sex from bottom to top. He lapped at her, swirled his tongue around her entrance, gathered and spread her essence. *Drank* her. A deep vibra-tion thrummed between her thighs when he growled against her cunt. She whimpered, pelvis twitching, but his fervent gaze and iron grip held her captive, and she did not want to escape.

And then his tongue was there—on her clit.

He licked and flicked the sensitive bud, echoing the movements of Kier's tongue on her nipple. Kier's hand kneaded her other breast, while Kayl's hands clutched her thighs, grazing her with their claws. The pleasure in her core coiled tighter and tighter. She rocked her hips, needing more—more pressure, more friction, more contact—but the twins kept her pinned in place.

Their tails joined in their ministrations, gliding along her skin, teasing and caressing. They traced paths along her arms and legs, across her belly and breasts, around her hips and backside, wrapped briefly around her ankle.

Her mates were everywhere, all around her, seeming to touch

every part of her body simultaneously and lighting up her every nerve with overwhelming sensation.

But even through that lustful haze, she understood what they were doing—the twins responded to her every reaction, no matter how small, adjusting their movements to push her pleasure to ever-greater heights.

Kier's fangs bit her breast, and Aileen cried out in pleasure-pain, throwing her head back and squeezing her eyes shut. He lifted his head and soothed the sting with his tongue. The air was chill upon her wet, hard, throbbing nipple.

Her thighs quivered, and her breaths came out in shallow pants. She dug her toes into the mattress and moaned. The pressure in her core expanded.

Kier traced the rounded shell of her ear with his lips. "Sing for us. Let us hear you, *na'diya*," he purred. "Let us hear your pleasure. Let us *feel* it."

"Kier," she whispered, dragging the blanket closer and turning her face into it. "Kayl..."

"Aileen," they replied, their voices reverberating into her.

"You are beautiful," Kayl said. Then his lips latched around her clit, and he sucked.

Rapture burst through Aileen, white-hot and blinding, as powerful as an exploding star. Her body tensed as roaring flames consumed her. A scream tore from her throat, a sound so primal, raw, and filled with pleasure that she barely recognized her own voice.

Kier buried his hands in her hair, and her cry was silenced as his mouth again descended upon hers. He shuddered, snarling against her lips, as Kayl lifted her ass to draw her more firmly against his mouth.

They held her trapped, Kier devouring her sounds of utter pleasure, Kayl devouring the liquid heat pouring from her core as he continued ravaging her cunt with lips and tongue.

She clutched Kier's head with one hand and grasped Kayl's with the other, writhing in their holds while her cries turned to whimpers.

The pulsing waves faded slowly, but the pleasure did not. Aileen's grip on the twins loosened as her body sank into languorous repose and Kier's kiss became more sensual, more tender, more loving. Delightful warmth saturated her. She trailed her fingers along the side of Kier's face, kissing him back until he withdrew.

Heart still pounding, she glanced down at Kayl. His eyes locked with hers as he nuzzled his cheek against her inner thigh. He slipped his tongue out, licking her glistening essence from his lips. The sight made her sex clench anew.

Despite how well-loved she felt in that moment, a vast emptiness remained inside her.

Looking at Kier, Aileen slid a hand down his body and wrapped her fingers around the hard length of his cock. Her eyes widened. His shaft was line with ridges on either side that were prominent even through the material of his shorts, and she couldn't stop herself from running her thumb along one of them.

Kier shuddered and hissed through his teeth, his face contorting with pain as he covered her hand and gently removed it from his groin.

Aileen frowned, brow furrowing. "I...don't understand."

He raised her hand to his face and brushed his lips across her knuckles. "This was for you, Aileen. We wanted only to give you pleasure."

"We will take our own when the time is right." Kayl smoothed his hands over her hips and waist, where he stroked her scar with a thumb. He placed a kiss on her clit; Aileen's breath hitched, and her pelvis twitched. The grin that spread across his lips was slow and devilish as his mouth dipped lower. "In the meantime, we—"

"I have decided to take a little for myself after all," Kier said, releasing Aileen abruptly. Before she could say a word, he shoved Kayl aside and took his brother's place between her legs. He eagerly dropped to his belly, cupped Aileen's ass, and dragged her closer, making her giggle. "It is my turn to enjoy our little mate's sweetness."

Kayl rolled onto his side and moved to lie beside Aileen, his grin having survived the encounter with Kier. "So long as I may hear her sing her pleasure again."

Aileen's already flushed cheeks warmed further. Smiling, she ran a finger over his bare chest, tracing the planes of muscle down toward his pelvis. She grinned when he caught her hand in a vise-like grip and halted it. She didn't miss the tremor than ran through him—or the long, thick outline of his cock visible through his shorts.

"Ah *na'diya*, you smell so exquisite." Kier hooked Aileen's legs over his shoulders and lowered his mouth to her sex.

She gasped; Kayl leaned in to claim her lips in a kiss, taking in her breath when she exhaled. His mouth moved over hers, and she tasted herself on his lips. That only excited her more.

Aileen immediately lost herself to the sensations, melting in Kayl's embrace as he took her in his arms to deepen their kiss. Kier's tongue moved in bold, wicked strokes, teasing her already sensitive flesh, but he did not make her wait long. Now it was Kayl who swallowed her cries as she reached her climax, and Kier who drank her essence.

Once the twins had had their fill and Aileen lay there breathless, Kier lowered her legs to the mattress, pressing kisses to her inner thighs as he did so. Then he crawled up to lie next to her again, turning onto his side and sandwiching her snugly between his body and his brother's. His arms cocooned her in warmth and strength, and the twins' tails coiled around her legs.

Despite all the other places they were now touching, there was no missing the hard lengths of their cocks pressed against her.

Aileen breathed in deep, taking in their mingled scents, and sighed contently. She rubbed her cheek on Kayl's arm and smoothed her hand up his chest. His heart thumped under her palm in time with Kier's against her back. She willed her racing heart to calm, to beat in sync with theirs.

Her lips stretched into a smile as her eyes flicked up to meet Kayl's. "I guess some dreams do come true."

But this had been better than their shared dream. Much, *much* better.

The twins laughed, each tightening his hold on her just a little. Kier's laughter was natural, rich, and warm. Kayl's was rougher, deeper, but no less genuine. Though their laughter ended, this closeness, this sense of...belonging, of *rightness*, remained. Aileen closed her eyes and simply let herself feel.

Kayl tipped his head down, pressing his forehead to hers. "Sleep, *na'diya*."

She hummed. "I don't want this night to end." But she already felt weariness weighing her down.

"There will be many more days and nights to come." Kier combed his fingers through her hair, grazing her scalp with his claws in soothing caresses. "Sleep, so you may dream of us some more."

TWENTY-FIVE

Gentle movement roused Kier from his slumber. He didn't open his eyes. He was enveloped in warmth, and the air he drew into his lungs bore the sweetest of scents. His muscles were languid, his heart at ease, his mind untroubled. If he was dreaming, why would he have wanted to wake?

That question was answered when Aileen stretched her limbs and let out a soft moan, her hand sliding over Kier's chest. She was tucked between the twins, her bare skin, warm and pliant after her slumber, touching theirs. Kier smiled. His tail twitched beneath the blanket before curling around Aileen's calf and ankle.

Aileen sighed, and her warm breath fanned across Kier's chest; she must've turned toward him sometime during the night. He thrilled in the feel of her body, in the serenity instilled by her presence, in the sense of completeness and love swelling within him while he and his brother held her in their arms.

Love...

Is that what this is? Kayl pulsed as he stirred on Aileen's other side.

Kier inhaled deeply, filling himself with her scent anew. Her usual fragrance, which had been irresistibly sensuous and alluring on its own, was only enhanced by the lingering perfume of her arousal.

Had it truly only been four days since they'd found her? Already, Kier could not imagine returning to a life without Aileen.

Yes. I think it is, Kayl.

Aileen smoothed her palm down Kier's torso, her touch sending tingles across his skin and making his stomach tighten as it trailed lower. Her hand paused at his navel.

Kier kept himself very still. He longed for her to continue her exploration, for her hand to resume its journey, but he could not ignore his uncertainty. The only sexual pleasure he and Kayl had ever received had been forced upon them. They'd been unwilling participants in acts which had, ultimately, been performed for their former master's satisfaction alone. Even now, lying beside their *na'diya* with her hands upon him, Kier struggled to hold back those dark recollections.

Lystai had not touched the twins because she'd wanted them to feel good, but because it had been another way to exercise power over them. Another way for her to control them. And that had been her greatest source of pleasure.

However much Kier and his brother craved Aileen's touch, they were still healing from what they'd endured. *She* was still healing from what she'd endured. All three of them were living in the shadows of their traumatic experiences.

And as right as their relationship felt, it was all still so new. He couldn't imagine how strange it must've been for a terran to consider becoming part of a *daevalis*—couldn't imagine how strange the concept of a *daevalis* must've been to her to begin with. The bond they were offering to Aileen was deeper, stronger, and more complete than anything known amongst her kind.

Once the twins opened themselves to her entirely, once they reached their climaxes with her, *within* her, the three of them would be bound. There'd be no going back from that. Kier and Kayl needed to know she was sure. They needed to know she truly wanted it.

Yet despite the twins' hesitancy, Kier had faith. Their bond would be made when all three were prepared in body, mind, and soul. Then their union would be...perfect.

Kier opened his eyes and glanced down at her face.

Aileen's attention was directed downward, toward her hand. Her brow was furrowed, and her lips were curled in a small frown. A whisper of her inner conflict seeped into him through their unforged bond.

Kayl, who lay with his chest against her back and his arm banded around her middle, also opened his eyes.

Bending her fingers into a loose fist, Aileen sighed and withdrew her hand. With careful, measured movements, she grasped Kayl's wrist, lifted his arm off her stomach, and settled it on the mattress behind her. Then she shifted, her beaded nipple grazing Kier's side as she pushed herself up into a sitting position.

Her fingers caught the end of Kayl's tail and gently unwound it from her leg.

"There's no easy way out of this sandwich," she muttered as she set about disentangling Kier's tail from her other leg.

It took a great deal of willpower for Kier not to laugh; even Kayl's lips curved into a smile.

Aileen rose, and the twins' mirth died as their eyes focused on her shapely hips and rounded backside. She didn't possess a tail or the long, lithe limbs typical of female daevahs, but that did not detract from the allure of her figure.

Those curves tantalized Kier, luring him in, demanding his attention. It wasn't that she was exotic—she was simply *perfect*. A pinnacle of beauty beyond his wildest imaginings.

Aileen was made for Kier and Kayl.

Watching her walk away, unclothed, was test of willpower far harder than the last; Kier yearned to leap to his feet, rush to Aileen, and take her hips between his hands; he yearned to run his palms over her thighs, to spread her legs and drink from her again.

His mouth watered at the memory of her taste.

But Kier wanted more than a taste. He wanted to know the bliss of sinking his cock into her hot depths, of her body greedily clutching his shaft, of her every little response to pleasure, however small, vibrating into him through their connected bodies.

He wanted Aileen to become theirs fully, and for them to be hers. He wanted all of her, in every way.

Before any of that could come to be, he and Kayl would have to tear down the barriers blocking them from forming that bond with their *na'diya*.

Aileen opened the shower and stepped inside. The water turned on shortly after the door was shut.

Kayl rolled onto his back, throwing an arm across his brow. *I share your struggle, brother*, he pulsed, his *aerys* strained. *But it will not be much longer.*

The sound of falling water filled the silence in the room, creating a soothing, unobtrusive ambience. Steam gathered on the shower's glass walls, soon obscuring the twins' view of Aileen.

Kier mirrored his brother's position. He was oddly aware of the distance between himself and Kayl, and he could not ignore how perfectly Aileen would fill that space. How perfectly she *did* fill that space.

Smiling, Kier shook his head. *What we shared last night...*

The twins' arousal had been a source of great discomfort while they'd tended to Aileen's needs, but Kier wouldn't have changed a thing. For the first time in their lives, he and Kayl had given such pleasure by choice, and they'd found immense fulfillment in the act. They would never have believed that they'd *want* to do so, or that their want would so quickly become a craving, a need, that they fought even now.

Even with our minds working together, we do not have the words to describe it, Kayl replied.

And that being the case...I cannot imagine how it will feel when we forge our daevalis *in full.*

Kayl let out a sound that blended a contented sigh and a carefree chuckle. Kier had never heard anything like it from his brother, not even as children.

Nor can I. But I long to find out, Kayl pulsed.

Kier's smile faded. *She longs for it as well, but...*

Kayl thumped the bedding with his tail. *But she is not yet ready. She does not know what it will mean.*

We are not yet ready, Kayl. We are the ones hesitating, not Aileen.

A flicker of anger crossed the psychic link, but it was anger directed inward. The twins had not lied last night; it had been about Aileen and her pleasure. In refusing to have their own desires seen to, they'd kept it about her—but they'd also spared themselves from facing their lingering uncertainties.

Soon, Kayl. We are almost there also. There is no shame in it.

That we have all come so far, so swiftly... Kayl sighed. *Part of me says I should not allow myself to hold on to this hope. That it cannot be real, that it cannot last.*

Shifting his arm, Kier raked his fingers through his hair. *Part of me says the same.*

You have been certain of her from the start.

Certain of her, yes. But of us? Kier let out a long, slow breath, turning his unfocused eyes toward the ceiling. *We convinced ourselves this would never come, that we could never have it. That part of me says this cannot be, but then I look up...*

Soft, lilting humming rose over the drone of running water in a simple melody, soon flowing into words in a language Kier and Kayl had never heard.

The twins lifted their heads off their pillows and looked toward the shower again. Aileen was merely a suggestion of pale skin and fiery hair through the fogged glass, all in gentle motion as she washed herself. Her voice echoed within the stall, building upon itself to emerge as something resonant, powerful, and utterly entrancing.

Kier's chest warmed, and that warmth coursed through his veins to flood every bit of his body.

"And there she is," Kier said.

That same warmth radiated from Kayl as the twins sat up. Kier bent his legs and rested his arms on his knees, while Kayl folded his legs and braced his hands atop them. Aileen's voice filled the room, and the twins felt her song in their hearts, their souls, and they knew this was real.

This wasn't a performance. She wasn't on a stage, wasn't entertaining anyone, wasn't pretending. The emotion in Aileen's voice wasn't feigned. The twins' mate was giving them as clear a glance into her soul as possible. She instilled every syllable with all the joy, passion, and longing in her heart, and even though the twins didn't understand her words, those emotions resonated with them.

Kier's tail swept back and forth across the bedding. "Our *na'diya* is radiant."

"She is," Kayl said softly. "Had anything gone differently, had we done as I wished, we would have lost her."

Shaking his head, Kier pried his eyes away from Aileen to look at his brother. "That is where your thoughts go, hearing her sing from her heart for the first time?"

Kayl's lips fell into a shallow frown. "I have my regrets, Kier. My shame. My failures weigh upon me, but none as heavily as those regarding her."

"I had thought we moved past that."

"Such is not accomplished so easily."

Kier sighed, swinging his attention back to the shower. "Perhaps not. Or perhaps you simply need more help learning to appreciate what we have now."

"My growing appreciation of her only intensifies the sting."

"Wrath. Vengeance." Kier turned his palms up and stared at them, noting the rough calluses, the faint scars. "We decided long ago to embody those things, to become them. But that decision never had to be final, brother. We can choose to be something else."

At the edge of Kier's vision, Kayl curled his fingers, digging his claws into his legs. "What can we choose to be? How do we choose it?"

Kier shrugged. "We choose to be hers. Her mates. Her *na'divali*."

"And if we do not know what that means?"

"We figure it out as we go. Together." Kier pushed himself onto his feet, lifted his hands over his head, and stretched. "We cannot move forward if we insist upon anchoring ourselves to the past. We do not have to forget, but we can let go."

Fixing his gaze upon the steamy shower stall, Kier strode forward.

"What are you doing?" Kayl asked.

"Moving forward, obviously." Kier flashed a grin over his shoulder as he caught the waistband of his shorts and shoved them down his legs. *We have a beautiful mate in the shower, naked and alone. Why are we sitting out here watching?*

Rınsıng away the last of the soap, Aileen faced the water. Her body slowly swayed as her singing drifted into a hum. The shower's heat suffused her, and the scents of earth, sea, and spice enveloped her. She greedily breathed them in.

Mates. I have mates.

She closed her eyes as her lips stretched into a smile.

Rivulets of water streamed down her body—a body thrumming with a song of its own. The memories of all those sensations lingered; she still felt the imprints of the twins' fingers upon her flesh, the pricks of their claws, the caresses of their lips, the lashing of their tongues against her sex.

Desire stirred within her, and she squeezed her thighs together. The experience had been unexpected, erotic, beautiful. It had been so much more than she could have ever imagined.

It had been her *choice*.

And that meant everything.

She'd wanted Kier and Kayl. She wanted them still. She only wished she'd been able to touch them and reciprocate the pleasure they'd gifted her.

Aileen smoothed her hands up her belly to cup her breasts. Her nipples were still tender, and the water falling upon the sensitive peaks sent a thrill straight to her core.

The shower door opened.

She gasped, jumping in startlement, and spun toward it.

Kier stood before her, grinning, with his hands high on the stall's frame and *every* delectable bit of his body on display.

Aileen's mouth went dry. Her gaze roved over the wide expanse of his chest, down the sculpted muscles of his abdomen, and followed his defined Adonis belt directly to his cock. His long, thick, erect cock.

Her eyes flared. His cock was teal at his scrotum, but the teal bled into purple toward the tip. That purple was more pronounced on the crests of the ridges lining the sides of his shaft. His cock twitched under her gaze.

Kayl stepped up behind him, just as naked and just as aroused.

Her eyes shot up to meet Kayl's before he slowly, seductively, boldly raked his gaze down her body. Something primal stirred within those blue and magenta depths.

The invisible tether linking Aileen to the twins pulled taut. Her heart fluttered in her chest, and her blood warmed, flooding her core with heat.

I want them.

I crave them.

I need them.

Before Aileen could find any words to say, Kier stepped into the shower, bent, and swept her into his arms. She squeaked, hands flying to his shoulders as he spun around, putting his back to the wall. He held her high against him, one hand flat on her back and the other clutching her ass. His velvety skin was warm against hers.

His grin curled into something absolutely devilish. "We were lured by a sweet, seductive voice." He stroked his tail up the backs of her knees and thighs, sending a thrill through Aileen and coaxing her to wrap her legs around his waist. That tail coiled around her calf.

Aileen chuckled and brushed a strand of hair from his forehead. "Were you?"

The door closed behind her. She glanced over her shoulder to see that Kayl had joined them, his long hair free of its tie and hanging down past his shoulders. He trailed the back of a claw along her spine. "The temptation was more than we could resist."

"Our wills are powerless against you, *na'diya*," Kier purred.

Aileen released a shaky breath as Kayl's claw ventured down, stopping at the cleft of her ass. Her sex clenched. "Is that what I am? Temptation? A siren luring her victims to their doom?"

Capturing her jaw, Kayl lowered his face to hers and skimmed his nose over her cheek and ear. "You are our temptation, Aileen, and so much more."

Kier brushed his lips up her jaw. "And if you are our doom, we go to it gladly."

Their low, sultry voices alone were enough to be her undoing.

Kayl tipped her face up and traced her bottom lip with his tongue. Her lashes fluttered closed, and her mouth opened in a soft sigh. With a low rumble, he bent closer, slanting his mouth over hers. The hot sweep of his delectable tongue sent a rush of fire through her veins.

More. Need more.

She lifted a hand from Kier's shoulder, looped her arm around Kayl's neck, tangling her fingers in his long hair, and pulled him closer. The kiss was all caressing lips and stroking tongues, a mesmerizing, unhurried ravishing of her senses. She easily fell under his spell.

Kier planted a tantalizing kiss at the hollow of her throat. He licked that spot and trailed his tongue lower until he captured one of her budded nipples between his teeth, making Aileen gasp. Her pelvis jerked against his abdomen, and her eyes flashed open as she turned her head to look at him.

He smiled before soothing her nipple with his tongue. "Will you let us pleasure you again, *na'diya*?"

"What if I want to pleasure you?" she asked, only to bite her lip and moan when Kier sucked her other nipple into his mouth. Each pull on the tender bud sent a pulse to her clit. Her sex clenched, and she thrust her fingers into his hair as she arched toward him, needing more.

Something stroked her slick sex in teasing swipes; it took her a hazy moment to realize it was Kayl's tail.

Kayl settled his hands on her hips and massaged her flesh. "Your pleasure gives us pleasure."

"But I want to..." It was so hard to think with desire clouding her mind. "I want..."

Kier released her nipple and placed a gentle kiss upon it. "In time, *na'diya*."

"Soon," Kayl said. "Trust us, Aileen."

"I do," Aileen whispered. "I trust you."

Their chests rumbled against her with low, deep growls.

Kier withdrew his hand from her back, slipped it between their bodies, and cupped her mons. "Ah, Aileen, you are so hot, so slick." He kissed her chest right over her heart as his fingers toyed with the delicate folds of her cunt. After gathering her slick from her core, he gently circled her clit with the pads of his finger, taking care with his claws.

Aileen sighed, tightening her thighs around his waist. All it took was a few strokes of his dexterous fingers to put her utterly under his control. She undulated her hips, unable to remain still.

Kier inhaled deeply and bared his teeth; his features were taut with desire, and his pupils had narrowed to slits. "I will never tire of your scent."

Kayl's chest pressed firmly against hers. Being caged between two big, strong bodies should've made Aileen feel small and powerless, should've made her feel trapped and afraid. But she didn't feel any of that with Kier and Kayl. She knew she was safe in their arms.

She knew she was...*loved*.

Aileen leaned back against Kayl. The thunderous beating of his heart vibrated into her. With a purr, he wrapped an arm around her and captured one of her breasts in hand, kneading the soft flesh. He pinched and pulled Aileen's hardened nipple, stoking her inner flames.

Kier's tail unwound and slithered along Aileen's leg. It followed a maddening path, leaving her skin ablaze in its wake, until it finally nudged her sex. Kier pushed the tip into her channel, stretching her, and withdrew it only the slightest amount before thrusting harder, deeper.

"Kier," Aileen moaned, her head falling back against Kayl's shoulder.

"I love how you say my name," Kier growled. He took her other nipple into his mouth and swirled his tongue around it, making her whimper and clutch at his hair.

His wicked tail pumped, pressing deeper and deeper, synchronized with the tantalizing rhythm of his fingers on her clit. Currents of pleasure coursed through her, gathering in her core.

As he trailed kisses up her neck and grazed her skin with his fangs, Kayl lowered his other hand, sliding it between her ass cheeks until his fingers reached her rosette. Her breath hitched, and her eyes widened when he stroked it.

"You are not daevah," Kayl said huskily, his mouth beside her ear, "but we can still take you as *na'divali* should."

"Together," Kier rasped.

The flash of uncertainty that had stricken her at his touch vanished as quickly as it had come. She wanted them. She wanted this.

Together.

Cupping Kayl's jaw, Aileen turned her face toward him and met his gaze. His eyes burned with an intensity that seared right to her soul. "Yes."

The tip of his tail brushed over her folds again, near to where Kier's was still thrusting, and gathered her essence. It withdrew and quickly replaced his fingers over her anus. Keeping his eyes locked with hers, Kayl firmly pressed his tail past the tight ring.

Aileen sucked in a sharp breath. There was a pain, a burning, a growing pressure as Kayl pushed farther in, his tail's shallow pumps stretching her more and more. Her brow creased, and her grip on the twins tightened.

Kier's fingers quickened on her clit, making Aileen squirm and whimper.

"We have you, *na'diya*," Kier whispered.

"I know," she rasped.

"Stay with us," Kayl ordered.

The pressure of Kayl's probing tail combined with Kier's thrusts and strokes to make Aileen's flesh tingle, and soon, the pain was paired with burgeoning pleasure.

It felt so foreign, so new, so deviant, so full, so...so...so...

Oh God, it feels so good.

Kayl was careful, gentle, but commanding in his touch. As her pain gave way to pleasure, he sped his thrusting tail. Though he didn't press much deeper, it was more than enough to awaken every nerve in her body and set them alight with pleasure.

She abandoned herself to the whirlwind of sensation. Moans emerged from her throat, ragged breaths tore out of her chest, and she could do no more than cling to her mates. Their tails pumped into her, their fingers stroked her, their mouths caressed her. They were the masters of her body, they were in control, and she entrusted herself to their keeping entirely.

"Let us hear your pleasure," Kier growled against her breast.

"Let us *feel* it," Kayl snarled, his hands flexing on her hips.

Aileen yielded to the scorching ecstasy mounting inside her. She moved against the twins in wild abandon, eagerly seeking more, and the twins gave it to her.

That internal fire roared, and she gasped in sweet agony as her body locked tight. Rapture flooded her veins. For a moment, she couldn't breathe, couldn't move, couldn't see. All she could do was *feel.*

And there, just at the edges of her consciousness, she felt *them.* Kier and Kayl. It was as though their souls were brushing against hers, as though their minds were almost touching, as though she could connect with them, become one with them, if only she could reach a little further, if only she could push through that last barrier.

Kayl shuddered against her back. "Just like that, *na'diya.*"

But that sensation was fleeting, and it slipped away much too soon, leaving her adrift on the churning ocean that was her climax.

"*Zor atkoshai,*" Kier growled. "I nearly felt you."

Kayl pressed his forehead to her temple. "Close. So close. *Ba'shanaal.*"

As the pleasure abated, Aileen floated down from the heights of her bliss and settled back into her own body, which felt deliciously heavy. She doubted that she could've kept herself upright in that moment, but she didn't have to worry—she was secure in Kier and Kayl's embrace, safe in their arms, cradled in their hearts.

Their tails stilled.

Aileen panted, quivering as water cascaded over their bodies. Her heart raced. She smiled, savoring the pleasure and satisfaction thrumming inside her.

But something was missing. She'd felt it, that hint of what it would be like to join with the twins completely. What she'd just experienced was only a shadow of what would come, of what they would share once they were bound. She anticipated that moment. *Yearned* for it.

Caressing their hair, she leaned forward and kissed Kier, then turned her head and did the same to Kayl.

She was exactly where she belonged.

TWENTY-SIX

"USE YOUR HIPS." Kier threw a few slow punches, emphasizing the motions of his hips as he did so. "That is what will lend power to your strikes."

Aileen nodded, her eyes fixed on Kier's bare abdomen as he moved.

Even without that glint of unmasked desire in her gaze, Kayl would've felt the flicker of arousal within Aileen—there'd been many such flickers in the ten minutes since their training session had begun.

Kayl folded his arms across his chest and leaned back against the wall. His tail dangled behind his legs, swaying lazily. He'd not been present during Kier's initial assessment of Aileen's fighting skills, but he'd received enough of his brother's memories to know she'd already shown significant improvement in her technique—largely because she hadn't had any technique to begin with.

But she did have determination. She'd said she had lost hope on Eternal Paradise, that she had let her dreams die, but clearly there was something inside her that had never succumbed to despair. That unyielding core had driven her onward through those horrid years, and it was stronger than ever now.

And it was just one of countless things about her that Kayl...loved.

They were in the final part of this journey, only a couple hours from their destination, and Kayl found himself wishing that weren't the case, that he and Kier could have Aileen all to themselves for a little longer. Wishing that these days of learning each other—of learning to simply *be*—would never come to an end.

Kier went through a sequence of punches, increasing the force and speed of each until his fists were making small whooshing sounds as they cut through the air.

Aileen's eyes widened as she dragged them up to watch Kier's arms. Those blue irises shifted back and forth rapidly, struggling to keep track of Kier's hands, but before long, she shook her head and met Kier's gaze, and a smile creeping onto her lips. "You're just showing off now, aren't you?"

Kayl smirked.

His brother snapped his hands back into a defensive stance before straightening, his own mouth stretching into a grin. A sheen of sweat stood out on his skin. "Perhaps. Are you suitably impressed?"

"Soon enough, Kier, she will realize just how insufferable your need for attention really is," said Kayl.

Aileen laughed, smile widening. "Not there yet."

Kier scoffed and braced his hands on his hips. "*Yet?*"

She turned away from Kier, assuming a fighting stance of her own. Kier was not the only one to take the opportunity to run his gaze down her body and slowly back up again. The arousal that shuddered through Kayl in that moment belonged not to Aileen, but himself and his brother.

Aileen had donned a pair of daevah-style pants which fit loose around her lower legs but were tantalizingly snug on her hips and backside. Her fitted top contained her breasts while leaving all else in view—her belly, her navel, the subtle scarring on her side, her delicate collarbone, her shoulders. And with her hair gathered and tied atop her head, her slender neck and the triangular tattoo on her back were also clearly visible.

She threw a few punches; Kayl could not tear his eyes away from her as she moved.

He'd never imagined feeling attraction to another person, or that it was even possible to get so close to anyone apart from his brother. Kier had always been there, and despite the hollowness the twins had harbored for most of their lives, having each other should've been enough.

But it never would be enough, never could've been. Kayl understood that now, and for all the failures, the frustrations, the lingering pain and anger, he wouldn't change a thing.

I am glad you have come to agree with me fully on that matter, Kier pulsed, shooting Kayl a glance.

I fear your ego will soon grow large enough to swallow the whole universe at this rate, Kayl replied. He lowered his arms and pushed away from the wall.

"Close, *na'diya,*" Kier said, standing beside her for another demonstration.

She watched intently as he went through another series of punches, partially mimicking his movements.

Kayl strode over to them, stopping behind Aileen. She glanced at him over her shoulder, her innocent smile belying the heat in her eyes. He reached around her, gently closed his hands over hers, and guided them into a slightly higher position.

When he shifted closer, pressing his body against hers, Aileen gasped. Her rounded backside nestled his balls, and immediate pressure built in his groin. The fire that ignited at his core was matched only by the heat radiating from her.

Kier released a huff. "I thought you were content to allow me to instruct her, Kayl."

"I cannot bear to watch our *na'diya* struggle under your lacking tutorship, Kier." Kayl leaned his head down, placing his mouth close to her ear, and said, "Balance. All things are about balance."

Though Kier snickered softly, he voiced no disagreement; neither did he mask the warmth pulsing from him through their link.

Aileen's heady scent filled Kayl's nose, at once soothing and wholly enticing. It reminded him of the fragrant fields of sweet grass through which he and his twin had run in their childhood, of the perfumed breeze during blossoming season, of that fleeting smell of sunshine-warmed skin. But there was something in it belonging solely to her, something uniquely *Aileen.*

Kayl released Aileen's hands and lowered his palms to her hips. He fought back a shudder, resisting the instinctive urge to curl his fingers and clutch her against his shaft. "Your strength, your balance, lies here." His heart quickened as he dipped his hands farther to hook them around her inner thighs.

Aileen gasped, and Kayl felt her pulse flutter. She angled her pelvis back, pushing her ass ever so slightly against his hardening cock.

The ghost of her taste skittered across his tongue. That memory weakened his knees, and very nearly broke his resolve. Images of her face, expression consumed by pleasure, flitted through his mind's eye. She'd been so tight around his tail. How divine would it be to actually mate with her, to feel her body bearing down on his shaft, greedily taking in more and more of him? How would it feel to be fully connected to her?

In the shower, they'd been only a whisper away from forging their bond. So close...and yet the twins had held themselves back. That wouldn't be possible for much longer.

Kier laughed. Kayl couldn't be sure whether it had been aloud or through their link, but it didn't matter; the nonchalance of the sound was undercut by overwhelming desire. Kier was struggling just as much as Kayl in that moment.

Clenching his jaw, Kayl spread Aileen's thighs slightly. She offered no resistance save the faint tremors that coursed through her body. Her breaths quickened, and her scent—the scent of her arousal —strengthened.

Kayl drew in a slow, deep breath, and somehow forced the words out of his throat. "Widen your stance just slightly"—his fingers twitched on Aileen's thighs, and his heart leapt in unison with hers— "and you may—"

An alarm blared, and the overhead lights flashed red. The sound pierced Kayl's desire, wrapped its claws around his heart, and squeezed.

It had only been days since they'd last heard that sound. It had only been days since Vrykhan's ship had nearly destroyed the *Fang*— and Aileen, Kier, and Kayl along with it.

Aileen tensed, tipping her head back to look at the lights before she twisted to face Kayl. "What's happening?"

Her fear bled into him in waves, matching the alarm's rhythm.

Kier snatched his holocom off a nearby exercise machine, unlocked it, and opened the alert message from the ship's computer. The information he read sizzled through the twins' psychic link.

Kayl's insides constricted, and his heart stilled.

"Cosmic storm," Kier rasped.

And based on what Kier had just read, this was by far the most intense cosmic storm the twins had ever encountered. The implications of that information blasted along their mental bond. Every possible outcome, every possible danger, triggered and explosion that shattered it into a dozen more thoughts, each more frantic than their progenitors.

"Four minutes," Kier said.

That meant no time to plan, no time to think, no time for hope or fear. Understanding passed between Kier and Kayl, requiring not so much as a single word. Their priority was clear—Aileen. Everything and anything to keep her safe.

"A cosmic st—" A started gasp cut off Aileen's words as Kayl swept her into his arms and hurried toward the door.

Kier moved ahead of his brother, slapping the holocom onto his wrist before darting through the doorway. He turned left to head for the cargo bay.

Kayl sped his pace, turning right once he entered the corridor. Aileen clutched his neck as he raced toward the cockpit. Red lights flashed along the hallway, drudging up memories he would sooner have forgotten; it was too reminiscent of the emergency lights in Eternal Paradise's docking bays when Kayl and his brother had escaped with Aileen.

When Aileen had been on the brink of death...

He gritted his teeth and pushed onward, not slowing as he entered the cockpit. All the holo screens were on and pulsing with warnings. Between the blaring alarms, his ragged breath, and his pounding heart, Kayl couldn't hear a thing.

Make her safe.

The thought was doubled, coming from his mind and Kier's simultaneously.

Kayl sat Aileen down on one of the chairs, grabbed the harness straps, and fastened them around her. Aileen's bright blue eyes were fixed on him, big and gleaming with fear and uncertainty, as he tugged the straps tight. The frantic splash of pink on her cheeks starkly contrasted her pale skin.

Kayl's heart ached. Though they had not a second to spare, he caught her face between his hands and pressed his mouth to hers in an impassioned kiss, vowing to himself that it would not be the last kiss they shared.

When he pulled back, their gazes met. The light in her eyes had changed; determination burned in her eyes, combating her fear. She understood the promise delivered by that kiss.

Aileen drew in a deep breath. Her nostrils flared with her exhalation, and she nodded.

Somehow, Kayl summoned the willpower to let go of her, turn away, and drop into the pilot's seat. He wrestled his harness on with one hand while he manipulated the controls with the other. New holo screens and readouts appeared before him.

The doors leading from the cargo hold into the lower maintenance deck were sealed, with their automatic and manual locks engaged. Kier would be moving on to the door separating the hold from the upper deck even now.

Mouth dry and muscles tense, Kayl flicked through screens and gauges, registering the information faster than conscious thought. His fingers moved of their own accord, silencing alerts, adjusting levels, and diverting power from systems that would be of no use in what was to come. He routed all the excess power into the energy shields.

And everywhere he looked, he was reminded that the *Fang* was operating at severely reduced capability. That there was so very little to work with.

Despite everything else demanding his attention, he still felt hints of her barely restrained fear through their unforged bond.

"Are there rainstorms on Earth?" he asked, glancing at her over his shoulder.

She nodded. Strands of her hair had fallen from their tie to dangle in her face, but she made no attempt to move them; her hands were clamped around the harness straps.

The ship's manual control interface came up in front of Kayl, visible in his peripheral vision. It was populated with a good number of warnings that had nothing to do with the approaching storm. "A cosmic storm is similar, but it is comprised of radioactive atomic fragments instead of water."

"So"—her tongue slipped out briefly to wet her lips—"it's nothing like a rainstorm?"

Kayl chuckled, though his amusement was shallow and short lived. "I suppose not."

Kier skidded through the cockpit entryway, halting himself by grasping the door frame. Aileen turned her head to watch as he closed the door and cranked the handle at the door's center, engaging the manual lock. A faint, brief airflow signaled the cockpit calibrating its pressurization.

As Kayl faced forward, Kier ran to hop the adjacent gunner's seat, drawing on his harness even as he brought up his own readouts and controls.

"This is all just precautionary, right?" Aileen asked with a hint of unsteadiness. "We'll be okay?"

"We will be okay, *na'diya*." Kier's voice was steady, confident.

They had to be okay. There was no choice. Their mate was in danger, and they would allow no harm to befall her. Kier slid his fingers over the controls on one of the screens, and the upper half of the cockpit's walls and its ceiling vanished, replaced by the view outside the ship.

Omega IV, their destination, lay ahead, still small with distance. It was varying shades of brown and gray interspersed with white clouds and hints of blue water. All around it stretched the inky black void, broken by pinpoints of light that were distant stars and the colorful clouds of distant nebulas.

Color flared through that holographic view—intense greens and blues like huge sparks, wavering and flickering wildly. The *Fang* trembled. New alarms blared in varying tones, and alerts flashed across the control screens.

It had begun.

"Is that normal?" Aileen asked, voice strained, as both the colors and the ship's shaking intensified.

"Perfectly normal," Kier replied.

Aileen's concern was as palpable as it was justified, and the twins longed to soothe her, to tell her there was nothing to worry about. Further words of comfort formed in their minds, but the twins did not speak them.

Telling Aileen they would be all right was not the same as saying there was no danger. The former was a promise, the latter a lie.

As though to demonstrate that danger, the *Fang* shook again, and a deep rumbling coursed underfoot. The display outside grew brighter and more varied; reds and violets joined in, pulsing in and out of the visible spectrum.

Kier's fingers flew over the controls in a blur as Kayl watched the shielding system readouts. The shield power levels fell faster with each new wave of the storm, and their integrity was fluctuating wildly. Even with Kier actively finding new sources of power to route to the shields, the levels would not stabilize.

The next flare of light was so bright that the holo windows automatically dimmed to compensate. The *Fang's* nose veered off course. The auto-navigation system switched on, attempting to correct the ship's trajectory. Kayl pinned the location of Omega IV's lone settlement, Navaire, on the display and disabled the auto-nav. He took the flight controls in his hands.

Is that wise? Kier pulsed.

Kayl glanced at Aileen. Her breaths came steadily but rapidly, her skin looked paler than normal, and she gripped the harness so tight that her knuckles were stark white. Her composure was tenuous at best.

I can guide us in manually, Kayl replied. *We need everything we can spare routed to the shield.*

Kier also looked back at their mate, and something softened in his expression. "We are with you, *na'diya.*"

"We face this together," Kayl added.

Somehow, she managed a smile; more surprising was that smile's genuineness. "Together."

Would that we could hold her right now, Kier pulsed.

We need but make it through this storm, and we may hold her all we wish, brother.

The ship rocked, and a spectacular spray of colors arced across the view holos. One of the screens in front of Kayl went dark, its projector cutting out for half a second before kicking back on.

The ship's power readings went out for an even briefer time; when they were restored, the levels dipped alarmingly, along with the shield's integrity. More screens around the cockpit flickered.

Just as abruptly as they'd plummeted, the power levels jumped back to near their prior values.

The shield integrity did not.

Under normal circumstances, the energy shield would've served merely as a redundant layer of protection from the storm. The ship's hull was more than enough to protect the passengers from the extreme radiation of a storm even this severe.

But the *Fang's* hull had been compromised since the *Azkazor* blasted a hole in it. The interior walls and doors weren't designed to block those cosmic energy waves, and wouldn't be enough to protect the twins and their mate.

The *Fang* bounced and twisted as the storm continued its assault. Muscles trembling, Kayl reoriented the ship time and again, battling the controls to maintain the course. Possibilities swirled around the edges of his consciousness, as numerous as the atomic particles battering the ship—infinite ways for this to end in disaster. Infinite ways for Kier, Kayl, and Aileen to lose everything.

Fortunately, his mental shield held—as did the *Fang's* energy shield. The planet ahead and the countless stars surrounding it spun and swung wildly through Kayl's field of vision, but he fixed his eyes on the waypoint, using it as his anchor, his center. The power levels continued their decline, falling ever faster as more and more energy went toward keeping the vessel on-course.

How long until entry? Kayl pulsed.

At the edge of Kayl's vision, Kier flicked through holo screens. *One hour, thirty-seven minutes, sixteen seconds.*

Kayl's hands tightened around the control sticks. *How large is this storm?*

After a brief delay, Kier's *aerys* came across the psychic link, heavy with concern. *It is surrounding Omega IV entirely.*

There was a chance the storm would pass before the shield failed. That was certainly possible, but it was highly improbable. And there was no question that the shield would falter well before the *Fang* reached its destination...at least at the ship's current speed.

They'd simply been riding the momentum the *Fang* had built from its last jump. Their supplies had been adequate for a five-day journey, so the twins had deemed it wise not to engage the engines and risk further system failures.

But the situation had changed.

Brother, Kier pulsed, *that would place immense strain on the already damaged engines and severely limit the power available to divert to the shield.*

Kayl stared at Omega IV, stared at the marker for Navaire, and extended his tail behind him. Its tip brushed Aileen's leg; he curled it securely around her ankle. It was the best he could manage now, the best comfort he could offer Aileen and claim for himself. Though he did not see it, he felt his brother do the same with her other leg.

For so, so long, Kayl had approached life with calculated detachment. He'd attempted to plan every step and anticipate every variable, even knowing that was impossible to accomplish. He'd carefully weighed potential risks and payoffs against the ultimate goal of revenge, protecting that goal as though it were the most fragile thing in the universe. As though it were the only thing that mattered.

But it had *never* been the only thing that mattered. Aileen had changed everything, but even before her, there'd been Kier. Now they were a triad...

And to keep it that way, Kayl would do anything.

He tightened his grip on the flight controls with one hand and pried the other away from them, dropping it to the engine control panel.

Kier and Kayl met each other's gazes.

"Are you certain?" Kier asked.

"No." Kayl glanced back at Aileen, as did his twin. Their eyes met, forming that sacred triangle, the outline of their *daevalis*, the whisper of what would come to be after they made it through this. He continued, "But we cannot await opportunity. We must make it for ourselves."

Aileen's laugh was real, though the fear remained in her eyes. "I'm not sure my mother was referring to life-or-death situations when she said that, but..." Her expression softened. "I trust you. Both of you."

Kayl coiled his tail a little tighter around her leg and faced forward. Once again, he fought to align the *Fang's* trajectory with their target.

I certainly hope we do not explode, Kier pulsed.

So do I, Kayl replied. He engaged the engine.

A new sound sprang to life amidst the noise of the jostling ship—a whirring hum, high-pitched and piercing. It vibrated through the floors, through the controls, through the air, vibrated into Kayl's flesh and down into his bones. It intensified in cycles, permeating everything; soon it was so high that Kayl couldn't hear it any longer, but the feel of it, the discomfort it induced, did not fade.

The ship's shaking grew more violent. Alerts blinked on the screens in front of Kayl, but he held his attention on the marker as he increased the power of the forward thrusters. The lights outside brightened, blocking out more and more of the view.

Easy, Kier warned.

Kayl continued sliding the throttle up. The screen monitoring the shielding system was again flashing, along with at least a dozen others. Half as many alarm tones blared from all sides, filling the thrumming air with jarring, discordant sounds. Other systems were failing, whole sections of the ship were shutting down.

Balance the power, Kier.

I am trying, Kayl.

Kayl pushed the throttle further. As the *Fang* gained speed, the planet ahead swelled, and the forces working to knock the ship off course strengthened.

Kayl...

Kayl gritted his teeth, which seemed likely to shatter due to the tension in his jaw and that maddening thrum coursing through everything. His nostrils flared with a heavy exhalation. *I am occupied, Kier.*

We have an engine overheating, and the life support system is losing pressure.

Kayl's hand did not ease on the throttle.

Fear pulsed from Aileen, mixing with the twins' fear; the blend was soured further by the vibrations, the noise, the flaring colors with their near-blinding intensity. The ship rattled all around, seemingly on the verge of coming apart.

Hold together. You must hold.

This is not how our journey ends.

All Kayl could see now was the indicator and the vaguest outline of Omega IV; everything else was wild light. The engine's thrum built into a chugging roar. On the lower edge of Kayl's vision, the gauges tracking the ship's power were pulsing, falling, flickering.

The universe was chaos, but Kayl clung to order, to control. The number and magnitude of the forces attempting to destroy his *daevalis* did not matter—he would not allow harm to come to his brother and their mate.

The *Fang's* speed increased, and the destination drew closer still.

Just a reminder, Kier pulsed through the cacophony, *we do need functional engines in order to slow down!*

The shield indicators strobed with alerts; failure was imminent. Warning icons blinked elsewhere; the engines were at the brink of failure, the power supply was nearly exhausted, everything that could go wrong was about to go wrong.

Without looking down, Kayl dropped a hand and brought up the flight interface on the display before him. Holographic lines traced paths amidst the spray of colors, marking the planet ahead, calculating the ship's current trajectory based on speed, indicated the distance and time both to entry and landing.

It was all very, very close.

Kayl...

Closer with every second.

"Kayl!" Kier said.

"I see, Kier," Kayl replied.

Hold on, na'diya.

Kayl reversed the thrusters. The ship quaked violently, the rattling and clanging drowning out the blaring alarms.

The ships forward speed plummeted.

"Our angle is too sharp," Kier said.

"I *see,* Kier," Kayl snapped. He relaxed his fingers, adjusted their positions, and took a tighter hold of the flight controls before dropping his eyes to monitor the ship's falling speed.

Kier growled and further dimmed the viewport display in anticipation of what was to come.

Kayl rotated the *Fang*. Kier's confusion rippled through their psychic link, but there were so many emotions crossing already that Kayl barely registered it. Battling the myriad of forces trying to either tear the ship apart or blast it off course, Kayl delicately altered their angle of approach. His thumping heart quickened with each passing instant.

"Kayl, we—"

"Reroute whatever you can into the shield," Kayl said, cutting off the reverse thrusters. He urged the *Fang's* nose up a little more; then they were out of time.

Fire flared across the view holos as the ship hit Omega IV's atmosphere. Orange, red, violet, white; the flames danced and sparked in a spectacle to rival that of the cosmic storm. The external vibrations ceased, leaving only the whirring hum of the engines.

And through that fire, Kayl saw hints of sparse clouds and land far, far below. This was not the lush, living landscape of his homeworld, nor was it the gleaming, radiant cityscape of Arthos, but it was solid ground—and it felt like he'd been so long away from solid ground.

Just ensure we do not meet that ground too enthusiastically, brother, Kier pulsed.

Alarms and warnings continued pulsing, blaring, beeping, but Kayl focused only on guiding the ship through the atmosphere, trusting his brother to handle anything else within their power to control.

A new warning flashed on the holo display—engine failure.

Everything into the shield, Kier. Now!

But Kier's hands were already flying at his controls, making adjustments faster than Kayl's eyes could trace. Fire continued battering the energy shield in that brilliant display. The absence of its roar was terribly pronounced in the relative silence; without the engines thrumming, the cockpit was almost uncomfortably quiet.

Aileen's panting breaths expanded in that quiet; only then did Kayl realize the alarm sounds had been muted by his brother. Their memory lingered in his ears regardless.

The flames diminished, allowing more and more of the planet below to come into view until finally they were gone.

"We are clear," Kier said with a relieved chuckle.

Kayl's lips curled into a grin. The planet's atmosphere would stop the worst of the cosmic storm, meaning the energy shield was no longer integral to their survival.

"Wow."

That single, breathless word from Aileen called the twins' attention back to her. She was staring at the forward view holo, her blue eyes wide and bright, her expression slack with wonder.

The twins turned their heads forward to follow her gaze.

Kayl's heart stuttered. Omega IV stretched out above them—or rather, below them, given that the *Fang* was upside down. Shimmering rivers and streams riddled the landscape, flowing through canyons and around hills and mountains that were dusted with sparkling flecks. Clumps of vegetation poked from the rough ground, concentrated around the waterways.

Far in the distance, Faladore Omega, the star the planet orbited, was nearing the horizon, its rays tinted in reds, oranges, and subtle violets. The shadows on the ground were lengthening before Kayl's eyes as night fell across the world.

Before meeting Aileen, Kayl would not have recognized such beauty.

No, Kier pulsed, *you would not have allowed yourself to. There is a difference.*

I do not appreciate the recent change in our dynamic that has left you correct more often than not, Kier.

Kier glanced at Kayl and grinned. *Another thing that has always been before your eyes, but you simply would not let yourself see.*

The *Fang's* nose dipped toward the ground.

"Umm... That's supposed to happen, right?" Aileen asked.

The planet swung around in the cockpit's holographic view until the *Fang's* passengers were looking straight down at the ground. Immense gravitational force pressed Kayl back against his seat as the ship plummeted, and his stomach flipped.

"It is a good sign," Kier said, voice strained.

"How's that?" asked Aileen.

"It means gravity is working."

Kayl shook his head and let out a ragged breath. "We shall keep that in mind when we hit the ground."

The ship began rattling again. Tufts of wispy cloud darted past outside, and Omega IV's surface, with those glittering specks lit up brilliantly by the setting sun, came closer and closer.

Aileen's voice quavered in time with the shaking ship. "And by *hit the ground*, you mean *land safely*, correct?"

"We will be fine," Kayl replied.

"That does not really answer her question," said Kier.

"No, it doesn't," Aileen agreed.

With a huff, Kayl cut power to the failed engines and engaged the antigrav drive. A deep vibration shook the cockpit, accompanied by a distant hum, but it was fleeting. A message flashed on one of the holo displays.

ANTIGRAVITY DRIVE OFFLINE. UNKNOWN ERROR DETECTED.

Kier spat a curse. Fighting the forces of gravity shoving them backward, the twins hurriedly flitted through various control screens, powering down all systems that weren't vital to safely landing. Kayl's heart hammered his ribs as though it were going to burst out.

"Can't you just...level it out? Pull up or whatever?" Aileen suggested, raising her voice to be heard over the increasingly loud clattering and rumbling.

"In atmosphere, that does not work without the antigravity drive," Kier replied.

A bead of sweat trickled down the side of Kayl's face. How long had he felt so hot? How long had his palms been clammy, his muscles stiff and burning?

Kayl hit the antigrav drive control again. The ship shook hard enough that his teeth would've clacked together were they not already gritted, but nothing else happened. The error message remained on the screen, but new text appeared below it.

WARNING—IMPACT IN 33 SECONDS. CORRECT COURSE IMMEDIATELY.

ENGAGING AUTOPILOT.

ERROR. AUTOPILOT SYSTEMS OFFLINE. REBOOTING...

"*Rebooting?*" Panic crept into Aileen's voice, surprising only in that it had taken so long to break through. "It doesn't mean—"

The holo screens lining the cockpit turned off abruptly, including the view ports, plunging Kayl, Kier, and Aileen into total darkness. Someone uttered a brief curse—*ja'skaal*. It might have been Kier, but it just as likely could've been Kayl.

Aileen's leg trembled, sending a tremor along Kayl's tail. The surge of fear that emanated from her poured ice into his veins.

"It did," she rasped. "It did. Fer fuck's sake."

The power flickered back on. Pale blue lights leapt to life across the console, designating the physical controls.

The words *REBOOTING SYSTEMS* appeared on the central holo screen, accompanied by a progress bar that was moving far too slowly.

Kayl swung his gaze toward his brother. "Kier, over—"

Before the word override could fully leave Kayl's mouth, Kier said, "Done!"

WARNING! MANUAL CONTROL ENGAGED. MANUAL CONTROL IS NOT RECOMMENDED DURING EMERGEN-CIES. PLEASE ALLOW—

Kayl dismissed the message with an angry slash of his claws and dropped his hand to the antigrav control just as the holo viewports came back on.

"*Zor atkoshai,*" Kier breathed.

"Oh shite," Aileen muttered.

The ground was still dead ahead, but much, much closer than

before. Kayl's body reflexively tensed for impact, stomach twisting into a jumbled knot and heart trying to leap out of his throat.

"Third time's the charm," Aileen intoned, voice trembling with hope and desperation.

Kayl slammed down on the antigrav control.

The *Fang* shuddered. Machinery whirred on the lower deck, thrumming with power, building to a droning whine.

One more message appeared on screen—*ANTIGRAVITY DRIVE ENGAGED.*

The ground was so close now that Kayl could have counted the individual pebbles scattered across it, could have counted the sparkling flecks dotting. Deep in his belly, something constricted so severely that he felt tingles in his fingers and toes.

Death. He was looking at death.

But death, along with all the universe's cruelty, could go fuck itself.

Before he could so much as suck in a relieved breath, he grasped the flight controls in both hands, braced his feet on the pedals, and did as Aileen had suggested—he pulled up.

His insides contorted, shifting into places they should not have been. The ship's nose leapt. Silent warnings flashed on the edges of Kayl's vision. He ignored them, leveling the ship a mere two meters off the ground.

The alien landscape now lay before Kayl, its rugged rock formations silhouetted by the setting sun. Nervous but relieved laughter bubbled from Aileen; it was echoed by Kier and Kayl.

Kayl finally inhaled as he guided the *Fang* over one of the wide canyons. The play of light and shadow on the landscape was beautiful, especially with those reflective bits everywhere. He welcomed the peaceful respite.

"Kier, remap our route to Navaire." Kayl scanned the horizon. "We will find a place to land near—"

Another alarm blared. The antigrav drive's whirring the faltered, and the ship's forward momentum faded.

"We are losing power," Kier said.

A torrent of curses swirled in Kayl's mind, so numerous that they smashed into each other and none of them emerged when he opened his mouth. A flick of his hand expanded the holographic view of the outside, making the cockpit floor seem to melt away.

"Oh God, that's terrifying," Aileen whispered, lifting her feet off the floor. Kayl did not relinquish his tail's hold on her leg.

The canyon floor lay below them, and its rock walls stood to either side. A stream with plant life lining its banks meandered along the bottom of the canyon. All of it passed in a blur as the ship hurtled forward.

"We are with you, *na'diya*," Kier said.

Kayl eased the *Fang's* speed, causing the vessel to shudder. The whine of the antigrav drive—one of many sounds that hadn't been typical before the *Fang* was damaged—intensified.

"Hold together," Kayl growled.

Kier grunted. "The *Fang* will hold."

Kayl's gaze fixed upon a spot ahead, where a bend in the canyon created a relatively wide, flat stretch of ground. He slowed the ship further; it bounced, rocking its passengers in their seats. Kayl somehow kept the *Fang* steady, guiding it through a gap narrow enough that its sides must have cleared the canyon walls by mere meters, easing it lower, lower...

Finally, the ship was lined up with the chosen landing zone. Kier lowered the landing gear; Kayl angled the *Fang's* nose up slightly and reduced the speed even more. Despite everything, they could make an easy landing, and then—

The holos went out, again filling the cockpit with darkness. All sound save the thundering of Kayl's heart stopped for an instant. Then his stomach lurched, and he felt gravity trying to wrench him up out of his seat.

They were falling.

The *Fang* hit the ground with a deafening crash; that sound, that impact, became Kayl's entire world. Everything shook violently, everything came undone. *He* was coming undone. That eruption of violence ceased as abruptly as it had begun, but the *Fang* continued sliding forward for a few more seconds, rocks and dirt crunching and crumbling beneath it.

Then there was stillness, silence.

Aileen coughed, and Kayl drew in a breath that burned his lungs. He hurriedly unlatched his harness and shoved himself off his seat, colliding with Kier, who was also rushing to Aileen. Their groping hands found her just before the emergency lighting came on, casting everything in a soft red glow.

Aileen's rounded eyes darted between Kier and Kayl ceaselessly. "Are you okay?"

"Are *you* okay?" the twins asked in unison, stopping their hands; each had one hand on her cheek and another on her knee.

She blinked. An eternity of silence passed in a single second, and then she made a sound—a snort.

Kayl and his brother exchanged a worried glance.

Aileen laughed. The sound came from her belly, came from her soul, and tears welled in her eyes as it went on. She reached for the twins as though to embrace them, only for her harness to stop her short. She grunted. That only made her laugh harder, and her tears finally spilled.

She dropped her trembling hands to the harness buckles and, with Kier and Kayl's help, freed herself. Then she threw herself against them, wrapping her arms around their necks.

"Yes," she rasped.

They embraced her tight, drawing in lungfuls of her scent; they were overwhelmed by relief, by the feeling of her in their arms.

"Yes." She buried her face against Kayl's neck and kissed it before turning toward Kier to do the same. "I'm okay. We are okay."

"We are," Kier whispered, clutching her closer.

Kayl had never been so afraid, even having faced death countless times. He'd never had so much to lose. But they were safe—his brother, his mate, his life, his *daevalis*.

He squeezed his eyes shut and pressed his face into Aileen's hair. "We are."

TWENTY-SEVEN

Aileen worried her lip and shifted her weight from one foot to the other. The cockpit was dark save for the crimson emergency lights, and standing inside it, alone, certainly wasn't easing her anxiety. Dragging a hand through her hair, she pulled off her hair tie and slipped it around her wrist.

Kier and Kayl had gone outside to survey the damage to the ship and scout the area. They had told her to wait until they confirmed it was safe, but after that terrifying crash, she didn't want them out of her sight. She wanted to cling to them so she could be certain that they were alive, that they were real, that this wasn't some dream, some nightmare, or...

Or the afterlife.

She rubbed her hands over her chilled arms. The action sent dull pain through her torso. Her whole body was sore, especially where the harness had crossed her chest.

Pain is good. You can't feel pain if you're dreaming or dead, right?

Aileen released a long, slow exhalation. "Totally not helping..."

She stared at the closed cockpit door.

Where were her mates?

Aileen turned and paced away from the door, glancing up at the blank, solid walls, wishing there was a window to see out of. "I swear, if we survived all this just for those two to get eaten by some monstrous alien beast, I'll...I'll..."

The *whoosh* of the door opening was thunderous in the otherwise silent cockpit. Aileen started, spinning toward it.

Kier and Kayl stood in the doorway, their heads slightly tilted, their mismatched eyes fixed upon her. Though they'd retracted their helmets, the twins were still clad in the segmented armor they'd donned before going out.

It was the armor they'd been wearing when they rescued her from Eternal Paradise.

"Are you all right, Aileen?" Kier asked as he stepped through the entryway.

Relief washed through Aileen. She hurried to Kier and threw herself against him. Her body hit his hard armor, triggering more of that aching in her chest, but she didn't care. She wrapped her arms around his neck and clutched him tight. "Just glad you're not being digested in some creature's belly."

Kier hugged her, letting out a chuckle. "As are we, *na'diya*."

"That is a strangely specific thing to be grateful for," Kayl said.

She grinned. "Well, there isn't much to do when you're waiting in the dark except let your mind wander through all the worst possible outcomes."

Kier drew back, moving a hand to her cheek. "How can it ever be dark when you shine so brightly?"

Kayl sighed. "Do you have a collection of lines like that stored on your holocom, Kier, or did you come up with that one on your own? This is not—"

Aileen waved a hand at him. "No, no. I like this. Keep going."

Smirking, Kier leaned down and tipped his forehead against hers. "Alien nights hold no terror for me, *na'diya*, for you are a beacon in the darkness, ever beckoning me to your side."

She kept her eyes locked with Kier's as she combed her fingers through the hair hanging at the back of his neck. "Careful, or you'll spoil me. I could really, *really* get used to this."

"Never shall I concern myself with the cold, for the thought of you is enough to enkindle a flame in my heart that will warm me through the deepest frost."

"*Ba'shanaal*," Kayl rumbled, pinching the bridge of his nose.

"Jealous, brother?"

"No, I simply realized where all this is coming from. Those Volturian dramas."

Even in the dim emergency lighting, Kier's blush was clear. "Perhaps my words were...inspired by those programs. *Loosely* inspired. But it is the feeling behind them that matters, is it not?"

Aileen laughed and rubbed her nose against Kier's. "It is. And I still love hearing them."

"Anything to make you smile." Kier pressed his fingers firmly to her lower back, drew her closer, and captured her lips with his.

Her eyes drifted shut as she succumbed to him. Her body grew languid, pliant, as his mouth caressed hers and sent tingles of arousal to her belly.

But it was over far too soon.

Kier released her and withdrew. A smile still played upon his lips as he stepped toward the door. "Come outside, *na'diya*, and—"

Kayl suddenly filled the space Kier had vacated. His eyes met hers, swirling with fire and hunger. He did not offer flowery words; he looped one arm around her back, tugging her against him, while his other hand caught her jaw and tipped her face toward his.

His mouth slanted over hers. Where Kier's kiss had been sweet and tender, Kayl's was fierce and passionate, claiming her with lips and tongue, stealing her breath and replacing it with his essence. The spark that had been ignited in her core roared to life. Aileen moaned, clutching at his armored chest. They'd shared pleasure with their mouths and hands, but she craved more. So, so much more.

"Words are fleeting, Aileen," Kayl said when he broke the kiss, brushing the back of a finger across her cheek. "What we three share is eternal."

And then he pulled away. Cool air swept over her tingling lips, making her shiver with want for his heat. She stumbled after him, having not realized just how much she'd been leaning into his hold.

Kier laughed; there was a wicked edge to the sound that further stoked the flames at Aileen's core. "Come outside. I am sure you'll be glad to get off this ship for a few minutes and breathe some fresh air."

Aileen blinked away her daze, cheeks flushing. She glared at the twins. "That was dirty and *so* not fair." She raked her hand through her hair, pulling it back from her face as she strode toward Kier. "I hope you both have blue balls."

The twins glanced at each other, then down toward their crotches, before returning their gazes to hers.

"You know they are not blue," Kayl said. "You have seen them."

"And there is little we can do about their color, regardless," Kier said. His smile took on a lopsided tilt. "Are you fond of blue?"

The reminder of their shared time in the shower sent a fresh rush of heat through Aileen. "It's an expression."

"And what is it meant to express?" asked Kayl.

"It means—" Aileen snapped her mouth shut. "You know what, you figure it out. But I'd better not be the only one suffering from it."

Kier and Kayl exchanged another confused glance. Aileen could almost feel the questions swirling through their minds and flitting along the psychic connection the two shared.

Though she took some petty satisfaction from their confusion, she couldn't stand there and watch them wallow in it. She stepped closer to them, smoothed one hand down Kier's forearm, the other down Kayl's, and asked, "So, are we going outside?"

Their answering smiles sparked a different sort of heat inside Aileen, this time around her heart.

Together, the trio exited the cockpit and walked along the corridor. It was strange to see the *Fang* like this; the emergency lighting created an ominous atmosphere, and though there was no damage visible in here, everything felt just a little...off. Of course, that was likely a result of the ship having come to rest at an angle, giving the floors a slight yet noticeable slope.

But that sense of wrongness helped Aileen realize what the *Fang* had become to her in her few short days aboard—a home. She knew that was entirely because of Kier and Kayl, but that didn't change the truth.

Her place was with the twins, and this ship was their home. At least for now.

They paused at the entrance to her room. Kayl went inside, emerging shortly after with a pair of boots she'd selected from the clothing storage a few days ago. She tugged them on, fastened their straps, and gestured for the twins to continue.

Kier preceded her, opening the door into the cargo hold. Cool air flowed into the corridor from the hold, carrying a faint odor—that ozone tang of fried electronic components. By the time she'd descended the steps, her nose was stinging. A few more meters and that sting had grown into a burn, spreading into her throat and lungs, forcing tears from her eyes.

Aileen stopped suddenly, pressed a hand to her chest, and drew in several ragged, rasping breaths. Her chest constricted; every breath *hurt*. It was as though she was on fire inside. Her heart thumped beneath her palm.

Kayl halted and turned toward her as Kier covered her hand with his, placing his other hand on her back. "Just breathe, Aileen."

"Can't..." she gasped. Her fingers curled, and her nails dug into her skin, clawing at her chest. She held her breath, unwilling to release that last, precious bit of oxygen. Her vision wavered.

Kayl took Aileen's face between his hands and leaned close, nearly nose-to-nose, commanding her attention. His voice was low and rumbling as he said, "Breathe. The pain will pass."

Aileen held his gaze. Fear demanded she hold that air in her lungs to avoid more pain, but her trust in her mates was stronger. She let out a shaky breath and drew in another, and then another. The burning lessened with each inhalation.

"Good, *na'diya*," Kier said.

Kayl stroked his thumbs over her cheeks. "Keep breathing. It is simply your body adapting to the alien atmosphere."

She'd forgotten the injections she'd been given before departing Earth—it had been years ago, in another lifetime. Before departing for intergalactic travel, all humans were given a compound that allowed their bodies to adjust to the varying environments they might encounter out amongst the stars.

Apart from the sting of the injector and a little itching for an hour or two, that compound had given her no reason to think about it again.

She was sure as hell grateful for it now.

"Better?" Kayl asked.

Releasing another trembling exhalation, she nodded.

"Good," said Kier, nuzzling her hair.

"You...felt this too?" she asked.

"No, we did not. Daevahs are differently equipped for such things." Kayl withdrew his face and raised a hand, tapping the side of his nose, indicating small slits.

"Our kind evolved to endure fluctuating levels of toxins in the air," Kier said. "Our ancestral homeworld was a harsh place at times. Our nose slits provide natural filtration. The Consortium's mutagens only made that trait stronger."

Aileen had wondered about those tiny slits, but it had seemed rude to point at someone's face and ask, *what's that?*

She took in another deep breath, this one without any pain at all, and let it out with relief. "I'm okay now."

With a gentle smile, Kayl released her face and took her free hand, positioning himself beside her. Kier kept hold of her other hand, moving to stand on her other side.

The twins walked forward with her, and now that she wasn't preoccupied with dying from poison air, she looked around.

Where the upper deck hadn't shown any signs of damage, the cargo hold was much different story. Panels had fallen from the walls and ceiling, bits of wiring dangled from overhead, and several of the floor panels were askew or bent out of shape. Some of the cots, which had been neatly stored along the walls, had come free. Their mattresses were scattered, their frames warped. And one of the storage lockers had opened, the clothing that had been inside now strewn about the space.

The trio continued to the ramp, where Kier took the lead to guide her across a particularly mangled section of the floor, and exited the *Fang*. Aileen hesitated at the bottom of the ramp, one of her boots hovering centimeters above the ground.

Kier gave her hand a gentle squeeze. "What is wrong?"

"I just... I passed through a few space stations before I ended up in Eternal Paradise, but I've never set foot on another planet. Only Earth. And, well, after being held prisoner for three years..." She looked at him. "I guess there's a part of me that's a little scared."

"Do not be afraid, *na'diya*," Kier said, offering her that heart-melting smile.

"We are with you," Kayl added. When Aileen glanced at him, she saw that intensity in his eyes, that fire, which said he'd fight the whole universe to protect her.

Aileen placed her foot down. The ground was solid and gravelly, crunching beneath her sole. Her fear gave way to burgeoning excitement. She watched her feet as she took those first steps away from the ship. There were little reflective flecks in many of the rocks, and they shimmered as she passed them. They were contrasted by the bits of dull, scorched metal and debris that had undoubtedly come from the ship.

But there was something else there, something that didn't quite make sense—a faint glow flowing over the ground in ever-shifting colors.

She lifted her gaze.

Aileen had expected cloying darkness, menacing shadows, and a harsh, unforgiving alien landscape. Yet she didn't notice the landscape at all in that moment—her full attention was drawn skyward.

The air fled her lungs as she beheld the sky. Countless stars glittered overhead, backed by inky blues and purples. Waves of light coursed in front of those stars, spanning the heavens as far as she could see. Streams of green and blue, pink and purple, red and orange, scintillating and flowing hypnotically.

Despite the terror of their final descent on this planet, there'd been beauty on display outside the ship. But this...this was on a whole different level. Lips parting, and she gazed up in wonder.

And it struck her then—she was on an unknown world, who knew how many thousands or millions of lightyears away from Earth, staring at a brilliant light show in the sky, and her parents weren't here to appreciate it. But for the first time since she'd lost them, that was okay. Because she carried their memories in her heart...and she wasn't alone.

We are with you.

Warmth bloomed in Aileen's chest and spread outward, permeating her from head to toe, wrapping her soul in comfort and security. In *love*.

Aileen squeezed Kier and Kayl's hands before looking at them, smiling. Their eyes were not turned skyward, but locked on her, shining with their own inner light.

"Beautiful," Kier rasped.

"Indescribably so," Kayl purred.

TWENTY-EIGHT

AILEEN SWEPT BACK the rogue strands of hair that had blown into her face and let out a huff. "Well... It could be worse, right?"

Kayl grunted. He stood beside her with his arms folded across his chest and his gaze settled on the *Fang*. Kier was on her other side, raking his claws across his scalp. Their tails swung restlessly, occasionally brushing the backs of her legs.

"I thought so last night," Kier said, "but seeing it by daylight has changed my opinion."

Kayl just grunted again.

Aileen tried hard to hold back her smile; she failed. By night, shadows had obscured the severity of the damage the *Fang* had sustained. The battered underside, loosened hull plates, and scorched metal hadn't seemed quite so bad.

But it was readily apparent now—the *Fang* wasn't going anywhere in this state.

Despite that, Aileen was happy. So what if they were stranded on an unfamiliar planet? They were alive, and they had each other.

She turned away from the ship. The *Fang* had come down on a bulging bend in a wide canyon. A stream passed by within meters of the ship's rear, close enough that water had partially flooded the deep groove torn into the ground by the crash.

The surrounding cliffs were tall and imposing, but they eased in both directions, becoming more like rugged hills. The rock on the ground and comprising the canyon walls was run through with those reflective flecks that sparkled depending on how the light hit them.

As beautiful as those flecks were, it was the plant life that truly made this spot feel special. There was far more vegetation than there'd seemed from above—not that the *Fang's* descent had afforded much time to absorb the sights.

Alien trees stood scattered along the stream, their dark trunks splitting into countless thin branches that wove into huge weblike clusters adorned with feathery green leaves. Clumps of grass and brush grew amongst the rocks all over. Their foliage came in varying shades of yellow and green with hints of crimson scattered throughout. Some looked soft as cotton, while others looked like they'd slice skin at the slightest touch. And there were flowers in a variety of vibrant colors, some growing in clusters with tiny blooms and small, delicate petals, others with long stems swaying in the breeze.

Aileen turned her face up and took in a deep breath. She'd almost forgotten what it was like to smell fresh air. The wind sighed around her, lifting her hair and fluttering her sleeveless white tunic, molding the diaphanous fabric to her body.

Aileen swept her arms outward. "Think of this as a great adventure! A...honeymoon."

"Even I can think of several better ways to be adventurous," Kayl grumbled.

"I have my doubts about that, Kayl." Kier turned his head toward Aileen, tilting it. "What is a honeymoon?"

She lowered her arms. "An Earth tradition. Basically, it's a romantic vacation a couple takes together after they get married."

Kier's brow knitted. "Married?"

"When humans join in a ceremony. It's, um, legal recognition that they're...mated, but it means so much more than that. Or it's supposed to, anyway."

Kayl frowned. "What does legality have to do with the bond between mates?"

"I guess it's like...a contract?" She winced.

The twins turned to face her fully, both wearing looks of confusion and dawning horror.

"Terrans must enter legal contracts to become mates?" Kier asked.

A low growl rose from Kayl's chest. "How could terrans have been invited to Arthos while following such barbaric practices?"

"It's not like *that*." Aileen sighed, drawing the end of her ponytail over her shoulder and running her fingers through it. "I'm really not explaining this well. There are instances where yes, marriage sucks, but it's a choice. It's not forced on anyone. And it can often go a long way in protecting a relationship and ensuring that two people can advocate and care for each other through any bad situations life might throw at them."

"I remain skeptical of this terran tradition," said Kayl.

"Does it not"—Kier lifted his hands, curling his fingers as though grasping at something unseen—"remove some of the wonder from a relationship? Reducing it to legalities seems so...reductive."

"And that statement was redundant."

"The question remains valid."

Aileen smiled and briefly glanced skyward. "You're just going to have to trust me when I say it's not all about legalities. Most marriage ceremonies are really about bringing friends and family together to celebrate the joining of a couple and the start of their lives together." She gestured at the twins. "How do daevahs become official mates?"

"Official?" Kier asked.

Her brow furrowed as she looked between the two of them. "Well, you both said I was your mate, and it's just something you *know*. Does that mean we're already mated after I agreed? Are we together-together? Is there a ceremony that needs to happen, or an exchange of vows?"

Kier grinned. "Ah, *na'diya*...there is an exchange involved, but it has nothing to do with words."

She frowned. "Then what? Do we just stare longingly into each other's eyes until we decide it's official?"

He laughed.

Kayl reached around Aileen and gave his brother a shove before locking eyes with her. "Males must mate their female to seal their *daevalis,* opening themselves heart, mind, and soul."

"Oh." Aileen blinked, and her cheeks warmed. "*Ooooh.*"

Not an exchange of words, but of...bodily fluids.

Well, obviously it was more than that, but the images playing out in Aileen's mind remained unchanged. Heat rushed through her, pooling low in her belly, and anticipation thrummed in her veins.

The things she'd already done with the twins had brought her to heights beyond her imagining. How would she hold herself together if they escalated things, if they took it to the next level?

Daevahs made their bond by bringing their bodies together. By sharing the deepest intimacy, by getting as close as possible to one another. By making love.

That sounds so much more romantic than exchanging vows.

And more...erotic.

She pressed her lips together. She wanted Kier and Kayl, wanted all of them, but sex was just one part of what they were talking about. To be their lover, their mate, to stare into their eyes and see their souls, to feel them all around and inside herself, to be one with them...

Aileen had always been a romantic at heart, but somehow, she'd overlooked the deep, meaningful role sex could play in romance. That wonder had been stolen from her, tainted by what had been forced upon her. After Eternal Paradise, she never would've dreamed sex could be the most beautiful, natural, spiritual thing shared between lovers—at least if not for Kier and Kayl.

"Aileen, are you all right?"

Kier's gentle but concerned voice snapped Aileen out of her thoughts. She blinked again, shaking away the negativity threatening to rise from her memory. "Yeah. Sorry. My mind wandered a little there."

And yet...

Frowning, she clasped her wrist, looked down, and dug the toe of her boot into the dirt. "Is that why we haven't...gone further? Are you unsure of me?"

"Ah, *na'diya*." Kier closed the distance between them, grasped her chin, and lifted it, forcing her eyes to meet his. "We have never been more certain of anything."

"You are ours." Kayl placed a hand on the side of her neck. His fingers curled, grazing her throat with their claws. "There is no question of our joining, no doubt. It is but a matter of time."

The twins brushed their tails up and down her legs, their touches maddening even through the fabric of her pants.

Kier settled his free hand on her hip and leaned closer. "But after all we have suffered, after all you have suffered, we...wanted to go slow."

"For our *daevalis* to be forged, all three of us need to be fully ready. Mind, body, and soul. No hesitation, no question."

"No more thoughts of the past, of the future." Kayl's fingers stroked her neck tenderly. "Only of us."

Kier brushed his thumb across her lower lip. "We all needed time to heal."

Tears stung Aileen's eyes as she looked back and forth between the twins.

Time to heal.

She slid her hands up to the backs of the twins' necks and drew them down, pressing a kiss to each of their mouths. "You have both healed me in more ways than you realize."

They gifted her with smiles—Kier's easy and warm, reflecting the depth of the passion in his eyes; Kayl's slower, a touch more solemn, but just as powerful for the glimpse it granted into his closely-guarded heart.

"When the right moment arrives, we will know," Kier said softly.

"And we three will be one," Kayl added.

The year Aileen turned sixteen, she and her parents had spent several months touring the western United States. Wyoming into Colorado, south to New Mexico, then onward to Arizona and California before hooking back eastward into Nevada. There'd been sights to see everywhere, and she cherished the memories she'd made, but one state stood out from the rest on that trip.

Utah.

Because something had happened there, something that had only happened once every few years—the McConnells had found themselves with an entire week of free time. No obligations to fulfill, no shows, no reason to travel.

They'd spent that week camping and hiking in the rugged Utah countryside, often along rivers and streams. They'd sung around campfires at night, had tried their hands at fishing by day, had explored and relaxed and simply enjoyed being alive. That week had been so special to them that her da had barely complained about his sunburn—at least not until he'd strapped on a guitar at their next show.

Omega IV reminded her of that part of Utah. Yes, the plants and rocks were different, and the sky wasn't the same shade of blue, but it had a similar feel. Both places gave her that sense of being in the middle of nowhere, with nothing but possibility all around.

Performing several times a day on Eternal Paradise had kept Aileen in shape, but hiking through rocky terrain still produced a burn in her muscles. She kept up with Kier as best she could as they followed the stream through the gently winding canyon. The sun steadily climbed higher into the sky, and the shadows cast by canyon walls and towering rock formations slowly shrank.

The temperature rose along with the sun, but Aileen enjoyed the warm sunshine on her skin, most of which was bare on her torso thanks to her low-cut, sleeveless tunic. After years of living in a tightly controlled environment—despite its tropical themes, Eternal Paradise had been kept at a steady twenty degrees Celsius—the heat was a welcome change.

I'll likely sunburn like my father if I'm out here too long.

Aileen smiled to herself. She recalled those times when her da had been as red as a beet after a long day in the sun, and how her mother would lovingly apply aloe to his burns, all while giving him a proper tongue lashing for not taking precautions *again*.

Kayl had said they'd crashed three and a half kilometers from Navaire. Aileen used to easily walk that distance while exploring whatever county fair she and her parents had been performing at on any given night. And now she had fresh air, expansive skies...and the twins.

A realization hit her—she'd thought about her parents without being pierced by that familiar pang of loss.

It's because of them. Because of my mates.

Aileen looked up at Kier and Kayl, and her heart swelled.

You have both healed me in more ways than you realize.

Those words couldn't have been truer. Not only were the twins helping Aileen overcome the trauma Saduuk had inflicted upon her, but they were helping her find happiness again. Helping her feel *love*. She would always miss her parents, but she felt like she was finally living again. She was finding joy in life, and more than anything, she longed to share that life with Kier and Kayl.

As though sensing her attention, the twins turned their faces toward her, each arching a brow. Aileen could only smile.

They always remained close enough to offer a helping hand or steady Aileen, assisting her whenever they had to climb sections of rock or cross the water. Their utter lack of jealousy still amazed her. Kier and Kayl didn't compete for her attention or affection, didn't glare at each other when one got to touch her, but the other didn't. They were just there with her. For her.

Before long, beads of sweat had gathered along Aileen's hairline and were trickling between her breasts and down her back. She and the twins hiked up an incline that brought them out of the canyon. The land leveled out, creating a base from which more of those stony hills and towering rock formations rose, casting long shadows. Vegetation dotted the landscape, some of it growing directly from the rocks. The wind remained a warm, gentle caress, the occasional gusts too weak to do more than kick up a little dust.

And in the distance lay Navaire, its buildings warped by the heat-shimmers pulsing from the ground.

The trio paused to drink some water before continuing, with the twins now flanking Aileen.

That first glimpse of their destination was bittersweet for Aileen. It meant their little journey was nearly at its end, that they would, hopefully, find the assistance they needed so they could be on their way. So they could start planning the rest of their lives. But it also meant a town full of strangers, it meant having to step out of the private reality where only Aileen and her mates existed.

Her *na'divali*.

Aileen glanced at the twins, and her heart clenched. It would've been a lie to say she didn't wish it could be just the three of them for a little longer. She didn't want these quiet, intimate moments to end.

It's not the end. This is just another step in our journey together.

Kier turned his head and caught her gaze. His lips stretched into that wide, mischievous grin that made her belly flutter wildly.

"Are you staring at us, *na'diya?*" he asked.

She chuckled. "I am most definitely checking both of you out. I just can't help myself."

Slowing her steps, she dipped her eyes to their backsides. The twins' clothing was loose and flowing, worn over those skintight bodysuits that hid their armor. Despite that, the fabric of their clothes sculpted to their asses as they walked, and the muscles of their broad shoulders and toned torsos were hinted at through their shirts.

There were so many features to admire, she couldn't keep her eyes on just one. "I must be one incredibly lucky woman to have two gorgeous, virile males protecting her."

"Ah, Aileen," Kayl rumbled, "your gaze is hotter than the sun."

"Well, if it bothers you that much…" Barely fighting back a grin, she averted her gaze and turned her face toward the sky.

He growled. "No. I would sooner burn to ash in your light, *na'diya*, than endure even a moment of darkness."

Aileen swung her gaze back toward him, eyes flaring, heart thumping. "I think that's my new favorite."

"Oh, come now, Kayl," said Kier, throwing his hands up. "You criticized me for using lines from those dramas."

Kayl's smile was downright wicked. "I spoke from my soul, brother. Not from a show."

"I told you I was merely inspired by the shows!"

Aileen's grin made her cheeks ache more than her legs did, but she wouldn't have changed it for anything.

"Speaking of the sun and burning…" She lifted an arm and studied her skin. "Your *na'diya* is going to get a sunburn if we're out here too much longer."

The twins' steps faltered, and Aileen walked past them. A hand clamped around her wrist, halting her abruptly, and tugged her back toward the twins.

"What did you say?" Kayl asked, scowling.

"That…I was going to get a sunburn?"

Kier frowned. "A sunburn? What does that mean?"

"Obviously a burn caused by the sun," Kayl snapped. He leaned his head down to examine her skin.

"We are tens of millions of kilometers away from this system's star"—Kier pointed skyward—"and protected by an atmosphere. How?"

Kayl's tail lashed behind him as he inspected the skin of her forearm, which was not yet showing an signs of a sunburn. "I am afraid I lack sufficient expertise in the field of physics to give you a satisfactory explanation, Kier."

"I was asking our mate, Kayl."

The ache in Aileen's cheeks deepened; she couldn't have stopped grinning no matter how much it hurt. She shrugged. "Ultraviolet light, I think? I'm no physicist either. It's just something that happens. It's especially bad for fair-skinned humans like me."

Just like that, both twins were staring at her again, their gazes intense. In unison, they asked, "How can we protect you?"

Before she could respond, Kier turned his back toward the sun, spread his arms wide, and stood on his toes in front of Aileen, taking up as much space as possible. His boots shuffled over the ground as he repositioned himself so his shadow fell across Aileen.

Meanwhile, Kayl had released her arm and was now untucking his tunic from his belt.

"Why did you not tell us before we left the *Fang*?" Kier asked.

She pressed her lips tight together to stifle her laughter.

"We cannot keep you from harm if we are not told of all the things that can harm you," Kayl said as he pulled his tunic off over his head, revealing the black bodysuit beneath.

"Maybe I just wanted you to undress for me?" Aileen said, running her gaze over him.

Kayl hesitated, narrowing his eyes. "You speak of burning in the sun, but you are teasing me?"

Aileen chuckled and leaned closer to him, pecking a kiss on his lips. "Because you are so fun to tease."

"Aileen..." Kier intoned. "This is a serious matter."

Kayl's tongue slipped out, running over his lower lip. Heat sparked in his eyes. "We may have overestimated the severity, Kier."

"Sunburns can be severe," Aileen said. "There are a few degrees of them. It's been over three years since I've been out in the sun, so I'll likely get a minor burn no matter what. But if I were to remain in the sun for an extended amount of time, especially without protection, it could get pretty bad."

Kier's frown deepened, and a crease formed between his eyebrows. "*Over*estimated, Kayl?"

Scowling again, Kayl flipped his tunic around and brought it down over Aileen's head. She chuckled as she slipped her arms through the sleeves. Of course, they were too long, and the tunic's hem hung to her knees, but the fabric was light and airy—and, best of all, it smelled like him.

She inhaled, taking in his spicy scent.

He shifted closer to Aileen and wrapped his arms around her. Aileen turned her head so that her mouth was close to Kayl's ear, but she held Kier's gaze. She lowered her voice and said, "I thought you two preferred taking clothes off me."

Kayl let out a shaky breath that was underscored by a low, delicious growl as he fastened his belt around her waist, yanking her a tad closer. "The sunlight can burn you when it touches your skin, *na'diya...*"

Kier closed the distanced between him and Aileen and leaned down. His eyes were vibrant, his pupils had narrowed to slits, and his ocean and earth scent enveloped her. His lips were a hair's breadth away from hers, and the heat that radiated from him was stronger than the sun's. Aileen's sex clenched, reminding her of that all too familiar hollowness in her core.

"But we can make you burn without touching you at all," Kier purred.

They both stepped away from her at once.

Aileen's breath left her in a soft whoosh.

Kier smirked triumphantly while Kayl clenched his jaw. They didn't hide the hunger in their eyes as they ran their gazes over her. As one, they turned, and continued walking ahead.

Aileen gaped at them before quickening her step to fall in line behind them. "You are both soooo not playing fair!"

"You started it," Kier said over his shoulder.

"Me? Kayl was the one taking his clothes off."

To her surprise, Kayl raised a hand to the neck of his jumpsuit, hooking his fingers beneath the collar. "I could keep going, if you would like."

Aileen came to a stop, brows raised. "Does that mean we get to play around a little?"

The twins halted as well, turning partly toward her.

Lashes lowered, she caught her bottom lip with her teeth and teasingly skimmed a hand down her neck, over her chest and abdomen, and past the belt Kayl had secured around her waist. She gathered the hems of the tunics and bunched them around her hips as she grasped the waistband of her pants and pushed down. "Cause I'm game."

The fires in the twins' eyes burned impossibly brighter. Kayl clenched his fists at his sides, muscles tensing and relaxing, and Kier's tail was practically wagging behind him. Their lips parted, and both let out heavy, hungry breaths.

Aileen paused and cocked her head. "Oh, but wait. That would mean I would be exposed to the sun." She tugged her pants back into place, let the tunics fall, and shrugged. "Ah well, maybe another time."

Kier and Kayl stared as Aileen walked past them; she managed to suppress her grin until they were behind her.

Their boots crunched over the dirt as they hurried to catch up to her.

"If your goal was to ensure that we are suffering as much as you, *na'diya*," Kier said, "you have succeeded."

"Overwhelmingly so," Kayl grumbled.

Aileen laughed and glanced at them over her shoulder. "You'll just have to make up for it later."

TWENTY-NINE

Aileen's view of Navaire sharpened as she and the twins neared the settlement. Most of its buildings were constructed with a pale, yellowish material that reminded her of adobe, though there was plenty of metal on display amongst them. One side of the town was dominated by larger, more advanced structures—one bristling with antennas and dishes, likely a communications array, and compound filled with hangars and huge loading equipment that must've been the spaceport.

The buildings were arranged along the edge of an immense pit, the bottom of which was out of sight until Aileen and the twins were much closer.

Kier said it looked like a quarry. The wind seemed stronger near the edge, and it made strange moaning sounds as it dipped into the pit and spawned small dust devils on the bottom.

The twins had told Aileen that Omega IV was a fringe world, an isolated planet with a single settlement that might well have been abandoned. She felt all that while she stood beside the pit. Felt hopes and dreams that had been crushed or discarded. Felt the abandonment, the loneliness.

She hoped it was all in her imagination.

They hurried onward, following the quarry around to the settlement.

A wide dirt road ran through the heart of Navaire, lined on either side by low buildings with metal-slatted windows. The entrance to the spaceport lay at the far end of the road, marked by a wide gate and three huge towers, which stood silent vigil over the quarry. Most of the metal in sight bore the distinctive patina of age and wear.

But this wasn't some old west ghost town.

Navaire's inhabitants were out and about—walking along the street, talking in front of buildings, working and living. A few of them tended alien animals the likes of which Aileen had never seen. One group was loading supplies into a hovertruck with a beat-up, weather-worn exterior.

The twins fell into place on either side of Aileen; together, they proceeded.

They'd not made it more than a few steps down the road before some of the locals noticed. After a few poorly concealed whispers, heads began turning. Doors opened here and there, and people emerged to look at the newcomers.

Aileen's heart quickened as more and more eyes fell upon her and her mates. She'd been a performer for her entire life. She'd been watched by more people than she could count, and had never been bothered by it, even if she still got nervous before getting on stage. But it felt very different to have an audience when you weren't performing.

Just another new location on the list, Aileen. No different than all the other unfamiliar places you've been.

Well, apart from the whole being on an alien planet in some far-flung corner of universe thing, anyway.

She smiled. Aileen had always enjoyed seeing new places and meeting new people. Saduuk had stolen that from her; for all the millions upon millions of diverse visitors who'd cycled through Eternal Paradise, Aileen's circumstances had never connected with any of them, had never been able to enjoy that diversity. She'd been a slave kept there to entertain Saduuk's guests and nothing more.

But that place was behind her. She was here, with Kier and Kayl, and she could choose how to approach this new life and face all the challenges it would bring.

The twins slowed as they neared the hovertruck, until Kayl placed a hand on Aileen's stomach, guiding her to a halt along with them. She glanced up at him, but he kept his gaze on the workers ahead.

Those workers wrestled a large crate up into the truck's bed, making it rock on its antigrav pads, before turning their attention to Aileen and the twins.

"Greetings," said Kier, moving slightly in front of Aileen as though to shield her. "Our ship requires repairs, and we need to replenish our provisions. Guidance would be much appreciated."

One of the workers, a muscular, scaled alien, brushed his hands together, wiping dust off his palms. "Your ship the one that blasted by last night?"

"Yes," Kayl replied.

Another of the workers, a thin, young kaital with large ears, blue skin, and big, black eyes, hopped down from the truck. "I told you it had to be them, Weyel!"

"Go let Ialle know," the scaled alien, Weyel, said over his shoulder to one of his companions, who nodded and hurried down the road toward a wide plaza. Turning back to the twins and Aileen, Weyel said, "We were convinced you crashed out there. Ialle's putting a rescue party together right now. Most of us figured it'd end up more a salvage mission than anything."

"With respect, we are happy you were wrong," Kier replied with a touch of dryness.

"Did you really make it through the storm?" asked the kaital, eyes wide.

The twins nodded. The excitement on the young kaital's face was almost as bright as the sun.

Weyel grunted, narrowing his eyes. "Your ship was already the talk of the town. Quite the show you put on. Knowing you survived, though... People will talk about it for months."

"They made it through the storms," the kaital said. "People will talk about that *forever*."

"All we did was almost not crash," Aileen said with a chuckle.

"Not much happens around here." Weyel was looking at Aileen now, studying her with an odd blend of confusion and concentration. He quickly shook off that expression and turned away, pointing down the road. "Take them to Ialle, Ardu. No point in standing around here."

Somehow, Ardu's face brightened. The kaital waved Aileen, Kier, and Kayl on as he started walking toward the plaza at a brisk pace.

"Thank you," Aileen said to Weyel as she and the twins set out after the youth.

The scaled alien nodded, looked Aileen over again with the same uncertainty and curiosity as before, and turned back to the hovertruck.

"I can't believe you made it through that storm," Ardu said, speaking so quickly that Aileen—despite her fluency in Universal Speech and her translator implant—almost couldn't understand him. He was moving in a sort of jogging sidestep, progressing toward their destination while keeping the twins and Aileen in view. "We saw all these colors flashing up there, and then fire and smoke, and this long, long streak going across the sky."

He moved his hand through the air in a very steep downward path. "Everyone thought for sure you were dead."

Aileen shuddered at the memory. That freefall before their landing had been...unpleasant. Maybe in a few months—or in another life—she'd be able look back and see the excitement of it.

Eh...probably not.

"We thought so too," Aileen said. "But our pilot is the best."

Kier glanced at her, smirking. "That may be a bit of an exaggeration, *na'diya*."

"Was it you?" Ardu's eyes rounded as they locked on Kier. "Oh, you have to show me some—"

"It was me," Kayl said flatly. "And there is no exaggeration."

Aileen's lips curled into a wide smile. Kayl wasn't prone to arrogance, and there was none of it in his voice now—only pure, unwavering confidence.

"You'd have to be the best to get through the storms," Ardu said.

Kier tilted his head. "Do those storms happen often?"

"The bad ones happen a couple times a year. We get smaller ones sometimes, but most people don't even notice those."

As they turned and entered the central plaza, Aileen let her gaze wander. The area was lined with more of those adobe-like buildings, but these were larger, a little better maintained, and less modular in design. Several looked to be shops. The largest of the buildings faced the quarry, and had a wide, sheltered porch spanning its front. Several locals were gathered on that porch, watching Aileen and her companions approaching.

A female broke away from that group and walked out to meet Aileen and the others.

The female was a dacrethian, like Almun from Eternal Paradise —tall, lithe, long of limb. But where Almun had been golden-skinned, she was a stunning amethyst, the color shifting into a light aquamarine along her throat and face. She wore a long, bright blue cloth around her neck and shoulders that trailed behind her like a cape, its fluttering adding an etherealness to her visage.

Ardu turned to face the dacrethian, gesturing excitedly toward Aileen and the twins. "It's them, Ialle! The ones who came down last night!"

Aileen and the twins had to tip their heads back as the dacrethian, Ialle, neared. Kier and Kayl were nearly a head taller than Aileen; Ialle was nearly a head taller than them. Beneath her cloak, she wore a long tunic in a deep, dark purple, secured at the waist with a wide, studded belt. The metal studs glittered with the same reflective flecks that seemed to be present in every rock on the planet.

Ialle came to a stop a few meters away from the group. She hooked the thumbs of her lower hands behind her belt and lifted one of her upper hands, smoothing it back over her hairless scalp. "I see that, Ardu. Head on back to Weyel and finish helping loading up while I acquaint myself with our visitors."

The young kaital frowned. "I don't want to miss any of this, Ialle. Weyel will be fine without me."

"Weyel needs you looking out for him, Ardu," Ialle replied without looking away from Aileen and the twins. "No one can read those tunnels like you, you know that."

Ardu's posture slumped. "Yeah, I know. All right. Guess someone will tell me about it later."

"I'm sure we'll see you around town, Ardu," Aileen said.

"Yeah." Ardu's smile returned, stretching across his face. "Yeah, you're right. Not like there's many places to go around here, huh?" That grin didn't fade as he waved and jogged back toward the waiting hovertruck.

"That was kind of you," Ialle said, tilting her head as she fixed her gaze on Aileen. "I'm Ialle. Navaire's duly elected arbiter, but only because these people keep voting me into office even though I told them I want to retire."

"We are glad to meet you, Ialle." Kier offered a slight bow, tail snaking back to hook around Aileen's leg. "I am called Kier, my brother is Kayl, and she is our mate, Aileen."

Aileen's heart leapt, and her belly fluttered. This trip to Navaire marked the first time she and the twins had interacted with other people together—the first time they'd introduced her as theirs.

She liked it. She liked it a lot.

The dacrethian's eyes widened, and she made a thoughtful hum as she studied Aileen anew. "Didn't know it was possible for daevahs to mate with...a whatever you are."

"I'm a terran," Aileen said.

"Can't say I've ever seen a terran. Or that I've heard of one, for that matter."

"We're kind of...new around the universe."

Ialle shrugged, turning her upper palms skyward. "As you might have guessed, we run a little behind the current trends here. Don't have many travelers coming through here." The dacrethian tilted her head, raking her gaze over Aileen. "And we've never had any like you, Aileen. You look...soft."

Is...that a bad thing?

Should I be offended?

The twins tensed, glancing at Aileen with brows low. Kier whispered, "Should we consider that an insult, *na'diya?*"

"I mean no insult," Ialle said. "You're just...different from what I'm accustomed to seeing."

Aileen blinked, following Ialle's gaze to look down at her own body before. The fabric of Kayl's tunic, padded by her own shirt beneath, molded to her breasts to make them look larger and more prominent than normal. Though comfortable, her pants were snug around her hips, ass, and upper thighs.

She flicked her eyes to Ialle. The dacrethian was tall and slender, with a seemingly flat chest and only the barest suggestion of flaring hips beneath her clothing. Her limbs were long and lean. Perfect.

That quickly, Aileen found herself battling a surge of self-consciousness. So many of the nonhuman species she'd encountered were so beautiful, so elegant, so exotic—and yet it seemed that all of them looked upon her that way.

Just like they had in Eternal Paradise. Just like they had before they'd offered Saduuk money to...to...

Aileen crossed her arms over her chest. Though everything was different—the place, the people, her manner of dress, her whole life—the memories and emotions from Eternal Paradise clawed their way to the surface.

Her throat constricted, and her heart sped. This was how she'd felt every time Saduuk had let prospective clients look her over, when he'd treated her like a piece of flesh to be rented out for a nightly rate.

Kier and Kayl stepped in front of her, forming a living barrier to shield her body from Ialle. Kayl's tail swept back, caught her free leg, and wrapped around it possessively.

Their attentiveness, thoughtfulness, and protectiveness chased those memories away. With the twins, she would never have to feel small and powerless again. She brushed her fingers lightly over their backs to signal her gratitude for their intervention.

"Our ship requires repairs," Kayl said firmly.

Ialle chuckled. "Yeah, I would imagine so. Doesn't explain why you're here, though."

Kayl glanced at his brother. "Was I unclear?"

"You're in town for repairs. That's clear enough. But the only travelers who come Omega IV are traders, fugitives, and bounty hunters." Ialle braced her upper hands on her hips. "You're not traders, because it's been the same three of them coming around here for the last fifteen years. So, you're either looking for a place to hide or looking for someone in hiding."

"We have not come to cause trouble," said Kier.

"Well, I'm glad for the reassurance. Consider my worries buried and forgotten."

Is she...being sarcastic?

Yes. That was some galaxy-class sarcasm.

"We really are here for repairs," Aileen said. "We kind of...ran into the storm unexpectedly."

The dacrethian laughed, studying the trio with open skepticism. "Unexpectedly? Your scanners should have been screaming the instant you entered the system."

Kier dragged his fingers through his chaotic hair. "Our scanners did detect the storm. About four minutes before we hit it."

The humor faded from Ialle's face completely. "You expect me to believe you survived the storm *and* a crash in a ship that couldn't even pick up the radiation until it was on top of you?"

Aileen arched a brow. "You think we'd fly straight into a cosmic storm for no reason?"

Ialle met Aileen's gaze. "Depends what you were running from. We've seen people try. And those rescue parties became salvage parties real quick."

"Our ship was fired upon by pirates," Kayl said flatly. "We would not have survived a second hit, so we jumped."

"Without a destination programmed," added Kier.

"We arrived in this system, our ship crippled. We patched up what we could to make the journey here. Our long-range communications and scanning systems were inoperative, so we did not detect the storm until it was too late to turn around."

"And even if we had turned around, our life support would've failed long before we could get anywhere safe," Aileen said.

"The only choice was to push through the storm," Kayl continued, "and hope we could breach the atmosphere before the shields failed."

"Or before the engines exploded," Kier said. "Either of which would have been rather unpleasant."

Ialle nodded. "I imagine so."

Kayl took a step closer to Ialle, tail unwinding from Aileen's leg but not breaking contact completely. "We did not come here to hide or to hunt. We came because there was nowhere else for us to go. We need repairs, we need supplies, and we need to send a message to Arthos."

"All of which we will pay for in credits," Kier added.

Ialle pressed her thin lips together, folded both pairs of arms across her chest, and dipped her chin. "It might be against my better judgment, but...I believe you. And if I'm truthful, I don't really care if you're criminals or bounty hunters." She looked each of the trio in the eye, one at a time. "Just don't cause trouble in my town."

Kier and Kayl both scanned the plaza; there were still plenty of townsfolk gathered around, watching, some of them talking in excited whispers.

"We will not cause trouble," Kier said.

"But we will not hesitate to defend ourselves and our mate should the need arise," Kayl added.

Ialle turned her head, running her eyes over the people as well. "Can't fault you for that. I think most people are too awed by you to want to start anything. Word of you making it through the storm has already spread. You're more likely to get begged for stories than harassed. Not much for entertainment around here."

"So...about the things we asked for?" Aileen said.

"I'll take you to Tallian, our mechanic." Ialle swung her gaze back to Aileen and the twins. "Can't promise he can fix your ship, but I'll let him determine that. As for supplies"—she extended an arm, pointing to a few of the buildings around the plaza—"our illustrious shops are open to you. I'll even talk with the shopkeepers to make sure they don't price gouge you."

"How kind of you," Kayl said dryly.

Aileen snickered, grasped his tail, and gave it a gentle tug. "Be nice."

Kayl started and turned his head toward her. His brows fell low, and he leaned down to rasp, "I will remember that when we make up for teasing you later."

Heat curled in her core, and Aileen squeezed her thighs together against a flare of desire. When it came to *later*, she didn't want nice; she wanted the twins to do every naughty thing they could imagine to her.

Kier cleared his throat, glancing briefly at Aileen and Kayl before returning his attention to Ialle. "And the message?"

The dacrethian unfolded her arms and turned her palms skyward. "Can't help you there, at least not for a few days. These storms knock out our long-range comms and scramble most geo-positioning equipment. They even mess with some of the automated mining equipment. That's a big part of why the companies that founded this colony eventually backed off. Storms are too unpredictable and too disruptive to operations.

"But it should pass in a few days." She curled her hands into loose fists and brought them all close to her chest, bowing her head in an almost prayerlike manner. "Then we can get a message out for you."

"Then I suppose we'll just have to wait out the storm," Aileen said, leaning against Kier and placing her hand upon his chest. She gazed up at him and smiled wide. "I'll enjoy spending that time with my mates."

Kier wrapped an arm around her, palmed her ass with his strong hand, and drew her against his body. He caught her chin and tilted her head back, looking down at her with a devilish grin. "And *we* will enjoy you."

THIRTY

IALLE LED KIER, Kayl, and Aileen across the plaza and between two of the shop buildings, gently brushing off the questions asked by the townsfolk they passed along the way. A three-meter-tall concrete and metal wall ran behind those buildings, separating the plaza from the spaceport. The large gate was open, one of its big metal doors having been detached and propped up against the wall. The dirt accumulated at its base suggested it had been there for a long while.

"Company used to keep tight security on the spaceport," Ialle explained as she stepped through the gap. "Can't blame them. Must've had billions of credits in goods and materials coming and going."

She paused to glance over her shoulder. "Mostly going, of course."

Kier scanned their new surroundings. Despite a misunderstanding or two, he found Ialle to be honest and charming in her own unique way, but he refused to let his guard down. It didn't matter how safe things seemed—the twins would always remain vigilant for the sake of their *na'diya*.

Like the rest of Navaire, the spaceport openly wore its age. The buildings seemed remnants of a bygone era. They were blocky and unadorned, with harsh, practical angles, but they stood with a sense of sturdiness and longevity. They'd been here long enough for their exteriors to be weatherworn and faded, and they'd likely remain standing for many, many more years after the twins and their mate departed.

The ground was covered in dirt with the same shimmering flecks that seemed to permeate the planet, but something about the feel of that dirt underfoot suggested that there was a firmer, artificial surface hidden beneath.

Ialle walked around an elevated landing pad. Kier glanced up at its underside as he passed, gently taking hold of Aileen's arm and guiding her away from the structure. The bare metal of the support struts was corroded and rough, and bits of metal and cabling dangled from beneath the pad itself, swaying in the wind.

Numerous hangars and landing pads filled the area, all in similar states of wear and disuse. Piles of junk—scrap metal, ruined electronics, mechanical components, and the husks of old vehicles—lay all over, much of it partially buried in the dirt.

Once they were clear of the landing pad, Kier turned his gaze to the left. The edge of the quarry lay a hundred and fifty meters away, its far side blurred by distance and heat haze. Three huge towers rose from that edge, each connected to an immense landing pad near its top. Thick support beams, reinforced by crisscrossing braces from top to bottom, held the structures aloft. Cables thicker than Kier's leg hung within the towers' framework.

Kier paused; Aileen halted beside him, and Kayl on her opposite side.

Again, Kier felt *time*. Those towers had been built to endure.

Freight elevators, Kayl pulsed.

Ahead, Ialle slowed to a stop and settled her gaze on the elevators. In a wistful tone, she said, "In the early days, those were running day and night, hauling up loads of faldrium from the quarry. Probably haven't been used in a good ten years."

Aileen tilted her head and swept some of her red locks out of her face. "Faldrium?"

The dacrethian nodded. "A rare mineral. They use it to make a lot of high-tech stuff. Apparently, it's a key component in most jump drive systems." A small smile played upon her lips. "All I really know is that it's what makes Omega IV sparkle."

Kier glanced at Aileen. She turned her face toward him, and her soft smile widened. He caught one of her hands in his and gave it a squeeze.

Beauty could be found in the most unlikely places—on remote frontier planets, within the coldest reaches of space, and on stage at a gaudy space resort and casino.

His *aerys* whispered in perfect sync with his brother's. *We are ready.*

He barely suppressed an excited shiver.

"Still have people who go down to extract faldrium, though they're pulling from the tunnels instead of the quarry these days. The traders pay decently for it when they come through, but what they buy is a speck of dust in the desert compared to what we used to ship out." Ialle hooked all four thumbs behind her belt and stared out over the quarry a little longer. "This town was something to see when it was bustling, but...the quiet suits this place better."

She waved them along and continued walking. Kayl strode after her. Kier and Aileen lagged, their eyes meeting again.

Aileen smirked, a playful light dancing in her gaze. "Just going to stare at me all day?"

Kier lifted her hand and lowered his head, brushing a kiss across her knuckles. "Perhaps. Are you going to stand there all day?"

She shrugged and leaned back, glancing at his backside. "Figured I'd take the rear. Enjoy the view a little."

"Ah, *na'diya*," he growled. That lustful haze only she could awaken settled over his mind, heating his blood and making his heart beat faster. "When we return to the *Fang*, we will ensure you are so awash with pleasure that you will not be able to form the smallest thought or utter the simplest word but for one."

"Oh?" She arched a brow and cocked her head. "And what word is that?"

"*More*," Kier purred. He loved listening to her cries of ecstasy, loved fulfilling her desires, but he loved it most when she begged for it.

He swung his tail, smacking it across her ass.

She started with a yelp, yanked her hand free of his hold, and used it to shield her backside as she took a few steps away. "You really do fight dirty."

What are you doing? Kayl pulsed. *Hurry along, so we may conclude our business here.*

Kayl was walking just behind Ialle, who was nearing one of the largest hangars—which also happened to be the only one open.

Coming, dear brother. Grinning, Kier stalked after Aileen. "I told you, *na'diya*, there is no such thing as a fair fight."

Her smile widened, and she darted off toward the others, the ends of Kayl's oversized tunic fluttering behind her. For an instant, Kier's playfulness was overwhelmed by a powerful instinct—the need to give chase, to capture his mate, to claim her.

He shook it off and slowed his pace, ensuring he did not catch up to her before she had reached Kayl and Ialle.

Kayl looked at Kier over his shoulder. *I would like to be included, brother.*

Barely containing a chuckle, Kier pulsed, *That comes as news to me, Kayl. Here I have spent our lives thinking you were much too serious to play.*

Kayl's eyes shifted to Aileen as she neared him, and his expression softened, that icy glare melting with the warmth of his longing and adoration. *That was before her.*

Those words echoed through their psychic link again—*We are ready.*

Ready to put the past aside. Ready to shed those traumas. Ready to trust themselves, to trust Aileen, and embrace their true destinies.

"Don't let the mess put you off," Ialle said as she led them through the hangar doors.

The hissing of a fusion tool and metallic clangs and groans sounded from deeper within the hangar.

Ialle raised her voice over the noise. "I know you don't exactly have many options here, but Tallian and his youngling are among the best."

Kier responded with a thoughtful hum, Kayl with a low grunt, as they and their mate studied the place. The hangar was large and spacious, likely sized to house the same freight ships that had been used to transport faldrium off the planet—not that any ships would fit inside now.

Spare parts and half-stripped vehicles lay all about in haphazard stacks and piles. The concrete floor was stained and littered with dust and debris, but tracks in the dirt marked the frequent lanes of passage. Various tools were scattered amidst the labyrinthine array of parts.

"I cannot tell if these vehicles are in the process of being built or being torn apart," Kayl said.

Ialle chuckled and shook her head. "Haven't had a new vehicle delivered in years. If not for Tallian scavenging parts from what's already here, there wouldn't be a functional vehicle on the entire planet."

The sound of metal hammering metal echoed off the walls, deep and resonant yet also high and piercing. Aileen winced as the sounds built upon each other; even Kier and Kayl found themselves gritting their teeth before long.

Cupping her hands to either side of her mouth, Ialle called, "Tallian!"

The banging grew louder still.

Ialle drew in a deep breath, shoulders and chest swelling, and repeated the name in a harsh shout that cut through the noise.

Someone snarled a curse, and a metallic object clanged on the floor. That was followed by a few more curses, muttered this time, and the scraping of metal over concrete.

"You all right, Tallian?" Ialle asked.

"I asked you not to do that anymore," Tallian replied. Though there was a gruff edge in his voice, it was softer and more refined than Kier would've guessed based on those muttered curses.

"Seems like the best way to get your attention."

"Or to get me to hurt myself. As much as it pains me to point this out, Ialle, you are capable of *walking* over here if you need to speak with me."

She snickered, shot an amused glance over her shoulder, and proceeded into the maze of parts and vehicles.

Kayl followed the dacrethian closely, with Aileen just behind him. Kier took up the rear, allowing himself to cease his vigilance temporarily so he could focus his attention on Aileen's backside.

Her hips swayed as she walked, and the way she had to move to avoid the obstacles in their path made her clothing sculpt to her ass perfectly. He clenched his teeth and held back a ravenous growl; he longed to tear those clothes off her and tease her rounded backside with his fangs.

"I can feel you enjoying the view, Kier," Aileen whispered without looking back.

He only grinned—and stared—harder.

"I want you to know that if I get lost in this mess, Tallian, the official succession laws have already been altered to force you to take my place," Ialle called.

"You had better make it through in one piece then, Ialle," Tallian replied. "If I were to succeed you as arbiter, your legacy would be forever tarnished."

"For making a bad choice in successor?"

"No, for choosing a successor who would show this town what competent leadership looks like."

The dacrethian laughed and paused, glancing from left to right before turning and proceeding forward. "Do you spend your days fixing things or sharpening that tongue of yours?"

Kier smiled to himself. The banter between Tallian and Ialle reminded him of the friends he and Kayl had made—of Thargen, Arcanthus, Drakkal, and the rest of Arcanthus's crew, who spent their time together tossing good-natured insults at one another. They'd welcomed Kier and Kayl into their group with such ease and warmth, had shown the twins what it was like to not be so alone.

It hadn't always been easy, and Kier knew his brother had struggled to connect with them and find his place, but it had been a good thing. Because despite his difficulties, even Kayl had opened up a little. Even Kayl had begun to thaw.

Without Arcanthus and the others being in the twins' lives, the past six months would've been so different. Kier and Kayl never would've gone to Eternal Paradise, never would've found Aileen. Never would've discovered their *na'diya*, their purpose, their happiness.

"I fear I may perish of old age before you arrive, Ialle," Tallian said, sounding far closer than before.

The dacrethian's head snapped to the side, and she let out a triumphant snicker. "There you are." She made one more turn, stepping around a stack of large, beat-up crates.

Kier followed his brother and his mate around the corner. They emerged in a more open space where some semblance of order had fought back the chaos. Workbenches and tool cases were arranged along two of the walls, with heavier equipment standing on the floor. A large lift at the center of the area held a rugged old hovercar over a meter in the air. The vehicle was partially disassembled, its pieces arranged neatly nearby— the smaller ones across a long, battered table, the larger on the floor.

Odd little trinkets were interspersed amongst everything—dangling chimes made of old bolts and scrap metal; wires bent into patterns and sculptures; tiny figures built from of bits of junk. All of it was painted in bright colors and demonstrated varying degrees of craft.

A tall robot stood beside the hovercar, arms raised to hold a piece in place. Its disproportionate body—elongated forearms, a blocky chest, wide, bulky feet, and a small head—was covered in chipped, mismatched paint.

Nearby the robot, a male uriti sat in a wheeled chair. His legs ended at mid-thigh, where his pants had been neatly sewn shut. His sleeveless shirt molded to his solid torso, accentuating his broad shoulders, powerful chest, and muscled arms. A sheen of sweat shone on his brown skin amidst smudges of dirt and grease. The short fur on his shoulders, forearms, and neck was a few shades darker, sprinkled with gray.

The uriti's flat black nose led to a forehead from which two sets of horns protruded. The central pair were thick, curving up and back over his head, while the other two swept to the sides and backward. His long hair was the same gray-streaked brown as his fur. It had been partly woven into a bundle of thick braids, all gathered atop his head in a knot.

Aileen gasped softly and, in a whisper so soft that Kier barely heard her, asked, "Oh my gosh, is he a faun?"

What is a faun? Kayl's psychic voice asked.

Kier shrugged. *The terran word for uriti, perhaps?*

The uriti's long, furred ears twitched. "You brought strangers."

"Aileen, Kier, and Kayl," Ialle said, indicating each of them as she said their names. "Now that they're no longer strangers, can we continue?"

Though Tallian's eyes were nearly black, they were far from empty; his gaze was heavy, keen, and piercing as he scrutinized the twins and their mate.

When Tallian's attention fell upon Aileen, Kier's fingers twitched, hands curling into fists, and his tail lashed from side to side. He'd never realized how difficult it would be to stand by while someone else looked upon his mate. He'd never realized just how sensitive his instincts would be to any threats, whether real or perceived.

It takes an immense amount of control, Kayl pulsed.

"You don't look like the usual sort who comes through town," Tallian finally said, leaning back in his chair.

Ialle nodded. "They claim not to be."

A crease formed at the center of Tallian's brow; that seemed about as much motion as it could manage given the horns growing from his forehead. "Is that enough to convince you these days? Perhaps you need to start spending time out of the sun."

Ialle snickered. "Perhaps you spend some time *in* the sun. You're always hidden away in this maze."

"I've told you many, many times over the years, Ialle"—he lifted a hand and gestured to a door on the back wall—"there is a rear entrance."

She shrugged. "I keep forgetting."

Tallian snorted, picked up the fusion tool from his lap, and placed it on the table beside him. Grasping the large rear wheels of his chair, he turned himself fully toward Kier and the others. He again flicked his gaze over the twins and Aileen. "What services do you require?"

"We need our ship repaired," Kier replied.

"I'm going to need specifics. Engine failure? Electronic components burned out? Hull damage? Jump drive no longer engaging?"

"Yes," Kayl replied.

Tallin blinked. "Yes to which?"

Kier couldn't hold back his smirk. "All of them."

"The jump drive may still be operational," Kayl said, glancing at Kier. "If it had power."

"And if it had power, it may blow up what is left of the ship."

Aileen made a quiet noise mimicking an explosion, spreading the fingers of one hand wide.

Kayl frowned. "We do not know that for certain."

"I hardly think that matters at this point, Kayl," Kier said with a chuckle.

Tallian drew in a long, slow breath, lifted a hand to his face, and scratched his forehead, directing his eyes toward the floor. "What manner of ship is it?"

"It is a combat-grade vaelyn reconnaissance craft," Kayl said.

"A highly modified vaelyn reconnaissance craft," Kier amended.

"You might've seen it last night, if you ever left this building," Ialle muttered, folding her arms across her chest and abdomen.

Eyes shifting back and forth but still downcast, Tallian nodded. He dropped his hand to his lap and tapped his thigh. "We'll take a look, but if it's a military grade ship and it's as damaged as you say, there may be little we can do."

Kier offered the uriti a shallow bow. "So long as it can fly and make a jump—"

"Preferably without exploding," Aileen added.

"—we will be satisfied customers," Kier concluded, grinning at his mate.

Tallian looked up, and an almost excited light sparked in his eyes. His lips curled into a smirk. "I won't promise anything, but even if I did...it's not like you can file a complaint if you explode."

"That's reassuring..." Aileen mumbled.

"Welcome to Omega IV," Ialle said with a laugh. "Doesn't get more reassuring than that around here."

Tallian spun his chair away, wheeling it toward one of the tool chests. "Bring your ship to the neighboring hangar, and we'll start assessing the damage first thing in the morning."

"Absolutely," Kier said. "If you could perhaps point us in the direction of the equipment required to haul said ship out of the bottom of a canyon and transport it three and a half kilometers into town, we will begin work immediately."

The uriti halted, posture stiffening.

Ialle's lips peeled back, and she let out a soft hiss through her teeth. "Unless you want it brought back in pieces..."

"I cannot say we'd be able to put those pieces back together again," Tallian said, snapping his chair back toward the others. He looked over Aileen, Kayl, and Kier once more as though assessing them anew, his eyes again hard. "I... I can send Shalla out to take a look. It'll get her away while I work on the quarry hauler Weyel's bringing in tomorrow. But hear me well"—he drew himself closer with several harsh turns of the chair's wheels and glared up at the twins—"you do anything to hurt her, and I will get this whole town out there to hunt you down."

"Shalla is your daughter?" Aileen asked.

Tallian narrowed his eyes, grasping the arms of his chair. "How do you know that?"

"Easy, Tallian," Ialle said. "I mentioned you worked with your youngling."

"That, and because of those." Aileen pointed at the handmade chimes. "I used to make my parents things like that too. Well, not like *exactly* like that, because I'm not that talented with a screwdriver and pliers, but...just little things."

As he ran his gaze over the trinkets, Tallian's expression softened. "She's been making them for me since she was small. She would find scraps around the shop and puzzle out ways to put them together. I used to joke with Veeani that the hangar would be filled from one end to another with Shalla's gifts before she reached adulthood."

Aileen smiled, a bittersweet gleam forming in her eyes. "We are not going to hurt her, I promise."

"She will be safe with us," Kier said.

"You have our vow," Kayl said.

"I appreciate that," Tallian replied, turning away again. "But I'm not going to send her alone, regardless. Triss!"

For the first time since the group had arrived, the robot moved, turning their small head to face Tallian. "You do not need to yell. I am standing fifty-seven point three-five centimeters away from you."

The uriti slapped the robot's leg. "You're going to accompany Shalla into the wilds to look at their ship tomorrow."

"I do not want to go," Triss said in a low, buzzing whine.

"You would think I had two younglings with the way you act. You're going."

Triss's arms lowered, and their torso turned toward Tallian. "But why? I have responsibilities here."

Tallian sighed, slouching back in his chair. "Tomorrow, Shalla is your responsibility. You will go where she goes."

"But it is too bright outside."

"Your optics will adjust."

"But there is too much dirt."

Aileen covered her mouth, muffling her laughter.

"We...should be going," Ialle said, easing toward the back door.

"Yes, you should," Tallian snapped, waving them away. "Leave the coordinates with Ialle. Shalla will be out tomorrow." He glared at the robot. "*With* Triss. I just need to make a few adjustments."

Barely holding back laughter of his own, Kier walked to the exit alongside his brother and mate. Ialle opened the door and stepped outside; the others followed her into the sunlight.

As soon as the door had shut, Ialle said, "I know it's probably hard to believe after that, but Tallian and Shalla really are the best."

The twins and Aileen exchanged glances with each other, mirth dancing in their eyes. A week ago, a situation like this would've been a crushing setback, and it would've left Kier and Kayl in dark moods. But Aileen had helped change all that. It was difficult to fall into a dark mood with her beside them.

With no small sampling of sarcasm, Kayl said, "We have nothing but confidence in him."

THIRTY-ONE

The smell of cooking meat wafted to Aileen before she even reached the canteen's entrance. Her mouth watered, and a pang of hunger struck her already grumbling stomach. She flattened her hand against her belly.

"I think my stomach is going to eat itself if we don't get food soon." Aileen shot a glance at her mates and hurriedly added, "Not literally."

Kayl scowled. "Why did you not tell us you were hungry sooner?"

"Because we were busy, and I figured we'd look for something to eat eventually."

Kier dipped a hand into his pocket, pulled out several ration bars, and fanned them out like playing cards. "I have had food the entire time."

She stared at the rations, face expressionless, before slowly shifting her gaze up to Kier's. "And how was I supposed to know you had food all along?"

With a nonchalant shrug, he returned the bars to his pocket. "You could have asked."

"So...you're saying that I should've just been in the mindset that my mate having his pockets stuffed with ration bars is completely normal, and it's on me for not anticipating it?"

Kier seemed to consider her question briefly, then offered

another shrug. "It would have prevented you from being hungry now."

Aileen arched a brow. "Have you ever heard of the silent treatment?"

"No," Kayl replied, pushing open the canteen door, "but we can check the medpod when we return to the *Fang* and determine if it is programmed in."

Kier frowned, and his brows fell. "I do not like the sound of it."

Yeah, that's kind of the point.

Aileen lifted her chin and faced forward, sealing her lips as she stepped into the building.

Though she did not look back at them, she felt Kier and Kayl immediately behind her. Their nearness made it hard to keep her gaze averted.

Come on, Aileen. You've got to have enough willpower to keep this up for more than a single second.

"Are you going to elaborate?" Kayl asked as the door swung shut.

Aileen didn't answer. It wasn't really about the food—she wasn't upset in the slightest. She just wanted to see how far this could go before they figured out what the silent treatment was.

Yet if she were honest with herself...maybe it was a little bit about feeling out of the loop so often. Kier and Kayl shared a link she couldn't imagine, shared their thoughts, emotions, their souls. They'd made such an effort to include her, to speak out loud when she was near, but they couldn't do so all the time—not that she expected them to.

She just wanted to be part of that. She wanted to truly join their *daevalis*, so there would be no more silence to endure.

The twins stepped up on either side of Aileen, settling their gazes upon her.

Kier's tail brushed her calf. "Aileen?"

Just think of it as a will-building exercise. Denying yourself the sight of them will only make it sweeter when you do look, right?

But...I could be looking right now....

"I can see that, Kayl," Kier rumbled. "I believe she is demonstrating the silent treatment."

She drew in a deep breath, crossed her arms beneath her breasts, and studied the canteen, making a point to look everywhere but at her mates.

The space was large and open, filled with numerous tables, both round and rectangular, that had stools lined up around them. All those tables and stools were attached to the concrete floor, which was crisscrossed by faded pathways that must've worn into it by foot traffic over many years. A bar counter stood toward the rear, backed by a wide window granting a view into the kitchen.

The place was reminiscent of a cafeteria at a factory, but it had much more character than that. The walls were decorated with all sorts of objects—paintings and pictures, framed pieces of faldrium, rusted tools, the claws, bones, and teeth of unfamiliar creatures, signs in various languages and stages of wear. Woven blankets and curtains finished out the wall décor, and living plants, just like the ones Aileen had seen along the canyon stream, sat in pots interspersed throughout the room.

The patrons were broken into small groups scattered around the tables; there had to be at least twenty of them eating and drinking, several of whom were now staring at Aileen and the twins.

"You're the ones that survived the storm, aren't you?" asked a silver-haired borian seated at one of the tables.

"And a crash," added a craggy faced bokkan.

"I heard you hiked a hundred kilometers through the wilds to get here and showed up without a speck of dust on you," someone called from closer to the back.

Kier laughed and shook his head. "The storm and the crash, yes. But it sounds as though the details of our hike have been somewhat exaggerated." He waved to the thin layer of dust coating his boots.

"Told you," someone else said.

"Your meals are on me either way," the borian declared.

Aileen flashed the borian a smile. "That's kind of you."

Grinning, he twisted in his seat to look at female borian behind the counter. "Whatever they want, Emai, put it on my tab."

Emai was Amazonian in stature, with one side of her head shaved and her blond tresses swept in the other direction. She folded her arms over her chest and gave the male borian a flat stare. "You realize you need to pay that eventually, right Orassic?"

He laughed. "You know I'll pay..." Leaning toward Emai, Orassic waggled his eyebrows. "One way or another."

Emai narrowed her eyes, but the corner of her mouth twitched up and a blush tinted her cheeks. "Yeah, you will." She stared at him a moment longer before shifting her attention to Aileen and the twins. Her expression softened, and she waved them over. "Come have a seat."

Aileen moved ahead of the twins, maneuvering between the tables until she reached the bar and slid onto a stool. There was another group seated at the far end of the counter—a groalthuun, a cren, an ilthurii, and an onigox. All four were male; all four were watching her. The friendliness and curiosity that had been in everyone else's stares seemed to be absent from those four.

She offered them an uncertain smile before Kier sat down to her right, blocking the group from her view. Kayl eased himself onto the stool to her left, sitting with his back straight and his shoulders squared; it was the sort of posture that could make your back ache just looking at it. But his head was turned to look past her, toward the other males.

Emai nodded at a board on the wall behind her. "The menu is small, but the food is good. Have your pick."

Aileen folded her arms on the counter and leaned forward, head tilting as she perused the menu. Unlike the flashy holographic menus at Eternal Paradise, this one would've been at home in an old-fashioned roadside diner back on Earth—it was essentially a chalkboard with half a dozen items listed. Though it was all written in Universal Speech, most of the words held little meaning for her, as the ingredients were unfamiliar.

"Whatever you recommend," Aileen said to Emai.

"The same," Kier and Kayl said together.

Emai stepped to the window. "Three zaberkii!"

"Got it!" came a reply from the kitchen.

Without hesitation, Emai snatched up three clean glasses and quickly mixed drinks inside them, resulting in pink and blue swirls reminiscent of cotton candy. She topped each with a wedge of pink fruit and set them on the counter before Aileen and her companions.

"That looks delicious," Aileen said.

"Desert nectar. Made from local addiva fruit. They're a favorite around here," Emai said as she wiped her hands on a cloth.

Aileen smiled and took hold of her glass, drawing it closer. Kier and Kayl were more hesitant; she didn't miss when they both glanced at the group of males sitting farther down the counter again.

"Is it alcoholic?" Kayl asked.

Emai nodded, mouth slanting into a smirk. "Don't hold your alcohol well?"

Gently, the twins slid their glasses back toward Emai, and Kier said, "We prefer to keep our minds clear. Alcohol tends to have something of an...echoing effect when two minds are linked."

One of the borian's eyebrows arched. "So...you get double drunk?"

"Something like that," Kier replied. "Water for us."

"No problem." Emai swept up the glasses and placed them on open part of the bar. "Two nectars, Orassic. Whether you take them or not, they're going on your tab."

Aileen picked up her glass, brought it to her lips, and took a sip. Sweetness blasted across her tastebuds. Her eyes flared. There was only a hint of alcohol, almost entirely overpowered by the fruity flavor. It'd been a long time since she'd had anything like it. She took deeper drink.

Orassic laughed, shaking his head. "Yeah, yeah. Female looks like she's enjoying it. If she doesn't drink them, I'll take them."

"Good?" Emai asked.

Aileen lowered the half-emptied glass and licked her lips with a smile. "*So* good."

Emai grinned and leveled a finger at Aileen. "Careful, or they'll sneak up on you. We'll have your food out shortly." She filled up two new glasses with water and set them in front of the twins. "Got a fresh batch of zaberkii just about ready. You three need anything, call out."

She walked away, leaving the trio to their drinks.

"Our female enjoys sweet things," Kayl said.

"So how could she possibly like you, Kayl?" Kier asked.

Aileen barely contained a laugh. Keeping her focus on her glass, she plucked the pink fruit from the rim and took a bite. Her eyelids fluttered against the onslaught of deliciousness. She assumed it was the addiva fruit Emai had mentioned; she was *definitely* going to have the twins buy some of the fruit before they left the planet.

Kayl picked up his water, sipped from it, and placed it back down gently. "She is struggling to maintain this silent treatment."

"That she has managed this long is admirable." Kier reached for her glass, wiped a drop of addiva juice from the rim with the tip of his finger, and lifted it to his lips. "But she will not hold out much longer."

From the corner of her eye, she saw him slip that finger into his mouth, his gaze fixed quite intently upon her.

"Sweet," he purred, leaning closer to her. "But not half as sweet as your nectar, *na'diya.*"

Aileen squeezed her thighs together as heat rushed to her core. All she could think of in that moment was the twins' heads between her legs and their tongues hungrily licking her cunt. She quickly took another bite of fruit.

Now Kayl leaned closer to her, hooking his tail around her shin and caressing the back of her knee with its tip. His breath was warm on her neck when he said, "Do you think she would remain silent while we drink from her?"

"Hmm. If we could convince her to allow us to quench our thirst..." Kier nuzzled her neck and flicked his tongue across her skin.

Aileen giggled, turned her face toward him, and gave him a gentle shove. "You're both impossible."

Kier grinned, eyes alight with desire and amusement. "Shall we declare victory, *na'diya?*"

She flicked a glance at Kayl, who was smirking. "For now."

"We will not gloat," Kier said.

Kayl's smirk stretched, and his gaze heated. "But we will be sure to celebrate. Later."

Aileen's cheeks flushed. "I am very much looking forward to later." She took another drink. The warmth in her belly intensified, spreading outward.

Soon enough, Emai returned with three steaming bowls. She placed them down on the counter in front of Aileen and the twins, handed out spoons, and headed off to continue her work with a confident stride. The zaberkii was a stew-like mixture with chunks of meat, chopped vegetables, and long, thick white noodles—or at lease what Aileen *hoped* were noodles—in a thick, dark broth.

The smell wafting from it was downright mouthwatering... And she was starving.

She took her first bite without even checking if it was too hot.

Though it was definitely on the warm side, it tasted too good for Aileen to care. She ate with a ravenousness that should've been embarrassing, but Kier and Kayl didn't remark upon it. They simply ate alongside her.

She pursed her lips and slurped up one of the noodles. Kier cocked his head, studying her mouth, and did the same. Broth spattered the countertop as the noodle flipped up and smacked his nose. He flinched, and Aileen covered her mouth with a hand as she laughed.

"That was not expected," he said, wiping broth off his face.

Aileen smiled. "I used to do it all the time as a kid."

Kayl brushed the back of his finger down her cheek. "We will never tire of seeing you smile, *na'diya.*"

That only made her smile widen and her heart thump faster. She looked back down at her bowl, absently stirring the contents with her spoon. It felt like a lifetime had passed since she'd been around people who made her content to just be herself, a lifetime since she'd not had to assume a role, to put on a show.

It also felt like a lifetime since she'd eaten real, homecooked food.

She and the twins continued eating, and there was nothing uncomfortable about the silence between them. It was good, it was right, it was soothing. She finished her first glass of desert nectar and started on a second glass; it was just too delicious to pass up. Her body was warm, languid, thrumming. That buzz was welcome after the crash and the hike out to the town had left her muscles sore and tired.

Aileen was only vaguely aware of boots shuffling on the floor nearby, and she barely registered the heavy footsteps drawing closer. She was too busy savoring the tender meat, flavorful broth, and sweet beverage, too busy reveling in the warmth her meal—and her mates— was stoking in her belly.

But she did notice that Kier and Kayl had stopped eating. She lowered her utensil. The twins' postures were tense, and their heads were turned in the same direction.

Those clumping footsteps were now directly behind her.

"So, you're the outsiders, are you?" asked an alien in a gruff voice.

Aileen glanced over her shoulder to see the goat-faced groalthuun leering at her. The other three males who'd been sitting with him at the far end of the bar were behind him, all staring at her, and Aileen's blood chilled under their hungry gazes.

"We are," Kayl replied flatly.

"I believe that was established when we entered." The evenness of Kier's voice belied the tension in his posture. "Perhaps you simply weren't paying attention?"

The towering blue cren with crimson eyes and hair tilted his head. "Impolite, aren't they?"

"I meant no offense," said Kier.

Aileen had never seen him so still; she was reminded of a tiger lying in tall grass, waiting to pounce on its unsuspecting prey.

"Of course you didn't," the groalthuun said.

"Pretty thing." The scaled ilthurii's tongue flicked out. "What is she?"

The fourth of their group, a massive onigox with bright green skin and four arms thick as tree trunks, grinned at Aileen. "Doesn't matter what she is. Only matters if her little slit is tight."

The groalthuun pressed a finger to her spine and trailed it down, making her skin crawl. She flinched away from his unwanted touch.

The ilthurii made a raspy, grunting sound that might have been laughter. "How much for a go with—"

Faster than Aileen's eyes could perceive, the twins spun around and surged off their stools. The groalthuun's hand abruptly withdrew as he and the ilthurii were knocked backward. Several sounds occurred in quick succession—grunts and growls, rustling cloth, shuffling boots.

"Seven thunders," Emai spat from near the kitchen.

By the time Aileen spun around, she could barely comprehend the scene before her. The twins had opened nearly two meters of space between Aileen and the group of males. The groalthuun was clutching his forearm, the ilthurii was sitting on his ass, tail caught between his legs, and the tall cren and even taller onigox were glaring at the twins.

Kier held a knife to the cren's throat; Kayl's blade was pressed to the onigox's groin, having already sliced through the larger alien's pants. They'd activated their armor in that space between heartbeats during which they'd acted. Kier's was hidden beneath his clothing save for the gloves and neck, while Kayl's segmented torso armor was fully visible, as Aileen was still wearing his tunic.

"Easy!" Orassic boomed as he and the canteen's other patrons hurried over.

Aileen's heart pounded against her ribs, its frantic beating permeating her body. The onigox and the cren lifted their hands into the air, fury gleaming in their eyes, but their companions were reaching for blasters on their hips.

"Don't you fucking dare," Emai growled. She leapt over the counter, landing amidst the combatants.

Seeing the female borian standing near the males only made Aileen realize how big the woman was herself. She was slightly taller than the twins, with a lean, athletic frame, and she bore herself without a sliver of fear despite being unarmed.

"Get your hands off your blasters," Emai commanded.

The ilthurii and the groalthuun continued staring at the twins, unmoving.

Orassic, who himself was nearly as large as the cren, strode up to the scene with his companions in tow. "Now, you damned fools."

Sneering, the groalthuun and the ilthurii obeyed, the latter slowly climbing to his feet.

"We were just curious," the groalthuun said.

"And I'm a volturian holo star," Emai replied.

The ilthurii clicked his teeth together and cocked his head. "You are certainly beau—"

"Just shut your fucking mouth," Orassic snapped.

Through all of this, the twins remained utterly still, their eyes focused on their enemies. Even their tails were motionless.

Orassic stepped between the twins, tugging back his long, silver hair. "You can lower your blades."

"Are you all right, Aileen?" Kier asked. His tail twitched, barely moving enough to perceive.

Aileen let out a quivery breath. "Yeah. Just a little shaken up."

Everything had happened so *fast*. Though she'd trained with Kier and Kayl over the last few days, she'd greatly underestimated their true speed.

I knew they were holding back with me...but I didn't realize just how much.

Is it wrong that I find that hot?

"Back away. Slowly," the twins said in unison.

Keeping their hands up, the onigox and cren eased backward.

Kier and Kayl straightened, lowering their weapons, but they neither retracted their armor nor turned away from their foes.

Aileen slipped off her stool and took a step toward them. Even though that was also a step toward the hostile males, it was comforting to be closer to her mates.

"I told you dust clods the last time you started trouble in here that it was your final chance." Emai jabbed a finger toward the exit. "You four need to leave, and if I see you around my place again, you'll be dealing with Ialle."

"Don't be like that, Emai," the groalthuun said.

The onigox grunted, the big fingers of one of his lower hands prodding at the torn fabric of his pants.

"We've been good customers for years," the ilthurii hissed.

"You occasionally pay for your drinks. That's about the only good thing I can say about you as customers." Emai strode toward the males. "Now start walking, or your sun-bleached hides will be the next thing I hang on the wall."

Baring his teeth, the cren wiped a drop of blood from his neck. "Choosing outsiders over us."

"Choosing decent people over you, more like it," Orassic said, shaking his head.

Clenching her fists at her sides, Emai growled, "Get. The fuck. Out."

The group of males retreated, casting hateful glares at the twins and Aileen.

"Better be on your way soon," the groalthuun said, "or this planet is going to eat you alive."

"Better hope we don't run into you again, more like," the onigox rumbled.

"Should you so much as look at her," Kayl snarled.

"There will be nothing left of you for Emai to hang on the wall," Kier finished.

With a few curses and insults, the males made their way to the door and stepped outside. The tension in the air began to ease immediately after their departure, though the tension in the twins lingered. Aileen closed that last bit of distance between her and her mates as Emai and Orassic turned to face them.

Emai tugged a few rogue strands of her hair back to the side, rasping her palm over her shaved scalp. "I'm sure it doesn't mean much, but I want to apologize for those fools. They're trouble on the best of days, but I think they're particularly irked today because they thought they'd be scavenging parts from your crashed ship."

"While Ialle and the rest of us took care of your bodies," Orassic added, his tone grave.

"It is not your fault," Kier said.

"Your intervention is appreciated," Kayl added.

Aileen reached out, placing one hand on the back of Kier's shoulder, the other on Kayl's. "Are you two okay?"

Slipping their knives away, they turned to face her. Their mismatched eyes brimmed with such emotion, such intensity, such fire. They swept in simultaneously, lifting her into a crushing embrace from both sides.

Aileen's surprised gasp was followed by a soft laugh as she looped an arm around each of the twins and squeezed as tight as she could, unbothered by the press of their hard armor.

Not for the first time, Aileen felt as though she were the most important thing in the universe—the most important thing in *their* universe.

Their grips were strong, clutching her close, but neither their strength nor their armor could hide the tremor that ran through them. Aileen brushed her lips across Kayl's temple before turning her head to do the same to Kier's jaw.

"I'd almost forgotten what romance looks like, seeing so little of it around here," Emai said.

Aileen's cheeks heated, but she clung to her mates until they finally lowered her onto her feet and eased back—though even then, they did not break contact with her.

"Oof." Orassic shook his head. "So you're just going to pretend there's nothing between us, Emai?"

Emai scoffed. "Whatever you and I have, Or, it isn't romance."

"Is that why you put the seven thunders to shame when I make you scream?"

Snatching a rag from her apron, Emai wadded it up and threw it at Orassic hard. She didn't watch the impact; her attention had already turned to Aileen and the twins. There was pink on her cheeks, but it was impossible to tell whether it had been produced by the confrontation or Orassic's comment.

"I'll take care of your food and drink while you're in town," she said, drawing her fists against her chest and bowing. "It's the least I can do after this."

"It wasn't your fault, Emai," Aileen said. "You don't have to do that."

"I don't, but I'm going to." She walked around the counter and lifted her hand in a dismissive wave. "Except for this meal. This one will still go on Orassic's tab."

Orassic laughed and shot a grin at Aileen and the twins. "Can't say I won't enjoy paying that off."

Aileen smiled at the borians' flirtatious banter, but when she turned to face Kier and Kayl, her smile faded. Their features were tight, their blazing eyes were focused solely upon her, and they exuded a predatory aura—one that ignited the flames of desire in her core.

Reaching up, Aileen cupped their jaws. "Are you okay?"

They shifted closer to her, armored fingers again flexing; she found she missed the bite of their wicked claws. Kayl's nostrils and nose slits flared with a deep inhalation as he lowered his head. His lips peeled back, revealing his fangs. Kier's tongue slipped out to trail over his lips. The heat radiating from the twins was overwhelming, intoxicating, seductive. Aileen's pull to them grew stronger than ever, and she felt herself sway toward them infinitesimally.

Kier groaned and turned his face away, releasing a ragged breath. "We...are fine."

Kayl squeezed his eyes shut and shook his head. Briefly, both twins tensed, and then they covered Aileen's hands with their own. Kier looked at her again, giving a smile that betrayed only a hint of strain. Kayl's smile was more subdued, but it widened when her eyes met his.

"We should finish our meals," he said.

Nodding, Kier guided her hand off his jaw. "If we mean to purchase supplies before returning to the ship, we ought not delay much longer."

Kayl lowered her other hand.

She knew something was off with them, that they were restraining themselves. She felt it—felt their desire pulsing at her through their tether. But this wasn't the time or place.

"Sounds good," she said.

Her worries fell away, if only for a little while, when the twins lifted her hands to their mouths and kissed her knuckles, their tenderness and warmth making her wonder if she'd only imagined the heated confrontation that had just occurred.

THIRTY-TWO

Fortunately, the group of males who'd harassed Aileen in the canteen were nowhere to be seen when she and the twins stepped outside. She hadn't let the encounter ruin her meal, thanks in large part to Kier and Kayl's steady, calming presences. It had helped that Orassic had left not long after the incident to speak with Ialle, whose role as arbiter, according to what Emai had said as the trio finished eating, was something like mayor and sheriff combined.

Navaire's few shops were all located near the canteen in the central plaza. The twins led Aileen first into Omega Mercantile, which served as the town's general store. The store sold local foods and produce, but it also offered goods obtained from offworld traders —prepackaged rations, drinks, and medical supplies, a variety of simple tools, clothing and survival supplies. The place had a little bit of everything.

They purchased some easy to carry rations, a few drinks that they didn't have on the *Fang*, a jar of addiva jam, and a cloak like Ialle's to help protect Aileen from the sun.

Next in the line of shops was something like a hardware store that also sold electronic components; they skipped it and stopped in front of the third store called The Glittering Cavern, where Kier and Kayl tilted their heads as they studied the eclectic front display.

Jewelry, trinkets, clothing, and décor crowded the little window, all of it with a handmade aesthetic that caught Aileen's attention.

When she looked up at her mates with wide, hopeful eyes, clasped her hands together, and asked if they could go inside, the twins simply smiled and waved her to the door.

The goods inside the shop were even more varied than those in the window. Portions of the room had been shaped to look like natural stone or wood, and there were several fountains scattered throughout that filled the air with the music of trickling water.

The shopkeepers, a pair of azheran sisters named Sira and Sala, welcomed the trio from behind the counter. They seemed delighted to have fresh faces in their store; they watched as Aileen and the twins glanced around, but their stares weren't the suspicious, put-off sort Aileen had seen from some shopkeepers back on Earth. These azheras had excitement in their eyes, like they couldn't wait for their new guests to discover the wonders on offer.

It made sense when Sira mentioned that almost everything in the shop had been made by the sisters.

The air was redolent of exotic flowers, spices, and fragrant smoke. A few of the scents were *almost* familiar, and fewer still were reminiscent of smells from Earth, but most were new to Aileen. Perhaps the blend was too much, too strong, but she loved it because there was something grounding about it, something natural. She happily filled her lungs with that air.

It served as a welcome reminder that she wasn't in an artificial environment out in space anymore. She was standing on a planet, there was a sun shining and wind blowing outside, and it didn't matter if it was all alien.

"Explore," Kayl said to Aileen, brushing a hand down her back and sending a thrill down her spine.

"Select anything and everything you want," Kier added, the pads of his fingers trailing from her elbow to her wrist in a tantalizing but fleeting touch. But the sensation he'd sparked on her skin lingered like it had been branded on her soul.

After an appreciative glance at her mates' backsides as they walked away to peruse the wares, Aileen let her gaze wander.

There were baskets filled with sticks of incense, bins nearly overflowing with interesting rock fragments, and shelves bearing rows and rows of faldrium chunks and other gems on little stands. One display case held dozens of carvings, a few made of wood but most of them stone. Woven tapestries and wall hangings, each bearing distinct patterns in varying colors, dangled from rods on the walls.

Aileen studied shelves full of candles that had been carved into different shapes and designs, some of which were colored and scented. She examined pieces of jewelry—necklaces, earrings, bracelets, torques, tiaras, rings and more—made from metals she couldn't identify, many of which bore pieces of faldrium as accents. Scattered throughout the shop were alien baubles and trinkets for which she had no names, almost all crafted from seemingly natural materials. They were all beautiful and had clearly been shaped with great care.

Maw would've loved this place, and Da would've worked whatever odd jobs he could find around town just so he could buy her anything she wanted from it.

Aileen smiled to herself. She and her parents had made so many memories in their time together. They'd gone on so many little adventures. For the first time in her life, she was beginning to realize just how short a while they'd really had with each other, but she could finally recall the joy of that time without being overwhelmed by sorrow.

That made her cherish those years all the more, and she was resolved to cling to every moment she had and was yet to have with Kier and Kayl all the harder.

Standing on her toes to see better, she scanned the shop for the twins. They were at the rear of the store with Sala, talking quietly as they examined something below Aileen's line of sight.

With everything that had happened in the last six days, with all the excitement and fear, all the passion and danger, it amazed Aileen that moments like these—these quiet, simple, mundane moments— were amongst those that shone brightest in her memory.

Cooking with Kier, sitting with Kayl in the cockpit and watching the stars through the holo windows, sharing meals, shopping...

Something her mother had said long ago rose from Aileen's memory.

All those big events in your life are important, Aileen. You'll remember them, and they'll shape you. But don't forget that all the time between those events can add up to so much more if you let it.

And wasn't that what her parents had demonstrated? Wasn't that the lesson they'd taught her simply by living their lives and loving one another?

"Thank you, Maw, Da," she whispered before continuing to browse.

The first thing to catch her eye—the first thing she wanted for herself—was a white dress. Aileen stepped closer to the garment and ran her fingers over the fabric. It stood out from the surrounding clothing thanks to the intricately woven designs covering it, many of which resembled Celtic knots. It looked like it had been crocheted, each piece meticulously brought together into a whole that stood as a work of art.

She ran her fingers over the designs with a smile before she pulled the garment down and draped it over her arm.

Her wanderings carried her back toward the front of the store, with a brief stop to pick out a few of the best-smelling bars of home-made soap. She found herself drawn to a set of shelves beside the counter that were filled with colorful blown glass containers reminiscent of perfume bottles. Though the little labels tied to each were written in Universal, most of the words were unfamiliar to Aileen.

Selecting a glittery, ruby red bottle, she removed the stopper, brought it to her nose, and smelled the contents.

"Mmm," she hummed as she closed her eyes. The sweet, mellow scent reminded her of coconut, which in turn made her think of crashing waves, sandy beaches, and how much she longed to visit the ocean again.

Definitely getting this one.

Placing her finger over the top, she flipped the bottle briefly, then rubbed the perfume onto her inner wrist. But the liquid didn't dry; it was oily and slick. Her brow creased. Maybe it was a scented oil?

A chuckle came from Aileen's right, drawing her attention to the azhera behind the counter.

"That is iyara extract," Sira said, her citrine eyes bright with mirth.

"I'm not familiar with that. It smells lovely." Aileen lifted the bottle. "What is it for?"

The azhera smiled, revealing her fangs. "It is used to aid in intimate pleasures. So everything...glides."

"Ohhhhhh." Heated flooded Aileen's face, and she chuckled

quietly as she rubbed her finger along her wrist, where the lubricant remained slick.

Yeah, definitely glidey.

Looks like I accidently found exactly *what I needed.*

Aileen peeked around the corner for Kier and Kayl, who were still speaking with the other azhera in back. She recalled their time in the shower together—the way they'd touched her, the pleasure they'd induced, her initial discomfort when Kayl had pressed his tail into her ass. But she recalled too the incredible, thrilling sensation of his tail filling her.

What would it feel like to have his cock inside her? What would it feel like to have both their cocks inside her at once?

More than anything, she wanted to experience that. She wanted to delight in the intimacy of joining with the twins at the same time, of feeling the three of them become one in heart, mind, and soul.

And body.

Aileen was ready to be theirs wholly.

And this little red bottle of wonders would help accomplish that.

She turned back to Sira and grinned. "I'll be getting this."

The azhera's eyes flicked briefly toward the twins, and her smile widened. Lowering her voice, she asked, "They are both yours?"

Aileen's expression softened. "Yeah, they are."

"Perhaps two bottles, then? I have heard daevahs are...attentive lovers to their mates."

The heat in Aileen's cheeks intensified, but so did her anticipation. "Ah, well, I guess I'll be getting two then." She plucked another red bottle from the shelf and set them on the counter along with the dress and soaps. "We do have to wait out this space storm, after all."

"Sometimes, blessing can be found in hardship." Sira lifted the dress carefully, letting it hang down. "This will suit you well, I think. If you need it altered, come in any time. Sala can adjust it however you wish."

"Thank you. It's a beautiful dress. Did she make it?"

The azhera nodded. "She makes most of the clothing and jewelry. My talents favor the oils, candles, and soaps." She leaned forward and whispered, "Though I am the better sculptor, whatever she might say."

Aileen laughed.

"Did you find something you want?" Kier asked from behind Aileen.

She started and looked up at Kier as he and Kayl stepped into place beside her. She caught her bottom lip between her teeth, glanced at the shopkeeper, and dropped her gaze to the red bottles. Would the twins know what was within them?

"Yes. A few things," she said, peeking back at her mates.

Sala stepped around the counter to join her sister, holding a cloth wrapped bundle in her hand. A knowing smile played upon her lips as she looked at the red bottles.

"As have we." Kier offered his hand to Aileen. "Shall we step outside and allow Kayl to pay?"

Aileen slipped her hand into his, and he drew her close as he led her to the door.

"Thank you!" she called over her shoulder before she and Kier stepped out.

They moved away from the entrance, and Kier released her hand as they stopped.

Drawing in a deep breath, Aileen swept her gaze across the plaza, taking in the sky, the buildings, the townsfolk going about their days. Despite everything, it seemed the town had quieted down since Aileen and the twins had arrived that morning. The trio still received curious glances, but there'd been more friendly waves and warm greetings than anything.

Beside her, Kier lifted his hands over his head and stretched. Aileen's eyes shifted toward him. His shirt pulled taut across his chest, accenting muscles that his clothing and bodysuit could not hide. His tail stretched out behind him briefly before falling into slow, easy swaying.

He turned his head, met her gaze, and smiled.

She smiled back. There was a smoldering light in his eyes. The heat at her core flared in response, and again she recalled the things they'd done aboard the *Fang*. She'd never imagined herself being so bold when it came to sex, but she wanted more—more of them. She couldn't wait to put her purchase to use.

And based on the look Kier was giving her, he was eager for more too. Just a little more fire in his gaze and she'd melt. She felt that pull toward him again; her whole body wanted to move closer to him, to touch him, to make love to him. His mouth twitched into a lopsided, roguish smirk, displaying one of his fangs.

God, she ached for him. For *them*.

But Kier shifted his attention away as he lowered his arms, scanning the plaza. "Discounting a few troublesome individuals, this is a surprisingly pleasant place."

"Huh?" Aileen blinked, dragging her mind out of the lustful haze that had settled over it. "Yeah. It is. Most of the people have been really kind."

He nodded, hooked his hands on his belt, and looked skyward. "They have been. Kayl and I have ventured to far more unpleasant places in far harsher environments. This is a welcome change. And the food at the canteen was quite good."

"It was." Aileen struggled against the urge to squeeze her thighs together. Why was Kier suddenly acting so...nonchalant? She strolled toward the edge of the dusty concrete walkway that ran in front of the shops and took hold of her wrist; her fingers brushed over the still lubricated patch of skin there, and desire quaked at her core.

She lowered her gaze and stepped forward, absently stroking her inner wrist. "So...are you, um..."

She felt Kier's eyes upon her. "Am I what, *na'diya?*"

"Are you..." She pressed her lips together. Why hesitate? She knew what she wanted, knew what was to come. And they'd already been intimate, hadn't they? So why the shyness? Turning to face Kier fully, she met his gaze. "Are you curious about what was in those bottles?"

"No."

Aileen's brows fell. "No?"

"No."

"Not even a *little?*"

That smirk still played on his lips, accompanied by a devilish glint in his eyes. "I already know, Aileen."

She gaped at him. "W-what? How?"

He closed the small distance between them, hooked an arm around Aileen's back, and tugged her body against his. His other hand caught her chin and angled her face toward his as he tipped his head toward The Glittering Cavern. "Because Kayl asked."

Oh, that is so not fair.

Her cheeks nearly burst into flame. She tried—and failed—to put on a neutral expression. "He did?"

"Yes," Kier purred, brushing his tail along about the curve of her ass. "And then he bought two more bottles."

THIRTY-THREE

Kayl slowed as he crested the rise. Omega IV's rocky landscape stretched out around him, its jutting rock formations and ridge lines casting lengthening shadows as the sun sank. The bits of faldrium scattered everywhere blazed like pinpoints of fire when the sun's rays touched them, creating a brilliant contrast between the deepening pools of gloom and the fading daylight.

The distant horizon from which the sun had risen was now shrouded by twilight. That darkening portion of sky danced with faint waves of color—the first visible rays of the cosmic storm, dulled by the lingering sunshine.

However different this harsh, rugged land was from the fields of long, soft grass and refreshing turquoise seas of the twins' home-world, it certainly did not lack in beauty.

He glanced back at Aileen, who was walking beside Kier. Before they'd left town, she had returned Kayl's tunic and, with a grin and a flourish, swept on her new cloak. So much of her body being obscured had only heightened the twins' hunger. But as the shadows had grown, she'd tugged back the hood and thrown the cloak wide open, uncovering her arms, her neck, her fiery hair.

Even in the shade, Aileen was radiant.

The ache that had awoken in Kayl on Eternal Paradise stirred low in his belly. His willpower had been frayed since he'd first seen Aileen, but today it was especially weak.

We are ready.

The twins had shared that thought repeatedly throughout the day—as they'd walked to Navaire, as they'd visited the mechanic, as they'd eaten and shopped, as they'd spoken to the locals. It had echoed in their minds while they'd teased Aileen, and it had nearly broken their resolve more than once. They'd returned to it, both consciously and subconsciously, over and over, and those words had reached a crescendo after the incident in the canteen.

They were ready. They did not want to spend another day with an incomplete *daevalis*. They did not want Aileen to suffer another day of being separated from them in any way. If nothing else, her silent treatment had made them painfully aware of that disconnect, of the missing voice in their psychic link, of how she must've felt when Kier and Kayl's *aerysi* communicated and she heard nothing.

"Almost there," Aileen said with a smile, tucking a loose strand of hair behind her ear. Her beauty was so natural, so effortless, so pure. It radiated from within and without, bathing the twins in its warmth and brilliance.

They could never have guessed such beauty would be part of their *daevalis*. Part of them.

Kayl returned her smile with one of his own as heat flared in his chest. He had counted every step since leaving Navaire; every millimeter traveled had intensified his desire, his anticipation, his need. "Almost."

As Aileen and Kier drew up beside him, Kayl matched their pace, and the trio descended into the canyon, following the stream. The rocky hills gradually rose into cliffs around them. Though most of the canyon floor was no longer touched by the sun, the flecks of faldrium all around glinted intermittently, and the stream shimmered as though emitting its own glow.

The sunlight striking the upper parts of the canyon walls bounced down, where it was refracted by the water and the faldrium lining the streambed, amplifying the scant luminescence. It looked like the cosmic storm had been cast down and isolated to the center of the canyon in a winding ribbon of color and light.

The way the reflected light danced upon Aileen's face and brought out the blue in her eyes was mesmerizing.

How would she look standing beside that stream unclothed, with that ethereal glow coursing over her bare flesh? How would she look stepping out of the stream with water droplets clinging to her skin, each one catching the light and sparkling like a distant star?

A little farther, brother, pulsed Kier. *We must keep control for mere minutes more.*

Despite his words, Kier's excitement and desire were no less pronounced than Kayl's, and their open link allowed all of it through undiminished, undiluted.

Kayl could not help but note all the spots along the streambank where three people could comfortably lie—or sit, kneel, stand, and crouch in any combination—with a blanket spread beneath them.

A blanket...or even a cloak...

He gritted his teeth and forced those thoughts back. Yes, he and Kier were ready, and yes, Aileen had conveyed her readiness too, but there was something to do first—a bonding gift. It was one of the few daevah traditions the twins knew from memory, and so it was the most important to them.

"How can we deny the existence of fate?" Kier had asked back in the azheran sisters' shop. He and Kayl had been examining the items they'd asked Sala to remove from a display case, one twin or the other glancing at Aileen every few seconds to ensure she wasn't drawing nearer.

Kayl hadn't had an argument to make. Though they hadn't chosen any of this—apart from forsaking vengeance to rescue Aileen —the gift they'd discovered here on this near-forgotten planet, in an isolated town of barely two thousand people, had been perfect.

Now that gift, bundled in protective cloth, lay nestled in the satchel Kayl had bought to carry their purchases, awaiting the moment when the twins and Aileen were back in their quarters aboard the *Fang*.

Tonight, the twins' *na'diya* would become theirs in every way.

Nothing had ever been so important to them, not even the revenge that had driven them for most of their lives.

"Despite a certain *incident*," Aileen said, drawing Kayl from his thoughts, "today was a good day. A really good day."

Kier brushed his tail down the back of her leg. "Every day has been good since we found you, *na'diya*."

Her answering smile was soft but vibrant, filled with affection and sincerity. "Every day with you two has been wonderful. But in some ways, today is the best so far."

Kier grinned. "The day is not yet over, Aileen."

She side-eyed him, her mouth slanting into a teasing smirk. "Kier, are you going to try to ruin it?"

He laughed. "Not at all."

Kayl moved closer to her and hooked his tail around her waist. "But we still have much to make up for."

She stopped, and a shiver coursed through her as she looked up at him. "Oh? You two think you can make it better?"

Kayl's cock twitched, straining against his bodysuit as his gaze dipped to her full, tantalizing lips. "Ah, *na'diya*," he rumbled, tugging her hip against him, "you have no idea of the pleasures awaiting you."

"Hmm..." She turned her body toward Kayl and leaned against him, eyes gleaming with hunger as she placed a hand on his chest. "We all know what's in those little red bottles, Kayl." She trailed her hand lower, following it with her gaze. Her voice was huskier as she continued, "I think I have some idea what awaits..."

Kayl shifted and dropped his hands to her hips, curling his fingers around her waist. The fabric of her cloak and tunic bunched in his hands. How easy it would have been to tear them off her...

She makes it difficult to deny our instincts, Kier pulsed.

Aileen turned her face away to look downstream. "Maybe we should hurry along?" Her eyes swung to Kier, drinking him in greedily before turning to Kayl. "I believe you both have some... making up to do?"

The *Fang* lay only a hundred and fifty meters away; their sanctuary, their home...the place where they would finally forge their *daevalis*.

His heart thumped, and fire spread through his veins, intensifying when his brother pressed in on the other side of Aileen and she tilted her head, allowing Kier's lips access to her neck.

Ready. We are ready.

Somewhere overhead, a pebble fell, clattering quietly amongst the rocks.

Kayl stilled. Electric tingles raced along his back, twisting his inner heat into something desperate and unsettling.

Such tiny sounds occurred often in wildernesses like this. It should not have been cause for immediate dread. And yet he was already moving to place himself between Aileen and the source of that sound when it repeated—even closer now.

Aileen made a soft, startled sound, arms falling away from Kayl as he spun fully toward the threat. His hand darted for the holocom on his wrist, and he swung his gaze toward the top of the canyon. Rustling clothing behind him suggested Kier was also in motion.

"You touch it, we shoot her," someone called from above.

The twins froze, fingers mere centimeters from their holocom controls, as their eyes fell upon the one who'd spoken—the groalthuun from the canteen.

The male stood at the edge of the cliff with a blaster rifle in hand, its barrel aimed down at the twins and their mate. He was ten meters up, hardly far enough to trust that he would miss.

The rage that had for so long dwelled in Kayl's heart roused and unfurled its blazing wings; its twin stirred within Kier.

Slightly farther downstream, a second figure moved to the cliff's edge with an old-fashioned gauss rifle trained on Kayl and his companions. A powerful tail curled behind the figure, and his long, thin tongue slipped out to flick in the air.

The ilthurii.

We have been inattentive.

We have been fools.

Kayl's rage ignited an inferno in his chest.

We have endangered our na'diya.

Two sets of heavy footfalls crunched across the ground behind Kayl. The uncomfortable heat on his back strengthened.

Fear rippled into him from Aileen, but it was wrapped around a solid, unshaken core of anger and defiance.

"Did you think we would let you just walk away?" someone asked in a deep, rumbling voice. The onigox.

They are pointing weapons at our mate, Kier pulsed, psychic voice trembling with fury.

Kayl clenched his jaw and bared his teeth. *Threatening her. Frightening her. Looking upon her.*

Those thoughts careened through the twins' mental link from both sides, repeating, echoing, building.

"Bag on the ground," the cren said, also from behind Kayl.

Kayl and his brother looked at their mate, who stood between them with eyes wide and skin paler than normal save for the splotches of pink upon her cheeks.

"Now, you fucking dustmunchers!" the groalthuun shouted.

Nostrils flaring, Kayl lifted the satchel off his shoulder and slowly laid it on the ground.

The gift. The bonding gift.

They will not take it.

Will not take her.

"Now hands up, over your heads," ordered the cren.

As one, Kayl, Aileen, and Kier raised their empty hands.

The twins brushed the tips of their tails along their mate's calves, hoping to reassure her, to ease her fear, to bolster her resolve. But their minds, their hearts, their souls, were ablaze. Their every instinct insisted that this was not right, that they needed to attack. That they needed to destroy any threat to their mate no matter the risk to themselves.

Yet somewhere deep inside, Kayl found his focus. He channeled all that rage and instinct, folding them upon themselves and compressing them over and over, forging them into something precise. Something deadly.

The approaching footsteps ceased a few meters behind Kayl and his companions.

Threatening our na'diya. *Looking upon her.*

"Turn around," the onigox commanded.

Defying the burning urge to set every muscle in his body into sudden, explosive motion, Kayl slowly turned to face the onigox. His brother and mate did the same.

The onigox was grinning, holding a large auto-blaster with the gaping barrel pointed directly at Kayl's face. His posture was otherwise nonchalant. Beside him, the crimson-eyed cren wore a grimmer expression and maintained a warier stance, holding his flechette pistol steady in both hands.

"Not so fucking smug now, offworlders?" The onigox took a step closer and tilted his head, eyes falling upon Aileen.

Reflexively, Kier and Kayl moved to shield her with their bodies.

"Do not move," the cren snarled, finger tensing on the trigger of his flechette pistol. A small red line on his throat, nearly matching the color of his eyes and hair, marked the bite of Kier's blade.

Again, the twins stilled, muscles going rigid with the unspent energy coursing through them. Their psychic bond expanded, overlapping their sensory inputs and further bridging their thoughts.

War raged within the twins. Reason battled instinct; restraint battled the need to act; concern battled anger. Though those forces were currently locked in a stalemate, Kayl knew that wouldn't last... and he knew which of them would emerge victorious.

That outcome needed to be delayed until the danger to Aileen was as minimal as possible.

The onigox raised one of his lower arms high and beckoned the ilthurii with his hand. "Come down, T'choss."

"You stay up there, Broerk," said the cren.

The groalthuun growled. "Why? You're *not* cutting me out of this, Jaggaan."

Jaggaan finally pried his crimson eyes from the twins and Aileen to glare up at Broerk, pistol swaying slightly off target. "Because we need someone keeping watch from above, you fool."

The ilthurii, T'choss, snorted. "And because you climb as well as a legless polgan."

Broerk spat a curse.

Kayl could not see T'choss, but the ilthurii was visible at the very edge of Kier's vision. The ilthurii slung his rifle across his back and swiftly climbed down the cliff face with the same ease he might've displayed during a leisurely stroll.

Once he was on the canyon floor, T'choss took his weapon in hand and advanced toward the twins and their mate. "You were right, Neroth. This was easy."

"Of course I was," replied the onigox. "They're like all offworlders. Arrogant and unaware."

"Sounds like projection to me," Aileen said, her voice starting uncertain but quickly gaining strength and steadiness.

The onigox returned his attention to her; Kayl and Kier barely held themselves in place.

Neroth narrowed his eyes, grin wavering. "And what's that supposed to mean?"

"It means your insult was pretty hollow coming from an arrogant cunt with no self-awareness."

Above, Broerk barked laughter; behind, T'choss echoed it with a rasping laughter of his own.

Jaggaan's expression took on a hint of ravenousness as he looked Aileen over. "She has spirit."

"We'll see how long that lasts," Neroth growled. "We'll see how long her body lasts too. Tiny, frail thing like her... That'll be a nice, tight rut."

Kayl's hands, still over his head, curled into fists. His claws bit into his palms, drawing blood, and he gritted his teeth so hard it made his jaw ache. Those sensations were echoed through his bond with Kier.

Our mate. Our na'diya. Ours. Ours!

"You will not touch her," Kier snarled.

"I won't?" Neroth released the foregrip of his auto-blaster, nestling the butt of the weapon against his bicep as he pointed it skyward, and stepped closer. "You having trouble understanding the situation here? You're outnumbered, outgunned, and outmatched in every way, little daevahs."

"Careful, Neroth," warned Jaggaan.

"Whatever," the onigox grumbled. He stopped immediately in front of Kayl, eyes burning. "T'choss, get the loud one's knife." Lowering his voice, he leaned down. "I'm going to use your knife to slice off your sack."

In his peripheral vision, Kayl saw T'choss coming up behind Kier. The ilthurii's sharp teeth were bared in a predatory grin, and he, too, had shifted his weapon into a one-handed grip, directing its barrel toward the ground.

Fury pressed against the twins' mental walls, assaulting the icy barriers Kayl had maintained for so long with blistering fire. The moment was so close...

Aileen glanced at Kier, then at Kayl, barely moving her head to do so.

Kayl couldn't know how much she sensed from him and his brother, couldn't know if it would be enough. Whether she read the twins' intent upon their faces or felt it from their hearts, she seemed to understand.

Her tongue slipped out, trailing across her lips. "What a fragile ego you have."

Neroth's brows fell. He shifted closer to Aileen and bent down further, placing his head just above hers. She looked so tiny compared to the hulking, four-armed alien, so delicate, but she didn't flinch, didn't look away or shrink back.

In his altered position, the onigox's body blocked Aileen from Jaggaan.

No better moment would come; Aileen had just created the best opportunity. Kayl and his brother shattered the last of the mental walls containing their fury.

T'choss reached for Kier just as Neroth lifted a hand toward Aileen's face. The onigox said, "Mouthy little *ji'tas*, isn't sh—"

Kier threw himself backward, catching the ilthurii's extended arm. Kayl slapped his hands down atop the onigox's lowered head. His claws raked Neroth's scalp as he grasped the onigox's hair in both fists.

Kier grabbed T'choss's wrist and wrenched on the ilthurii's arm. Bone cracked. That same instant, Kayl dragged down on Neroth's head and leapt off the ground, driving his knee into the onigox's face.

The onigox and his companions cried out and cursed.

Our mate.

Neroth reeled, staggering aside. As Kayl landed, he hooked Aileen's waist with his tail and tugged her into the cover provided by both his body and the onigox's. She let out a startled sound before ducking low to make herself as small a target as possible.

Beyond Neroth, Jaggaan swung his pistol toward the only exposed target—Kier.

Kier slammed his back against T'choss's chest, pinning the gauss rifle between their bodies, and spun, dragging the ilthurii around.

The cren's flechette pistol went off with a roar. Superheated fragments of metal sparked bright orange in the deepening shadows, striking the ilthurii's back.

T'choss hissed and growled, his pained sounds mingling with the sizzling of his burning flesh. Jaggaan uttered a horrified curse.

"I don't have a clear shot!" Broerk yelled.

Kier's eyes flicked to the clifftop. The groalthuun had braced his blaster on his shoulder and was aiming down at the group, eyes wide.

"Fuck," Neroth snarled, swinging a huge fist at Kayl.

Kayl twisted aside to avoid the blow, again shoving himself off the ground, and drove all his weight down on the hunched onigox's head. Neroth's powerfully built torso turned gravity against him; he toppled forward, crashing to the ground.

Landing on one knee beside Neroth's head, Kayl released his foe's hair and swept his hands down. His claws shredded his pants on both thighs.

Kier drew his knife from the hidden sheath on his thigh, released

T'choss's broken arm, and spun. The knife traced a gleaming arc through the air, slicing clean through the ilthurii's throat. Before the wound had even opened, Kier took hold of the hand with which T'choss still grasped the gauss rifle.

Kayl's hands found what they sought—the grips of his knife and pistol. He tore the weapons free of their concealed holders.

"I killed T'choss," Jaggaan said, bewildered.

"Fucking shoot them," Neroth boomed, slapping three hands on the ground to push himself up onto his knees. That fourth hand still held his auto-blaster, which he was swinging toward the twins—toward Aileen.

Kier turned the ilthurii's gauss rifle toward the top of the cliff and pressed T'choss's finger down on the trigger. Several high cracks echoed through the canyon—the sounds of the rifle's projectiles breaking the sound barrier.

As rocks shattered and cracked near Broerk, sending him to take cover, Kayl thrust his knife into Neroth's arm, halting the onigox's auto-blaster.

They threatened our mate.

Neroth snarled and swung his left arms back at Kayl. A growl rose from Kayl's chest as he threw himself into a roll, dodging the onigox's thickly muscled arms and ripping his blade free.

The onigox cried out again and pulled his injured arm away, rolling onto his back. Kayl braced his feet on the ground. At the edge of his vision, he saw Jaggaan fighting to steady his trembling weapon, eyes darting between Kier and Kayl repeatedly.

Kier fought the collapsing ilthurii's weight to realign the gauss rifle, dragging it toward the cren. Kayl launched himself into another somersault, this time over the onigox. He lashed out with his blade during the roll. The honed tristeel edge cut through fabric and flesh as easily as it cut through the air.

The onigox let out a hoarse scream. As Kayl landed on the ground, Neroth clamped his lower hands over his groin, dark blood gushing from between his fingers.

That scream seemed to jar the cren from his stupor. His finger squeezed the trigger of his flechette pistol.

Kayl's arm darted up. His blaster went off with a whine; the ilthurii's gauss rifle fired simultaneously, creating a sound like two stones striking one another.

A plasma bolt sizzled through the cren's face, shearing off one of his tusks, and a small hole appeared in the center of his chest. Blood misted the air behind him. The cren's flechette pistol swung wide just as it roared again, spraying its glowing-ember projectiles into the canyon wall.

One of Neroth's huge hands caught Kayl's arm and squeezed, the grip crushing enough to break Kayl's hold on his knife.

The onigox rasped, "You fucking—"

Kayl bent his arm across his chest, aiming the blaster at Neroth.

Neroth's eyes widened. Kayl destroyed them—along with most of the onigox's face—with three quick shots.

One for each part of our daevalis.

The onigox's torso remained raised off the ground briefly, his ruined, smoking head upright with the blacked hole that had been his face gaping at Kayl. When it fell to the ground, the onigox's hand fell with it.

The twins both looked at Aileen, who was huddled on the ground with her hands over her head, terribly still.

Kayl and Kier's hearts pounded.

Be all right.

She must be all right.

Kayl shoved himself onto his feet; Kier shoved the dead ilthurii away.

Aileen lifted her head, her terrified eyes scanning her surroundings until they fell upon the twins. Her relief was visible. "Are you both okay?"

She began to rise.

Before either Kayl or his brother could move closer to their mate, a too-familiar sound came from above—the rattling of disturbed rocks.

Aileen stilled, her gaze whipping in that direction. "*No!*"

Broerk, silhouetted by the setting sun, stepped to the edge of the cliff and aimed his blaster rifle down. He shouted something. Neither Kier nor Kayl understood the words; all their attention was on their mate.

Again, fear surged over Kayl's rage. Anger could not serve as armor for their mate, could not shield her from what was about to happen.

So we must be her shield. Now, and always, the twins pulsed as one.

They leapt toward her, fingers working in midair. Armored segments formed out of their bodysuits, rapidly encasing the twins' bodies. They landed over Aileen as their helmets sealed around their heads.

Broerk opened fire.

Plasma bolts rained from above, a searing torrent that battered the twins' armor. They braced themselves over and around Aileen, covering her entirely as the impacts of those bolts shook them. The brothers were only distantly aware of those impacts, only distantly aware of the blaster's high-pitched, thumping whines, of Broerk's wordless, echoing shout.

But they could not ignore Aileen's body beneath theirs. They could not ignore the tremors coursing through her, could not ignore her desperate, panting breaths or her frightened cries.

They could not ignore the pangs in their chests that came in response to fear.

Dirt and rock sizzled around them as it was struck by plasma, sending smoke and steam into the air. The displays in their helmets flashed with heat warnings. Kayl felt warmth building on his back despite the armor's shielding and the bodysuit's insulation, but it could not compare to the fire in his core, the fire in his soul.

He is trying to kill her...

They failed to take her, so now he is trying to kill her.

Kayl clutched the grip of his blaster tightly enough to make his hand tremble. Would nowhere be safe? Would there always be another battle to fight, more blood to shed?

We will always fight for her, the twins' *aerysi* pulsed. *Anything for her. Everything for her.*

The plasma bolts ceased suddenly. The auto-blaster's whine was replaced by a fleeting sound that was as subtle as it was distinct—the crackling hum of a power cell failing.

Kayl and his brother shoved themselves upright, Kier dragging the blaster from his thigh holster as he moved. They pivoted on their knees, spinning toward the cliff, pistols raised. Their weapons were on target before their helmet displays had even marked the hostile gunman.

The barrel of Broerk's auto-blaster was glowing orange with heat, and smoke curled from the power cell compartment. The groalthuun attempted to eject the cell only to yank his hand away with a hiss.

His eyes flicked down. "Oh, fu—"

The twins' blasters fired so quickly that the succession of shots sounded like a single, high droning. Blue-white plasma bolts bathed the canyon wall in their soft glow, creating deep pockets of dancing shadow across the stone.

If Broerk cried out, his voice was swallowed by the sound of the blaster fire.

Within seconds, dozens of bolts had hit their marks. The groalthuun finally fell backward and out of sight, but not before glowing embers had flaked away from his charred flesh to drift lazily on the breeze until they cooled and faded from sight.

Together, the twins let the blasters fall from their hands, retracted their helmets, and turned back to their mate.

"Are you hurt?" Kier asked.

Aileen launched herself at them, arms wide as though to wrap the twins in an embrace. Kayl caught one of her arms, halting it, while Kier caught the other.

She looked between them with confused, watery eyes. "What's wrong?"

"Plasma heat," Kier rasped.

The strain of holding back, of not taking her in their arms, was nearly too much for the twins, even with their willpower combined. Chaotic thoughts tumbled through their link.

Ours. She's ours.

Make her ours.

They tried to kill her.

Almost lost her.

Ours.

Kayl clenched his jaw, and his tail lashed the ground behind him.

"Are you both okay?" she asked, body trembling. "Please tell me you're okay."

"Fine," Kayl replied through his teeth.

"Are you hurt?" Kier repeated. He and Kayl spread Aileen's arms wider to get a better look at her, frantically raking their eyes over every inch of her body. Other than a few green strains on her pantlegs from the vegetation, there were no marks upon her.

"I'm fine. Scared as hell about you two, but I'm fine." She peered past them, toward the bodies on the ground. "Are they all dead?"

"Not dead enough," the twins growled.

They raised their holocoms, checking the readouts for their suits. The heat had dispersed. Without a moment's hesitation, they retracted their armor, released Aileen's wrists, and threw their arms around her, drawing her into a tight embrace. She hugged them and tipped her forehead against theirs.

"I thought I was going to lose you," she whispered, fingers digging into their backs as her hold tightened.

"Never," they replied. "*Never*."

But they'd almost lost her. In the short while they'd known Aileen, she'd faced a lifetime's worth of danger. That she'd come away from most of it unharmed was miraculous, but that was not enough. Kier and Kayl needed to do more. They needed to preempt those risks. They needed to...

Need to complete the daevalis.

The fires inside the twins had not diminished. Those flames were ravenous, growing larger with each heartbeat, but their source had changed. They were fed by desire, by need, by instinct, by choice—their choice to embrace their *na'diya* fully and become one with her.

But more than anything, that fire was fueled by love.

We should return to the ship, Kier pulsed. *Too exposed here. Too dangerous. And I...I cannot control myself much longer.*

Kayl's fingers twitched, claws catching in the fabric of Aileen's cloak. He yearned to tear all that cloth away from her, to bare her skin, to behold her beauty and revel in it, worship it, ravage it.

Nor can I, Kayl replied. *Let us be swift.*

The twins released Aileen, Kier withdrawing from her entirely. As Kayl slipped an arm under her legs and scooped her off the ground, Kier retrieved their fallen belongings. Aileen held tight when Kayl stood up.

Her delectable scent filled Kayl's nose, fanning the flames within him to even greater heights. He barely suppressed a shudder; Kier did not suppress his.

Kayl and his brother raced toward their ship.

THIRTY-FOUR

Aileen clutched Kayl and kept her eyes on Kier, afraid to look away. Everything had happened so fast. Throughout the entire confrontation, her only thoughts had been for her mates. And she'd been...helpless. Anything she might have done to assist the twins could've resulted in death, whether her own by inadvertently getting in the way, or Kier and Kayl's by distracting them at a vital moment.

But they'd survived without a scratch.

Even after training with them aboard the *Fang* and seeing their speed in the canteen, Aileen had been utterly unprepared for just how deadly Kier and Kayl were. She knew they'd fought their way out of Eternal Paradise, which had been invaded by God knew how many pirates, but she'd been unconscious through most of that.

Her mates were lethal, efficient, and...breathtaking.

She pressed her lips to Kayl's jaw. His grip on her strengthened.

Though it felt like an eternity had passed, it couldn't have taken the twins more than half a minute to reach the *Fang*. Kier had remotely lowered the ramp, only half of which touched the ground thanks to the ship's angle.

Kayl bounded onto the ramp without missing a step. He darted through the cargo hold and up the stairs, reaching the entrance to the upper deck before the ramp had fully shut behind them, and continued forward. The doors along the corridor darted by, no longer bathed in the red glow of the emergency lights, no longer quite so foreboding as they'd been after the crash.

He halted only when he reached the cockpit. Kier hurried past them as Kayl, muscles tense, lowered Aileen onto her feet. She heard Kier drop several objects onto the chair, and she turned her head to see him bent over a control console with a single small holo screen in front of him.

"There is enough to spare," Kier said.

"Then turn it on," Kayl replied.

Their words were strained, raw, and hurried.

Kier's fingers flew through commands on the screen. "Short range bioscanner is active."

"Nothing will harm us here," Kayl said, catching Aileen's chin and turning her face back toward him. "You are safe, *na'diya*."

Eyes locked with Kayl's, she touched her fingers to his cheek. "I know."

Aileen always felt safe with them, and she knew they'd protect her from any danger. She just didn't want them to do so at such great risk to themselves.

His fingers flexed on her chin, grip almost becoming painful, before he dropped his hand and pulled away from her. He stalked toward his brother. With the pair standing side by side, the tension in their postures was even more pronounced—heads bowed, shoulders squared, fists clenched, tails erratic and stiff.

Aileen kicked off her boots, removed the cloak from her shoulders, and draped it over one of the chairs. She frowned as she watched the twins, waiting for them to tell her what was going on inside their heads, to share their telepathic conversation with her, but neither of them said a word. Neither of them even looked at her.

"What is it?" she asked.

Their muscles tensed further, and the swinging of their tails faltered.

"Kier?" She took a step closer to them. "Kayl?"

As one, the twins growled and turned to face Aileen. They fixed their fierce, mesmerizing gazes upon her, their eyes so bright that they seemed to give off their own light. Their pupils had narrowed to predatory slits.

"We need you, Aileen," they rasped.

The breath fled her lungs. Kier and Kayl's features were bestial and ravenous, and *she* was what they hungered for. Desire unfurled in her core, and her sex clenched, pulsing with an ache that only the twins could soothe.

Her hands dropped to her sides, gathering the hem of her tunic.

No more waiting.

Aileen had spent her entire life waiting for her mates. The wait ended now.

She drew the tunic off over her head and tossed it aside, and her tank top swiftly followed. Her nipples hardened in the open air. Heart fluttering wildly, Aileen hooked the waistband of her pants with her thumbs and pushed them down, letting them pool around her feet. As she straightened, her long, loose hair fell around her shoulders.

Completely bare, she met them twins' gazes again. "I need you too."

Their eyes were fixed upon her with blistering intensity. Her belly fluttered with excitement. The twins stalked toward her, and she drew in a shaky breath, but she was not scared.

Their outer clothing succumbed to their claws as they moved; they shredded the fabric and tore it away with the same ferocity they'd shown their enemies. The hidden seams on their bodysuits parted, revealing their broad, tantalizing chests. They tugged the material off and cast the suits to the floor.

They'd worn nothing underneath.

Aileen's gaze roved over their lithe physiques—over the planes and valleys of their muscles, over their long, toned limbs, over their narrow waists and Adonis belts, which were like arrows pointing to their erections. Naturally, she followed those arrows, drinking in the sight of their throbbing shafts with those prominent ridges.

The pressure in her core expanded, but it was oddly hollow. She yearned to have the twins inside her, to feel those ridges as they thrust in and out of her body, to be filled by them.

When the twins finally reached her, they pulled her into their arms—Kier at her front, Kayl at her back. The heat of their bodies surrounded her. Their tails brushed up the backs of her calves and curled to tease her inner thighs, and their hands roamed her body, moving along her shoulders, down her arms, and over the curves of her hips. Aileen's breath hitched when Kier's fingers skimmed her chest. Her breasts swelled in response, feeling heavier and achier than before, and she leaned closer, craving more of his touch.

"Please," she whispered as she settled her hands upon his chest.

His lips drew back, baring his fangs, and his growl rumbled beneath her palms as he cupped her breasts in his rough hands. He massaged her flesh with a mixture of reverence and covetousness, coaxing a sensual sigh from Aileen's lips.

Kayl swept her hair over one shoulder. Gripping her hips, he pressed a kiss to the center of her back. She shivered. His breath warmed her skin, and tingles spread through her as he placed another kiss upon her back, and another. She saw it in her mind—he was kissing each point of the triangle love knot tattooed there.

Aileen drifted on a sea of pleasure, her breaths matching the rhythm of Kier's clever hands. Her eyelids fluttered, only to flare when Kier pinched her nipples hard enough to make her clit twitch.

She caught hold of his wrists and gasped, "Kier!"

He grinned, rolling her nipples between his fingers and thumbs. "I never tire of hearing my name from your lips."

Heat gathered between her thighs, and she squeezed them together, seeking to alleviate the growing ache in her core.

Kayl's tail glided up her calf. When it reached her knee, it curled around her leg and continued up, creating delightful friction on her sensitive skin that made Aileen shiver. She couldn't resist as he forced her thighs apart, didn't want to resist as it crept higher still. Finally, it reached the apex of her thighs, and Kayl pressed it to her sex.

Aileen's breath hitched. That simple pressure built her need impossibly fast, impossibly high, and she would've gyrated her hips to claim more were Kayl's hands not holding her firmly in place.

Kier sank onto one knee, placing his head level with Aileen's chest. He breathed in deep, his nostrils and nose slits flaring, and exhaled with a growl.

"You smell so sweet, Aileen." Kier's warm breath teased her nipple as he moved his mouth close. His wicked tongue flicked out, tracing a circle around the swollen bud. "So fucking sweet."

She rasped another word—whether it had been *more* or *please* did not matter. Their meanings were the same.

But Kayl's tail dropped away and hooked around the middle of her thigh, tugging her legs farther apart.

"You want more?" Kayl asked, his mouth beside her ear. Brushing his nose through her hair, he slid a hand from her hip to her belly, flattening his palm over it. The tips of his claws grazed her pelvis.

Her sex clenched in anticipation. That hand was resting so, so close. Letting out a shaky breath, she nodded.

"You *need* more?" Kier purred before scraping a fang across her nipple; her grip on his wrists tightened as a tremor coursed through her.

It wasn't enough. God, it wasn't enough.

"More," Aileen begged, arching into his touch.

Kayl's hand dipped. He cupped her sex, fingers gliding between her slick folds, and hissed. "She is so wet for us."

"Mmm." Kier closed his lips over her nipple and sucked, lavishing its tip with his tongue. He released it to say, "Now I want to hear her sing."

He drew her nipple back into his mouth as Kayl pressed a finger deeper, its pad brushing her clit.

Aileen's head fell back against Kayl, her fingers delved into Kier's hair, and she gasped, overwhelmed by the sensations. Kayl circled and stroked her clit, his movements falling into the same rhythm as Kier's mouth to strike her with pulse after pulse of pleasure, each more powerful than the last.

Kayl slipped his other hand into her hair, cradled the back of her head, and turned it to expose her throat. He kissed her there, grazing her skin with his fangs before he captured her mouth with his. Firm and commanding, his lips led hers in an intimate dance; his tongue soon joined in, demanding she part her lips and allow it entry.

Kier removed his mouth from her nipple. The cool air was a delightful shock against the wet bud, quickly replaced by the heat of his callused fingers as he moved his mouth to her other breast. Fangs, lips, and tongue worked together to assail her with pleasure, every jolt coursing directly to her core.

Kayl sped his finger. Ecstasy struck her in waves, like the ocean lashing the shore before a storm, faster and faster, harder and harder, making her breaths heavy and erratic. Her knees buckled. She leaned back against Kayl fully. Only his strong body and firm hold kept her upright, and she poured her gratitude—along with her consuming need—into her kiss.

Her body quivered, and her essence dripped down her inner thighs.

She was so close, *so* close...

Kier's mouth left her breast. He trailed small, scalding kisses down her abdomen. Growling, Kayl dropped his hand from her hair to palm her breast in his brother's absence, squeezing and holding her against him like he'd never let go.

Kier caught her hips between his hands. His lips continued downward, over her belly, across her pelvis, closer, closer... Kayl's fingers spread her cunt wide, and then Kier's mouth was *there*, tongue flicking over her clit before he latched onto it.

Aileen tensed, releasing a hitched, broken noise, and for an instant, there was nothing. She was suspended in time—no sound, no feeling, no thoughts. But even in that void, there was Kier and Kayl. Her mates.

The universe came rushing back, and she cried out, tearing her mouth from Kayl's as pure, powerful pleasure swept through her. She threw her arm back, curling it around Kayl's neck while keeping the other in Kier's hair; she needed to hold on to them, couldn't stand without them.

Kier caught her legs behind her knees and draped them over his shoulders. He clutched her ass, lifted her cunt closer to his mouth, and lapped greedily at the liquid heat flowing from her before thrusting his tongue into her center.

"Yes," Kayl said in her ear as he took over stroking her pulsing clit. "Sing, *na'diya*. Sing for us. Let us hear your pleasure."

Her core convulsed and her toes curled against Kier's back as a tidal wave of ecstasy crashed into her. Her hips bucked of their own accord, her body desperately seeking—*needing*—more. It was almost too much already, and yet it wasn't nearly enough. It would never be enough.

The twins did not relent.

She panted, moaned, and whimpered, all the sounds escalating in pitch.

Brow creasing, Aileen caught her bottom lip with her teeth and looked down her body at Kier.

He met her gaze. His eyes burned with passion and pleasure, but there was a shadow within them, cast by a deep, tortured yearning.

Something went taut within Aileen; it began in her chest, around her heart, but spread swiftly in hot, electric arcs until it suffused her. Every bit of her was straining toward the twins, responding to the call of their souls. Desperate to become one with them. She'd felt it before, but never so strong, never so sure.

Kier's pupils dilated and contracted back to slits.

Aileen knew without any doubt that Kier and Kayl felt the same pull toward her, that her soul was calling right back to theirs.

Kier lifted his head. Her essence glistened upon his lips. His tongue swept some of it into his mouth, and the heat in his eyes intensified.

"You are ours," he said in unison with his twin. Their voices wrapped around her, firm, commanding, loving, and thrilling, heightening that inner pull.

"Yes," she breathed. "I've always been yours."

Kier closed his eyes. He and his brother shuddered, and low growls rose from their chests. When he opened his eyes again, they glinted with primal possessiveness. He lowered her legs from his shoulders.

Kayl withdrew his fingers from her sex, and Aileen's gaze followed his hand as he brought them to his mouth. He closed his lips around them, sucking as he pulled them free. His chest vibrated with a groan.

"Give me our mate," Kier said as he lay back on the floor.

Lifting Aileen, Kayl settled her upon Kier's stomach with her knees to either side of him and his hard, pulsing cock nestled against backside.

Kier immediately reached up, cradled the back of her head, and drew her down, crushing his mouth to hers. Aileen slapped a hand on the floor and moaned as he devoured her, his tongue leading hers in a sultry dance. She tasted herself upon his lips.

His tail wound around her waist, and his hands glided along her body to frame her hips. The scrape of his claws over her skin sent a thrill through Aileen, coaxing her deeper into his slow, intoxicating kiss.

Kier guided her hips up and shifted beneath her.

When he lowered her down, the head of his cock pushed past her entrance. She moaned. Kier broke their kiss and hissed through his teeth, staring up at her with half-lidded eyes.

"Aileen," he rasped.

He lifted her up and pulled her down again, pushing his shaft deeper, and Aileen felt every one of those ridges as they stretched her, as they glided along her inner walls and left no part of her channel unstimulated.

Aileen's sex clenched around him, her body eager for more, eager to take him fully. Her limbs trembled, threatening to give out. Her need was too great. It was too much for one person to withstand, too much for one person to survive.

And it still was not enough.

Kier's claws pricked her flesh as he tightened his grip. With a final, driving thrust, he buried himself inside her completely.

Aileen gasped. Her sex contracted around him as a brief, shallow orgasm sent a rush of a heat through her.

Kier tipped his head back and shuddered as he gritted out, "*Fuck...*"

The way he'd uttered that word instilled her with a sense of power. *She'd* caused that reaction in *him*—this fierce, deadly being who'd saved her, who craved her.

Aileen ground against him. She needed him even deeper, needed the friction, needed to feel those ridges striking her pleasure points, needed to see her mate lose control—but he held her immobile.

"No," Kier growled, clamping a hand on the back of her neck. "Not yet."

Aileen dropped her forehead to his shoulder, breathing in his scent. His cock pulsed inside her. All she wanted was to move, to feel his shaft pumping in and out of her. All she wanted was to revel in this blissful, torturous connection between their bodies. Had she not been so aware of herself, of him and Kayl, of everything, had she not been so utterly *present*, she might've sworn she was in the grips of rhapsodic heat.

She moaned. "I need... I need..."

Oh God, she needed Kier and Kayl so badly she burned.

A hand settled upon her back, smoothing up her spine. Aileen arched into its touch. That only sent Kier's cock deeper.

"Patience," Kayl murmured as he dropped his mouth to her shoulder, caressing her skin with his lips. And then he was gone.

"Easy for you to say," Kier replied in a husky, unsteady voice. "You are not yet inside her."

"But I feel her through you."

Something cool and wet dripped between her ass cheeks, and a coconut-like fragrance washed over her. Kayl growled as he squeezed her ass and spread her wide. An instant later, Aileen felt his touch *there*. Her breath hitched as the pad of his finger circled her rosette, spreading the lubricant, gently pushing it inside her.

"Kayl," she whispered, anticipation rippling through her.

"I am here, *na'diya*," Kayl rumbled. More of that liquid dripped onto her.

Kayl's finger withdrew, replaced by the blunt head of his cock. His hands circled her waist, and he pushed forward, nudging his shaft inside her.

Aileen stiffened at the burning stretch, turning her face against Kier's neck as a foreboding chill ran down her spine. She squeezed her eyes shut. For an instant, a dark shadow from the depths of Aileen's memory crept along the edges of her consciousness. Kayl went still.

"Breathe, Aileen," Kier crooned. He moved his hands and tail over her skin, petting her soothingly, lovingly, and pressed a kiss on her head.

"Open your eyes," Kayl said. "It is us. *See us.*"

"We have you. We will always have you."

Aileen opened her eyes and inhaled, willing her body to relax as she drew in the twins' mingled scents—earth and sea, sandalwood and spice. She would not let those memories ruin this for her. Would not let her past come between them.

She curled her fingers into Kier's shoulders. "I know."

Kayl stroked his thumbs over her lower spine. He drew his cock back and pushed it forward again until she felt herself close around the first of his ridges. It hurt, but she breathed through it, keeping her body relaxed.

His grip on her waist tightened. He pumped slowly, sinking deeper inside her little by little, allowing her to stretch around him, allowing her body to accommodate to him. All the while, the twins spoke to her, comforted her, their tails caressing her body.

Aileen panted and whimpered as whispers of pleasure overcame the pain with every stroke of Kayl's cock. He was stimulating nerves she never knew existed, enhancing the sensations already sparked by Kier. She slipped her tongue out and ran it up Kier's throat.

"Ah, Aileen," Kier moaned, raising his chin.

With a fierce snap of his hips, Kayl plunged into her fully, eliminating whatever distance had remained.

Aileen cried out and bore down upon the twins. She'd never felt so stretched, so full, in her entire life, and it was *glorious*. It was right. It was exactly what she'd craved with them from the beginning.

One. We are one.

Heat descended upon her back as Kayl leaned over her. One of his hands curled around her throat, forefinger and thumb cradling her jaw, and he lifted her head off Kier's shoulder. At his guidance, she sat up; Kier's cock sank deeper still. Aileen and Kier moaned.

Kayl tipped her head back and dropped his mouth to her neck, kissing, caressing, nipping, biting. Goosebumps prickled her skin as a thrill swept through her. Those strong fingers then turned her face toward Kayl's. He captured her lips with his own and tilted his hips, his ridges sliding just a little farther into her. He swallowed her breathy cry.

When Kayl broke the kiss, he snarled, "Ours."

THIRTY-FIVE

Pleasure enveloped Kier. For a single moment that felt like an eternity, he could do nothing more than hold his breath and wait for that pleasure to destroy him. It came from his body—from every point of contact with Aileen, especially his cock, which was sheathed in her tight, wet heat. It came from every tiny movement of Aileen's body. It came from her, whispers emanating from her very soul and coursing along the spiritual tethers that connected her to the twins.

But it also came from his brother, unhindered by any mental barriers.

Sol'Kier Sevris and Sol'Kayl Kortanis were as one. Their minds shared all; their pleasures and pains compounded, every sensation doubling, their mate's scent twice as powerful as it filled their lungs. The pressure built by their ecstasy, built by their need, their instincts, their anticipation, was also wildly enhanced.

Neither of them should have been able to withstand those sensations.

Their *aerysi* pulsed together.

Our mate. We are inside our mate.

Ours. She is ours.

We are hers.

Kier released a slow, ragged breath through his gritted fangs and looked up at Aileen. Her lips were parted, a hair's breadth from Kayl's, and her half-lidded eyes shone with lust and need. Her full breasts beckoned him, their swollen tips reddened from his attentions, and wisps of her hair hung about her shoulders in disarray.

She was radiant.

"Such a sight exists nowhere else in the universe," Kier said.

Kayl loosened his hold on her jaw enough for her to look down. She met Kier's gaze.

Kier's fingers flexed on her hips, their pads pressing into her soft skin. He smoothed his palms up her sides until he cupped her breasts. "Nothing is more beautiful."

"And she is ours." Kayl brushed his lips just beneath her ear; Kier tasted a hint of her salt and sweetness on his own tongue.

She reached up to cradle the side of Kayl's face and settled her other hand over Kier's heart. "And you are both mine. My *na'divali*."

That bit of movement from her sent ripples of pleasure through the twins, but the physical sensation could not compare to what her words made them feel.

Kier and Kayl had spent their whole lives knowing that something was missing, that their *daevalis* was incomplete. They'd always been aware of it, but neither realized until this moment just how immense that void had been.

And this little terran was the one to fill that space. She was the one who'd finally triggered the healing their souls had so desperately needed, the one who'd brought them closer than had ever seemed possible.

Seal the bond, one of the twins pulsed; it mattered not which.

There was no more denying that instinct. No more delaying it. Aileen was theirs, and they would not wait another instant to form the bond.

The twins moved in unison, Kier returning his hands to Aileen's hips to guide her as they pumped into her. Their rhythm nearly faltered immediately. The pleasure was overwhelming, beyond anything they'd imagined possible, especially when her body clenched and sought to draw their cocks in deeper. Aileen's scent was heady, infused with her essence, surrounding the twins in a cloud that urged them on harder, faster.

All that friction and pressure grew and grew, and ecstasy crashed through them in strengthening waves. They felt every bit of her, felt her flesh molding to their ridges, caressing and squeezing, stimulating every millimeter of their shafts.

Ours.
She is ours.
Meant for us, made for us.

"Aileen," they rasped. Her name left their lips as a plea, a prayer, a promise.

"Need more," Kier said.

Kayl scraped his fangs along her neck. "More, *na'diya*. More."

The twins sped their pace, their panting breaths drawing yet more of her sweet scent into their lungs.

Aileen arched her back, lips parting with a moan as her thighs quivered around Kier. Kayl released her neck and dropped his hand to her waist, just above Kier's, and used that new grip to slam her down onto them faster still.

"Kier... Kayl..." she breathed.

Her brow creased, and she fell forward, her weight coming down upon the hand she had on Kier's chest. She lowered her other arm, reaching back to grasp Kayl's waist, and moved her body with theirs, matching their rhythm perfectly.

Her altered position allowed them to sink even deeper into her tantalizing heat. She curled her fingers, nails digging into their flesh as she quaked around their cocks.

She opened her eyes, their pale blue filled with desperation as they met Kier's gaze. "Please. I can't... Oh God, it's too much."

"Not enough," Kayl growled, quickening their rhythm further to match the racing of their hearts.

Pleasure wove through the twins, permeating every fiber of their being, but it retained that torturous edge. Everything within them was building to that peak, to that single instant that would redefine them forever, to that moment when they would clutch eternity in their hands.

But they had not reached it yet.

Their sacks ached, filled near to bursting with seed. That ache raced along their shafts, deepening with every thrust, with every scrape of Aileen's nails, with every breathy moan and whimper she released. Her desperation for release was theirs—all those desires, needs, and sensations swirled together in a storm at their cores, becoming so much stronger than the sum of their parts.

Strongest of all was that pull, that unseen force drawing them inexorably to Aileen. The twins were closer to her than ever now.

They could feel so much more than her pleasure; they could almost hear her thoughts flitting just outside their psychic link.

The tethers were there, running between their souls, nearly touching—they but needed a spark that would fuse them together wholly and forever.

Ours, ours, ours. Make her ours.

Claim her.

All of her.

The twins' breaths came short and shallow, while their movements grew only more savage. Aileen's cries escalated, punctuated by the twins' snarls and grunts as their bodies teetered on the precipice beyond which awaited rapture defying imagination.

"Need you," Kier rasped.

"Need to feel you," Kayl groaned.

"All of you," they said.

They drove into her hard. Her muscles tensed, and a shudder ran through her from head to toe, but climax eluded the twins and their mate.

"Open to us," the twins commanded.

The twins gritted their teeth as Aileen leaned more of her weight forward, pressing her budded nipples to Kier's chest, and undulated her hips faster. Kier's hands clenched her hips, and his tail stiffened. The way she moved, the way her sex encased him, the way it stroked him, was maddening in the amount of pleasure it induced.

The psychic link binding Aileen to them thrummed. Tiny points of light, like distant stars glittering in and out, danced in the twins' vision. They felt Aileen's pulse racing, felt the breath rasping in her lungs, felt the sweat trickling over her skin.

So close.

More.

"Let go," the twins urged. "Welcome us in."

Aileen's eyes shut, and her mouth opened with a soundless cry. Her entire body tensed, clamping down on the twins' cocks, and her thighs squeezed Kier tight. That impossible pressure swelled infinitely; the twins' linked minds reeled, barely holding together, as the entire universe trembled around them.

And then everything burst.

The twins were swept into a maelstrom of sensation, minds torn to pieces and scattered across the cosmos. Ecstasy coursed through their veins at the speed of light, suffusing their every cell, swallowing their beings.

Their eyes closed, and color obliterated the darkness behind their eyelids. Teal, purple, magenta, blue, and red, coalescing to form their bodies—to form their mate's body.

They felt her completely; they were her, and she was them. Her mind, her sensations, her memories and hopes and dreams, all of it swirled together in a torrent along with every bit of Kier and Kayl. They felt her body down to its smallest piece as though it were their own, felt her breaths as though taking them into their own lungs, felt her pleasure and her pain, and through her, they felt themselves.

Nothing separated them—body, mind, and soul.

The twins' seed erupted from their cocks, filling Aileen, and her essence flooded from her core. Three voices cried out in overwhelming pleasure, layering with each other to form one voice, one song.

All three were powerless but to ride the intense waves, their bodies moving out of sheer instinct, driven by forces too primal to control. They could not open their eyes, but they saw each other clearly. They glowed with those colors, with that radiance. Their souls glowed, forever forged as one.

The twins' *aerysi* rose together in perfect harmony.

Our daevalis *is forged.*

Our bond is eternal.

The colors faded, and the twins' awareness of themselves slowly returned. It felt like their bodies were materializing from the ether. Tingles pulsed over their skin, spreading heat, and gravity reasserted itself; their limbs were languid and heavy, but neither twin relinquished his hold on Aileen.

Their throbbing cocks remained buried deep inside her, and her inner walls quivered around Kier's shaft. Sweat, seed, and Aileen's essence slickened their flesh, and the scent in the air belonged to all three of them, spiced with sex.

Aileen lay limp upon Kier with Kayl leaning over her, her breath coming in shallow pants against Kier's neck, tickling his skin. Her heart thumped in time with theirs.

Her *aerys* pulsed in Kier's head.

Oh, my God. I died. I'm dead.

What a way to go.

That was... That was...

Bliss.

"You are not dead, *na'diya*," Kayl rumbled, nuzzling the back of her neck and brushing his lips over her skin.

The twins eased their grip on her as a sense of serenity spread through them, coaxing the lingering tension out of their muscles—it was Aileen's serenity, her comfort.

Mmm, I love it when they kiss me, she pulsed.

"I'm not?" she muttered.

Kier grinned and turned his face down, kissing her forehead. *You are not.*

"I feel like I'm in heaven any—" Her breath caught. "That...that was your voice. In my head."

Her mind-voice raced. *I heard him! Oh my God, I heard him. In my head. In my head. In my head.*

"You did hear him," Kayl said.

She stiffened between them. *Wait...*

Kier and Kayl pulsed in unison, *Yes,* na'diya. *We can hear you too.*

Excitement blasted from her. *We're bound? Bound. We're—* Aileen lifted her head and looked at Kier, her smile stretching wide. "We're bound? It worked?"

Now it was Kier who stilled, staring into her eyes. Gone was the pale blue he loved so much. A vibrant blue starburst surrounded each of her pupils, bleeding into bright magenta around the edges of her irises.

The same colors that were in the twins' eyes.

Kayl pushed himself up and grasped her chin, leaning aside as he turned her face toward him. He let out a slow breath through his nostrils. The affection radiating from his heart was mirrored exactly in Kier's.

Lifting a hand, Kier cradled the side of Aileen's neck, stroking his thumb across her cheek. "We are bound, Aileen. It worked."

And the twins had never felt so complete. So at peace.

THIRTY-SIX

AILEEN BLINKED AT HER REFLECTION. Starburst blue and magenta eyes stared back at her. She leaned closer, turning her head from right to left, and blinked again.

Is this a trick?

Is it temporary?

How did this happen? Was it magic?

Was it...sex magic?

They're beautiful! But it's so...strange.

They're my mates' eyes, but mine. Kind of.

They are still your eyes, Aileen, Kier said in her mind.

Kayl's voice came next. *And it is not magic. It is our* daevalis.

"Shite!" Aileen started, her hands catching on either side of the sink. It wasn't that the twins' voices were loud, but they were new.

They were *inside* her head.

And those voices had been inside her head since she and the twins made love the night before. The earth-shattering, mind-blowing sex had culminated in an indescribable moment during which she'd truly been one with her mates—she'd felt herself in their bodies, and them in hers. She'd marveled at the aftermath, during which their thoughts had been shared freely, mind-to-mind. But the day's events, paired with all that overwhelming pleasure, had taken their toll soon after, and Aileen had succumbed to exhaustion.

She'd woken once during the night, cuddled between Kier and

Kayl on their makeshift bed. They must've carried her into their room after she'd passed out.

Everything had been so quiet, so peaceful. So right. And somehow, she knew it wasn't just her experiencing those feelings. They had come from the twins, too, flowing freely along their new bond to amplify the serenity, the rightness, the love.

Everything had been *perfect*.

She'd drifted off to sleep again, only to be awoken most recently by the call of nature. Her internal clock had suggested it was early morning, but Aileen hadn't been sure whether she could trust it—the days on this planet were definitely shorter than those on Earth. It could've been midday for all she knew.

Gently as possible, she'd slipped out of the twins' embraces and padded to the loo. Every muscle in her body ached dully, especially her more intimate parts. She'd realized as she sat on the toilet that the twins must've cleaned her up, because her skin wasn't crusted with the copious amounts of bodily fluids that had been another result of that mind-blowing sex. That they'd taken the time to care for her in such a thoughtful way was touching.

After peeing for what had felt like twelve hours without pause, she'd cleaned up and washed her hands at the sink.

That was when she'd first looked into the mirror, when she'd first seen her eyes. And she'd probably been staring at them for a good five minutes by now.

How could it not have been magic? People's eyes didn't just change, at least not without some sort of medical procedure or colored contact lenses. And it wasn't like her eyes were the only things that had changed.

We would have warned you, na'diya, *had we known it would happen,* Kier said in her mind.

Daevah females take on the eye colors of their mates when their daevalis is forged, Kayl explained. *They have colorless eyes until that bond is made.*

We did not think it possible for your eyes to change, Kier continued. *But it is natural, Aileen. It is part of...us. Part of what we three have made. These pulses of thought, this open flow of feelings, your eyes—it is all natural, all part of our* daevalis.

Natural? Seems like magic to me, Aileen thought, brow

furrowing as she concentrated. *Did that work? Did they hear me? The sex was definitely magic. Oh God, was that magic...*

You do not have to shout, Kier replied with a chuckle.

Aileen pouted. "I wasn't shouting." *How can a thought be a shout?*

Kier's psychic voice was still laced with amusement. *By being quite loud.*

It wasn't loud in my head, she thought. *I just...focused on it.*

One in the same when it comes to telepathy, Kier pulsed.

Is it? I... How? If I think in a shout, it's not a shout, but if I think hard, it is?

When you are done, na'diya, *we will speak face-to-face,* Kayl said.

Face-to-face.

She'd been that way with Kier as he'd pumped his cock in and out of her cunt, and Kayl... Her body clenched at the memory of the twins inside her, of how they'd filled her, of their bodies moving in unison and the indescribable pleasure they had wrought.

Aileen squeezed her thighs together as a delicious ache bloomed in her core.

A low growl, echoed in two voices, sounded in the back of her mind.

Aileen... Kayl's psychic voice intoned.

Unless you mean for us to burst into the lavatory, na'diya, *ease your thoughts,* Kier said.

Embarrassed heat flushed through her, and she covered her face with her hands. *Well... Well maybe you should stop reading my thoughts!*

We are not going to close ourselves off to you, Kayl replied firmly.

She could almost feel Kier smirking before he said, *And we are not reading your thoughts. You are projecting them to us.*

Aileen frowned. *I'm not meaning to.*

Come to us, na'diya, they gently coaxed.

She took a deep breath and released it in a slow exhalation, which sent wisps of her hair flying to the side. She tucked them behind her ear.

After everything they'd shared, why was she suddenly so shy to see them?

Because everything is...different.

She was now connected to them in a way that was so profound, so surreal, so impossibly intimate, and it left *everything* bared. Even if it had only been for an instant, the twins and Aileen had known each other entirely when their souls had joined, down to the tiniest detail. So what if that knowledge had been fleeting? It had happened; they'd seen *all* of her.

And she'd seen all of them. Though the specific memories had long since faded, she'd experienced all their suffering and pain, all their years of being slaves, all their loss and anger and rage. There'd been spots of happiness, specks of comfort, and all the bad had been quickly blasted aside by the overwhelming joy and pleasure of their joining, by contentment so immense it seemed endless, but the negative hadn't been erased.

It was part of Kier and Kayl in the same way Aileen's traumatic experiences were part of her. But those experiences seemed so much smaller now, so much weaker, because their weight was being carried by three hearts.

She exited the loo and returned to their shared bedroom. The twins were still in bed, right where she'd left them. Kayl was sitting up with a corner of the blanket draped over his lap and his hair, uncharacteristically tousled, hanging loose around his shoulders. Kier was reclining on his side with his head propped on one hand and a knee raised, covers cast aside.

Neither had dressed.

And it wasn't like she had either.

"Umm...hi." She caught her lower lip between her teeth and grasped her elbow, feet turning in as that shyness return tenfold. But that self-consciousness didn't stop her from raking her gaze over her gorgeous mates.

Why did they have to look so sexy, even right after waking up? That mussed hair, those bedroom eyes... All that delicious skin and muscle just waiting to be licked.

Kier's cock twitched, hardening before her eyes, and Kayl groaned, pressing a hand over his lap.

"It is going to be difficult to do anything but mate with you, Aileen, if you continue projecting such thoughts," Kayl said.

Kier laughed, tail lazily thumping the bed. "Is that a bad thing, brother?"

Aileen grinned as she stepped closer to them. "I mean, I wouldn't be averse to it..."

The twins' gazes fixed on her, gleaming with hunger.

"Nor would I," Kier purred.

"We have not even showered," Kayl said distractedly, eyes dipping to Aileen's sex. "And we should be teaching you to control your *aerys*, Aileen."

She didn't know what her *aerys* was, but she couldn't bring herself to worry about it just then. The open desire in the twins' stares—desire she could *feel* radiating from them—obliterated whatever nervousness she'd experienced only moments prior.

Aileen lowered herself onto the makeshift bed and crawled toward Kayl, eyes locked with his. She stopped before him, smiled, and ran a finger from the base of his throat up to his chin. "You could teach me while we shower."

And we could do so many other things. So many pleasurable things...

A shudder ran through Kayl, and a spark of pleasure arced from his core directly into Aileen's. He released an unsteady breath, took her hand in his, and brought her fingers to his mouth for a kiss. His tail brushed her outer thigh.

Kier eased up behind her, gathering her hair and sweeping it over her shoulder. His hand continued down her back until finally settling over her hip. The twins tensed, and a pang of guilt struck Aileen, but it was not her own.

"Ah, *na'diya*," Kier said, "forgive us."

Aileen's brow furrowed as she looked back at him. "Forgive you for what?"

Keeping their touches light, they guided her upright on her knees. She followed their movements with her gaze as they gently ran their fingers and palms over her skin, their touches lingering in all the places she had little bruises and scratches. When Kier's hand paused at her hip, heat flooded Aileen's core; the bruising there matched his fingers perfectly.

Kayl moved a hand to her neck, trailing the pads of his fingers up and then across the underside of her jaw. "We did not mean to be so rough."

Why are they sorry? I loved that they were rough. I loved that they let go. I want that again. Here. Now. In bed. In the shower. I want their hands on me, their claws scratching me, their teeth biting me, and their cocks—

"Easy," Kier said with a chuckle.

Aileen groaned and dropped her hands to her sides. "I can't help it."

Kayl's claws teased her jaw. "Our mate is insatiable."

Her lashes fluttered as she leaned into his touch. Every sensation was heightened since they'd bonded, making even the slightest contact between their bodies a thrill.

"Mmm." Kier's tail slipped between her thighs and grazed her sex, gliding through the essence already gathering there. "Is it not our duty to ensure our mate's needs are met?"

Aileen's breath hitched, and she shivered. *Oh, oh yes.*

"Our duty"—Kayl tore the blanket away, baring his ribbed, throbbing cock—"and our pleasure."

She barely had time to take the sight in before Kayl grasped her by the hips and dragged her onto his lap with her legs to either side of him. That quickly, there was nowhere for her to look but into his heated eyes. He shifted his hold on Aileen, lifted her pelvis, and dropped her down atop him, burying himself to the hilt in her willing body.

Aileen flung her head back with a gasp. Electricity sizzled along her every nerve, infusing her with sensation.

So big. So full. The ridges! *Oh, God, he feels so good.*

Kayl dipped his head, skimming her throat with his fangs. *So tight. So hot.* Ba'shanaal, *our mate is perfect.*

Keeping his hold on her, Kayl lay back; the change in position eased him even deeper inside her. His pupils were thin slits lost in swirling seas of blue and magenta.

Kier placed a hand on Aileen's back and guided her torso down, fingers curling just enough for the tips of his claws to prick her skin. The fronts of his thighs bumped the backs of hers as he positioned himself behind her.

Aileen arched her lower back. *Yes. Yes. I need him inside me. I need them both.*

He brushed the tip of his cock around her rosette, spreading that cool, slick lubricant they'd bought in town. "And you have us, *na'diya*," he purred, pushing into her. "Here in bed."

"And in the shower." Kayl slid his fingers into her hair to cup the back of her head.

Aileen moaned, toes curling and fingers clutching Kayl's shoulders.

The twins drew back simultaneously. When they thrust into her again—scattering her thoughts and sending blistering ecstasy through her veins—they growled, "And we have you."

"So...YOU'RE saying I shouldn't think?" Aileen asked, arching a brow as she drummed her fingers atop the mess table.

Kayl smiled; the expression was warm and easygoing. This was an entirely new version of the male she'd first met. "No, Aileen. That is not what I mean at all."

For someone so precise in his actions, he certainly is failing to be precise in his explanations, Kier pulsed.

Aileen grinned; that grin only widened when Kayl rolled his eyes at his brother. Her body was abuzz in the aftermath of their lovemaking, which, true to the twins' words, had occurred first in their bed and then in the shower.

The water wasn't nearly the hottest thing in the shower this morning...

No, it was not, Kier agreed.

Aileen's cheeks flushed as she shifted atop the chair. The hard surface made her all the more aware of how thoroughly her mates had pleasured her.

"Perhaps a modicum of focus would be beneficial?" Kayl said, tapping a claw on the table.

Aileen let her gaze dip to where the open collar of his loose tunic revealed his sculpted chest muscles—and the bite mark she'd left between his neck and shoulder during their first round this morning. "Oh, I'm focused."

She felt a flash of desire from Kayl, and she didn't miss the hint of purple darkening his teal cheeks. But he reigned in his emotions quickly.

"Learning to control your *aerys* is important, Aileen," Kayl said.

Aileen dragged her gaze away from Kayl's chest. "Okay. And my *aerys* is...?"

Kier's telepathic response was gentle. *It is the voice of your mind, of your soul. It is your essence, your being, in a form that can speak directly to ours. Your aerys is you in your purest form.*

That's a lot for one little word, she thought. *And it's kind of…beautiful.*

It is, Kier replied.

"But the connection between our *aerysi* requires balance. Your thoughts are…" Kayl turned his hand palm up and curled his fingers, grasping for words.

She traced the tip of a finger along a crease on his palm. "Filled with sexy fantasies about my mates?"

His blush intensified. "You are not supposed to take delight in tormenting me, Aileen."

She chuckled and leaned in to press a kiss to his lips, smoothing back a strand of his hair that had escaped from its tie. "I'm teasing you, Kayl. It's a…good kind of torment." She sat back. "You and Kier have been in each other's heads your entire lives, but this…this is all so new to me. I'm happy. *So* happy."

Happier than I've been in my entire life. So happy that I'm afraid this is all just going to disappear, like it's too good to be real.

Kayl's eyes softened. As clear as though he'd spoken aloud, his voice resonated in her mind. *It is real. We are real. We will not disappear, Aileen.*

She looked away as tears stung her eyes, dragging a hand through her hair. Just the thought of the twins being taken from her made Aileen's heart feel like it was being ripped to shreds. "You can't promise that. No one can."

"Yet we promise it all the same," Kier said from the doorway. His footsteps were silent as he walked over to her. He placed the items he was carrying on the table and seated himself beside her. "No one in all the universe will fight as fiercely as we two to remain with you, Aileen."

Why does this hurt so much?

Aileen looked up at Kier. "I know I'm being…" She shook her head and let out a small laugh. "I'm being ridiculous. I know."

"No, *na'diya*." Kier stroked his hand over her cheek.

Kayl brushed the back of a finger down her arm and wound his tail around her leg. "Since the moment we recognized you as our mate, we have struggled with fear."

"The fear of you coming to harm, of losing you. You are not alone in this."

Aileen smiled, sniffling, and blinked her tears away. "I know I'm not. I know we've all experienced loss. But I just..."

...love you. I love you. I love you both so much, so deeply, so wholly, that my soul aches with it.

Her eyes flared.

Oh shite! No, no, no! This...

"This isn't how I wanted to tell you," she hurried to say, gaze flicking between them, cheeks flaming. She propped her elbows on the table and buried her face in her hands.

Why couldn't I have blurted it out while they were inside me? That would have been more romantic than this!

Kier chuckled. "Ah, *na'diya*." He took hold of her right hand, drawing it away from her face. "We know. You have shown it to us in countless little ways."

Kayl grasped her other hand, gently pulled it away, and laced their fingers together. "The way you look at us. The way you speak to us. Your concern and thoughtfulness, your self-lessness."

"We hope that we have shown it also," Kier continued. "But if it has not been clear..."

They lowered their faces, brushing their noses against her hair and skimming her ears with their lips. They both said, "We love you, *na'diya*. With the entirety of our hearts, minds, and souls. We love you."

Warmth bloomed within Aileen, and she smiled wide. She turned her face first toward Kayl, then Kier, granting each a soft, lingering kiss, taking her time to caress their lips.

The love Aileen and the twins felt for each other echoed through their new bond both in words and raw emotion, strengthening, blossoming, growing.

And despite their stirring arousal, this was enough. Just being there together, being close, was enough.

Eventually, the twins lifted their heads, and Aileen glanced at the table for the first time since Kier had joined them. He'd set down a tray with several of the oval, pita-like breads they'd purchased in town, along with the jar of addiva jam.

She grinned and picked up the jar, wiggling it in the air. "You know you're going to have to stock up on this stuff before we leave, right?"

Kier chuckled. "As much as you want."

"Then we'd better make extra space in our food storage."

The shelves upon shelves filled with jars of addiva jam that appeared in her mind's eye must've projected to the twins, because they broke out in laughter.

They ate, making short work of the bread and going through half the jam in the process. Aileen hummed appreciatively as she licked the last bit of jam off her thumb. Had there been more bread, she probably would've kept eating—and she was pretty sure she'd already had more than either Kier or Kayl. Apparently, her mind had been so shattered by sex that she hadn't realized how hungry she'd been.

Aileen hummed contently and leaned against Kier, rubbing her cheek on his arm. "So good."

She wanted nothing more than to spend the day alternating between lazing about and having wild sex with her mates.

God, I'm turning into a sex fiend.

It's them. It's always been them.

Kier snickered. "You are blaming us?"

She peeked up at him and smiled. "Definitely."

Kayl brushed strands of hair from her cheek, drawing her attention toward him. "There was something else we purchased in town."

"We meant to give it to you last night," Kier said.

Images flashed through the psychic link, carried on a swell of rage —the thugs who'd attacked them on their way back to the ship. In a few short seconds, Aileen experienced the battle anew, but from the twins' perspectives. She felt their anger as though it had been her own...and she supposed it was.

"Obviously, things did not go according to plan," Kayl said dryly.

He and Kier reached into their pockets, each removing a cloth wrapped bundle that fit on his palm.

"The daevah tradition is for *na'divali* to give their *na'diya* a joining gift." Kier brushed his thumb across the cloth, tracing the object inside. "That is what we intended."

Aileen's heart skipped, and those butterflies returned to her belly, but there was a hint of panic in their fluttering. "You got me a gift?"

I didn't get anything for them. Is a na'diya *supposed to gift her* na'divali *something as well?*

Their warm, gentle laughter eased her immediately. They each took one of her hands and guided them onto the table; their holds were firm but soothing, and she loved the feel of their calloused palms against her skin.

"A *na'diya* is not expected to gift something to her *na'divali*," Kayl said, "though she is free to do so if she chooses."

Kier's lips curled in that roguish smile that made Aileen's knees weak. "And what gift could surpass that which we have already received?"

"What gift have you received?" she asked.

You, their voices whispered in her mind.

Her chest swelled with the love pulsing into her through that psychic link, with the affection radiating from their touches, with the calm induced by their nearness. They leaned against her from either side, resting their cheeks on her hair.

"This is why our fathers chose to fight in their last moments," Kier said softly.

Kayl released a low hum. "Though they had been peaceful their entire lives, anyone would deem *this* worth fighting to the death for."

Aileen could've happily sat there between the twins all day without complaint. Even her excitement for the gifts still resting on the twins' palms wouldn't have been enough to move her from that spot. But Kier and Kayl soon straightened—far too soon, in her opinion—and released her hands.

She kept her hands on the table. Her belly was right back to fluttering, and it took a surprising amount of willpower to keep from drumming her fingers in anticipation as her mates took the corners of their respective cloths between forefinger and thumb.

Their hands paused.

"That we found something made by daevah crafters here, so far from everything, was a wonder," Kier said.

Again, their voices whispered in her mind.

Fate. It was fate.

You are our fate, Aileen.

Kayl turned his face toward her, a small smile touching his lips. "It was perfect."

As are you, their psychic voices said.

Aileen's eyes again misted with tears, which she fought to hold back.

The twins drew back the cloths. Each bundle contained a metal cuff bracelet. The twins settled the cloths, bracelets still atop them, on the table.

The daevahs delicately picked up the bracelets and held them for her to see. Their silvery metal had a subtle, opalescent sheen as it shifted under the light. The cuffs were woven from numerous metal strands that came together to form intricate whorls, all culminating in a single gemstone inlaid upon each bracelet.

Those stones shifted their colors, just like the metal, depending on how the light hit them. On Kier's bracelet, that change was from a soft aquamarine to a deep teal, the underlying greens and blues alternating as the stone was turned. Kayl's went from lilac to indigo, with dark blue creeping in at points. The polished gems had been shaped into perfect spheres—they were like otherworldly pearls.

The twins took Aileen's forearms in hand, lifted them from the table, and slowly slid the bracelets onto her wrists. The metal was cool, contrasting the warmth of the twins' touches to raise goosebumps on her skin.

This was like a wedding ceremony. This was like the groom—grooms—putting the rings on their bride.

Aileen's chest constricted. She turned her wrists, allowing the light to play upon the bracelets, in utter awe of the exquisite, shifting colors.

"They're beautiful," she said.

The twins smiled, their joy flowing straight from their hearts to mingle with hers.

"There is more," Kier said before he and his brother unfurled the cloths again, revealing two more cuffs—identical to the bracelets they'd just gifted her but for their larger size. Kayl placed his onto his right wrist; Kier placed his onto his left wrist. The cuffs fit perfectly just behind their holocoms.

Just when Aileen didn't think her heart could get any closer to bursting with love, the twins placed their hands beside hers, bringing the cuffs together, and the stones on all four bracelets lit up, emitting soft glows in their natural colors.

"The gems are called mesmureen," Kayl said. "They are cherished by our kind."

"When they are brought close together, they shine for each other," Kier added.

"We thought of you when we saw them."

"You...and us."

The twins hooked her pinkies with theirs, binding their hands together in the smallest, simplest, most heart-melting way. Voices speaking as one, they said, "You make our souls shine, Aileen. Since the moment we came close to you."

There was a high-pitched noise. It might have come from Aileen's throat, which was so tight she couldn't possibly have formed any words. She burst into tears.

A rush of thoughts, emotions, and memories flooded her mind. Foremost was happiness. She'd never imagined such happiness was possible, even though she'd seen it from her parents, even though it had been there, right in front of her face, for most of her life. She finally knew what it was like to have what her parents had had.

And she would *never*, ever let it go.

But she couldn't help thinking of where she'd been—of the years she'd spent lost and alone, the years she'd spent trapped on Eternal Paradise. She had thought she would never escape Saduuk. She'd thought she would die in that place, broken, abused, and forgotten.

Yet here she was. Alive, free, loved. Her every fear had been dispelled, and her every dream, even those she'd thought dead, had come true. Because of them. Because of her mates.

They'd saved her. And so much more than that, they *loved* her.

She tried to speak, but it only forced a choked sob from her throat and fresh tears from her eyes. So she threw her arms around her mates' necks, hugging them tight, and thought.

I was drowning in a sea of darkness, and you two were the light that guided me ashore. You make my soul shine, my na'divali.

The twins wrapped her in their arms, pressing their cheeks to her hair and coiling their tails around her legs. She was enveloped by their bodies, by their warmth, by their love. They whispered soothing words and endearments as one of them smoothed down her hair and the other rubbed her back.

A rapid alarm blared from the twins' holocoms.

Aileen started; Kier and Kayl stiffened. They withdrew quickly, raising their holocoms to check the flashing alerts. The twins met each other's gazes, expressions suddenly hard.

She didn't need to ask what was happening—they shared it with her through their bond.

There was a vehicle approaching the *Fang*. A large one.

THIRTY-SEVEN

KIER LEANED his shoulder against a jutting piece of the canyon wall and peered out from behind it. The vehicle was not yet in sight.

He clenched his jaw, swallowing a flare of anger and protective-ness—forty meters ahead was the site of last night's battle. Forty meters ahead lay the corpses of the males who'd tried to take Aileen, who'd tried to kill her. Wild beasts had gnawed upon the remains during the night, but the sun seemed to have chased those creatures away, leaving only death behind.

Had friends of Neroth's group come in search? Kier and his brother would not hesitate to kill to defend their mate, but...

He hated that they were apart from Aileen again. He hated that she was in the cockpit with the blast door sealed while he and Kayl were out here, waiting to face another threat. He hated that Aileen had received mere days of safety and security before being plunged back into danger.

Please be careful, she pulsed, not for the first time.

We will, na'diya, the twins replied in unison. *Be at ease.*

Tch. Yeah, because that's so easy.

Despite everything, Kier grinned; the expression was unfortu-nately fleeting.

Most of all, he hated that Aileen's mind was again occupied with worry, especially after the *very* pleasant morning they'd shared. She deserved peace.

They *all* deserved peace.

The marker in his helmet's display continued ticking down the meters as the vehicle drew closer. It was moving along the canyon floor, approaching from the direction of Navaire.

Were they friends of the fallen, or local law enforcement coming to bring Kier and Kayl to justice for what had happened? Though the twins had acted in defense of themselves and their mate, they'd been to many places across the universe where authorities would side with locals regardless of the circumstances. Ialle and the other townsfolk didn't seem like the type...but people often acted differently once blood had been shed.

I see it, Kayl pulsed, opening his vision to Kier.

Rather than doubling, however, his vision tripled—and that third input was from inside the *Fang's* cockpit, where most of the control consoles and screens were dark.

The view from inside the ship wobbled, and Aileen's hands came into it as she slapped them down on a console to steady herself. Her *aerys* quavered. *Oh. Ohhh...that is... Woah. That is disorienting. How are you doing that? How do I... Oh, I might be sick...*

Kier's brow furrowed. *Aileen, are you seeing through our eyes?*

Yes. Yes, I am. I— Oh, please, Kayl, don't move your head that fast.

I am sorry, na'diya, Kayl pulsed.

We will close it off to you, Aileen, Kier thought. *We do not want to cause you discomfort.*

No! She replied hurriedly, closing her eyes. *No. I just need a moment. I want to see. Maybe...maybe I can notice something you don't and be helpful in some way. Oh, God. I feel like I'm going to fall off the ship if I take a step...*

Psychic voice concerned but firm, Kayl pulsed, *You do not need to be helpful, Aileen. Just safe.*

Maybe this is a way to do both? Please. I'm feeling better already. You won't even notice I'm here. I'll be quiet, and if I distract you at all, you can close it off.

Her next thoughts were softer, drifting from just beneath the surface of her conscious mind. *Let me help. They have to let me help. I can't just stand here and wait, not knowing. Can't stand here while they're in danger...*

The twins could never be unaware of their mate. Never. Even if she never spoke or thought another word, they would always notice her.

Very well, na'diya, Kayl pulsed.

We will not deny you, Kier added.

From his perch lying atop the *Fang,* Kayl could see down to the next bend of the canyon, around which a large hovertruck had just turned. The vehicle was as worn as the others they'd seen in Navaire—faded, flaked off paint, mismatched exterior panels, and heavy tristeel bars, battered by sand and sun, welded on the front and sides. But it looked solid regardless, perfectly balanced on its antigrav pads.

It was built like an armored transport from a few hundred years ago—rugged and reliable, its metal-plated exterior enclosing a large bed that could've been carrying twenty people for all the twins knew. The tinted windows hid the driver and any other occupants from view.

Kayl shifted the railgun, training the crosshairs on the truck's forward antigrav assembly. *If it draws much closer, I will disable its drive.*

The twins' view through Aileen's eyes moved from one end of the cockpit to the other and back again as she paced. Her unfiltered thoughts tumbled through the psychic link. *Oh, God. I hope they're careful. Please be careful. Please be careful.*

Kier adjusted his hold on his blaster and sank low, keeping his gaze on the vehicle. *It is all right, Aileen.*

Calm, na'diya. We will be fine, but you must be calm, Kayl pulsed gently.

Aileen nodded, locks of red hair bouncing at the edges of her vision.

Calm, she echoed, slowing her steps. *Calm. Caaaaaaalm. Just be calm Aileen. Think of waves lapping on a tropical beach, a warm breeze, lush fields of heather...*

Her psychic voice gradually faded, and again Kier smiled, albeit briefly. She was learning quickly. He could not help but take pride in that, though he wasn't sure he if wanted her to gain full control of her *aerys.*

It was nice to have someone in his head who wasn't quite so restrained as Kayl.

Focus, Kier, Kayl snapped through the psychic link.

With a grunt, Kier returned his attention to the matter at hand.

The hovertruck slowed as it neared the scene of the shootout. It was just close enough now for Kier to make out the faint hum of its antigrav drives. He slipped his finger behind the trigger guard, lowering his left hand to reach for his second blaster, which was at his hip.

The hovertruck stopped. It remained in place, quiet and still but for its barely perceptible swaying in the air. Kier's hand closed around his second blaster. He felt his brother's finger poised on the trigger of the railgun, ready to fire.

The antigrav drive's hum intensified slightly as the vehicle sunk closer to the ground. One of the doors swung open, and a person hopped down from the cab.

Ialle was immediately recognizable by her violet skin and blue cloak, but the blaster rifle in her hands prevented the twins from taking any comfort in her arrival. She held a hand over her eyes and scanned her surroundings; Kier reflexively leaned farther behind the rock.

Do you happen to recall how good the average dacrethian's eyesight is, Kayl? Kier pulsed. *Because she is looking right toward you.*

I have altered my position. I am no longer in her line of sight, Kayl replied.

If Ialle had spotted either of them, she made no indication. With the barrel of her weapon angled down, she stepped forward carefully, studying the scene laid out before her. She stopped beside one of the bodies—the cren—and toed it with her boot, lips falling into a deep frown.

Kayl's thought came through the link, measured and with no apparent emotion. *This is a troubling development.*

Ialle is a good person, Aileen pulsed. *I don't think she's going to start shooting or anything.*

You know that from meeting her one time? Kayl asked.

I don't know it, but...I felt it. Most of the people we met yesterday seemed like good people.

I felt it too, Kier thought. *I will go speak with her.*

She is armed, brother, Kayl pulsed.

And I am armored, brother. Kier released his second blaster, pushed away from the cliffside, and lowered the first blaster to his waist. The mag holster engaged, locking the weapon in place on his hip.

We cannot guess what she will—

Calm, Aileen pulsed, cutting off Kayl. *You're covering Kier from above. If anything goes wrong, you'll both be all right.*

The thoughts that followed were undoubtedly ones she hadn't meant to share. *Please be all right. You two had better be all right. Oh, God, did I really just encourage my mate to walk* toward *someone with a* gun?

Kier pressed his lips together, barely containing his laughter.

What is there to laugh about, Kier? Kayl demanded.

A great deal, it would seem. Kier stood up and retracted his helmet. *For now, it is simply that I love our* na'diya *a little more with every thought she shares.*

Aileen's mind-voice replied quickly, *I'm not trying to share everything!*

We know, Aileen, Kayl replied gently. *You have done nothing wrong.*

Nothing at all, Kier pulsed. He stepped out from his cover.

Ialle was crouched beside the ilthurii, holding the scaled body up on its side as she examined the wounds on its back. She flicked her gaze toward the cren—or, more likely, toward the flechette pistol still clutched in his hand.

Kier approached her, keeping his hands away from his blasters.

The door on the other side of the hovertruck's cab burst open. Kayl pulsed a warning as the occupant leaned out of the cab and braced her gauss rifle between the door and the frame, aiming it at Kier.

"Thought I told you to—" Ialle began.

"Stop there!" the new female called. She was a young uriti with warm brown skin, large purple eyes, and long, silvery hair. The two sets of horns rising from her forehead were delicate, their pale bone bearing a faint violet tint.

Kier stopped, turning his palms outward.

She looks even more like a faun than her father, Aileen pulsed. *She's beautiful.*

"—stay in the truck," Ialle finished flatly.

I have a clear shot, Kayl pulsed.

Kier and Aileen's *aerysi* rose in unison. *Do not take it!*

But she—

No, Kayl, Kier pulsed.

That's Tallian's daughter, Aileen thought. *That's Shalla.*

"He was creeping up on you, Ialle," the uriti said.

"I was not creeping," Kier replied, frowning.

"Yes, you were." Shalla tipped her head to the side, gesturing toward the canyon wall. "You were hiding behind the rocks."

"Yes...and then I stepped out into the open and approached in full sight."

"It's all right, Shalla," Ialle said, letting the ilthurii drop onto the ground. A small cloud of dust rose around the body.

Shalla's eyes narrowed, and her long ears drooped slightly. "He's probably the one who did all this, and you're telling me it's all right?"

"He did do this. Him and his brother." Ialle braced her lower hands on her knees and pushed herself upright. She tipped her rifle back over her shoulder and waved toward the *Fang.* "Who I'd guess is watching from somewhere over there, right?"

"Correct," Kier replied. "Can you blame us for our caution?"

Placing her lower hands on her hips, Ialle swept her gaze around the scene, again studying the bodies and the melted dirt and stone scattered around them. "Probably not. I'll wait until after you tell me what happened to give you a definitive answer."

"We will gladly explain everything." Kier nodded toward the uriti, whose rifle was still trained on him. "Preferably without weapons at the ready?"

Ialle sighed. "Shalla..."

The uriti's eye shifted, looking past Kier, and rounded. The barrel of her weapon dipped, and her jaw slackened briefly. "Is that the ship?"

Kier glanced over his shoulder. "Yes, it—"

Shalla ducked back into the cab, slammed the door, and set the hovertruck into motion. The passenger door, which had been left open, slammed shut with the vehicle's momentum.

"No, it's all right, Shalla," Ialle muttered. "I couldn't possibly need any help here."

Kier turned so he was perpendicular to the dacrethian and the *Fang,* looking from one to the other and back again. "Should we be concerned?"

Ialle ran a hand over her smooth scalp and shook her head. "Tallian says she's better at his job than he is, and I agree. She's brilliant. It's just that her mind seems to work a little too quickly sometimes, and she tends to get a little overly focused on anything related to mechanics or electronics. It's a wonder her and her father have even remembered to feed themselves in the years since they lost Veeani."

Kier closed off the extra sensory inputs from his *daevalis* and squeezed his eyes shut. When he blinked them open, it took his mind a moment to readjust to seeing only through his own eyes again. He felt immediately more grounded, but he also felt...more alone.

"Veeani...she was Shalla's mother?" he asked.

"Yeah." A sad light crept into Ialle's eyes. "Shalla was young, but not nearly young enough to forget. Veeani would be proud of her, though. Always was."

He couldn't shield himself from the sorrowful pang that struck his heart.

Fortunately, he was jarred from his thoughts before he could fall into reminiscence about his own parents when Kayl pulsed, *She is bringing that vehicle very close to the ship, Kier.*

Well, she is here to fix it, Kayl, Kier replied. *Do you expect her to do so with her bare hands?*

Aileen's amusement rippled through the psychic link. Kier stopped himself from smiling; to do so might not have seemed appropriate to Ialle, given the circumstances.

Kayl, you may come down, Kier pulsed, *and Aileen, you may come out if you would like.*

Her *aerys* came in a flurry. *Thank goodness that's over. How is worrying so exhausting? Was I really pacing that much?*

That torrent was followed by a far more deliberate pulse from her—*Be out in a minute.*

The corner of Kier's mouth twitched up despite his best efforts.

"Anyway"—Ialle gestured to the body at her feet—"we should probably address this before much more time goes by."

"They ambushed us as we were returning to our ship," Kier said, moving closer to her. He pointed to the clifftop. "The groalthuun and the ilthurii were up high, while the other two must have followed us down into the canyon. I believe they choose to attack once our ship was in sight."

The dacrethian's eyes flicked to each of the three corpses on the ground, then up to the top of the canyon. "I assume Broerk's up there?"

"Whatever remains of him, yes."

"I swear, a skeks with half its head blown off would have more brains than this lot did." She looked over Kier, who was still clad in his armor. "You three all right? Aileen wasn't hurt?"

The very thought of Aileen being hurt sparked anger and fierce protectiveness in Kier, but he kept them down in his belly, where they were unlikely to accomplish anything. "Thankfully, we emerged unharmed."

Ialle let out a humorless snicker. "Don't know if that's a testament to how dangerous you are, or how incompetent they were."

"You mentioned they have caused trouble before?"

"Yeah, they have. Usually some arguments, trying to push people around. Bullying their way into salvage rights. Few fist fights here and there, but they were usually broken up quick enough." She jabbed a thumb toward the big onigox. "Neroth was the worst of them. Biggest person in town, and he liked to throw it around. But usually, they were just bitter drunkards who didn't do any real harm."

Kier let out a long, slow breath through his nose. "They certainly tried to in this case."

"Wow," Shalla said from near the *Fang*.

Kier glanced in her direction to see the uriti out of her vehicle, standing before the crashed ship with her head tipped back. The *Fang's* ramp was lowering, but by the way she moved her head, she wasn't focused on that as much as she was the entirety of the *Fang*.

"They never went this far before." Ialle's voice called Kier's attention back to her. Her frown deepened. She closed the distance between her and Kier and lifted her three empty hands as she bowed her head, fingers splayed and palms skyward. "I should've done more, Kier, especially after Orassic told me what happened in the canteen. I should've kept a closer eye on them."

For the first time in what felt like a long while, Kier thought of the mission he and his brother had begun fifteen years ago—the task they'd believed to be their purpose.

They'd spent so long blaming themselves for the terror Vrykhan had sown across the universe, had felt responsible for all the dead, all the enslaved. They'd carried that weight upon their shoulders, and it had driven them to bitterness, emptiness, hopelessness, and isolation.

He could not fathom that a week ago, he and Kayl had only lived only for Vrykhan's death. So, so much had changed since then.

Everything had changed.

"Their crimes are not yours," Kier said softly. "You are not responsible for the choices they made."

She chuckled; like her earlier snicker, it was devoid of humor. "But I am responsible for protecting our people. That includes any outsiders who come through town."

"Your kindness and hospitality have been greatly appreciated, Ialle. We are more grateful than we can express. And if it is any consolation, we were not in town when they attacked."

Ialle lowered her hands and lifted her head, the corner of her mouth ticking up ever so slightly. "Guess I'll take what I can get."

Aileen's psychic voice whispered in Kier's mind, clearly without her intending for it to do so. *She has hooves! And a cute little tail! Oh my God, uriti are gorgeous. It's like they stepped out of myth!*

Based on her thoughts, Kier could only assume that Aileen had emerged from the *Fang*.

"I'll have to get some people out here to clean this up later. That's not going to bother you?" Ialle asked.

Kier shook his head.

"All right. Might be some questions back in town, but I'll make sure word gets out that you were justly defending yourselves. Everyone knows what these four were like. Don't think they'll be too surprised by it." She lifted her chin toward the *Fang*. "We probably ought to get over there and make sure Shalla doesn't get carried away."

They turned to the ship and walked toward it side by side. Kayl and Aileen stood at the base of the ramp, watching the hovertruck shake and sway as Triss struggled to get down from the enclosed bed. Shalla was already standing beneath the ship, near the hole that had been blasted into it by the *Azkazor*, with several armored panels already removed and laid on the ground at her feet. A mess of dangling wires obscured her face.

"We were not expecting you this morning," Kier said to Ialle.

"Decided to ride out with her. More for Tallian's sake than Shalla's." Ialle shrugged her upper shoulders. "And a few people mentioned hearing shots out in the wilds last night. Usually, it's just someone hunting the polgans that come out when the shadows start getting long, but...figured I'd tackle two things with one trip."

As Kier and Ialle arrived, Triss finally landed on the ground with a heavy *thunk*. Dust kicked up around the robot's large, unwieldy feet. "It is as though being forced to come here was not enough of an indignity."

"I'm sure you'll get over it," Ialle said, grinning.

"What's taking so long, Triss?" Shalla called. "Get over here and give me a hand!"

"I am a highly advanced artificial intelligence," Triss said in the flat tone they seemed to use for everything. "I should be given tasks that make use of my vast computing power."

Shalla stepped aside just before a large metal component fell out of the *Fang* and landed heavily on the ground where she'd been standing. "Highly advanced is a bit of an exaggeration, don't you think? I need you for your brawn."

Triss trudged toward Shalla, steps as heavy as the fallen part. "I do not feel appreciated."

Brows low, Kayl glared at Kier. "She is tearing the *Fang* to pieces."

"Into more pieces, you mean?" Kier pulsed.

"Everything was kind of ruined already, wasn't it?" Aileen asked. "She can't really make it much worse than it was."

Ialle folded her lower arms across her abdomen. "Did she even introduce herself before she started?"

"Nope," Aileen replied with a chuckle, tucking a few loose strands of her hair behind her ear as she observed Shalla. "She just hurried right past us and started digging in."

She trotted like a deer, Aileen thought. *It was so graceful, so adorable.*

"That doesn't belong here," Shalla muttered as she reached up into the *Fang's* hull. She tugged out a small electronic component with bits of wiring dangling from it, turning it in her hand as she examined it. A tiny orange light on the side faded out and did not come on again. Shalla tossed the piece aside.

"She is just throwing parts all over the place," Kayl said in a low voice. "It does not even look like she knows what she's removing!"

Smirking, Kier tilted his head and dragged his fingers through his hair. "To be fair, we don't know what most of those parts are ourselves."

With her blue-and-magenta eyes sparkling, Aileen put a hand over her mouth to hide her smile.

"I do not find this amusing." Kayl's voice was rawer than he normally allowed in front of other people. "This is our home."

Aileen's smile instantly vanished, and a flood of guilt and concern washed over Kier.

Kier walked to his brother and curled a hand behind Kayl's neck, touching foreheads with him. "I know. This ship means as much to me as it does you, brother. But it is beyond us to fix it. We must trust Shalla."

"That is difficult," Kayl rasped.

"It is. But know that we will always have a home in each other." Kier looked at Aileen and smiled. "In our *daevalis*. I will stay with Shalla and oversee her work. Perhaps you might find some way to pass the time with our *na'diya?*"

"You are sending us away?" Kayl asked.

Kier chuckled. "I am simply sparing you from the stress this is clearly causing." He flicked a gaze toward Shalla; the mess around the uriti seemed twice as large as it had been a moment before, and now Triss was also reaching up to tear parts off the ship.

"Chaos is not your preferred element, Kayl," Kier said, meeting his brother's gaze again.

Kayl frowned and searched Kier's eyes. "Very well, Kier. Perhaps this is the most opportune time to teach Aileen how better to defend herself. To continue her training."

Kier lifted his head and tilted it slightly. "That...is a wonderful idea. Not necessarily what I was thinking when I made my suggestion, but a wonderful idea all the same."

"Not exactly what *I* was thinking when you made your suggestion, either," Aileen muttered, briefly looking disappointed before she smirked. "But I guess our little sparring matches do tend to end with all of us on the ground..."

THIRTY-EIGHT

KAYL HELD the blaster pistol out to Aileen on the palm of his hand. It was one of the smaller models he and Kier used when they needed to carry a concealed weapon, and thus seemed the logical starting point for her. He'd led her downstream and around a bend in the canyon, leaving the *Fang* out of sight and the sound of clanging parts and banging tools distant enough for him to ignore.

Aileen stared at the blaster, one of her delicate eyebrows arched, as the breeze swept through her hair and fluttered the skirt of her green dress. "So when you said training, you meant *training* training."

He raised a brow mirroring her expression. "As opposed to?"

"You know..." She shrugged and gestured vaguely at Kayl, raking her gaze over him. A bit of fire glittered in her eyes. "*Training.*"

Her thoughts flowed into Kayl's mind. *Body training. Hot bodies. His hot body pressed up against mine, arms around me, breath on my skin...*

"Aileen..." Arousal flared at his core, coaxing a low growl from his chest. His heart pumped pure heat into his veins; it spread slowly, like molten lava. He was not oblivious to such innuendos—especially not after a few days with his sensual terran—but he had to tamp down the excitement they normally sparked.

At least for a little while.

He gently closed his fingers around the blaster, lowered it, and stepped nearer to Aileen. Placing his free hand on her cheek, he gently guided her face up toward his. "Tell me, *na'diya*... Yesterday, when those males accosted us at the canteen, how did you feel?"

She frowned, and a little crease formed between her brows. The flutter of emotions that came from her—accompanied by flashes of memory—nearly broke Kayl's heart.

"Violated. Then scared. Helpless," she said.

"And when they attacked us last night?" he asked softly.

I thought I was going to lose my mates, she pulsed.

Aileen dropped her eyes and covered his hand with her own, clutching it. The mesmureen on her bracelet glowed softly. "Terrified. And helpless again. More than that, though. Completely powerless." Her tongue slipped out to wet her lips; normally that would've driven Kayl mad with desire, but now it only made him all the more aware of her distress.

"I know I haven't trained with you two very much, but I feel like I've learned a lot in that short time," she said.

He stroked his thumb across her cheek. "You have, *na'diya*."

"But none of it mattered. Not one damn bit. What good does it do me to know how to fight if everyone is twice my size and ten times as strong?"

"Ah, *na'diya*," Kayl rumbled.

We will always protect you, Aileen, no matter what, Kier pulsed.

Kayl tipped his forehead to Aileen's. "Against any danger, any foe. Anyone or anything that means you harm will have to face us."

Aileen flattened her palms on his chest. *But you might not always be there.*

Kayl's jaw muscles ticked, and his chest constricted. He and his brother shared the same longing in that moment—to promise that they would always be there, that they'd never be apart, even for a moment, but how could they, knowing it wasn't true?

The helplessness that knowledge filled them with was not unlike what Aileen had experienced yesterday.

Aileen smoothed her hands up Kayl's chest and cradled his jaw. For a moment, she just stared into his eyes, her gaze swirling with all those helpless, overwhelming emotions. Then she pulled him down. Her mouth collided with his, claiming it with crushing urgency. She dropped her hands and curled her fingers, clutching his shoulders as her eyes closed. But her thoughts were open.

Need them.
Love them.
Please don't ever leave me.
Can't lose them.
Never! the twins pulsed.

With a growl, Kayl dropped his hands—one of which still held the blaster—to her hips and slid them back to her ass, pulling her against his body. She was all soft curves against his hard planes, and he wanted little more than to tear away their clothes, to eliminate those barriers, so he could feel her warm skin on his.

He tilted his head and slanted his mouth over hers, kissing Aileen deeper, harder. She moaned, reciprocating with equal eagerness. It was hot and wet and raw, sending a blaze of yearning through him.

But this kiss was more than desire. It was born of desperation, longing, and love.

Aileen broke the kiss. She pressed her forehead to his while their panting breaths mingled. "I don't know how I'm going to survive sharing such strong emotions with the both of you. Sometimes it feels like they're going to consume me."

"I know, *na'diya*," Kayl rasped. "For many years, I allowed myself only to feel the rage I locked in my heart. I shielded myself and my brother from everything else. I let nothing in. This is overwhelming, disorienting, sometimes frightening, but I would not change it. I would never change it. I want to feel *everything*, Aileen. With you."

Aileen smiled, and a rush of warmth, happiness, and affection enveloped Kayl.

I would say it is a deep regret that we did not open ourselves to all this sooner, Kier pulsed, his *aerys* uncharacteristically solemn, *but I do not think it was possible before you, Aileen.*

"You have brought us together. You have made us whole," Kayl said.

"I hadn't realized just how much of a void I had inside me until we came together." Aileen tilted her head back, opened her eyes, and pressed a light kiss upon the tip of Kayl's nose. Her smile widened into a grin. "Now teach me how to shoot so I can protect my mates."

Kayl smiled, and his tail swung with just a bit more enthusiasm than usual. "Let us begin with you learning to protect yourself, *na'diya*."

He withdrew from Aileen, though releasing his hold on her was a greater test of will than he could've expected.

Focus, Kayl, Kier pulsed with no small amount of smugness.

I am occupied, Kier. Kindly keep your thoughts to yourself unless there is an important matter requiring my attention.

Aileen laughed.

Kayl's brow furrowed. "What?"

"You two bicker in your heads just like you do out loud," she replied. "It's pretty funny to know that this back and forth has been going on the whole time, even though I couldn't hear it. But...it's also endearing."

And it is endearing that you have been arguing with yourself in your head all along, Aileen, Kier pulsed.

She blushed and combed her hair back from her face. "It's perfectly normal to talk to yourself."

Kayl lifted his free hand and brushed his knuckles across her cheek. "We would not know. We have never had the luxury."

She smiled and caught his hand, kissing his fingers. "It's often lonely. I don't recommend it."

"Well, *na'diya*, you will never be alone again." A corner of Kayl's mouth crept higher. "And I am sure Kier will see to it that you never experience silence again."

Kier snorted through their link, and Aileen laughed.

But the weight of the prior day's events settled upon Kayl quickly, dulling his amusement. He lifted his hand and opened his fingers to reveal the blaster. "Regarding our reason for being out here, Aileen... You will often find yourself physically outmatched, but we would not have you feel so helpless. This is the equalizer."

Her gaze fell upon the weapon. Her smile faded, and that crease reappeared between her eyebrows. "It seems so small. Like it couldn't possibly make a difference."

Kayl didn't take his eyes off her—the little terran who'd changed everything for him and his twin. She wasn't a warrior. She possessed no experience, no significant training, no applicable skills. But he did not doubt she had it in her to fight.

To fight for what she loved.

"Small things can often make all the difference, Aileen." He slipped his hand out of hers, grasped her wrist, and guided her hand down to the blaster.

Aileen carefully closed her fingers around the grip. As Kayl released her wrist, she lifted the blaster from his palm. Her pointer finger moved to slip behind the trigger guard.

"Like this," Kayl said, drawing his own blaster from his hip. He angled the weapon sideways so she could see and laid his forefinger along the side of the trigger guard.

Tilting her head, Aileen mimicked his hold. All the while, she kept the weapon pointed away and down; that alone was more awareness and discipline than most people who'd never handled such a weapon demonstrated.

"Finger on the trigger only when you mean to shoot," Kayl continued, "or the tiniest twitch could mean disaster."

He placed his empty hand on her forearm and slid it down slowly toward her hand. He could not ignore the little bumps rising on her skin in the wake of his touch. "Think of the blaster as an extension of your arm. Where you point, it will shoot."

She took in a soft, shaky breath, gaze following his hand intently. "That seems too simple, doesn't it?"

Finally, his hand reached hers, covering it. "I have recently come to understand that most things are quite simple. Simplicity can be daunting...but it can also be good."

"Mmhmm," she hummed distractedly. *He has such sexy hands...*

Focus, na'diya, Kayl chided gently, fighting a smile.

"Sorry!"

He tried to shut out the flickering desire coming from her, but his own had already sparked deep in his belly. He turned his face away from her, scanning the area, before shifting her hand to aim the blaster at the chosen target. "You see the boulder there? The one jutting from the base of the cliffside, twenty meters away?"

Her hand tensed beneath his. "Yes."

Moving his thumb to the safety, he switched it off. "Shoot it."

A faint tremor coursed through Aileen's arm as she slid her finger behind the trigger guard.

"Just squeeze the trigger," he encouraged.

She did so tentatively. The blaster went off with that high whine that was punctuated by a soft *thump*. Aileen started, but fortunately the plasma bolt had already left the weapon, striking the center of the boulder to leave a glowing orange ring that was already leaking molten rock.

Shite! her psychic voice blasted.

"Woah," she breathed.

Kayl smiled and released her hand, which swayed immediately, dipping lower. She looked at him, arching a brow. The blush staining her cheeks did not help him restrain his desire.

"Shoot the same boulder," he said, gesturing to it. "Hit as near to the first shot as you can."

"Okay. I can do that." She lifted the blaster again.

I think, she pulsed softly.

Aileen pulled the trigger. Having anticipated the result, she flinched just before the blaster fired, disrupting her aim enough to send the plasma bolt into the ground two meters short of the boulder.

"Maybe I can't?" She winced, glancing at him from the corner of her eye.

"You can, *na'diya,*" he replied.

Kier echoed those words through their psychic link.

Kayl returned his blaster to its place on his hip and moved a little closer to her. It took everything in him not to touch her. "Try again. Respect your weapon and what it is capable of, but do not fear it."

She nodded and extended her arm again, adjusting her fingers on the blaster's grip. Her shoulders rose with a deep breath. She fired.

The plasma bolt went wide of its mark, melting a shallow groove on the left side of the boulder, near the top. More than a meter off-target—but so much closer than her first attempt.

Aileen lowered the blaster and looked at Kayl. "I meant to do that."

He smirked. "Did you?"

"I really did."

"Of course you did, *na'diya.* I am sorry for doubting you."

He totally knows I'm lying, she pulsed. *Why bother trying? They can hear my thoughts. You're listening right now, aren't you?*

I would never dare intrude upon your thoughts, Aileen.

Her lips twitched, and laughter burst from her. "Smartass."

"I will be sure to ask Kier whether that is an insult or a compliment," he replied.

Kier's *aerys* came through the link immediately. *I believe—*

"Later," Kayl said. "I will ask later."

Fine. It is not as though I have nothing to do, Kier replied. *Hmm...*

I do not believe that part will fit back in that spot now that it has been torn out.

Kayl sighed and returned his full attention to Aileen.

Aileen pecked a kiss on his cheek. "The ship will be fine." She waved toward the boulder and raised the gun. "How do you two make this look so easy?"

"Practice. Far too much practice." But he would not allow himself to dwell on the past, to reflect upon the circumstances that had driven the twins to take up arms. That all of it had ultimately led to Aileen was enough; the rest did not matter.

He moved behind her, hooking an arm around her middle and flattening his palm on her belly. He didn't miss her little intake of breath. Using his arm to keep her steady, he placed his leg between both of hers and nudged them a little wider.

"Um, Kayl?" she asked. *How the heck am I supposed to focus like this? Oh God, his body feels so good. And he smells good too.*

Concentrate, Aileen, he pulsed. But when he inhaled, the air that filled his lungs was perfumed with her scent, and his own focus nearly wavered.

"Begin with a solid base." He touched his free hand to the back of her arm and slightly adjusted its angle. "Every tiny movement of your body"—*do not think of being inside her, of feeling her slightest trembling, feeling her heartbeat, her every breath*—"will affect your aim."

"So not helping," she singsonged, glancing back at him.

"If you would but turn your thoughts to our lesson, Aileen..."

"You're not so innocent." Cheeks somehow darkening further, she looked ahead. "Okay. I got this."

Focus, Aileen, she pulsed. *Just focus. Focus on your target, that big ass boulder sticking straight out. How hard can it be? Don't focus on how nice his cock feels against your ass, or how much you love having his arm around you, or how his voice makes your cunt wet.*

He growled, long and low, and squeezed his eyes shut as desire flooded him with unbearable heat. His lips peeled back of their own accord, baring his fangs. Before he could stop himself, he dipped his head and nipped at the spot between Aileen's neck and shoulder.

Aileen squealed, arching into him, and giggled. Despite the playfulness of her reaction, Kayl felt arousal radiating from her core. It washed over him in a wave strong enough to make him shudder.

"Aileen..." he intoned.

"Okay! Okay! I'll focus!" she cried with laughter.

His tongue flicked out to sample the taste of her soft skin. She shivered.

Our na'diya *is quite the distraction,* Kier pulsed with humor.

And you two are double *the distraction,* she countered.

Neither Kayl nor Kier could argue that.

They continued training as the sun climbed higher into the sky. Kayl showed her the blaster's various functions—the safety, the power cell chamber, the charge override. He demonstrated how to eject the power cell and replace it, coached her on her breathing and her grip. And between those little lessons, he had her shoot at the boulder. Each time she fired, he offered praise and encouragement, offered advice and correction. His hands seemed to be on her constantly; the excuse of adjusting her stance or her aim was too good to pass up.

Her confidence slowly grew, and her aim slowly improved.

When she started to display reasonable comfort with the weapon, he showed her different ways to hold it depending on the situation—she wouldn't want her arm fully extended if her target was extremely close. Before long, she'd demonstrated enough improvement that he had her switch to a more distant target.

With each touch they shared, the heat in their bodies grew. All those fleeting brushes of his fingers against her skin, of his body against hers, of his breath on her hair or upon her neck, built upon each other. All those small things coalesced into something much greater.

Into something increasingly difficult to ignore.

As Aileen next took aim at her target, Kayl dipped his head and grazed her shoulder with his lips, breathing in her delicious scent, which was heady with her arousal.

Enough, she pulsed, engaging the weapon's safety. *This isn't training, it's seduction. And I can't take it anymore.*

Dropping the blaster, Aileen turned, caught Kayl's face between her hands, and pulled him down into a fierce, hungry kiss. Kayl's eyes flared, but his surprise was short lived. Letting the walls in which he'd contained his desire crumble to dust, he banded his arms around Aileen and drew her close, returning the kiss with equal fervor. He craved his little human mate with every fiber of his being.

She caught his bottom lip with her teeth, sending a jolt of pleasure straight to his cock, before she sucked it into her mouth and soothed it with her tongue. His fingers flexed, clutching her closer as his chest rumbled.

How unfair that you two get to enjoy one another while I watch our ship get disemboweled, Kier pulsed.

Aileen dropped her hands to Kayl's shoulders and released his lip, trailing her mouth along his chin, jaw, and behind his ear in a succession of scalding kisses. Each of those kisses made his heart beat a little faster and his blood burn a little hotter.

His cock strained against the confines of his bodysuit, permeated with the dull, maddening ache of his need.

It was your suggestion, Kayl replied.

Mhmm, pulsed Aileen.

We will open to you, Kier, Kayl continued. *Share this with you.*

Tempting as that may be, I must refuse. I will continue supervising our mechanic for now... But I will take some time of my own with our na'diya *later.* Kier's words were suffused with playfulness, bearing not a shred of jealousy. But before either Kayl or Aileen could respond, Kier threw up a barrier, cutting himself off from their psychic link.

What loss or emptiness Kayl might have felt at that was immediately curtailed by Aileen, who licked along the collar of his bodysuit.

"How do you open this?" she asked, her breath warm on his skin.

Kayl lifted his chin and moved a hand to his collar, pressing his thumb to the seal control at the top. The instant the material parted, Aileen had her fingers beneath the seam, and she yanked the suit to either side, baring Kayl's chest and shoulders in one motion. And then her mouth was on his neck.

"*Na'diya,*" he purred.

She kissed the hollow at the base of his throat, palms sliding along his arms as she pushed his sleeves down. "I love when you say it like that."

His skin tingled beneath her hands, and his breaths became ragged. For all they'd done together in the last few days, she'd not once been so forward, so bold. She'd never been so direct in taking what she wanted.

Old memories clawed at the edges of his mind. Aileen's forcefulness was nothing like what Kayl and his brother had been subjected to as slaves, but he could not help thinking of it. Their former master had taken from them whenever she'd pleased—she'd torn off their clothes, touched them, used them, had made them feel violated in every way. She'd been in control of their every interaction until they'd finally ended her.

Aileen wrapped her fingers around Kayl's wrists and rested her forehead on his chest. She trembled against him. "We're making new memories." Her voice was soft, though there was an angry bite to it that was amplified in her psychic voice. *That fucking bitch.* "If you ever want me to stop, I will. I swear. I will stop right now if you need me to."

"I know, Aileen," he rumbled, brushing his lips over her hair and breathing in her heady scent anew. "Do not stop. Not now. I am burning for you."

"Oh, thank God, because I'm dying for a taste of you." She pushed his sleeves past his wrists, freeing his arms. The material of his suit folded down, catching around his waist as it caught on his tail.

The warm sun on his bare skin could not compare to the heat of Aileen's touch, to the fire in her eyes, to the inferno roaring at his core.

Placing her hands on his hips, Aileen grazed her lips down his chest. She scraped her teeth across his skin and nipped his pec. He groaned and cupped the back of her head, threading his fingers through her hair. She sucked, licked, and bit, offering his chest the same attention he and Kier had given her nipples, ravishing him with pleasure-pain.

"*Zor atkoshai*, Aileen," he rasped, tail lashing behind him as he stared down at her. "Your mouth is more wicked than I had imagined."

Aileen peeked up at him and grinned. "You think this is wicked?" Beginning over his heart, she left a trail of kisses down the center of his abdomen, speaking a word between each press of her lips. "I plan to use this wicked mouth"—she reached his lower belly, where she pulled down his body suit and grasped the base of his hard cock as it sprang free—"here."

He sucked in a sharp breath and shuddered, fingers flexing and claws grazing her scalp.

Aileen stroked her fist up his length, her palm gliding over his ridges, then back down. Though her hand was small and soft, her grip was firm and sure, and it instantly increased the pressure within him tenfold. Seed gathered at his tip. His hips twitched with the urge to buck, to create more of the sweet friction that would launch him to his climax.

And Aileen's eyes were fixed upon his shaft with such hunger...

"*Na'diya*," he rasped.

She leaned forward and flicked her tongue over the tip of Kayl's cock, gathering his seed. "Mmm..."

Kayl hissed as a shudder wracked him.

Then she closed her lips around his shaft.

He threw his head back and snapped his eyes shut. She sucked, taking his cock deep into the heat of her mouth, stroking its underside with her tongue. That tongue teased every nerve in his body through his shaft—every stroke tensed a new muscle with a wave of pleasure, sent a new jolt of sensation through his limbs and back to his core.

He forced his chin down and fought his eyelids open, locking his gaze on her. He wanted to watch. Wanted to see her. Wanted to stare into her eyes as she did this to him, for him.

Aileen's blue and magenta starburst eyes were bright as she looked up at him. For a moment, she stilled with those full, pink lips stretched around his cock, her stare keeping him rooted in place. Then she drew her head back. *Slowly*.

The deliberate drag of her lips and tongue made Kayl's back arch and coaxed a choked sound from his throat. His knees nearly buckled when she squeezed his base again.

"Aileen," he growled. He knew other words, he must've known other words, but apart from her name, only one would come out. "*Fuck*."

She moaned. That sound—so small, so inconsequential—vibrated along his shaft, underscoring the waves of pleasure she induced with a low, relentless thrum. His tail stiffened, and he reflexively moved his other hand to her hair, grasping the strands in both fists.

"Do not stop, *na'diya*," he commanded.

Mmm, I won't, she pulsed as she worked his length. Her mouth glided up and down, its rhythm matched by her pumping fist at the base of his shaft. *You taste so, so good.*

He drew in a deep breath. Her scent had shifted, now infused with her arousal. *Need to feel you. To taste you.*

Kayl bent his tail, swinging it between his legs. Its tip brushed the inside of her knee. He guided it higher, under her skirt and along her inner thigh. The heat he sensed from her intensified the closer his tail drew to her sex.

Finally, his tail reached its prize. He pressed its tip against her slit. Aileen whimpered. Her flesh was hot and wet, slick with her essence, more of which trickled out as he slid his tail along her parted folds. Her rhythm wavered. The small, muffled cry she released around his cock speared him with utter ecstasy and made his entire body tense.

"Fuck," he repeated, taking in another breath through his gritted fangs. He forced his tail away from her sex.

She gyrated her hips toward his retreating limb, but he did not stop its motion. It rose beside Aileen, moving toward his face, until he dipped his head and extended his tongue to lick her nectar off the tip of his tail.

He groaned long and deep before slipping the end of his tail into his mouth and sucking off every last trace of her essence. It slid down his throat, warming him from within and spreading that pleasure even more thoroughly.

"Delicious, *na'diya*. So sweet. So fucking sweet." Kayl dropped his tail and hooked it beneath her skirt again. "Make more for me. Come for me."

As his tail again brushed her sex, Aileen rose higher on her knees and spread her legs farther apart, granting him easier access. He pressed into her entrance, her essence easing his entry.

Once more, she wavered, grasping his backside for support as she swayed, her nails digging into his flesh. She pulled her mouth off him, breathing heavily.

"More, Kayl," she whispered, peering up at him, that hunger in her eyes only intensifying. "More." And then her mouth was around him again.

He plunged his tail deep, pushing it to the back of her channel. Aileen's pleasure coursed into him. Her walls fluttered around it, and fresh nectar spilled from her to trickle along his limb and down her thighs.

She cried out around his cock. *Oh God! Yes!*

You belong to us, Aileen. He withdrew his tail almost completely before forcing it back in as far as possible with a pump of his hips. *You are ours.*

Yours, she pulsed.

Aileen quickly recovered her rhythm, and Kayl matched it with his tail, pumping in and out of her as she worked his shaft with her mouth and hand. Each time she slid her lips forward, he released a low snarl. Each time she drew back, a flash of pleasure made his body tremble and sway toward her as though afraid she would pull away.

Each time he thrust his tail into her, she moaned. Each time he began to withdraw it, her thighs quivered, and her pelvis dipped as though to follow him.

Kayl's breaths quickly grew ragged, and the rest of the universe faded into nothingness. Aileen was his sun, ecstasy was his heat, and her eyes, intent and lustful, were his nourishment. She was all he needed, all he wanted.

He tightened his hold on her hair and guided her faster as he pumped his hips, unable to hold back. The pressure within him was overwhelming, torturous, and he needed relief. But he didn't want this to end, didn't want the pleasure to peak and then fade.

Kayl said her name again, his voice dragging it out into an exaltation, a plea, a benediction. That pleasure built and built, rising rapidly but steadily.

Though he had set their pace, Aileen quickly demonstrated that he was not in control. She hummed; she twisted her fist as she pumped; she undulated her tongue and used its tip to lavish his every ridge, to tease his slit. Each little ministration was a surge of rapture, an overload of sensation. And the way her sex clamped greedily around his tail only made his enjoyment grow exponentially.

There was nothing in the universe as alluring and arousing as Aileen's pleasure, and its effect was infinitely stronger now that they were bound and he could feel it directly.

She rocked her hips in time with his thrusts, and her moans around his cock escalated, vibrating through his shaft. Pleasure coiled tighter and tighter in his core, wrapping around Aileen's shared pleasure, layering and layering...

Kayl's rhythm faltered as his back arched again and his muscles contracted. The explosion threatened for an agonizing eternity, and he brimmed with a pressure that would surely blast him to pieces, that would break his mind and leave nothing of behind. Just when it became too much, when his breath hitched and his teeth clenched and he couldn't even make a sound, he burst.

He let out a roar as his seed erupted in Aileen's mouth, hips bucking reflexively, desperately. Ecstasy rocketed his mind out into the cosmos, forcing his eyes shut.

Aileen clutched his ass, and her body tensed. Throat convulsing, she drank his seed, pumping and sucking, whimpering around his cock. Her legs quivered, and her movements grew erratic. He felt her resisting her own climax as she sucked his shaft dry.

"Come for me, Aileen," he snarled.

She tore her mouth from his cock with a cry and rode his tail. "Kayl, I...I... *Ah!*"

Her sex contracted around his tail, and a flood of liquid heat spilled down his limb and over her inner thighs.

Keeping his tail in motion, Kayl caught her jaw, dropped onto his knees, and angled her head back, capturing her mouth with his, taking her sweet cries into himself. She threw her arms around him, holding tight as she succumbed to her climax. Her ecstasy washed through him and rekindled his own, mixing with it, intensifying it.

Kayl cradled Aileen as she shuddered through the rapture bursting form her core. He slowed his tail, and soon slid it out to leisurely circle her clit, easing her down from those heights. As he did so, he kissed her with tenderness and affection.

"Kayl," she breathed after breaking their kiss, tipping her forehead against his.

"Ah, *na'diya*," he purred, "you have consumed me."

She hummed and smiled. "Mhmm. Damn right, I did."

His smile mirrored hers, and he laughed. A few days ago, he might not have understood her meaning, but nothing was the same anymore.

He gathered her up against him, and she wrapped her legs around his waist, trapping his hard cock between their bodies.

Aileen rested her head on his shoulder and kissed the bite mark she'd branded him with earlier. "I really enjoyed this training. We should do it again sometime."

"We shall. Very soon." He nipped at her ear. "You still have much to learn, Aileen. You will need a great deal of training, I am sure."

She grinned and chuckled. "*Lots* of training."

I really, really love them, she pulsed.

And we love you, Aileen. More than words alone could ever express.

THIRTY-NINE

Shalla strode into the cockpit and stopped at the central console, dropping her hands to her hips as she dragged her gaze over the darkened controls and holo projectors.

Kier quickened his stride to join her. Despite standing over a head taller than the adolescent uriti, he'd found it difficult to keep up with her as she'd prowled the *Fang*, poking into systems and tearing apart components.

Triss, in contrast, had maintained a slow, unwavering pace, their plodding steps currently echoing along the corridor far behind Kier. The robot had caught up to Shalla only on a few occasions, always just in time for the uriti to finish what she was doing and flit off to another spot.

"Never see anything this nice around here," Shalla said, "or this new."

Kier came to a halt beside her. "Have you or your father ever worked on anything like it?"

She tapped the manual controls, bringing the central console to life. The instant the first holo screen appeared, she flicked through the menus with her fingers. Her reply was both distracted and dry. "I just said we never see ships like this."

Fortunately, a lifetime of being Kayl's brother had greatly reduced the effects of such tones upon Kier; he simply shrugged it off. "Can you repair it?"

Shalla brought up another screen and entered a set of characters —a holocom ID. Before Kier could ask what she was doing, she initiated a call, and the main holo projector blinked on.

Tallian's upper half materialized in the projection. Brows low and mouth downturned, he glared at his daughter. "Shalla. Home. *Now.*"

She folded her arms across her chest. "No."

Tallian bared his teeth and expelled a growling breath. "Get in the truck and come home immediately."

Shalla arched a delicate brow. "Was my initial response not clear enough, Father?"

His jaw muscles bulged, and the cords on his neck stood out. "Ialle told me what happened out there. I will not have you alone with them. I will not have you in danger."

She huffed and angled her face down toward the controls, but not before Kier glimpsed a chink in her stoic expression. As she entered commands on the holo screen, she said, "If Ialle told you what happened, you already know the daevahs and the terran were attacked. They defended themselves."

"They're dangerous, Shalla, and we don't know them," Tallian replied, his words low and strained.

With an awkward smile, Kier lifted a hand and waved. "One of them is standing right here."

Tallian didn't look away from his daughter. "I know."

She sighed, shoulders drooping. "Any time I leave, I'm in danger. Any time I stay, I'm in danger."

"Our shop is safe," Tallian insisted.

Shalla laughed, meeting her father's gaze. "If Triss plants their foot too heavily one day, everything you have stacked in there will come crashing down atop us."

"That's something of an exaggeration, Shalla..."

"And part of why you sent me out here to begin with is so you could work on one of those damned haulers without me there. Maybe you could explain to me how *that's* safe?"

The male uriti's features contorted with pain. "Shalla, you know why... Why I don't want you here when... It's not—"

"Father, you agreed to help these people. You trusted them—and me—enough to have me take care of it."

"Before I knew of this attack, Shalla. Before I knew—"

"*Rhunai*, please. I know this is difficult."

At that first word, Tallian's expression softened, and the light in his eyes took on a wistful glint.

Kier felt like an intruder upon a conversation that should've been private.

Why did Kayl and Aileen get to have all the fun while Kier dealt with all this?

Because you sent us off, Kayl pulsed gently.

Kier's brows fell. *Have I mentioned how much I despise it when you are right, Kayl?*

No, because that would be a lie.

Zor atkoshai, Kayl, there you go again.

Aileen's laughter bubbled through the psychic link, high and carefree. *We'll be in soon, Kier. You won't have to deal with it alone for much longer.*

"Damn it, Shalla," Tallian rasped.

"I'll be fine, *Rhunai*," Shalla said. "I promise."

The words Aileen had spoken to Kayl not long ago drifted into Kier's mind, echoing with her pain and fear.

You can't promise that. No one can.

"We will do all we can to keep her safe, Tallian," Kier said. "As fiercely as we defend our mate, we will defend your daughter."

Only then did Tallian look at Kier, face immediately sterner, gaze immediately heavier. "If anything happens to her, daevah, anything at all, I will find a way to destroy you. Even if I have to turn Triss into a mechanized suit so I can run you down myself, I will find a way."

"I do not want you inside me," Triss said from the cockpit's entrance.

Shalla smiled. It was the first time Kier had seen her do so, and it changed her completely. She dropped her face again and tapped something on the holo screen. "I'm sending you a connection to the ship now, *Rhunai*. Review the diagnostics for me."

"I have reviewed the diagnostics," Triss said, stomping across the threshold, "and provided my analysis."

"Getting another opinion, Triss," Shalla replied.

"I did not give you an opinion. I am a machine. I provide only facts."

"That's questionable." Tallian looked to something off to the side, eyes intent.

Ah, Kayl, you are going to love this, Kier pulsed. *It is just as chaotic as Arcanthus's crew.*

Kayl groaned through the psychic link.

Who is Arcanthus? Aileen asked.

An associate of ours, Kayl replied.

With a thoughtful grunt, Tallian turned his body and extended his arms, hands clipping out of the range of his holo recorder. "You inspected the power couplings going into those auxiliary systems?"

"Yes, *Rhunai*," Shalla replied.

"Comm lines are still in place? Nothing severed?"

"Internally they are mostly intact, but the long-range comms array was destroyed. Had to attach a signal booster just to connect with you because of the storm."

The air in the room shifted subtly, briefly flowing toward the *Fang's* aft. Faint footsteps sounded at the far end of the corridor.

"Perhaps the power reserves are simply too low..." Tallian raised his arm again, manipulating something out of view. "First priority is to ensure the power system is still closed so we can increase the charge and run full diagnostics with all systems reporting."

"Already started," Shalla said, "but I can't go much further without picking up parts. Triss, can you send *Rhunai* the images you recorded?"

Sensing the nearness of his *daevalis*, Kier turned his head toward the doorway.

Kayl and Aileen entered the cockpit, hands clasped, mesmureens glowing faintly on their bracelets. Their clothes and hair were disheveled—not that Kier understood how a one piece, form-fitting body suit could *get* disheveled. Sated heat lingered in their eyes, and their lips were curled into small smiles.

Kayl's roar had echoed through the canyon like the triumphant call of a wild beast. Their current appearance only confirmed what that roar had declared—they'd shared unimaginable pleasure while they were away.

Kier smirked as they walked over to him. *Clearly the two of you trained quite hard.*

To his delight, Aileen's cheeks flushed. She tugged down the fabric of her dress and smoothed a hand over her hair, taming some of the tousled locks. But his delight shifted unexpectedly when flashes of what Kayl and Aileen had done sizzled through the psychic link, blasting Kier with heat and arousal.

Curling his hands into fists, Kier willed his tail to still and let out a long, slow breath. *Oh, you two are cruel to tease me when I can do nothing about it.*

Just think of it as building anticipation, Aileen pulsed.

"Huh." Brow furrowing, Tallian tilted his head. He muttered, "A highly modified, combat-grade vaelyn reconnaissance craft ..."

Aileen stopped beside Kier and brushed her hand down his arm until their wrists were together. Their mesmureens glowed aquamarine, and his heart swelled with affection. But that fire still burned deeper within him, its flames stoked by those at Aileen's core.

Her lips stretched into a grin as she glanced at him from the corner of her eye. *I promise, Kier...the wait will be worth it.*

He touched the end of his tail to her calf and slowly slid it up her leg. *If I get you at the end, I will endure any wait,* na'diya.

"Is this everything, *Cheya?*" Tallian asked, calling the attention of Kier and his companions back to the holo.

"Everything I can currently get to," Shalla replied. "Some of the ship is inaccessible because of the way it crashed. I'll need the big antigrav jacks to get it off the ground and finish checking everything."

"Which means I will have to load and unload them," said Triss.

"We all have our roles to fulfill, Triss."

"How do I apply to have my role changed?"

Kier and Aileen chuckled; Kayl smiled.

Tallian turned his face toward the trio, looked them over, and sighed. "I know better than to ask how you obtained a ship like that, and I don't really want to know the circumstances that brought you here with it." He shook his head, and again his eyes softened. "But despite everything, there's a part of me that wishes I were out there too, seeing it with my own eyes. Touching it with my own hands. Veeani would've..."

The uriti's expression fell, and his nostrils flared with a heavy exhalation.

"Easy, *Rhunai,*" Shalla whispered. "We just need to focus on the job."

He cleared his throat and quickly reclaimed his composure. "Yes. The job. Ialle assured me your credits were good, but something like this..."

"Whatever the cost," Kier said, "we will pay it."

"Within reason," Kayl amended, eyeing his brother.

Coiling his tail around Aileen's leg, Kier turned his head toward his twin. "I suppose you have access to an intergalactic pricing guide we can reference to determine whether their fees are reasonable?"

"I do not need a guide to—"

"Okay." Aileen stared up at Kayl until he met her gaze, then did the same with Kier. Once both twins had their eyes upon her, she said, "We'll figure everything out together later."

There's no need to argue in front of them, her *aerys* added.

"Right," Kier replied.

Kayl nodded. "Mhmm."

Aileen turned her face back toward Tallian. "You were saying?"

The uriti let out a gruff laugh and shook his head. "I'm aware that I may be difficult at times—"

Shalla, who'd returned her attention to the holo screens lower on the console, snorted. "Understatement."

"Thank you, *Cheya*," Tallian grumbled. "But for what it's worth, I offer my word—my rates are fair. I'm aware of your situation, and I know you've no other options, but I do not believe in taking advantage of misfortune to line my pockets."

"You have our appreciation for that," Kier said.

"The real problem," Tallian continued, "is parts. Your ship is highly advanced, and as you might've noticed, Navaire is not exactly awash in modern tech."

"Can you fix it?" Kayl asked, swinging his gaze from Tallian to Shalla.

Tallian glanced at his daughter and dipped his chin.

She nodded and drew in a deep breath. "I'm going to have to improvise quite a bit, and my father will have to fabricate replacement parts as is possible. It's going to look bad while we're working —*very* bad—and when it's done, it's still going to look bad. But it will fly, and it will jump you to somewhere you can get everything properly replaced."

Shalla looked at the trio, expression flat. "And you *will* need to get proper repairs done before long. I learned from the best, but there's only so much I can do without the right parts."

Hope spread through Kier, Kayl, and Aileen, creating a sensation not unlike warm sunshine on their skin. It was a relief that the *Fang*, their home, could be repaired. The freedom of being able to take Aileen anywhere in the universe would be most welcome.

But all the same, leaving this planet—the place where they'd bonded, where they'd become one—wasn't something any of them were in a hurry to do.

"Understood," Kier said.

"How long will it take?" Kayl asked.

Shalla lifted a hand to her face, rubbing her fingers on her cheek and leaving a little smudge of grease there in the process. "Four, five days. Depends on whether you three can be helpful."

Kier snickered. "If by helpful you mean stay out of your way, I am sure we can manage."

Aileen looked between Kier and Kayl, her delight pulsing through their link as she swung their entwined hands back and forth. "Like I said...honeymoon!"

FORTY

Aileen lifted her hair off her shoulders, letting the breeze cool her neck. The sounds of clanging metal, hissing fusion tools, and a clomping robot had been the prevalent ambience over the last three days. Shalla's progress on the repairs was unreal, even when accounting for the assistance from Kier, Kayl, and Triss. The slight uriti moved quickly and efficiently, bouncing from task to task without missing a step.

She'd ordered the twins around that first day, frequently checking on their work. What she'd seen must have satisfied her, as she'd soon taken to assigning them particular tasks and leaving them to it for hours at a time.

Aileen, on the other hand, was useless when it came the repairs, but she'd insisted on helping however she could. Thus, she'd become the official gofer. When someone had their head—or in some cases their entire upper body—poked into some compartment or tight space, she was the one who'd fetch the tools that were just out of their reach or run off to the hovertruck to find a part that Shalla had been patient enough to describe in great detail.

She'd taken it upon herself to keep everyone fed and hydrated, and she had even stopped Triss a few times to clean dust and grime off their optics. And as she'd hurried about the work site, the *Fang* had slowly come back together. That was even more impressive considering just how much of the ship Shalla and Triss had disassembled at the beginning of the process.

Despite the young uriti's warning, the repairs she'd completed looked clean and professional, even if the sheen and color of the replacement parts didn't quite match up to the rest.

They were getting close. That was exciting; for the first time in so long, it felt like the universe would be open to Aileen. Like she could go anywhere, see anything. And the best part? She'd get to share the adventures to come with Kier and Kayl. Her *na'divali*.

Aileen drew her hair over a shoulder, stretched her legs out in front of her, and leaned back against cool boulder, focusing her eyes upon her mates' backsides. They were standing beneath the ship, twenty meters away from her, with their arms over their heads as they sorted through a seemingly infinite number of wires. Even in the shade, the air was warm, and they'd both removed their shirts.

She wasn't about to complain about that.

Their teal skin glistened with sweat, and their toned muscles flexed alluringly as they worked. Though the twins' pants were loose around their legs, the fabric hugged their asses, especially whenever they bent down to retrieve a tool.

Aileen grinned. It was the best show she'd seen in years.

Have I told you two how sexy you are while you work? she pulsed.

They turned their heads simultaneously, looking at her over their shoulders.

The corner of Kier's mouth twitched up to reveal a fang. *Lounging around while we work, na'diya?*

It's healthy to take regular breaks, she replied, *especially when the view is so eye catching.*

Warmth blossomed in her chest, flowing straight from her mates —it was their satisfaction, their pride, their sense of being appreciated and wanted.

The twins turned back to their work. Kier stretched his arms out over his head, arching his back to jut his ass toward her. He wiggled his tail.

Aileen chuckled.

Though she still hadn't mastered the skill of controlling her thoughts, it had grown easier over the last few days. She'd learned to spare her mates from most of her mental ramblings. It was difficult sometimes, but the difficulty was worth it for the occasions when she could open herself to the twins completely and share every bit of herself without shame or fear of judgment—like when they made love.

And we would have it no other way, Kayl pulsed.

Aileen smiled. *Guess I didn't keep those thoughts very well contained, huh?*

You need not hide your thoughts from us at all, Aileen, Kier pulsed soothingly. *You will develop control in time. Your ramblings do not bother us.*

She ran her gaze across the *Fang*'s belly. There were still holes in the hull, still armored plates lying on the ground with various parts atop them awaiting installation, but Kier and Kayl were the only two working down here. Flattening her hands on the boulder, Aileen pushed herself up, pausing to brush the grass from her leggings.

"Is Shalla still inside?" she asked.

"I believe so," Kier replied over his shoulder. "She was in the hold when I saw her last, with most of the floor panels torn up."

That had to have been at least an hour ago. Aileen turned toward the ramp and frowned. "I'll go check on her and bring her a little something to eat. She gets so hyper focused, she'd go an entire day without stopping to even breathe if no one told her to."

"Very well," said Kayl. "We will likely be here long after you are done."

Aileen grabbed a ration bar and a canister of water from their bag she'd set beside herself.

"Indeed." Kier bent his arm to flex his bicep. "We will be waiting to resume the show for you."

She chuckled, and as she made her way toward the ramp, she called over her shoulder, "As long as I get a private show later!"

The cargo hold was noticeably cooler than outside, even coming from the shade. Just as Kier had said, most of the floor panels had been removed and were separated into two groups—a neat stack of undamaged panels and a haphazard pile of misshapen ones. But Shalla was nowhere to be seen, and the hold was quiet.

Picking a path along the underfloor supports, Aileen crossed the hold. The door leading into the upper deck was closed, but the passages on either side of the stairs stood open. Aileen paused beside one of those entryways, turned her head, and listened.

From somewhere deeper in the bowels of the ship, she heard the dulled buzz of a distant fusion tool.

Aileen followed the sound into the narrow underdeck corridor. She'd seen inside most of the large compartments lining both this corridor and its counterpart on the opposite side of the ship, had gazed upon the complex components they held, and hadn't bothered asking what most of it was. If the family van had been too complex for her to help her da repair, she doubted she'd understand any of this.

But give me a song and I can break it down for you note by note.

Yeah, because that's definitely a lifesaving skill.

She finally found Shalla up in the nose of the ship. The uriti was sitting at the edge of a hole in the floor, practically doubled over to lean into it, her fusion tool bathing her in its bright, strobing light. Triss stood on the other side of the hole, holding a large blaster turret in their arms—undoubtedly the turret that had formerly occupied the hole.

Aileen stopped in the doorway and called Shalla's name.

The uriti seemed not to have heard, but Triss's head spun toward Aileen. "Shalla, Aileen is here."

The fusion tool buzzed and hissed for a couple more seconds before falling silent. Shalla lifted her head and looked toward Aileen. Her cheeks were smudged with dirt and grease, and several strands of silver hair had escaped from the knot atop her head. Her brows rose over her goggles.

"Hey." Aileen lifted the ration bar and water canister. "Brought you something to eat and drink. Thought it'd be a good time to take a break."

Shalla cocked her head. "Thank you, but I just ate."

She leaned back into the hole again.

"Shalla," Triss intoned.

"What?" the uriti asked without looking up. The fusion tool sparked back to life.

Triss raised their voice to be heard over the tool. "Your last meal was this morning as we drove here. You have not eaten in six hours, twelve minutes, and twenty-three seconds. Twenty-four seconds. Twenty-five se—"

Aileen swept into the room. "That's right! Break time it is." She stopped at the floor gap, right across from Triss, and sat on the floor, legs crossed.

Shalla turned off the fusion tool again, braced a hand on the edge of the hole, and sighed. "I suppose I should eat."

"Yes, you should," Triss replied. "Does that mean I can finally put this down?"

Sitting up straight, Shalla frowned at the robot. "It isn't as though your arms can get tired."

"No, but I can get bored."

The uriti waved indifferently. "Fine. Do as you will, Triss."

"Yay," Triss cheered in their flat voice. They bent at the waist, placed the turret on the floor nearby, and turned to clomp toward the exit.

"But only until I call you back!" Shalla shouted as Triss stomped into the corridor. She shook her head, tugged off her thick leather gloves, and lifted her goggles away from her eyes.

Aileen chuckled. "They're like a kid."

Shalla snorted as she placed her gloves on the floor beside her. "I've said that myself, which always prompts my father to remind me that—"

"You are a kid too."

The uriti ducked her head. "Yeah."

"Well, as an adult, I am here to provide." Aileen held out the ration bar. "This is food. *Fooooood.* We eat food regularly to stay alive."

Shalla laughed softly and took the ration bar from Aileen. She cupped it in her hands and stared at it, crinkling the wrapper absently with her thumb. "The way these things taste, they make it easy to forget about eating."

"I know, right? Sometimes it's like chewing on dirt. You'd think in a universe advanced enough to build things like this"—Aileen gestured at the surrounding ship—"that they'd at least find a way to make ration bars taste good."

"I suppose it's about the nourishment in the end, isn't it?" Shalla turned the bar over and delicately tore the wrapper open. With a wrinkle of her adorable deer-like nose, she took a bite.

Aileen set the water canister down beside Shalla. "Here. It'll help wash it down."

"Thanks," Shalla said around a mouthful. She picked up the canister, opened it, and drank.

"So how long has your da been a mechanic?"

Shalla tilted her head. "Da? You mean my father?"

"Yeah, sorry. Da is what I called my father. You also call yours *rhunai*?"

With a small smile, Shalla nodded. "I do. He's been a mechanic all my life, and for a long time before I was born. He and my *rhana*—my mother—opened the shop in town together. She used to work with him. He sometimes says"—she dropped her voice an octave—"even when I had legs, Veeani ran circles around me."

Aileen chuckled, but her humor quickly faded. There was a sorrow in the young uriti's voice that Aileen recognized all too well, and it made her heart ache. "Your mother isn't around anymore, is she?"

Shalla's smile fell, and she shook her head. "She died when I was eight years old."

"Do you mind if I ask what happened?"

"I don't mind." Shalla glanced up at Aileen with large, violet eyes. "It was a long time ago... Those braids in my father's hair... They're part of an uriti tradition. One for every year spent apart from your mate. One braid for every year they're gone. There'll be eight of them soon enough. She's almost been gone for as many years as I knew her.

"And it's never gotten easier for him. I think he relives it, every day..."

Aileen had been devastated at the loss of her parents. She couldn't even begin to imagine the agony of losing her mates. She'd known the twins for a little over a week, and life without them already seemed impossible.

"She and my father were working on one of the haulers from the quarry," Shalla continued. "They didn't realize that the power couplers were substandard and had corroded inside. The specs for those haulers, sent straight from the company that founded the colony, claimed those couplers would last for centuries. *Rhunai* says they were likely cutting corners to save some credits, since they'd invested so much into the operation already. Anyway, when they recharged the power cells, the engine...exploded. *Rhunai* lost his legs in the blast. *Rhana*..."

"She didn't make it."

Shalla shook her head. "I was doing my lessons while they worked. That morning, I had hugged her and said goodbye, and she had smiled at me. She had such a beautiful smile. But I never thought... I never thought that would be the last time I'd see it. The last time I'd see her."

Tears stung Aileen's eyes, and her chest constricted. She knew what that was like. God, did she know... And even dealing with it as an adult, she'd been utterly devastated.

What is wrong, na'diya? Kayl pulsed.

Kier's voice joined his brother's in her mind. *We feel your sorrow. Your loss.*

I'm talking to Shalla, Aileen replied. *I'm okay. Don't worry.*

Aileen reached out and settled her hand upon Shalla's arm. The uriti looked up, eyes glossy with tears.

"I understand your pain. I lost my parents too," Aileen said.

Shalla's brow knitted. She lifted an arm, brushing away tears with the back of her hand. "You did?"

"I did. Just like you, I said goodbye, thinking I'd see them again when they returned from their trip. But there was an accident, and they...they never came home. And I grieved for a long time and felt lost." Aileen tucked the dangling strands of Shalla's hair behind her long ear. "You never forget their absence, and it hurts for a long, long time. But eventually you realize that all the good is still there too. All those memories you made. And you learn to hold those so much closer to your heart.

"Your mother is gone, but your father is still here. You both have memories of her to share and hold onto forever. More than that, you both have many, many more memories to make together. So the two of you need to make sure you don't spend every minute mourning— or with your head stuck in an engine." Aileen's eyes dipped. "Or in a hole full of wires and mechanical doo-dads."

Shalla sniffled and laughed. "I would like to spend more time with him."

"Tell him. I'm sure he'd love to spend more time with you too."

"I will tell him." Shalla fiddled with the ration bar, swinging her legs. "He always finds something for me to do elsewhere when he's dealing with one of those haulers, but we do work together a lot. Build things, take things apart, put things back together again. I truly enjoy it, and he does too. But I think...maybe we both put too much into it because *Rhana* is gone. Maybe...we're both trying to make up for her absence, to fill in the void she left behind."

"Well, at least now you know you're not the only one doing it. I did it too, for a long time. I wandered through galaxies trying to find what was missing, never realizing that the hole in me wasn't there just because my parents were gone. But don't worry. You *will* find the missing pieces someday, Shalla, and everything will come together."

Shalla smiled and settled her hand over Aileen's. "Thank you for the food, and for the conversation. This was nice. I know you aren't comfortable with machinery and electronics, but...you're quite good with people. With...how people work. Not how they work biologically, of course, but—"

Aileen smiled. "If you ever want to talk, I'm all ears."

The uriti drew back, brow low as her eyes flicked over Aileen. "You only have two ears, and they are rather small. Was that one of your terran figures of speech?"

Aileen laughed. "Yeah. It is. It just means that I'm more than willing to listen."

Shalla smiled.

"But...I am still your adult provider, and right now, I say you need to finish that ration bar."

With a whining groan, Shalla lifted the ration bar to her mouth and took a bite. "Fine. But that doesn't mean I'm going to like it."

Aileen grinned. "As long as you eat it."

She sat with Shalla for a little longer, chatting as the uriti finished the ration bar and most of the water, and then took her leave. As she stepped back into the corridor, she heard Shalla speaking into her holocom, telling Triss to return—and the robot's replies, made staticky by the comm, telling her that they did not want to.

Aileen smiled when the uriti resolved the dispute by telling Triss they could choose any job they wanted to do next, with Shalla acting as the robot's assistant—once the turret was done, of course.

When Aileen reached the cargo hold ramp, she found Kier and Kayl standing at its base. With the sunlight directly upon them, their skin was vibrant, those purple stripes complimenting the teal perfectly. They turned to look up at her, offering her smiles that were completely different from one another and yet so similar in their love and affection. Their eyes were so bright, so intent, so caring.

Her love for them was staggering in its power, equaled only by the love she felt from them.

Aileen strode down the ramp, threw her arms around the twins, and held them tight, squeezing her eyes shut.

They embraced her back.

"*Is* everything all right?" Kayl asked quietly.

"Have I told you two that I love you?" she asked.

"Many times," Kier replied, "and we have felt it every moment. But we never tire of hearing it."

She drew in a deep breath, relishing the twins' mingling scents. "I love you."

"And we love you, *na'diya*," they replied. "More than should be possible, we love you."

FORTY-ONE

AILEEN SMILED CONTENTLY as Kier ran his claws through her hair, grazing her scalp and gently working out the little tangles. She lay with her head upon his chest, facing skyward; Kayl lay beside her with his head resting on her belly. His hand was intertwined with hers, his thumb tracing delicate, soothing circles on her wrist.

The twins had set out blankets on the ground and built a fire as the sun had set, inviting Aileen and Shalla to join them for a meal roasted over open flames. There'd been laughter, talking, and delicious food—especially delicious after so many of those ration bars over the last few days. But Shalla had soon departed, not wanting to be out too late.

Though Aileen and her mates had become fond of the young uriti, they welcomed the time alone.

The cacophony that had come as a result of the repair work was done for the day. No more banging and clanging, no more hissing and buzzing, no more curses from Kier as he pinched a finger or gave himself a shock. All the sounds that remained were natural—the crackling of the fire, the sighing of wind through rocks and canyons, the soft burbling of the nearby stream, and the rustling of vegetation in the breeze.

And overhead was...the universe. The cosmic storm rippled through the sky in brilliant colors, though it was noticeably dimmer than the night Aileen and the twins had arrived on Omega IV. That just meant the stars were more visible; countless points of light twin-kled across the heavens, each representing a celestial body so immense that it was almost unfathomable for them to look so tiny.

And they were so different from the stars Aileen and her parents used to gaze up at back on Earth.

Before long, Aileen and her mates would leave this planet to travel between those stars, heading to...

To where? Where will we go, what will we do, when infinite possi-bilities stretch before us? How will we choose?

"Are you not supposed to be relaxing, *na'diya?*" Kier asked gently.

Kayl let out a low hum. "It is difficult to look at the stars and not wonder such things, Kier."

Aileen looked at Kayl. Unlike her, he kept his mind so controlled, choosing which of his thoughts were shared through their psychic link. She stroked his finger with one of her own. "What are you thinking, Kayl?"

"The same as you, Aileen. I wonder where we should go, what sort of life we should make. For so long, we had but one purpose, and saw no future for ourselves beyond it. But we have a future now, with you."

Kier chuckled. "And we find ourselves overwhelmed by choice."

"You said the *Fang* was your home," Aileen said.

"It is."

"Do you have another elsewhere? A place you go when you're not hunting?"

"We were always hunting," Kayl replied.

Aileen frowned. She'd lived in a van for most of her life, always traveling from one place to another, and that van had been her home. She and her parents had made it a home. But they'd chosen it out of love—love for each other, love for music, for performance, for seeing as much of the world as they could in the time they had been gifted.

And that made it so, so different from the lives the twins had led. Their lives had been empty, lonely, driven by revenge, by hatred and pain. She couldn't blame them for it, not at all... But her heart hurt for them.

"If you could choose anywhere for us to make a home, where would you choose?" Aileen asked.

They were silent for what felt like a long while, and though they did not directly share their thoughts, she felt their minds working, felt hints of their emotion as they considered her question. All the while, they continued their little ministrations—Kier combing her hair, Kayl brushing her wrist.

"Tilara," they finally said in unison.

"Our homeworld," Kier added.

She smiled. "Describe it to me."

"All we have are distant memories," Kayl said. "We have not seen it since we were small."

Kier stilled his hand, flattening his palm on her hair. "But even then, our words would not do it justice."

"Would you try anyway?" she asked.

"Hmm... Perhaps we may do better." Kier shifted his hand, gently sliding it down to her cheek. "Close your eyes, *na'diya*."

Aileen turned her face into his touch, kissed his finger, and closed her eyes.

At first, there was only darkness behind her eyelids. She felt the twins, physically and psychically, surrounding her, and the air she breathed, while tinged by the fire's smoke, was laden with their scents.

Though she didn't immediately realize it, the air changed. A sweet scent rose above all the others, an *alive* scent, sprinkled with the perfume of exotic flowers. Then light banished the darkness.

She was standing on a low hill, overlooking a wide, rolling field of tall, blue-green grass that swayed in the breeze. Clusters of flowers grew amidst the grass, their petals in deep reds, purples, and blues, their shapes varied and lovely. The sky overhead was a beautiful blue that shifted toward green on the horizon, dotted with tufts of white clouds.

The landscape turned—or rather, her mind's eye turned. The gentle hills led down to a wide beach with lavender-tinted sand. Tall trees with long branches and blue-green leaves stood along the edges of the beach, with bunches of yellow fruit reminiscent of lemons growing toward their tops. Birdlike creatures soared over the beaches and waddled across the sand, picking at unseen morsels on the ground.

And the water...

The sea stretched out as far as she could see, its clear turquoise waves lapping the shore. On the distant horizon, the sea blended almost seamlessly with the sky, giving her a sense of infinity.

A warm breeze flowed over her skin, bearing a hint of sea salt and carrying the sounds of children laughing and playing to her ears.

The vision turned further, giving her a view along the coast, where the ground rose into low cliffs. A sprawling village ran from the beach up onto those cliffs, its buildings blending pale wood, lavender stone, and bits of glinting metal and glass. There were daevahs of many colors outside, talking, working, living, their children running along the stone-paved roads and through the long grass.

Home.

She felt the word more than she heard it, felt it flowing from the hearts of her mates, and she felt all the yearning and sorrow and joy that came with it.

For a moment, Aileen imagined building a family here. She imagined Kier and Kayl's faces lighting up with happiness. She pictured herself walking along the beach barefoot with her mates, watching their children laugh and play in the sand and water, pictured all of them sitting around a bonfire, listening to the waves as they played music and sang beneath the stars.

We will make it our home, Aileen pulsed, her longing mingling with theirs.

So long as we are with you, we are home, na'diya, the twins thought in unison. *But Tilara...*

Perhaps it is time we return, Kayl pulsed.

Perhaps it is time we start there anew, Kier added.

The vision faded slowly, like mist burning away under the morning sun, but the place they'd shown Aileen lingered in her heart. Her imagined family lingered there too, ghosts of a future that might or might not ever come to pass. Ghosts of future for which she yearned from the depths of her soul.

She opened her eyes. Omega IV's sky stretched out above her, nothing like the sky the twins had shown her and yet beautiful in its own way. What did the stars look like on Tilara? What were the sunsets like, the sunrises?

"All beautiful," Kayl murmured. "Doubly so were we to watch them alongside you."

"And to see the wonder on the faces of our younglings as they witness such sights for the first time... That would be bliss, would it not?" Kier asked.

Aileen blinked, only then realizing that Kayl had propped himself up on his elbow to look down at her, and Kier had lifted his head to do the same. The firelight set their eyes aglow, and within those blue and magenta depths there burned a new want, a new need. A new instinct.

They'd never planned for a future—neither the twins nor Aileen had thought they'd have one. Yet now the idea had arisen, an idea so right, so pure, so compelling, and she knew it was as embedded in their hearts as it was in hers.

Kier's hand brushed one side of her face, Kayl's the other.

"A family," Kier rasped.

Kayl let out a soft breath, sliding his hand down to her stomach. "With our *na'diya*."

"How can we come to want something so much, so quickly, when we have never given it thought before?"

"Because we chose this." Kayl's expression was solemn and still so full of adoration. "We chose a second chance to live, chose Aileen. We chose love."

Aileen's belly fluttered, and hope swelled in her heart, but...

Her chest constricted. How could she give what all three of them so clearly desired? "I'm not a daevah."

Kier turned his face toward hers, kissing her forehead. "And yet we are bonded, *na'diya*."

"But that's our minds. It's...psychic. That can't just make everything else"—she waved toward her pelvis—"work biologically."

"You were injected with a compound when you left your homeworld, were you not?" Kayl asked.

"Yes, to give us a resistance to disease and allow us to adapt to new atmospheres."

"But it allows many species to adapt to more than that," Kier said. "We personally know one terran who is carrying the child of a sedhi, and we have heard of many more who have been impregnated by other species."

Aileen's eyes widened, and that hope rekindled. "It's possible? For us?"

"We do not know for certain, Aileen." Kayl's nostrils and nose slits flared with a huff. "Daevah reproduction requires the seed of both males simultaneously."

"Our seed needs to bond," Kier added, "or it will not take."

"So you'd both need to..." Aileen's brows rose as she recalled how full she'd felt with the two of them inside her vaginally and anally, but for their ridged cocks to be in her sex at the same time... "Both at once?"

They nodded.

Her core clenched with sparking arousal. She wanted that. She wanted them inside her, wanted their seed, wanted their babies. She wanted it all.

But not yet. Not until they found the place where they'd settle down. Not until they found the place that would be their home.

Tilara. With its beautiful lavender sands, turquoise ocean waters, fields of fragrant grass, and colorful flowers.

Aileen reached up and cupped both of their faces. "When we're ready. I want to experience everything in this lifetime with you."

"When we are ready," they agreed.

Kayl said, "We have time to live, *na'diya*. Time to learn, to decide. To love each other."

"And there is much we would do with you before we have younglings," Kier purred.

"Well, until then..." Grinning, she trailed a finger down the twin's chins until she hooked the collars of their tunics. "I say we explore the things we can do together to their fullest."

Images flitted through her mind—fleeting, lurid imaginings of all the things she wanted to do with them, all the things she wanted them to do to her. Fire roiled in her core, triggering a deep, throbbing ache.

Low growls rose from the twins, rumbling into Aileen through their bodies. Her inner flames leapt even higher, instantly multiplied by her mates' desire.

Aileen sat up and pulled Kayl toward her until their mouths connected. His fingers delved into her hair and took hold, keeping her in place while his lips ravaged hers in a demanding, hungry kiss. And she gladly succumbed to the sweet invitation of his tongue. Aileen moaned and clutched at his shoulder as she slid her other hand down Kier's chest.

Blood rushed to the surface of her skin, making it prickle with awareness, and heat pooled between her thighs.

Another hand captured her jaw and turned her face, stealing her from the savagery of Kayl's kiss. Her eyes met Kier's for but an instant before he swooped in and claimed her mouth as his own. Unlike Kayl's punishing kiss, Kier's was sultry, coaxing, lingering as though he were savoring her taste. Their tongues twined and danced, their lips stroked and caressed, their breaths blended into one. Every second of it lulled her deeper and deeper under his spell.

When he rose, she moved with him, getting onto her knees. Her hands worked in unison with Kier's and Kayl's, tugging at fabric and unfastening buttons in a lustful haze until no barriers remained between their bare skin.

Kier drew back and brushed Aileen's hair from her face, staring intently into her eyes. "You are so beautiful."

Kayl kissed the side of her neck, making her shiver, "So radiant."

Ours, their voices said in her mind.

Flattening his palm to her back, Kayl bent Aileen forward until she was on her hands and knees. Her hair fell over her shoulders. His hands trailed down her spine and over her hips, his claws leaving fiery lines in their wake. Her nipples hardened, turning into achy little points.

Aileen sighed, keeping her eyes riveted upon Kier. He'd knelt before her, one hand wrapped around his erect shaft, slowly stroking. A bead of moisture gathered at the tip of his cock. She licked her lips and captured her bottom one with her teeth. The memory of Kayl's delicious seed spread across her tongue; more than anything, she wanted to pleasure Kier in the same manner. More than anything, she craved his taste.

Kier's hand paused. "Do you want this, *na'diya?*"

Kayl's callused hand smoothed over her ass and slipped between her thighs. His fingers delved into her slick folds. A growl rumbled in his chest.

So wet, so needy, his voice pulsed.

Moaning, Aileen arched into his touch. "Yes."

Kier shifted closer until he was directly before her. He cupped her chin and stroked his thumb over her lower lip before angling his shaft toward her. "I am yours."

She reached up and curled her fingers around his cock. It throbbed in her grasp, and more seed trickled from its slit.

Kier's lips drew back in a snarl as he released himself and buried his fingers in her hair. "Take me into your mouth, sweet mate."

Kayl found her clit and circled it. He kept his touch light, coaxing, unhurried, until she was rocking her pelvis in time with his ministrations.

There was something primal about this. There was something wild about making love in the open, beneath the stars, exposed to the wind and bathed in the heat of a fire.

Aileen whimpered and leaned forward, sliding her fist down to the base of Kier's shaft to massage his sack. Looking up at Kier, she dragged her tongue along the underside of his cock from balls to tip, licking away the seed that had gathered there. His salty-sweet flavor heightened her hunger for more.

His body tensed, and he hissed. "Aileen..."

Before he'd finished saying her name, Aileen closed her mouth over him. She took him in deep, moving her lips over every ridge, stroking the sensitive underside of his shaft with her tongue, taking as much of him as her mouth allowed. She sucked as she drew back, and Kier's pleasure echoed in her core, combining with her own.

He grunted, and his fingers tightened in her hair as his other hand cradled her jaw. "*Ba'shanaal!*"

His psychic voice followed his exclamation. *Did not know this would feel so good. Ah,* na'diya, *do not stop.*

She didn't plan to. Aileen wanted to experience his every little reaction, wanted him to lose control, to fill her mouth with his seed. She glided her lips up and down, again and again, and pumped her fist in time with them.

All the while, Kayl stroked her clit. Awash with sensation, she undulated her hips, her breath quickening. Kayl's finger wound her need tighter and tighter until she was nearly vibrating with it. Her slick dripped down her inner thighs.

Aileen panted through her nose and strengthened her grip on Kier's shaft as he pumped his hips. *Kayl... Please...*

"You need more, na'diya?" Kayl asked, moving his finger to carefully circle her entrance. "Do you need me here?"

Yes. I want you inside me, she begged.

"Then I shall do as my mate commands." His hand left her,

replaced not a moment later by the blunt, probing tip of his cock. He pushed inside her with a gentle nudge, his passage eased by her slick.

Aileen groaned and arched her back, bearing down upon him. Kier growled and bucked. More seed seeped from him, and Aileen sucked it down eagerly.

"Fuck," he snarled.

Kayl drew his hips back.

Aileen's sex clenched around the emptiness he was leaving in his wake, and she nearly cried out at the loss, at the hollowness. *No! Please, plea—*

Gripping her hips, Kayl thrust forward, burying himself deep in her body.

Aileen gasped. There was a flicker of pain, but it was swiftly replaced by a flood of heat and that wonderful fullness. Her inner walls clutched his shaft, seeking to deny his escape, taking him deeper.

"Ah, *na'diya...*" Kayl groaned. His fingers flexed, and his claws pricked her flesh. "I feel you. I feel so much of you."

He pumped shallowly at first, as though trying to stretch her around him. But then he withdrew again, slower than before, farther than before, making her blissfully, torturously aware of every one of the delicious ridges on his shaft. Aileen's limbs trembled.

"Now let me feel *all* of you." Kayl slammed back into her so hard and deep that it stole her breath.

He did it again, and again, and again, his thrusts increasingly brutal, increasingly bestial, each one making Aileen cry out around Kier's cock. But in her thoughts, she begged Kayl to go faster, harder.

Pressure built in her core, fueled by her expanding pleasure.

Kier grasped her hair with both fists and pumped his hips in sync with his brother's movements. Her jaw ached, but she didn't care; the snarls and grunts that punctuated their every movement were worth it. This pleasure—*their* pleasure—was worth it.

Her mates were worth it.

They moved faster and faster, their cadence becoming one of ruin—it would tear her apart with ecstasy beyond comprehension, would leave nothing of her behind, and she welcomed it. She was already lost in a maelstrom of sensations shared between her and her lovers, and she craved more, more, more.

But she would take Kier and Kayl with her.

The moment came with explosive force. Three souls cried out in rapture. Three bodies convulsed, overcome by pleasure. Everything Aileen, Kier, and Kayl felt was felt as one. Everything was shared.

Kayl surged into Aileen a final time as his cock jerked, filling her with jets of hot seed. Her inner walls constricted around his shaft, her core cramped with pleasure, and she moaned. But the sound was cut short when Kier's seed spilled down her throat. She swallowed every drop, pumping her fist to take everything he could give.

Breathing heavily, Kier withdrew from her mouth and crumpled to the ground. He cupped her face, looked into her half-lidded eyes, and kissed her.

"Aileen," he whispered after breaking the kiss. He pressed his forehead to hers.

Aileen smiled and caressed his cheek, her thumb tracing the marking there. Her racing heart felt as though it would pound right out of her chest, and her body was sore in the most pleasurable way.

Heat blanketed her back as Kayl leaned over her. He trailed kisses over her tattoo and along her spine, massaging her hips to soothe away the throb left by his crushing grip. He rasped, *"Na'diya."*

Kayl carefully withdrew from her, making her shiver as those ridges slid along her inner walls one last time. His seed seeped out of her, but before it could go far, he used the pad of his finger to push it back in.

She shuddered anew. The act was so feral, so possessive. It was as if he wanted nothing of his to escape her—as if Kayl's seed marked her as his.

Then, gently, the twins eased her down, lying to either side of her with arms, legs, and tails intertwined, enveloping her with their warmth and solidness.

"No matter what stars we lie beneath," Kier said.

"No matter what galaxies we venture to," Kayl continued.

"We will love you more with each passing moment," they said together, their hands and tails brushing her skin. "You are our home."

FORTY-TWO

Shalla reached into the opening in the ceiling and glanced over her shoulder at Kayl, Kier, and Aileen. Though the young uriti kept her expression neutral, a glimmer of excitement brightened her violet eyes. "Ready?"

Kayl nodded, while Kier and Aileen responded simultaneously with an enthusiastic, "Yes!"

Lips twitching up at their corners, Shalla faced forward. Her arms moved as her hands worked inside the compartment.

"This is degrading," Triss said.

"You're being helpful," Shalla replied.

Triss was kneeling on the cockpit floor, torso bent forward, with Shalla standing on their back. The depressions built into the robot's hard metal casing looked very much like footholds, and the adolescent uriti currently had her hooves planted in the uppermost set.

The robot's small head turned slowly to look back at Kayl and the others. "I possess many valuable and critical skills."

"You do," Aileen said, smiling softly. "We've seen you putting them to excellent use over the last few days. Thank you, Triss."

Kier grinned, leaning back with his hands propped on a control console. "But right now, it seems like your most valuable skill is being a self-aware stepladder."

"And yet you are still more useful now than Kier has been

through this entire process," Kayl said, folding his arms across his chest. But he couldn't keep the smirk off his face for long.

"Might want to take cover, Shalla," Aileen said, shaking her head. "Shots are being fired all over the place in here."

Shalla stretched her legs and balanced precariously on the edges of her hooves, reaching deeper into the opening. Despite all their complaining, Triss straightened their torso slightly, granting Shalla some extra reach. The uriti craned her neck, and the upper half of her head disappeared into the compartment.

"And"—the uriti grunted softly, arms tensing, before a click sounded within the compartment—"done."

The cockpit came to life all around. Holo screens and displays blinked on, the countless buttons and controls lit up, and the central console projected a star map of the local system.

The *Fang's* computer populated all those displays with the same message—*REBOOT INTERRUPTED. RECOVERING... DIAGNOSTICS AND SYSTEM SCAN IN PROGRESS...*

"Feels like it's been forever since I've seen it like this," Aileen said, smiling warmly as she ran her eyes around the cockpit.

Kier followed her gaze with his own. "I had nearly forgotten how excessive it is. I do not know what half of these controls are for..."

"I suppose it is good, then, that I am our pilot," Kayl said.

Kier leaned closer to Aileen, put a hand to the side of his mouth, and loudly whispered, "He does not know what most of them are for either, *na'diya*."

Kayl rolled his eyes.

Shalla withdrew from the compartment. She bent forward, and Triss passed the ceiling panel to her. It snapped back into place when she fitted it over the opening and pushed up on it.

Kayl turned to the nearest display, watching characters flit across it as the ship assessed itself. His tail flicked from side to side, and he drummed a finger on his bicep, willing the process to hasten.

Undoubtedly, Kier's impatience had begun to affect Kayl. They'd been around one another far too much during their lives.

You cannot blame me for this, Kier pulsed as he and Aileen joined Kayl in front of the screen.

Can't blame me either, Aileen added. *Even if I can be impatient sometimes, too.*

Kier's smile stretched into a grin. *It is more unnatural that Kayl was never impatient before.*

You are both wrong, Kayl replied, tail swinging a little faster. *I can blame* both *of you, and my prior demeanor was perfectly natural.*

Kier snorted.

Shalla's hooves clomped on the floor when she hopped down from Triss's back, though her steps were quiet as she walked over to join the others. She said nothing, but Kayl could almost feel the anticipation radiating from the adolescent.

And it would've been a lie to say he wasn't brimming with anticipation of his own, especially since it was being wildly amplified by Kier and Aileen's excitement.

The trio had faced challenges on Omega IV, yet their time here had been...magical. It had greatly surpassed anything Kayl had thought possible, so much so that most of it felt more like a waking dream than reality. Particularly last night, when he and Kier had made love to their mate in the open air as countless stars and the final waves of the cosmic storm glimmered overhead. A significant part of Kayl was reluctant to leave this planet—and he knew this planet would never leave him.

He would forever cherish this world as the place their *daevalis* was made.

Aileen caught Kayl's right hand and Kier's left hand; the stones on their wrist cuffs glowed in delight for their closeness. The trio's hearts thumped in unison.

This moment...this was the culmination of days of hard work, of sweat and aches, of fingers getting pinched between metal panels and heads being bumped on the walls and ceilings of compartments never designed for people to fit inside. Everyone here had toiled to reach this moment, and while it would not have been possible without Shalla, Triss, and Tallian, it would never have been finished so quickly were it not for the twins and Aileen.

This was the future. The *Fang* was a gateway that would lead them to anywhere in the universe. All they needed to do was open that gate.

Next time, Kayl, I suggest you either better shield your thoughts or come up with a better metaphor, Kier pulsed.

Have you ever paid any attention to your own thoughts, Kier? I assure you, they—

Aileen gave their hands a squeeze. *We're supposed to be having a moment.*

The twins smirked. Their excitement remained undiminished, but at heart, they knew it didn't matter what the report would say. So long as they had their mate, they would have happiness.

The characters continued flitting across the screens, cycling through hundreds of data points in the time it would've taken Kayl to read only one.

Then, quite unceremoniously, it was done. The completed diagnostics report appeared on one of the central displays, and all the other screens were slowly populated with their usual readings, gauges, and controls as, one by one, systems that had been deactivated for days came online.

Kayl and the others turned their attention to the report.

Aileen tilted her head, brow furrowing. "It's probably just me, but I have no idea what I'm looking at."

Bracing a hand on the console, Shalla leaned forward, squinting at the text. "It's not just you."

The twins laughed.

Kier gently withdrew his hand from Aileen's and shifted over to his usual position at the gunner's seat, bringing up a command screen. "That is because it is all written in *Tal'sin*."

Aileen regarded Kier for a moment before giving Kayl a questioning look.

Smiling, Kayl said, "It is the native language of our people. This is the Daevah alphabet."

Even in digital form, the characters were flowing and artistic, created with delicate curves and angles. He'd learned to read and write those characters long, long ago, and it felt like just as long since Kayl had seen them.

Shalla nodded, standing up straight. "Ah. System was rebooted and defaulted to its original language."

Kier tapped a few options, and the text on the displays changed to the simple, uniform characters of Universal Speech. "Better?"

Crossing her arms over her chest, Aileen stared at the report. "Worse. At least before it looked pretty. Now it looks bland on top of not making any sense."

Once their next bout of laughter faded, Kayl and Shalla perused the report, quietly discussing the items that came up, while Kier and

Aileen stood by, watching with expressions of greatly exaggerated gravity.

"Well?" Aileen finally asked, chin cradled in the crook of her hand as she stroked her cheek with her index finger.

Kayl shook his head. "You are both ridiculous."

Kier raked a hand through his hair. "Alas, but we are forced to such extremes to counteract just how boring you are, brother. It is the only way to balance our *daevalis*."

"I see you still confuse boring and responsible, Kier."

"Some of the auxiliary systems are still running at limited capacity." Shalla, who was still studying the report, swiped her fingers through the holo to scroll the text. "Power converters are operating at reduced efficiency, so you'll burn fuel a little faster than normal, but the cores are charging and distributing within spec, even if it's on the lower end. Jump drive's stable. Benefit of crashing on a planet with faldrium in every speck of dust, I guess. Arc cores in the shield generator were changed out, so you'll have shields, but they're not going to hold through much more than breaching atmospheres, so, you know...don't go getting into any more space battles and you'll be okay until you can get this stuff swapped for better parts."

"And...that's all good, right?" Aileen asked.

Chuckling, Shalla glanced at Aileen and smiled. "All things considered, yes. It's good."

"It will fly," Kayl said. His spirit was already soaring; the *Fang* was operational. The universe was theirs. All they had to do was choose their next destination, and...go.

Our first destination should probably be Arthos, Kier pulsed. *It is where we are most likely to find the parts required to properly fix the ship, especially if we enlist Arcanthus's aid.*

Kayl groaned inwardly. He'd never enjoyed crowds, and years of chasing pirates and slavers into the dangerous, neutral-territory cities and space stations they frequented had left him even less tolerant of anywhere with large numbers of people. The Infinite City was noisy, dangerous, unpredictable...

I've always wanted to see Arthos, Aileen pulsed, smiling at Kayl. *They say it's one of the wonders of the universe.*

Letting out a huff through his nose, Kayl pulsed, *For you*, na'diya. *For you, I will endure Arthos again.*

Kier's tail slapped the back of Kayl's leg. *Stop being overly dramatic, brother.*

Can I be blamed for wanting to have Aileen to ourselves?

The faintest blush appeared on Aileen's cheeks, accompanied by a spark of heat that rippled through the psychic link and sank low in Kayl's belly.

Kier looked upon their mate with a glint of hunger in his eyes. *No. Who needs the rest of the universe when we have her?*

Aileen pressed her lips together and let out a long, slow breath. A stern expression settled over her face. *You two need to behave yourselves. We have company.*

Fortunately, Shalla had returned her attention to the report, perusing the information while navigating command menus on a secondary screen. After a short while, she lowered her eyes and said, "So, I was thinking..."

A delicate frown played upon Aileen's lips. "What is it, Shalla?"

"You probably won't believe when I say this, but..." Shalla wrung her hands, the gesture reminding Kayl of just how young she was. "For all the work I've done fixing up stuff like this, I've never actually flown in a spacecraft before. I mean, I have a hoverbike me and my father fixed up for when I have to go check machinery outside town, but that's not..."

The uriti lifted her gaze and ran it around the cockpit, throwing her arms out to indicate the *Fang* in its entirety. "That's not *this*."

"Are you asking for a ride?" Kayl inquired flatly.

"Well, you need to test it anyway, don't you? And I should be on the test flight in case anything needs to be adjusted. We can just go to town! I'm sure my father would love to see this ship firsthand, and he can doublecheck everything, just so you know—"

Kier dropped into his chair with a chuckle. "You could have just asked directly."

The uriti beamed. "Really?"

Kayl eased down into the pilot's seat. It was both comforting and strange to be sitting there again; it felt like an eternity had passed since the crash. But the controls before him were the same as ever, and he found himself quite eager to get the *Fang* into the air again.

He glanced up at Shalla. "What of your hovertruck?"

Purple eyes wide with excitement, Shalla sat down in one of the secondary seats. "Triss can drive it back."

"But I want to fly too," Triss said from the rear of the cockpit.

"Didn't you go up with Garlahan when he had to repair the geolocation satellite a few months ago?" Shalla asked, eyeing the robot.

"That was for work. This is not fair."

"I'm doing this for work too!"

"You are doing it because you want to."

"Um, not to interrupt," Aileen said, "but will Triss even fit into the cab of that truck?"

Shalla waved dismissively. "They can jack in from the back. Drive it remotely."

"I am not licensed to operate vehicles," Triss said. They had risen from the floor, back still turned toward the others but head facing them.

"No one on this planet is licensed, Triss," Shalla replied. "The local government operates on a *do what you want until you lose a hand and Ialle scolds you* system."

"Fine." Triss's head slowly spun away, and the robot stepped forward, ducking through the cockpit entryway. "But do not expect me back soon."

Dragging a hand down her face, Shalla said, "I swear *Rhana* was having a laugh when she programmed you, Triss."

"Perhaps if I was treated better, I could have a laugh too." The robot's clanging steps moved away along the corridor, though they little reduced in volume—almost as though they were purposely walking more heavily as they went.

"Are they going to be okay?" Aileen asked as she took the remaining seat and reached back for the harness.

Shalla snickered. "Yeah. Triss knows how much they're appreciated. Problem is that they're just like everyone else in Navaire—bored to the point of having to create their own entertainment."

Kayl arched a brow. "They entertain themselves by acting like that all the time?"

"And you thought I was bad, brother," Kier muttered.

"You are," Kayl replied as everyone drew their seat harnesses over their shoulders.

"Triss is kind of...my best friend," Shalla said quietly. "I'm even the one who gave them their name. Sort of."

"Sort of?" Aileen asked gently.

"Yeah." The uriti laughed to herself. "I was really young when my parents built Triss. I knew robots were made of metal, and as far as I knew back then, all metal was tristeel. But...I couldn't exactly pronounce tristeel. I guess I used to say it like *triss-teel*. And that's what I called the robot they were building."

The twins smiled softly, and Kier said, "Which became Triss."

Shalla nodded. "It's foolish, but..."

"It's not foolish at all. I love it," Aileen said.

The young uriti smiled self-consciously, cheeks darkening. "We ready to fly?"

Aileen buckled her harness and settled her hands on her lap, drawing in a deep breath. "Yeah. I might be experiencing a little PTSD, but let's do this."

Kier snaked his tail through the cut out at the base of his seat, brushing it over Aileen's shin. "Worry not *na'diya*. The ship is far more likely to explode than it is to crash."

"It is not going to explode," Kayl and Shalla said simultaneously in equally firm tones.

On the screen that displayed a schematic of the ship with all its entryways and ports, the icon representing the rear ramp changed to show that the ramp was closed. Triss had disembarked.

Aileen laughed. "Not sure whose confidence is more inspiring." She reached forward with both hands, but the harness halted her well before she could touch the twins. Kier and Kayl reached back, meeting her hands halfway, and twined their fingers with hers.

With a smile so warm and bright that it melted Kayl's heart, she pulsed, *I can't wait to begin our lives together*.

FORTY-THREE

The *Fang's* engines hummed as Kayl took the flight controls; the ship itself seemed just as eager to fly as its passengers.

Aileen glanced at Shalla. Though the young uriti was gripping the shoulder straps of her harness tightly enough to make the tendons on her hands stand out, her violet eyes were wide with eagerness, and when she noticed Aileen looking at her, she grinned.

Kier touched something on the console in front of him. The walls —from the tops of the consoles and up—along with the ceiling, faded away, replaced by an unhindered view of the shadowy canyon walls and darkening sky outside the ship.

"If Shalla did her job, we should not feel anything," Kier said.

The *Fang* rose, guided smoothly by Kayl's precise touch.

Aileen's stomach fluttered as the rock walls seemed to slide away; seeing the movement without feeling it created a disorienting disconnect between body and mind.

Kayl sped their ascent. Towering cliffs, rock formations, and mountains flitted through the view holos until all that remained immediately visible from Aileen's seat was the sky, all deep reds and oranges on the horizon but bleeding into purple and blue overhead.

With another flick of Kier's fingers, the floor also vanished.

Now Aileen's stomach outright lurched, and her heart made a frenzied attempt to claw its way into her throat. She still felt the floor, solid as ever, beneath her boots, but again there was that pesky disconnect between what she felt and what she saw.

Far, far below was the stream beside which she and her mates had spent the last few days; there was the gouge left in the ground by the *Fang's* not so graceful belly flop; there was the canyon that had swallowed up their ship—and it all looked so small.

Shalla laughed. The sound was equal parts nervous and delighted.

Then Kayl shifted the throttle, and the *Fang* accelerated forward. Omega IV sprawled out below them. The setting sun cast long, deep shadows across the rocky landscape, but everywhere the sun touched, flecks of faldrium shone like glittering fire.

The view was gorgeous—especially because they were not currently in the process of crashing.

At least she really hoped they weren't.

Kayl looked at Aileen over his shoulder. His smile was warm and reassuring. *We are not crashing, na'diya.*

And even if we were, Kier added, smirking at Kayl, *my brother has much more experience with it now. The next crash will be far better than the first.*

Though his brows fell and he pressed his lips flat as he regarded his twin, the smile did not fade from Kayl's eyes.

Chuckling, Aileen returned her attention to the view.

This world was just as beautiful as it had been when Aileen and the twins had first arrived during another sunset.

She realized it then—they'd come full circle. Not just regarding their time on this planet, but...in life. Aileen was no longer alone. She'd found the love for which she'd so long yearned. She'd found a family as affectionate and quirky as the one she'd lost years ago. Her travels had taken her farther from home than she'd ever imagined possible, yet oddly enough, in going so far, she'd finally come home.

The twins smiled at her. Their love flowed freely through their bond, and she sent hers back to them. The shared emotion didn't diminish in the slightest when Kier and Kayl faced forward again.

Aileen looked at Shalla again. The girl's eyes, still rounded, were now in constant motion; she seemed determined to take in the entirety of the expansive view at once. And Aileen's heart turned to complete mush when she realized the uriti had lifted her hooves off the floor—it was as though Shalla were imagining herself flying instead of the ship.

"We should push the *Fang* a little, brother," Kier suggested with suspicious innocence.

"You are correct, Kier," Kayl replied. "We must test its performance under stress if we truly wish to take measure of Shalla's work."

"You don't have to." But Shalla's gaze was practically glowing as it darted back and forth between the twins.

Kayl opened the throttle further.

Aileen felt the slightest pressure push her back against her seat as the ground below became a passing blur.

With Aileen and Shalla laughing and cheering, Kayl put the *Fang* through a series of increasingly complex maneuvers; flips, rolls, dives, and turns so tight they must've defied the laws of physics. At one point, he brought them lower to the ground and wove the ship between several of the tall, pillar like rock formations.

"All right, all right!" Aileen cried; her cheeks ached from smiling so much. "You're not testing anything, you're just showing off now."

"Now?" Kier asked pointedly.

"I am simply employing my considerable skills," Kayl said as he leveled the ship and turned toward Navaire.

The town lay beneath the darkest part of the sky, with the night's first visible stars twinkling on the horizon just beyond it. The lights along the streets and on the buildings gave the place a completely different feel than it had during the day—it seemed somehow warmer, somehow more inviting. A bright refuge in a world of encroaching shadow.

Shalla activated the holocom on her wrist. "I'll let *Rhunai* know we're coming in."

"Where should we land?" Kayl asked as the *Fang* banked wide around the town.

"Spaceport," Shalla replied distractedly. "Huh. No connection."

"Lingering effects of the storm?" Kier suggested.

"Maybe. But comms should've been up by now, even without signal boosters." Shalla frowned at the screen of her holocom for another moment before glancing up and pointing. "Bring it right into there. Me and Triss opened it up for you this morning."

Kayl guided the *Fang* through a smooth descent, reducing the ship's speed, and turned into the relatively empty hangar Shalla had indicated.

Apart from a jarring shake as the ship settled onto its landing gear—which Shalla said must've been the result not of her work but pilot error—the landing was perfect.

Aileen smirked at Kayl. *Much better than last time.*

Kayl's hands moved quickly as he powered down systems, and his tail rippled with a hint of restlessness. His mind-voice was laced with wicked promise as he pulsed, *I will remember all these little slights,* na'diya, *and I shall be sure to account for each later.*

Kier let out a soft sigh, unbuckled his harness, and stood up. *Please do save it for later, brother. You are only torturing all three of us otherwise.*

The others released their harnesses and stood as well. As they filed into the corridor, Kayl pulsed again, his *aerys* more serious now.

Do you have your blaster, Aileen?

Aileen glanced at him over her shoulder, brows falling low. *Should I?*

With a frown that suggested he didn't like his own answer, he replied, *Yes. Hidden, like I showed you. I do not believe we need to go so far as to put on our armor, but...*

But it is best if we are all armed while off the ship, Kier finished.

Aileen nodded. She wasn't a fan of having to walk around with a blaster strapped to her leg, but she'd have been a fool to disagree with the twins. Anything could happen at any time, and she wanted to be armed not only to defend herself, but her mates.

"I'll be right back. Just have to grab something." Aileen slipped into their room to hurriedly don the thigh holster Kayl had given her, ensuring the blaster was snugly in place before rejoining her companions.

Shalla was beaming as they disembarked. Once she was on the ground, she hurried off under the ship, checking the armored plating that had been replaced. Aileen and the twins awaited her near the base of the ramp.

"Looks good," the adolescent said as she returned. "And thanks."

"Thank you, Shalla," Kier replied, offering an uncharacteristically formal and yet wholeheartedly gracious bow. Kayl mimicked the gesture.

"Yeah, thank you so, so much," Aileen said.

Shalla's cheeks flushed. "Just did my job. Anyway, I should go and—"

Aileen's eyes flared as a sudden idea struck her. "Are the shops still open?"

The uriti's brow furrowed. "Maybe for a little longer? Most of them close not long after sunset, I think."

"Okay, so we need to hurry."

In identically confused voices, the twins asked, *"Na'diya?"*

Aileen put on her sweetest smile and held up a palm to them. "Could I have some credits? Please?"

Don't think. Don't think, Aileen.

But this is thinking.

This doesn't count!

Kayl frowned. "Was the landing rougher than it seemed? Aileen does not seem to feel well."

"I'm fine," she replied with an exaggeratedly offended glare. "I just have an idea, but it's meant to be a surprise."

Don't think, Aileen. Don't you dare think about it again, not even for a second.

"Quite an interesting technique," Kier said with a chuckle.

"I want to get something for Shalla and Tallian before we leave."

Shalla waved her hands. "No, Aileen, you don't have to—"

"I don't have to," Aileen said in a gentle but firm tone, "but I *want* to." She met the twins' gazes. "I also want to get something for you two. But I'd like that to be a surprise, which is hard when you can literally read my mind."

"Ah, *na'diya*," Kayl rumbled as he and Kier each placed a hand on one of her cheeks. They brushed their thumbs over her skin, grazing it with their claws.

"You do not have to get us anything," Kier said.

Kayl added, "But we will cherish anything you do."

Kier's mouth slanted into that charming, mischievous smile as he fished a credit chip out of his pocket. "Especially if mine is better than Kayl's."

Aileen laughed, closing her fingers around the chip he laid upon her palm. The twins stepped back.

Aileen swung her gaze to the young uriti. "Come on, Shalla. We're operating on a tight schedule."

The delicate crease between the uriti's brows deepened. "You want me to go...shopping?"

Aileen nodded. "With me."

"With you."

Again, Aileen nodded. "Shopping. With me."

"Now?"

"Right now."

The girl began to say something—Aileen chose to believe it would've been *okay*—but she didn't have a chance to finish before Aileen grabbed her hand and tugged her along. On the way out of the hangar, Shalla managed to slow Aileen just enough to slap the control button that closed the huge bay doors.

With the twins close behind, Aileen led Shalla across the spaceport yard. The piles of parts and old vehicles were unsettling beneath the darkening sky. Though the floodlights standing everywhere gave of strong white light, shadows as thick as ocean fog clung to the junk and debris.

Aileen quickened her pace—not because she was uneasy, not at all. It was just because she really wanted to get to the shops before they closed for the night.

Can't even successfully lie to yourself, Aileen.

How are you going to stop yourself from letting this little surprise slip? It's—

She shot a nervous glance at back at her mates. Their eyes were keen, but they kept their expressions neutral, giving nothing away.

Fortunately, the lights were still on inside the stores when Aileen and her companions entered the plaza. Keeping hold of Shalla's hand, Aileen hurried to The Glittering Cavern.

"So...we will wait out here for you?" Kayl asked.

Aileen looked at Kayl to find him standing on the walkway that ran in front of the buildings, his stance uncertain—like he'd paused mid-step and didn't know how to proceed.

Kier slapped a hand down on his brother's shoulder and dragged him back. "Now who's being overly dramatic? We will resupply while Aileen sees to her business. I do believe our *na'diya* wants the hold filled with addiva fruit before we depart."

"Yes," Aileen said with a chuckle. "Yes, she certainly does."

And do not forget to purchase another bottle or two of the iyara extract, Kier added with a grin that made Aileen laugh even as it injected heat into her core.

The twins walked toward the general store; Aileen and Shalla entered The Glittering Cavern.

Sala was standing at the counter. She bared her fangs in a smile that was somehow friendly and warm. "Welcome back, Aileen. I am glad you decided to return."

Aileen waved. "I've been wanting to come back for days. Everything in here is just so lovely."

"Thank you. Our ancestors would take pride in such praise. If—" The azhera's catlike eyes fell upon Aileen's companion, and they widened. "Is that Shalla? Tallian's cub?"

"Yes, it's me," Shalla said, offering an anxious smile. From the side of her mouth, she muttered, "Not a cub, though."

If the azhera had heard the girl's comment, she made no indication. Sala said, "I haven't seen you in here since you were knee high. Be welcome!" She pressed a hand over her chest. "My heart is now full."

"Thanks." Shalla walked farther into the shop, eyes downcast.

Aileen moved up beside her, placing a hand on the girl's arm. "I'm sorry, Shalla. If you're not comfortable here or you just want to go, it's okay. I understand. I know I was maybe a little over enthusiastic..."

"No." Shalla shook her head. "It's fine. Really."

Frowning, Aileen tipped her head toward the door. "We can go."

Shalla huffed and drew to a halt. "I...don't want to go. It's just that... This shop was my mother's favorite place in town. She used to bring me in here all the time. But since she died, I...haven't come."

"Oh, Shalla. I'm so sorry. I had no idea." Aileen gently squeezed the girl's shoulder.

"You couldn't have known. This place just makes me think of her, and that's...hard."

"Me and my parents used to travel all over our world, singing and playing music together. Those songs were our lives. Music is what brought them together, and they loved it so, so much that they shared it with me too. But when I lost them, I didn't think I could ever sing again, because every note would remind me of them."

The uriti's eyes were so innocent, so vulnerable in that moment. "So what? You just learn to live with the pain?"

"You do. That's all you can do. But eventually, you remember that the things they loved should be sources of joy, not pain. I realized that I couldn't go on without music, because it was so much a part of me. And when I sing those songs that my parents taught me, I'm closer to them than ever. That feels a little sad, but it also feels really, really good."

"I don't know if I can do that."

"You already are, Shalla." Aileen moved to stand in front of the girl. "Your mother loved mechanics and engineering and all that stuff, right?"

Shalla nodded.

"Well, you still do that and enjoy it."

"But *Rhunai* does it too."

"And it's great that you share that with him. It's something you all had together. But you're allowed to enjoy other things as well. Things that were just for you and your mother." Aileen gestured at the surrounding shop with her free hand. "You're allowed to look at this place and see your mother, and it's okay for that to be sad. But you can also look at it as something you and her both loved, a place where you made memories and shared joy. Your mother would want you to be happy."

Releasing a slow, heavy breath, Shalla ran her gaze around the shop. A small smile crept onto her lips. "You're right. It can't all be engines and antigravity drives, can it?"

Laughing, Aileen withdrew her hand from Shalla's shoulder. "It *can* be, but that doesn't mean it should be. Now"—she rubbed her hands together and grinned—"let's get moving. It's been a long time since I went shopping with a friend, and I plan to help you make up for a lot of lost time, but I doubt Sira and Sala are going to want to keep the shop open all night."

FORTY-FOUR

Kier couldn't help but grin when Aileen and Shalla emerged from the shop, each carrying a sturdy cloth bag laden with goods.

With a hint of self-consciousness in her smile, Aileen peeked up at him with a self-conscious smile. "Did you two...hear anything?"

"You kept remarkably quiet," Kier replied. "I did not much enjoy it, if I am honest."

Kayl snickered. "He said that you may be my match when it comes to the psychic silent treatment."

Aileen's smile took on a mischievous slant. "You know, I might have to side with Kayl. You are definitely the more overdramatic one, Kier."

"Ah, to be so frequently and mercilessly wounded by the ones I hold dearest." Kier shook his head and sighed. "Would that my love were returned in kind."

"That just proves my point." Aileen closed the distance between her and Kier, stood on her toes, and pecked a quick kiss on his lips. "Never change, my *na'dival*."

Kayl glowered at Kier, who responded with a smirk.

All the while, Shalla stood watching with a little crease between her delicate brows.

"So he is rewarded for such behavior?" Kayl asked.

When Aileen only replied with a half-shrug and a nod, Kayl lifted a hand and clutched at his chest. "I fear our time apart has left me bereft, *na'diya*. Surely my heart shall crumble to dust without the power of your love to bond its shattered pieces together."

Aileen stepped over to him, grasped his tunic, and tugged him down into a kiss that lingered at least twice as long as the one she'd given Kier. Once she withdrew, Kayl grinned like a fool.

Kier scoffed, folding his arms across his chest. "I do not see why his reward should be greater than mine."

"Oh, those weren't rewards," Aileen said. "And I only kissed Kayl longer because he's more likely to be upset."

The twins eyed her. "Upset about?"

"I *might* have gone a little overboard." She lifted her bag slightly; behind her, Shalla put on a nervous smile.

"Overboard?" Kayl arched a brow. "Is that not when—"

"She means she spent more credits than she should have, Kayl," Kier said. "Just when I believe he has made progress... At any rate, do not concern yourself, Aileen. We are not upset."

"So you can all really read each other's thoughts?" Shalla asked, drawing everyone's attention.

Kier cocked his head. "Is that what you have been thinking about this whole time?"

"I just can't imagine it." The uriti glanced from Kayl to Kier, and then finally settled her gaze on Aileen. "Sorry. With as much as they go back and forth, you probably never have a moment's peace."

Aileen laughed.

Kayl huffed through his nostrils. "Moving on. We are going into the parts shop for a quick look. There are items aboard the *Fang* that we would like to replace, if possible, before we depart in the morning."

Tilting her head, Aileen looked over the twins with a heavy gaze. One of her delicate eyebrows arched. "My dear, sweet *na'divali*... I can't help but notice a concerning lack of addiva fruit on your persons. Are my eyes deceiving me? Maybe you have some very deep pockets you hid them in?"

Between Aileen still masking her thoughts and her saccharine tone, Kier couldn't determine the emotion underlying her words. Surely, she'd spoken in jest.

Hadn't she?

The twins exchanged a glance from the corners of their eyes; Kayl was no more certain than Kier.

"We arranged for the shopkeeper to deliver fresh produce to the *Fang* in the morning," Kayl said carefully.

Kier added, "Including what I believe you terrans would refer to as a *fuckton* of addiva."

Aileen regarded him thoughtfully. "A fuckton, huh? Well, as long as it's a metric fuckton, it should be just about enough."

"I..." Kier's brows fell, and he absently tugged at the loose braid hanging near his ear. "Is there a significant difference between the two?"

"Yes," she replied gravely—but that seriousness cracked a moment later, giving way to laughter and a bright smile. "However much you bought is perfectly fine. In fact, knowing you two, it's probably too much."

"Nothing is ever too much for our *na'diya*," Kayl purred, brushing the backs of his fingers down her forearm.

A little shiver ran through her. "That is definitely not true, but I'll allow it. Anyway..." She turned to face Shalla. "Did you want to go into the parts shop with them?"

The uriti's lips peeled back, displaying her flat white teeth, and she let out a slow, hissing breath. Sliding the straps of the bag over her forearm, she again tried her holocom, only to receive another *NO CONNECTION* message. "I want to, but I really should get back to my father. He'll be wondering where I am, and he's probably tried to call."

"I'll walk with you," Aileen offered. "We can show everything to your da and give him those gifts."

"Really? I mean...you don't have to."

Aileen chuckled. "I want to. Besides, I wouldn't know what a single thing was in that shop. Give me a *guitar* and I can string it blindfolded and tune it by ear, but mechanics..." She shook her head.

Kier's heart warmed. His adoration and admiration for Aileen grew with each day. She was playful, kind, considerate, passionate, humorous, and gracious. She knew her limitations, was aware of her shortcomings, but she never let them stop her. She embraced them as part of herself. No shame, no feelings of inadequacy. That she'd been a slave not even two weeks ago, that her hope had been crushed, seemed impossible.

She had so quickly grown into *herself*, and she was exactly what the twins always had—and always would—need.

He'd watched his mate with wonder and pride as she'd connected with Shalla. Aileen's easy demeanor and intuition had helped the adolescent open up, had helped her smile and laugh; the Shalla who'd first come to the *Fang* days ago was not the same Shalla standing before them now.

When the twins and Aileen had younglings of their own—if they ever could—Kier would love seeing her interact with them. No children in all the universe could ever have a better mother than theirs would.

"Is that all right with you two?" Aileen asked, jarring Kier from his thoughts.

He realized only then that he and Kayl had been staring at her with dreamy, far-off expressions on their faces.

Kayl recovered his wits first. "Yes."

"Perhaps when you are through, we can meet at the canteen for a meal?" Kier suggested.

"Yeah, you probably should," said Shalla. "Emai mentioned that you haven't taken her up on the free meals. I think she said something about feeding you so well you wouldn't be able to get off your stool without assistance."

"Well, I certainly do not want to invoke Emai's wrath."

Aileen smiled. "Sounds good to me."

"Perhaps I can convince my father to get out of the shop for once, and we can eat with you?" Shalla's tone had just a hint of hopefulness, a hint of guardedness.

"I think that would be lovely," Aileen threw an arm around each twin, bumping Kier's back with her bag, and hugged them. "See you soon."

They embraced her in return.

It is not as though we will not be with you, Kayl pulsed.

You cannot be rid of us that easily, Kier added.

Wouldn't dream of it. She chuckled and squeezed them a little tighter. *But I'll still miss your presence.*

After the trio withdrew from each other, Aileen and Shalla set out toward the spaceport, and the twins watched their mate leave. They both felt that tug at their hearts, at their souls, urging them to follow her, chastising them for letting her out of their sight. But she was so happy, so *alive*. How could they have told her no?

When the universe had only just opened to them, how could they deny her anything?

They stepped into the parts shop, where Kier forced himself to peruse the hardware rather than acknowledging that the tether between their souls was lengthening, stretching, tightening. That Aileen was getting farther away.

The twins soon found their way to the back of the shop, where dozens of bins held a variety of hardware in varying shapes and sizes, some of which had clearly been salvaged for resale.

Kier pulsed, *Just had to come in here, did we?*

I want to replace the valves on the drink dispenser, Kayl replied, not looking away from the parts before him. *I tire of having to clean a mess whenever I get a drink.*

I have shown you a hundred times how to avoid making a mess, Kayl.

And I have told you we should not have to resort to realigning the nozzle and tilting the entire machine to avoid spraying liquid everywhere.

Their bickering continued after Kayl selected a set of parts, which Kier insisted were the wrong size. Using their hands as makeshift rulers, they debated the width of the valves, the length of the nozzles, and eventually found themselves arguing about the color of the dispenser's handle.

I definitely made the right choice, Aileen pulsed, her smirk evident in her *aerys*.

While clearly, I did not, Kier replied.

"I will return to the ship, pull out the parts, and bring them back here to show you, Kier," Kayl said, brandishing a polished valve control on one hand. "This is the right size."

The door to the shop opened, and someone entered with hurried footsteps.

"Did those daevahs happen to come in here?" the newcomer asked the shopkeeper. The speaker was panting lightly, but their voice was familiar.

The twins straightened and turned their heads toward the front of the store, but they could see neither the shopkeeper nor the newcomer due to the aisles of shelving.

"Yeah, they're in the back." The shopkeeper chuckled. "Was

about to go see if they needed help. They've been looking at those valves for quite a while."

The newcomer was hurrying toward the twins before the shopkeeper had finished speaking, rapid steps moving along a side aisle. A young, lanky kaital with blue skin and big, black eyes skidded around the corner and staggered to a halt as he saw the twins.

"Ardu?" Kier placed a hand on the youth's shoulder to steady him. "What is wrong?"

"Ialle needs you," Ardu said breathlessly. The first time the twins had come to town, the kaital had been thrumming with excited energy, but a shadow lay over that energy now.

Unease pooled in Kier's gut. "What happened?"

Ardu shook his head. "A ship came into the spaceport."

The twins exchanged a look, brows furrowed.

"Yes. The repairs were completed on our ship," Kayl said. "We relocated it to the spaceport at Shalla's suggestion."

"Not yours. There was another, landed a few minutes ago. They made it to the canteen before Ialle could talk with them, but she's in there with them now."

Something rippled through the twins' psychic link, something dark and creeping.

Though Kayl shared his brother's unease, none of it came through in his voice as he asked, "Why send for us then?"

Kier leaned down, putting his face closer to Ardu's and catching the youth's gaze. "Has anyone been hurt?"

"No, no one's hurt." The kaital took in a big gulp of air, which seemed to calm his nerves, if only slightly. "She told me to find you because the newcomers asked about you."

Kier's heart stuttered. That dark thing swept into his chest, twisting around his insides and spreading debilitating cold. Thoughts rocketed back and forth between the twins, a thousand possibilities, a thousand considerations, but all those thoughts led to one name—Vrykhan.

They could not have found us so quickly, Kayl pulsed. *It was a blind jump, and the Fang is untraceable. For all they know, we could be anywhere.*

I do not know what you would like to hear, brother, Kier replied.

That it is not possible.

I will not lie to you.

What's going on? Aileen pulsed, psychic voice heavy with concern. *I feel your panic.*

Without a word, Kier and Kayl tossed the parts they'd been holding back into their bins and strode toward the door, sharing what little they knew of the situation with Aileen.

You are in Tallian's hangar? Kayl asked.

Yeah, we are. Just got inside, she responded.

Kayl's mind-voice took on a commanding tone. *Remain inside until we come for you.*

It was answered by another swelling of concern from Aileen.

Fear not, na'diya, Kier pulsed gently. *All will be well.*

He longed to tell her that they were just overreacting, that their fear was unwarranted, but the dread gathering in his stomach said otherwise.

Kayl shoved the door open. As he and Kier exited the shop, he pulsed, *Do you still have your blaster, Aileen?*

Her trepidation was palpable as she answered. *Yeah. It's hidden, just like you said. I'm not...not going to need to use it, am I?*

We will do all we can to ensure you will not, Kier replied. *You need not be afraid,* na'diya.

Only prepared, Kayl added.

All right. I feel like I'm always telling you two this, but really—be careful.

Kier gave the only response he could. *Nothing will keep us from you.*

I'm holding you to that.

The twins stalked toward the canteen side by side, hands dipping toward their blasters. They shielded Aileen from the maelstroms inside themselves as best they could. Foremost amongst their emotions was their old, dear friend, rage.

Ardu's footsteps sounded rapidly behind the twins, but he seemed unable to match their determined strides. His voice was thin when he called, "Wait! Slow down!"

Would Kier and Kayl ever know more than the most fleeting peace? Had they been cursed as children, doomed to lives rife with pain, suffering, and violence? They'd long since wearied of such an existence; now that they had Aileen, they outright rejected it. How many more times would their old life try to drag them back?

If it is them, Kier pulsed, *if it is* him...

It ends here, Kayl replied. His tail lashed behind him, its every movement harsher than the last.

You know what happened the last time we just charged in, Kier.

I do. And this time we will finish what we begin.

As they neared the canteen's entrance, Ardu said, "Ialle asked me to—"

"We must see to this matter, Ardu," said Kier.

Kayl grasped the door handle and cast a heavy glance at the young kaital. "Stay outside."

Ardu's eyes were huge and pleading. "But she wanted me to tell her when you got here."

"We will tell her." Kier dropped his hand, swept aside the layered fabric of his clothing, and grasped the blaster holstered at his hip. He tugged it free.

"*Before* you went in."

Drawing his own blaster with his free hand, Kayl pulled the door open.

Kier stepped through without hesitation. Blaster raised, he swept his gaze across the space, absorbing the details without conscious thought. He'd expected an all too familiar scene—locals on their knees, held at gunpoint by leering pirates. Vrykhan perusing the *merchandise*. But the canteen was almost deserted save for two groups—Emai and Orassic sitting with their backs against the bar counter and Ialle at one of the tables with two guests.

His brother moved up behind him, covering the angles Kier was not. The twins froze.

That is not right. I cannot be seeing whatever it is my mind thinks I am seeing.

Kayl managed only one word—*How?*

Ialle turned her head toward them, eyes rounding. She slapped two hands on the table and shoved herself onto her feet, throwing her arms wide. "Easy. No need to shoot up Emai's place."

"Especially not after we just cleaned up," Emai called from the counter.

The twins were vaguely aware of Ardu entering behind them, largely because Ialle's gaze flicked past them before she put on a decidedly *what-the-fuck* expression.

"Ah, there they are! Do you two always make such dramatic entrances?" asked one of Ialle's guests. The gray-skinned sedhi's yellow *qal* marks glowed dimly, his black and yellow eyes were intent upon the twins, and his silky, violet robe was parted to expose his sculpted torso. His lips were slanted in a smirk.

"No," Ialle said, her stance stiff as her eyes shifted from the twins to the sedhi. "When they came to town a few days ago, they just walked in like normal people. Without weapons drawn."

The burly vorgal seated beside the sedhi barked a laugh. Jagged scars covered one side of his head, and his short tusks jutted from his wide grin. The tattoo on his cheek marked him as part of the elite vorgal military, the Vanguard. "Not how they introduced themselves to me."

"What the fuck?" Kier rasped.

"I could ask the same thing," Arcanthus replied.

"Me too," said Ialle. "You two want to lower your blasters? If there's some conflict here, we—"

"No conflict," Thargen said. "They're just so fucking overjoyed to see us that they're speechless."

"Yeah, sure looks like joy to me," the dacrethian muttered.

"You two just going to stand there all fucking night?" Thargen thumped the tabletop with a fist. "We don't have all night to waste."

"Indeed," said Arcanthus, bending a cybernetic leg and bracing it over the knee of the other. "Really, it's all right. You can lower your weapons. You might even be so bold as to put them away, but that's all up to you."

"What the fuck?" Kayl said.

"You two have really summed up the evening's events." Ialle looked from the twins to Arcanthus and Thargen again. "Maybe some explanations are in order here?"

"Told you already"—Thargen scooped a handful of a cracker-like snack from a bowl on the table and shoved it into his mouth, crunching it as he continued—"we're basically best friends."

"You fought alongside them in *one* battle," Arcanthus said.

"Yeah. But it was a really fucking good battle."

"Well, I've spoken with them regularly over the last six months, well beyond the purview of the arrangement I made with them."

"Not exactly sure what that means," Thargen replied, taking another handful of the snack, "but if I remember right, that arrangement only happened because I introduced them to you."

Moving slowly, Ialle picked up a mug from the table and raised it to her face. She peered inside, then sniffed at its contents. "Emai, how strong did you make this drink tonight?"

"It's not the drink," Orassic said with a chuckle. "It's...whatever in the seven thunders this is."

Arcanthus swung his leg down and rose from his stool, spreading his arms. The robe dangled to either side, leaving his loin cloth to do all the work of covering his private parts. "It's a happy reunion."

Feeling oddly numb, Kier lowered his arm, and the blaster nearly fell from his nerveless fingers. Beside him, Kayl did the same. They both asked the question Kayl had posed through their link moments before. "How?"

"Well, I suppose that's progress," Ialle muttered before taking a long, long swig of her drink.

I'm...having trouble telling just what it is I'm feeling from you two, Aileen pulsed. Her *aerys* was a perfect blend of concern and confusion. *Everything all right over there?*

Kier nearly laughed aloud, and he couldn't stop himself from shaking his head. *It...is an unexpected friend. Arcanthus. And we cannot tell what we are feeling either.*

Shock. I believe it is shock, Kayl pulsed.

A torrent of relief flowed from Aileen. Thankfully, it eased the twins' shock and fought back the numbness that had gripped them.

We are still trying to make sense of this, Kier thought, *but know we are safe,* na'diya.

Kayl added, *And we will see you soon.*

Good, Aileen replied. *I can't wait.*

Arcanthus's smirk faded as he lowered his arms and strode toward the twins. The hard expression that settled on his face was unlike any the twins had seen from him—though it certainly fit what they knew of his history in the slave pits and the deadly skills he'd developed as a result.

"Before I get into how, my friends, let me say that I am *extremely* disappointed in you." Arcanthus's voice dropped low. "The arrangement we made was a mere formality. You are ostensibly part of my little organization, and you happen to have helped save the lives of two people I hold very dear. I've come to hold the both of you quite dear, as well, despite your efforts to prevent me from doing so." At that last bit, Arcanthus quite pointedly looked at Kayl.

"I asked you not to go into Eternal Paradise alone," he continued, "because there are two of you, and while you're quite skilled, your target had a fucking army at his disposal. If you damned fools hadn't cut off communication, you would've known that we were on our way to help."

Arcanthus moved closer still, eyes shifting from Kayl to Kier and back again repeatedly—with that third eye on his forehead doing the same in reverse. "You have been fighting for a noble cause, but it is not a fight I want you to die for."

Kayl huffed through his nose. "We have always been willing to—"

Arcanthus raised a finger, silencing Kayl. "I don't care. You're willing to die, that's fine. But I am not willing to remain idle while you run off to do so alone."

"Me neither," Thargen called.

"We were not alone," Kier said.

"I am not going to argue semantics with you, my friends," Arcanthus replied. "You were together. That still counts as alone to me. If you had taken the time to hear me out, perhaps we would not be on a fringe world twenty million light years from civilization, with me having spent the whole damned trip here wondering whether we were going to find you dead or alive."

Ialle folded her lower arms across her abdomen, resting an upper elbow on her forearm. She took another sip of her drink and glanced at Thargen. "So...is the sedhi like their adopted father?"

Arcanthus glared at her. "I am not that much older than them."

"Just a lot more sensitive," said Thargen.

With a comically heavy sigh, Arcanthus shook his head. "None of this has gone according to plan."

Somewhere within the twins, a realization had occurred. Kier had felt it for a long while—ever since they'd met Thargen and his terran mate, Yuri—but only now did it truly come into focus. Arcanthus and his crew had welcomed Kier and Kayl into their home, into their lives, had accepted the twins despite their eccentricities, their stubbornness, and their tendency to shun assistance.

For too many years, Kier and Kayl had been in constant motion, relentlessly hunting, but as far as their lives went, they'd been static. They'd been stuck. They'd never moved past being frightened, angry children who couldn't trust anyone but one another, who couldn't let anyone in.

Thargen and Arcanthus had helped the twins take their first real step toward changing. Their first real step in overcoming the past and finding a new family after being alone for much, much too long. Had it not been for their experiences with this sedhi, his mate, and his crew, the twins might have had far more difficulty in accepting Aileen as their mate and embracing her as wholly as they had.

"We are sorry," Kayl said, bowing slightly and placing a fist over his heart.

Kier copied the gesture. "And we are glad to see you."

"And as though everything else wasn't enough," Arcanthus said, "now you're arguing wi— What did you say?"

Smiling, the twins repeated their words.

Arcanthus braced a hand on his hip, stroking his chin with the other as he regarded the twins. "That is...odd. Usually, everyone argues with me for much longer than necessary before ultimately conceding. You've skipped a few steps."

"We should not have gone into Eternal Paradise alone," said Kayl.

"And we should not have cut off communications," Kier said. "But we do not regret what happened."

How could they, when minutes of delay might've meant never finding their mate? Waiting for help could have led to Aileen's capture or death. Even knowing all they did now, neither Kier nor Kayl would've chosen differently.

"Well, I..." Arcanthus deflated slightly. "Thank you. And I am happy to see you both alive and well."

The twins nodded. After they holstered their pistols, Kier pointed at the table, where only Thargen remained sitting, still munching on his snacks. "Now, Ar—"

Arcanthus wagged a finger. "Ah, ah, ah. We are with *new* friends, Sol'Kier."

Kier narrowed his eyes. "Sit down, *Alkorin*."

"And explain *everything*." Kayl's tone was as firm as the sedhi's had been earlier.

"So assertive." With his usual smirk back in place, Arcanthus sauntered to the table, the twins keeping close behind. He dropped onto a stool and leaned forward, propping his elbows on the table. His expectant gaze settled upon the twins as they sat across from him.

"It does not comfort us when you are silent," Kayl said.

"Comforts me." Ialle stepped away from the table. "Just make sure these two don't make any trouble, and—"

"Sit, Ialle." Though his voice retained its natural charisma, Arcanthus had spoken with an underlying air of command.

The tall dacrethian paused. "Listen, sedhi, I only had two goals here. One was to make sure you aren't a danger to the town. The other was supposed to be giving Kier and Kayl a chance to get away in the case that you and your vorgal friend came here with ill intent toward them. As long as you behave, none of this is my concern—or my business."

"You certainly have a quaint, quiet little town here, arbiter," Arcanthus replied. "I do not doubt that is due in no small part to your leadership. So please, for the sake of your people, sit and listen."

At the counter, both Emai and Orassic's expressions darkened.

Ialle kept her features neutral and her tone even despite the nature of her next question. "Are you threatening my town, sedhi?"

Arcanthus shook his head.

She stared at him for several seconds longer. Then, spitting a curse, Ialle returned to the table, folded her lower arms across her chest again, and gestured for Arcanthus to speak.

Embers of foreboding smoldered in Kier's gut. "How did you find us?"

"Ah, yes, the untraceable ship. It was a simple process." Arcanthus turned his palms toward the ceiling and shrugged. "Some months ago, I installed a tracking device on the *Fang*."

"You *what?*" Kayl growled.

Kier clasped his hands together and placed them atop the table, forcing himself to breathe slow and steady. The twins' anger was justified, but if they allowed the emotion to take control, it risked tapping into their deeper fury.

Arcanthus flattened his hands on the table. Despite his limbs being made of metal, they seemed to be instilled with a strangely organic tension. "Tragedy and near-tragedy have befallen myself and my associates far too many times. So, recently, I have made a deliberately more proactive effort to curtail would-be tragedies."

"That gives you no right to install a tracking device on our ship with neither our knowledge nor our consent," Kier said.

Kayl's tail lashed behind him. "That is a deep violation of what trust we had shared. It was wrong."

Again, Arcanthus leaned forward, and the table creaking softly beneath his weight. "Perhaps we should debate ethics another time." His gaze flicked toward Ialle. "When we are able to more openly discuss the actions we have *all* taken in pursuit of our particular goals."

Ialle threw back her head, dumping the remainder of her drink into her mouth. Then she held the empty mug up in Emai's direction and wiggled it.

"You said we're closed, remember?" Emai asked.

"Doesn't mean the drinks should stop," Ialle replied.

Arcanthus's third eye tracked Emai's movement as the borian walked behind the counter and grabbed a fresh mug, but his other eyes remained on the twins. "Even without the tracker, which I must add was broadcasting on a very secure, highly encrypted channel through your ship's also very secure, highly encrypted comms array, I knew you were going after him. That's why we left immediately after I gave you the information."

Ialle smoothed a palm back over her head. "Normally I wouldn't ask for specifics, sedhi, but you're being really, really vague."

"The twins have spent most of their lives hunting a notorious and very dangerous pirate. Information I uncovered suggested he would be at a particular location at a particular time. Fully aware that they intended to do something rash, I gathered some of our mutual friends and attempted to rendezvous with Sol'Kier and Sol'Kayl before they got themselves killed.

"Our dear twins will have to fill in the details of their little adventure, but as you can see"—Arcanthus waved at the Kier and Kayl—"they survived despite their best efforts, and I failed despite mine."

"Ah." Ialle studied the twins with new curiosity, as though again taking their measure.

"Following us to Eternal Paradise is easy enough to explain," said Kier, frowning, "but how did you find us here?"

Arcanthus snickered. "Didn't pay even a bit of attention, did you? The tracker."

Kayl's brows fell. "Which you said was broadcasting through the *Fang's* communications array."

"Correct."

"The same communications array that was inoperative before we even made the jump to this system."

"Yes. That is where speculation comes in, so you will have to bear with me."

"Please"—Kier unclasped his hands to turn a palm up—"speculate to your heart's content."

"I assume your ship was damaged." Arcanthus waited for the twins to nod before continuing. "The tracker was still transmitting, but said damage caused that signal to broadcast openly. The protections afforded by the ship's encryption and security were essentially gone, blasting an indecipherable but detectable signal out into the cosmos."

Jaw muscles ticking, Kayl drew in a slow, deep breath.

Kier dragged a hand through his hair, barely noticing the scrape of his claws against his scalp. "We had a signal being openly broadcast. From our ship."

Emai strode over, eyeing Arcanthus as she passed a fresh drink to Ialle. The dacrethian took the mug, threw it back, and drained at least half of it in a single draught. The borian braced a hand on the table and leaned upon it heavily, making it clear that she wasn't going anywhere.

Arcanthus barely afforded Emai a glance. "That is my theory, yes."

"A signal that anyone could have detected," Kayl said through his teeth.

"Yes. I accessed comms equipment from around the universe, pinging countless nodes in search of the slightest blip that could've been your signal. It was like trying to find a particular drop of blood on the floor of a fighting pit. That's the point at which I grew convinced you were dead."

Thargen laughed. "Told you they wouldn't fucking die."

Arcanthus waved the vorgal off. "But after a long, long search, we detected the signal from this system. That signal promptly went out again. Yet I would not be deterred, so on we chased. I imagine it was that nasty cosmic storm that knocked out the signal right after I located it."

Orassic joined them now, holding a dark bottle in each hand. He slid one across the table to Thargen. "Yeah, the storms tend to do that."

Ialle said, "They interfere with the satellites and comm arrays. Doesn't matter how much we boost a signal, it's not making it off-planet during those storms."

"That make sense," Arcanthus replied. "It also explains why the *Azkazor* hadn't yet approached the planet when we first entered the system."

Kier's insides twisted into knots. "What did you just say?"

"Right." Arcanthus drummed his fingers on the table. "Well, that openly broadcasted tracking device signal might *possibly* have been what the pirates used to track you to this planet."

Ialle's eyes flared. "Are you saying there are pirates on Omega IV?"

"*Ja'skaal*, Alkorin, why would you not *begin* with that information?" Kier demanded.

Arcanthus waved his hands placatingly. "Easy, easy. I already have people working on it, all right? I'm taking care of it."

"Taking care of it?" Kayl asked, pushing up from his seat. "Alkorin, the *Azkazor* is a battle cruiser with dozens of drop ships, hundreds of guns, and a crew numbering in the thousands!"

Kier also sprang from his seat, pacing away from the table. His heart raced, pumping fiery blood through his veins, and his chest was tight. Between his mind and Kayl's, there wasn't a shred of silence or stillness to be found.

"That's never stopped you two from charging right in, has it?" Arcanthus asked, shifting his weight onto one elbow. "I have my best people on it and th—"

"Except for me," Thargen said.

"Right. But you understand, Thargen, that you're reserved for less delicate matters."

The vorgal grinned. "Fuck yeah."

"And those people have matters well in hand," Arcanthus continued. "The *Azkazor* is in orbit, and I am tracking its exact location. Additionally, I've hacked into their communications and have been monitoring them. They're a particularly quiet bunch, it seems, but I do know they've only landed one drop ship somewhere well outside town. An advance scouting party, if you will."

"What is wrong with you, sedhi?" Ialle cupped the sides of her head with all four hands. "A force like that... This town doesn't stand a chance if those pirates launch a raid. They'd take whatever they want from us."

"They would take you." Kayl's voice was deep, raw, unapologetic. "They would take you and every other person in this town they could sell for even a few credits."

"And then they would take everything you own, erasing the lives you've made here," Kier said.

"Excellent job reassuring the local authorities, my friends," Arcanthus said.

"She does not need to be reassured, Arc, she needs to be informed."

"Fuck," was all Ialle managed to say, arm muscles flexing subtly as she pushed in on her head from both sides. "*Fuck.*"

Arcanthus tipped his head back, sweeping loose strands of his long, black hair between his curved horns. "Please, everyone, it is all under control. They most assuredly plan to raid the town, but not until after they've located our esteemed twins here. And their raid will not succeed, regardless."

"You'll forgive me, sedhi, if I don't have the greatest confidence in your promises," Ialle said scathingly.

"That's fair. But as I've mentioned, you will eventually come to understand that I am right."

Plans coalesced, collapsed, and reformed in the twins' minds. Knowing that a battle cruiser filled with savage pirates lurked somewhere overhead was intimidating, but they'd spent their lives preparing for this. Though they'd longed for a clear shot at Vrykhan, they'd understood the likely reality—that they'd have to battle through droves of pirates to reach their target and have their revenge.

And even if their burning need for vengeance had diminished, the twins were ready to deliver it now more than ever—because they had Aileen to protect.

Though Navaire didn't contain nearly as many innocent bystanders as Eternal Paradise had, the situation was far from ideal. Vrykhan and his pirates would not hesitate to abuse any advantages they could find. That meant no one in town was safe—whether as slaves, hostages, or living shields, Vrykhan would use them.

"You need to get your people somewhere sheltered," Kayl said.

Kier nodded, hand dropping to his blaster. "Preferably somewhere you can defend with a small force."

"The tunnels," Orassic said before taking a swig of his drink. Though his expression was still hard, he seemed largely unshaken.

Ialle nodded. "Our best chance. But if they cause a cave in…"

"We have a lot of people who know the underground," Emai said. "The pirates would have to collapse half those tunnels before we ran out of ways to escape."

"As long as we have Ardu with us"—Orassic nodded toward the waifish kaital, who still stood near the canteen's entrance, looking uncertain—"we'll be all right."

"The pirate's scouting party only took position after it started getting dark," Arcanthus said, rising from his seat. "If you're going to move your people, Ialle, do so as discreetly as possible. The pirates may well accelerate their plans if they see the populace fleeing."

"Right." Ialle activated her wrist holocom and initiated a call. "No connection?"

As she attempted to make the call again, Emai and Orassic tried their own holocoms; they all received the same message. Just like Shalla had earlier.

"Storm's been over too long for this to still be an issue," Orassic said.

Arcanthus sighed. "The pirates have very likely knocked out intergalactic comms and jammed local comms."

Fresh rage roiled within Kier. How many times had this sort of scenario played out, and in how many places? "It is how Vrykhan operates. Isolate a settlement, ensuring there will be no help…"

"And then attack with brutality and speed," Kayl said.

Ialle growled a curse before pointing to Emai, Orassic, and Ardu. "You three, come with me. We're going to have to spread the word the old-fashioned way. Kier, Kayl, be careful." The dacrethian frowned at Arcanthus. "We make it through this, sedhi, and you're buying the entire town a round of drinks."

Arcanthus snickered. "I had assumed that me saving your lives would've been payment enough, but fine, dacrethian. I'll buy a round of drinks for the entire town. Would you like meals thrown in with that?"

Emai glowered at him. "You going to cook all that food?"

Thargen slapped a hand down and shoved himself to his feet, making the table shake even though it was bolted to the floor. "I'll cook."

"Let's forget the food, then," Ialle said. "Come on."

She and the other locals hurried to the door, Orassic nudging Ardu along with them.

Kayl fixed an intense gaze upon the sedhi. "Should you have any more information, Alkorin, now is the time to share."

"As I said, they've been relatively quiet on their comms. They took position on a rise just outside the spaceport, and they already seem to be marking targets." Smoldering anger crept into his normally smooth tone. "They mentioned a terran entering a hangar just a few minutes ago. These slaving skrudges never miss an opportunity to take a terran. The profit is too high."

The fear that had assailed the twins upon learning of a recently arrived ship was nothing; it had been a whisper of cool air, a negligible shiver down their spine, a few bumps raised on their skin. But the fear they experienced now...

It was utter consuming—black, frigid, and impossibly heavy, it wrapped around them and paralyzed their every muscle, turning their marrow to ice.

"What is it?" Arcanthus asked, tilting his head. "I've never seen that look on either of your faces."

Thargen growled. "But I recognize it."

Arcanthus might never have frowned as deeply as he did in that moment. "Me too."

"You know the terran," Thargen said.

In raw, strained voices, the twins replied, "She is our mate."

FORTY-FIVE

"ALL THIS..." Tallian shook his head. The little crease that had formed between his brows was identical to the one that sometimes formed between Shalla's.

The table before him, which Shalla had cleared of parts and tools with a frantic energy, was now haphazardly piled with a variety of items—dresses, blouses, pants, woven scarfs, a reversible cape that was tawny on one side and a rich forest green on the other, decorative hairpins and combs, a delicate silver chain with tiny dangling charms and a violet stone that had wound perfectly around Shalla's horns to fit like a tiara.

There were numerous fragrant soaps and scented candles, two bottles of perfume—which Aileen had been sure to confirm was, in fact, perfume—and a leather satchel with intricate patterns pressed into it. To one side stood several jars of vibrant paint.

The young uriti had said Triss was well past due for a fresh paint job, which Aileen had agreed, and had selected several different colors to allow Triss their choice.

The crown jewel of Shalla's treasure hoard was the battered metal tray perched precariously atop everything else. She'd upturned a cloth sack and poured an assortment of crystals and stones onto the tray as she'd excitedly explained, with voice raised to overcome the clattering, that she planned to incorporate them in the little trinkets she created.

Aileen hadn't lied about overdoing it. She'd known it as she and Shalla had added items to their pile in The Glittering Cavern, had known it long before their haul had become so...excessive. But every time she'd told herself no more, she'd looked over to see the elation on Shalla's face as the adolescent tried on clothing or jewelry, and Aileen's resolve had crumbled.

She didn't regret her decision. It had felt like...like a mother-daughter experience, the sort that neither Aileen nor Shalla had enjoyed in years. The sort that they'd both sorely needed.

There was no replacing Veeani, but helping Shalla recapture the joy of shopping with her mother, even only faintly, only fleetingly, was priceless. And for just a little while, Aileen had felt closer to her maw.

"Well, it's a bit much, isn't it?" Tallian asked, looking first at Shalla and then Aileen.

"Really, it's fine," Aileen replied.

Shalla smiled pleadingly.

"We shouldn't accept this." Tallian rubbed a large, callused hand over his cheek. "Your daevahs agreed to pay in credits."

The adolescent uriti's smile crumbled.

"Oh, no. Please, Tallian, I didn't mean to give you the wrong impression," Aileen said hurriedly, raising her hands in a placating gesture. "None of this is meant as payment."

Tallian's gaze shifted to his daughter, and the wariness in his expression gave way to guilt. "What is it meant to be then?"

"Gifts."

His brows angled down toward his nose. "Do all terrans give such excessive gifts to strangers?"

Aileen shrugged. "Some do, I guess. I'd say it's definitely not typical, but it's not unheard of."

He leaned an elbow on the arm of his wheelchair. "So why now? Why my daughter?"

"You don't need to be so hard on her about it, Father," Shalla said, her voice strong and steady. "Aileen's a good person, and so are the twins."

"Ah, *Cheya*," he rumbled. "I'm just trying to protect you."

Shalla sighed, but a small smile crept back onto her lips. "I know, *Rhunai*. But I *can* look out for myself too. At least somewhat."

Tallian snorted. "Every time I think about that, I feel suddenly older."

The exchange warmed Aileen's heart. Such relationships between father and daughter were precious, and they made her think of her da, with all the bittersweetness that came along with it.

"I wanted to do this because Shalla is amazing," Aileen said, smiling at the girl. "She's brilliant, talented, and so, so driven. I don't know anything about fixing spaceships, but I'm pretty sure it would've taken most mechanics twice as long to finish the work she did on the *Fang*."

Cheeks darkening, Shalla looked away.

"And her joy is just...it's uplifting." Aileen combed her fingers through her hair, sweeping it back. "So I wanted to do something for her. Not just in thanks, but because she deserves all the happiness she can get."

The gruff elder uriti's expression softened, his eyes still on Shalla. "You're right, Aileen. My daughter is amazing."

Shalla met his gaze. "Thanks, *Rhunai*. You're not so bad either."

He laughed, and one of those small braids—which Shalla said he'd woven in remembrance of his mate—fell in front of his ear. With a carefulness almost bordering on reverence, tucked it into the knot atop his head. "I'd say your amazingness was inherited from me, but you favor your mother much more. And that's a good thing for you."

"About *Rhana*..." Shalla looked down again and frowned, though the expression seemed more thoughtful than sad. "There's one more thing to show you, Father."

She reached into the bag that had, only minutes ago, been filled with half the items spread on the table, and withdrew a small box carved from pale wood. As she carefully set the box down and opened the lid, she said, "This is for you."

Tallian watched as his daughter removed a chain necklace from the box. She stooped down, and he leaned forward, allowing her to clasp the chain around his neck. He delicately lifted the pendant dangling from the necklace and stilled, staring at it with an unreadable expression.

Meanwhile, Shalla took a second necklace out of the box, identical to the first but for the pendant's design being flipped. She moved to put that chain around his neck too, but Tallian caught her hand before she could.

The pale red stone set in each pendant glowed softly now that they'd come so close to each other.

Aileen couldn't help but think of the bracelets on her wrists—and of her mates.

There were no words to rightly express her gratefulness and relief that their fears had proved unfounded. Kier and Kayl were okay. There wasn't going to be another fight, and she wouldn't have to stand by, helpless and consumed by worry, as they battled elsewhere.

She yearned for the moment when the stones on her bracelets would glow again. The moment when she could draw her mates into her arms and tell them that she wasn't sure if she'd ever let them out of sight again.

She tightened her hold on her own bag just a little, which held the only item that wasn't for Shalla or Tallian. It held Aileen's gift for the twins. And though she couldn't completely silence the whisper of doubt in the back of her mind—which told her the twins would think the gift foolish, pointless—she was more excited than anything to give it to them.

"Your mother loved these mesmureens," Tallian said, voice low and thick. "She always said—"

"That they are like magic." Shalla smiled, eyes shimmering with tears.

"Magic. Their glow, their colors...and that they ended up here, so far away from where they were formed, but still find comfort in each other...all magic."

Aileen's chest constricted; Tallian wasn't only talking about the stones. He saw his own story in them—his story with his mate.

"The bracelets Aileen and the daevahs wear reminded me of *Rhana*. I wanted you to have something to remind you of her too."

Tallion cupped Shalla's cheek. "Ah, my *cheya*... I already do."

Tears stung Aileen's eyes.

"But why two?" Tallian asked.

"One for you, and one for *Rhana*," Shalla replied. "And while you wear both necklaces together, the stones will glow, and you'll know she is with you."

Tallian let out a slow, heavy breath. Eyes glistening, he gently freed the necklace from Shalla's hold, took it in both hands, and clasped it around her neck. He covered the chain with his palm, his big hand stretching across the girl's collarbone from shoulder to shoulder. "Now *we* will always know she's with *us*."

Not going to cry. You are not going to cry, Aileen.

The uriti's hugged each other, and Aileen's heart ached in the best of ways. Though she'd only spent a few short days on Omega IV, her memories of this place were filled with instances like this—people coming together in love. Of course, everything she'd shared with Kier and Kayl would always be foremost of those memories, but there was so much more than that. Navaire's people would leave an impression upon Aileen forever.

The twins had saved her life, freed her from slavery, and loved her so, so fiercely. And the people here had shown her compassion and warmth, which had been rare things in Aileen's life for such a long time.

"Don't think this'll get you out of your work tomorrow," Tallian grumbled, smiling.

Shalla chuckled. "Why would I want to get out of work?"

The two finally withdrew from one another, and the glow of their mesmureens gradually faded.

"We're going to eat at the canteen with Aileen and the twins, *Rhunai*." The young uriti looked her father over and frowned. "You should clean yourself up. Perhaps change your shirt."

He laughed and shook his head. "See? You're all the reminder of Veeani I need."

"I'm not joking."

"Oh, I am aware of that, Shalla. When did I indicate that I wanted to—"

Panic blasted into Aileen's mind, dragging along a fear so strong and cold that it staggered her and stole her breath. She dropped a hand onto the table to steady herself.

"What's wrong?" Shalla hurried over to Aileen.

Aileen lifted her hand—in which she still held the bag—to her temple. Overwhelming emotion had flowed through the psychic link before, and it was usually euphoric, but this...

This was unlike anything she'd ever experienced. It was too much. Thoughts tumbled into her mind from the twins, but they were so frantic, so jumbled, that she couldn't make sense of them.

"Aileen?"

She barely heard Tallian. *Please, Kier, Kayl. I can't... I don't know what's happening.*

Na'diya. Their voices growled that word in her head, filling it with that icy fear, with a fiery urgency.

They are coming for you, Kier pulsed.

Her eyes widened. That warning should've been too vague for her to understand, but those words acted as a cipher, decoding the chaos that had preceded them, and everything clicked into place.

Vrykhan, the tretin pirate who'd enslaved the twins as children and killed their parents, who'd terrorized, murdered, and abducted countless thousands, who'd mercilessly attacked Eternal paradise over a personal squabble with Saduuk and had nearly killed Aileen, was *here*.

"Oh, God," Aileen rasped, hardly aware of the words leaving her mouth.

"Is it Kier and Kayl?" Shalla asked. "Are they hurt?"

Lock the doors and hide, Kayl pulsed. *Now!*

We are on our way. Despite his attempt at reassurance, there was a hard, desperate edge in Kier's *aerys*.

Aileen opened her mouth to speak, but her chest was so tight that she couldn't get out a sound. Her eyes darted from Shalla to Tallian; they both wore looks of concern, though the elder uriti's was much more wary.

Vrykhan wouldn't stop at killing the twins. What he'd done on Tilara and Eternal Paradise stood as proof of that. Shalla and Tallian, Emai and Orassic, Ialle, Ardu, Weyel, Sira and Sala—*everyone* in this town was in danger.

"Lock the hangar," Aileen breathed, turning toward the rear exit. "We need to—"

The back door burst inward with a great bang, part of the latch flying off and clattering on the floor.

Aileen started, bumping back into the table, and Shalla let out a startled gasp.

Angling his body so his broad frame could fit, a large bokkan stepped through the doorway. Three other aliens entered behind him. All wore mismatched pieces of armor that were painted and adorned with trinkets that granted them a primal, ruthless visage. Each carried a holstered blaster on their belt and a long, cylindrical weapon in hand.

Aileen's heart quickened; those long weapons were shock staves, just like Eternal Paradise's security team had used to subdue violent or unruly guests—and uncooperative *employees*.

Tallian rolled his wheelchair forward with a few powerful shoves, placing himself between the newcomers and Shalla and Aileen. "Is there a reason you saw fit to break my door?"

One of his hands eased behind his chair, and he waved Aileen and Shalla away.

The twins' voices had never been so loud in Aileen's mind. She felt everything from them—their heartbeats, racing even faster than hers; their panting breaths; their boots slamming against the ground in rapid succession as they sprinted toward her; their every volatile emotion. They called her name, but not with their voices, not with their minds—with their *souls*.

A female volturian with short hair and a scar across her cheek not unlike the one on Aileen's side stepped forward. "That's her. Saw one of the daevahs carrying her right before the other shot me."

"You need to leave," Tallian said, shifting himself closer to the pirates—and closer to a worktable that still had several tools laid upon it. "We're closed for the night."

"Whole town is closed," said the grinning male borian with a spiked strip of hair down the center of his head. "Forever."

"Take the females," the volturian commanded, "and remember, the warlord wants the terran unharmed."

"What about the cripple?" Asked the fourth alien, who had a brown carapace and an insect-like face.

The volturian snickered. "Worthless."

The twins' *aerysi* continued blasting Aileen's mind, and Tallian was waving his hand urgently, but Aileen couldn't move. She was painfully aware of the blaster strapped to her thigh, of the concealed slit on her pant leg that would allow her to access the weapon.

Could she use it? Would it make a difference? With four pirates, all armored, and only ten meters separating her from them...

The already tense air crackled with a new, electric energy that made the small hairs stand up on Aileen's skin. She wasn't sure what happened first, wasn't sure if the pirates darted forward because Tallian snatched a big wrench off the worktable, or if their sudden advance had prompted him to grab the tool. She only knew that everything surged into terrifying motion.

"Run!" Tallian shouted, throwing his chair into the path of the oncoming pirates.

Run! the twins yelled telepathically at the same instant.

Aileen didn't think—she just moved. Catching one of Shalla's arms, she ran for the labyrinth of parts that separated Tallian's workspace from the hangar's bay doors, dragging the stunned adolescent along.

"No," Shalla breathed, resisting Aileen. "*Rhunai!*"

Tallian snarled. Aileen glanced back to see him swing the wrench, striking the insect alien in the face. A dull crack and an undulating, agonized hiss punctuated the blow. Then the borian was there; his fist connected with Tallian's cheek.

The volturian and the bokkan charged after Aileen.

Gritting her teeth, Aileen tapped into all the strength she could muster and yanked Shalla forward. The sounds of struggle continued behind them. Tallian grunted, and the wrench again struck flesh. A shock staff buzzed, and the male uriti cried out in pain.

"*Rhunai!*" Shalla called again.

"Go!" Tallian roared.

The female volturian spat a curse, and furniture and tools crashed onto the floor.

Just before Aileen and Shalla reached the scrap maze, she glimpsed Tallian. The cords of his neck stood out, his teeth were bared, and his hair was coming undone, but he'd knocked down the insect alien and had tripped the volturian. The borian was struggling with him; Tallian had caught his opponent's wrist in one powerful hand, holding the shock staff at bay.

Dread and guilt wrapped their claws around Aileen's heart and squeezed. She needed to go back and help, needed to...

Needed to get Shalla to safety.

The bokkan batted aside the table where Shalla's purchases had been arranged as though it weighed nothing and charged forward.

Aileen plunged into the maze. She had no idea how to navigate it, no idea where any path led. All she had was a beacon to guide her —the inferno that was the twins' fury and fear, drawing steadily nearer like an approaching storm. Every turn she made was made to move toward it, toward them.

And to keep Shalla moving *away* from the danger behind them.

Tallian snarled again. The sound was followed by pained grunts and curses. More objects clattered to the floor, and the volturian snapped, "Shock him again."

The crackle of the shock staff was cut short by a tremendous crash near the spot Aileen had entered the scrap maze. Metal and parts slammed onto the floor and against each other hard enough to make the ground tremble under Aileen's feet.

"Not going to get very fucking far," the bokkan called.

Metal groaned, creaked, and crashed on concrete. The noise was deafening.

Fuck me, that's one way to get through a maze.

Shalla braced her hooves on the floor and tensed her every muscle. Aileen's shoulder screamed in protest as she was jerked to an abrupt halt.

The junk piled all around swayed and rattled as the bokkan bashed his way closer. Aileen cast a desperate, questioning glance back at her companion.

The adolescent shook her head firmly and gestured in the opposite direction from which Aileen had been running.

Aileen gave in to Shalla's lead as the chill of her dread deepened and spread. The young uriti tugged Aileen along, moving at a startling speed through narrow gaps between towering piles of trembling scrap.

Another massive crash, this time followed almost immediately by another, then another; the bokkan had triggered a chain reaction, and now the piles of scrap were like falling dominoes rushing toward Aileen and Shalla with increasing speed.

Clenching her jaw, Aileen focused on Shalla, focused on keeping her legs moving, focused on anything but that growing fear. They would get out of this. She'd get Shalla to safety, meet up with Kier and Kayl, and go back for Tallian. Everything would be—

Chaos engulfed Aileen, obliterating her senses with a cacophony so immense that it could only have been created by the world being torn asunder around her.

THE DIN from the hangar reached a ground-shaking peak. The bangs, booms, clangs, and groans blended into one overwhelming sound that echoed across the night sky and vibrated in Kayl's bones, making his heart skip several beats.

Aileen!

Somehow, Kayl sped his pace, and Kier kept right alongside him. The only thing to surpass the frenzied rhythm of their boots striking the ground was the thunderous drumming of their hearts.

How could a journey that had taken only minutes at a leisurely stroll feel as though it lasted an eternity at a sprint?

Up head and to the right stood Tallian's hangar, still two hundred meters distant. A faint cloud of dust rolled out through the open bay doors, gradually dissipating as the particles settled on the spaceport strip.

Aileen! Kayl's *aerys* repeated, this time in unison with his brother's.

A thousand thoughts clawed at the edges of the twins' minds, bolstered by a thousand terrifying, paralyzing possibilities, a thousand doubts, a thousand reckless courses of action. A thousand vows to ensure Vrykhan and his pirates paid for this with every last drop of their blood. But both twins held those thoughts back, both kept their minds as quiet as possible despite the emotions roaring inside them.

I...I'm all right, Aileen pulsed, psychic voice shaky. *At least I think so.*

The twins' relief couldn't fight back the tide of rage and fear upon which their souls were being swept away. All their willpower was focused on running; every shred of their beings was turned toward reaching their mate.

Almost there, Kier pulsed. *Almost.*

Neither twin noticed the breath sawing in and out of his lungs or the burning, constricted sensation in his chest and throat, neither noticed how his frantic pulse throbbed through his entire body.

One hundred and fifty meters.

Just a little farther. A little farther and—

"Fuck," Thargen growled from somewhere behind Kayl.

"Fuck indeed," Arcanthus said, voice uncharacteristically strained. "Get down!"

Keep running. Keep running. Forward, only forward, must go forward, must—

The hum of an antigrav drive made Kayl's skin prickle, especially since it came from behind him.

He and Kier glanced over their shoulders. They glimpsed a ship speeding toward them—a rugged, military-style dropship, the sort used by many armed forces across many galaxies to land troops and materiel on planetary surfaces.

A pair of free-moving turrets outfitted with plasma cannons jutted from the craft's sides. The cannons were angled toward Kayl and his companions.

"Ja'ska—"

Before the curse had finished leaving Kayl's mouth, the cannons lit up, bathing the sides of the ship with blue-white light. Thargen and Arcanthus surged forward with bursts of speed, each tackling one of the twins.

Kayl hit the ground with Arcanthus atop him just the deep thump-whine of the cannons reached him. Huge plasma bolts darted overhead, striking the ground only meters away and melting large holes in the strip. A second pair of shots sounded, striking close enough for a fleck of molten stone to land on Kayl's hand. Hissing through his teeth, he snatched his hand back and pressed it to the dirt beneath him.

The dropship passed overhead slowly. The antigrav drive's thrum resonated down to Kayl's marrow, building an unbearable pressure in his skull that would surely split it open. Those cannons drooped as though to target Kayl and his companions, but they did not fire again as the craft continued toward Tallian's hangar.

Still grasping his blaster in one hand, Kayl clawed at the ground, struggling to drag himself forward. But Arcanthus pressed his weight down atop Kayl; between his larger frame, augmented skeletal and muscular systems, and cybernetic limbs, the sedhi was *heavy*.

"Get off me," Kayl snarled.

Arcanthus grunted as, despite the disparities between their size and strength, Kayl nearly bucked him off.

"Listen to me, daevah," Arcanthus said. "We need to take cover, now."

Not far away, Kier battled Thargen's hold. The twins' minds grew increasingly frantic as the thoughts they'd been holding back began to break through.

No. No, Aileen, no! You need to get out of there, go back.

Need to get to her. Have to get to her.

Kill them. Will kill them all.

Have to go! Let go!

Every drop of blood. Every drop of Vrykhan's blood.

Aileen! Aileen, Aileen, na'diya, *be safe, be safe, please—*

Calm, Aileen pulsed, mind-voice thin but steady. *I'm alive. You're alive. Calm. I know you'll get here. I know.*

Rage quaked in the twins' cores, rage, and guilt, and helplessness, because she was in that hangar, and they were here. They weren't with her. They weren't protecting her *now,* when she needed them the most.

The dropship spun around as it touched down in front of the hangar, pointing its nose—and its plasma cannons—toward Kayl and the others. Large doors swung up on the sides, making the craft look like a beast that was raising its wings in a display of prowess.

Armor-clad pirates leapt out of the open doors, their boots kicking up dust as they landed. Most of them immediately turned toward Kayl.

Growling, Kayl angled his blaster on the ground and fired several quick shots toward the pirates. The plasma bolts looked pathetic compared to what the dropship had produced. Somewhere to the side, Kier also fired. The burst of projectiles struck armored chests and shoulders, and pieces of deflected plasma fell to create ember-like flecks of orange on the ground. One of the pirates dropped; another cried out in pain.

"This way." Arcanthus hooked an arm around Kayl's torso and dragged him up.

The pirates returned fire. The twins and their companions ran to the cover of a scrap pile near the center of the strip, ducking low behind the wreckage of an old hovertruck.

Kayl's fist tightened around the grip of his blaster. Plasma bolts hit the other side of the scrap pile, but there was too much metal between for them to penetrate.

The twins and their companions continued firing at the pirates, but their weapons would do little against armored opponents from such range apart from slow their advance.

"Guess they're serious," Thargen said.

"Because the tretin battle cruiser they have in orbit didn't already tell you that?" Arcanthus asked.

The emotions swirling through the twins grew more powerful than ever. Kayl and his brother struggled for control, struggled to view the situation with logic, with clarity, rather than through the lens of their fury.

They could not get to Aileen if they were dead.

"Our mate is in that hangar," Kier said. "We need to get to her *now*."

Arcanthus shifted his position, peering through a gap in their cover. "Well, only about thirty or so pirates to fight through to get there."

Thargen cocked his head to the side, cracking his neck. "A good warmup."

We do not have time for that, Kayl pulsed.

We have few options, Kayl, his brother replied.

Kayl activated his holocom. A few practiced flicks of his fingers brought up the automatic flight controller for the *Fang*—which could not connect to the ship. He growled. "Arcanthus, can you override their jammer?"

"Remotely? No. They're likely using a manually operated device." Arcanthus pointed toward the pirates. "And that device is very likely on their ship."

"And the only thing we have with enough firepower to take it out is the *Fang*," Kier said.

"Which we cannot call because of the jammer." Kayl let out a slow, harsh breath through his nose. A hundred curses danced on the tip of his tongue, and not one was sufficient to sum up his feelings.

"Sotera all over again," Thargen grumbled.

"Remember," someone shouted from near the dropship in a gravelly, malicious voice that was chillingly familiar to the twins, "I want those fucking daevahs *alive*."

"Well, that's to our advantage," Arcanthus muttered.

But Kayl barely heard him; he and Kier were occupied with sending frantic telepathic messages to Aileen.

Get out, you need to get out.

Get out of there. Run, Aileen. Run!

FORTY-SIX

THERE WAS STILL so much noise everywhere—the bokkan and his companions tearing through the debris, drawing steadily closer to Aileen; shouts and blaster fire from outside; a low hum resonating off the hangar walls in the strangest, most unsettling way; Kier and Kayl's voices in Aileen's mind; the sound of Aileen coughing up the dust she'd breathed in.

Everything had gone to shite.

But Aileen could only focus on one thing just then, and it was what kept her moving despite the burning in her chest and the rawness of her throat, despite the dull aches throughout her body, despite the approaching danger.

She'd lost Shalla. The uriti's hand had slipped from Aileen's when everything had come tumbling down around them, and now Aileen didn't know where the girl was, and it was dark and dirty and... What if something had happened, what if—

Calm, she reminded herself. She needed to keep that word in mind, needed to cling to it like it was her life preserver and she was adrift on a violent sea.

Aileen reached out and felt around in the darkness for any sign of Shalla. She was woefully aware of time—each second was an eternity in the tomb-like space created by the falling scrap, but each was also so incredibly fleeting. Every moment meant the people hunting her drew a little closer, and now the twins, her mates...

They were in trouble too. A lot of trouble. She'd seen flashes of the dropship landing through their eyes, had felt their panic. She'd seen the pirates hopping off the craft, the blaster fire. Her belly churned with dread.

They'll be okay. They'll be okay, she chanted in her head again and again, keeping the thought to herself.

"You really made a fucking mess of this," the male borian grumbled as more parts were tossed aside somewhere nearby.

"Shalla," Aileen whispered hoarsely.

"I'm all right," Shalla rasped from somewhere to Aileen's left.

"Leave the cripple," the volturian pirate said. "We need to get to the terran."

Aileen crawled toward Shalla's voice. Beams of light breaking through the wreckage afforded her glimpses of the twisted metal and debris around her as she moved. Thankfully, the wall of scrap to her right had held, creating a tunnel-like space for several meters in either direction.

A big, violet eye, staring at Aileen through the gap between a pair of heavy tristeel plates, caught her attention.

"Keep going," Shalla said.

Aileen hadn't thought it possible, but her heart quickened. "Are you stuck?"

"No, but I'll have to find another way around. You need to go, Aileen. They're coming for you."

Reaching out, Aileen slipped her hand through the gap. "I can't go without you."

The girl squeezed Aileen's hand. "You have to go get help. Right, right, left. That's the way."

Somewhere amidst the maze—not at all far enough away—metal groaned as though being bent, and the bokkan grunted with exertion.

"Go," Shalla said. "You need to go."

Aileen's father had once told her that doing the right thing was rarely easy, and that it required a lot more self-awareness than most people realized. She'd been too young at the time to truly understand what he'd meant.

She understood now.

Everything in her wanted to help Shalla, everything in her refused to leave the girl alone. But reality didn't care about what she wanted. She and the uriti were separated by thousands of kilograms of scrap metal and parts and were being hunted by four dangerous pirates, all but one of whom was much larger and stronger than both Aileen and Shalla.

Doing the right thing sometimes meant recognizing your limitations and thinking past them to find the best solution—and the best solution here was for Aileen to draw the pirates away from Shalla and Tallian, buying the uritis time to escape, and then, hopefully, reach the twins before Vrykhan's thugs caught up to her.

"Get to your father and get him somewhere you can hide, Shalla," she said, withdrawing her hand from the gap.

"Stay alive, Aileen."

The twins' thoughts blared in Aileen's mind, so frantic and charged with emotion that they threatened to paralyze her. Their distress, fear, and rage assailed her unrelentingly. She gritted her teeth and focused on here and now.

All that mattered was getting out of here alive and finding her mates.

Swallowing thickly, Aileen continued forward. As soon as she was able, she pushed herself to her feet and stumbled into a run.

Right, right, left.

She took the first right turn quickly, having to steady herself by touching a hand to the scrap wall—which thankfully held up. A few more hurried strides brought her to the next turn.

Ahead and to the left, the junk piles opened up again, and the light spilling through that gap was different. It was the bright, pure glow of the floodlights from the spaceport yard. Somehow, Aileen moved her legs faster.

Get out. Get help. Help. Need help.

My mates are close. They'll help.

Run, Aileen. Run!

Please. Tallian, Shalla...they need help.

Get out of there, Aileen!

Him, it's him. Ja'skaal...

Hope Tallian is all right. Hope Tallian is alive.

Help, help, someone help.

Run. Have to run. Have to—

Some of those thoughts hadn't been hers, but her mind was so messy, so chaotic... The twins were close. *Very* close. A hundred meters, two hundred; she wasn't sure how to determine distance with psychic senses, but they were so near it hurt.

A shadow fell across the opening just as Aileen turned the corner.

Her eyes flared, and her icy fear finally penetrated to the center of her heart. It was too late to stop, too late to change course. She skidded straight into a huge, hard wall of muscle, and the wind burst from her lungs.

No! No, no, no!

The thought came from her, from Kier, from Kayl; it was all of them, their minds, their hearts, their souls, crying out at the cruelty of fate.

Aileen staggered backward, catching herself by grasping a metal bar lodged in the scrap pile.

And Vrykhan grinned down at her, his sharp-toothed expression so predatory and threatening that it would've made a shark shite itself. He wore only a skirt made from studded strips of leather with a red cloth around his hips, cinched by a wide belt from which hung the largest blaster pistol she'd ever seen. His bare torso was powerfully muscled, covered in more scars than she could count.

Somehow, the fact that he wasn't wearing armor only made him more terrifying.

"Looks like I'm not the only one who survived my wounds back at Saduuk's shithole," the tretin said in a deep, rumbling voice. He stepped forward, darkness falling over his face—but two of his four eyes glowed through the shadows, their malicious crimson focused directly on her.

Aileen backed away, her legs weak, her breaths short and shallow. The blaster hidden on her thigh weighed a thousand kilos; she couldn't have drawn it if she'd wanted to.

Her heart raced. A burning sensation crept over her side, sinking deeper and deeper, but it somehow only made her colder.

Shot me. He shot me. Almost killed me. He...

Run.

Before she could move, one of Vrykhan's huge hands darted out and clamped around her throat.

Acting purely on instinct, Aileen clutched his thick wrist with one hand and pried the metal bar free with the other. She swung it as hard as she could, hitting his arm just above the elbow. He grunted, and his devilish grin widened.

When she swung again, he caught the bar in his free hand, wrenched it from her grip, and threw it aside. It clanged on the concrete floor and rolled away. He dragged her closer and lifted her off her feet.

Aileen's other hand took desperate hold of his in a vain attempt to relieve the pressure on her neck.

"No one is getting away this time," Vrykhan growled. He raised Aileen until her face was level with his and leaned forward.

All she could make out of his features were those two glowing eyes, those wicked teeth, those jagged horns.

A demon. He's a demon straight from hell.

Her nails dug into Vrykhan's flesh, but he seemed not to notice.

The tretin studied her eyes and let out a derisive snort. "They mated you, *ji'tas*? And it worked... No wonder people pay top credits for you terran vermin."

As he tightened his grip, Aileen clawed at his arm and kicked her legs, but she couldn't loosen his hold, couldn't relieve that crushing force, couldn't do anything. Her vision blurred, darkness encroaching around its edges.

"Aileen!" the twins roared, their voices echoing in both the night air and her mind.

Their senses opened to her. Through gaps in different pile of scrap, she saw the ship that had landed in front of the hangar. She saw the pirates, at least thirty strong, who'd poured out of the craft. She saw the blasters and shock staves in their hands. And she saw, horrifyingly, the hangar's open bay doors.

She saw Vrykhan, made small with distance, from behind. Saw her own thrashing legs beyond his body. Saw a shock of her dirty, tousled red hair.

Sorry, she pulsed. *Sorry. Love you. So sorry.*

"I know you fuckers can hear me," Vrykhan growled, leaning closer still until his nose bumped Aileen's. "I know you're here. You want your little terran? Come get her." He strengthened his grip, and black spots danced across Aileen's vision. "She won't stay fresh for long."

All the fury and fear in the universe flooded Aileen in that instant. It filled her with fire, with ice, it consumed her, it tore her apart and pieced her together. It was beyond words; it was soul-to-soul. It was the twins, it was their *daevalis*, declaring war upon the entire universe.

And it was not enough to stop Aileen from succumbing to darkness.

Sorry, she repeated. Then she knew no more.

FORTY-SEVEN

KIER COULD NOT DRAW BREATH. He could not move, could not think. All he could do was watch. Their mate, their Aileen, their *na'diya*...

Their life.

No! Kayl's *aerys* cried.

The pirates were hunched around the armor-plated hull of their dropship, passing out tranq guns, net launchers, bindings, and slave collars. Before long, the suppressive fire Kier and his companions were creating would prove inadequate, and their enemies would come for them.

He knew that, but he didn't care. His attention was fixed on the scene beyond the ship.

Vrykhan heaved the unconscious Aileen over his shoulder. Her limbs dangled, her hair fell to obscure her head, and her mind remained silent. Utterly, frightfully silent.

Kier had not felt so helpless since he was a child—since he'd watched Vrykhan murder his mother and slaughter his fathers. Now he was here, so far removed from that night both in time and space, and he was a powerless observer again.

For the second time, he was watching Vrykhan take *everything* from him.

Sorry.

Aileen's *aerys* echoed in his head, coaxing his heart to resume beating and his lungs to finally draw in the air he so desperately needed. For a fraction of a second, he'd thought it had been her, but no. It had only been a memory, had only been the ghost of her voice, of her raw, heartfelt, despairing apology.

Now equipped with the sort of nonlethal weaponry they employed to capture prisoners, the pirates remained around their ship, most of them kneeling to present smaller targets—trusting that their armor would protect them from this range.

Vrykhan turned toward the dropship. Two of the tretin's eyes—the eyes the twins had injured—shone with malicious red light.

What awoke in Kier and Kayl then was familiar to them—wrath; vengeance; the deep-rooted rage they'd harbored in their hearts for nearly three decades. But it was stronger than ever because Vrykhan had taken Aileen. He'd taken their *mate*. Because for her, they would fight across the cosmos. For her, they would tear reality apart. They would do anything—*everything*—to get her back in their arms.

The tretin extended his powerful arms to either side, settling his gaze on the pile of scrap behind which the twins and their companions were positioned. "You're outmatched in every way, little daevahs. Surrender."

He took everything from us, the twins thought.

Now we will take everything from him. His other eyes. His arms, his legs. His grin. His ships and his crew.

His whole fucking life.

"I suppose it would be silly to ask whether you two are wearing your fancy armor, wouldn't it?" Arcanthus asked.

Thargen grunted. "Who needs armor? There's maybe forty of them. Those fuckers are doomed."

The twins' cores shuddered with overwhelming emotion. Their need to spill blood reached an unimaginable height. But they clutched at control, willing another memory of Aileen's *aerys* to pulse back and forth along their psychic link—*Calm*.

It was not easy, not by any means, and it was not sustainable. Yet they needed to hold onto at least a shred of calm until the time was right.

"They will die," Kier said, gaze still fixed on Vrykhan.

"Every one of them," Kayl continued, voice as cold as the void of space.

"But he has our mate. Any move we make puts her at risk."

Arcanthus swept his tail across the ground, scraping up dust, as he tapped a finger against one of the derelict hovertruck's side panels. "We need but delay them. If we can prevent him from doing her harm for a little longer…"

The twins glanced at Arcanthus from the corners of their eyes.

"Does this relate to you having everything under control, Arcanthus?" Kayl asked.

"Your tone implies a lack of faith, Sol'Kayl."

But that was wrong, wasn't it? Because despite the twins having dropped out of contact, despite them having raced toward what should've been their deaths without so much as thanking Arcanthus for the information and aid he'd provided, despite there being no reason for Arcanthus to have thought the twins survived their visit to Eternal Paradise, Arcanthus was here. Thargen was here.

Even without the twins asking, they'd come to help.

"When this is all done, we will have a very long conversation about boundaries and consent," Kier said, "and about how we could have avoided some problems had we been more open with you. But we do trust you, Arcanthus."

"And we should have put all our trust in you much sooner," Kayl added.

Arcanthus's lips curled in a roguish smile. "I did not expect our reunion to be so heartwarming."

"Good, now you three hug so we can fucking kill these bastards," Thargen said.

Kier and Kayl turned their gazes ahead again. The pirates waited patiently, most of them still within the shelter of the dropship with their weapons directed toward the twins. Their discipline was admirable; it was no wonder Vrykhan and his crew had managed to have such long, destructive careers. Once the pirates chose to advance, they would very quickly overwhelm the twins and their companions.

"The longer you resist, the harder this will be for your terran *ji'tas*," Vrykhan boomed. He reached back over his shoulder, grasped Aileen's hair, and pulled her down. The toes of her boots barely touched the ground as he held her up by her hair.

Kier's fingers curled, claws scraping the metal upon which his hand was braced. All that fury, held in his heart for so long…it had concentrated into something primal, a force that he would not be able to contain once he unleashed it.

The same rage thrummed inside Kayl. Together, the twins walled it off behind icy mental barriers, hoping they would hold against the immense heat.

Vrykhan turned Aileen to face the twins, making her feet drag across the ground. "She's so tiny, so soft. How much do you think she can endure?"

Aileen's eyelids fluttered; her mind brushed against the twins', her consciousness flickering.

Anything to save her. *Anything.*

"How long do you need, Arcanthus?" Kayl asked.

The sedhi raised his wrist, and a small holo screen projected from his cybernetic prosthesis. "Everything is nearly in place. It should be a matter of minutes."

"The fuck are you two thinking?" Thargen demanded. "Even I know charging out there is a stupid move, and that's usually my go-to."

"He wants us alive," Kier replied. "Vrykhan is not one to bluff."

Arcanthus's eyebrows fell, and his yellow eyes were scrutinous as he looked over the twins. "You do realize, of course, that he likely only wants you alive so he can kill you?"

"We know."

"But if we do not surrender, he will harm our *na'diya* further," Kayl said.

He and Kier loosened their holds on their blasters, letting the weapons rotate around their trigger fingers until the barrels were angled downward.

Thargen shook his head. "Craziest part of this whole thing. You two with a terran mate."

Arcanthus turned that scrutinous gaze onto the vorgal. "Because the tretin warlord with a personal vendetta against our friends and his army of pirates about to raid a settlement are totally mundane?"

"Typical Tuesday."

"Do you even know what Tuesday is, Thargen?"

"Of course I do. It's"—the vorgal lifted a palm, shrugging one shoulder—"some terran shit."

Kayl released a slow breath. "I am finding it difficult to believe that you will not squander whatever time we are about to win for you."

"Nonsense. Only the utmost professionalism from us, Sol'Kayl," the sedhi replied with a smirk.

"Last warning," Vrykhan shouted.

Pain arced through the psychic link—stinging scalp, burning throat, aching neck. The twins' tenuous control faltered. Gritting their teeth, they stood up straight, raised their hands over their heads, and walked out from behind their cover.

"Try not to get shot," Thargen said.

Arcanthus snickered. "Excellent advice from someone who seems to get shot every other Tuesday."

"Must be my magnetic personality attracting all kinds of stuff."

The spaceport yard stretched out before the twins. The dropship sat a hundred meters away, its antigrav drive humming, surrounded by pirates. A great number of weapons were now aimed directly at the twins.

Vrykhan displayed his teeth in a grin that bore no humor, no satisfaction, no smugness; there was only hatred and anger in the expression. Only evil. "Weapons on the ground."

Aileen groaned, reaching up to grasp her hair as she struggled to plant her feet on the ground; Vrykhan held her just a little too high.

Everything within the twins protested. Their hearts and souls cried out, demanded they fight, they slay, they avenge and protect. With jaws clenched and chests tight, they tossed down their blasters.

Malevolent snickers and chuckles rippled through the pirates. Undoubtedly, they believed their guaranteed victory had just become easier.

The tretin swung Aileen in front of himself and strode forward. She whimpered, half-stumbling, half-sliding, powerless to withstand the strength of Vrykhan's extended arm. Her eyes were open now, her wavering vision locked on Kier and Kayl.

Her fear—fear for their safety—blasted into the twins.

No. No, not like this, she pulsed. *Please. You have to go, you can't just give yourself to him.*

It will be all right, na'diya, the twins replied in unison.

"Come join us," Vrykhan said. "We've been waiting too long to catch up with you. Don't make us wait any longer."

Tension coursed through the twins' muscles as they walked. Each step closer to the pirates was a step closer to capture, to pain, to death...but it was also a step closer to her.

Vrykhan halted beside the dropship and leaned his head down so that predatory mouth was far, far too close to Aileen's neck. His free hand grasped her chin, keeping her face directed at the twins. "Watch, *ji'tas*. Watch what they've earned for themselves. And when that's done..." His long, pointed tongue slipped out, trailing along the top of her ear. "They'll watch what they've earned for *you*."

Aileen shuddered and cringed; the twins bared their teeth in snarls, their strides faltering as they battled the urge to charge at the tretin. No one touched their mate, especially not like that. No one threatened her. Not without retaliation.

Not without death.

Several of the pirates moved away from the dropship, fanning out as they approached Kier and Kayl. One of them asked, "You want us to put them down, warlord?"

"No. That would spoil the fun, wouldn't it?" Vrykhan purred into Aileen's ear, coaxing another shudder from her.

"What about their friends?" another asked.

Vrykhan turned his face forward, eyes shifting to the place where Arcanthus and Thargen were still positioned. "If they so much as poke their heads out, you reduce that scrap to a pool of molten metal."

The plasma cannons on the dropship shifted.

"That's rather rude, isn't it?" Arcanthus called.

"Afraid we'd win a straight fight?" Thargen asked with a laugh. "Didn't realize tretins were such cowards."

"Not helping," Kier and Kayl said through clenched teeth.

Vrykhan straightened. "Don't worry. Everyone will get their turn." Those two glowing red eyes settled on the twins with laser focus and, somehow, his grin grew. "You want to fight, don't you? It's in your postures, in your eyes. It radiates from you. What was it? I killed your family and sold you into slavery?

"Now look at you. Strong, effective fighters. Warriors. A hundred intergalactic governments have chased me for decades, but no one has caused as much difficulty for me as you two little daevahs. The only reason you've made any difference is because of me. You are strong because of me."

The tretin yanked up on Aileen's hair, and she cried out, grabbing at his hand as her feet left the ground entirely. The twins squeezed their fists, claws drawing blood from their palms.

"But *I* am the conqueror," Vrykhan growled, "and just as I made you, I can destroy you. You won your freedom. You should've accepted that as enough. You should've contented yourselves with surviving. When you chose to come after me, you chose death."

The twins' rage was a swelling force in their chests, pressing outward with exponentially expanding pressure, threatening to burst any second. Their hearts pounded, and a tornado of memories rampaged through the backs of their minds.

Their feet came down with immense weight as they stopped; it was the weight of destiny, of inevitability. No matter what they might have done, Sol'Kier Sevris and Sol'Kayl Kortanis would always have arrived at this moment. Their fates were tethered to Aileen—but they were tethered to Vrykhan also.

It was well past time for that last tether to be severed forever.

"Val'Aeral Vuros, Val'Aekan Aegis, Nei'Yari Solara," the twins intoned, their voices carrying into the night sky. Heat coursed through their veins, and their hearts quickened, but just a little of that internal pressure eased.

"They made us," said Kier, "and you killed them."

"So we shaped ourselves," said Kayl. "*Sin kortanis ayar*; for I am vengeance."

"*Ys sevris ayar*; and I am wrath. We forged our strength. It was not given to us."

Kier snickered as he and his brother ran their gazes over the pirates. "Your strength is hollow."

Kayl's eyes fell upon Vrykhan. "A conqueror who preys only upon the weak and defenseless is merely masking his own weakness."

The corners of Vrykhan's mouth twitched down, and his long, powerful tail lashed behind him. "Let's see how much fight is in you. Ravagers! Fists and shock staves. Make them feel every bit of pain they've inflicted on our comrades. Make them suffer for every wrong they've done us."

"No!" Aileen cried. She pressed her trembling lips together and stared at her mates with watery eyes. *You need to run. They're going to kill you. Just go! I can't... I can't lose you too.*

Nothing, na'diya. *Nothing will keep us from you,* the twins responded.

Flicking on their shock staves, the pirates advanced, spreading farther apart to encircle the twins.

Kier and Kayl assumed fighting stances, standing back-to-back. Their hearts slowed, each thunderous beat rattling their ribs with pent up wrath, and their conscious thoughts fell silent.

One of the pirates chuckled. "Some sport before work."

"Not sport," another said. "This is justice. Just like the warlord promised."

"And justice means we do this nice and slow," a third pirate said.

"Justice?" Harsh, humorless laughter bubbled up from Kier's gut. "Your like has no concept of justice."

Kayl's tail bumped the side of Kier's leg and stilled. "But we will gladly instruct you."

"Try to keep up."

The pirates charged.

Kier and Kayl burst into motion. They blocked, dodged, and deflected a torrent of attacks from all sides, their limbs moving in blurs. And they lashed out with attacks of their own—fists and feet, elbows and knees, heads, tails, claws, and teeth, each strike a brutal retort to their enemies' aggression.

Pirates staggered, stumbled, and tripped, grunting and cursing as the twins' frenzied defense repelled their assault.

Kayl's knuckles connected with a cren's jaw, cracking a tusk. Kier drove his heel into the side of a borian's knee. The joint popped and bent sideways. When Kayl caught a volturian's extended arm, Kier hammered his elbow down on the limb as his brother wrenched upward. The volturian's scream swallowed the sound of breaking bone.

The twins acted as one, perfectly coordinated in every movement no matter how subtle or overt. Yet it wasn't enough; most of their blows struck armor plates, knocking enemies backward or off balance but inflicting little damage. The same was not true of the hits the pirates managed to land on the twins.

Despite the adrenaline coursing through Kier and Kayl's systems, they felt everything. They felt their bodies being slowly battered and bruised. They felt the static buzz of shock staves drawing near to their skin, felt the electric charge in the air.

They felt Aileen. And through her, they heard Vrykhan speak.

"Imagine the things they could've done. The wealth they

could've won, the empire they could've forged, if they had even a single shred of intelligence."

"They're going to end you, you fucking cunt," Aileen rasped. Her voice held steady, and it dripped with venom like Kier had never heard from her. But beneath that semblance of defiance, her mind reeled, and her thoughts were chaos.

She battled her fear, her anger, struggling for the calm she'd urged her mates to seize. That she'd succeeded to any degree was a wonder, because she was still in the clutches of a monster, forced to watch as her mates were swarmed by at least a dozen enemies. She knew that a flick of Vrykhan's claws across her throat or a sharp twist of her head would mean her end.

And yet her only concern was for the twins. It flowed from her in waves, bolstering Kier and Kayl, lending them new strength, pushing them harder, faster.

But that concern wasn't enough either.

So long as Vrykhan had her, the twins could not win this fight. They could not allow themselves to do what was necessary, because he would hurt her. He would *kill* her.

"Some of you terrans certainly like making threats." Vrykhan dropped his hand from her chin, banded his thick arm around her chest, and tugged her back against his body. "It's a shame you're all too small and frail to act upon those threats. But I'm not, *ji'tas*. I do not make idle threats. I make promises."

Something hard struck Kier's right leg. The pain of the impact was immediately eclipsed by an electric jolt that locked up every muscle in the limb. Fire raced along his nerves, down to his toes and up into his hips and lower back.

Kayl swung around behind his brother and threw a lightning-fast kick, striking Kier's assailant on the chin. As the pirate fell backward, the shock staff dropped from his hand.

The instant that electric current ceased, Kier's leg buckled, and he fell onto one knee.

AILEEN'S HEART QUICKENED, and her soul cried out as the pirates redoubled their efforts.

Digging her nails into the tretin's forearm, she watched as her mates fought against impossible odds, using every part of their bodies as weapons. Determination and love radiated from them, but their fury—so deep, so powerful—remained muted.

She needed to get away from Vrykhan. That would enable her mates and their allies to act without restriction, without the fear of her being harmed in retaliation. But she didn't know how to accomplish that.

Distract him. Try to find an opening...or make one.

"So this is justice?" she asked, mouth dry. "Sending your crew to have their asses kicked?"

"You say that as though your daevahs are winning," Vrykhan purred, voice vibrating into Aileen. "For every blow they land, your little males will suffer ten more."

In the nearby hanger, someone shouted, "Where the fuck did the uriti *ji'tas* go?"

They haven't found Shalla. Shalla's safe.

We need to be safe. My mates...

Aileen tugged down on his arm, which didn't move so much as a millimeter. "Funny how it always seems to be the biggest monsters who buy into that eye-for-an-eye shite, but never apply it to themselves."

"Eye for an eye?" Vrykhan grunted. "I like that. And your males happen to owe me a couple eyes, don't they? What do you think, terran? Should I take an eye from each or just leave one blind?"

With her voice so full of rage that it no longer sounded like her own, Aileen said, "I want you to remember your philosophy when I shoot you. Remember that you're owed the pain."

But she couldn't entirely block out the imagery forced into her head by his words. Her stomach churned, and she let out a trembling breath.

Kier and Kayl were holding on. But how much longer could they last? They'd been bloodied, beaten, and shocked, and still they fought, fueled by the strength of their *daevalis*. How long would that be enough? And what good was that strength if it only applied to them protecting her? What good was it if she couldn't protect them too?

Please. Whoever is listening, whatever is listening, help us. Cut us a break.

The universe, to her startlement, responded—or at least one of the twins' friends did, from behind the pile of junk.

"Everything is set!" That sounded like the sedhi, Arcanthus. "And I just wanted to add that the two of you are doing an excellent job. Keep it up!"

Another growl rumbled in Vrykhan's chest. "What the fuck are you talking about over there?"

"Why would I tell you?" Arcanthus asked. "That would spoil the surprise."

"How about I have you blasted to ash?"

"What an inelegant solution. Exactly what I'd expect from a tretin."

Not what I had in mind when I asked for help. Really, really not what I had in mind.

"Now!" Vrykhan roared, releasing Aileen's hair to jab a finger toward the scrap mound. "Blow them the fuck up!"

"Warning." Triss's voice rang out across the yard. "Obstacles detected in roadway. Recalculating route."

Vrykhan turned toward Triss's voice, which had come from behind and to the right—the direction of the spaceport's main entrance. "Now what the fuck is hap—"

A familiar hovertruck with a weatherworn finish and mismatched exterior parts sped across the strip toward the pirate dropship, the hum of its antigrav drive having been drowned out by that of the idling spacecraft. The tretin drew a blaster from his hip and fired a burst of plasma into the truck's cab.

The vehicle's speed and trajectory didn't waver.

Several of the pirates who'd hung back to watch the spectacle of the twins being mobbed snapped their heads toward the approaching vehicle, but most were too late to react.

The truck spun at the last second without changing direction, gliding sideways over the ground. A rapid succession of heavy thuds marked the vehicle striking at least a dozen pirates who'd been in its path; their bodies were swept aside like dust by a broom.

With a crash to rival that of the scrap avalanche from earlier, the hovertruck slammed into the side of the dropship. Parts, sparks, and dust that glittered with motes of faldrium flew into the air. Aileen squeezed her eyes shut and turned her face away as bits of debris rained around her.

Loosening his hold on Aileen and shifting her aside, Vrykhan stepped forward. "Fuck!"

She opened her eyes and glanced over the scene.

Electricity arced from damaged components in the twisted, smoking wreckage. Debris blanketed the ground, far more than seemed possible even from two large vehicles, and the bodies of at least ten pirates lay scattered amongst it. Several bloody, broken survivors moved amongst the ruins, groaning in pain and bewilderment.

Thank you. Thank you, thank you, thank you.

But the twins were still caught in their struggle, their fight having devolved into a wrestling match with half a dozen opponents. Many of the pirates who'd swarmed them stared at the crash scene in shock and anger.

Arcanthus popped out from behind his cover. "As much as I feel like I should take credit for this, it was not part of the plan."

That didn't matter. It didn't matter at all. Sometimes opportunities were given; sometimes they were made. And, once in a while, one led to the other.

She had one chance to put everything the twins had taught her to use. One chance to give *them* the opportunity to do whatever was necessary to end this. To give them the opportunity to fight.

Aileen, no! He will hurt you, the twins pulsed in alarm. *He will kill you!*

Her reply came with a calm and surety that surprised even her. *And if I do nothing, he'll kill us all.*

Aileen...

Though there was concern and trepidation in their psychic voices, something else came on the heels of it, something that filled her heart and then spilled outward to flood her body—belief. Their belief in her. Their support, their impossibly deep love.

You got this, Aileen, she told herself. *Super simple. Just going to escape the gigantic demon warlord who's holding you hostage and then go for a nice sprint past however many pirates survived that crash so you can get to friendly people. All super simple.*

Annnnd I'm mentally rambling again.

Aileen clenched her jaw, took in another breath, and used the slack Vrykhan had inadvertently afforded her to spin toward him. As she moved, she thrust her right knee up and pushed off the ground with her toes.

Her knee connected with the tretin's groin hard enough to make her kneecap ache, though she was sure he didn't have armor on beneath his leather skirt.

His powerful thighs closed around her knee, trapping it, and his hand darted up to grab a fistful of her hair at the back of her head. When her weight came down, her left foot couldn't quite reach the ground, and so her hair took the majority of the burden again.

She hissed, and tears stung her eyes. Grasping her hair with her left hand, she dropped the right to her thigh.

Vrykhan turned his face down toward her.

Alarm blared from the twins.

Calm. Calm. Calm.

Not over. Not done.

"I usually have an appetite for a spirited *ji'tas*," Vrykhan said through those terrifying, pointed teeth. "Forgive me if I'm not in the fucking mood. What did you think this was going to accomplish? Give my slit a tickle and see if you can win my favor?"

"Not quite," Aileen grated as her fingers probed the leg of her pants, searching, searching, desperately moving the fabric around.

He stared at her for a second that stretched on into eternity, and she thought she would fall into those evil red eyes, that she would be swallowed by them. Then he turned his head toward his pirates, raised his blaster, and snarled, "No more games. Kill the fucking daevahs!"

Aileen's fingers hooked the slit on her pants. She forced it open and reached through, turning all her willpower toward keeping her hand steady despite the thundering of her heart as she grasped the blaster holstered on her thigh.

She placed her finger on the trigger. "Eye for an eye."

Vrykhan looked back at Aileen; she pulled the trigger.

Searing pain blazed along her thigh, and fire flared on her pants, instantly leaping to the tretin's pelvis. He growled in pain. Aileen squeezed the trigger again, and again. Two more plasma bolts struck Vrykhan near the first. The stench of scorched flesh and the tang of plasma filled her nose.

The tretin roared and threw Aileen away.

Her breath hitched; for an instant, she was soaring, weightless, untethered.

No, not untethered. Never untethered. Because her mates were there, her *na'divali*, and they would be connected to her no matter what. Only they could make her feel like she was floating and yet utterly grounded at the same time. Only they could make her feel like everything would be all right when things were at their direst.

She hit the ground hard, the impact blasting up her tailbone before her momentum carried her onto her back and into a roll. The wind burst from her lungs for the second time in a few minutes, and her chest burned. She tumbled across the hard ground, getting scraped and bruised, and finally came to a stop on her belly.

A single thought entered her mind, oddly serene despite everything.

At least my pants aren't on fire anymore.

Aileen! the twins called in her mind, their voices stronger, clearer, and more focused than before.

As she pushed herself up from the ground and fought to take in a breath, her mates unleashed their rage.

FORTY-EIGHT

Aileen was hurt.

Aileen had escaped Vrykhan's hold.

Those two facts tore along the twins' psychic links in a firestorm as the icy prisons that had contained their rage shattered.

None of the chaos that had unfurled around them mattered. Their pain made no difference; the crash held no significance. Their only priority was clear.

Aileen is hurt.

Aileen is free.

She needs us. Our mate needs us.

The twins' minds became one, driven purely by instinct, by primal fury. No more restraint. No more mercy.

The twins shifted their positions abruptly, reversing their resistance to the pirates grappling with them. The pirates fell, several of them landing atop the twins in a jumble of limbs, grasping hands, and buzzing shock staves.

Kayl and his brother had already drawn their knives before the pirates came down fully. Jolts of pain seized their muscles more than once during the struggle, but they kept their weapons in constant motion, the blades punching through narrow gaps in armor and finding unprotected body parts to slice and stab. Blood ran hot over the twins' hands and splashed their faces.

Their foes growled, swore, and cried out, groaned and grunted and expelled ragged breaths. But even when the pirates eluded the bite of the twins' blades, they could not escape the raking claws, the hammering elbows and knees, the constricting tails.

"Fucking take them out!" one of the pirates outside the struggle yelled.

Aileen...

Aileen needs us.

Coming. We are coming.

Killing.

Killing them all.

"Thargen!" Arcanthus called.

"About fucking time," the vorgal snarled.

Kier tore a shock staff from the hands of a dying pirate, shoved himself out of the writhing pile, and smashed the weapon across the face of an oncoming enemy. The staff broke with the force of the blow, spitting sparks; the pirate spat blood and teeth.

But two more of the pirate's comrades were just behind him.

Arcanthus darted past Kier from behind. The hardlight sword in the sedhi's grasp lashed out too fast for anything to be seen of it but a yellow blur.

One pirate's head toppled off, while the other's throat gaped with a wide slash—like a second mouth—that poured blood.

And still more came.

Kayl dragged himself out from beneath a corpse and kicked, slamming his boot into the ankle of another attacker. As the pirate fell, a huge form flew over Kayl and landed heavily upon the pirate, crushing bones.

Laughing, Thargen cleaved his pinned foe's skull with a chop of his hardlight axe. Another pirate swung at the vorgal. Thargen's second axe severed the attacker's arm at mid-forearm.

Tearing their knives and claws free from the flesh of their enemies, the twins stood up. Their gazes immediately fell upon their mate.

Aileen had managed to get onto her hands and knees, her red tresses hanging in her face as she struggled to catch her breath. Hers was the only pain that broke through the flaming barrier of Kier and Kayl's rage, the only pain they felt.

Vrykhan remained far too close to her, only ten meters away, down on a knee with his torso hunched forward. His weight was braced on one arm, which was pressed down atop his blaster. Wisps of smoke rose from his groin.

"Warlord?" a pirate called from the hangar—the female volturian who'd been chasing Aileen. She emerged from the scrap mess at the front of the hangar with the borian and bokkan close behind.

Chest heaving with his ragged breaths, Vrykhan lifted his face. "Get the fucking terran!"

The trio of pirates locked their gazes on Aileen and hurried toward her.

Closer to the wrecked dropship, nearly a dozen more pirates were still on their feet, tossing aside their tranq guns and net launchers to draw blasters, knives, and energy blades.

They were obstacles in the twins' path, deserving of only destruction.

The hovertruck's back doors burst open. Several of the nearby pirates spun, reflexively firing their weapons at the figure that emerged.

Bolts struck Triss's chest and arms. Molten plasma dripped off their metal casing, but none of the shots seemed to have penetrated. The robot's small head turned, optics sweeping across the pirates. "Why are you shooting me?"

Arcanthus clenched his right fist. A circular hardlight shield formed on the back of his wrist, the same yellow as his sword and *qal*. "Go to her. We'll take care of what's left."

The twins charged toward their mate.

More weapons fired, casting blue-white flashes across the debris-littered yard, and Thargen laughed with delight. In Kayl's peripheral vision, he saw Arcanthus's shield expand, pulsing as plasma bolts struck it and dissipated, and then the sedhi was amongst his foes with blade swinging. Thargen rushed in not far behind.

Two pirates with energy blades leapt into the twins' paths, their eyes wild.

The twins dispatched their opponents much like they might've swatted away irritating insects, barely noticing the blood pouring from the wounds they'd opened before moving on at even greater speed.

Aileen. Na'diya. *We are coming.*

I know, she pulsed, *I know.*

Kier and Kayl's rapid strides devoured the distance between

them and Aileen, but the pirates from the hangar had been closer. The borian reached Aileen seconds before the twins could have, bending down to reach for her.

No such thing as a fair fight, Aileen thought. She swung her arm up, throwing a handful of dirt into the borian's face.

"Fuck!" The borian turned his head away and flinched back.

Kayl's hand snapped forward, releasing his knife. The weapon flipped in the air, blood-soaked tristeel glimmering under the floodlights, and lodged in the borian's shoulder.

The pirate grunted, bumping into the smaller volturian who'd been close behind him and knocking her off balance.

Aileen dropped flat on the ground the instant before the twins leapt over her and drove their knees, with all their weight and speed behind them, into their foes. The borian and volturian fell; the twins landed atop them.

"Fuck you," the volturian rasped, thrashing beneath Kier as she reached for the blaster on her hip.

Kier caught her throat in one hand, slammed her head on the ground, and plunged his knife into her eye. Kayl grasped the hilt jutting from the borian's shoulder and twisted it. The borian threw his head back, howling in pain. Kayl slashed his claws across the borian's exposed neck, tearing it apart.

The bokkan, still several meters away, spat a curse and tugged a blaster pistol off his belt.

Kier reached for the volturian's blaster, ripping it free of its holster.

Before he could raise it, the center of the bokkan's chest burst outward, spraying blood and bits of bone and tissue. The pirate dropped his weapon as the telltale crack of a gauss rifle echoed across the spaceport.

With a soft, confused grunt, the bokkan fell dead.

Behind him, atop a scrap heap in the hangar, the twins spied Shalla. Her silvery hair stood out amidst all the dark, discolored metal. She lowered her rifle, violet eyes wider than ever, and released a breath that made her shoulders tremble.

The twins spun back toward their mate, the blaster falling from Kier's fingers. Aileen pushed herself up. Kayl caught her arm and helped her. Before she was even fully upright, she and the twins caught each other in a desperate, crushing embrace.

An onslaught of thoughts and emotions erupted in the twins' minds, but foremost was relief, carried upon the pulsing waves of their love.

Ours.

Ours.

You are ours, Aileen. Our na'idya. *Ours.*

We have you.

They withdrew from her not out of want, but need, and quickly examined her wounds. Their hearts refused to slow.

Cuts. Scrapes. Patches of battered flesh that would become dark bruises soon enough. But worst of all was the long yet thankfully shallow plasma burn on her right leg, running from mid-thigh to knee. She flinched and hissed through her teeth when Kier pulled the singed cloth away from the wound.

"Ah, *na'diya...*" Kayl rumbled.

They needed to get her to the *Fang*, to the medpod. Needed to clean and treat the wound on the way, needed to ease her pain. Needed to—

Aileen placed one hand on Kier's cheek, the other on Kayl's. Her eyes were filled with worry for the wounds they'd received. "I'll live." She looked past them, and her gaze became hard. "But this isn't over."

The twins followed her gaze with theirs.

Vrykhan was still there, ten meters away, face contorted with pain and malice. His crimson eyes, both natural and cybernetic, blazed at the twins. His fingers tightened around the blaster still pinned under his hand.

"I remember now," the tretin growled. "Tilara. Your fathers had the same expressions as you before I killed them. They were like insects, crushed under my boot."

The fury at the twins' cores resurged. In their minds' eyes, they saw the faces of their parents, their friends, their neighbors. They saw the faces of the many, many slaves they'd rescued, and the many more for whom they'd been too late. They saw their own faces. They saw Aileen's face.

The weight of destiny bore down upon them. Their bodies felt suddenly heavier, their movements felt slower, time itself seemed to crawl. Everything had led them to this moment, and this moment was crucial to everything that would follow.

This had been inevitable.

The powerful muscles in Vrykhan's arms flexed, making the tendons on his hand stand out. He pushed off the ground and brought his blaster up; somehow, the twins knew he was aiming for Aileen alone. They knew he intended to make them suffer—to let their souls be picked apart by the pain of loss until there was nothing left.

Kayl's hand darted to Aileen's thigh, grasping the blaster still holstered there.

Kier's hand darted to the blaster he'd dropped on the ground.

Aileen ducked down, and the twins threw themselves in front of her as they brought their weapons up. The pressure in their chests grew with each passing microsecond. Everything they held dear hung from a single, delicate thread, and Vrykhan meant to cut it.

Three blaster shots went off simultaneously, their sounds blending into one.

A bolt struck the ground in front of the twins, melting a long groove that ended mere centimeters from their knees.

Vrykhan released a strained exhalation. Fresh tendrils of smoke flowed from a pair of holes on the center of his chest—holes so close together that their edges overlapped. His lips quivered, peeling back farther, his arm fell, and his shoulders slumped.

"*Vurocht eshe*," he snarled in the harsh language of his kind. "*Vurocht ahk.*"

War upon you. War upon all.

The tretin's blaster trembled upward again.

The twins fired again and again. Plasma bolts darted across that ten-meter space, their blue-white light making Vrykhan's shadow dance behind him.

When the twins ceased fire, the tretin's arms and legs were riddled with plasma wounds, and several new holes had been burned through his abdomen. His cybernetic eyes flickered and dimmed. The blaster fell from his fingers, and he collapsed, landing heavily on his side before rolling onto his back.

Kayl and his brother glanced back at their mate. Aileen's eyes were wide, her breaths were rapid, and her heart was racing, but she'd suffered no further harm.

Remain here, Kayl pulsed.

Feel us, Kier added. *We are with you, now and always.*

She nodded, and her love, already so pure and bright, intensified.

The twins rose and stalked toward the tretin.

Vrykhan's tail groped for his fallen weapon, moving slowly, weakly. One of his hands lay motionless on the ground; he'd managed to get the other to his belt, where he struggled to remove something from a small pouch.

"Still...lost," he rasped. Though his voice was filled with hatred, it had lost its power. He released a harsh, choked sound that might have been laughter. "Even with me dead...you...still...lost."

Vrykhan's fumbling hand managed to free the item from his belt. Kier fired a single shot, striking the tretin's wrist. Vrykhan's fingers twitched, and the item fell from his grasp, rolling across the ground with a clink of heavy-duty glass.

A single-use injection of ulturine.

Kier stopped the rolling vial beneath his boot and pressed his weight down, crunching it. Kayl kicked the tretin's fallen blaster away.

Vrykhan laughed again, and a black, sludgy substance bubbled from his mouth. "Always more. Too many...for you." The tretin wasn't looking at the twins, who halted just out of his reach to either side of him. His gaze was directed skyward...and he was grinning.

"Oh, God," Aileen breathed.

The twins' hearts stuttered; though they dared not look away from Vrykhan, their bond with Aileen showed them exactly what she saw.

Far above, the pale form of the *Azkazor* was visible in the night sky. It was still in orbit, but that it could be seen at all was testament to its size and intimidating presence. But the pirate battle cruiser wasn't the reason for Vrykhan's laughter or the shock that had gripped Aileen and the twins—those reactions had been caused by the dozens of ships speeding toward the spaceport, all of them trailing fire and vapor.

Thudding footsteps marked Triss's approach. Arcanthus and Thargen, both spattered with blood, accompanied the robot.

"Triss, go help Shalla and Tallian out of the hangar," Kayl said.

"They are in trouble?" The robot's blocky torso turned, and some of their internal components whirred and clanked. They plodded off toward the hangar far faster than the twins had seen the robot move during their days working together.

"Too late," Vrykhan growled. "You should've...brought a fucking army. That's what's coming...for you."

"As much as I'd hate to be a contrarian," Arcanthus said as he stepped up beside Kier, "you're wrong. I find a small, precision force more effective in a great many scenarios. Such as this one."

"Dead. They are going to crush...all of you."

"*They?*" Arcanthus glanced skyward and tilted his head.

Kier and Kayl each lifted a brow, regarding the sedhi with confusion.

"We need to go, Arcanthus," said Kier. "We need to get everyone to the *Fang.*"

Vrykhan chuckled. "Yes. Flee...cowards."

"A little self-reflection might've benefited you in life," Arcanthus said, looking down at the tretin again. "Being stubborn about dying isn't bravery. All of us have done that. And those dropships"—he pointed upward—"aren't filled with your precious pirates."

"Bluffing won't...help you, sedhi," Vrykhan rasped.

"My dear friends said you aren't one to bluff. I believe it. You're a simple creature, after all. I'm quite capable of bluffing, but know this, Vrykhan—I have no need to."

Understanding fell into place in the twins' minds. They weren't sure how Arcanthus had managed it, but they knew he wasn't lying. There were no pirates coming to avenge Vrykhan. This wasn't a single battle won; this was the end of the war.

"Think you can...intimidate me?" The tretin kept his gaze directed at the night sky. His grin had wavered, but it crept back now.

Arcanthus produced something from his belt, holding it out on the palm of his cybernetic hand—a small detonator with an ergonomic grip and a flip-up trigger guard. He held the device to Kier.

As Kier accepted it, Kayl stepped around the fallen tretin to join his brother.

"I assumed the two of you would like to do the honors," Arcanthus said, his tone solemn. "It was your years of hunting, dedication, and sacrifice that made this possible. It is time to free yourselves from the hunt."

Kier and Kayl stared down at the detonator. It was hard to believe all this could be so simple, that it could end so abruptly. But they did not doubt Arcanthus.

They looked back at Aileen. She'd regained her feet, favoring her wounded leg, and now stood watching them intently.

"We were already freed from this hunt," Kayl said.

"We will be glad to no longer have its shadow looming over us regardless," said Kier.

Aileen drew in a deep breath and nodded. *End it.*

Kier flicked up the detonator's guard. He lifted his hand to Kayl, and they put their fingers on the trigger together. Their thoughts were as one.

It is done.

They pressed the trigger.

High overhead, the *Azkazor* erupted in a burst of light. The immense battle cruiser, which had terrorized the universe for decades, was gone in the blink of an eye. The blast spread outward like an expanding star, debris flying in all directions. But even the trails left by the debris flickered out before long, and the light faded.

Nothing remained in the place the battle cruiser had occupied but the starry night sky.

"The fuck... The fuck did you..." For the first time, there was fear in Vrykhan's voice. There was panic.

The twins raised their blasters. They fired half a dozen shots each; every bolt struck its target—Vrykhan's face.

The tretin's body tensed for an instant and then fell, limp and unmoving.

Kayl and his brother stared down at Vrykhan's ruined face. In that moment, it was like only a day had passed since they'd first encountered him. They'd felt so powerless and insignificant then, and the tretin had been so big, so impossibly strong, so insurmountable. They'd been helpless children, and he'd been an unstoppable force of pure evil.

Now Vrykhan was a lump of smoldering meat. Now...he was nothing. Exactly as he should have been all along. The twins would never again have to look up at him. He would never again make them feel small and afraid. He would never again instill them with hatred, would never again have a hold on their lives.

No one would ever have to fear this tretin again.

The air overhead hummed with antigrav drives, and the twins finally looked up to see the dropships arriving. The first of them passed directly over the twins and their companions before touching down smoothly only a few meters away. Another joined it, then another, and another, and soon the dropships were landing all over, filling the spaceport and spilling into the surrounding area.

Reflexive tension rippled through Kier and Kayl as the ramp of the first ship lowered, but they did not raise their weapons.

Dozens of people were packed inside, easily twice as many as had been on the ship that delivered Vrykhan to the spaceport. But just as Arcanthus had said, they weren't armed and armored pirates. Their clothes were dirty and tattered, and though their species were widely varied, they were tied together by a common trait—they all had slave collars clamped around their necks.

All but two, anyway. A pair of females, a sedhi and an ilthurii, wove through the crowd to descend the ramp side by side. The sedhi had an auto-blaster slung over one shoulder and a wide crimson sash tied around her waist.

The twins knew the pair, though it had been months since they'd parted ways—Vireesi and Fyr'ta, the sedhi and ilthurii who'd been amongst the survivors the twins had rescued from Sotera along with Thargen and his terran mate, Yuri.

Kayl's lips parted. He'd meant to speak, yet not a sound emerged. Even his bond with his twin was silent; Kier was equally speechless.

"They weren't pushovers, but between whatever magic you worked on their systems, your crew, and the Raiders, they didn't stand a chance," Vireesi said as she and Fyr'ta reached the base of the ramp, looking past the twins.

"It would not have been possible without your aid," Arcanthus replied.

"Well… Once a Crimson Raider, always a Raider, right? Fuck slavers. Especially these tretins."

Fyr'ta brushed a hand over Vireesi's shoulder, and she twined her tail with the sedhi's. She was looking directly at the twins. "And we could not decline the call to help after all you have done for us, Sol'Kier and Sol'Kayl." She dipped her head in a respectful bow.

Kier attempted to speak but managed little more than his brother had. "I… We…"

"Hey Vireesi. Fyr'ta," Thargen called cheerfully.

"Thargen." The female sedhi smiled and tilted her head. "How is it you're covered in blood every time I see you?"

"Typical Thargen," Arcanthus said.

"You are not so clean yourself, sedhi," Fyr'ta said.

"You've caught me at an inopportune moment," Arcanthus replied. "I assure you, this is not typical for me. Though I am fond of crimson."

Aileen laughed. She didn't know these people, hadn't even been introduced to them, but her response to their interactions was pure laughter, brightened by relief and joy and a simple but powerful sense of just...being alive. Despite her limp, she rushed to the twins and threw her arms around them. They embraced her, body and soul.

More of the dropships opened their doors and ramps, revealing more slaves, more sedhis with crimson cloths tied to various parts of their bodies, and several more members of Arcanthus's crew—the female ilthurii, Sekk'thi, and the cren, Kiloq, Koroq, and Razi.

When had the twins' hearts ever been so full? When had they ever felt so...weightless? So unburdened?

"I'm so glad you're okay," Aileen breathed, clutching the twins tighter.

"You are safe now," they replied. "That is all that matters."

"It's done. It's all done, right?"

They withdrew from Aileen only enough to look at her face. Her pale skin was smeared with dirt that had been cut through by sweat, her hair was a mess, and lips were dry. But her eyes, which glimmered with unshed tears, were so, so vibrant, so alive, so filled with love. She'd never been more beautiful.

"I was wrath," Kier said softly, tossing his blaster down.

Kayl dropped his weapon as well. "And I was vengeance."

"But now, we are yours and yours alone," they said together. "And our only fate is to love and protect our *na'diya* with every bit of ourselves."

She shifted her arms, placing a hand on each of their cheeks, and brushed her fingers across their skin. "Heart, mind, and soul, I am yours, my *na'divali*."

They drew her closer, each kissing her slowly, tenderly, gratefully before wrapping her in an embrace that none of them ever wanted to end.

The long, painful road that had forged their *daevalis* had been traveled. The hunt was over. And after so, so long, their lives had finally begun.

They'd found their fate, and they would never let her go.

FORTY-NINE

"Even during those early boom years, we never had half this many people in Navaire," Ialle said with a hint of wonder.

"A glimpse of what could've been," said Orassic. "And I'm glad things didn't go this way. I like the quiet."

Emai folded her arms across her chest. "That's why you take any opportunity to talk to every person who steps through those doors?"

"I'm just being friendly!"

Aileen chuckled. The residents of Navaire were good people. Their interactions reminded her so much of her da, who'd excelled at striking up a conversation with pretty much anyone to make them feel welcome and at ease. Though she hadn't known these people for long, Aileen was going to miss them—especially Shalla—and she hoped that, someday, she and the twins could revisit this place.

Of course, we can, na'diya, Kayl pulsed from beside her.

She looked up at him and smiled.

Anywhere you would like to go, Kier added. He stood behind Aileen with his arms around her and his chest pressed firmly against her back.

Arcanthus leaned back on the counter, smirking. "It warms my heart to know that such banter seems to be the norm for most groups of friends. We're not so strange, are we?"

"We are not," replied Kier, brushing his cheek on Aileen's hair. "But I cannot speak for you."

Aileen tightened her loose hold on his forearms and snuggled against him. The canteen was absolutely packed; so was the plaza, the shops, and the spaceport. Navaire was nearly overflowing with the people Arcanthus's team had rescued from Vrykhan's ship.

After returning to the *Fang* to tend to the wounds they'd suffered in their battle with the pirates, Aileen and the twins had hurried to assist with the slaves.

No. Not slaves. Not any more than I am, or the twins are. They're...refugees.

Yes, Kayl pulsed. *Refugees, looking forward to a new beginning. A new future.*

His tail slipped around her leg, squeezing gently. It still amazed her that such a touch could be exactly what was required at any given moment—it could be a source of strength; a thrilling tease; a soothing caress; a quiet reassurance.

Right now, it was the latter, because goodness knew she and her mates were far too exhausted for anything more strenuous than lying down and falling asleep.

They'd spent hours alongside Arcanthus and his crew removing hundreds of slave collars. Of course, Aileen hadn't known a thing about the computer programs required to break the digital locks on said collars, so she'd helped in a different way—applying first aid to skin that had been rubbed raw by those collars and guiding the weary, bewildered refugees onward in the process that Ialle had hastily thrown together to get everyone settled.

Despite the people of the small town having only just been under threat of being raided, kidnapped, or killed by pirates, they'd quickly rallied to help the refugees. Ialle's leadership had been decisive, and Aileen had found it especially impressive because the dacrethian had not once hesitated to ask for help or turn to those who knew better than regarding the particulars of their hasty operation.

If Aileen had held any doubts before, they'd been banished through the night—Navaire would've fallen apart years ago without Ialle. She'd balked at being elected arbiter, but clearly, she was the perfect fit for the role.

There'd been blankets and clothing to pass out, sleeping places to arrange, and so, so many people in need of guidance and a friendly face. The small town's infrastructure and supply stores had been pushed well beyond their limits, but the townsfolk had worked through every problem with a rugged determination and a dedication to aiding the refugees.

It helped that Arcanthus's crew had filled a couple of the dropships with supplies from the pirate battleship—primarily food, but there'd been some other essentials. The extra stores from the *Fang* had already been passed out as well.

The situation wouldn't be tenable for long, but things would hold until aid arrived from off world.

Here in the canteen, locals mingled freely with refugees, passing out and sharing food and drink. The kitchen had been operating nonstop to prepare enough food for everyone to have some, and Aileen was amazed that Emai could even stand upright at this point. The borian had been a whirlwind of motion all night, aiding in the kitchen, overseeing the logistics of getting enough supplies brought in to accommodate everyone, delivering food and drinks, cleaning messes and clearing tables. Aileen had done her best to help with the serving and cleaning, and her legs felt like jelly now. Without Kier's support, she wouldn't have been standing upright at all.

The sun would soon rise, and she doubted that anyone in town had slept. The approaching sunrise was likely to bring a lot of snoring.

The longest night of Aileen's life was nearly done.

It had begun with such joy and carefreeness, and had so swiftly descended into terror and violence, but hope had won out in the end. Hope and cooperation; compassion and kindness.

Vrykhan was dead, and he would not cast a shadow over this. He would not bring these people down for a second longer.

Your legacy is not in killing him, Aileen pulsed gently, looking up at Kier and then aside to Kayl. This *is your legacy. It's the people you've helped, the lives you've saved. Mine included.*

Ah, na'diya, their *aerysi* rumbled. Kayl leaned in close, tipping his chin onto her head, and Kier squeezed her a little tighter.

You saved our lives as well, Kayl replied.

We would have thrown them away if not for you, Kier added.

She responded by letting her love flow freely along their link, and she smiled to herself as the twins reciprocated. Their *daevalis* was so warm, so full, so...perfect.

"You're not like any Raider I've met, Alkorin," said Vireesi, the female sedhi who'd landed on that first dropship of refugees. She slipped an arm around Fyr'ta's waist and drew the ilthurii close.

"I'm not like any anything you've ever met, I'd venture," Arcanthus replied.

Aileen's smile widened. She'd only just met the twins' friends amidst all this chaos, and there'd barely been time to learn anything beyond their names, but they seemed like good people. And how could anyone not smile in Arcanthus's presence?

Remember, na'diya, *you are* ours, Kier warned.

Aileen laughed. *Oh, I know it, Kier. He is charming, but you two...you are everything.*

We are, Kayl replied, his tail sliding higher, *and you are everything to us.*

The female sedhi chuckled. "True. And so, I think the next round of drinks for the Raiders is on you, isn't it?"

"It's the least I could do," Arcanthus said.

Fyr'ta snickered. "Shall you make it two rounds then?"

"Everyone always wants a little more," he grumbled. "Shall I just buy the whole establishment and give everything away for free?"

"It's not for sale," Emai growled.

Kayl caught hold of Aileen's hand and lifted his head. "The operation you conducted was impressive, sedhi."

"Improvised," Arcanthus replied with a nonchalant wave. "I merely employed a lesson I learned long ago and hoped for the best."

"And what lesson was that?" asked Kier.

"Do not be afraid to ask for help," the sedhi replied flatly, leveling a pointed look at the twins. "None of us can tackle everything alone. This matter especially. So, I sought aid from the most competent force I knew."

"A former Crimson Raider and her retired friends," said Vireesi with another chuckle.

The vorgal, Thargen, laughed huskily. "Told you it was worth introducing you."

"Yes, well... I've never let good sense stop me from exercising my right to complain," Arcanthus murmured. His third eye flicked over to Shalla and Tallian, the later of whom was staring at him.

Aileen turned her gaze toward the uritis as well. She'd nearly sobbed in relief when, shortly after the dropships had landed, Triss emerged from the hangar with Shalla beside them and Tallian in the robot's arms. Despite being battered and bloodied, Tallian had been alert and energetic, and had proven it by pounding on the robot repeatedly and grumbling about being carried.

After receiving medical attention, the male uriti had insisted on helping however he could, so long as his daughter remained well within sight.

That demand had been quite reminiscent of one the twins had made after Aileen emerged from the medpod on the *Fang*—she'd not been allowed out of their sight for the rest of the night, and she had no complaints about it. She didn't want them out of hers either.

"Do you require something, uriti?" Arcanthus drawled, turning his face fully toward Tallian. "You've been staring awfully hard for quite some time."

Tallian grunted, brows falling low.

Shalla rolled her eyes in the most human-teenager way possible and nudged her father with her elbow. "Just ask him, *Rhunai*."

Arcanthus tilted his head. "Ask me what?"

"Nothing," Tallian replied.

"He's curious about your legs," Shalla said plainly.

"*Cheya...*"

Shalla braced her hands on her hips, regarding her father. "Did you not just hear what he said about asking for help? Come on, Father. Swallow that pride before you choke on it."

Tallian shook his head, expression softening. "Shalla, that—"

"Was overly harsh? Well, I—"

"Was exactly what your *rhana* would've said."

"I... Um. Well. She would've been right."

"From what I understand, Tallian, you've managed to keep everything in this town running despite a dearth of parts and materials," Arcanthus said, stepping closer. "Your robot, which I must assume was hand-built, was functional enough to turn the tide of the battle earlier. Why haven't you done anything about your legs?"

Tallian's nostrils flared with a heavy exhalation. "I have my reasons, sedhi."

"Because he puts everyone else first," Shalla said, frowning. "And I think because it reminds him of my mother. Like...it'd somehow be disrespecting her memory to help himself."

"No," Tallian said hoarsely. "It's... She died. She's gone. This is what I must bear."

"You don't have to, *Rhunai*."

"You really don't," Arcanthus replied, his tone gentling significantly. "I'll take care of it. I need but take a few scans, and I can have something custom made for you."

"I've no need of charity, sedhi," Tallian replied.

"It's not charity," Arcanthus said firmly. "You have taken very good care of my friends. I would like to repay that."

"They've already paid, and—"

Scowling, Shalla elbowed her father again.

Tallian sighed. "Thank you, Alkorin. I...I would greatly appreciate it."

Aileen smiled again; by now, she'd smiled so much that her cheeks were, ridiculously enough, the sorest part of her body.

A week ago, a month ago, a year ago; she *never* could've imagined life would bring her here. She never could've guessed at the twists and turns things would take. And she never would've believed that the happiness she'd found here could be possible.

"We should go rest soon," Kier whispered. "You are already too tired to walk, and we are nearly too tired to carry you."

"Nonsense, Sol'Kier," Kayl said, shaking his head. "I will never be too tired to carry our *na'diya*. I will always find the strength."

"Have I been mistaken all along, brother? Are we in competition after all?"

"I would hope not, if only for your sake."

"How thoughtful of you."

Aileen laughed.

"Aileen?" a familiar voice called over the din of conversation. "Aileen!"

Aileen's heart skipped a beat. That soft, melodic voice was out of her past, and she hadn't heard it in a lifetime...but that lifetime hadn't even been two weeks ago, had it? She quickly searched the room. Her eyes immediately landed on the lavender-skinned volturian approaching through the crowd.

She's alive. Oh my God, she's alive.

Elation and relief struck Aileen, and tears burned her eyes. "Tulaya..."

Sensing her need to go to the volturian, Kier dropped his arms, and Aileen raced forward, embracing Tulaya as soon as she was within reach. The volturian hugged her back.

"I'm so glad you're here. So glad you're safe." Aileen squeezed the woman tight. "I didn't know if the pirates had taken you, or if you...or if you'd been killed."

Tulaya let out choked laugh. "I thought you were dead. When I saw you get hit on that platform..." A shudder ran through her. "That was the last time I saw you before I was taken." She drew back, tears trailing down her cheeks. "How did you survive? Did they take you too?"

Aileen shook her head and smiled. "My mates saved me. I would have died if not for them."

The volturian's eyes flared. "Mates?"

Aileen looked toward Kier and Kayl and smiled. They stared back at her with adoring intensity, and their love flooded her chest with warmth.

I take it you like it when I claim you as my mates? she pulsed.

Kier grinned. *Very much so.*

"The daevahs?" Tulaya turned back to Aileen and peered into her eyes. Her breath hitched. "Your eyes! I...I did not know such a thing was possible."

"Me either. But apparently fate has a way of making anything possible."

Though the time since Aileen and Tulaya had last seen each other was short, it had taken its toll on the volturian. She'd always been willowy with gentle curves, but she was far thinner now. Her skin lacked its normal luster, her eyes were dulled, and even her *qal* had dimmed. The dark circles beneath her eyes spoke of the woman's exhaustion.

Tulaya took hold of Aileen's hand and smiled softly. "I am happy for you."

Aileen gave Tulaya's hand a squeeze. "Where will you go from here?"

"I... I have not thought about it," she said, oddly distracted. Something subtle brightened in her eyes. "It almost...does not feel real. To be free. To be..." She turned her head, fixing her gaze upon a figure approaching through the crowd—a huge cren with slate-gray skin, electric blue eyes, and disheveled, snow-white hair with several long braids hanging down his shoulders and back.

Razi—one of Arcanthus's friends. And while every cren Aileen had met was tall, Razi was easily the largest she'd ever seen, not just in height but in his powerful build. And yet even given his size and his undoubted formidability as a fighter, there'd been an undeniable calm and gentleness about him from the start.

"Loaded up," he said to Arcanthus in a deep, rumbling voice as he neared. "Whenever you're ready."

Arcanthus nodded.

"Do you plan to leave already?" asked Kayl.

"Not just yet," Arcanthus replied with an easy shrug. "But it's best we aren't around when authority figures start showing up to help these people get home."

The conversation continued, but Aileen couldn't pry her attention from Tulaya. The female volturian was staring at Razi with an intensity that Aileen wouldn't have believed possible from her back at Eternal Paradise. But of course, they'd all had their parts to play in that place, and that had typically necessitated meek, submissive demeanors.

What little defiance Aileen had shown had certainly cost her, and Tulaya had always warned her against it.

Razi turned his head toward Tulaya. His eyes widened, and the contrast between his black sclera and those vibrant blue irises seemed to heighten. Slowly, his lips curled into a smile around his curved, three-centimeter-long tusks.

Tulaya's *qal* came to life, taking on a white glow brighter than Aileen had ever seen from her.

The big cren's expression shifted, lips parting slightly, brows lifting, and pupils dilating.

"I..." Tulaya said breathlessly.

Slowly, Razi turned to fully face her. The volturian's fingers grasped Aileen's hand tighter, trembling faintly, and Aileen could just make out Tulaya's racing pulse through that touch.

"Is everything all right?" Aileen whispered, frowning.

The cren hunched down, putting his face closer to Tulaya's eye level, but he drew no closer. Each of his movements was careful, almost delicate, belying his stature. "Have you eaten?"

Tulaya blinked, and her tongue slipped out to run across her lips. Her *qal* brightened a little more. "Have I...?"

The way Tulaya's *qal* was reacting...

Volturians had been one of the first species to have open relations with humans, and so their culture was one of those most familiar to

Aileen's generation. It had bled into human pop culture in so many ways, especially entertainment—volturian movies and music had been incredibly popular for most of her youth.

Qal usually glowed like that in reaction to a volturian's mate.

"Easy," the big cren said, lifting his palms and offering a tentative smile. "We'll go nice and slow, okay? I'm Razi. What's your name?"

Only then did Aileen realize everyone nearby was watching the scene unfold. They all knew, didn't they?

Formality cannot mask the truth of the soul, Kayl pulsed.

Aileen recognized the saying; it was a volturian proverb that had been widespread on Earth. But it had always been about this, about *qal* and soul mates.

"I..." Tulaya backed away from Razi, her breath quickening. "I... I'm sorry, Aileen, I have to go." She spun around suddenly, her trembling fingers slipping out of Aileen's hold, and hurried into the crowd, which swallowed her immediately.

Razi's hands twitched forward as though to reach for her, but he gave no chase. He clenched his jaw, expression hardening, and stood upright, staring in the direction Tulaya had fled. That hardness on his face didn't hide the glimmer of pain in his eyes.

"Well damn," Thargen said.

Arcanthus slapped the vorgal with his tail.

"I meant that sympathetically!"

"Perhaps you must work on your tone then," said Sekk'thi, the female ilthurii from Arcanthus's crew.

"Magama's flailing teats, I'm capable of fucking sympathizing with a friend," Thargen growled.

Arcanthus slapped Thargen with his tail again.

Razi didn't seem to hear them; he was still staring after Tulaya. "I do something wrong?"

That look in his eyes made Aileen's heart ache. She longed to go after her friend, but knew that Tulaya needed time alone. Needed an escape. "No. No, you didn't. She just...she's been through a lot, Razi."

"She went from one master to another," Kier said, his voice low. "And now she is suddenly free."

"It is an overwhelming time for anyone." Kayl's voice was also low, but his tone was gentle, and he regarded the big cren with deep emotion in his mismatched eyes. "As you surely know, Razi."

Razi nodded, a far-off light entering his gaze. "I do know."

Aileen stepped forward, placing a hand on the cren's thick arm. "She was stuck in Eternal Paradise for longer than me, and as much as I suffered there, Saduuk put her through worse."

Razi nodded. His nostrils flared with a heavy exhalation. "I'm going to double check the ship."

Thargen's brow furrowed. "But you just—"

Now both Arcanthus and Sekk'thi hit the vorgal with their tails.

Glowering, Thargen snatched a drink off the bar and guzzled it down. "You're lucky I don't have a fucking tail."

"I'll find you soon, Razi," Arcanthus said.

The big cren nodded again and walked away without a backward glance.

"We are going to take our leave as well." Kier moved into place on Aileen's right and offered his arm.

Kayl came up smoothly on her left, holding out his arm as well. "We are claiming some much-needed time to ourselves."

Aileen slipped her arms through her mates'. She couldn't help but recall the first time they'd done this, when they'd escorted her to the first meal they'd eaten together.

"That's all you've had this whole time," Thargen protested.

"And would you be standing here right now if Yuri had come along?" Arcanthus asked with a smirk.

"Fuck no," Thargen replied without hesitation. "In fact, I'm going to have a few words for Drakkal and Urgand for staying behind when we get back."

"Such as what, vorgal?" Sekk'thi asked. "Thank you?"

"They are there safeguarding your mate," Arcanthus said.

"Yours too," Thargen growled. "Doesn't it drive you crazy?"

"Every moment. But given her pregnancy, it comforts me that she is with my head of security and the only qualified medical practitioner on our staff."

"Pfft." Thargen waved a hand dismissively. "That's sure a fancy fucking way to say *medic*."

Kier shook his head. "We will speak with you after we have rested, sedhi."

"Yeah, *rested*," the vorgal teased.

Arm-in-arm, the twins led Aileen through the crowd. By the time they reached the spaceport, the pain meds had long since worn off, and all three felt every ache in their bodies—and in each other's. But it was a satisfying sort of pain. It had been earned by difficult work and perseverance, and when it faded, it would leave them closer—and their bond stronger—than before.

The first hints of light glowed on the horizon as they neared the hangar housing their ship. Before they could move any closer to the *Fang*, their attention was caught by plodding footfalls drawing steadily closer.

The trio turned to find Triss approaching them. The robot held a cloth sack in one hand.

"Aileen. I was coming to look for you," Triss said. "Now I have no reason to apply my advanced search algorithm to do so."

Aileen chuckled. "How are you, Triss?"

"I am the same." Their small head dipped to look down. "But there were nearly several new ventilation ports melted into my casing."

The robot's metal chest bore scorch marks and melted indentations courtesy of the pirate's blaster fire, but thankfully, nothing had gone through Triss's outer casing.

Triss raised an arm with a mechanical whir, holding the bag out to Aileen. "I wanted to give you this. We found it under the scrap in the hangar. Shalla said it was yours."

Aileen's breath hitched. It was the bag from The Glittering Cavern—the bag that contained her gift to the twins. As she accepted it from the robot, she said, "Thank you so much, Triss. I must've lost it when everything fell, and I... I haven't even thought of it since then."

"I am sorry, Aileen. It does not seem the object inside fared well."

The hint of sorrow in the robot's otherwise flat voice might've been in Aileen's imagination...but she couldn't be certain.

Lowering their arm, Triss stepped back. "Thank you for helping Shalla. Goodbye."

The robot turned and departed unceremoniously, kicking up little clouds of dust with every thumping step.

Frowning, Aileen hefted the bag. Its contents rattled softly. Her frown deepened. She positioned herself to block the bag from the twins' view with her body and opened it, peeking inside.

"What is wrong, Aileen?" Kayl asked as he and his brother stepped closer to her.

She reached into the bag and scooped out some of its contents on her palm—broken and splintered pieces of pale, carved wood, a scrap of velvety cloth, and tiny electronic parts that had surely fit together before the bag had been crushed. Her shoulders slumped. "It's ruined."

"It is all right," Kier said softly. "It was only a thing."

"I got it for you two as a belated joining gift. It was...a music box."

"We have you, *na'diya*," they soothed, wrapping their arms around her.

As tears misted her eyes, the twins took hold of her hands, guiding her to dump the broken parts back in the bag. Then Kier took the bag from her hold and tossed it down. They turned Aileen to face them.

"We will not end our day like this," Kayl said as he and his brother wiped the tears from her face.

Aileen's gaze flicked toward the sky again, which was just a little lighter than before. She drew in a steadying breath, brushed away a lingering teardrop, and nodded.

Without a word spoken between them, the trio walked to a scrapped hovertruck nearby and helped each other climb onto it. The roof of the vehicle's cab was just tall enough for them to see over the wall ringing the spaceport.

Kier and Kayl held her from either side as they settled down atop the cab. She breathed them in, letting their scents wash over her, and as she exhaled, she sang.

There were no words—just her voice, weaving a sweet, simple melody that grew deeper and more powerful as she opened her heart and poured everything into the song. All her happiness, all her love, that sense of belonging, of fitting, of completeness, it all came through. Her pain was there too. But the loss and suffering she'd endured only made everything else stronger.

When she finished the last note, it lingered in the air, echoing across the alien landscape as though it would carry on forever and ever, long after Aileen could no longer hear it.

"*Na'diya*," Kier breathed. She sensed the tightness in his chest, the overwhelming swell of emotion—it was the same as what she sensed from Kayl.

And the strongest of those emotions was their love for her.

"That was the gift," she said quietly. "That was what I recorded in the music box and wanted to give to you. I know it doesn't mean anything, but—"

"Ah, *na'diya*," Kayl rasped, stroking his fingers down her cheek, "it means everything."

"You put into song what we would never be able to put into words." Kier's tail curled around her hip and settled across her lap. "Hearing the music of your soul, Aileen, straight from your lips...we could imagine no greater gift."

And with those words, her disappointment vanished.

"I don't think I'm ever going to let you two go," she whispered, snuggling against them.

The twins held her a little closer as all three turned their faces toward the horizon to watch the sun emerge and cast its brilliant glow across the rocky land. The clouds were vibrant reds, oranges, and violets, forming a palette of natural beauty that shifted as the sun climbed.

Aileen's heart rose with the sun, and despite the weariness of her body, her spirit soared. "We're free."

Kier placed a gentle kiss atop her head. "And the sunrise has never been so beautiful."

"But it is not half as beautiful as the next," Kayl said, catching her chin in his fingers and tipping her head back.

The twins were both looking at her, their eyes more vibrant than the sunrise, their love warmer than the rays of sunshine upon her skin.

"Nor the one after that," Kier said, smiling. "Each sunrise with you, *na'diya*, will eclipse the last."

EPILOGUE

Kayl closed his eyes and drew in a deep breath, filling his lungs with warm, salt-kissed air. He'd done so more times than he could count since arriving here, and his wonderment had not faded—this air was so familiar, so soothing, so *right*, even after all these years.

Home.

He opened his eyes. The turquoise sea stretched out before him, its gentle waves washing up on the pale purple beach in endless succession. But for a few specks of cloud near the horizon, the sky and the water blended almost seamlessly together. When Aileen had first glimpsed this view through the twins' memory, she'd seen infinity.

Kayl couldn't help but see the same now. Infinity—unrestricted possibility.

Coming back to Tilara had been...difficult. It had taken time for the twins to work through their painful memories, time for them to reach the understanding that pain was such a small, small part of what they'd experienced here.

One night; they'd had one night of agony here, one night of terror. And it had left deep, undeniable wounds on them...but it could not cancel out all the days and nights that had come before it. They would no longer let that single terrible night darken all the good that had preceded it, would no longer let it overshadow all the other memories they had of their parents.

So, after several weeks with Arcanthus and his crew on Arthos, the twins and their mate had decided to make this trip. To seek real peace. To seek their home.

And what they'd found here...

His gaze dipped, falling upon the two figures in the water. Aileen and Kier were floating on their backs, the former with her red hair fanned out around her head, their bodies swaying with the sea's easy rhythm. Kier's tail was coiled around her waist, ensuring she wouldn't drift far. After too many sunburns, which Kayl was convinced had pained him and his brother more than her, her skin had taken on more of the little brown spots she called freckles.

They suited her. And the twins had enjoyed discovering all the new ones that had appeared on her delectable body.

Even now, with her eyes hidden behind the dark glasses she'd taken to wearing most days, she radiated happiness. And her happiness was met with Kier and Kayl's elation, swirling and building into something bigger and bigger. Something beyond words.

She'd flourished here on Tilara. The twins had flourished also. But most of all, their *daevalis* had flourished.

Kayl knew they would've found happiness anywhere, but the closure of being back here was invaluable. Because they hadn't returned to abandoned, decaying ruins.

They'd returned to find a living town.

Itheria wasn't the same as they remembered—nothing ever could be—but the town of their youth was still here. It had been almost surreal to walk into Itheria and see so many daevahs gathered together, and then to have some of those daevahs look at the twins, look *close*, and with delight and wonder ask if they were Sol'Kier and Sol'Kayl.

The town had not died out. The people had not died out. There'd been survivors that night, there'd been many villagers who'd escaped the raid. And those people hadn't fled Tilara. They'd remained here, rebuilt Itheria, and carried on to honor the memories of their friends and family who'd been lost.

They had become stronger.

The twins' trip to the memorial that had been erected upon a rise overlooking the ocean—overlooking eternity—had been cathartic. The twins had been unable to hold back their tears when they'd found the names of their parents, written together in the sacred triangle, as was daevah custom, on the memorial plaque. Removing their own names from that plaque had brought more tears, but it had also reminded them that they were alive. They were free.

They had their *daevalis*.

And after two months here...they didn't plan to go anywhere. The life they'd made in Itheria with their *na'diya*, this simple, quiet life, was exactly what they wanted. It was exactly what they deserved.

Are you going to spend all your time staring at the water in deep contemplation, or are you going to join us, brother? Kier pulsed, lifting his head to glance at Kayl.

Aileen's lips curled into a smile, but she did not lift her head. *I like it when he's in deep contemplation.*

At least I know our mate appreciates me, Kayl replied.

It's the only time I stand a chance of sneaking up on him, Aileen continued.

Kier laughed, and Kayl couldn't suppress a smile. He'd never felt so light, so unburdened, so unbothered. So—

His holocom chimed with an incoming call.

"You brought that with you?" Kier released a frustrated sound and dipped his head under the water.

Kayl chuckled, lifted his wrist, and accepted the call.

Arcanthus's holographic form appeared from the projector. "How pleasant to see my favorite daevah." He put a hand beside his mouth and whispered, "Don't tell Sol'Kier I said that."

"He already heard you," Kayl replied.

"It's all right. He knows that he's actually my favorite."

"Did you need something, Arcanthus?"

The sedhi leaned his elbow on something—likely his desk—and propped his chin on his hand. "I just wanted to see how everything was going out there. I was contemplating a visit with Samantha some time after our little one is born, and was wondering if you've furnished that guest room yet."

Kayl flicked his gaze toward the water. Aileen and Kier stood waist-deep now, waving and mouthing silent shouts for him to hurry. Kayl's smile broadened as he ran his gaze over his beautiful mate's body, which was nearly unclothed save for the small top and bottoms she called a bikini. "Unfortunately, I am currently occupied, Arcanthus. I must go."

"You're shirtless and outside," the sedhi replied flatly. "You're lounging on the beach again, aren't you?"

"I would have expected you to know that, as you are so skilled at keeping track of us."

The sedhi's brows fell. "Sometimes I question whether you having developed a sense of humor is a good thing."

"Then I shall allow you time to consider it." Kayl rose from his chair and unfastened the holocom from his wrist.

"You're really going to end the call on me? Haven't you learned anything after all we've been through?"

Kayl laughed, holding the holocom on his palm. "I have, Arcanthus. We will call you later."

"That's not what I—"

Kayl's thumb brushed through the icon, ending the call. He silenced the holocom and tossed it into the bag he and his companions had used to bring their belongings to the beach. He paused for a moment, studying the instrument leaning against the bag—Aileen's guitar. Its shaped and polished wood had a beautiful grain, and her clever fingers could coax such lovely sounds from its strings.

Itheria's villagers had come to love it when Aileen would play her guitar and sing. Children would sometimes sneak away from lessons and chores if they heard her, and adults seemed more than willing to set their responsibilities aside to hum and sing along with her songs. By now, they'd even learned the words to several of her terran songs.

It had proven to be another way in which their hearts grew ever fuller.

Kayl strode across the sand to join his mate and his brother, each step easier than the last.

Aileen lifted her sunglasses onto her head as Kayl stepped into the surf. "I'm proud of you."

Kier quirked a brow. "Why, because he terminated the call a little more politely than usual?"

"No, because he's really taken nicely to relaxing." Her eyes trailed over Kayl's body from head to toe and back up again. Slowly. "It suits you, Sol'Kayl."

"You know how I feel about you using my full name, *na'diya*," Kayl purred as he stalked toward her.

She grinned, brushing a finger back and forth across her chest.

Droplets of water trickled beneath her breasts. "Hmm... You'll have to remind me."

He lunged across the last bit of distance separating them, splashing water into the air that broke the sunlight into faint rainbows. Aileen giggled, backing away, but he caught her before she could escape, lifted her up, and spun her about.

Kayl grinned. Clutching his shoulders, she laughed; her eyes were alight as they stared down into his.

When he stopped, Aileen's smile softened, and she tucked the strands of his damp hair behind his ear before brushing his cheek with the backs of her fingers.

I love seeing you two smile, she pulsed.

Kayl loosened his hold, allowing Aileen's body to slide down him. He relished the feel of her skin against his, of the hardened points of her nipples brushing his chest through her thin top, of the bloom of arousal pulsing from her core into their psychic link.

"I will always have a smile for you, *na'diya*," he said huskily.

Kier moved into place behind her, gathering her hair in his hand and guiding her head to the side. He skimmed his lips over her shoulder and kissed her just beneath her ear. "As will I."

Kayl's senses rippled as their psychic bond expanded, pushed outward by their growing arousal. He was already losing himself in the sensations, in the emotion, in their *daevalis*, but he held on just long enough to look into Aileen's eyes.

Speaking with one voice, he and Kier said, "You are ours, Aileen. Heart, mind, and soul. Forever."

Kayl slanted his mouth over hers and let the spark of pleasure ignite and carry them to ecstasy.

AUTHOR'S NOTE

If you made it this far, all we can say is...thank you! From the bottom of our hearts, thank you so, so much. We seriously cannot expression how grateful we are. We truly hope you enjoyed accompanying Kier, Kayl, and Aileen on their journey of healing and finding love.

Have you heard authors say how they put their blood, sweat, and tears into their books? Yeah, well, we definitely felt it with this one. But despite the hardships and complications along the way, we love the outcome. And we are so thankful for all our cheerleaders (you amazing readers and authors, you!) who have supported us throughout this process. And please, if you could take a moment, we'd love it if you could leave a review. <3

You might be wondering what's next for the Infinite City? Well, if you caught that bit at the end, yes, it's our quiet, grim, volturian-soap-opera-loving cren, Razi! The bad news...there's going to be a bit of a wait. We have multiple books to write before we revisit the Infinite City, but we WILL come back!

Be sure to join our newsletter and/or our Facebook Reader Group for updates, commissioned art, and to just chill.

His Darkest Craving

His Darkest Desire

ALIENS AMONG US

Taken by the Alien Next Door

Stalked by the Alien Assassin

Claimed by the Alien Bodyguard

Saved by the Alien Crime Boss

STANDALONE TITLES

Claimed by an Alien Warrior

Dustwalker

Escaping Wonderland

Yearning For Her

The Warlock's Kiss

Ice Bound: Short Story

ISLE OF THE FORGOTTEN

Make Me Burn

Make Me Hunger

Make Me Whole

Make Me Yours

VALOS OF SONHADRA COLLABORATION

Tiffany Roberts - Undying

Tiffany Roberts - Unleashed

VENYS NEEDS MEN COLLABORATION

Tiffany Roberts - To Tame a Dragon

Tiffany Roberts – To Love a Dragon

ABOUT THE AUTHOR

Tiffany Roberts is the pseudonym for Tiffany and Robert Freund, a husband and wife writing duo. The two have always shared a passion for reading and writing, and it was their dream to combine their mighty powers to create the sorts of books they want to read. They write character driven sci-fi and fantasy romance, creating happily-ever-afters for the alien and unknown.

Sign up for our Newsletter!
Check out our social media sites and more!
http://www.authortiffanyroberts.com